Texas Billionaire Brides Series
by
Roz Lee

TABLE OF CONTENTS

The Backdoor Billionaire's Bride

USA Today Bestselling Author

ROZLEE

Acknowledgements

I have many people to thank for bringing this story to life.

First, I have to thank my family for putting up with me and my neurotic mood swings when I'm writing. That includes our rescue dog, Bud, and our rescue grand dog, Scout, who made sure I got plenty of cold, fresh air during the long days that went into writing this story.

A special thanks to my husband for helping me plot the story on one of our long drives. P.S. – This one is done. We need to take another road trip!

The Backdoor Billionaire's Bride might never have been completed without the New Jersey Romance Writers who cheered me on during JeRoWriMo. I needed someone to hold my feet to the fire as much as I needed to know I was not alone in my struggles to get words on paper. For all my fellow 30K'ers, I owe you one.

To Karen and Diane—thank you both for reading and giving me your honest opinion. It fills my heart to know I have friends I can count on.

To my editor, Laura Garland, thank you for knowing where the commas go.

PART ONE

A successful marriage is an edifice that must be rebuilt every day.
Andre Maurois

CHAPTER ONE

K. Ford Adams ran his fingers along the edge of the massive wooden desk. Generations of Adamses had run an empire from this very spot, and now it was his turn—whether he wanted it or not. And, he definitely did not want.

His father was gone. Kenneth Adams had appeared in good health up until a few days ago when a heart attack had taken him from his family, his business, and his town, at the youthful age of fifty-eight.

Butte Plains, Texas, would miss the elder Adams. The third generation born and raised in the small town, Ken Adams had been loved and respected by everyone.

As the single-largest employer in Butte Plains, the town had been built around his family's factory generations ago, so naturally, the employees would be curious about the person taking the helm. At least that's what he told himself as he looked around at more than a century of memories cluttering the office. Nothing much had changed over the years. Each Adams to sit at the desk added their own achievements to the collection, but none had ever removed anything.

Everything from a yellowed photograph of his great-grandfather breaking ground on the original building, to a plaque declaring his father as Employer of the Year in Butte Plains, an honor bestowed only one month ago, lined the walls. What would become of it all once he sold the business? All the memories would need to be packed away and, most likely, stored in the attic of the family mansion along with all the other junk collecting dust there.

He didn't want to think about what would happen to the stuff once his mother passed. Three years her husband's junior, Helen Ford Adams, hopefully, had many more years on earth. He'd leave worries of what to do with the house and its furnishings for later. He had enough things on his plate—like figuring the company's value and finding a buyer. The sooner he converted the assets into cash to provide for his mother's remaining years, the sooner he could return to his own life—and get the fuck out of Butte Plains. Again.

Nothing remained for him here. Never had been.

An image popped into his head—a woman dressed in a trim black suit, a smart hat complete with some sort of net veil shielding the left side of her tear-ravaged face as she listened to the preacher's softly-spoken graveside prayer for Kenneth Adams's eternal peace. She'd looked familiar, but then again, he'd once known everyone in this town. It could have been anyone from his past, though he couldn't think of a single female with as much beauty and grace as the mystery woman possessed.

It didn't matter if he knew her or not, her tears had been genuine, marking her as someone special in his book. Ford didn't want to follow in his father's footsteps, but he had loved and respected the man. Ken Adams had been an excellent father, instilling values, passing on wisdom, and encouraging his son to follow his dreams, even if they took him away from Texas and the family business.

Ruthlessly shutting down thoughts of the mystery woman and how she knew his father, he turned his attention to the one modern thing in the office—a state-of-the-art computer. He remembered the day, a few years ago, when his father mentioned the new office manager had insisted he learn to work the computer system. The year before, all the company's records had been converted to digital files, and this new employee had been determined to drag Ken into the present century. The man had gone along reluctantly, but, from later accounts, he'd taken to the new technology with an ease that spoke of his intelligence.

Since the desk dated back to a century before computers, Ford put the keyboard in his lap, and pushed the Enter key. A password prompt appeared on the flat-screen monitor. Ken Adams's greatest weakness, if he had one, was his love for his wife and son. Every pass code, from the factory's alarm system to the keypad for his home garage-door opener was one of two words. Ford smirked as he typed his mother's name in the blank box.

"So much for security," he mumbled as the blank screen gave way to a program his father had left open. Chuckling to himself, he swiped at tears blurring his vision. When his sight cleared, he leaned back in the chair and moved the next card on the deck to its appropriate place on the Solitaire board. He couldn't stay in Butte Plains and run his father's company, but he could finish this last game for the man who had taught him to balance work and play.

~~~

Following the touching graveside service for her boss, Becky Parker couldn't bring herself to drive up to the family's mansion for the traditional wake. She'd had about all the heartbreak she could stand for one day, and confronting K. Ford Adams today wouldn't do anyone any good. Everyone she talked to seemed confident the heir would embrace the family mantle and come home to steer the helm of Adams Manufacturing. She knew he would not.

Ken Adams had spoken of Ford often, and with great affection, but he'd also known his son had no interest in the family business. Ford was an only child, so, following family tradition of passing down from father to son, the place had become his—whether he wanted it or not. Which meant the company would go on the
~~~

auction block. Or worse—Ford could flat-out close the plant. Butte Plains was struggling enough. Closing the factory would be the last nail in the coffin lid for the small west Texas town she loved so much.

Out of respect for the other workers' grief over losing a beloved friend and employer, Becky had thus far kept her Negative Nellie thoughts to herself. But if she came face-to-face with Ford in the mood she was in, she didn't think she'd be capable of keeping her mouth shut. She'd been brought up better than to cause a scene at a wake, so she'd wait until she had Ford alone before she told him what she thought of a man who would turn his back on his neighbors.

Steering her car in the opposite direction of the Adams's home, she headed toward the one place she knew she'd be alone today— her office. The plant had been shut down so all the employees could attend the services, but she still had work to do. Payday was coming up, and she needed to figure out how to go about transferring funds into the payroll account. There would be legal wrangling to get it done since Ken had always handled money transfers himself. Ford could probably do it, but she didn't want to bother him yet. It might be days—weeks—before he decided to see about disposing of his responsibility, and the factory workers couldn't wait until he got his shit together to be paid.

She absolutely refused to believe this paycheck might be the last any of them would receive from Adams Manufacturing.

Pulling into the vacant parking lot, she eyed the barren planter boxes dividing the rows. The daffodils would be poking their heads up soon, followed closely by the tulips and those other flowers she could never remember the name of. She made a mental note to contact the landscaper and see about having fresh mulch put down before the weeds got out of hand. She parked in her usual spot, extricated her purse from beneath the hat she'd worn to the funeral then exited the car. Approaching the front door, she froze. The seam between the double-glass doors sat off-kilter. Certain she'd secured it the night before, she glanced over her shoulder. Someone had unlocked the door, but her car was the only vehicle in the lot.

Had one of the other workers come by and forgotten to lock up when they left? It certainly wouldn't be the first time the building had been left open. Everyone in town knew there wasn't anything worth stealing in the place, no money, and very little with any resale value—so not worth the trouble if a person meant to make an easy buck. The real, but very small, threat was vandalism. The machinery inside had all been custom built to do what it needed to do. Replacing any part would take time and money. Wholesale destruction would put them out of business. Becky made a mental note to remind everyone with a key to make sure they locked up next time then reached for the door handle. No need courting disaster, especially since disaster already loomed over their heads in the form of one K. Ford Adams.

After locking the door behind her, she made her way through the silent lobby to the hallway leading to the executive offices. She turned the corner, stopping cold at the sight of light shining from the open doorway at the end of the hallway. From Ken Adams's office. Only one person—besides her—had the right to be in the boss's office, and he was receiving mourners at his mother's home across town.

Who the hell would invade a man's office on the day of his funeral? Remembering the empty parking lot, she sighed. *Whoever it is, they're gone. Might as well see what damage they've done.*

Stopping in her office next to Mr. Adams's, Becky noted nothing out of place. Her computer sat in its usual place. If they'd burgled, they'd done a piss-poor job of it. Leaving her purse, she rounded the corner into the adjacent office and came to an abrupt halt.

"Holy crap!" Her hand flew to her chest to calm her runaway heart.

The last person she'd expected to see sat behind the ancient desk. At her exclamation, he glanced her way then tossed the keyboard on the blotter and leaned back in Mr. Adams's chair. Other than catching a glimpse of him at the funeral, she hadn't seen the younger Adams in over a decade, but she'd recognize him anywhere. Ford was the spitting image of his father, and—holy cow—sexy as hell. Her image of him as Ebenezer Scrooge faded fast. "Ford," she gasped. "I mean, Mr. Adams. What are you doing here?"

He scrubbed at his face with both hands in a gesture that spoke to the strain he must be under. Dropping his hands to the desktop, he glanced around the room. No matter what he decided to do with the company, the man had just lost his father and it showed in the lines bracketing his eyes and mouth. Her heart softened toward him. "In case you haven't heard, I'm the new owner."

"Yes. Of course." She willed her breathing to even out. "I meant…. I assumed you'd be at the house."

"I could only take about five minutes, then I had to get away." He gestured absently. "Figured no one else would be here."

Becky nodded. She could relate. When her father passed, she'd hated every minute of the wake. If she'd been able to find a way to escape, she would have. She gave Ford props for doing what he needed rather than bowing to antiquated traditions.

She tossed aside her plan to get a head start on the payroll situation. She'd leave him to deal with his grief. "Oh. Well. I'll go, then. Didn't mean to interrupt." She took a step backward.

"Becky Jean?" He unfolded from the chair.

She didn't remember him being so tall—over six feet, she guessed. He'd shed his black suit coat and rolled up the sleeves of his white dress shirt. A black-and-silver striped tie hung loose, drawing her attention to the triangle of golden skin his open collar exposed. Her mouth watered. An image flashed in her brain of her slowly licking him there.

Becky licked her lips instead then bit her lower lip, just to be on the safe side. If she remembered right, Ford had been sort of nerdy in high school. *There's nothing nerdy about him now.* Not. One.

Damn. Thing. *God, what is wrong with me?* She hadn't had much experience with instant lust, but she knew it when she felt it. And boy, did she feel it from the roots of her hair to the tips of her toes — and in every erogenous zone in between. Even if the man hadn't been her new boss, he'd still just lost his father — a man he loved. She couldn't think of a single thing more inappropriate than lusting after Ford. Drawing a mental line, she shoved her wayward thoughts behind it.

"Don't go." Her body responded to the baritone command, freezing in place, melting at the core. "It is Becky Jean, isn't it?"

"Um… it's just Becky now."

Though his eyes still looked sad, his smile appeared genuine. "I knew I recognized you! Saw you at the service." His smile dimmed. "Thanks for coming, by the way."

"It was the least I could do." She meant the comment with every fiber of her being. She'd started with the company in high school, working afternoons and weekends boxing products for shipment in order to save for college. As an undergrad, she'd spent her summers on the assembly line, a jump in pay she needed to continue funding her degree. A week after her college graduation, her father had been diagnosed with inoperable lung cancer. Her family needed her. And with her brother, Colin, a sophomore in high school, she'd had no choice but to put off looking for a job in marketing in a big city. She'd returned home, and to the assembly line to help pay her father's staggering medical bills. Soon after, Ken Adams learned about her situation and offered her the job of office manager. The pay hadn't been enough, but it went a long way to easing her family's burden. In her eyes, Ken Adams had been a saint, and she would not let her attraction to his son get in the way of doing what she could to keep his factory open.

"Hey. What are you doing here anyway?" he asked.

God, even the way his eyebrows knit together was sexy. *Snap out of it, Beck. Now.* "I… uh…. Payroll has to go out this week. I thought I'd… you know, get the ball rolling."

"You work here."

"I manage the office."

He turned his gaze to the desktop. He flicked the keyboard keys with his index finger. "You're the one who got Dad on the computer."

She counted bringing the elder Adams into the twenty-first century as one of her major accomplishments. Remembering the struggle, she smiled. "Guilty as charged."

When Ford returned his gaze to her, pain clouded his eyes, but a tiny smile lifted one side of his mouth. "I tried for years to get him online. I'm grateful you managed to convince him. We kept in touch via Skype and email."

"I didn't know about the Skype."

Ford shrugged and went back to flicking the keys. "Doesn't matter."

But it clearly did. He sat, turning his attention to the computer monitor. He seemed to shrink right before her eyes. "I'll look into the account situation at the bank. I'm guessing money needs to be transferred into the payroll account?"

"Yes. By day after tomorrow."

"I'll take care of it." His voice rumbled with conviction and dismissal.

"Thanks." She backed out of the doorway. He looked as if the world rested on his shoulders. "It can wait until tomorrow."

"I'm sure it can, but I need something to do."

"Okay. Well." She bit her lip again. "I'll be in my office. If you need anything."

He glanced at her, appreciation shining past the pain. "Thanks, Becky Jean."

He'd come here to escape the sympathy of others, but she got the oddest impression he still needed to hear it. "He was a good man. Lots of people are going to miss him."

His Adam's apple bobbed. He dipped his chin, acknowledging her comment then turned his focus to the computer screen. Becky slipped into her office, leaving him to deal with his grief in his own way.

CHAPTER TWO

Ford stared after Becky Jean. He'd heard the same sentiment a thousand times since he'd returned to Butte Plains earlier this week, so why did he have the feeling that, coming from her, the eulogy held a hint of warning? Was she implying *he* wasn't a good man? *Why would she think that?*

Chalking the uneasy feeling up to grief and fatigue, he clicked the computer keys. No matter what he did with the factory, the workers needed to be paid. He'd never worked a day in the factory, but he knew how businesses operated. He just needed to figure out which account usually funded payroll and arrange with the bank to make the transfer—then he could get on with gathering the necessary financial statements needed to entice someone to buy Adams Manufacturing.

As he clicked through his father's personal files, his mind kept returning to Becky Jean Parker. He had a hard time reconciling the steaming-hot woman from the cemetery with his long-ago recollections of the girl he remembered from school. She'd been a mouse, sitting at the back of classrooms, never saying a word he could recall. He could count on one hand the number of times he remembered interacting with her, and none of those had been particularly memorable. She hadn't run with any of the popular crowds, hadn't played sports, hadn't attended the high school dances or other social functions. She'd been more of a ghost than a mouse—invisible, but there if you bothered to look.

He hadn't bothered to look.

That's not entirely true. There was that one time….

He'd shown up at the local photography studio to have his senior portrait made and she'd been there. Waiting his turn, he'd peeked to see who had the appointment ahead of him, and been shocked to see Becky Jean perched on a stool, smiling for the camera. She'd been wearing one of those black drape things leaving her slim shoulders bare. Her red hair hadn't yet mellowed to the subdued auburn it was now. The curled ends had lain against her chest, drawing attention to the swell of generous breasts. A Mona Lisa smile graced her glossed lips, and her eyes had sparkled with intelligence.

Only he knew the reason for the slightly pained smile he'd worn in his senior portrait. He'd had a raging hard-on the entire photo session, all because of Becky Jean Parker.

Ford shifted, his dick as hard today as it had been back then. For years, he'd chalked up his response to teenage hormones, but seeing her, talking to her today, proved nothing had changed. She still stirred his blood in inappropriate ways.

As of today, Becky Jean worked for him. He absolutely wouldn't take advantage of an employee. No way.

Another image came to mind—Veronica Ramsey. The younger sister of his business partner, Scott, she was beautiful and sophisticated. They'd been friends and fuck buddies for over a year. When he'd told her his father had passed away and he had to make the trip home for the funeral, she'd expressed her condolences, but hadn't offered to accompany him. He'd momentarily considered *asking* her to but figured if he had to *ask,* then he didn't want her there anyway. He'd begun to question if he even wanted her in his life. When it came down to it, they had little in common. Where he preferred to share a drink with a buddy or two, she preferred a party—the bigger, the better. Born into a life he'd never dreamed of, she'd dazzled him from the beginning, but it didn't take long for him to see past the glitz. Once he had, he'd been surprised to see how empty her friends' lives were. He wanted more for himself, but Ronnie wouldn't take "no" for an answer.

He forced his attention back to the payroll situation. He had no business admiring anything about his new office manager. Becky Jean was his employee. She, and all the others, would expect to be paid this week. His father would kick his ass if he let them down.

An hour later, Ford had learned two things. He couldn't sell the company, and he wouldn't be leaving town anytime soon. Neither realization made him happy. In fact, they pissed him off.

Sitting back in the leather desk chair built to fit his father's frame, not his, he scrubbed both palms over his face. Tension he'd been holding in his shoulders all day felt like cement blocks weighing him down. Why hadn't his dad said something? How had the situation gotten this critical without Ford suspecting? Did anyone know? The employees? If anyone did, it would be the office manager.

Sitting up, he bellowed, "Becky Jean! Get your ass in here right this minute!"

Barreling around the corner, eyes wide, the woman skidded to a halt in the doorway. "What?"

"That's all you've got to say? *What?*" He stood, knuckles digging into the oak desktop. "Where did the money go?"

Her eyes narrowed, her brows knit together. "Money?" One hand white-knuckled the doorframe.

"Umm. The petty cash is in the safe in my office?" Her voice trailed up and off.

"I'm not talking about the petty cash, and you damn well know it. Where. Is. The. Money?"

"I don't… uh…. What?" She swallowed hard, let go of the doorframe, and tugged the hem of her suit jacket down. Squaring her shoulders, she glared at him. "Is there a problem, Mr. Adams?"

"Fuck, yeah! I mean… yes, *Becky Jean.*" He emphasized her

name, infusing as much civility as possible into his cold-as-steel voice. Two could play this dignified business game. "There *is* a problem. There isn't enough money in all the company accounts *combined* to meet this week's payroll. I want to know where it went."

All the blood drained out of her face, and she reached for the doorframe again. Her hand missed, but her shoulder caught, preventing her from falling. Ford rushed to her side. Wrapping an arm around her waist, he guided her to one of the green leather visitor's chairs. Hoping his father hadn't broken with Adams's family tradition, he scooted around the desk and opened the bottom left drawer. Seconds later, he pushed a tumbler of Tennessee's finest into Becky Jean's palm. "Here, drink this."

He held the glass steady while she sipped at the amber liquid. Making a face like she'd sucked a lemon, she pushed the glass away.

"Yeck!" She wiped her lips with the back of her hand. "What is that?"

"Whiskey." He finished the two fingers with one swallow and rose to refill the glass—which he downed before returning to sit on the edge of the desk, with yet another two fingers of courage. Ford sipped at his third glass of whiskey, letting the first two work through his system while he studied the woman in front of him. Her eyes looked lost, but at least the color had returned to her cheeks. If she'd known about the company's financial troubles, she did a hell of job playing innocent. Which made his father a better actor than he'd given him credit for. In their weekly conversations, the man had given nothing away concerning the dire financial situation.

"What the hell has been going on around here?" He congratulated himself on sounding close to reasonable—thanks to the alcohol dulling the sharp knife of betrayal.

"I don't know." She seemed fascinated with her hands twisting in her lap. "Is it that bad?"

"Yes. It's that bad." No wonder his father had a fatal heart attack. Ford was about to have a coronary himself. "What happened to the cash flow? From what I can tell, Dad has been dipping into his personal accounts to keep this place running for quite some time." Which meant his mother didn't have a penny to her name. *Shit.*

Becky Jean turned her face up to his. Even her misery didn't dim her beauty. "I swear I didn't know. Mr. Adams — your father — insisted on doing the books himself."

"But the factory is still churning out product, shipping out orders. Or did I miss something in the production schedules?"

"We are shipping orders. Not as many as we did a few years ago, but we have clients."

"How many clients?"

"One."

"One?" Yep. He'd follow his father into an early grave. "What happened to the others? Adams Manufacturing used to be the leading supplier, worldwide, of baby bottle nipples."

She shook her head. "We've been losing market share for a few years. With the movement toward breastfeeding, people aren't buying as many baby bottles as they used to."

Any other time, he would have enjoyed watching her face flame at the mention of breastfeeding, but his present situation had trampled his libido into submission. "What about the agricultural market? Aren't people still milking cows?" For as long as he could remember, their largest contracts had been for the teat cup liners used in milking machines. Not glamorous, but it paid the bills.

"It's China's fault."

"China?"

"We can't compete with their prices. Dairy farmers are just like everyone else. They don't care where the product comes from as long as they save a buck."

Shit. "The agricultural market was the cash cow, so to speak."

"Yes. Farmland Supply didn't renew their contract this year, not for any of the products we supplied them."

He mentally ticked off the products he remembered—teat cup liners, rubber gloves, bottles, and nipples for hand-feeding orphaned and sick livestock and zoo animals. They'd supplied the large farm retailer with those and more for as long as Ford could remember. "So what *are* we producing?"

"Baby bottles and nipples, and not nearly as many of those as we used to."

"China?"

She nodded. "Yep. Your father hired an independent lab to analyze the Chinese products, see what they're made of. He was hoping to launch an advertising campaign to undermine consumer confidence in their products and shift the public back to products made here in the U.S."

It was something, but without the agricultural component, Adams Manufacturing was doomed to fail. "Whose idea was that? The lab thing?"

"Mine." She sighed. She'd appeared sad at his father's graveside. Now, she looked defeated. "It was too little, too late, wasn't it?"

"Yep." He finished off the rest of his drink, savoring the smooth burn making its way down. He stood, circled around to his father's chair, and sank into it. From the moment he'd comprehended the scope of the problem, he'd known what he had to do. He forced himself to say the words. "I'll float the payroll out of my own pocket until I can figure out what to do with the— What's left."

"You're going to close the plant." Her voice held resignation rather than surprise.

He stared into the bottom of the empty glass then set it carefully in the center of the desk. Raising one eyebrow, he asked, "What choice do I have?"

"I don't know. It's just so many people depend on their jobs here. The whole town depends on Adams Manufacturing. This is going to hurt so many people." She made it sound as if he'd said he planned to kick every puppy in town and drown all the kittens, too.

"I don't want to, but unless you can come up with a way to keep this place running, and to turn a profit then I don't see I have any choice. It's already bled my father, and his widow, dry." Visions of his mother moving into his spare bedroom formed in his head. *Good God.* "If I let it, it'll do the same to me. I don't see what the difference is between closing in a few weeks and closing a few months down the road when I run out of money, too."

She brightened. "You've got enough money to keep the plant open?"

"Hold on a minute." He held his hand up in stop-right-there signal. "I've worked damn hard for my money, and I'm not going to throw it down a dry well and hope it turns into water. I'll contact the few remaining clients we have and negotiate final production numbers to get us out of our contracts. Once we fulfill those orders, we'll shut down for good."

She deflated, but at least she didn't look like she might faint this time.

"I have to think about my mother, Becky Jean. I've got to salvage whatever I can of all this" — he swept his arm out to indicate the business — "for her." He had to be careful or they'd both be wearing paper hats and flipping burgers before the year ended.

"What about the employees? The people who work here don't do it because it's the most fun they've ever had. They do it because they have families to feed."

"I'm not a puppy kicker, Becky Jean!" Fuck, he was back to shouting. He cleared his throat and tried again. "If I could see a way to make this place turn a profit, I'd do everything in my power to keep it open."

"No, you wouldn't." She straightened her spine. "You had every intention of selling this place, or closing it down when you came here. Don't even try to deny it. I'm not stupid. You were looking for an excuse, and you found one." She stood, her outrage making her seem taller, and, damn his libido, sexy as hell. "Go ahead. Shut the plant down. Put all these hardworking people out of a job. This town is hanging on by a thread anyway. The Adams family built Butte Plains. It's only fitting an Adams be the one to cut the last thread."

Pausing in the doorway, she drew her shoulders back and, lifting her chin, delivered her parting shot with the precision of a sniper. "You'll find a pair of scissors in the center drawer."

He jerked the drawer open, found the scissors—a big, sturdy pair, at least a century old. Holding them aloft, he worked the handles, enjoying the metallic rasp of the blades sliding against each other. "Snip snip," he said loud enough to carry to the next office. She answered with a disgusted groan, followed by a door slammed shut.

Dropping the weapon of mass destruction to the desktop, he buried his face in his hands. He'd never seen a more alluring sight than Becky Jean with her panties in a wad. He'd be wise to keep an eye on sharp objects when she was around, but the probability of her doing him bodily harm didn't keep him from imagining all her passion channeled into more pleasant activities.

This is so not the time, ole buddy. Once again forcing his thoughts away from Becky Jean and the way her shapely ass looked as she'd beat a hasty retreat, he made a mental note of all the things he had to accomplish before he could close the doors on Adams Manufacturing and get back to his life.

Grabbing his suit coat off the back of the chair, he called out as he passed the office manager's closed door, "I'm going to the bank. I'll be back." With a little luck, his father had another account not listed on the company computer system. Maybe he'd set up a trust for his wife, or invested funds in something. Maybe he had a safety-deposit box full of cash. Stranger things had happened.

CHAPTER THREE

You're positive?" he asked the stout man who'd been his father's banker for decades. "There are no hidden assets?"

"No, son. I'm sorry. I argued with your father many times over the last few years regarding his use of personal funds to keep the plant running, but he was adamant the place needed to stay open."

Why? Ford couldn't begin to follow his father's train of thought—beggaring himself so the few remaining employees could keep their jobs.

"I refused to lend him money, hoping he'd come to his senses and close the place down, but he was determined to forge ahead. Said he was working on the problem and it was only a matter of time before he had what he needed to turn the place around."

The lab reports on the Chinese products. Too little, way too late. "He had a plan, but I'm afraid it wasn't much of one."

"I'm truly sorry, Ford. Your father was the best of men." He shook his head. "He was my friend as well as my client. This town is going to miss him."

Ford fought the tears threatening to fall and cleared his throat. "That's very kind of you to say." He stood on weak legs and extended his hand across the solid oak desk. "Thank you for taking the time to see me today, Mr. Wheeler."

They shook hands. "If there's anything I can do for you...?"

Ford paused at the office door. "Lend me a few million?" he asked with a smirk.

"Anything but that," the banker said.

So much for hidden assets. The extent of Ken Adams's savings appeared to be the jar on the corner of his dresser where he deposited whatever change he found in his trouser pocket at the end of the day. Rough estimate — ten dollars, minus the fee the bank would charge to count and roll it.

Retracing his steps back to the factory, three blocks south then four blocks east, Ford paid little attention to the businesses he passed along the way. His stomach rumbled, reminding him he'd missed lunch and he'd had no appetite for breakfast. Thinking to grab a sandwich at Marge's Diner, he stood on the sidewalk, stunned, looking in the window at the vacant interior. The establishment had been a fixture in Butte Plains dating back to his grandfather's days. Seeing it gutted, the familiar lunch counter and Formica tabletops gone, shook him almost as much as finding out his parents were on the brink of bankruptcy.

Turning from the disturbing carcass of a once-thriving business, he glanced up and down the block. Many of the stores he'd taken for granted as a kid were empty shells. With most of the shops closed, the place began to look like a ghost town.

What the hell happened?

Forgetting everything except his empty stomach for a minute, he made a left instead of a right, hoping to find another of his favorite eating establishments still in business. He almost jumped for joy when he spied the neon *Open* sign in the window of the Hanson's Bakery. His mouth watered for one of Mrs. Hanson's ham-and-cheese croissants. As he pushed the door open, his stomach growled again. Perhaps he'd have two of the delicacies.

Mrs. Hanson smiled at him from behind the ancient counter. Nothing had changed here, which he immediately recognized as part of the town's problem. People were drawn to new and shiny, not outdated and dull, no matter how good the food.

"Ford," the older woman said, her sympathy grinding against his last nerve. "I'm so sorry about your father. He was a good man."

"The best," he answered automatically. Hoping to change the subject, he pointed to the top shelf in the display case. "Can I get two of the ham and cheese, and a soda? To go." He could eat and walk at the same time.

She grabbed a square of waxed paper and reached into the display case. "I couldn't make it to the funeral — didn't have anyone to mind the shop. I sent some pastries up to the house, though."

"Thank you," he said.

"Mr. Hanson passed three years back, and our Bobby and his family moved to Dallas. I'm thinking of closing up and moving, too. I miss my grandkids something awful."

Bobby graduated a year behind Ford, as he recalled. "Why'd Bobby move?"

"Not much need for electricians around here." Mrs. Hanson talked while she bagged his food. "He got a degree in electrical engineering and went to work for Matthews Electric." Ford recognized the name. They operated out of a big warehouse about a mile from Adams Manufacturing.

Pausing with her hand in the cooler, she asked, "Regular or diet?"

"Diet."

"He looked for work around here after Matthews closed, but —"

"Matthews Electric closed?" They'd been the second-largest employer in Butte Plains in their day.

"Been nearly two years, I guess." She pushed buttons on the ancient cash register. "A lot of people left town, looking for work. 'Course your father took on as many as he could, but he didn't have much use for electricians and such."

That explained the heavy payroll numbers he'd noticed a few years back in the records. The numbers had evened out as, he supposed, most of those people found other jobs or moved away.

Like Bobby Hanson. "Are those turkey and cheese?" he asked, pointing at the display again.

"Yes, and I've got one pepperoni left."

"Give me one of the turkey ones, too. And another diet soda." Talk of his failing company reminded him Becky Jean had arrived shortly after he had, which meant she probably hadn't had lunch either. If she didn't want a croissant pocket, he'd eat it himself.

Butte Plains had always seemed so stable. Staid and dull, but stable. He'd never thought of it declining the way it obviously had. There wasn't a damn thing he could do to turn it around, but the idea of the idyllic, yeah, it had been a great place to grow up, town disappearing made him sad. It must be doubly hard for someone who lived here to watch it happen.

He knocked on Becky Jean's office door, trying the handle before she had a chance to answer. Pissed off as she'd been, at least she hadn't locked him out. Stepping inside, he took it as a good sign she didn't attack him with a letter opener. Instead, she turned hopeful eyes his way. He set a firm look on his face and shook his head. "No go. No hidden accounts. No safety-deposit box full of cash." He held up the bakery bag. "However, Mrs. Hanson had some stuffed croissants left. Ham or turkey?"

She pushed some papers to the side. "Turkey."

He tossed one of the parchment wrapped delicacies her way, unwrapping the other for himself. "Diet okay?" He set a bottle on her desk blotter. "Did you know Matthews Electric went out of business?"

"Uh-huh," she said around a mouthful of pastry. "Along with Roma's Pizza, the skating rink, the bowling alley, and the Majestic."

"Shit. The Majestic?" He'd taken his first date there to see *The Matrix*. The outing had been his first and only date with Katelyn Roberts. The girl had zero appreciation for good films.

"Among others. Those are the ones I can think of off the top of my head." They ate in silence for a while. "Remember Herschel's Appliances on Main?" she asked.

Ford nodded. "Closed?" he asked, though he already knew the answer. He'd seen the empty retail space earlier.

"Walter Construction?" She took a bite of her stuffed croissant. "Closed?"

Becky Jean took a sip from her soft drink then swallowed. "Yep. You remember Scooter's Plumbing, don't you? They had those trucks with the cartoon characters on them?"

"They're closed, too?" *Fuck.* "What hasn't closed? That might be a shorter list."

"Hanson's Bakery is still open." She glanced at the grease-stained bag on her desk with the familiar logo printed on it.

"I hate to tell you, but she's thinking about closing. Wants to move closer to Bobby. Apparently, he has a wife and kids now. Did you know about that?"

"He married Chrissy Matthews."

His eyebrows rose. "Didn't her dad own Matthews Electric?"

"Yep. Didn't make any difference. There wasn't enough business around these parts to keep the doors open, so he was left without a job, just like everyone else." She wadded up her empty wrapper and tossed it in the bag. "I'm sorry to hear about Hanson's. I'm going to miss that place."

"Me, too." What was he saying? Unless she closed up in the next few weeks, he wouldn't be around to miss the woman's tasty concoctions.

Becky Jean finished off her soda, collected all their trash, and tucked it into the wastebasket behind her desk. She rocked back in her chair with a sigh. "So, what's next?"

"Damn if I know." He leaned forward, resting his elbows on his knees. "I can't think right now. I arranged to move enough funds out of my personal savings to cover this week's payroll. Tomorrow, I'll call my wealth manager and see about converting some investments into cash. I'll need to see all the accounts receivable and a summary of what we owe—taxes, utilities— anything else you can think of."

"You look beat. Why don't you go home, try to get some rest?"

He stood and made his way to the door. He couldn't ever remember being this tired. "See you tomorrow?"

"I come in at eight."

Noticing he'd left the lights on in his father's office, he reached for the switch. "Damn. Forgot to turn off the computer." Visions of an electric bill he couldn't pay danced before his eyes. He'd just powered down the system when he glanced up to see Becky Jean standing in the doorway.

"I didn't see your car out front when I came in. How did you get here?"

"Walked." Christ. Why did she have to be so damn beautiful? He caught himself looking at her left hand. No ring. No husband. No fiancé. *Not my business.* Which reminded him he needed to call Ronnie and tell her he wouldn't be back in time for the museum opening she had her heart set on attending. Maybe Scott would accompany her. He made a mental note to ask his best friend if he could fill in for him.

"Come on. I'll give you a ride."

He vaguely remembered she lived on the opposite side of town from his parents. "It's out of your way. I can walk."

She headed toward the front of the building. He followed, admiring the way her ass swayed from side to side with each step she took. "Nope. Remember the Wilsons? They moved to Florida. I rent their house."

He knew the house she spoke of. It sat at the base of the hill his parent's house occupied. "They moved to Florida? When did this happen?"

"About the time you graduated from college, I guess. Bobby Hanson rented it for a while."

"Then he lost his job and moved to Dallas."

"Yep. I moved in when the Hanson's moved out."

For a town that never seemed to change, it seemed everything had changed. With opened eyes, he noticed what he hadn't seen before. Businesses boarded up, weed-covered parking lots, broken out windows, and *For Sale* signs in front of empty houses were like pickets on an ancient fence—close together and falling down.

"I'm staying in the gatehouse," he said as the car wound up the long drive.

"Why?"

He glanced at the woman driving. "Seemed like a good idea at the time. Besides, I brought work along." Or he hoped he had. The 3D printer he'd had shipped should have been delivered today. He'd planned to use the time away from the office to work on some ideas of his own. With everything going on, he doubted he'd have time. Getting his mother out of the financial pit she didn't know she was in would take all his time in the foreseeable future.

"What kind of work do you do?"

"I design things for people."

"What kind of things?" She stopped in front of the gatehouse, put the car in park, and turned to face him.

"People come up with ideas, things they want to build but don't have a clue how to go about it, or don't have the resources to create a prototype. I work with them, take their concepts, and turn them into reality." He liked what he did—he'd actually made a shit-ton of money at his job. But it kept him so busy he rarely had time to do what he wanted—to develop ideas of his own. A few days with nothing to do but help his mother put her life in order and sift through offers to purchase the company had sounded perfect.

"You can make a living doing that?"

He smiled. "I've made more than a living at it. Lots of times, inventors don't have capital to pay upfront for my services, so I take a percentage of sales once the product goes to market. If the item sells well, it can be extremely lucrative."

"Wow. I went into the wrong line of work."

"Office managers don't usually bring down the big bucks." She certainly hadn't. He'd noted her salary in the payroll records.

She shrugged. "My degree is in marketing, but my dad got sick and had to leave his job. So when I graduated, I stayed home to help out. Your father promoted me from line supervisor to office manager. The boost in salary allowed me to help my parents. I've been there ever since."

"How's your dad?"

Her shoulders sank, and he knew before she said the words. She'd lost her father, too.

"He passed away last year. His life insurance paid off the house. Mom still has her part-time job at the nursing home. It's enough for her to live on."

"I'm so sorry."

"It gets easier," she said, though her body language said she was lying through her teeth.

He tried to recall her parents, but if he'd ever met them.… Not a single memory surfaced. "I doubt that," he said, turning to look out the passenger-side window. A large cardboard box sat on the front step—the perfect excuse to end what had become an awkward conversation. "Looks like my package arrived." He reached for the door handle. "Thanks for the ride."

"Not a problem." She cranked the engine before he had both feet on the ground.

"See you in the morning," he said as he closed the door. She made a neat three-point turn and disappeared around the curve in the drive. He made a mental note to stay away from the subject of her father's passing. There had to be a story there, he was sure of it, but he had enough problems of his own to solve without borrowing more.

After lugging the printer into the house, he placed a call to his office in New York. Scott's disappointment rang through the line when Ford informed him he needed to stay in Texas for a month or more. Fortunately, his friend understood obligation to family and agreed to take his sister to the museum opening in Ford's place.

Ronnie had been less pleased to hear his news than her brother. Who would escort her here or there? Fuck if he knew. He had *real* problems to deal with. Ford didn't tell either of the siblings the extent of his financial troubles. Scott would have understood, but Ronnie wouldn't. He often wondered how the two could be related. Scott had no intention of relying on his trust funds for the rest of his life. He had talent and drive, where his sister simply… didn't. Scott possessed enough tact not to ask questions, and Ronnie appeared too busy worrying about her social calendar to think to ask him why. Soon, the whole world would know why he'd stayed in Texas, but he hoped by then he'd have better news to impart.

The thought of the big, old building his great-grandfather had built no longer bearing the Adams's name hit him hard. The feeling didn't make any sense. He'd known all along he wouldn't keep the company. Selling would be ideal, but that option no longer existed. He might be able to unload some of the machinery once they closed. He made a mental note to check into the possibility in the next few days. Maybe there was some kind of auction house he could contact to handle the sale for him. If not, the scrap value of the metal inside the plant had to be considerable. He could keep a few of the employees on to dismantle the equipment.

He added *call salvage yards* to his mental to-do list. Surely, someone would haul the scrap off for a cut of the value. *Then* he could put the buildings up for sale, but given the number of empty storefronts in Butte Plains, his kids, if he ever had any, would still be paying taxes on the property long after he'd departed the planet. He made another mental note to see what the taxes actually were, and if he could get them reduced once the place fell into disuse.

Before turning in for the night, he called his mom. He knew he'd been a shitty son, leaving her to deal with the swarm of mourners on her own, but of the two of them, his mother had the social skills to handle the situation. The daughter of one of the wealthiest families in the county, she'd been born to play hostess to throngs of people. She fussed over him, worrying as usual about her only child instead of focusing on herself then informed him she and her sister Florence would be fine alone in the house overnight.

He wished her good night then slipped into bed.

Instantly, an image of Becky Jean Parker flashed into his brain. He'd made the mistake of mentally undressing her earlier, and the image refused to go away. Every time he closed his eyes, he saw her shapely body on display. Physically, the two couldn't be more different. Ronnie liked to tell people her tall, lean form and small breasts attributed to her runner's body, even though her idea of running meant hurrying to grab the last barstool in a crowded restaurant.

Ford considered himself something of an artist. He created drawings and models in his mind and on paper then turned them into sculptures. Useful sculptures, but the point remained, his brain saw what his eyes couldn't. He didn't need to see Becky Jean undressed, his brain calculated the information his eyes collected and translated it into an image he knew would be pretty damn close to the actual thing.

Given the proportions of the image, his body couldn't help but respond. He'd have to be dead not to react to large breasts, a trim waist, and a heart-shaped ass. God, how he'd love to get his hands on her ass. His palms itched to feel her soft, pliant skin beneath his hands. He'd take his time, committing the details to memory then he'd part her— *Shit!*

He could not be thinking about what he wanted to do to Becky Jean's ass. He had other things he should be thinking about, like figuring out how to tell his mother she couldn't afford the luxuries she took for granted.

Helen Ford had come from money and married into money. The Ford family fortune had taken an unfortunate turn back in the 80s when her father and brothers had sunk, literally, everything they had into an offshore drilling rig. A good portion of their money, in the form of twisted metal, constituted a man-made reef at the bottom of the Gulf of Mexico. It had become quite the attraction in recent years for the scuba diving set. What money hadn't sunk with the drilling platform had gone to clean up the oil spill, and to settle the resulting lawsuits. Only Ford's trust fund, set up by his grandparents years ago, had escaped untouched. If it weren't for the tax issues involved, he'd sign it over to his mother. The interest on the principle had paid his college tuition and given him a start in life, but he'd never relied on the money for his day-to-day living. Shortly after graduation, he and his roommate established their own business. In less than a year, he made enough to live on. The following year, he requested the interest on the principle be put back into the account instead of being paid out to him.

He'd managed to accumulate considerable wealth on his own. He didn't need his trust fund. He made another mental note to ask his wealth manager about the possibility of transferring the trust to his mother. But that would have to wait until the factory had been dealt with. No way would he let hungry creditors have access to his trust fund if he could help it. Nope. It would be just fine, right where it was.

CHAPTER FOUR

Becky had always wanted a house with a porch, and now she had three outdoor living areas to choose from. The house she rented might not be the prettiest residence in Butte Plains, but it suited her perfectly. The wraparound porch began in the front, traversed the south side of the house, ending on the east side outside of the kitchen. She enjoyed nothing more than watching her backyard come alive each morning while she sipped her first cup of coffee. The birds and squirrels going about their business usually held her attention, but not today.

She'd had a difficult time getting to sleep the night before, and when she'd finally succeeded, her dreams had bordered on nightmares. Her life was changing, and once again, she had no choice in the matter. She'd had no alternative but to help her parents and younger brother get through her father's illness. The decision had been the right one at the time. Staying in Butte Plains after her father passed away had been easier than trying to start over. Too much time had passed since her college graduation to try for a job in her chosen profession — or so she told herself. Colin had graduated from high school and announced he wouldn't be going to college. He'd packed his guitar and a duffel bag of clothes and hopped the first bus to Nashville, where he'd achieved his dream of being a musician, and more. He'd written a couple of hit songs for other artists and sang lead for a band that was building momentum daily.

She didn't begrudge him his success, but on days like today, she wished fate and circumstances hadn't taken her choices away from her. If not for her father's illness, she might have found a job in a big city, become something more than office manager for a failing company. Becky faced the harsh reality.

In a few months, she would be out of a job, and nothing remained for her in Butte Plains. Her mom would be fine, but if she wanted, she could move, too. She wouldn't have any trouble finding a job in a nursing home in a big city.

What will I do? Office managers are a dime a dozen in big cities.

I could look for a job in marketing.

Yeah, and start at the bottom with all the kids with their shiny new degrees and probably a couple of summer internships under their belt.

As much as she wanted to blame Ford for her predicament, she couldn't. He'd done what she had wanted to do—he'd made a life for himself outside of Butte Plains, and she understood why he would want to get back to it. Maybe if the factory had been in good financial shape, she could have talked him into letting her run the place, but, under the present circumstances, he had no choice but to shut down. If she were in his shoes, she'd do the same thing. But understanding the situation didn't stop her from wishing for a way to keep the place open. She would survive, even if it meant moving to a big city, but concern plagued her about the other employees.

Manufacturing jobs were drying up across the country as businesses outsourced production to China and Mexico. Most of their workers had lived in Butte Plains all their lives. They had extended families to consider, too. She couldn't help but think about the head of their shipping department, Todd Carver. His elderly mother lived with him, and she knew for a fact his neighbors helped keep an eye on her while he worked. Moving would be a major upheaval for Todd and his mother.

The more she thought about it, the more determined she

became to convince Ford to keep the plant open as long as possible. There had to be some way.

Practicing her impassioned plea in her head, she wished the birds pecking at the birdfeeder a good day and went inside to get dressed.

~~~

Her new boss pulled into the parking lot as Becky got out of her car. She chalked his punctuality up to his desire to put Butte Plains in his rearview mirror as soon as possible. Waiting beside her car for him to join her, she thought about the man who had starred in her dreams last night. Sometimes he'd been the sexy seducer, making her body sing, then he'd be the monster raining terror on her quiet little world.

If she were to draw the man of her dreams, he'd be Ford Adams. She'd always been drawn to tall, dark, testosterone-overloaded men. If he had an ounce of compassion in his bones for his new employees, she might consider acting on her attraction, but he didn't, so she wouldn't. Then there was the part about him being her boss. She'd checked for a wedding ring, and his father would have mentioned his son becoming engaged. So, unless he had a girlfriend back home….

The expiration date on their professional relationship couldn't have been stamped in more indelible ink, so there wouldn't be any *real* harm in sleeping with him. It wasn't like he could promote her from unemployed to employed. Only her scruples stood in the way of a fling with the sexiest man in Butte Plains.

She didn't do flings. She'd had a brief relationship with a guy she'd met in the library her sophomore year of college. The chemistry between them had been off the charts, but David had been immature, skipping classes in order to party. He'd flunked out of school the spring semester and moved home to Colorado. Last she'd heard, he'd become a ski instructor at one of the smaller
~~~

resorts in the winter, living off his parents the rest of the year.

Her scruples were there for a reason—to protect her from doing stupid things.

Damn scruples.

"Good morning." She shaded her eyes from the morning sun with a hand to her brow.

"I don't know what's good about it."

She opened her mouth to say it was a good day because she'd woken up on this side of the grass—an old joke her grandfather on her mother's side had been fond of—but thought better of it before the words passed her lips.

Unlocking the door, she ushered Ford in ahead of her. She punched in the alarm code then flicked on the overhead lights. "Someone's grumpy this morning." He had a right to be. He'd buried his father yesterday, and today he had to begin the steps to shut down the business his ancestors had built. Nothing to be happy about in either of those things.

"Didn't sleep well." He stalked off in the direction of his new office.

His grumbled remark gave her the opening she'd been hoping for. She caught up with him as he sat down at his desk. "Did you come up with any ideas to keep the plant open? You know, a lot of good people are going to lose their livelihoods. Families are going to suffer. People are going to have to move to find other employment. Kids are going to have to change schools. And—"

"Forty years of darkness! Earthquakes! Volcanos! The dead rising from the grave! Human sacrifice, dogs and cats living together… mass hysteria!" He powered up the computer while he ranted. "I get it, Becky Jean. I really do, but I'm fresh out of ideas."

She shook with the need to pummel him. How dare he make fun of the situation? She clenched her fists at her sides and unclenched her jaw. "I can't believe you're quoting *Ghostbusters*! You might think this is all a joke, Mr. I've-got-plenty-of-money, but I can assure you, the people who depend on their jobs here will *not* think closing the plant is funny."

Slamming her office door didn't bring the satisfaction she'd anticipated. Becky crumpled into her desk chair and lowered her forehead to her arms folded on the desktop. She didn't know what came over her, but when he'd begun quoting from one of her favorite movies, applying a scene she'd always thought hilarious to the present situation, she'd lost it. Every bit of civility she possessed flew right out the window.

So, so stupid.

She revisited the last few minutes, wondering how she could have prevented the scene from happening. Things had started out on an even keel. A pleasant good morning from her. A not-so-welcoming reply from him, making his mood apparent.

She'd goaded him. Poked the bear, and the beast had lashed out.

Great. Just great.

She owed Ford an apology. Just, not yet. Her outburst couldn't have improved his mood, and it hadn't improved hers, so waiting awhile—a year or so—would be a good idea. Give them both time to cool off.

~~~

Ford stared at the empty doorway. His ears still rang from her tirade, and his brain remained fixated on the image of her ass, walking out the door.

"Down, boy," he cautioned his cock. "Can't have her."

He'd lain awake most of the night, contemplating his next moves, trying to come up with another solution to his problem besides shutting down operation of the factory. After finally drifting off to sleep in the wee hours of the morning, he'd dreamed of making love to Becky Jean and woken with a boner he'd had no choice but to take care of in the only way available to him.
~~~

He hated to start the day jacking off, but the hand job and a cold shower made it possible for him to function. He'd been celibate too long, and he'd had a thing for Becky Jean in high school, even if had only lasted a day or two.

Well, a week. It had taken him a week to shift his lust to Cindy Price. She'd offered to give him a hand job behind the castle on the seventh green at Put Around Mini-golf. He'd taken her up on the offer and escorted her to prom in payment. They'd called it even after getting it on in the backseat of the limo on the way home. Last he'd heard, Cindy had gone to junior college in the next county and married some cowboy she'd met when the rodeo came to town.

Ford shook his head to clear it. He owed Becky Jean an apology. He'd let yesterday's revelations overwhelm him, and in so doing, he'd forgotten how this would affect her. No matter what happened, he had a job to go back to, but she wouldn't. She'd thought highly of his father, her tears at the funeral were proof enough, and even though her job was just as temporary as everyone else's, she seemed more worried about the other employees than about herself. She had a college degree, and she seemed reliable enough. She'd find employment somewhere. Most likely she'd have to leave Butte Plains. She'd blame him, but hell, none of this was his fault.

He'd do the best he could for her, and for all of them. But he wouldn't make promises he couldn't keep.

He picked up the phone, intending to call the office next door to remind Becky of the reports he needed. When his door opened and she stepped inside carrying an armload of folders, he set the receiver back in its cradle. "Ms. Parker."

"Mr. Adams." She placed the folders on his desk and stepped back. "I'm sorry. I was out of line earlier." Backing toward the door, she continued, "Those are the reports you wanted. They're on the server, but I thought you might need them printed out for… the bank?"

He offered her a weak smile, accepting her apology and her

peace offering. "Thank you." He thumbed through the stack, opening the one marked Accounts Payable. "This will be very helpful."

"I don't know what this month's utilities will be, but I included copies of our bills for the last three months to give you an idea."

"Becky. I owe you an apology, too. Quoting a silly comedy, under the present circumstances, wasn't appropriate. My only excuse is I'm under a lot of stress. The words just came out. I'm sorry."

"It was my fault. I pushed your buttons. I understand you're focused on the immediate need to shut down, but I wanted you to see the broad picture, too. I was insensitive. You're dealing with the loss of your father—now, all this."

"We're both under a lot of stress. This can't be easy on you, either. I appreciate your concern for the workers, and believe me, if I could do anything to prevent this from happening, I would." He shook his head. "I lay awake last night trying to come up with options."

"Nothing?"

"Nope. Not a thing."

Becky Jean bit her bottom lip, and her eyes glistened with unshed tears. *Fuck.* Time to get her out of there before he did something stupid like try to console her. Recalling the dream he'd had once he'd fallen asleep last night, touching her wouldn't be a good idea, not even to offer comfort. He cleared his throat. "Thank you for these." He tapped the stack of folders. "I'll look them over before I have to leave."

She nodded again. "The reading of the will at two o'clock?"

"Yes. How did you know?" He'd gotten a phone call this morning from his father's attorney notifying him of the reading.

"Mr. Trumble called a few minutes ago. He said I should be there."

"Why?" He couldn't imagine why she'd be invited. Wills were private, to be shared only with the interested parties.

"He didn't say, and I was too shocked to ask. Maybe it has something to do with the running of the company. It's the only thing I could think of."

Ford shrugged. "Could be. And since you're the office manager...." He didn't believe her excuse for a second. A cold sliver of unease slid along his spine.

She shifted her feet, her gaze landing everywhere but on him. "Umm." She bit her lip again, and a sudden and unwanted urge to taste her lips hit him. Ford mentally pushed the thought away.

"Something else, Becky Jean?"

"Yes, sir. Everyone else is here — all the office staff."

He sat back. He knew exactly what she wanted. Nothing good could come of telling the employees how temporary their jobs were. "There's no need in stirring the hornet's nest just yet, do you think? Let's keep this to ourselves until we have a plan — a day or two at most. No use in everyone panicking before we have something concrete to tell them."

"You're right, of course. A couple of days won't make any difference in the grand scheme of things."

"My thoughts, exactly." Only a day or two could make all the difference — he should know. Look at all that had happened to him in the last few days. He'd gone from a successful businessman in his own right to a puppy kicker and dream destroyer in the blink of an eye.

Becky Jean backed out of his office. He braced for another slammed door. Hearing nothing, he relaxed. If he planned to get this thing done, he needed her on his side, or at least not fighting him.

CHAPTER FIVE

Ford saw his mother off with a kiss to her tear-stained cheek. Aunt Florence would see her safely home. They all needed time to process what had just occurred in Mr. Trumble's office. He couldn't imagine what his father had been thinking when he'd drafted his will, but he damn sure needed to find out. Turning to his car and the woman waiting next to it, he clenched his jaw to prevent making rash statements he'd hear repeated back in court proceedings later on. Who was Becky Jean Parker to his father? Ken Adams wouldn't have done what he'd done for just anybody. Several possibilities ran through his head—none of them acceptable or fathomable. His father wasn't that kind of man. He just wasn't.

Calling on his best manners, he held the passenger door while Becky Jean slid into the passenger seat. She remained quiet on the ride across town, giving him time to run through his options. The will stipulated the factory had to remain operating for one year before it could be sold. They'd need money to make payroll, purchase supplies, pay utilities and taxes. He had some savings, but not enough to last an entire year unless they scaled staff and production back to the barest minimum. The will hadn't said anything about what capacity the factory had to run—just that it had to run.

Becky Jean would be pissed about laying off employees, but unless she paid the extra wages herself then the cuts would be made. The way things stood, her salary would be coming out of his pocket which, in his mind, meant she had zero say in who he fired in order to keep her ass out of bankruptcy. Which brought him back to how he was going to come up with the necessary funds.

If push came to shove, he could sell his house in New York. Since he'd restored the historic home, he'd been approached more than once with offers. He'd bought it because it reminded him of the house he'd grown up in, only in need of repair. Half a million dollars later, the property had turned into a showplace. Letting go of it would hurt, but he could always buy another house. Thoughts of selling brought him around to the house in Butte Plains he owned 50 percent of—the one his mother lived in. He couldn't sell it out from under her, but he could mortgage it. He'd have to tell his mother the precarious nature of her financial situation in order to get her signature on a mortgage, but it might not come to that. For the moment, he'd prefer to keep her out of the loop. Mired in grief, he didn't need to distress her more with things she couldn't do anything about. There had to be another way. He'd start with trying to find a way to turn a profit.

"When we get back, get me a sample of every item we currently have in production, and every item we have produced in the past… say ten years. No. Make it twenty-five years."

"What for?"

"We have to keep the factory operating for the next twelve months. In order to do that, we need to turn a profit, even if it's only a dollar. Maybe if I see what we've got to offer, I can come up with a way to make us profitable." He nearly bit his tongue off on the word *us*, but until a court decided differently, he had to include Becky Jean in the equation.

"Tell what's her name in receivables to get on the phone. We need to collect every outstanding invoice owed us. Start with the most recent and work back from there."

"Her name is Angela."

He'd met the rest of the office workers before he and Becky Jean left for the reading of the will but couldn't remember their names. "Doesn't matter what her name is. What matters is cash flow. We need income. Anything over six months old, tell her to discount it by 10 percent if they pay in the next ten days."

"Okay."

"Thanks to Dad draining every account he had, our payables are in decent shape. We can't afford to piss off our suppliers. No supplies equals no production. No production equals no income."

"I get it."

He ignored her snide remark. He didn't have time to soothe hurt feelings, not if he meant to prevent this Titanic from sinking and taking them all down with it. "Just get me those product samples, ASAP."

"Yes, Your Highness."

Ford braked hard at the stop sign, taking his anger at her snippy tone out on the brake pedal. Eyes focused straight ahead, he unclenched his jaw enough to speak. "Unless you have come up with a way to get us out of this mess then I'd appreciate you not getting your panties in a wad over the direction I'm taking. At least I'm doing something." He might be high-handed, but he didn't see he had any other choice but to take charge. He let up on the brake then applied slow, steady pressure to the accelerator pedal when he'd much rather smash it to the floor and drive until Butte Plains, Adams Manufacturing, and Texas disappeared in his rearview mirror, becoming nothing but an unpleasant memory.

Becky shifted in her seat. Her heated gaze seared like the West Texas sun on an August day. "You make it sound like I'm not doing anything," she huffed. "I've done everything you asked so far, haven't I? And, in case it hasn't occurred to you, I can't afford for this company to go under. It was one thing to lose my job when it closed. As part owner, if it closes now, I'll lose everything. I'll do whatever it takes to keep the place running for the next year. I don't see as I have any choice."

No, she didn't, and neither did he. They were partners in this mess until a court decided otherwise, and the legal process could easily take more than the year they needed to stay in business. Like it or not, he needed her help for the next twelve months.

"Glad to hear you're onboard." He actually liked the way she'd found her spine. He'd been worried about her—the quiet, devastated woman she'd become following the bombshell bequeath wasn't the Becky Jean he'd come to know. "Do we have a marketing person?"

The shift in the conversation caught her off guard. She faced forward again, though the vacant look from before had vanished. "No. I've sort of been doing the job—what little there is to do."

"Congratulations, Ms. Parker. You've just been promoted to marketing director. I'd give you a raise if I could."

"But…. I…. What?" She huffed out a breath, and her pale cheeks colored.

How would her other cheeks look with a bit of color? *Don't go there, Ford. She's your business partner. Remember the lawsuit she's likely going to file. A sexual harassment complaint won't help you any.*

"We have to sell our product. Since we can't lower our prices to compete with foreign manufacturing, we're going to have to come up with a marketing plan to convince retailers and consumers our product is worth paying more for."

"We haven't gotten any results back from the lab we hired to analyze the foreign-made products."

"Cancel the lab report. See if we can get a partial refund. We'll—*you'll*—have to think of something else to convince people to buy our product."

He pulled into the parking lot and followed Becky Jean inside. At the reception desk, she went straight ahead instead of turning down the hall to their offices.

"Where are you going?" he called out.

"To the factory floor. You want product samples, I'm going to get you pr—" As she opened the heavy steel door, noise from the production line nearly drowned out her last words.

He spun his key ring around his index finger then pocketed his keys and headed toward his office. The contrast of her soft curves surrounded by the industrial machinery shouldn't be so intriguing, but it seemed everything about Becky Jean Parker intrigued him.

~~~

Becky grabbed a sound-muffling headset off the rack by the door and put it on. She'd welcome the din of machinery in motion, but drowning out the racket going on in her head wasn't worth losing her hearing over. She'd have to find another way to silence the turmoil of the last few days.

On the heels of the shock of her boss's sudden death came grief and the stress of being at the helm of Adams Manufacturing until his son arrived to take over. Seeing Ford again after all these years had been another shock. He'd been good-looking—in a geeky sort of way—in high school, but man, oh man, had he changed! The last decade had been good to him in a way it hadn't been with most of their classmates. Riding in the car with him had been a mistake. There had been no escaping his scent in the confines of the sporty rental. Not even the smell of melting rubber and heated plastic on the factory floor could drive the memory of his woodsy, all-male scent from her nostrils. Lord, she'd wanted to strip naked and rub herself all over him. Still wanted to. Damn it all to hell.

Then, to top it off—Kenneth Adams had left her half of his half of Adams Manufacturing! Heaven only knew what Mrs. Adams thought. And Ford. Did they think something had gone on between her and the late Mr. Adams? By the way the lawyer had looked at her when he read the part of the will pertaining to her, he'd certainly thought so. Neither Ford nor his mother had said anything, but they must have been thinking it. Hell, she'd be thinking it if it were anyone besides her in this position.

She had to find a way to assure them she hadn't been carrying on an affair with Kenneth Adams. He'd been kind to her, for sure,
~~~

but he'd never… and she'd never….

No. She wouldn't go down that road. It was just too weird to think about. Ken Adams had been like a father to her, giving her a job when she needed one, never once asking for anything but a solid day's work from her. She'd loved him, but not for the reasons his lawyer seemed to think.

Touched beyond belief Mr. Adams had thought to include her in his will, she couldn't credit the position she currently found herself in. Part owner of Adams Manufacturing. An equal partner with Ford Adams. Well, a minority partner given he controlled his mother's 50 percent, too. Once again, her life had taken a path she hadn't chosen for herself.

One year. Twelve long months before they could sell or close the business. Which meant they had to keep it running, because God knew, her share of the business's debts far outweighed her personal assets. She had to do everything possible to keep the factory going, and, at the moment, that meant hitching her wagon to Ford's, no matter which direction he decided to head.

She grabbed an empty box from shipping then made her way through the warehouse, dropping one of each style product into the box. Waving to the dozen-or-so people hard at work, she made her way to the front offices. After replacing the hearing protection back on the rack, she stood for a minute, welcoming the sound of normality before opening the door and stepping back into the chaos her life had become.

At the sound of Ford's voice, heavy with frustration, Becky halted short of his office. "Can we talk about this later?" A short pause. "Because I'm busy."

Torn between wanting to drop the box of products he'd requested over his head and not wanting to pry into his personal life, she faltered in the hallway then headed toward her own office.

"You think I want to stay here for a year? Fuck, Ronnie. You know me better than that."

Becky stopped cold. *Ronny? Who the heck…?*

"Listen, I really am busy. The sooner I get this figured out, the sooner I can come home." He'd lowered his voice so, giving up all pretense of not eavesdropping, Becky leaned closer to hear his next words. "Yeah, yeah, I know. I'll call tonight, and we'll talk about it then."

Ford's gay? What the hell? It would certainly explain why he'd chosen to live so far away from where he'd grown up. She imagined it would be easier to start over someplace new than to explain to the people he'd grown up with. There were some narrow-minded people in Butte Plains, but they were the minority. Still, she could see where it would be easier to live an alternative lifestyle as little fish in a big pond instead of a big tuna in a goldfish bowl.

Her arms ached, reminding her of the reason she stood outside his office to begin with. In light of her new knowledge, the thoughts she'd been having in regards to Ford's hotness seemed ridiculous. He was taken—and gay. She laughed at the old cliché? All the good ones were either taken or gay. Just her luck. Not that she had ever had a chance with the man—or wanted a chance with him. Boyfriend in New York or not, Ford would be leaving as soon as possible. In the meantime, they had to find a way to keep Adams Manufacturing running for the next year.

Fear gripped her gut, and she leaned against the wall, willing the pain in her belly to go away. Ford and his mother would sustain huge losses over the next twelve months if the factory didn't show a profit, but she would lose everything. And like it or not, and unless she found a way to decline her inheritance, she had little choice but to help Ford turn the company around.

After taking a few deep, calming breaths, Becky straightened her shoulders and stepped forward.

CHAPTER SIX

"Here."

Ford sat back while Becky Jean placed their current and past products in a line across the front of his desk. She was pissed, still or again, he didn't know which. Did it matter? Not one little bit, he decided. It didn't even matter if she was pissed at him or her situation or both. She could stand in line with everyone else in his life wanting to tear a strip of hide off him. Neither Scott nor Veronica had taken his news well. They both wanted him back in New York. He could handle all his obligations to his east coast business from Texas, but, for the next year, Ronnie would be on her own, socially. Her brother would do his duty as escort for the most important events, but Scott didn't enjoy the social whirl the way his sister did.

He didn't want to think about what Ronnie would do without him there for the next year. A beautiful woman, she had a need for others to prove it to her on a regular basis. They'd never agreed to be exclusive — not that he cared if she slept around. It would take a stronger man than he to keep Veronica in line. He wasn't up to the job, and he knew it.

Fuck. He had needs, too. The next twelve months would be hell — in more ways than one. Forcing his attention back to the woman in his office, he studied her. Her movements were jerky —

telegraphing her anger—yet the emotion looked good on her. Her cheeks bloomed with color, and her eyes sparked with fire.

She had passion best channeled into something besides anger. He knew what he'd like to channel it into, but since he had no intention of bedding her, he'd settle for getting her ass in gear to keep him, and his mother, from bankruptcy. He didn't want to admit it, but he couldn't do it alone. He needed Becky Jean's help. But before they went any further, they needed to talk about something else. He'd seen the look on the lawyer's face, knew deep down what the man had been thinking. He should have called him out on it, but without knowing absolutely for sure….

He leaned forward, got down on eye level with the assortment of baby bottles, nipples, and flashlights. "What happened to the flashlight business? Everyone needs a flashlight."

"Can't you guess?"

"China?"

Placing a hand to her chest, she sighed dramatically. "I feel so much better knowing my business partner is such a genius." Tossing the empty box into the corner of his office, her glare dared him to make something of her smart remark.

He reminded himself she had plenty of reason to be angry and let it go.

"Anything else?" she snapped.

"Nope. Just the things we talked about in the car."

"You mean the things you ordered me to do? *Those* things?"

Studying the array of basic items lined up on his desk, he nodded. "Yes, those things. The sooner we implement our plan, the better."

"You mean the less of your own money you'll have to put into the company."

"I could demand you put in 25 percent, but since you don't have it…. Or am I mistaken?" If she were a cartoon, there'd be a thundercloud hanging over her head. The blush of anger on her cheeks grew to an inferno. His question may have been a low blow, but he could go lower. He *would* go lower. She stepped back from his desk. "One more thing before you go."

"What?" She practically vibrated with anger.

He dove low, went in for the kill. "Were you sleeping with my father?"

The blood drained from her face, and, for a second, he thought he might have to leap over the desk to catch her before she hit her head against the chair standing between her and the floor. Coiled to move, he relaxed when she pinched her lips tight, straightened her shoulders, and torpedoed him. "Fuck you, Ford Adams."

Turning on her heel, Becky Jean strutted out of his office, her perfect heart-shaped ass swaying like a sailboat on rough seas.

Bang!

The pictures on his wall shook. If she kept slamming her office door, he'd have to call someone in to reinforce the door and the walls of his office.

Well, there's your answer. She hadn't been his father's mistress — not that he ever really believed his dad would cheat on his mom — but others would think it. Did think it. He'd make a point to set Mr. Trumble straight the next time he saw him, and, as soon as he could, he'd find a new lawyer. One who knew what the word discretion meant.

With the image of Becky Jean's ass burned on his retinas, Ford turned his attention back to the products on his desk. They were all serviceable and essential to different segments of the population at various times. Demand for the items certainly hadn't dropped. As far as he knew, babies were still being born, human, bovine, and otherwise. Breastfeeding craze aside, water and juice didn't come from breasts, so mothers were still buying and using bottles and rubber nipples.

He picked up one of the bottles, turned it over. Nothing on the bottom. Everything made outside the U.S. had to be stamped with the country of origin. He remembered a while back a big movement to buy products stamped *Made in America*. It wasn't much, but they could capitalize on the trend. Maybe even get a mention on the morning talk show behind the story. He made a note on the legal pad at his elbow to see about having the label added to the bottles and their packaging. His new marketing director could put some feelers out to the news networks, see if they could run a story. He smiled, realizing he'd just added public relations to Becky Jean's new duties. She'd fume about the added work, but she'd do it.

Imagining her tuning up to rip him a new one had him hard as a post. Again. He glanced up from his notes, and his gaze landed on the giant nipples designed for hand-feeding livestock. His gaze traveled down the line to the teat liners for milking machines.

A chill chased up his spine. He grabbed both items, studying them with new interest. "Huh." He slipped the teat liner over the giant-sized nipple then set his creation on the desk. Maybe he'd been approaching this from the wrong angle. Instead of trying to push the products they already had, maybe they should consider a *new* product. Something nearly everyone he knew had at least one of.

People were still having babies. Which meant they were having sex. And everyone knows, *sex sells.*

He reached for his legal pad, ripped off the top sheet of notes, wadded it into a ball, and tossed it toward the empty box in the corner. Opening the center drawer, he pushed aside the scissors earmarked for cutting the last thread holding Butte Plains together, and found the set of drafting pencils his father always had at hand.

When he finally looked up from his drawing, he realized how quiet the office had become. The low hum and rumble from the machinery had ceased. He strained his ears for the sound of voices in the other offices. Nothing. He glanced at his watch, noting the late hour. Everyone would be gone, and he should be, too. He'd promised to visit with his mother this evening, and since he'd been scarce ever since the funeral, he needed to fulfill his promise to her.

Grabbing his suit coat, he shoved his inspiration into one of the pockets then picked up the pad containing his sketches. He'd have plenty of time later tonight to transfer his drawings to his laptop. And, if he had any luck, he'd get to try out his new 3-D printer this evening. They'd need a prototype in order to make an injection mold for the new product.

He shut off the lights in his office and headed out. A thin band of light showed beneath Becky Jean's door. He tapped lightly then turned the knob.

"You still here?"

Becky glanced up at the man filling her doorway. It had taken most of the afternoon for her to calm down, but seeing him standing there smiling at her as if he hadn't accused her of having loose morals a few hours ago, brought the anger back to the surface. "Apparently," she said through gritted teeth.

"Look, I'm sorry about earlier. You had to know I would ask. And just for the record, I never, not even for a second, thought you and my dad…. Well, he wouldn't have, and, in the little time I've known you, I'd come to the conclusion you wouldn't have either."

"You insulted me, and your father, Ford. I don't know which made me angrier."

"Both, I hope. Once word gets out about his will, others are going to think it."

The blood drained to her toes again, leaving her light-headed. She dropped her forehead to the desk, silently begging the room to stop spinning.

"Becky Jean. Are you okay?" Ford's big hand rubbed a circle on her back. Jiminy, his touch shouldn't feel as good as it did.

"I'm fine." She managed to sit up. He removed his hand and sat on the corner of her desk as if he owned it. "Your mother doesn't think…?"

His eyebrows knit then relaxed. "No. I'm sure she doesn't. She and my dad were always thick as thieves. Admittedly, I haven't been around much in the last ten years, but I'm sure nothing changed. They always had a marriage I envied. A love like theirs doesn't come around often."

"I couldn't bear it if your mother thought—" She shook her head. "The others don't matter."

"They matter to me." The words were spoken so softly, she couldn't be sure she heard right. Before she could ask him to repeat them, he bounded off her desk and headed to the door. He stopped and turned to her. A big smile on his face, he looked like a kid who'd just found a stash of cookies.

"What?" she couldn't help but ask.

"I've got an idea. It could be something big."

His excitement reeled her in. She wiggled in her seat, anticipation chasing away all other thoughts. "Well? What is it?"

"Can't tell you yet. I will. Soon. Gotta Go."

Becky stared at the empty doorway. How dare he dangle hope in her face then leave her hanging? Grabbing the nearest item on her desk, she held her stapler aloft, poised to throw it through the door. When his head then his body filled the space, she sighed and put the missile down.

"Hey? Do you cook?"

"Y-yes. A little. I'm no Julia Child, but I can boil water." She narrowed her eyes. "Why?"

"'Cause I need to eat. If you'll cook tonight, maybe I'll let you see what I'm working on later. Deal?"

She tried to picture Ford in her little kitchen, sitting at the table she'd found at the Methodist Church thrift store, and just couldn't do it. "You want to come to my place for dinner?" she squeaked.

"No. You come to mine. Bring food. I don't think there's much in the fridge. Anything will do. I'm not picky. See you in say, an hour?"

"Um." If there could be anything worse than him being in her kitchen—it had to be her in his.

"Good. Great!"

Once again, Becky Jean stared at the vacant doorway in disbelief. What had she just agreed to? "Don't forget to turn the lights off when you leave," Ford shouted from the end of the hall.

Becky raised her middle finger. "Fuck you, Ford Adams."

She would need to wash her mouth out with soap if this kept up. She'd used the F word twice today *and* made an obscene gesture. Neither was her style, yet she couldn't really regret either transgression. They'd fit the situation, which went to prove how different her circumstances were today from all the previous days of her life.

~~~

Elbows on the granite countertop at the Adams's gatehouse, Becky stuffed a forkful of spaghetti in her mouth and chewed. Since her arrival, she'd exchanged less than a dozen words with Ford. He seemed to be in geek heaven, typing on his laptop computer, muttering under his breath, and occasionally letting go with some choice curse words. She'd fixed a simple meal of spaghetti and meatballs with a salad and garlic bread then proceeded to eat by herself.

She swallowed then spun her fork in the long noodles again. "Are you going to eat? You know, I could have stayed at home and done the same thing."

Ford turned his intense gaze on her. "A few more minutes, Becky Jean. I've almost got it."

"Got what? Are you going to tell me what this is all about?"

"In a minute. Trust me, Becky Jean, this is good. Stupendous. Best idea I've had in ages." He returned his gaze to the computer. Having no clue as to the quality of his previous ideas, she had nothing to judge this one by—provided he ever got around to sharing it with her.

Becky took another bite then washed it down with a sip of some very good wine she'd found in the wine rack above the sink. When she'd asked Ford about opening it, he'd answered with a grunt, never even looking up. Surely no one would leave a special
~~~

bottle of wine in a rarely used gatehouse. But, what did she know of rich people's habits?

Shrugging, she refilled her glass. It turned out to be damn good wine and shouldn't go to waste.

"Voila!"

At Ford's triumphant shout, Becky nearly jumped out of her skin. "Geez, Ford. Give a girl some warning. I almost spilled my wine."

"Pour me a glass, will ya? I'll be right there."

She reached for the glass she'd set out for him over an hour ago. "Are you going to tell me what's going on?"

He had moved to the kitchen table where he'd set up a 3-D printer. "Soon, Becks. Real soon." He slid a memory card into a slot on the printer. With his index finger poised in midair over a red button, he smiled at her. "Here goes nothing!"

As soon as he punched the button, the printer whirred to life. Fascinated, Becky watched as the machine spit droplets of black goo onto a small platform. She'd heard about 3-D printing technology, but she'd never seen it in action. "What are you making?"

He admired his creation in the making for a few seconds then joined her at the eat-in bar. Nodding at her almost-empty plate, he asked, "Any left for me?"

She obviously wasn't going to get any answers until Ford decided to give them, so she filled a plate and slid it in front of him. He dove in, eating like a starved man. While he ate, she kept her eye on the object slowly taking shape across the room. Like playing *Wheel of Fortune*, she needed more clues before guessing. After a few minutes, Ford slowed to a normal pace.

"We've been looking at this all wrong, Becks."

"How do you mean?"

He sipped from his wine glass then set it down. "We've been trying to figure out how to make a profit by selling products we already have."

"We can hardly make a profit selling things we don't have," she pointed out.

"True enough. But I'm talking about new products. Something we can retool for at a minimum cost and be ready to ship in less than two weeks' time."

"What makes you think we can sell this mystery product and make a profit?"

"Ah hah!" He stabbed his pointer finger toward the ceiling. "Not we." He turned his index finger toward her. "*You*. You're our new marketing director. You're going to sell it. Leave the profit making to me."

The fine hair on the back of her neck stood up. If he'd been sure she would go along with this, he would have come right out and told her his idea instead of being so secretive. She glanced at the printer. The object remained unidentifiable. "What, exactly, do you think I'm going to sell?"

CHAPTER SEVEN

"The first-ever, lock-in-place butt plug!"

Her insides turned to ice while, inexplicably, heat infused her skin. She didn't need a mirror to know her face had turned tomato red. Her gaze automatically went to the printer dripping plastic droplets onto an ever-growing pile. Could the item really be…? She had no idea. She'd read about their use in a few steamy romance novels, but she had no firsthand knowledge of the devices.

"You can't be serious." Needing to steady her nerves before she went ballistic on her business partner, she reached for her wine, brought the cool glass to her lips, and drained it.

"I'm dead serious, Becks. It won't take much to retool one of the machines to make them. We'll keep packaging to a minimum — a plastic bag with a cardboard header. We'll earmark the first five hundred as free samples, which you'll send out, worldwide, to wholesale adult toy distributors. I tell you, this will work. People will buy this product."

"Are you insane? First, this is Butte Plains. If we start making… those *things*" — she nodded toward the printer — "all our employees will quit. Second, I don't know anything about the adult toy industry. I wouldn't know where to start if — and that's a very big *if* — I were to agree to your ridiculous plan and we could convince our people to produce the… things."

"First," he mimicked her not-quite-business-like shrieking voice, "our employees will make what we tell them to make if they want to keep their jobs. If they quit, then what is the unemployment rate in Butte Plains? Ten? Fifteen percent? We'll replace them. Second, you're a smart woman. I'm sure you've heard of the Internet. It shouldn't take you more than a few hours to acquaint yourself with the major adult toy wholesalers."

She barely heard what he said after he called her smart, but evidently, her subconscious had been listening. She caught up quickly. "Even if we could accomplish a miracle turnover, do people buy those *things*?"

"The adult toy industry is huge, Becks."

"I wouldn't know." She forced her thoughts away from the cute pink vibrator she kept in her nightstand for those times when she needed release in order to remain sane. Ford might be right about sex selling, but she'd never in a million years let him in on how lonely she'd been since returning to Butte Plains. Some things a girl had to keep to herself.

"Trust me, sex sells."

"Even if it does, what makes you think your… *item* will sell?"

"Mine locks in place. It's a huge improvement over anything on the market today." He got up and crossed to where the printer put the finishing touches on his creation. "There will be some assembly required before packaging. I've already contacted Scott about the locking mechanisms. He designed one a couple of years ago for a project that never went anywhere. He's willing to let us use it for a few pennies royalty on each unit sold. He's sending me a case of them by special messenger to try out. They'll be here tomorrow."

"Who's Scott?"

"My best friend and business partner. He's an incredible designer in his own right. Luckiest day of my life was the day we were assigned as roommates at MIT."

"Oh." Did Ronny know about Ford's relationship with Scott?

Maybe they had a three-way going on or something. *Not my business.*

Becky gathered the dirty dishes and put them in the sink. Leaning back against the counter, she gazed at her insane business partner's back. He had one thing right—they needed to do something different, but did they have to dive ass first into the adult toy manufacturing business? Turning, she rinsed the dishes and put everything into the dishwasher. When she spun back around, Ford stood in front of the table, his new creation in his hand.

"It doesn't look any different on the outside. The locking mechanism will be what separates it from the run-of-the-mill variety." He flipped the item over, examining it from every angle.

"I just don't see it working, Ford."

"Have you ever used a butt plug?"

Heat rose to her cheeks. "No. I've never even seen one."

"You through there?" He nodded toward the kitchen prep area.

"Yeah. Why?"

He set the plug on the counter. "Come on. It's time for us to take a field trip."

"Where are we going?" she asked, sinking into the soft leather seats of his luxury rental car.

"Don't ask."

"I don't like this, Ford." She reached for the door handle.

"Okay, okay." Before she could bolt from the car, he cranked the engine and drove down the driveway. "There's an adult store out on the Interstate. I saw it when I drove in from the airport."

She knew the place—by sight only. "You can't be serious."

"I wish you'd quit saying that. I'm dead serious, Becks. I appreciate what you and my dad were trying to do, but the fact is we need to change course, and fast. We're headed straight for the iceberg. If we hit it, we're all going down. You, me, my mother, all our employees."

He painted a grim picture, but, in truth, she'd seen the same one hanging on the wall. But there had to be another way.

"If you've got a better idea, this is the time to speak up."

Damn him for being logical. "No. Sadly, I don't have any idea at all, much less a better one."

"Then give me the benefit of the doubt here, Becks." He pulled into the blessedly empty parking lot and cut the engine. "There are thousands of these stores across the country. They're springing up in malls and respectable neighborhoods, too. Many are women-owned businesses. You should like that."

"Impressive." *Not.*

"Come on. Let's go inside."

"No."

"Come on, Becks. Consider this your first class in Marketing to the Adult Toy Industry 101."

She rolled her eyes at him. "What if someone sees us? What will they think?"

"I hope you do see someone you know. It will help convince you normal people are buying this stuff. As for what they'll think… well, I suspect they'd wish they could help you with whatever it is you're buying tonight."

"I'm not buying anything."

"Just wait until you see what they have to offer. You might change your mind."

"I hate you."

"No, you don't."

"Yes, I do." She reached for the door handle. "I'm going to go inside, but only so I can gather enough information to point out the errors in your plan."

Ford placed his hand on the small of her back and guided her through the aisles toward the back of the store where a flashing neon sign said *Anal Play.*

"It's okay to look around, Becks."

"I don't want to look around."

"Sure you do. This is the kind of place you can't *not* look around. It's like an old-time carnival—filled with oddities you're drawn to even though you know you shouldn't be."

Damn. Why did he have to be right all the time? She'd already spotted several things she wouldn't mind taking a closer look at, but Hell would freeze over before she'd admit being curious. "Let's just do what we came to do and get out of here."

"Sure you don't want to look around?"

"Positive."

They stopped in front of a wall display covered with butt plugs of every size and color imaginable.

"They're identical to the one you just printed." *Except for that one. And that one.*

"Yes, they are." At the sound of Ford's voice, she tore her gaze away from the one with electrical wires attached. He took one down for closer examination.

He held it up, end first. "See? Where this one is solid on the end, mine has a hole in it. The locking mechanism will go right there."

She scanned the wall. "None of these have locks?"

"Nope. A design flaw I'm going to correct."

"Seems to me, if a lock was such a good idea, someone else would have come up with one. And, have you considered there could be a reason none of these have locks?"

"Like what?" He took a large pink one down.

"Like, it's a bad idea, for reasons I can't even begin to think of."

He turned his gaze to her and smiled. Something inside her flared to life. She took a step back. *He has a boyfriend. He has a boyfriend.* Maybe if she reminded herself enough times she'd believe it.

"You've never tried to keep one of these things in, have you?"

No. "Have you?" God, she did not want to go there, not with Ford.

His smile turned to a smirk. "I plead the fifth. But I can see I need to convince you of the superiority of my product." He reached for a shopping basket from the stack of them in the corner.

"You'll need something small at first." He dropped a package containing a slim, pink plug in the basket.

"Ford!"

Two more, in successively larger sizes landed in the basket. "Look, Becky Jean, if you don't believe the product is the best on the market, you won't be able to convince the buyers to give it a try. This is Market Research 101 — know the competition."

Damn. Why did he have to be right? Again. "I didn't say I would market this thing."

"You will. Once you try it, you'll see." He tossed in two more styles then headed off down another aisle. Becky followed, cringing when he stopped at the section containing personal lubricants. She pretended not to read the labels while he searched the shelves. Eventually, he picked two different ones and added them to his shopping basket. "One more thing," he said, moving off again.

He stopped in front of a rack near the checkout counter. "Cleaner," he said, tossing a large bottle with a pump-style lid into the basket. "Anything you want to look at while we're here?"

"Absolutely not," she lied. She eyed an interesting display of vibrators nearby. While Ford paid, making small talk with the cashier, she pretended not to look at the various battery-operated boyfriends. She'd ordered hers years ago from an online retailer, but she wouldn't mind having one of these new high-tech ones.

"All set," he said, coming up behind her and putting his hand on the same spot it had been before. Heat radiated off his palm to the small of her back. The gesture felt intimate, and so good she almost forgot to be mad at him.

He ushered her to the car and opened the passenger door for her. She climbed into the seat, relieved to have gotten in and out of the store without being seen. As Ford went around the back of the car to get to the driver's side, another car pulled into a parking space a few over on his side. Becky sank as low as possible and thanked the universe for poorly lit parking lots. To be on the safe side, she turned her face away and hid behind her hand.

Hurry. Hurry. Hurry. The sooner they got out of there, the better.

"Hey, Mr. Boggs. Nice to see you again." Ford's voice pierced the car door.

Crap! Mr. Boggs had been the principal at the high school forever. Everyone in town knew him, and he knew everyone. Thank Heaven she'd made it to the car before he drove up!

"Good to see you, too. How's your mother doing?"

"She's holding up. Thanks for asking."

"Sad thing, your father going so young. We're all praying for you, and your family, son."

"Thank you, sir."

"Gotta hurry," Mr. Boggs said. "It's our anniversary this weekend. Gonna pick up something special." His voice got closer as he approached Ford's car parked directly in front of the entrance to the Adult Emporium.

"How many years have you been married?"

"Twenty years since Sharon said, 'I do.' Gotta keep things fresh, you know? Well, of course you know. You're here, aren't you?"

"My regards to Mrs. Boggs, sir."

The driver's side door opened. Ford slid into the seat and tossed the shopping bag into her lap. "Coast is clear. You can sit up."

"Did he see me? Do you think he knows?"

"No, he didn't see you, unless he has X-ray vision, and what, exactly, would he know?"

Once they'd cleared the parking area, she sat up and fastened her seat belt. "Not funny," she said, tossing the bag to the backseat.

"Look, he didn't see you, and he has no idea what I had in my bag." He chuckled. "I bet Mrs. Boggs is going to have a mighty fine anniversary. Don't you?"

"I have no idea."

"You do realize they have sex, don't you? They have three kids. Or is it four?"

"Five."

"You don't say? How old is the youngest?"

"Two."

Ford's laughter filled the car.

No longer in danger of being discovered, she could see humor in the situation. "Okay, so they've had sex."

"At least five times in twenty years," Ford added, helpfully.

"Okay. You win. People have sex, and some of them buy… toys. But I'm still not convinced this thing of yours will sell."

"You'll sell it, Becks." He parked at the curb in front of her house and reached in the backseat. He plunked the heavy shopping bag into her lap. "Try the smallest one first. See how long you can keep it in doing normal stuff."

Nothing she could say would sway him, so she changed the subject. "My car is at your place."

"I'll pick you up in the morning. No use both of us taking our cars to work since we live so close."

He had a point. Besides, as long as he paid for the gas, why should she argue? She opened the door and prepared to step out. "What time?"

"Seven thirty okay? We can pick up breakfast at Hanson's and you can fill me in on how your market research is going."

"I'm not going to try these." She clutched the bag in her hand as she got out. "See you in the morning."

Before the door closed, Ford said, "Lube, Becks. Lots of lube!"

~~~

If he'd ever thought about what Alice must have looked like when she hit the bottom of the rabbit hole, he now knew. The expression on Becky Jean's face when she stepped inside the Adult Emporium had been comical. She appeared ready to turn and try
~~~

to claw her way back out. Only his hand on the small of her back kept her from doing so.

Oh, and her expression following his conversation with Mr. Boggs? *Priceless.* Becky Jean riled so easily, and damn, if pushing her buttons hadn't been the most fun he'd had in years.

At the gatehouse, he set his prototype on the dresser in the bedroom while he undressed and showered. As he passed by later on his way to bed, he picked it up. He'd made it a good size. Not small, but far from being the biggest on the market. Silicone would make it light and pliable, adding to the comfort while allowing the stretch needed for the locking arms to work properly. It would be easy enough to make it in a variety of sizes, even one small enough for a beginner.

An image popped into his head of Becky Jean wearing his invention. He didn't have anyone else in Butte Plains he could trust to test the prototype, so she'd be the first to try it out. He imagined turning the key, locking the plug in place then examining the device to make sure it seated properly. God, he wanted to help Becky Jean with the plug, and more, but he couldn't. Maintaining a professional relationship had to be a priority. He'd get Adams Manufacturing back on its feet, then they could sell it. He'd go back to his life, and Becky Jean would move on. If they made something of this new product, perhaps her 25 percent would amount to enough to set her up in a new life away from Butte Plains.

Thinking about Becky Jean dating — getting naked — with some guy made Ford grind his teeth. For Christ's sake, she'd never used a butt plug! What did she know of the world and the perverts inhabiting it? She needed someone to lead the way, show her the delights to be experienced without destroying her moral compass. It couldn't be him, though, so he'd best put those thoughts out of his head.

He admired her loyalty to the employees and to the town as a whole. The success of his recovery plan depended on her sense of responsibility and her desire to help the people she cared about.

She would do her best to market his invention, but in order to do so, she had to understand how revolutionary it was.

When he'd stopped by to see his mother earlier, she'd given him his dad's phone, and he'd transferred the contacts he'd deemed essential over to his own. He'd made sure to transfer Becky Jean's first. Picking up his phone from the nightstand, he searched out her number and made the call. It rang several times before she answered, sounding breathless.

"I hope nothing slipped out when you ran to catch the phone," he said, easing into his favorite tease-Becky-Jean mode.

"What do you want?" she asked, her tone indicating she hadn't forgiven him for taking her to the sex-toy shop.

"I wanted to see if you needed any help with your market research."

"I'm doing just fine without your help."

He smiled at the admission she let slip.

"I told you I wouldn't try the… products, and I'm not."

He swallowed the laugh bubbling up. He'd let her have her little deception. "You're not, huh? Do you think it's too difficult to insert them on your own? Because, if you do, I stand ready to assist. All you have to do is ask."

CHAPTER EIGHT

Becky slid gingerly into the passenger seat of Ford's fancy car, acknowledging his chipper greeting with a grunt. Their shopping adventure the previous evening, plus her embarrassing experience with a few of the items they'd purchased made him the last person she wanted to see.

"I need my car back." Somehow, knowing she had the means to put distance between them whenever the mood struck mattered a lot this morning.

"You can pick it up this evening."

She didn't expect him to be so agreeable. After he'd called last night while she'd been trying out the smallest of the items he'd purchased, and having little success keeping it in place, she figured he'd be hammering her with questions this morning. The fact was, he hadn't made her uncomfortable.

"What's wrong?"

"Nothing's wrong."

"Something is. I thought you'd want to know the results of my market research, but you haven't even asked."

"Nothing is wrong. You hung up on me last night, so I thought it best to drop the subject."

"You don't want to know if I tried one of them or not?"

"I know you tried at least one. You know as well as I do, in order to judge our product against the competition, you are going to have to try all of them. You *could* ask someone else for their opinion, but I don't see you running around town asking people to fill out a survey in regards to their experiences with butt plugs."

That he knew her so well didn't make her any happier. "You know darn well I'm not going to survey anybody. For your information, I tried some of the competitors' products, and you were right, they don't function as well as one would expect them to."

"How are you going to sell butt plugs when you refuse to say it?"

"You still have to prove to me you have a superior product. Until then, there's nothing to sell."

"Point taken." He parked then walked around to open her door. "I printed two more last night." He held up a plastic grocery bag. "As soon as I get the shipment of locking mechanisms, I can show you how this is going to work."

Unlocking the front door, she entered with Ford on her heels. She disengaged the alarm and followed him down the hallway to their offices. He paused before entering his. "The locking mechanisms will be here today. In the meantime, I'm going to get Owens in the machine shop working on a mold. The sooner we turn out a complete unit, the better."

"I suppose so." She still wasn't sold on the idea of a new product, especially given the nature of the item Ford had come up with. "I'm going to see how Angela is doing with the receivables then go over our outstanding bills with Carla to see if we can prioritize the bills. Maybe we can delay paying some of them. If need-be, I can call some of the creditors, explain about Mr. Adam's death. It could buy us a little time. We've paid well in the past, so we have that going for us."

"You could check out wholesalers, too. I'd like to see a list of places we can approach to carry our new product. The sooner we get it in their online catalogs, the better."

She might just get through this crazy partnership if they kept things on a professional level. "I'll see what I can do."

Sometime later, Ford popped his head in her office door. "Come on! There's someone I want you to meet."

He hurried off before she could question him. Shaking her head, she glanced at the clock on the corner of her desk. She'd been working steady for over three hours.

"Break time," she mumbled, pushing away from the desk. Raised masculine voices floated down the hall, drawing her out of her office.

Ford and another man she didn't recognize stood in reception, beaming at one another like loons. She hung back, watching the obvious reunion. Who was this man? She knew everyone in town, and if he'd attended Butte Plains High School, she would recognize him. He appeared to be Ford's exact opposite. He was blond where Ford had dark hair. His skin had the flawless quality of a Norse god where Ford's skin leaned more toward golden sunset. Her partner dressed to the nines—suit and tie every day—where the newcomer wore aged denim and a NY Giants T-shirt. Equal in height to Ford, the man was undeniably handsome, but she had no trouble tearing her gaze away from him.

In the week since Ford's return to his hometown, he'd had little to smile about. Seeing his face transformed in genuine pleasure damn near took her breath away. His eyes sparkled with life, and the laugh lines bracketing his mouth made her knees weak.

"Ah, man, it's good to see you."

"You, too," the god replied. "Ronnie said to tell you to get your ass back, ASAP."

Ford's smile dimmed. "I'll be back when I can, you both know that."

"Yeah, we know."

"I miss my life there." As if he willed the sad thoughts away, his smile returned. He clapped the newcomer on the shoulder. "I'm damn glad to see you, though."

Stepping forward, Becky cleared her throat.

"Becky Jean!" Arm around his friend's shoulders, her partner turned to her. "Look who I found!"

The Giants fan punched Ford's midsection. "Who found who? I'm the one who flew halfway across the country to see what the hell is taking you so long."

Becky squirmed under his appreciative gaze.

"And now I know."

He separated himself from Ford and approached, hand outstretched. "I'm Scott Ramsey, and you must be Becky Jean."

Ford's business partner. Not what she expected, though she couldn't say exactly *what* she'd thought the man would be like. He was too pretty and in too good a mood to hold his scrutiny of her body against him. She took his hand. "Nice to meet you. You're the partner I've heard so much about?"

"He's been talking about me?"

"Truthfully?" She raised one eyebrow.

"By all means. Tell me what this reprobate has been saying." He glanced over his shoulder.

Leaning against the reception desk, arms crossed, Ford smirked.

"Well, he's hardly mentioned you."

The newcomer laughed. "I knew it! Out of sight, out of mind." He leaned in and placed a kiss on Becky's cheek. "It's a pleasure to meet you, Becky. We've heard a lot about you."

"We?"

"Me and my sister, Veronica — Ronnie. Ford told us all about you, but I see he left out the part about you being gorgeous." He glanced over his shoulder at her new partner, who shrugged off the criticism.

Ronnie. Not Ronny. A woman.

"Enough." Ford straightened. "Did you bring the locks?"

So much for giving the newcomer the third degree. She had no business prying into Ford's personal life anyway. She'd learned all she needed to know—Ford was taken. Did it make any difference his significant other turned out to be a woman instead of a man as she'd incorrectly assumed? It shouldn't, but it did. Whatever fledgling thoughts she'd had about her sexy new partner were inappropriate in more ways than one.

"I did." Scott motioned to a box on the corner of the reception desk. "Decided to bring them myself instead of trusting them to an overnight carrier."

Ford scooped the box into his arms. "You didn't have to go to the trouble, but I'm glad you did. Come on. Let me show you what I'm working on." He led Scott toward the factory floor. "I'm dying to see if this works."

The roar of machinery filled the air as the two men disappeared through the door like two little boys with a new toy, leaving Becky behind shaking her head.

"Are there more like him in New York?"

Becky startled at the other woman's voice. She'd all but forgotten about the girl seated behind the high desk. "You mean, Mr. Ramsey?"

Carolyn had been manning the front desk at Adams Manufacturing during the day and taking night classes at the county community college since she graduated from high school three years ago. Lord knew what she would do if she lost her job. Becky Jean's gaze lingered on the door the two men had disappeared through and sent up a silent prayer Ford's idea would work.

"Holy cow, Ms. Parker. He's gorgeous."

Becky wasn't at all surprised by the receptionist's remark. Other than Ford coming home, this Ramsey fellow had to be the first fresh bait to swim in the Butte Plains pool in forever. The sharks would be circling him in no time. Innocent little Carolyn didn't stand a chance.

Becky resisted the urge to roll her eyes. Yeah, the man was good-looking, but his Scandinavian genes had nothing on Ford's

Texan ancestry. "Wipe the drool off your chin and finish up the time-sheet logs, will you?" Becky turned back toward her office.

"Sure thing."

She did roll her eyes at the exaggerated sigh the girl let out. *Geez.*

When Ford appeared in her doorway, she glanced at the clock, surprised to see she'd worked through lunch and most of the afternoon. "Did you need something?"

He stepped inside and shut the door. "I have something for you." He set a butt plug on her desk then stepped back. "Ta da! The first-ever, lock-in-place butt plug!"

Up until the moment he set the lump of molded plastic on her desk, she'd been in a state of denial about the new direction he wanted to take the company, but with the evidence front and center, those days were over. She pasted a smile on her face. "Wow! You work fast."

"Not me. Owens is a genius. The man can make anything, I tell you. I gave him the prototype first thing this morning, and voila! Here's the finished product." Pete Owens kept the machinery running, sometimes by miraculous methods. He either deserved a raise, or to be drawn and quartered. She didn't know which.

Becky stared at the obelisk. She hadn't given its size much thought when she'd seen his prototype, but she'd never worn one, either. With the experience behind her, she viewed Ford's new invention with trepidation. "I didn't remember it being so large."

"It isn't as big as some of the ones we bought last night."

True enough, but she hadn't tried any of the larger ones. She'd been uncomfortable enough with the ones she had tried, and since they all appeared to be constructed in much the same way, she saw no point in trying the others. "I'm not putting that thing inside my body."

"Yes, you are." He picked it up, turning it so she could see the protruding end of the device. "Let me show you how it works."

"No need. I'm not going to test it for you."

He'd produced a small key from his pocket and inserted it in the lock embedded in the base. "Once it's fully seated, just turn the key." He continued to talk, completely ignoring her protests. "This lock Scott designed is genius, and this is the perfect application for it. See the way the arms on the lock expand outward creating a shelf-like effect?" He made a ring with his thumb and index finger, encircling the smallest part. Becky shuddered, imagining the thing inside her.

"Once the lock is engaged, the only way to remove the device is with the key." He inserted the key again and turned it. The locking arms retreated and the plug returned to its original size. "Come on. Let's go home. I can't wait for you to try it."

"I'm not trying it."

"You are trying it." He picked her purse up from where she'd left it on the corner of the desk, stuffed the sinister-looking device inside, and headed toward the door. He acted like an overgrown child sometimes—there was no reasoning with him.

Becky closed the file she'd been working on and rose. "I want my car back."

"Sure thing. We'll go to my place, you can put the plug in there. I'm can't wait to hear what you think of it."

She knew where she wanted to put the plug, and it wasn't where Ford thought. Besides, she didn't really need to try it, did she? The difference appeared obvious, and in theory should work. She hoped it would be enough to convince people to buy it.

"What did you do with your friend?"

"Scott? Said he was tired. He's chillin' at the bed & breakfast over on Maple Street."

"Roseanne Meadow's place?"

He shot her a look she couldn't decipher then went back to watching the road. "The Yellow Rose? I thought Roseanne and her parents moved to Florida when we were in high school."

"They did, but her grandmother left her the old Victorian, so she came back, fixed it up, and turned it into a B&B. She's been having a tough time of it, like everyone else in town. If things don't pick up, she'll probably have to close the doors soon."

"I remember. You two were friends back in the day, weren't you?"

"Yeah. We stayed in touch, sort of, after she moved. It's been nice having her back in town."

"I'm sorry her business isn't doing well. I dropped Scott off earlier. It looks like a nice place."

"It is. She used to serve high tea there on Sunday afternoons, but she stopped about two years ago, I guess. Times have been hard on the town."

Ford grunted a response. What did he care if the town folded in on itself like an armadillo? In a year's time, maybe less if they got the plant turning a profit, he'd go back to New York where his biggest problem would be deciding which restaurant to eat at before he and his girlfriend took in a Broadway show.

They pulled into his driveway, and Becky made a beeline for her car. "See you in the morning," she called out, fishing the keys out of her purse.

"Wait! Aren't you going to come in, give the new product a trial?"

"No. I'm not. I told you I wouldn't, and nothing has changed my mind." She climbed in her car, tossed her purse into the passenger seat, and cranked the engine. As she pulled away, she caught sight of Ford standing next to his car, watching her drive away. She absolutely would not do what he'd asked her to. No. Way. In. Hell.

CHAPTER NINE

Determined not to dwell on thoughts of Becky Jean trying out his new invention, and all the process entailed, Ford walked up the long drive to his mother's house. She'd called earlier and invited him to dinner. He'd explained about his friend being in town, and requested a rain check, but when he'd called to see what time to pick Scott up, he'd said the owner of the B&B had offered to fix him something so he could call it an early night. If Roseanne was anything like Ford remembered her from a decade ago, he figured his buddy had more going on than a quiet dinner and early bedtime. The guy definitely had a way with women.

Even though Ford had begged off earlier, his mother wouldn't turn him away. Helen Adams always prepared for company.

He had a few things he needed to ask her in regards to the estate, and he wanted to hear her reaction to finding out her husband had left a significant portion of the company to a young, female employee. He knew beyond a shadow of a doubt nothing had been going on between his father and Becky Jean, but no matter what assurances he'd given his new partner, he wanted to make sure his mother agreed. He had yet to come up with a tactful way to broach the subject when his mother solved the problem for him.

"How are things going with Becky? She seemed shocked at the reading."

Ford searched his mother's face for any sign she harbored ill will toward Becky Jean and found none. "That's an understatement. I take it you knew all along?"

"Your father discussed it with me years ago when her father became ill. I agreed it would be a nice thing to do."

All kinds of possible reasons for the bequeathment to be the right thing to do flitted through his mind—none of them good. God, could Becky Jean be a half-sister? *Shit!* Given the thoughts he'd been having about her, the idea made him sick to his stomach. "What do you mean?"

"It means just what it sounds like."

He sure as hell hoped it didn't, but he kept the thought to himself.

"I had been dating Jess Parker when I met your father. In fact, if he hadn't brought me to a dance at the Community Center, I wouldn't have met your father. Kenneth and Susannah were there together. I took one look at Kenneth and knew I would marry him one day. Jess took one look at Susannah, and practically forgot my name. I left with your father and Jess left with Susannah."

He'd never heard the story of how his parents met, or if he had, he didn't remember. His father and Becky's mother? Becky Jean and he were the same age. It didn't take a genius to figure it out. He couldn't understand how his mother could be so nonchalant about the fact her husband had recognized an illegitimate daughter in his will. Appetite gone, he dropped his fork and sat back.

Helen Adams pointed her butter knife at him. "Ford Adams! I know what you're thinking, and you'd better get it out of your head this minute." His mother's scolding voice shook him out of the funk he'd sunk into. "I led your father on a merry chase, but Jess and Susannah married right away. They didn't have Becky Jean until years later. Your father said he could never repay Jess for taking me to the dance. Providing for his widow and daughter was the least he could do, and I agreed."

Ford dabbed at the sweat dotting his brow then placed his

napkin back in his lap. Several years ago, leaving Becky Jean a percentage of the company would have been a nice thing to do, but today, not so much. Ken Adams had set out to do something good and inadvertently destroyed any chance Becky Jean had of financial success—unless Ford pulled a miracle out of a hat—or shoved one up the ass of every adult in the United States. More than ever, the pressure to turn Adams Manufacturing around weighed on him.

"She's a lovely young lady, don't you think?"

He recognized the tone of her voice. He'd have to nip his mother's matchmaking in the bud if he wanted to have any peace. He cut his mother a look meant to squelch her meddling. "I'm sort of seeing someone, Mom. Besides, Becky Jean is a business partner."

"Who is the person you're seeing, and why haven't I met her?"

He spent the next ten minutes dodging his mother's bullets. He'd never once considered bringing Veronica home to meet his mother. They didn't have a meet-the-parents kind of relationship, but he'd gladly throw his fuck buddy under the bus to shut his mother up.

He sighed with relief when, halfway through dessert, his phone rang. Glancing at the screen, he excused himself from the table. "Gotta take this—work." Out of earshot, he accepted the call. "Hey, Becky Jean. Everything alright?"

"No. Everything is not alright. Get down here. Right. This. Minute." Her angry tone immediately conjured an image of her cheeks flaming with color, her blue eyes shooting lasers at him.

"Where are you?" Visions of the plant going up in smoke filled his mind.

"My house. Now, Ford. If you aren't here in five minutes, I'm going to hunt you down and murder you with my bare hands."

Okay. So the plant hadn't burned to the ground. "What's going on? I'm having dinner with my mother."

"I don't care if you're having dinner with the queen herself. Get here, pronto."

Ford pulled the phone from his ear. How had she managed the equivalent of an old-fashioned phone hang-up with her touch-screen cell phone?

"Neat trick." He stuck his head in the dining room. "Sorry, Mom. Gotta run. Something's come up." Before she could protest or inquire as to the nature of his emergency, he headed for the door. Not bothering to stop at his place, he took off down a path he'd frequently used as a kid when he walked or rode his bike into town. Where the driveway wound back and forth up the grade, the path cut a straight swatch down the face of the butte, ending up on the alleyway running behind the houses on Becky Jean's street. Without thinking, he knocked on her back door.

"Becky Jean? It's me, Ford."

He heard her stomping through the kitchen then the door swung open. He'd seen hornet's nests look less volatile. He took a precautionary step back.

"It's about damn time you got here." She grabbed a hold of his sleeve and pulled him inside, slamming the door shut behind him.

"I came as soon as I could." True. Nothing short of a jet pack strapped to his back would have gotten him there sooner. "What's wrong?"

"I'll tell you what's wrong, mister. This thing you invented is wrong!" Her face red, her shoulders drawn up tight, she looked ready to explode.

"Calm down." He reached for her, intending to guide her gently away from the kitchen and the block of knives on the countertop, but she jerked out of his reach. For the first time, he noticed the pink Texas Rangers T-shirt and denim cutoffs she wore. Damn, he'd never found the wholesome girl-next-door style to be sexy before, but she rocked the look.

"Don't touch me!"

Hands in the air, he tried his best to appear harmless. "Why don't you tell me what's going on? I can't fix what I don't know."

"The thing you invented," she said through gritted teeth.

"The butt plug?"

"Yes, you idiot. The…. It's stuck." He thought it impossible for her face to get any redder, but he'd been wrong.

"Stuck where?"

She crossed her arms in front of her and tapped her bare foot. Her cotton-candy-pink toenails momentarily distracted him. "You know where." Her voice came out so small he surely misheard.

"You mean?" He glanced down to her hips then back up to her face. Tears tracked down her cheeks and her bottom lip trembled.

"Yes. I got it in, but once I removed the key, I can't see to get it back in. I tried and tried…."

All humor gone, Ford stepped tentatively forward, arms open. She flung herself against his chest. He closed his arms around her, holding her while her tears soaked his shirt. "I tried to call Roseanne, but she's not answering her phone."

"There, there. It's going to be all right." He rested his chin on top of her head and patted her back, inhaling her intoxicating scent—simple and clean—not even a trace of the expensive perfume Ronnie favored, and often made him sneeze. He had no business being attracted to Becky Jean. She wasn't his type, but the more time he spent with her, the less it seemed to matter. Knowing he would soon see and touch her ass set his blood to a slow boil.

"Why couldn't it just slip out like the others?"

Grateful they were back to talking business, albeit sex-toy business, he smiled at the confirmation his design worked. Gloating, however, didn't seem like a good idea. "Is it uncomfortable?" Severe discomfort could explain her panicked state and signal a design flaw that would end any chance of his plan working. But the opportunity to see her ass made the experiment worthwhile.

"No. It's…. I…. When Roseanne didn't answer, I didn't know who else to call." She sniffed and hiccupped at the same time. He gave in to a crazy impulse and kissed the top of her head.

"Give me the key."

"I don't want to."

"Not ready to take it out?"

She socked him in the ribs.

"Ouch! Why did you hit me?"

"You deserved it for putting me in this situation. I hate you."

He was dying a slow and painful death—torn between wanting to gloat and howl at the success of his invention and wanting to see what he had no trouble at all imagining. But first he had to calm his test subject down. "No, you don't. You hate the position you're in, and I completely understand."

"This is all your fault."

Ford rubbed his chin on the top of her head. "I take full responsibility for your predicament." He held her for a few moments, waiting for her to calm. If she didn't stop trembling, he'd never manage to fit the tiny key into the lock mechanism, and he figured he'd only get one shot at it before she murdered him.

"You can't tell anyone about this."

He knew men who liked to talk about their conquests, but he'd never been one of them. The way he saw it, if a woman let him see or touch any part of her, he owed her the favor of keeping the details to himself. "I promise. Not a word to anyone."

"Okay, then."

When she didn't move out of his arms, he asked, "Where's the key?"

She loosened her hold on him and stepped back. Without making eye contact, she turned and headed down the hall. "I left it in the bathroom. Come on."

Ford filled his lungs, holding the air in as long as possible before letting it out in a *swoosh* before following her sexy ass down the hallway. This sure beat the hell out of dinner with his mom.

She led him through a bedroom he presumed to be hers to a large, modern bathroom. Someone had updated the century-old house to include the trendy en-suite. They'd done an excellent job blending vintage and modern together. Knowing how difficult the effect was to accomplish, he appreciated it even more. "Nice," he said.

Becky Jean glanced over her shoulder at the bathroom. "Oh. Yeah, Bobby and Chrissy put this in. I love the way they used modern touches but kept the vintage feel of the house."

"Me, too. If I didn't know better, I'd think it had been here since the house was built."

"I didn't ask you here to admire my bathroom."

Ford laughed. "Sorry. I recently finished a complete remodel on my house in New York. I did something similar there." She didn't share his amusement. He wiped the smile off his face and held out his hand. "Key?"

She dropped the tiny piece of metal into his palm. "No looking at anything else. Don't touch anything you don't have to. Are we clear?"

"Perfectly."

She dropped her shorts and bent over the counter, providing him with his first up-close-and-personal view of the ass that inspired him to create the plug in the first place. The sight of those perfect globes were enough to bring him to his knees, but add in the three-inch strip of black plastic wedged between them, and he held onto his good intentions by the thinnest of threads.

"Are you going to use the key today?"

"Huh?" He jerked his chin up. Their gazes met in the mirror and held, and, for a second, the ground beneath him shifted. Her contradictions baffled him. Brave and confident, yet vulnerable. The urge to make her his in the most elemental way hit him in the solar plexus. He sucked in a sharp breath.

"Ford!" Her gravelly growl had to be the sexiest thing he'd ever heard, but it snapped him out of the lust-filled haze he'd become lost in.

He took a step forward. "Yeah. One sec."

His fingers were numb, probably from lack of blood since most of his supply had diverted to his groin the second she dropped her drawers. He fumbled around trying to get a grip on the tiny key. "We need to make the heads on these keys bigger."

Becky Jean made a sound — part sigh, part groan — and wiggled her butt. "Just get on with it, will you?"

"Okay. Got it." He dropped to one knee behind her. "Is it okay if I touch you? I mean… I need to part… can't see."

"Just do it!"

Ford willed his hands not to shake. As careful as a man handling a bomb, he parted her cheeks enough to see the lock mechanism. "Here goes." With a little push, he slid the key home then turned it 180 degrees counterclockwise. "There."

Rising, he wiped a bead of sweat from his brow. "All done. You can do the rest yourself, can't you?"

"Yes."

He made it as far as her bedroom before he had to stop and lean against the wall for support. It had taken every ounce of self-control he possessed to walk out of Becky Jean's bathroom without doing something monumentally stupid. Like remove the plug and replace it with his cock. He managed to hold onto his control, but the feel of her skin and the erotic image of the toy he'd created with his own hands seated between her cheeks would stay with him until his dying day. And, at the rate his heart raced, he could die any minute.

The sound of running water reminded him he needed to get the hell out of his partner's house, but his legs were in no shape to carry him anywhere just yet. Besides, he'd feel like the worst sort of human if he didn't hang around long enough to make sure she hadn't suffered any ill effects from the untested device. Thinking he could have caused her harm sent a bolt of fear through him. Eventually, the door opened and Becky Jean stepped out. Other than a rosy flush to her cheeks, she appeared to be fine.

"You okay?"

She slicked her hands down the sides of her denim shorts. "Fine. I'm fine. No harm done. Sorry I panicked."

Relief loosened the glue holding his feet to the floor. He pushed away from the wall and smiled at her. "Understandable, under the circumstances."

"I suppose so. At any rate, your device works." Her gaze darted around the room as she spoke, eventually coming around to land on him. "You know what you said about making the key bigger?"

"Yeah." He held up his hand, fingers spread. "It's a little small for someone with big hands."

"Well, I got to thinking, what if we made a key with a flat head on it, sort of a thumbscrew design that would stay in all the time. So, if someone used the device solo, like I did, they wouldn't have the issue of trying to get the key back in. All they'd have to do would be turn the thumbscrew."

After all she'd been through, she still had the wherewithal to find a way out of the situation she'd found herself in. Amazing. "I think it's a great idea. I'll ask Scott to design one as an option."

Becky nodded. "Good. Good. It would solve the problem, then."

He didn't want to leave. He wanted to pull her into his arms and hold her, tell her how special she was, do all the things to her he'd envisioned over the last few days. But he couldn't. They were business partners — a fact he'd do well to remember. "I'd better be going."

She walked him to the back door.

"See you in the morning."

Every step back to the gatehouse was pure torture.

CHAPTER TEN

"Where were you last night? I called the B&B and your cell phone and got a recording." Becky eyed her best friend across the antique oak table in the kitchen of The Yellow Rose.

"Sorry. Ford's friend is staying here. He's… demanding." Roseanne picked a potato chip off her plate and snapped it in two. Something seemed off about her friend, but Becky couldn't put her finger on the change. Usually attentive to every detail, today she seemed… distracted.

"So demanding you couldn't answer your phone? What if it had been an emergency?"

"Was it?" She jerked her gaze to Becky as if checking for visible injuries.

Becky shrugged. "It seemed like it at the time." She'd never forget the moment she realized she couldn't get Ford's invention out of her body without help. When she hadn't been able to reach Roseanne, she'd contemplated calling her mother and dismissed the idea as beyond insane. For a brief moment, she'd considered driving to the twenty-four-hour emergency clinic, but scrapped the idea as soon as she realized she'd have to sit in the car in order to get there. Ford had been her last, and only, resort.

"Everything's okay?"

"Fine. Just fine." *Ford has seen my ass, up close and personal, but, no biggie, I'm good.* She'd come over on her lunch hour to vent to her best friend, but for whatever reason, she wanted to keep what had happened the previous evening to herself. The night had been embarrassing, but the way Ford had handled the situation made her want to hoard the moment. Once she'd calmed down enough to tell him why she'd demanded he come over, he'd been wonderful—tender and not at all condescending, as she had expected him to be. After she'd bent over the bathroom counter, he'd inserted the key, disengaged the lock then left her to remove the plug herself. The expression on his face when she found him lounging outside the bathroom door had been… complicated. She'd lain awake most of the night trying to decipher what it had meant, and come up with absolutely nothing. Until she made sense of it, she'd rather keep the incident to herself.

"Tell me about this Scott guy. He didn't seem like the demanding sort when I met him yesterday."

"Hon, you have no idea."

Becky finished the salad she'd brought for her lunch while her friend listed off the demands made by her Yankee guest. None of it sounded particularly out of line to her. Water on the bedside table, turndown service. Other than the request for a specific brand of coffee, it all sounded like things any guest might expect from a Victorian B&B. She didn't say it out loud, of course. She'd never tell her friend how to run her place of business any more than Roseanne would tell her how to make baby bottle nipples. Instead, she let her friend vent. Scott Ramsey couldn't be the first demanding guest Roseanne had played hostess to, and he wouldn't be the last.

Besides, Becky had her own problems, of which she couldn't speak. She and Ford had yet to tell the employees the severity of the situation, and until they did, she had to keep the details to herself. She trusted Roseanne not to say anything, but the woman clearly had enough on her plate without worrying about the last major employer in town closing its doors. And, lord knew, she didn't want to talk about what had happened the night before. If

Roseanne had answered her phone, it would have been different. Ford's involvement would have ended with him asking her to try out the plug—something she could explain away as the crazy idea it had been. Even if the plug turned out to be the best thing to ever happen to the adult toy market, she didn't see how it could to save Adams Manufacturing. How many could they sell, anyway?

As soon as she'd finished her lunch, Becky snapped the lid back on the plastic container she'd used to transport her lunch and pushed back from the table. "As lovely as it is here, I've got to. Things to do, you know?"

"What's Mr. Ramsey doing here, anyway? Is Ford leaving soon?"

Becky couldn't tell her about the locking mechanism without mentioning Ford's big idea to save the company, so she settled on a version of the truth. "They're working on some sort of project together. As to Ford leaving, I don't see that happening anytime soon."

"Why not? You were so sure he wouldn't hang around."

She shrugged. "He has no intention of staying a day longer than he has to, but things are… complicated."

Roseanne narrowed her eyes. "Define complicated."

What the heck? It'll be common knowledge soon enough. The terms of Mr. Adams's will would become public through probate proceedings, and the struggle to keep the plant open wouldn't go unnoticed by the employees. "Mr. Adams left me 25 percent of the company."

"What?!"

"Calm down." Becky held up a staying hand.

"How can I calm down? You're rich!"

"Whoa! Whoa." She shook her head. "I'm on the brink of losing everything, and so are Ford and his mother. The company is broke."

Her friend's enthusiasm hit the proverbial iceberg. "What's going to happen to all the people who work there?"

"Unless Ford pulls a miracle out of his hat, we're all going to lose our jobs, but I'll also be on the hook for my share of the debt. I know Mr. Adams intended to do something nice for me, and, a few years ago, it would have been. But for the last year or so, we've been holding on by a thread. I only found out yesterday how thin the thread really is."

"And there's nothing you can do?"

Becky explained the terms of the will and how she had no choice but to go along with whatever idea Ford came up with. "Ford has an idea for a new product he thinks might at least keep us in business for the next year, and he asked Scott to help him with it. If we survive the year? Who knows?"

"Wow."

"Tell me about it. My life's become one long, crazy roller coaster ride."

"That's what you wanted to talk to me about last night? I'm so sorry I wasn't available to you. I feel like a jerk."

"No, please. Don't give it another thought. I was just feeling a little down last night." She pasted a smile on her face. "I'm better today. Talking to you helped."

"Is there anything I can do?"

"No. Just keep this to yourself for a while, okay? No need upsetting everyone in town until we've explored every avenue open to us."

"My lips are sealed." Roseanne stood and began to clear the table. "Any idea how long Mr. Ramsey is going to be here?"

"As long as it takes, I guess." Becky stood. "I've got to get back."

Roseanne wrapped her in a warm hug. "Call me if you need anything."

"I will."

~~~
~~~

Becky sorted through the stack of message slips she'd picked up from reception on her way in. They couldn't hold off telling the employees much longer. It had been weeks since they'd shipped out the first batches of their new product to suppliers around the globe, and they hadn't heard a peep out of any of them. She'd put off everything she possibly could to cut costs to the barest minimum, including ordering the mulch for the parking lot dividers. The spring bulbs had done their thing and been replaced by knee-high weeds. If not for the cars parked there daily, passersby would think the place abandoned. *Great curb appeal.* She pitied the Realtor who had to sell the place looking the way it did.

Something had to change — soon.

The first three messages were from suppliers they'd delayed paying, no doubt wanting to remind her the three-week deferral they'd requested would end soon. She'd have to ask Ford about providing more funds. Confident orders for his toy would come in, Ford insisted on continuing to produce the item, in an attempt to save face with their employees and the town, she'd named the *Safeguard Backdoor Locking System.* As a result of the aggressive production schedule, they were running desperately low on materials, and unless they paid their suppliers, they'd be shutting down *all* production soon.

She set the dun calls aside and read the last of the messages. Recognizing the name of one of the largest wholesaler's they'd mailed product samples to, her heart tripped and her skin tingled. Could this be it? Could they have actually made a sale? Ever since the night she'd had to ask Ford to help her remove his invention, she'd known he was right — it would revolutionize the butt-plug industry. *If* they could get anyone to buy it, and so far, she'd had no success in that area.

It had to happen. Ford had poured money into the project for additional molds and to retool several of the machines no longer in use to churn out their new product. Everyone but a skeleton crew assigned to complete the last orders of baby bottle nipples were assembling and packaging products for which they had no orders.

Scott, Ford's friend and business partner from New York, had sunk a lot of money into the project, too, providing the locks free of charge in hopes of making his money back, and then some, once the product began to sell. He'd offered to train the people on the assembly line, and for reasons Becky couldn't fathom, remained in town. *Probably waiting to see if any orders are going to come in.*

Becky read the short, uninformative message again. Maybe they just wanted to ask questions. She opened a file folder, pulled out the sheet she'd prepared with all the talking points for their new product. "There's no time like the present." Lifting the receiver, she dialed the number listed on the pink message slip.

~~~

"Ford?" Becky knocked on his open office door then stepped inside. "Got a minute?"

He put down his pencil and rocked back in his chair. "Sure. What's up?"

He'd been working on a new design the last few days, and seemed to have lost track of routine things—like shaving and combing his hair. *He looks like he just climbed out of bed.*

She had no business thinking about a sleep-tumbled Ford. They had a purely professional relationship that, due to the nature of the business, included him seeing her naked ass on one occasion—but it had been a one-time occurrence, and an emergency to boot. Nothing remotely similar would happen again. Becky wouldn't be seeing his adorable disheveled countenance across the bed, so best to quit imagining it. Besides, as soon as they put Adams Manufacturing back on an even keel, Ford would start looking for a buyer for the share of the company he controlled. He'd been clear from the beginning about his desire to go back to his life in New York, and she couldn't blame him. Butte Plains didn't rate a dot on most maps. The nightlife here consisted of high school
~~~

football games in the fall and catching lightning bugs in the summer. The pace of life was two steps behind slow and getting slower with each passing day.

She closed the door and approached his desk. "I have good news and bad news. Which would you like first?"

"Might as well start with the bad." He sighed and held his hand out for the paper she extended to him. "Don't make me read it, just tell me."

"We're running extremely low on raw materials. If we don't pay some of our suppliers, we're going to have to scale back our production of the *Safeguard Backdoor Locking System.*"

"Bottom line?"

She named a figure that made him whistle. He dropped the paper on his desk. "And the good news?"

"We *need* more raw materials."

His brows knit as he stared up at her. "Isn't that the same as the bad news?"

"No. It's the opposite of the bad news." She could barely keep the smile off her face, but she loved turning the tables on Ford. "See?" She handed him another sheet of paper. As he read, his face relaxed then his lips curved upward in a tentative smile.

"Tell me this isn't a joke."

"No joke. I just got off the phone with the head buyer. They want fifty-thousand units as soon as we can ship them. I promised ten thousand a week for the next five weeks with a promise to fill the order faster if we could manage it."

A giant smile split his face. "You did it, Becky Jean. You really did it!" He jumped up, rounded the desk, and threw his arms around her, lifting her off the ground with a whoop they probably heard in Dallas. She laughed right along with him.

After printing out the purchase order the buyer had emailed to her, she'd danced around her office until she'd been able to control her expression. Seeing Ford this happy filled her with joy. She laughed and hung on as he spun her around until she became dizzy.

"This calls for a celebration." He set her down then went back to his desk. Chest puffed out, he produced a bottle and two glasses from a lower drawer. "Tennessee's finest," he said, removing the top.

She laughed and accepted the tumbler with a splash of amber liquid.

Ford lifted his glass in the air. "Out with the old, in with the new," he said. "And, to the latest incarnation of Adams Manufacturing."

They tipped their glasses together until a crystal-clear *clink* rang out. Becky sipped at her drink while Ford finished his in one gulp, then refilled it and downed the second helping. They were a long way from being out of the woods, but this first order did warrant a celebration. She tipped the rest of her drink back. Coughing as the liquid burned its way down, she held her glass out for a refill.

"We did it, Becky Jean." They'd done significant damage to the bottle of Tennessee's finest. Ford had called Scott to let him know, then drank a toast to his best friend whose locking mechanism was the true success behind the new product. Never mind it had taken Ford's genius to marry his design with a lock with no other practical application. Several drinks later, he'd waxed poetic about Becky's marketing skills.

If anything reeked of donkey doo-doo, his statement did. She'd named the product, slapped a bunch of them into boxes, and shipped them off to adult toy suppliers then prayed they'd see what Ford saw—the chance to make a fortune.

She still didn't believe more orders were imminent, but Ford thought differently, and for the time being, she chose to believe him. For the first time since the reading of Mr. Adams's will, the doom of bankruptcy seemed less certain.

"To butt-plug wearers everywhere," she said, lifting her glass.

"Here! Here!"

PART TWO

Marriage is an adventure, like going to war.
Gilbert K. Chesterson

CHAPTER ELEVEN

Four months later….

"It's a good idea, Ford." Becky paced in front of her partner's desk and refused to back down. "The *Home Shopping Network* is huge. They've proven the marketing strategy works."

"So, why not let *them* sell our products? I don't see why we need to stick *our* necks out."

"I thought you were all about innovation. This should be a no-brainer, partner of mine. Thanks to your creative mind, we have several products on the market, and more on the drawing board. Our Internet sales are through the roof on our site, and on the sites we distribute to."

"If sales are so good, then I don't see any point in expanding into something we know nothing about."

"Sales are good, but they could be better." Becky planted her feet and glared at her stoic partner. "Ever since the *Safeguard Backdoor Locking System* hit the market four months ago, we've become known for our innovation in the adult toy market. Internet stores are a dime a dozen. Everyone with a computer and a garage to stock inventory has one. Yes, those are profitable for us, but think about it. We would have our own cable network where we sell our own brand directly to the public. We could sell advertising to all those Internet stores, as well as to the brick-and-mortar stores. I don't see a downside to it."

Ford rocked back in his chair, a sure sign he was softening. Since becoming business partners, she'd learned to read him well. Becky tamped down her enthusiasm. The biggest hurdle would be getting Ford to agree to establish the first-ever adult cable shopping network and, in her estimation, by far the easiest task ahead of her, given her plans.

Elbow braced on the arm of his chair, he brushed the knuckle of his index finger over his bottom lip. She would not allow the unconsciously sexy habit to distract her as it always did. This was too important.

"You're talking about a huge monetary investment. We'd have to hire studio space, professionals to produce the show, spokespersons to sell the products, plus we'd have to set up a fulfillment center separate from our current wholesale distribution center. None of which would be cheap. Can we afford it?"

She had answers to all his concerns, but with Ford, she had to take it one step at a time or he'd dig in his heels. She shifted the focus back on him. "Don't you even read the reports I put on your desk?"

"I'm supposed to read them?"

Shaking her head, she plopped into one of the twin leather guest chairs facing his desk. Lord, he could be exasperating sometimes. "I read the ones you put on *my* desk."

"I don't write reports." The samples of various plastics, notebooks, and drafting supplies strewn across the top of his desk testified to the truth of his statement. The crumpled grease-stained sandwich wrapper occupying one corner could have been today's lunch or from last week. She made a mental note to sneak the cleaning staff in as soon as possible.

"Yes, I know. However, when you come up with a new product, I at least take the time to look at it." She'd also personally tried every one of his inventions, but she'd keep the information to herself.

"I don't have time to read every report that comes across my desk, Becky Jean. I trust you to inform me if something needs my attention, but otherwise, I don't want to be bothered. I'm happy with my role as head of product development." He lifted a sketchpad then dropped it. Becky blanched at the particles of dust dancing under the glow of his desk lamp.

Ever since Ford's former college roommate turned business partner had returned to New York two months ago, Ford had focused his attention on designing new, innovative products. "Is Scott coming back?"

"I don't think so. Why?"

"Just wondering. He stayed longer than necessary the first time, which made me think he had other reasons for hanging around." Reasons like Roseanne Meadows. The town grapevine had buzzed with rumors about those two the entire time Scott had stayed at the B&B. Becky had asked her friend more than once about her guest, but Roseanne always shifted the conversation to Ford and Becky, and since she had no intention of discussing her obsession with her new business partner, what little she knew about the Yankee and the owner of The Yellow Rose was stained with grape juice.

"He needed to get back. We have clients, plus he wanted to hire someone to take my place for a while."

The reminder of Ford's temporary residence status plunged an ice pick straight into her heart, but she masked the hurt with a smile. "You mean you're replaceable?"

"Apparently. Or so Scott believes." He waved the insult away. "We've been thinking about hiring an apprentice, somebody straight out of college. This is as good a time as any."

"Well, we all appreciate you stepping in here, and your dedication to the company, but it's important to stay abreast of our financial status, don't you think?"

"Like I said, if we have cash flow problems, I'm sure you'll let me know."

She added hardheaded to her list of Ford's personality traits. "To answer your earlier question—yes, we can afford to undertake this new project. In fact, I don't think we can afford not to. Someone is going to do it. It's only a matter of time, Ford. It's a natural move for the most innovative company in the adult toy market."

He sighed again and rocked forward to cross his forearms on the desktop. Becky hid her victory smile and waited for confirmation of what she already knew. She had him.

"What do you need from me?"

Yes! She did a mental fist pump. "I'll have the documents on your desk tomorrow at the latest. Sign them and get them back to me. That's all I need." *For the time being.* She'd spring the rest of it on him once she'd sealed the deal and he couldn't say no.

"Okay." He reached for his drafting pencil. "Can I get back to work?"

"Sure." As she stood, their gazes met and held for a breathless moment before she remembered he was her partner and the spark of interest she thought she saw in his eyes had to be her overactive imagination. Forcing her mind back to business, she straightened before heading toward the door. Recalling the reason she'd come to see him in the first place, she gripped the doorframe and faced him. "Thanks, Ford. This is the right thing to do. I know it." He waved her on her way with a grunt indicating he'd already shifted his focus back to his drawing—further proof her eyes and her mind had been playing tricks on her. The only thing Ford was interested in was whatever deviously naughty toy he was designing.

She hadn't lied. His innovative designs had catapulted Adams Manufacturing into the adult toy market with the force of an all-out assault. Their competitors had scrambled to come up with products to gain back market share and failed miserably. They could no longer sit on their well-padded asses. If they did, the competition would catch up and eventually overtake them. She had no intention of letting that happen.

When *Home Shopping Network* had come to her with an offer to feature their products in an exclusive late-night showcase, she'd been flattered, but she'd also seen the possibility in the idea. If the popular home shopping network thought they could sell their products, then there was money to be made. Why not make it themselves?

She'd done her research before presenting the idea to Ford. It would be less expensive to rent studio space, but they already had an entire building not being used. The red-brick structure she had in mind had been the original home of Adams Manufacturing and had been deemed structurally sound by the people from the state historical society who had come out to see if it qualified for listing on their registry. Renovating the space would cost them up front but, in the long run, would be an investment in the future and a feather in the cap for Butte Plains. Once completed, the building could be home to a new state-of-the-art studio with plenty of room for offices and the distribution center Ford had correctly listed as an expense. Removing the cost of land and constructing a new building out of the equation made the start-up bottom line a nice shade of pink instead of bright red.

Until the new studio could be completed, she planned to begin production in the conference room in the present building. Some soundproofing would be necessary to prevent rumblings from the factory bleeding into the sound feed, but the renovation wouldn't cost much. Besides, she fully intended to start small. No sense dumping a lot of cash into what she had to admit could be a bit of a risky venture. No one had ever attempted to sell adult toys on television. The concept might be a complete flop, but she didn't think so. She knew marketing, and the success of various niche home shopping networks told her this one would be well received by the buying public.

Especially if you had a sexy-as-sin person hawking the wares. And Ford Adams was *sexier* than sin.

~~~
~~~

Ford had to admit the conference room turned studio looked pretty good. Not fancy, but thanks to the magic of television, the viewing public would never know. The part of it they would see had clean lines, and above all, looked classy.

"Is it worth all the noise you had to endure the last few weeks?"

Ford hadn't gone along with the idea of launching their own adult toy shopping show easily, but he'd seen the miracles Becky Jean could achieve when she set her mind to something. If she said it would work, then it would work. He turned to his business partner. "It looks good."

"That's all you've got to say?"

God, he loved to push her buttons. When riled, she turned a becoming shade of red, and Lord, if the sight didn't set his blood on fire.

He had no business toying with her, though. He'd long since decided their professional relationship wasn't enough to keep him from taking what he wanted, but every time he thought about acting on his desires, something happened to remind him his stint here would end soon. The last time he'd spoken to Ronnie—over a week ago—she'd pumped him for information about when he would find a buyer for the company and get the hell out of Dodge. He'd reminded her Dodge was in Kansas, not Texas. She hadn't been amused.

Truthfully, he'd begun to like it here. He was having more fun than the law allowed, as his dad used to say, designing sex toys and watching his company grow. His company. Not his dad's, not his family's. *His.* Yes, he'd built on the bones of the ones who'd gone before, but in all fairness, there hadn't been much left. He'd take partial blame for the condition he'd found the company in. If he'd returned to Butte Plains after college, he might have helped his father turn the company around before things became desperate. If his father had asked, he would have come. But Ken Adams knew his son, and, in keeping his difficulties to himself, he allowed Ford to seek his own happiness.

He'd be eternally grateful for the opportunity. His dad had been one in a million.

So, coming to the realization he wasn't exactly bored with his life in Butte Plains came as a bit of a shock. He'd yet to decide if he wanted to stay permanently. He still had eight months before he could sell out, so he didn't need to make a decision until then. And, if he did decide to keep the place, Becky Jean had proved more than capable of running the entire shebang without him being present. He could design products anywhere in the world. If they needed him in the initial stages of product development, he could pop back in for a while.

Looking around the room once again, he admired Becky Jean's ingenuity. She'd made something out of nothing, and done it in record time. "How deep are we into this project?"

"I put the expense report on your desk this morning." She had, and he'd glanced at the bottom line, but telling her so would make her suspicious. She thought he didn't read the constant stream of financial reports she sent his way, but that wasn't entirely true. He read the bottom line on all of them, if not the details. He'd never told anyone about the second mortgage he'd taken on his house in New York. Those first couple of months had all but drained his personal reserves. Thanks to their success with the *Safeguard Backdoor Locking System*, he'd paid off both mortgages on his home, and he once again had financial reserves. Becky Jean Parker had as much to do with it as anyone. Adams Manufacturing had gained solid financial ground, thanks to her marketing skills and her ability to be everything to everybody. The earning potential of the company was through the roof, the cash flow robust, and their debt low. Now would be the perfect time to look for a potential buyer.

So, why are you still here?

He'd asked himself the question a million times, and the only answer remained—he was having fun. He was designing for himself for the first time in his professional career, and he had the means to watch those designs leap from the page, become reality then go out into the world for millions to enjoy. One day, he'd have to go back to the business he'd built with Scott right out of college, but for the time being, he owed it to himself to enjoy the life he'd dreamed of since he drew his first invention at the age of seven.

He glanced at the woman who made it possible for him to do nothing but draw all day. Becky Jean solved problems across the spectrum—from production snafus to missing paperwork. Everyone, including him, relied on her. "You did?"

"You know I did." Her tone made it clear she'd lost all patience with him. He needed to come clean.

"Yes, I know. I read the report. You've kept the cost down on the project, and I appreciate it. I'm not entirely convinced this is going to be a success, but at least we won't lose our shirts on the deal."

"High praise from you," she said.

"It looks like you've got everything under control." He ran a hand over one of the boxes containing lighting equipment that had arrived earlier today. "Your report listed the technical people you hired, but I didn't see a spokesperson. Haven't been able to find anyone?"

It was one thing to stand in front of a camera and talk about cookware or jewelry, and quite another to talk about butt plugs. Not to mention, finding someone to fill the role in Butte Plains seemed an impossible task.

"Uh… no. I mean, yes."

Her stammering made the hairs on the back of his neck stand on end. Everything from the flush of her cheeks to the way she pretended interest in the papers on her clipboard told him she had something to hide—something he wasn't going to like. "Which is it?"

"Which is what?" She wandered around the room until she'd maneuvered a stack of boxes between them.

He hadn't seen her this nervous since the night she'd called him to her house to help her remove the prototype of the *Safeguard Backdoor Locking System*. "Becky Jean."

"It's the right thing to do," she pleaded. "The demographic research suggests more than 75 percent of all adult toys sold are purchased by women."

He'd read the same statistic somewhere. Probably on one of the reports she'd sent his way. "So? What does that have to do with our spokesperson?"

"Well, it needs to be a guy."

He didn't like the leading way she'd ended her statement. "I don't care if the person is male or female, as long as they can sell our products."

"Good!" She smiled the biggest smile he'd ever seen then made her way out from behind the wall of boxes. "It's all settled, then."

"Wait," he said, putting himself in between her and the door. He could almost feel the weight of the boulder dropping out of the sky, aimed straight for him. "What's settled?"

"Our spokesperson, of course. You'll be perfect."

Wham! Splat! She'd played him like a fiddle. He raised both hands, palms out. "Whoa. Back the wagon up, little lady. I am not going to go on TV to sell butt plugs."

"Well, someone has to, and who knows the *Safeguard Backdoor Locking System* better than you?"

Logic wasn't going to work on him. Not when it came to making a fool of himself. "That's not the point, and you know it. I'm a product development engineer, not an actor."

"Who said anything about acting? Remember when you were trying to sell me on the idea?"

He nodded, recalling how difficult she'd been to win over. In the end, it had been the product, not anything he'd said that had convinced her to jump on the bandwagon.

"You convinced me, and I'd wager the phones will be ringing off the hook with women wanting to buy anything you're selling."

"Don't bet the company on it, Becks." He used his most menacing, don't-fuck-with-me voice. He trusted her judgment regarding their business, would do anything she said—within reason. This was *not* within reason. Not even close.

"I'm not, but even if I did, it's a safe bet. No one is more passionate about your designs than you. Our sales took a noticeable jump after the article about you appeared in *Texas Monthly*. And, at the risk of inflating your already-considerable ego, you aren't bad to look at. The female audience is going to eat you up."

He stored away the fact she thought he was good-looking for another time and concentrated on the more pressing matter. "What about the male audience? Don't they matter?"

"Truthfully? Not as much. Women do most of the purchasing in this country. They're the ones we have to appeal to."

"As a male of the species, I'm offended." *And screwed.* As usual, she knew her facts.

"Get over it, Ford." She glanced over her shoulder at the boxes. "The technicians will be in this afternoon to set everything up. We'll have a dress rehearsal at six this evening. If everything goes well, we'll go live next week."

"Live?" Out of necessity, he'd long ago gotten over his aversion to public speaking, but live television? Not his idea of a fun time.

"For now. If sales warrant, we'll invest in taping equipment, but until we see if this is going to work, our shows will be live broadcasts."

He closed his eyes and counted to ten. He wished he'd put his foot down on this project when he'd had the chance. "What if I say no?"

She huffed out a breath. "Look. You wanted me to keep expenses down, so I have. I've compromised on everything, including the studio I really wanted. On-air talent is expensive."

"How expensive?"

She named an hourly wage he could barely comprehend.

"You're shittin' me."

"I wish I was. Plus, the agents I spoke to all insisted on lengthy contracts. I want this to work, but I'm realistic, too. We're launching to a small, localized market. It could flop, and I don't want to be on the hook for any more than we have to be."

He couldn't fault her for being practical. She was a hell of a businesswoman and a marketing genius. Adams Manufacturing was lucky to have her. *He* was lucky to have her. For better or worse, they were in this together. She'd left him little choice. "I'll agree on one condition."

"Anything you want."

For the first time since she'd sprung her crazy-assed idea on him, Ford smiled.

~~~

I can't do this. Standing on the mark the director indicated, Becky couldn't ignore the testosterone tower next to her. Since Ford had taken to wearing jeans and worn-out MIT T-shirts to work—something she blamed on his friend Scott—she'd almost forgotten how breathtaking he looked in the tailored suits he'd worn when he first returned to Butte Plains. Between his distracting presence and the display of butt plugs on the table next to them, she was as nervous as an armadillo crossing a six-lane freeway during rush hour.

Anything you want, her conscience mocked. *Whatever possessed you to say such a thing?*

"I'm ready. How about you, Becky Jean?" Ford's deep voice held a hint of mockery, too. And why wouldn't it? She'd opened the door, and he'd walked right through, dragging her into the pit of humiliation she'd dug for herself.

"Ready as I'll ever be, I guess." She wiped her sweating palms on her skirt.

"This is a rehearsal. It doesn't matter how you look," Ford said.
~~~

Easy for you to say, Mr. Perfect. "Still no reason to be a slouch."

"Just relax," Justin said. The kid just graduated college with a degree in filmmaking, and he was eager to put it to use. The idea of being on the ground floor of something as innovative as the *Adult Shopping Show* appealed to the young man. Even the pittance she'd offered him hadn't discouraged him from accepting the job as producer/director/master-in-charge of getting them on the air. "Everything is on the teleprompter but feel free to improvise."

"I think I'll stick to the script," Becky Jean said.

"Not a problem. It gets the message across."

It should. She'd written it herself.

It took over an hour to get through the half-hour segment. Justin continually stopped to adjust the lighting and remind them to relax. Remind *her*, she amended. Despite his initial resistance, Ford proved to be the natural she'd predicted he would be. She was the mess.

"You should do this alone," she said as they wrapped up the second run-through.

"Oh, no you don't," Ford said. "If I have to do this, *you* have to do this."

"I'm worse than Lucy Ricardo trying to sell Vita-Meata-Vegimin."

"You'll be fine," he stated with a finality that said he wasn't going to let her off the hook.

"I'm going to remind you, you said that when social media starts lighting up with scathing reviews of our show." As she stomped off the set, she wished she'd never had the idea in the first place.

CHAPTER TWELVE

Becky Jean had to be the worst spokesperson he'd ever seen, but Ford knew exactly how to fix the problem. He didn't know shit about teleprompters, but, being mechanically gifted, he could figure out most anything. Arriving early to the makeshift set, he disabled the reading device. Without it as a crutch, Becky Jean would be obliged to interact with him instead of just reading scripted lines. She'd never had any trouble telling him exactly what she thought, so, he reasoned, if he could keep her attention focused on him, she'd forget all about the camera and the audience, and things would go much smoother. He hadn't convinced Justin, but the younger man agreed to give it a shot after Ford added another percentage point to the man's commission off sales made through their new 800 number.

"Don't let on you know this is a setup or she'll walk," he cautioned their jack-of-all-things-television.

"My lips are sealed, Mr. Adams."

"Seeing as we're partners in crime, why don't you call me Ford?"

The kid nodded. "Ford it is. You really think your partner is going to be able to pull this off?"

"If there's one thing I know about Becky Jean, it's she can do anything she sets her mind to. Just remember, no matter how mad she gets, keep the cameras rolling."

"Whatever you say, Ford."

Becky Jean breezed in. Earlier in the day, she'd had on a cute dress that reminded him of summer picnics. The suit she'd changed into screamed cock-block. If she buttoned up any tighter, her eyeballs would bulge out.

"Oh, hell, no."

"What?" She stopped in her tracks. "Is something wrong?"

"Where'd you get the Mary Poppins' suit?"

She glanced down at herself. "Nordstrom's in Dallas. Why?"

"It's hideous." Judging by the color in her cheeks, he'd pissed her off and he hadn't uttered a single lie. "Is it the same one Lucille Ball wore in the Vita-Meata-Vegimin commercial?" It damn sure could have been. It was that ugly.

She lifted the skirt thingy hanging over her hips. "Peplums are very much in style, I'll have you know."

"You wearing something under that hideous thing?"

Her mouth opened and closed like a fish as she absorbed the insult and contemplated her answer. "Of course."

Just as he'd thought. Buttoned-up Becky Jean would have more than one layer of armor. "Then take it off. Style or no style, the jacket has to go."

She turned to Justin, silently asking his opinion. The younger man didn't miss a beat. He shook his head. "I'm with Ford. Take it off."

"Well, I never—" She removed the jacket, then hung it carefully on the doorknob. "Satisfied?" She spread her arms wide to show off a silk blouse. It wasn't anywhere near as ugly as the suit coat, but it still screamed uptight bitch, not sexy woman.

"It's not great, but it's better." Ford motioned her over to her spot beside him. They would open with a wide shot of the two of them then narrow to a close-up as the two introduced themselves and welcomed viewers to their new show. Later, they would move to the display table and spend the last twenty minutes talking about today's product — the *Safeguard Backdoor Locking System.*

Becky Jean had done a credible job with the script she'd prepared for the sabotaged teleprompter, but it had nearly bored Ford to death. If they had any chance of this network idea working, they were going to have to grab any viewer's they had by the short hairs and refuse to let go.

He fully understood his plan could backfire. Becky Jean could walk out and leave him there to woo customers all by himself, but he didn't think she would. He needed it not to happen. If he had to subject himself to public ridicule, she would, too. They were partners, after all.

She placed her feet precisely over the X taped on the floor. "Let's do this."

Ford glanced at the clock. Less than a minute to airtime. He exchanged a look with Justin then turned his gaze on Becky Jean. "Hmm. Something is still not right."

"Really? I look perfectly fine. Nobody's going to be looking at me anyway."

Oh, he begged to differ. Yes, the women would be looking at him most likely, but they'd be curious about Becky Jean. They weren't just selling butt plugs, they were selling sex. And though he thought she oozed sex appeal no matter what she wore, present suit notwithstanding, the viewers, all two of them, he suspected, didn't know his partner as well as he did. Therefore, something had to change.

"Which is why we need to do something different. No one wants to buy a butt plug from someone who looks like their ass is so tight nothing short of a jackhammer could drive a wedge of plastic up it."

Color flooded her cheeks, and her mouth fell open in horror. Moving quickly, Ford reached for the top button on her blouse. Despite its tight-ass appearance, the fabric was the softest silk. Under different circumstances, he wouldn't mind feeling it slide against certain parts of his body. His fingers slipped, but he managed to release the top two buttons before Becky Jean recovered from his shocking statement. By then, it was too late. The fabric fell in a soft V from her collarbone to the top of her cleavage. Bedroom ready, he'd call the look. *Perfect.*

"On the air in Three. Two. One," Justin counted down.

Ford faced the camera and plastered a smile on his face he'd used countless times to charm women out of their panties. Slipping his arm around Becky Jean's waist, he tugged her to his side. "Good evening, ladies and gentlemen, and welcome to the ASS — *The Adult Shopping Show.* I'm K. Ford Adams, and this is my partner, B.J. Parker." He smiled down at Becky Jean who looked sexy as sin with her cheeks flushed and her lips parted. He hoped the audience would interpret the anger simmering in her gaze for another sort of passion. Before she found her voice, Ford rushed on with the detailed instructions he'd memorized from the original script. Business was business, and the viewers, if they had any, needed to understand how the ordering process worked.

Keeping his arm snug across her back and his fingers digging into her hip, he ushered Becky Jean to the display table, talking to the camera all the way.

"B.J. and I want you to know every product we recommend has been tested by us and deemed worthy of adding to your bedroom collection. And all our products come with a money-back guarantee. If the product doesn't live up to your expectations, simply return it for a full refund within thirty days of purchase."

He stopped behind the draped table where an array of butt plugs lay artfully arranged to showcase the item from all angles. After the initial release, sales had warranted production of the plug in various sizes from a slim, beginner model to a fist-sized one for the more advanced ass-play crowd. Across the board, the line represented the lion's share of their earnings.

"Tonight, we want to introduce you to a revolutionary new product — the *Safeguard Backdoor Locking System.*"

She was going to kill him. Right there on local television. Becky thanked heaven the projected viewership for the eleven-thirty-to-midnight time slot on the small regional cable network amounted to about a dozen people. With any luck, ten of those had already fallen asleep, leaving only two witnesses, and Justin, to convict her of murder.

Ford's voice droned in her ears as he explained to the camera what made his butt plug better than all the others on the market. No one knew the item better than the man who had designed it, and his expertise came through in his confident tone of voice. Every woman out there would be hanging on his every honey-and-testosterone-laden word. As she'd suspected from the beginning, he didn't need her. They were twenty minutes into the half-hour show, and she hadn't uttered a single word.

"B.J., honey, you've tried the revolutionary new *Safeguard Backdoor Locking System*. Why don't you tell the viewers what you thought of the product?"

What the hell? He didn't really expect her to endorse his butt plug, did he?

Rage washed through her, making her see red. The two viewers who were still awake would know she'd tried not only his invention, but several of their competitors. She really was going to kill him, but first, she'd give him what he wanted.

"Go ahead, honey. How did it compare to others you've tried?"

Remembering her humiliation at having to call him to help her remove the plug, she smiled up at him. "I'd be happy to, Ford." Facing the camera, she began. "Ladies, I have tried the *Safeguard Backdoor Locking System*, and let me tell you, the operative word here is 'locking.'" She picked up the medium-sized sample and pointed the base toward the camera. "Justin, can you get a close-up of this, please?

"There, ladies. See how tiny the key is?" She looked into the camera lens. "We've all fumbled with trying to fit a key into a lock in the dark, and know how impossible it is even with a key the size of your car or house key. Now, imagine this product is in place, and you want to remove it. There is no way you're getting this out on your own. Once it's in, and the lock is engaged, it isn't going anywhere until your partner inserts the key for you."

"And, there you have it, folks!" Ford took the plug from her hand and held it up triumphantly. "A glowing testimonial from B.J. Parker! Thanks for watching, and remember, the number is 1-800-BUT-PLUG. We're K. Ford Adams and B.J. Parker for the *Adult Shopping Show*, saying good night, and sleep tight. See you next week. Same time. Same channel."

He tugged her close and planted a kiss on the top of her head just as Justin chirped from behind the control panel, "And, we're out!"

Ford's hand slid from where it rested on her hip, and she had to grab the table to steady herself. She hadn't realized how much she'd been relying on him to keep her upright during the show.

"Great job, Ford. And, Ms. Parker, you were awesome!" Justin bounced with his enthusiasm.

"Are you insane?" She directed her tirade at Ford. "What happened to the script?"

"The teleprompter broke just before you got here. We figured you'd have a coronary, so we decided not to tell you and just wing it."

"Wing it?" She might be irrational, but his winging it had gone too far. "How dare you tell the whole world I've tried the… the *System*?"

"I didn't exactly tell the *whole world*, Becky Jean. You said it yourself. The viewership for this time slot is practically nothing. So what if two or three people know? None of them know you."

"They might!" She stomped to the door and grabbed her jacket off the doorknob. Jamming her arms into the sleeves, she faced him. "What if my mother is one of the people who saw the show?"

He shrugged, and she looked around for something to throw

at him. Seeing nothing she could easily pick up, she shook her head in frustration.

"For what it's worth, Ms. Parker," Justin piped up, "I thought it went very well. Better than rehearsal, and the sparks flying between you two was awesome. Heck, you had me wanting to call in, and I've already got the samples you gave me."

"Thanks, Justin," she said, ashamed she'd ranted at Ford in front of an employee. "I'm glad you found the spectacle entertaining."

A knock sounded on the door. Becky spun around and opened it. The young woman she'd hired to work the switchboard overnight in case orders actually came in stood there with a worried look in her eyes. "Yes, Camille, what is it?"

"Ms. Parker, ma'am. Uh…. Could you maybe take a few calls? Kim and Lisa are answering calls as fast as they can, but people are hanging up."

"People are calling in?" She couldn't believe it. "How many calls have come in?"

"At least a hundred, and those are the ones I could answer. If this keeps up, you're going to need a bigger switchboard and a lot more order takers."

"We'll be right there," Ford said over Becky's shoulder. "Can you patch calls into our offices?"

"Sure. Just let me know when you're ready." Becky stared at the girl's retreating back.

"We'd better hustle. Justin, can you take a few calls, too?"

"Sure thing." As the technician pushed past her, she thought she heard him say, "Who would have thunk it?"

She sure hadn't.

CHAPTER THIRTEEN

"Whoowee!" Roseanne fanned herself. "Talk about hot. Your show was H.O.T. hot last night, girlfriend."

"Please," Becky pleaded across her friend's kitchen table. "Can we not talk about the show?"

"Why ever not?" Roseanne plunked two sweaty glasses of iced tea on the table to go with the chicken salad sandwiches she'd prepared for their weekly lunch date. "You are gorgeous, always have been, and Ford… well, he's about the sexiest thing to ever come out of this little town. But the two of you together? Bam! The chemistry between you two is explosive."

Becky lifted the slice of homemade multi-grain bread to examine the chunky chicken goodness underneath. Two lengthwise pickle slices, also homemade, topped the mound, just the way she liked it. For someone who'd never had any culinary training, Roseanne had become a fabulous cook. "You saw rage, not lust. You are right about one thing — there was almost an explosion. I came within an inch of blowing my top, right there on set."

"Really? Do tell, my friend."

Becky replaced the bread on her sandwich with a sigh. The crazy number of orders that came in overnight had gone a long way toward calming her anger. Ford had been right, but damn if she would admit it to him. However, she could tell Roseanne. As they downed their sandwiches and cold drinks, she told her friend what had transpired the night before.

"But the show went off without a hitch, or so it appeared from my end," Roseanne said.

"If sales are any indication, then you're right. We're looking at adding more phone lines to handle the calls."

Her friend shook her head. "I still can't believe you sell sex toys for a living. What does your mother think about it?"

Becky shrugged. "She almost had a heart attack when I told her, but she'd rather me sell sex toys than move to Dallas, or farther away, to find a job."

"Your mother always has been the practical sort."

"Yeah, she is. However, she's still after Colin to get a regular job." She curled her fingers into air quotes around the word regular.

"How's your brother doing? Is he still playing at that club in Nashville?"

Becky's younger brother, Colin, had never been interested in going to college—much to their parent's disappointment. Right out of high school he'd packed his belongings and the guitar he'd made in eighth grade woodshop into the beat-up truck he'd saved all his life for and struck out for the bright lights of Nashville. Determined to make it as a country singer/songwriter, he'd lived like a pauper for years before obtaining a measure of success shortly before their father's passing.

Becky rose to place her empty plate and glass in the sink then leaned against the counter. She needed to go back to the office but was reluctant to do so. "Yeah. He signed a record contract earlier this year. According to him, he's on his way to stardom. I guess we'll have to wait and see."

"That would sure be something, wouldn't it?" Roseanne placed her dishes in the sink, too. "Tell him I said hi, next time you talk to him."

"I will. He says he misses Butte Plains, wants to live here when he makes it big. But for the time being, Nashville is his home."

"Well, I hope all his dreams come true. If talent is what it takes, he's got it in spades."

Becky couldn't argue with her assessment. Her brother had always been gifted when it came to music. He was a genius with wood, too. She counted among her most prized possessions a jewelry box he'd made for her in high school. If music didn't work out for him, he could easily make a living as a craftsman. "I'll tell him you said so," she said, heading for the back door. "Thanks for lunch, and for letting me rant. Same time next week?"

Back in her office, Becky sat at her desk doing her best to stay awake when a blur of pink breezed past her door leaving the faint scent of gardenias behind. Even when her husband had run the company, Helen Adams had been an infrequent visitor to the plant, but she'd been there enough times for Becky to recognize her, even if her unique perfume didn't give her away.

"Ford Adams!" Yep, Helen Adams had arrived, and she wasn't happy. Scandalous news spread faster than a brush fire in Butte Plains. "Tell me what I just heard at the Dippity Do isn't true."

Becky imagined her partner leaning back in the new ergonomic desk chair he'd insisted on purchasing. This one didn't creak the way his father's had, but she'd committed Ford's new mannerisms to memory. Sometimes having a steel-trap mind could be a liability.

"Good to see you, too, Mom. Have a seat." Ford's voice carried through their open office doors.

She didn't envy her partner the job ahead, but it had been his decision to not tell his mother about her precarious financial situation or fill her in when things began to turn around. Ford's days of withholding information had come to an end.

"What is the meaning of this, Ford? Do you have any idea what they're saying about Adams Manufacturing?"

"I've got a pretty good idea." She couldn't miss the frustration in Ford's voice.

"Is it true? Are we making…?"

"Sex toys? Yes, we are. And we're making a lot of money.

Money we desperately need."

Becky experienced a twinge of guilt for eavesdropping on the conversation, but she wouldn't miss this for the world. Mrs. Adams owned 50 percent of the company. If she pushed Ford to sell her portion immediately, which could be done since her husband hadn't imposed any restrictions on what she did with her shares, everything they'd worked for would be lost—just as it appeared they might survive the year.

Becky had never envisioned herself selling sex toys, but she *had* imagined bringing Butte Plains back to life, and she could see it slowly happening—all because Ford Adams had designed and built a revolutionary sex toy. Since they'd first begun production of the *Safeguard Backdoor Locking System*, they'd tripled the number of people they employed, and many were locals who had been out of work for years. This morning, she'd approved the hiring of a dozen more phone operators. The print shop making the headers and instruction sheets for their product packaging had recently expanded into a larger building and doubled their workforce. Their success was a perfect example of a trickle-down economy in action.

She had to give her partner credit, he didn't mince words with his mother, telling her straight out about the condition he'd found the company in, mentioning that desperate times had called for desperate measures. When she argued the indecency of their products, he argued the indecency of bankruptcy court and seeing his mother move to an apartment complex and flip burgers to pay the rent. Mrs. Adams quieted down after the reality check. Becky's heart hurt for the woman who, other than burying her husband, had never suffered a hardship in her life.

When other women of her generation were out making their own way in the world, Helen Adams had chosen the path of wife, mother, and social butterfly, relying on her husband to provide for her. If the threat of destitution didn't scare her straight, nothing would do it.

Becky crept to the door to better hear the woman's response.

"But really, Ford. You said it yourself—the company is doing better, so can't we go back to producing decent products?"

"No, we can't." He patiently explained the shift in the market to cheaper imported goods, as well as the decline in demand for the products they'd been making for the last several decades. Then he reminded her of the ways the company had adapted over the last century, pointing out this latest change to be one more of those shifts. "I don't know how much longer I can stay here and do this, Mom. I planned to sell the company from the beginning, but there's no market for a dying industrial plant. To be honest, if Dad hadn't insisted the plant had to operate for a year before I could sell my portion, I would have been gone months ago."

"Why on earth would you want to sell?"

"I think it's the only solution. Scott and I worked hard to get where we are. He's been great about me being here, but I'm neglecting my partnership with him. I need to get back before he loses patience with me."

"Adams Manufacturing is your *legacy*. I can't believe you would consider selling it."

Go, Mom!

"I don't see any other choice. There's nothing for me here."

"I'm nothing?"

"You know that's not what I mean. This town has been dying for ages."

Rustling fabric and the casters on Ford's chair rolling across the rubber mat alerted her to the mother and son standing. Becky hustled back to her desk and ducked her head, pretending to read the report in front of her. A narrow band of pink appeared along the edge of her doorway where his mother had stopped.

"I don't know if I can ever hold my head up in this town again anyway. Maybe I'll go with you when you go back to New York."

"You know you're welcome to come live with me in New York or anywhere else I might go, but this is your home. Your friends are here."

"I can make new friends, but you're the only son I've got."

Becky held her breath as the older woman stormed past her door. She'd had enough experience with parental guilt to make her feel a little sorry for Ford. His mother wouldn't make it easy for him to walk away from what she perceived as his familial obligation. But, unlike Becky, Ford would never cave to his mother's wishes. He'd be out of Butte Plains on the next bus if he found a buyer today.

"You heard?" At the sound of his voice, she glanced up. Shoulder propped against the doorframe, he looked as defeated as he sounded.

"Heard what?"

He snorted. "No need to play innocent, Becky Jean. I know you heard every word."

"Not every word." She had missed a few. Maybe. "I thought you handled it well."

"So well she'll probably end up living with me in my house back East."

"That would be bad?"

He shrugged. "Not bad, but this is her home. She wouldn't know anyone there. She'd be miserable."

"She has a lot to think about. Give her some time to adjust to the way things are."

His lips lifted on one corner. "You're a good person, Becky Jean. My dad knew what he was doing when he hired you."

Becky stared at the empty doorway long after her partner vacated it. She couldn't decide if she adored the man for his kindness to his mother and hated him for his disregard for the company bearing his name, and the town it meant so much to. Every time he talked about going back to his life on the East Coast, a gaping hole opened up in her midsection. His mother would eventually come around, but Ford seemed resolute. He would leave, and Becky would be wise to guard her heart so it didn't go with him.

~~~

Numbers don't lie, but they do tell a story. Of all the things Becky had learned in her economics classes, that one statement stuck in her mind as she looked at the sales reports on her desk. She'd have to speak with Ford about finding a way to increase production of the *Safeguard Backdoor Locking System*. Sales from the initial broadcast had simply floored her, but she'd forgotten about the local network's plans to tape and replay the show throughout the week.

They'd gone live on Wednesday evening. By Saturday, eleven other small markets had called wanting to get in on the action. In other words, they were an overnight success.

Even the astronomical numbers she had before her didn't lessen her anger at the way Ford had manipulated her. Everyone around town called her B.J. these days… then snickered behind their hands. She knew exactly what they were thinking. B.J. stood for blow job. Her humiliation knew no bounds.

Gathering the papers she needed to discuss with her partner, she took a deep breath to steady her nerves. Ford could be incredibly agreeable on some things, but on others… nothing short of dynamite would make him budge. It would be a shame to blow such a nice-looking male specimen to bits, but if it took an explosion….

She knocked on his open door. "Ford? Got a few minutes?"

"For you, B.J.? Always." He tossed his drafting pencil on the desk and rocked back in his chair.

"I've told you not to call me that," she said, plunking into one of the old green leather visitors' chairs. She'd thought Ford would want to change everything about his father's office, but so far, he hadn't moved a thing, except to arrange a place to display samples of all their past and present products. He'd said potential buyers would like seeing how the company had evolved over the last
~~~

hundred or so years.

No doubt their current success would bring a host of interested people to their door. If she sold her share, too, she'd have enough money to start over someplace else. Maybe open a small marketing firm of her own. Not that selling sex toys meant she had the knack for selling anything else, but she had more credibility than she'd ever had before.

"You have to admit, the nickname turned out to be a stroke of genius, Becky Jean. B.J. Parker is a *YouTube* success."

"We're on *YouTube*?" A stab of horror turned her insides to ice.

"Yep. Our first episode has gone viral. I owe you an apology. I never thought this television network idea would work. You're a marketing genius."

"I don't know, Ford. Maybe we should quit while we're ahead." She handed him the latest sales figures. "Sales jumped through the roof this week. I honestly don't know how we're going to meet the demand. And if the same thing happens with the next product we showcase?" She bit her bottom lip as he scanned the reports. "I think we might have bitten off more than we can chew."

Ford tossed the papers on his desk. "Nonsense, Becky Jean. We can handle this."

"Not without adding another shift to the factory. We'd have to hire more workers, including supervisory personnel. Our expenses would increase, too. Longer hours means higher utilities."

"How long would it take to hire and train a second and third shift of workers?"

"*Two* new shifts? Are you crazy?"

"I don't think so, but thousands of people are waiting for their *Safeguard Backdoor Locking System*." He smirked at the name she'd given his locking butt plug.

"Laugh all you want, but I was right about the name. It adds a level of respectability to the product."

"And it looks good on the new sign out front." He'd insisted on hanging a new sign on the front of the building. *Adams*

Manufacturing. Home of the Safeguard Backdoor Locking System. Guard your assets with the best. She'd argued against the assets part, but he'd pulled his majority-shareholder card, and she'd had no choice but to back down.

"I can't even imagine what your father would say if he knew."

"He'd be proud as hell. The Adams family has weathered wars, depressions, recessions, and advances in technology to stay in business this long. We did what we had to do, Becky. He'd be proud of what we've accomplished."

She tried not to read anything into him calling her Becky. From the first day, he'd insisted on calling her Becky Jean or Becks, and then B.J. Never once, until today, had he called her by her preferred name. "He might be proud we found a way to stay in business, but I can't help but think he would have preferred we do it with a more respectable product."

"Careful. You're beginning to sound like my mother."

"She was right, you know?"

"Maybe, but we did what we had to do."

She couldn't argue with his logic. Ford's ridiculous invention had brought the company back from the brink of bankruptcy, and done it in record-breaking time.

"Which brings us back to these orders. We have to fill them. We don't have any choice."

She sighed. She hated admitting he was right. "It's going to cost a fortune to increase production."

He steepled his fingers under his chin and stared at the computer monitor that barely clung to the corner of his desk. Like all the others in the building, the screensaver was a rotating montage of photos depicting the front of the building from various angles. She smiled at the one interior shot of all the employees on the factory floor, smiling and waving at the camera. Already outdated, it would be more so if they added production shifts. Soon they'd need a football field to hold everyone and a drone to hover over to take the photo.

Ford's voice snapped her attention back to their latest problem. "Remember, we make a lot more money off the direct sales orders. The extra cushion will offset a good portion of our investment in running an expanded production schedule."

She nodded and shifted, trying to find a more comfortable position. Would he even notice if she replaced his ancient visitors' chairs with something new? "True, but what happens when we feature another product next week? If we have an equal response, how are we going to meet the demand?"

Ford's gaze bored into her. "I have every confidence in you, Becky. You'll find a way."

The sincerity in his voice washed over her like a warm summer breeze, lifting her spirits and melting her resistance. "I'll ask our new HR person to start calling applicants she has on file. If we can't find enough workers, we'll advertise the positions. In the interim, we can expand the first shift an hour or two. It will cost us in overtime wages, but the increase will be less than the cost of new hires."

His smile warmed her. "I knew you'd find a way. Don't worry about the numbers. The orders are going to keep coming in." He glanced at the latest sales report again. "Have you looked into transforming the original factory building into a home for the *Adult Shopping Show*?"

"I have the plans I'd initially drawn up and a few estimates. The historical society voted to allow most of the interior renovations, provided we don't significantly change the exterior."

"I suppose putting ASS on a sign out front is out of the question."

She sighed at the old argument. "Yes, I'm afraid it is. You'll have to settle for *Adult Shopping Show* on a discreet, street-level sign."

He shrugged off her dismissal of his ridiculous proposal. "Let's get hopping on those renovations. As I said, your idea is pure genius. It's already exceeded my wildest dreams, and it's only going to get bigger."

That's what she was afraid of. It was time to make some changes. "About the show," she said, placing another stack of papers on his desk. "I think we should find a real spokeswoman to replace me."

He didn't even glance at the headshots the Dallas talent agency had sent over. "Why would we do a fool thing like that? I didn't sell all those units. *We* sold them, Becky Jean. You and me. Look at the comments on *YouTube* if you don't believe me."

"You tricked me into saying those things," she accused.

"Maybe so, but your backhanded endorsement convinced people to buy the product and cemented in their mind that you and I are more than business partners. They want to see more, and they want to hear you endorse the product."

"You expect me to actually try everything we showcase?"

He nodded. "Yep, *and* endorse it. I promised our viewers we wouldn't bring them a product we hadn't personally tried and found to be worthy."

"Don't you mean you promised them *I* would try the products?"

He shrugged. "It's not my fault they assumed we would be trying them out together."

God, if only we were. She squelched the thought. Having those images in her head during a show would render her incapable of speech. "Aren't you even going to look at the models who want the job?"

"It would be a waste of time, and you know it." He dropped the photos in the wastebasket beside his desk. "Which product are we featuring this week?"

"I don't have a clue," she said, rising to leave before she suggested he help her try something out.

"I suggest we go with the *KeyP Me Safe Light.* Increasing production on the tiny flashlights will be fairly easy."

The small personal vibrator that doubled as a key

ring/flashlight hadn't gained the same popularity as the locking butt plug. It could use a marketing push. It amounted to a variation on the flashlight they had been producing with a few add-ons easily outsourced to people in the community to assemble off-site. "I'll come up with a script for the show and get it over to you so you can read it before we go on air."

"Just send me a list of the talking points. We did okay without a script last time."

Easy for him to say. He wasn't the one who'd made a fool of himself, blurting out very personal and private information. "You aren't going to goad me into confessing I've used this thing."

"I won't have to because you *are* going to test it and tell the audience about your experience. If you don't, I'll make something up myself."

She clenched her fists. "You wouldn't!"

"I would, and I will." He picked up his drafting pencil and shuffled papers, searching for whatever he'd been working on when she came in. "Call me this evening if you need help using the *KeyP Me Safe Light*. That's the kind of research I excel at."

She made it to the door before he stopped her. "Oh, and check out the *YouTube* videos. You'll see what I mean."

CHAPTER FOURTEEN

"Is all this really necessary?" Becky eyed the extensive makeup palette spread across her kitchen counter. She should have known better than to ask for Roseanne's help.

"Yes, it is." Her friend rearranged the assortment of paints and creams, most of which Becky couldn't identify. "Amy did a great job on your hair, and the dress we picked out is killer. All you need is a little makeup, and Ford Adams won't know what hit him."

Amy Kilgore, former classmate and present owner of Dippity Do, had done a fantastic job on Becky's hair. The new layered cut made the most of her natural curls while framing her face in the best possible way. Thrilled with the outcome, she'd made an appointment for the following week to have her hair styled before the next show, too. "I don't want to hit him. I just want him to notice me." Becky closed her eyes while Roseanne smeared some kind of lotion stuff on her face.

"Trust me, he's going to notice." She put the cap back on the tube and tossed it aside. From another tube, she squirted a dot of pale liquid onto her fingertip. Brush in hand, she tilted Becky's head back. "Hold still, will you? We've got to get this done, pour you into your dress, and get you there in time for the show."

"Preaching to the choir." Becky twitched her nose. "That tickles."

"Shut up. Artist at work here."

Aware of the minutes ticking by, she tried to remain calm, but the closer she came to actually carrying out her plan to bring Ford to his knees, the more she doubted she should. "Am I doing the right thing?"

"No doubts, girlfriend. The man deserves to be taken down a peg or two after the way he tricked you on last week's show."

When Roseanne came at her with another brush, Becky closed her eyes again. She didn't know why it bothered her so much if Ford thought her uptight, but it did. And she'd made up her mind to change his opinion.

Becky closed her mouth while her friend drew a line beneath her lower lashes. As soon as her hand lifted, she asked, "What if he doesn't notice?"

"He's gonna notice. He'd have to be dead not to. Take my word for it. Lips open, honey."

Becky parted her lips. While Roseanne worked her magic on them, Becky envisioned Ford's face when he saw her. Maybe, for once, he'd see her as a woman, not just his business partner. What kind of relationship could he have with this Ronnie woman? Ford had been in Butte Plains for half a year, and she'd yet to make an appearance. If she had a guy as gorgeous and great as Ford, no way would she let him wander off on his own for months. Ford had never given Becky reason to believe his affections were up for grabs, but his actions didn't speak of a commitment to his long-distance relationship. Besides, she had no intention of trying to steal Ford. He'd deliberately insulted her. Today's makeover was payback.

"There. All done." Becky grabbed the hand mirror Roseanne held out to her. "What do you think?"

"Oh, wow." The woman staring back at her couldn't be her.

"Like it?"

Becky turned her head from side to side, admiring the transformation from all angles. "You're a genius, Roseanne. Where did you learn to do this?"

"Lonely hours spent watching *YouTube* videos."

Becky set the mirror aside. "Business has been that bad?"

"My occupancy rate last year was less than 20 percent. Thank goodness I own the house outright. I'm only paying utilities and the small loan I took out to convert the property into a B&B. As long as I do all the cooking and cleaning myself, I can get by with renting the occasional room."

"Then I won't waste any more of my time feeling guilty about the length of time Scott spent here. I'm sure the extra money helped."

"Sure did." Roseanne got busy stashing everything back into the plastic shoebox she'd used as a travel case for today. "Is he coming back?"

Becky didn't miss the wistful tone of her friend's voice. Even though she complained about Scott's overbearing ways, anyone who knew Roseanne well could see she'd fallen hard for the Yankee and had been devastated when he returned to New York. "Maybe. I'll make sure he stays at The Yellow Rose if he does."

"Thanks." She secured the lid on the box. "Let's get you into your dress and on your way. At least one of us should get what she wants."

~~~

Ford tossed the script for the *KeyP Me Safe Light* show in the wastebasket without reading a single word. They'd tried going the scripted route, and it had been a dismal failure. He had no idea if Becky Jean had tried out the product, but he'd find out soon enough. Ever since their conversation earlier in the week, he'd been thinking about how to play it if it became clear she hadn't tried it. He hadn't tried it either, but he knew what the tiny little device could do, and he had plenty of experience with similar items. If necessary, he'd point out the unique features of their pocket
~~~

vibrator then launch into a monologue about how much fun it had been to use it on B.J.

Becky Jean would be sure to turn varied shades of red, which the viewers would incorrectly interpret as embarrassment. They'd sell thousands of units, and no one would be the wiser except him. He'd be watching his back for the foreseeable future, but the sales would be worth sacrificing his safety.

"Hey, Justin," he said, looking around their tiny studio. "I can see our co-host isn't here yet."

"We've got time. She called about an hour ago to say she'd gone home to change clothes for the show. I sure hope she doesn't have any more suits like the one she had on last week."

"I hear you," Ford said as he adjusted his tie. "It worked out though."

"Sure did. A few more weeks like the last one and I can pay off all my student loans."

"That would be nice." He propped his hip against the display table. "I know what you said when we hired you, about this being an opportunity to get in on the ground floor of something with real potential. And honestly? I thought you were nuts."

"If we'd gone on the air last week the way B.— Ms. Parker wanted, we would have been sunk. The woman has vision, but she can't act."

Ford chuckled at the accurate description. "This whole thing was her idea, so yeah, she has vision. I think once she sees the public doesn't want robots selling them sex toys, she'll be onboard with this fly-by-the-seat-of-our-pants style."

"Are you saying you threw out this week's script, too?"

"Yep."

"Thank you, God."

"You're welcome, but just Ford will do." He kept a straight face until Justin caught the joke and burst into laughter. They were both brushing tears from their eyes when the door opened and Becky Jean stepped inside.

No. Not Becky Jean. *B.J. Parker* walked through the door.

Her auburn hair hung in loose curls around her shoulders—the complete opposite of the tight bun she'd worn earlier. Her makeup was heavier than he'd seen her wear, but flawlessly done. Her eyes sparkled, and the shade of red on her lips matched the dress hugging each and every one of her generous curves. His rational mind knew the garment would pass the HR test for work-appropriate clothing, but damn, it had to be the most unconsciously sexy thing he'd ever seen. The clinging red number screamed look but don't touch in a way that made his fingers itch to peel it off her.

Justin's low, appreciative whistle snapped Ford out of his lustful haze.

"Sorry I'm late." She tossed her purse on one of the conference room chairs lining the walls out of camera range. "My hair appointment ran late."

"Damn, B.J.— I mean, Ms. Parker. You look—"

"Perfect," Ford interrupted before the younger man said what both of them were thinking. "You aren't late. We were just talking about the videotaping equipment you ordered."

Justin gave him a puzzled look but took up the conversation. "In addition to taping during the day, we'll be able to do several weeks' worth of shows in a short period of time. As it stands, we only get one shot at doing it right, but once we start advance taping, we can edit out blunders."

Ford joined Becky Jean on their designated spots.

"Jacket on or jacket off?" she asked.

Hell, he hadn't even noticed the dress had a matching jacket. She dropped the short blazer off her shoulders to reveal the sleeveless dress beneath. His brain leapt into action, conjuring up images of all the ways he could assist her in removing the cover-up. "On. Leave it on." *For now.*

"If you say so. I like the dress either way." She shrugged the fabric over her shoulders then pulled her hair free from her collar and smiled at Justin. "I don't think I'll be as nervous when we can edit out mistakes. If I'd known how popular the show would be, I would have purchased the taping equipment in the beginning."

"You've got nothing to worry about, Ms. Parker. A few mistakes make you human, and people relate to flaws."

She laughed. "Well, they must, because we made plenty of mistakes last week. If we stick to the script tonight, it should go better."

"About the script—"

"Did you try the product, Becky Jean?" She didn't need to know he'd decided to ditch another carefully worded script in favor of pushing her buttons on live television. Nothing good could come of it, but good things did happen when she responded to him without artifice. Last week's sales were proof enough.

"No, I did not," she said. "I've used flashlights and key rings before."

He raised an eyebrow at the one function of their product she'd left out. "Have you ever used a vibrator?"

Color bloomed on her cheeks. "I have a massager. Does that count?"

He had no business imagining the things popping into his head. "I suppose it does." *Lord, she's going to be the death of me.* He glanced at the clock—thirty seconds until air-time.

"On your spots," Justin said. "Ford, a little closer to Ms. Parker."

Ford moved closer. She always smelled good, but maybe because she'd been to the salon to get her hair done her scent seemed more tantalizing than ever. Every breath he took made him more aware of the Siren standing next to him. And like every wise sailor, he knew he needed to steer clear.

Justin held up five fingers. "On in five. Four. Three. Two. One." He pointed his index finger at them.

"Good evening, folks. I'm K. Ford Adams, and this is my partner, B.J. Parker. Thanks for tuning in tonight." Ignoring the exasperated vibes coming from his partner, he thanked everyone who placed orders the previous week then mentioned the availability of the *Safeguard Backdoor Locking System* for those who hadn't yet ordered. After repeating the 800 number, he turned to Becky Jean.

She jumped in on cue. "Tonight, we'd like to introduce you to one of our newest products, the *KeyP Me Safe Light*."

Ford followed her lead, moving to the display table. He took up the dialogue, describing the tiny vibrator in his own words while B.J. held one of the miniature marvels up for the camera to capture. So far, she'd gone along with his non-scripted version of the show—mostly because she had no choice on live television. Lifting the small device from her palm, he prayed she'd go along with his next idea.

"Ladies and gentlemen, last week we promised we wouldn't show you a product we couldn't personally recommend. And since I have it on good authority B.J. has not tried out the *KeyP Me Safe Light*, I feel obligated to show you, and her, the benefits of this little jewel."

"Oh no!" Becky Jean placed her hand on Ford's chest to hold him at bay. She shook her head. "No. No. No. No. No."

"Just a little demonstration for our audience, B.J." He smiled at the camera then back at her before moving to stand behind her. Placing his hands on her shoulders to keep her from running, he addressed the viewers. "In case you don't know, B.J. is the Marketing Director here at Adams Manufacturing. She works hard at her job, and I often see her at her desk, late in the day, rolling her head, trying to loosen the tight muscles in her neck. Sound familiar to anyone out there? I thought so," he said amiably, hoping to draw the audience, and Becky Jean, in. He'd only guessed she rolled her head to reduce stress, but from the way she turned to glare at him, he'd nailed her behavior.

"Though there are many uses for the *KeyP Me Safe Light*, this is one of my favorites." He held his hand up to show the key ring around his middle finger and the mini-flashlight/vibrator lying along the length of the digit. With a flick of his thumb against the switch embedded in the end, the device hummed to life.

"B.J. seems a little tense right now. Let's see if we can fix you up." Before she could get a protest past her lips, he brushed her soft-as-silk hair over one shoulder and pressed the humming cylinder to her racing pulse. She moaned as he worked the vibrator up and down her slender neck. No words were necessary. The way her body responded to the sensual massage said it all.

Ford crooned soft words in her ear, imagining what it would be like to have her beneath him, to feel her body respond to his in bed. He shouldn't have to share her responses with anyone, let alone the entire world. If this episode proved anything like the first one, millions of people would be witness to Becky Jean's surrender.

No woman had ever turned to putty in his hands the way she did. Knowing they were not alone, he still couldn't bring himself to stop. Slipping his hand lower, his lips followed the path he'd blazed. His hand trailed down the slope of her neck to her shoulder where he pinched her jacket between his thumb and index finger, slowly easing it off her shoulder.

He managed to repeat the process on the other side, but when he eased back to see what he'd done, the sight of her bare upper arms trapped in the confines of her jacket nearly sent him to his knees. Giving himself a mental shake, he removed the jacket. Just her jacket. Nothing more. But there was something about the demure neckline of her sleeveless dress, it made removing the outer garment seem like a sensual act.

He'd been inside his share of clubs where the dancers had no problem removing what little clothing they wore while moving provocatively. None of those shows had ever affected him as much as seeing Becky Jean's bare arms.

Thanking the heavens the viewing audience couldn't see him below the waist, he smoothed the vibrator along the length of her right arm, massaging and caressing every inch of skin. When he reached her hand, he stroked each finger before pressing the digits together. As he dragged the toy from fingertip to palm, her fingers closed over his like tulip petals folding in for the night.

Becky couldn't take her eyes off Ford's hands. One of hers lay in his open palm while he did all manner of wicked things to it with the vibrator attached to the middle finger of his other hand. She should be taking Ford to task for ignoring the script again, but from the moment he'd swept her hair off her neck, she'd forgotten why she should be pissed at him. When he touched his lips to her neck, she'd turned into a puddle of goo and lost the ability to think at all.

Yes, the vibrator hummed over her skin, but she couldn't blame it for her mental shutdown. No, she blamed it entirely on Ford. Sure, the tiny trembles made her skin tingle, but they were overshadowed by the feel of his hand trailing along behind, leaving fire in its wake.

"B.J.?"

She tore her gaze away from her fingers clamped down on Ford's. Dazed, she studied his face for clues.

"What do you think of the *KeyP Me Safe Light*?"

"Huh?"

He smiled so bright it was like looking into the headlamp of an oncoming train. Something in the back of her mind told her to run, but the message got lost somewhere between her brain and her feet. She stood rooted to the spot, staring up at Ford, their hands intertwined, her heart thumping out an erratic beat. He spoke to someone — not her.

"There you are, folks. If that's not a raving endorsement of the product, I don't know what is! Remember, the number is 1-800-BUT-PLUG. Operators are standing by to take your order."

"And, we're out!" At Justin's triumphant shout, Ford yanked his fingers from Becky's grip, severing their connection. She shook her head and a bead of sweat trickled down her temple. The young tech went around shutting off the hot lights. "Tonight was even better than last week. Man, oh man, we're going to make a fortune if this keeps up."

"I think you may be right." Ford held something out to her. Becky stared at the lump of red fabric for a moment before reaching for it. "Sorry about dropping your jacket on the floor, but I didn't know what else to do with it. Put the dry-cleaning bill on the production expense report. In fact, I think we should add a clothing allowance to the expenses."

Becky jammed her arms into the sleeves and resettled the jacket on her shoulders. She felt shaky and not at all in charge of her faculties. As the lights dimmed, she shivered in the suddenly cool air.

"Are you all right?" Ford took her by the elbow and led her to the nearest chair. She dropped heavily. "You don't look so good."

"Thanks." She glanced up at him. "I'm fine, just got a little overheated, I think."

"When you're ready, I'll drive you home."

She grabbed her purse and stood. "That's not necessary. I can drive."

"You might be right" — he took the purse from her hands, slung the strap over his shoulder then reached for her elbow again — "but why take chances when I have to go past your place anyway?"

"I suppose." She couldn't think when Ford touched her, couldn't muster up the wherewithal to tell him to mind his own business. "We should check in with the phone bank, make sure they have it covered."

"We hired a dozen people this week and installed enough lines to handle the load, plus an elaborate call-holding system. They don't need us distracting them."

She acknowledged the truth in his statement. They'd spent an exorbitant amount of money on the upgrades as well as converted the old supervisor's office on the production floor to accommodate the new order takers.

CHAPTER FIFTEEN

Ford snuck another glance at his passenger. Becky Jean hadn't said a word since they'd left the factory. He'd hoped some fresh air would do her good, but in the glow of the passing streetlights, she appeared as dazed as he felt. He couldn't leave her alone in her present condition. He'd worry himself sick if he did.

She waited for him to open the car door for her—another sure sign she wasn't herself tonight. For a moment, she reached out to take his offered hand, but snatched hers back before their fingers touched.

Ford stood back, allowing her to stand under her own steam. He followed her to her door where she dug in her purse, eventually producing a key attached to a *KeyP Me Safe Light*. He glanced around, but all he could see in the weak light coming from the porch light were a few clay pots with some sort of flowers bubbling out of them. Her hand shook, but with the aid of the flashlight on her keychain she managed to fit the key in the lock. In case she had ideas about leaving him outside, he trailed close behind her, pausing to remove the key from the lock and shut the door.

As she stepped out of those fuck-me pumps that had been driving him insane for the last hour, he reminded himself he'd brought her home in order to care for her, not to take advantage of her.

When she slipped the jacket off her shoulders and tossed it on a nearby chair, he fisted his hands in his pockets and reminded himself he had no business thinking about how soft her skin had been beneath his fingertips.

And when she turned and faced him, eyes dark with arousal, lips parted in invitation, he forgot everything except how much he wanted to kiss the beautiful woman standing before him.

He closed the distance separating them in two strides. Her scent overwhelmed him. Out of necessity, he'd blocked it out on the set, but they were alone here so he opened himself to her every nuance. Her beauty went beyond the physical. There was a wholesome quality about her that made her radiant in a way he'd never seen before. It both intrigued and scared the hell out of him. He'd never been attracted to wholesome. All the women in his life had been worldly and sophisticated—complicated. They played the relationship game on the same terms he did—without any expectations.

Becky Jean had expectation written all over her face.

He planned to leave Butte Plains as soon as he could find a buyer for his and his mother's share of the factory and negotiate a fair price. Becky Jean deserved someone who would stick around. Someone who would give her the fairy tale.

Before he did something they'd both regret in the morning, he took a step back. Becky Jean followed. He lifted his hands, intending to push her away, but moving with purpose, she wrapped her hands around his head and drew his face down to hers. Her lips were warm and pliant, her kiss more experienced than he would have believed. She nipped his lower lip. He gasped and opened for her.

Damn. Her tongue swept in, dueling with his. His blood turned to molten lava slaughtering cells in his upstairs brain. Thinking with his downstairs brain, he cupped her ass and dragged her hard against him. She was soft in all the right places, and fuck if he didn't want to take everything she offered. Her fingers tickled the pulse at his throat then went to work on the top button of his shirt. The fastener slid free. Cool air brushed his skin bringing sanity with it.

"Whoa." Backing away took every ounce of decency he possessed. There were at least a million reasons not to peel her out of her dress and sink into her warmth. They were business partners. Never mind she was the hottest thing west of the Mississippi. She didn't strike him as a casual sex type of woman. "We have to stop, Becky Jean." He held his hand up — a stop sign between them.

If he'd actually thrown a bucket of ice water on her head, he couldn't have done a better job of breaking the spell between them. Becky Jean blinked a few times then focused her gorgeous blue eyes on him. Another blink washed away the last traces of arousal, replacing the tender emotion with anger. Cold. Hard. Anger.

Ordinarily, he reveled in pushing her buttons, riling her up to see blue flames in her eyes and a rosy blush on her cheeks, but her anger tonight was different. Sharper. Deeper. If looks could kill, he'd be wearing a toe tag.

"Go, Ford." She pointed at the door. "Get out of my house."

"I'm sorry, Becky Jean, but you know as well as I do—"

"That you're a snake oil salesman? Because you are." She pointed at the door again. "Get out. Now."

"Can't we talk—?"

"About the way you seduced me on camera? About the way you touched me? About the way I—"

The way you felt in my arms? The way your skin feels like satin and your hair feels like silk? The way that dress makes me want to tear if off to see your luscious curves? The way I think about you morning, noon, and night? The way I wish to hell we weren't who we are? "About us?"

"There is no *us*, Ford. There's me, and there's you. For a minute there, I lost my head. Thought *maybe* I was wrong." The vixen who'd all but attacked him had disappeared, replaced by the shy and all-too innocent woman he'd come to admire.

He'd gone too far during the broadcast, let his desire for her show, and they were both going to suffer for his mistake. "I'm sorry." He inched toward the door. "I'm really sorry."

He knew he should be thanking her for throwing him out of her house. She'd done the right thing. He'd done everything she'd accused him of, and more. As he drove up the hill to his temporary home, he cursed himself for a fool. Not once since Becky walked into their makeshift studio, glammed up to the nines, had he given a single thought to the consequences of acting on his desires. He'd allowed his hormones to overrule his common sense, and Becky had suffered for his stupidity. He owed his partner an apology.

~~~

Oh. My. God. Becky fell face-first on her bed. She'd wanted to prove to him she wasn't some backwoods mouse—that she could be sexy and sophisticated like the women he undoubtedly dated on the East Coast. For once, she'd wanted him to look at her with desire in his eyes. The dress, shoes, and makeup she'd let Roseanne talk her into had done the trick. She'd turned the tables on Ford, saw the way he'd looked at her when she entered their makeshift studio. His eyes nearly popped out of his head, but he'd turned the tables right back on her, reducing her to a puddle of goo in front of God-only-knew how many viewers. And she'd fallen for his seduction. Fallen so hard she'd flung herself at the man, even knowing he couldn't offer her more than a romp in the sack.

"He didn't even offer a quick tumble," she reminded herself. She rolled to her back, refusing to shed a tear over Ford Adams. *Face it. He doesn't want you. You're nothing more than his business partner. Maybe his relationship with Ronnie is more serious than I thought.*

He'd been right to push her away. Girlfriend or not, Ford would eventually leave Butte Plains, and she had nowhere else to go. They'd turned the company around, so it was only a matter of time before he started looking for someone to buy him and his mother out. As strange as his relationship with Ronnie seemed to
~~~

her, he did have a life to go back to, and she had… nothing.

Her 25 percent of the company grew in value every day. Eventually, it would be worth something — at least enough to keep her going until she found something else to do with herself. Because she couldn't see retaining her portion once Ford sold. Potential buyers would probably want the whole thing anyway, which meant in order for Ford to sell, she would have to, as well.

Was it wrong for her to wish he'd stay? The elder Mr. Adams had known the importance of his business to the town and done everything in his power, except ask his son to come home and help to keep the place open. He'd be proud of what Ford had accomplished in so short an amount of time, but he'd also be rolling in his grave if he knew his progeny's plans to sell. She knew in her heart he'd hoped a year would give his son enough time to realize Butte Plains and Adams Manufacturing were home and decide to stay.

She'd known from the beginning falling for her new partner would be a stupid thing to do, and, after tonight, she also knew she'd ignored her own advice. But for a hot minute when he'd been wrapped around her, bombarding her senses with his lips, his sneaky, seductive words, and the damn vibrator he created, she'd let herself believe he felt something for her, too.

Talk about stupid. She set the gold standard for idiocy.

~~~

Becky ducked into the ladies' room for one last check before her interview. Not a hair appeared out of place, but her tidy hairdo did nothing to quell the butterflies in her stomach. In the weeks following the humiliation of throwing herself at Ford and being rejected, she'd dedicated herself to her job, building an entire network on the foundation of their flagship program, the *Adult Shopping Show*. Months of work had gone into converting the original building into a home for the new network. The expanded
~~~

facilities would allow them to branch out to a full schedule of prime-time and weekend shows, each with a different theme. Talks were underway to feature their competitors' products during the less popular time slots.

Thanks to Ford's creative genius, their product line had expanded exponentially. He complained about not being able to design fast enough to keep up with her marketing plans, but they both knew the opposite was true.

Right this minute, he was doing an interview in one of the new studios with *Forbes* Magazine. A reporter from *Cosmopolitan* waited for her in yet another studio. Afterward, she and her partner were going across town to meet a Realtor about purchasing an abandoned warehouse in order to expand production. They were also looking at a few locations near the Interstate to become a new distribution hub. To say they were busting at the seams would be an understatement.

The previous week they'd hired the same architect who had designed the remodel of the old factory to draw up plans for an extension to the current offices so they could get rid of the portable units brought in to house their newest employees. Her marketing team had increased from one — her — to half-a-dozen-plus underlings. The accounting staff outnumbered every other department except factory workers and the direct sales team.

Becky made a mental note to talk to Ford about his ideas regarding the phone order takers. Outsourcing to India would save them money, but hiring a company out of Dallas to pick up the slack would keep jobs in Texas, if not in Butte Plains. He might not care about creating jobs locally, but she did.

"We're ready for you, Ms. Parker."

Becky gave herself a mental shake and followed the intern down the hall.

Ford leaned against the wall outside the door and listened in on Becky Jean's interview. He'd done at least a dozen in the last few months, but this was her first, and to hear her tell it, her last one. She'd only agreed because the magazine's editor insisted their female readership wanted to hear her success story, not his.

A feminist to the core, he'd let Becky Jean believe she'd badgered him into all manner of equal opportunities for women within their company, but he'd fire every man on the payroll if he could replace them with women as intelligent and driven as his partner. His design set them on the right course, but without Becky steering them along the path, they'd probably be no better off than they were the day of his father's funeral.

The woman deserved her day in the limelight.

"Hey. The receptionist said I'd find you here."

Ford smiled and gave Scott a guy hug. "Did you come to drag me back to New York?"

"No, man. You got a good thing going here, and the new guy is working out okay. He's so good I've actually had some time to work on a few projects on my own."

Even though Ford had made a lot of money designing for other people, while working for others, he'd missed letting his imagination run wild. "I hear you, buddy. I never knew how much I missed the creative process until I got to do it full-time. What kind of stuff have you been working on?"

He knew that smile. Scott had always been a big kid, unable to hide his enthusiasm. "You still have an office?"

"Sure do." He didn't know why he was standing out in the hall anyway. Becky Jean didn't need his help. The woman could take care of herself. He waved his hand, signaling Scott to follow. "Come on."

Ford shrugged out of his suit coat. After hanging it on the back of his chair, he removed his tie and popped the top button on his shirt. Feeling as if he could breathe again, he turned his attention to his guest. "Ronnie didn't come with you?"

Scott shook his head. "Sorry. I tried, man, but she's adamant she isn't going to set foot in this *hick* town. Her words, not mine."

He searched his heart for the disappointment he'd become used to, and found resignation instead. He'd heard the insult before and thought the very same thing a time or two himself, but he'd never heard it from Ronnie. She was too diplomatic for that. The woman was a pro at saying something without saying anything. Her unique ability made her a favorite in her social circle. No party could be complete without Veronica Ramsey.

If she thought Butte Plains a hick town, what must she think of him? He plastered a smile on his face. "Makes me wonder what she sees in me."

"It's always been a mystery to me," Scott said with a laugh. "I always thought she had good taste then she took up with you. Shattered my image of my little sister."

His former roommate knew him better than anyone else on the planet, yet he never said a thing when he'd asked Ronnie out. Ford had taken his friend's silence as approval. "Trust me. Your sister is far from being the saint you led me to believe her to be."

"Hey, I never said she was a saint. Personally, I don't know what you see in her. She can be a brat when she wants to be."

Her holdout on coming to Butte Plains being a perfect example. "Tell me about it." He shuffled a stack of financial reports to the side of his desk. "So, what brings you back to Hicksville?"

His friend beamed. "I have something I want to show you."

"Yeah? You been spending company time designing something on your own?"

"Don't tell the boss, but yes, I have." He dug in his pocket. "See what you think."

Ford turned the prototype over, examining it from every possible angle. "This is incredible." He'd never seen anything so lifelike. "How much is it going to cost me?"

"What makes you think I'm willing to sell?"

He put the object back in its box then rocked back in his chair. "You wouldn't have brought it to me if you didn't want to strike an agreement with Adams Manufacturing."

Scott nodded. "You got me there. Never crossed my mind to take it anywhere else."

Ford tried to contain his excitement. Coming to terms with Scott on this project would put them at the top of the heap in the adult toy market. He couldn't afford to let the opportunity get away from him, but he also knew his friend was shrewd enough to know what he had. He'd come to Adams Manufacturing first out of loyalty and friendship, and if Ford had anything to say about it, he'd still have a loyal friend when the negotiations were done.

"There will be a ton of cost to get it into production. The first hurdle will be figuring out how to mass produce it. Then there's packaging and marketing."

"Not telling me anything I don't know."

"It's worth more than I can offer up front. Adams Manufacturing is expanding fast. Lots of cash is coming in, but lots is going out, too. Would you be interested in a percentage agreement?"

"Only if I can personally oversee every step from creating the molds to designing the packaging."

"From New York?"

"From here. The new guy we hired is doing a great job. So good, I can't believe we didn't hire someone years ago." Scott cleared his throat and fidgeted in his seat. If Ford didn't know better, he'd mistake his college roommate's actions for nerves. "I could stay as long as it takes."

He'd seen the reports from the company he co-owned with the man sitting across from him. The kid they'd hired to take up the slack while Ford revived his family's business was some kind of genius, it seemed. He had yet to meet the guy, but Scott, and the bottom line, didn't lie. But he couldn't imagine why the born-and-bred Yankee would want to spend months in Butte Plains, Texas, when he could easily turn the project over to Ford's team and just sit back and collect his profits — of which there would be a shit-ton of once this product became available to the general public.

"Running away from something? Is what's her name getting too close?" He'd lay odds a woman had something to do with his friend's contract condition.

"You mean Solange?"

"Is she the runway model?"

"Yeah, but this has nothing to do with her. A lot of work went into creating this product, and I want to make sure the consumer gets the best possible version of it."

"And you don't trust me to see to it?"

"You know that isn't true. Look around you. You've got your hands full as it is. I have the time and the expertise to spearhead this project. Can you say the same?"

Scott had him there. "I've got the expertise, but you're right about the time. And the plant is running at capacity. As a matter of fact, Becky Jean and I are supposed to go look at some real estate this afternoon. We're thinking of opening another production facility—among other things. Wanna go with us?"

"You bet. I've got to drop my bags off at The Yellow Rose. Pick me up there?"

CHAPTER SIXTEEN

"Boy, am I glad that's over." Becky Jean sank into the same chair Scott had vacated a half hour earlier. "I don't know how you do it."

"Interviews?" He shrugged. "I can't stand them, but the director of marketing and public relations keeps insisting I do them." He smiled, driving home the barb.

"Okay, okay. I get the message, but you're swimming with the big fish now. People want to know who you are, where you came from. It's good for business."

She had a point, but he didn't like speaking about his personal life to strangers any more than she did. "Speaking of business...." Ford pushed a rectangular box toward her. "What do you think of this?"

"Another one of your designs?" Becky reached for the generic container. His groin tightened as a blush crept up her neck to her cheeks—a response he could have predicted. After all this time in the adult toy business, the products they sold still flustered her.

He reined in his libido. "Nope. Scott created it. He's willing to enter into a partnership agreement with us to produce and market it." He leaned forward. "Go ahead. Pick it up. See what you think."

Becky lifted the lifelike toy from its resting place. Seeing her hands on the replica male appendage caused his real one to ache. God, what he wouldn't do to feel her fingers wrapped around his cock. It had been a hell of a long time since a woman had touched him.

"Silicone?"

He forced his attention to the spec sheets Scott had emailed him. "According to the specs, the inner core is a simple rubber compound. The outer layer, or skin, if you will, can be either latex or silicone. The prototype is latex."

"Some people are allergic to latex." Holding the base in one hand, she wrapped her other hand around the shaft and tugged. The outer layer slid over the core, rising up to cover the head then retreating. He swallowed hard, imagining her fingers wrapped around his flesh, moving up and down his shaft. "Feels very lifelike."

Fuck. He did not want to think about how she came to have that knowledge.

"True." He almost wept with relief as she placed the prototype back in the box. "I'm thinking silicone is the way to go."

"How much does he want?"

Her color had returned to normal since they'd moved on to discussing money. Everything would be great if his dick would do the same. "I told him we would discuss it this afternoon. I invited him to go warehouse shopping with us."

She stood and turned. His gaze landed on her perfect ass. It seemed like forever since he'd helped her remove the prototype of the *Safeguard Backdoor Locking System,* yet the images of her sweetly rounded globes remained fixed in his brain, popping up at inappropriate times—like right then. He remained seated as she moved to the door.

"Give me a minute and I'll be ready to go."

He was ready to go right then, but not in the way she meant. He needed a minute to wrestle his body under control enough to be seen in public. "Take your time."

~~~
~~~

Becky locked the bathroom stall door. Wrapping her arms around her middle, her fists clenched tight, she dropped her forehead to the cool metal. *Holy smoke, what the hell?*

It's business. It's not personal. It's a product. *Something to sell. It's what marketing people do.*

No matter how she spun it in her head, she couldn't shake the images her mind created when she'd held the remarkably lifelike dildo in her hands. Granted, her experience with the real thing amounted to one, but if memory served her, Scott's creation was a near-perfect replica of a generously sized penis. Right down to the satin-smooth skin and ridged muscle underneath. It just lacked the ability to ejaculate.

"No. No. NO! Don't go there."

"Ms. Parker? Are you okay?"

Stifling a groan, Becky lifted her head. "I'm fine, Carolyn, but thanks for asking." Straightening the jacket on her red suit-dress, she stepped out and approached the wash basins. "Can you tell Mr. Adams I'll be right out?"

"Sure thing." The young receptionist turned to go then stuck her head back in. "Mr. Ramsey is back."

She pumped soap onto her palm and stuck her hands under the automatic faucet. "So I heard." The crush Carolyn had for the handsome Yankee apparently hadn't abated in the months since she'd last seen him.

"He sure dresses up the place, don't you think?" Before she could answer, the door swung shut behind the infatuated girl.

"If you say so," Becky mumbled, waving her hand in front of the sensor on the paper towel dispenser. Poor Carolyn didn't stand a chance, she feared. She couldn't thank Ford's college friend enough for bringing them the revolutionary new product, but he could have sent the item by courier instead of hand delivering it. She suspected the man had his reasons for coming back to Butte Plains, and they had everything to do with her friend Roseanne.

The owner of The Yellow Rose B&B refused to talk about the Yankee, which said a lot about the two of them. She'd seen the way they looked at each other when they thought no one would notice. There was something going on between them—she just didn't have a clue what.

Carolyn's misplaced infatuation gave Becky something else to think about besides her growing interest in her business partner.

"Good luck," she said to her reflection. "You're going to need it."

She took a deep breath and opened the door.

~~~

"Sorry to keep you waiting," Scott said, scooting into the backseat of the SUV Ford insisted the company purchase so he could turn in his rental. "I had a few issues to discuss with the innkeeper."

"I'm sure Roseanne will bend over backwards to make your stay as pleasant as possible," Becky said.

"I'm sure she will." He smirked.

Becky turned in her seat to glare at him. "You know, she asked if you were coming back. I got the impression she might be looking forward to your return, but I'm rethinking that."

Scott smiled. "It's good to know she missed me." When Becky opened her mouth to let him have it, he held a hand up to stop her. "Simmer down. Ms. Meadows and I understand each other perfectly. I'm demanding as hell, but I also pay very well. No doubt my fat pocketbook is the reason she wanted me to return."

"You wouldn't be her first demanding customer." She faced forward. "If you're going to be difficult, it's only fair you pay accordingly."

"Believe me, she earns every penny."

Ford stopped at an intersection and looked over his shoulder at his friend. Was that disapproval or something else? Before she
~~~

could question the two of them, Ford accelerated through the intersection. "Where to first?" he asked.

"The first stop is over on Muleshoe. The Realtor said he'd meet us there."

"Wasn't that place a leather goods factory at one time?" Ford asked.

Focusing on their mission, Becky nodded. "I believe so. Mr. Ferguson said he thinks most of the old machinery is still inside, which could be a problem for us."

"Sounds like a great opportunity," Scott said from the backseat.

"To do what?" Becky scanned the printout of the listing. "What on earth would we need for a leather factory?"

"You're already making sex toys. Why not create a line of leather goods for the people using your toys?"

"He has a point, Becky Jean. We could also make our own line of whips, floggers, restraints—you name it." He glanced over his shoulder again with a smile for his friend. "Nice thinkin', buddy."

Becky groaned. "Great. That's just what we need, to take on another project when we can barely handle the ones we're juggling now."

"I didn't say we were going to buy the place. We've got to see it first. If the equipment is there, we'd have to see if we could find some of the former employees, see what would be involved in getting the place up and running again. It would mean more jobs for more people."

Damn. He knew she couldn't resist an opportunity to add more jobs to the local economy. They passed a diner that had reopened last month. From the looks of the vehicles parked outside, business couldn't be better. "McCrae's is open again."

Ford hummed his agreement. "I heard Mrs. Hanson decided to hire a manager so she could retire." A few months ago, they'd instituted lunch time staff meetings on Wednesday's. Ordering stuffed croissants from the local bakery insured attendance more often than not. Knowing the bakery would remain open meant he wouldn't have to come up with something else to lure their employees to the meeting.

"She told me she wanted to spend more time with Bobby's kids since he and Chrissy moved back home."

"He's a top-notch electrician. Did a good job on the wiring for the remodel of the old building."

"He said his father-in-law is so grateful to have his daughter and grandkids back, he's letting Bobby run his new business out of the old Matthew's Electric building free of charge."

"I'm happy for Bobby, but I kind of hoped we could rent or buy his building ourselves. It would be perfect for our new production facility."

"This place sure has changed since the last time I saw it," Scott said as they passed a truck loaded with building supplies unloading in front of another eatery that had closed years ago. "Have you seen all the stuff opening up along the freeway? Amazing."

"Business is booming in Butte Plains." Becky couldn't keep the smile off her face.

"It's good to see," Scott said.

"Did you notice the new hotel going in? Should be done in a few more weeks. Next time you come down, you won't have to stay at the B&B if you don't want to."

"Yeah, I saw their sign. As long as The Yellow Rose has a room for me, I think I'd prefer to stay there. The level of service is excellent. Can't get that at a chain."

"No, you can't," Ford agreed.

Their agent, Sam Ferguson, waited for them when they pulled into the overgrown parking lot of what once had been Butte Leather Goods. Becky sighed. If the parking area reflected the interior, this place needed more than a cosmetic facelift.

An hour later, she climbed back in the passenger seat. As soon as Ford started the engine, she cranked the air conditioner to full blast and adjusted every vent she could reach to blow on her.

"Hey, greedy much?" Ford claimed the center vent closest to his side for himself.

"How do you people stand this heat all summer long?" Scott complained from the backseat.

"You get used to it," Becky said.

"Fuck," he said before he bent his face over the vent blowing air from the center console into the backseat.

"What did you think?" Ford pulled out of the lot right behind the Realtor's land yacht.

As soon as Sam had opened the big bay doors, letting the bright summer light shine where it hadn't in nearly a decade, the two grown men flanking her had become little boys on Christmas morning. She'd seen the awe etched on their faces and known the only discussion would be over how soon they could sign the papers. Nevertheless, she had to try. "It's a disaster, Ford. The place has more rodents in it than machinery, and it has a *ton* of machinery."

"More like ten tons."

Becky shot Scott a death look then turned to Ford. "I get it, I really do. It's a challenge, but it will still be here in a year or two."

Ford shifted his gaze to the rearview mirror. "Maybe if we had a partner. Someone to share the start-up expense and do most of the work? Say… in return for a bigger share of the profits on the new toy?"

"What? Are you insane?" Becky punched Ford's arm.

"Ouch! Why'd you hit me?"

"How much of an investment are you thinking?" Scott asked.

"We put up 70 percent. You put up 30 percent, and we kick you another 2 percent of the profits on the toy in exchange for you running the place. We split the profits the same way, 70/30.

Becky's head spun as the numbers they were talking grew to staggering proportions. They'd gone from zero credit at the bank to an almost-open-ended credit line, but adding a leather factory to their expansion list would test their limit.

"Make it 5 percent on the new toy and you have a deal."

"Five it is." Ford smacked the steering wheel with the heel of his hand in celebration.

"Oh. My. God. You are beyond insane." She glared at Ford's smugly elated face.

"Maybe," Ford said, "but you love me anyway."

Becky turned to gaze out the side window — anything to keep Ford from seeing the truth in her eyes. He'd been joking, but love was no joke. If she allowed herself to think about it, she knew she'd find herself well on her way to being hopelessly in love with the man — so she refused to think about it.

A few minutes later, they parked next to Mr. Ferguson in front of what had once been a vegetable-packing plant. Becky took one last breath of chilled air before sliding her feet to the sweltering, cracked asphalt and followed the men inside. At least someone had kept the place clean and critter-free.

Ford and their new partner in the leather business couldn't have cared less about the warehouse, but it was exactly what Adams Manufacturing needed in regards to size and location. "The price is above market value," she said. "We'll take it for 20 percent less than the asking price if the seller covers closing costs." She cocked an eyebrow at the Realtor who moonlighted as the Mayor of Butte Plains. "And I assume all applicable permits and zoning issues will be forthcoming from the city?"

"Yes, ma'am. I'll see to it." She shook hands with the older man. "The Buford family has been sitting on this for at least ten years. I think they'll jump at the offer."

She dug a business card out of her purse. "Call me as soon as you hear back from them. We'd like to expedite the closing. We've already ordered machinery. We'll need to get our people in here as soon as possible to get started on the infrastructure."

"Not a problem, B.J. — I mean, Ms. Parker."

Ignoring his embarrassing slip, Becky led the way out, waiting by the car door while the men secured the warehouse door. It had been a hell of a day, and it wasn't over yet. She still had to test the toy she and Ford would be endorsing on the show they planned to tape the next day.

She'd managed to effectively test the other toys they'd featured in the last few months. As a single woman, she'd had a passing acquaintance with dildos and vibrators, so similar toys were simple enough for her to test. After the second week when Ford had broken her down on television with a simple, tiny vibrator, she'd learned her lesson and wouldn't admit to testing. If she hadn't tried it, they didn't hawk it on the show. Having her own opinion of the merits of the devices they sold gave her a measure of control since Ford refused to work with a script.

Despite her promise to herself to never ask for Ford's help again, she found herself in a predicament of her own making. She'd thought she had plenty of time to work up the courage to test one of their newer products, but they were scheduled to tape the segment tomorrow, and she'd yet to get up the nerve to test the product. She tensed just thinking about attaching the tiny clamps to her nipples. She'd done her research, even tested them on her pinky finger. She simply couldn't see herself being able to attach them to a more sensitive area. She needed help, and besides Roseanne, who'd claimed to be unavailable tonight, the only person she trusted to help her was the one person she had no business asking.

He'd been the perfect gentleman about the incident with the butt-plug prototype, and she'd appreciated his restraint at the time. Then he'd rejected her after she practically threw herself at him after their second live broadcast. Message received. He didn't want her. Whether his rejection had to do with her or the mysterious and conspicuously absent Ronnie, she didn't know.

Still, she needed his help, so she'd set her feelings for the man aside, suck up her courage, and ask for his assistance with the clamps. She wouldn't throw herself at him again, but if one thing led to another, she wouldn't say no. If that made her a bad person, then so be it.

They dropped Scott off at The Yellow Rose with a promise to discuss their new joint venture the following day. They were nearly back to the office before Becky got up the nerve to say what she'd been rehearsing in her head for the past few days.

"I need you to come to my place tonight. Use the trail from the top of the butte down to my street. I'll let you in the back door."

He'd parked in his reserved spot right next to her car but kept the engine running as he turned to her. "You want me to sneak to your house tonight?"

"Yes." She nodded once. "We've given the town enough to talk about. They don't need to see you on my doorstep after hours."

"And, why, exactly am I going to be on your back doorstep this evening?"

"I need… help. With one of the products we're showcasing tomorrow."

He frowned, and she could practically see him mentally going through tomorrow's taping list. A wide smile split his face. "The nipple clamps."

She nodded again. "I've never…. I don't know…. Hell, Ford, I'm afraid if I get them on, I won't be able to get them off. When I think about it, I imagine myself rolling on the floor in agony and my hands shaking so hard I can't remove the damn things." Nothing but the truth there. The idea of testing the clamps by herself scared her spitless.

"You want me to help?"

"Don't look so damn happy about it. You're the reason I have to test them in the first place, so it's only fair you have to give up your evening to help me." More truth. If he hadn't insisted she endorse every product, she wouldn't be in this mess.

"Why not ask one of your girlfriends? I bet Roseanne would help."

Roseanne had claimed she had other plans for the evening—

and she'd made the claim before the nipple clamps were even mentioned. "She's busy tonight."

"Lucky for you, I'm available to assist you." He cut the engine and opened his door. "I'll be there with bells on. Oh, wait! You'll be the one wearing the bells."

The heat flooding her system had nothing to do with the summer sun beating down on her body as she followed Ford to the front door. Images swam through her brain like mirages — enticing yet untouchable. Tonight, they'd be real. Her breasts grew heavy as she imagined Ford's hands on them, his fingers flicking the tiny bells dangling from her nipples. The pain would be bearable because the expression on her partner's face would mirror the pure lust inside her. At least she hoped so.

Ford opened the front door for her. The new chime they'd had installed to announce visitors sounded like a gong to Becky's ears.

"Bells on," Ford said, with a smile.

Becky made an indecent hand gesture only he could see. His laughter followed her down the hall to her office. It was going to be a long afternoon.

His casual comment earlier in the day echoed in her brain. *You love me anyway.*

Yeah, she did. With every passing day, she fell a little bit more in love with her business partner. Intellectually, she knew better, but her heart refused to listen to her brain, and she'd given up trying to make it. Tonight, she'd follow her heart, and if it led her down a road of broken dreams, then she'd patch together what she could and move on. Life was too short to live with regrets.

CHAPTER SEVENTEEN

In an effort to burn off nervous energy, Ford jogged to the base of the butte then back up again—twice—before continuing along the path running behind Becky Jean's house. If running in the late-summer heat didn't kill him, the wait to get his hands on her would. Walking out on her the night she'd kissed him had been the right thing to do, or so he'd believed then, but as time wore on, he'd come to view the move as one of the biggest mistakes of his life.

He didn't know exactly when he'd stopped thinking about Ronnie, but it had happened. In the time he'd been away from her, the distance between them had become more than just miles. Whoever had said absence makes the heart grow fonder clearly didn't know what they were talking about. They rarely spoke these days, and when they did talk, the conversation lacked dimension. She hadn't been sitting at home alone, pining for his return. Her social calendar was as busy, if not busier than ever, and her interest in his day-to-day life had shrunk to zero.

With every passing day, Ford became more certain he wanted to stay in Butte Plains.

Ever since the night of their second live show, he'd wanted another chance with Becky Jean. He'd gone too far on set, driven her home, and made the monumental mistake of kissing her then walking out when she responded with more ardor than he'd expected. Maybe if he'd apologized the next day…. But he'd never found the words. What could he have said, anyway? *I wanted to fuck you six ways to Sunday but was afraid you'd want to marry me?"*

Just what every woman wanted to hear.

He'd known then she had feelings for him. Becky Jean didn't invite a man to her bed if she didn't feel something for him.

He'd thought at the time it was nothing more than lust on his part, but time had shown him the error of his ways. He'd never met a more amazing woman. She could do anything she set her mind to, and do it well. If he ever made it to her bed, he'd be the luckiest son of a bitch on the planet.

His lungs heaved as he came to a stop on Becky Jean's back porch. He took a moment to remind himself to play it cool, no matter how hot his blood ran for her. Sure, she'd responded to him like crazy on set, but as soon as the on-air light dimmed, so did she. He'd never taken advantage of a woman before, and he wouldn't start with Becky Jean. But… if she gave any indication tonight was about anything other than business, then all bets were off. He'd learned his lesson about pushing her away, and he wouldn't make the mistake again.

She answered the door wearing the shortest shorts he'd ever seen and a sleeveless blouse with buttons down the front. Her auburn hair fell in a waterfall of curls from a band on the crown of her head. She looked fresh and sweet and sexy as hell in a girl-next-door way that made his lips dry and his legs weak.

Shit. I'm in so much trouble.

"Get in here." She grabbed his arm and yanked him inside. "Did anyone see you?"

"What?" He could hardly breathe much less comprehend her meaning. Being this close to her, knowing she'd invited him there to get closer, messed with both his brains. Seeing her in her innocently sexy outfit awakened every male cell in his body, but it was her touch that destroyed him.

He closed his eyes and pinched the bridge of his nose while he puzzled out what she'd said. "I don't give a rat's ass if anyone saw me."

"Well, I do. You know how people in this town talk."

"Let them talk," he said, advancing on her. It seemed like he'd been waiting forever for this opportunity, and somewhere between reasoning with himself on her back porch and feeling her hand on his arm, he'd come to a conclusion. He'd waited long enough. He had to find out if the chemistry between them was as strong as he thought. Memories of the kiss they'd shared all back at the beginning of summer haunted his dreams.

He'd take full responsibility for the lost time, but he couldn't clamp her nipples and not touch her in other ways. Fuck, if he didn't prepare her properly, she'd never be able to take the pain anyway. Scott had always been more into that sort of thing than Ford, but he knew his way around the toys. Knew there could be nothing pleasurable or erotic about them if the person wearing them wasn't aroused.

For the first time since their fateful night, he let his desire for her show in his eyes.

Becky Jean took a step back. He took a step forward. His blood pounded past his ears on its way south as the expression on his prey's face changed from worried outrage to something infinitely more enticing—lust. She could play it cool all she wanted, but her body betrayed her. Her gorgeous blue eyes darkened to pools of desire, inviting him to swim in their depths.

"Ford."

"You knew what would happen when you asked me to come here tonight." He'd had his moments of doubt, but no longer. She'd thrown the pass with every intention of him catching it.

"We shouldn't do this."

"Maybe not," he conceded, closing the distance between them slowly, giving her ample time to change her mind. She stood statue still until he came close enough to catch her scent in his nostrils. Her signature fresh, clean scent and another more earthy one hit him square in the libido—arousal. "But we're going to do it anyway, aren't we?"

Her gaze met his. Her pink tongue darted out to wet her lips. "Yes," she whispered.

He wedged one foot in between hers then slid an arm around her waist and pulled her softness within an inch of his hard body. Leaning in, he brushed his lips over the shell of her ear. "Want to know what I'm going to do to you?"

She shivered in his arms. "Wha-what are you going to do?"

God, he loved the breathless quality of her voice. Flexing his arm, he tugged her closer. "I'm going to taste you. All over. I'm going to kiss every inch of you, starting right here." He covered her lips with his, stealing her gasp before plunging his tongue in to capture her groan.

She tasted like chocolate and fine wine, sugar and spice. And everything nice he'd ever dreamed of.

He traced her curves with one hand while the other remained on the small of her back, anchoring her to him. When she arched, pressing her breast into his palm, it was all he could do to keep from tossing her over his shoulder and hauling her to the nearest flat surface. She made him caveman crazy with need.

Breaking the kiss, he searched her face for any sign he'd misunderstood her actions. She gazed up at him, eyes dark with passion, her lips swollen and parted. Every labored breath pressed her hard nipple into the flesh of his palm.

"I've wanted you for so long," he whispered against her lips. "I can't wait to taste you." He nibbled along her jaw until he found the throbbing pulse in her neck. Her head fell back, allowing him better access.

Pressing his mouth to the spot, he inhaled deep. Out of self-preservation, he'd taken to holding his breath around her. Her scent drove him insane. Hell, it drove him up the wall and clawed at his gut every damn day.

Her nails dug into his shoulders. "The clamps."

"We'll get to them, I promise."

Reluctantly, he released her breast and worked on the buttons standing between him and her body. He had to see her, touch her. Now.

"I want to make you as crazy as you make me. I want to hear you beg me to let you come then I want to sink into your heat over and over again until neither one of us can remember who we were before."

She groaned, and he took the sound as permission to continue.

He slid the last button on her blouse free then went to work on her shorts. As soon as the zipper gave way, she wiggled her hips, sending the fabric to the floor. He leaned back to look at her.

Every man had their own personal definition of beauty, had an image in their mind of what it should look like. Gazing at the perfection before him, he realized how inadequate his imagination had been. It wasn't just the two perfectly formed globes encased in ivory lace or the indentation of her waist or the way her hips flared out to create the ideal place for his hands. It wasn't even the soft mound hidden beneath a scrap of fabric. It was all of her — the entire package — the way she championed others, the way she rose to every challenge, the way she used her incredible intellect to make the most of a situation. He'd learned from others how she'd sacrificed her ambitions for her family when her father became sick. Once she had the chance to put her education to use, she used it to help others. Adams Manufacturing had grown like a monster octopus with a dozen legs — not because of greed, but because she wanted to create more jobs for the people in her community. She had single-handedly rebuilt Butte Plains.

"You're beautiful." He'd said the words to women before, but he'd never meant them more. "So damn beautiful."

She ducked her head as if the compliment embarrassed her. He put his index finger beneath her chin, compelling her to look at him. "Those are just words, Becky. Let me *show* you how beautiful you are."

Her body trembled under his hands, and, for a heartbeat, he thought she'd changed her mind, and this would be all he'd ever have of her. Then her lips curved upward in a quivering smile, and his heart twisted itself up in knots. Afraid to move, he held still while she gathered the hem of his T-shirt and tugged. "Yes to all of it, but I want to see you, too. I've waited too long."

Christ almighty! "Not so fast." He wrapped his fingers around her wrists, stopping her from undressing him. He wanted to feel her skin against his more than he wanted his next breath, wanted to feel her mouth on him, but he also wanted to take his time. She deserved more than the fast fuck on the kitchen counter his dick wanted. "I want this to be good for you, and the only way I can is for you to let me take charge. I'm not a Dom… I don't always have to have my way, but I'm so close to the edge, if you touch me, it's going to be over before it begins."

He could practically see the wheels spinning in her head as she sized up the situation. If she said no, he'd do all he could to see to her pleasure before his, but he didn't like the odds he'd leave them both wishing they'd never gotten naked together. He was about to plead his case again, when she sighed and he knew he had her.

"What do you want me to do?" she asked.

"Nothing. Just feel." He nodded toward the shipping box bearing the Adams Manufacturing logo sitting on her counter. The shows scheduled to tape this week were all about their new line of bondage play gear. He could hope…. "What have you got in there?"

She glanced at the box. Her mouth opened, but no words came out. He almost smiled, but thought better of it. He reached for the box. "Let's take this to the bedroom, shall we?"

She crossed her arms across her middle. "Ford." His name sounded like a warning on her lips.

He tucked the box under his arm and lied through his teeth. "Product research, Becky Jean. That's all."

"You won't do anything I don't want to do?"

"Swear." If he'd learned anything about his business partner in the last few months, it was she wasn't a prude. Shy. Private. But she'd try just about anything once. He'd be surprised if she tried the nipple clamps again after tonight, but who knew?

"Okay then, but I want a safeword."

There was the Becky Jean he knew, practical to the bone. He nodded, anything to get her moving. The sight of her nipples straining against the lace of her bra drove him insane with need. "Choose."

"Pickle. That should do it."

"Pickle it is." She wouldn't need her safeword, but if having a way out gave her comfort, he would go along. "Let's go."

He followed her up the stairs and down the short hallway he remembered from the last time he'd been in her house. Memories of the plug he'd created seated between her sweet ass cheeks had never been far from his mind since the night she'd called him to help her remove it. God, what a night. Dragged from dinner with his mother and aunt by Becky Jean's frantic call, he'd been out of his mind with worry until he got to her house and found out she'd panicked because she couldn't get the key in to release the locking mechanism on the plug. He'd been both amused and proud — of her for trying the thing, and of himself for creating the toy. As monumental as the test had been for the company, the memory of touching her skin eclipsed everything else in his mind. He'd lost sleep thinking about touching her ass again — hell, touching *any* part of her.

After a quick glance at the contents of the box he'd carried upstairs, he set it on her dresser and turned to find Becky Jean standing halfway between him and the antique four-poster bed occupying the center of the room — her arms at her sides as if she dared him to look his fill. He took the challenge, cataloguing every inch of her from her full lips to her toes curled into the braided rug. Fuck, he'd never seen a more beautiful woman. He had to believe she remained single because of the dearth of eligible men in Butte

Plains, because who in their right mind wouldn't want her in his bed every night? She belonged to him tonight, a circumstance he planned to take full advantage of.

"Take off the bra." He held his breath while she reached behind her to undo the back clasp. Held it while she extricated her arms from the straps. Held it while the lace garment fell away from her front to reveal the most perfect breasts he'd ever seen. When his lungs began to burn, he exhaled in a rush. "God almighty, Becks. Look at you."

"What?" Her brows drew together, and she looked down at her chest then back up at him. "Ford?"

He couldn't claim to be a virgin, had seen more than his share of breasts, but he'd never, never been this undone. She would be the death of him. He forced his gaze to her eyes. "They're perfect, Becks."

"They're boobs, Ford. Everyone has them."

"Not like those." He couldn't wait to get his hands and lips on them.

"I'm dying here. Are you just going to look, or are you going to put the clamps on?"

The clamps. Mention of the reason he'd been granted this opportunity in the first place brought him out of his trance. "We'll get to those." He motioned with his hand. "Panties. Off." *Me. Caveman. You. Obey.* He was losing it. Fast.

She hooked her thumbs in the waistband, bent, and pushed the tiny scrap of fabric past her hips. As she straightened, she tossed the garment off to the side. He didn't know where — didn't care.

Becky Jean was all woman, from her generous breasts to the flare of her hips to the thatch of red hair at the juncture of her thighs. Blood he desperately needed to deliver oxygen to his brain diverted to his groin, making him glad he'd changed out of his jeans before coming to her house. The jock strap he'd worn had lost the battle with his dick, but he could live with the discomfort.

His heart thundered, trying to keep up with the demand from

his libido while ignoring the one organ he needed to remain functioning. He would not fuck up this opportunity by going caveman on her. Which meant he had to rein in his impulses. *Breathe. Come on, Adams, man up.*

He licked his dry lips with his even-drier tongue. He needed a drink, and he knew just where to get one. "On the bed," he said. "We need to try these cuffs out." He spun around to dig in the box for the restraints he'd seen earlier and prayed Becky Jean would do as he said without question. One brush of her hand and he'd explode. In order to do anything for her, he'd need to insure she couldn't touch him.

When he turned back around, he sent up a silent thank you to the gods for looking out for him. Becky Jean lay spread-eagle in the center of the bed—waiting for him to secure her wrists and ankles to the bedposts. He'd never seen a more inviting scene. He tore his gaze away from her torso. *Focus.* With numb fingers, he unbuckled one of the smaller cuffs then fastened it around her right wrist. "Too tight?" he asked, using his index finger to test the fit. These were the best they offered at the moment, a light, durable nylon fabric lined with flannel, it sported a single buckle fastener. He owned heavier wristwatches.

"No," she said, examining the product with her other hand. "I've been wanting to try these on ever since we started carrying them. It's pretty comfortable, actually."

"You'll tell me if anything changes, won't you?"

"Count on it." She lifted her arm over her head, and he fastened the cuff to the short nylon strap he'd looped around the bedpost.

As he worked his way around the bed, fastening her ankles, he tried to focus on the task at hand instead of the treat awaiting him and not the feel of her skin beneath his fingers or the delicate floral scent he'd come to associate with her. And he sure as hell tried to block out the musky tones of her arousal that awakened the primal male in him.

When he'd secured her left wrist and confirmed she experienced no discomfort from the restraints, he finally allowed himself the luxury of looking at her.

"Fuck, Becks."

She wiggled her ass, pulled and tugged at the four-point restraints, testing her limits and obliterating his. He'd never wanted a woman the way he wanted this one.

He pulled his shirt over his head and tossed it across the room. "You're fucking beautiful."

He put one knee on the edge of the mattress. His gaze met hers.

"Ford." She strained toward him. Everything he had hoped to see on her face was there—desire, need. "Please."

Her softly spoken plea grounded him. He had her right where he wanted her, open and trusting. He wouldn't let her down. "I've got you, Becks." He stroked a strand of hair from her cheek, allowed his thumb to linger on her lower lip. "I'm going to make you feel good, I promise."

She closed her eyes and moaned, rocking her hips up—an invitation he had every intention of accepting. But first, he wanted to know everything about her.

CHAPTER EIGHTEEN

Becky's body dipped and rolled with the motion of the mattress as Ford climbed over her, situating himself between her legs. He still had too many clothes on, which seemed completely unfair and, yet, erotic as hell. Bound to the bed, she felt powerless, until he stretched over her and ground his erection against her throbbing mound, and she understood the power she held over him.

"This is what you do to me, Becks. You're so fucking beautiful, inside and out." He flexed his hips, letting her feel the hard steel of his erection beneath his shorts.

Becky shifted, seeking the contact she needed, but groaned when the restraints prevented her from doing so.

"Relax, baby." Ford pressed her into the mattress with his body flush on hers. His hands traveled along her arms until he twined his fingers with hers. His mouth hovered over hers. "I'm going to see to your every need. I promise."

"Ford," she sighed as he peppered her face with tiny kisses that made her toes tingle.

"Becks. My Becks. Say you'll let me love you." He nibbled at her earlobe.

"Yes, God, yes," she moaned.

At her acquiescence, he crushed her lips with his. She tensed for a second then his tongue demanded entrance, and she opened for him. Slowly, he melted every bone in her body, seduced her with mouth and tongue until his breath became hers and hers, his.

When he broke the kiss, she strained to follow then sagged against the mattress as he forged a path of wet kisses down her neck... then lower.

"Oh God, Ford," she cried as he tongued one nipple then the other. She arched her back, begging him to take more. He obliged, taking a tight bud into his mouth and sucking hard. A bolt of white-hot heat shot straight to her core. She moaned, and if not for the weight of his body and the restraints binding her, she would have rocketed into orbit.

He pulled her breast taut, grazed his teeth over the aching tip then released her with a *pop*. He let out a delighted chuckle, but before she could verbally brain him for his childish behavior, he bent and took her other breast into his mouth. Becky sucked in a tight breath and held it as he gave this nipple the same lavish treatment he'd bestowed on the other. Her lungs burned by the time he let go and chuckled again at the audible release.

"Fuck, Becks. I could do this all night, but we've got toys to test, don't we?"

Huh? Becky struggled to keep up with his train of thought. He leaned over, reaching for something on the bedside table. The ringing of tiny bells jump-started her brain a mere second before he sat back on his knees. The sight of the nipple clamps in his hands sent a cold chill racing across her skin, which only made her nipples tighter.

"I've only used these things once before," he said, testing the tweezer-like jaws on the tip of his finger. His gaze met hers, the heat immediately chasing away her fear. "These are for beginners."

He took her left breast in hand, squeezing and plumping it. He flicked his thumb over the hardened bud, making her squirm. "They're still going to hurt like hell, Becks, but I promise to make this good for you. Do you trust me?"

She'd never seen the correlation between pleasure and pain. Didn't understand the concept, but she had Ford Adams promising to make her feel good. How could she pass up the opportunity? She nodded. "Do it."

He bent and took her nipple into his mouth again, sucking until she writhed beneath him. Before she could comprehend his intent, he released her, pinched the tip between his thumb and forefinger, stretching her skin. Mid-gasp, the clamp bit into her skin, stealing her breath. Her fingernails dug into her palms, and she burrowed into the mattress, tried to dig a hole with her shoulder blades to escape the excruciating pain. She bit her lip muffling her screams. Tears slid down her cheeks.

Somewhere amidst the pain she recognized Ford's voice. "Breathe, Becks. Breathe." And his hands, stroking her from rib cage to mound, his thumb brushing her clit over and over again. "You're doing good, Becks. So good. Use your safe word if you need to, baby."

His hand kneaded her other breast—preparing it for the same torture, yet she couldn't force the word past her lips to stop him.

His lips closed over her nipple. She whimpered. Her pussy clenched with need. He moved swift and sure, as if he'd done this a thousand times—and maybe he had. She didn't want to think about him making some other woman crazy enough with need to let him do this to her.

Before she could analyze what she recognized as jealousy, he tugged on her nipple. She cried out, arching her back then digging her shoulder blades into the down comforter in an effort to escape. The pain stole her breath and blanked her mind. Her safeword floated to her lips, dying there as Ford stroked her again. Directing the pain, focusing it to a tiny point.

"So good, babe. Fucking beautiful. Ride it, baby. Gonna make you come. I promise."

Her breasts were on fire, yet the real pain seemed to be between her legs. *Please. Please.* She raised her hips, begging for relief, for release. She never knew need could hurt so much. "Please." She formed the word with her dry lips, but had no idea if sound had accompanied it.

A brush of warm air on her pussy warned of his intent. The first swipe of his tongue along her slit had her straining to get away. Too much. Too painful. Too wonderful.

Then his hands were under her ass, lifting her. He fastened his mouth to her pussy, and she lost it. The orgasm tore her apart, smashed her to bits, and through it all, he rode her pussy, licking, sucking, biting, until she collapsed into a wrecked and sniveling mess.

"Baby. Look at me." Ford's hand on her cheek, wiping away the snot and tears broke through to her. She managed a weak smile for the beautiful blur above her. "Good girl. You're doing fine, Becks."

Her lip trembled as she fought back another round of tears.

"Happy tears?" he asked.

She managed to nod.

"Ready for another O?"

Is he crazy? She'd never been a multiple-orgasm person anyway, and after the one she'd just had? He could try, but success seemed impossible. She shook her head. Ford laughed and stroked her face again.

"Hang on, babe." As he adjusted her hips, sliding them up onto his thighs, three things registered in her endorphin-drugged brain. He'd released her ankles, he had removed his clothes, and stretched one of their new road hazard red *Safe Sheaths* over his cock. How long had she been out of it?

Something big and hard pressed against her entrance. "Perfect," he said. "I'm sorry, Becks. They say they hurt worse coming off than they do going on."

She struggled to make sense of his words, had only begun to decipher the code imbedded in them when he reached for the clamps. At his touch, pain ricocheted through her then the insistent pressure on her nipples disappeared. Her brain registered relief for a nanosecond before blood rushed into deprived tissues, the blinding pain levitating her off the bed. In the same instant, Ford entered her. The stretch and burn of his possession, magnified by the sensation in her nipples, pushed her over the edge into another orgasm, taking what remained of her, flinging it out to the universe.

She cried out and gripped the nylon bands around the bedposts, anchoring the top half of her body while Ford held her thighs in his strong arms, holding her open for his thrusts. As she came down from the highest high ever, she opened her eyes. She'd never seen anything as beautiful as Ford with his head thrown back, his jaw clenched in ecstasy. The muscles in his arms and chest, coated in a sheen of sweat, flexed as he pounded in to her, seeking his own release. His big cock stretched her tight, but her body adapted, took every inch of him, so when he became impossibly bigger, she noticed. Seconds later, he ground his hips against her like he was trying to dig a tunnel to her heart. A curse exploded from his lips at the same moment his shaft pulsed inside her. She welcomed his weight as he collapsed on top of her like a broken construction crane.

"Fuck, Becks. I think you killed me."

~~~

The first rays of sunlight peeked through the blinds when Becky slipped out from under the heavy arm pinning her to the mattress. Ford slept the same way he lived his life—with everything he had. She lay on her side, taking in his relaxed form. She'd spent most of the night learning every detail of his body, down to the small scar on his shin, the result of a bicycle accident when he'd been ten, he'd said. He'd returned the favor, slowly cruising up and down her body, more than once. Her nipples were still sore from the clamps, and probably would be for a while. The pain had been unbearable until he'd distracted her in the most
~~~

amazing way possible. Her nipples were uber-sensitive and every touch to them telegraphed need to a spot between her legs. She smiled, knowing she'd carry the reminder of their night together with her for some time.

Ford snored, then rolled to his back. The strip of handmade Irish lace edging on the top sheet pulled up to his abdomen emphasized his raw masculinity in a way she decided he wouldn't appreciate, but she sure did.

Before she gave into the temptation to wake him and beg for a repeat of last night, she slipped out of bed. Wrapped in her old terrycloth robe, she took care of her morning needs then headed to the kitchen.

Her shirt and shorts lying on the kitchen floor brought a blush to her cheeks. God, she could still feel the solid weight of him pressing her into the mattress. He'd ignited a fire inside her that had both consumed and transformed her. He'd set the bar so high no other lover would ever come close to matching him. Maybe once the memory of his touch had dimmed she might be interested in another, but she couldn't see far enough into the future. Maybe then she'd look for someone she could spend her life with. Someone who shared her love of home and family, someone who wanted to put down roots. Someone who would love her as much as she loved... Ford.

A sharp pain in the region of her heart made her gasp. She clutched the edge of the counter to steady herself. *Shit.* She'd gone and fallen in love with the man. There was no maybe about it, and ignoring her feelings wouldn't make them go away.

How could you? He's not your forever man. She'd known the truth from the start, but when he'd accused her of knowing what would happen when she invited him over to help her with the clamps, she couldn't deny it. Somewhere in the back of her mind, she'd known, or at least hoped.

The clothes she'd been wearing when he arrived were right where she'd left them on the kitchen floor—a sure sign she'd lost her mind. She picked them up and folded them into a neat stack on the corner of the counter.

Destined to get her stupid heart broken, she had no one to blame but herself.

As she started the coffee, she considered her options, quickly deciding she had none. She mentally steeled herself for what she had to do.

She needed to get Ford out of her house, and fast. If he didn't want to take the trail back to his house, she'd have to find a way to sneak him out to her car for the ride up the hill. The rumors about her and Ford's father were without foundation and had evaporated as untruths tended to do, but if someone saw Ford leaving her house in the wee hours of the morning, the news would burn up the Butte Plains grapevine before the diner switched the breakfast menus for the lunch specials. Not only would her mother be embarrassed, she'd get ideas in her head about rose-covered arbors and wedding vows. Last night had one-night stand written all over it.

"So, this is where you are."

At the sound of his gravely, morning voice, Becky turned from mindlessly staring at the stream of black liquid trickling from the coffee maker. Ford stood in the doorway with her grandmother's lace-trimmed sheet wrapped low on his hips. She had an insane urge to run her palms over the scruff darkening his jaw. Lord, if their customers could see him this morning…. "Huh?" *Smooth. Get a grip.*

"I woke up to an empty bed." He crossed to the coffee pot, opened a couple of cabinets until he found a mug. The brewer conveniently chose that moment to spew the last drop into the carafe. He filled a cup for her, then one for himself. He leaned against the counter and eyed her over the rim of the cup. "You aren't regretting last night, are you?"

How the hell did he expect her to think with so much of his skin showing? "Uh. No." She shook her head in answer to his question and in an effort to jolt her brain into functioning. "Not at all. I was just thinking."

He took a sip of his coffee, smiling as he lowered the mug. "About?"

She shrugged. "About how to get you out of here without anyone seeing you leave."

"I see." He set the cup on the counter and started opening cabinets again. His back proved as magnificent as his front. The play of muscles as he went from one cupboard to the next made her mouth water and her fingers itch to touch. "Do you have anything to eat? Cereal or something?"

He looked over his shoulder. She pointed to the left.

"Pantry. I should have milk in the fridge, but I'd give it the sniff test first." She couldn't remember the last time she'd been to the grocery store.

Her guest slapped two bowls of dry cereal on the table, sniffed the milk before pouring. He unceremoniously tossed her a spoon before digging into his breakfast as if he'd been denied food for a week. Skeptical of the expiration dates on both ingredients, Becky toyed with hers until her companion came up for air.

"'s good," he said, nodding at her bowl. "You should eat."

She stirred the soggy flakes. "I'm not much of a breakfast person." *But I could eat you.* She forced the wayward thought away before she gave into temptation and the thought a reality.

He glanced at her. "It's the most important meal of the day." He took another bite then shook more dry flakes into his bowl. "Besides, you're going to need your strength."

"For?"

He waggled his eyebrows. His wicked smile told her exactly what he had in mind.

"No." She held up a staying hand. As much as she wanted to strip her grandmother's sheet off his body and take him up on the offer of more mattress calisthenics, she couldn't think of a worse idea. Her heart would never survive another round with him. Plus, they had a business to run. "We've got to be in early today, remember?"

His expressive brows knitted in confusion as he puzzled out her comment. "Oh, yeah. We're signing papers on the new property today."

"And taping three shows."

"That, too."

Ford scooped the last flakes out of his bowl, downed them then rose to take the dish to the sink. "I'd rather stay in bed with you. I enjoyed last night."

"About last night… I sort of forced myself on you. I'm sorry."

"You didn't force anything on me. If anyone's to blame, it's me." He leaned on the counter, his ankles and arms crossed. He could be intimidating, even wearing nothing but a sheet. "You needed help testing one of our products. Actually, we managed to test several of them, if memory serves. I'm always available to help with testing, research, or whatever you need." The matter-of-fact way he offered his services reminded her last night had been nothing more than sex for her partner.

She squared her shoulders, causing her bathrobe to drag across her sore nipples. Stifling a gasp, she dug deep for the strength to resist his offer. "I'll keep your generous offer in mind. In the meantime, you should leave before the neighbors see you."

Ford held his ground for the longest then casually straightened. "We aren't through, Becky Jean." He headed toward the bedroom.

She needed to be careful and not read too much into his words. Last night had been fun, but Ford didn't belong to her, no matter how much she wished differently. They'd made a mistake, taking their relationship outside the realm of strictly business, and no amount of chalking it up to product research would make it right. A shiver danced along her spine. Morning-after regrets were a bitch.

~~~

Out of breath from his mad dash home, Ford slammed the back door of the gatehouse. He snatched a water bottle from the fridge, downed it in one long pull then braced his hands on the counter, willing the cold liquid to douse the fire burning in his gut.

He'd come within an inch of dragging Becky Jean back to bed and keeping her there for the rest of the day. He'd had a lot of sex, but last night had been off-the-charts hot, the best ever.

He could still hear those little gasps she made every time he filled her. And he'd never forget the breathless way she said his name when she came. Hell, no woman had ever given him as much as she had, not even Ronnie. Especially not Ronnie.

Shit. Ronnie. Their relationship had been dead for months, but they'd never acknowledged as much. Hell, how could they when they rarely spoke? He made a mental note to talk to her soon, make it clear they were through.

Popping a pod into the coffee maker, he rinsed the mug he'd used the previous morning and placed it under the spout in time to catch the first drip. While the beverage brewed, he recalled every minute in Becky Jean's kitchen.

He'd been distracted by the thin V of skin showing between the lapels of her robe she'd put on when she got out of bed. The sight of her mussed hair had taken him back to the night before when her hair had spilled across the white pillow case and tangled with the lace edging.

He blew on the steaming cup of coffee then took a sip while he fished a protein bar out of the open box on the counter. He couldn't imagine not holding Becky Jean again, not sinking into her welcoming heat, losing himself in her incredible blue eyes. She was the most caring, genuine person he knew, and she deserved better than him.

He arrived at the plant to find Becky Jean already hard at work, looking sexy as hell in another of those suits capable of inciting a
~~~

riot. "Good morning, Mr. Adams," she said. "Taping begins at ten this morning in the new studio. I've put a new proposal on your desk. I'd appreciate a response no later than the close of business today."

Damn. Seeing her in her prim-and-proper business-woman mode turned him on. Memories of just how un-businesslike she had been in bed the night before were gasoline on a bonfire he had no chance of putting out. He'd have to be careful, or he'd be consumed by the conflagration. He returned her polite smile with one of his own. If she wanted to pretend she hadn't begged him to do wicked things to her last night, he'd let her. For now. "Good morning to you, too, Ms. Parker. I'll read over your proposal, but I'm certain whatever you have in mind is in the best interest of Adams Manufacturing." He stepped into the hall then leaned back into her doorway. "See you at the taping."

The proposal met his every expectation. While increasing payroll, adding more shows featuring products from other manufacturers would add to their bottom line without stretching their capital reserves the way the new facilities they'd committed to would. Becky Jean had been wasting her time as an office manager. The woman had a head for business like no other he'd ever seen—which turned him on like crazy. The way she said *spreadsheet* got a physical reaction from him every damn time.

CHAPTER NINETEEN

Becky waved Amy away. "That's fine," she said, examining her hair and makeup in the mirror. She could do her own makeup, but they could afford to hire someone to come in on taping day, and the extra money her former classmate earned allowed her to hire a part-time person in her salon. "I think I'm done. Why don't you see if Ford needs anything?"

Amy met her gaze in the mirror. With an understanding look, she patted her on the shoulder. "I don't know how you do it."

"Do what?"

"Go on television with Ford week after week to sell sex toys and not jump his bones. It must take nerves of steel."

Becky turned and made a beeline for the rack of dresses the owner of the new downtown boutique had sent over for her. Three hung facing out for today's tapings. "Ford and I are business partners." She fingered the multi-colored silk she planned to wear during the nipple-clamp show. When she'd tried it on, the fabric had skimmed her curves in a gentle caress reminding her of the way Ford had touched her face, soothing away the pain and stealing another piece of her heart.

"I'm just sayin', you two are H.O.T. on screen together. It's no surprise your toys are selling like hotcakes."

"Sex sells." Becky fell back on her standard answer.

175

"Remember, the blue dress first then the pink block print. The watercolor silk is last," she said. "No one would blame you if you hooked up with him. You know that, don't you?"

No. She didn't know any such thing. She'd been on the wrong side of the grapevine before, and she didn't want to be there again. "This is business," she repeated. Maybe if she said it enough times, she'd begin to believe it herself.

"Whatever you say, girlfriend." She opened the dressing room door. "I'll check on Ford, then take a break. Text me when you're done with the first show. The pink is going to require a few changes in your makeup to keep you from looking like a clown."

Becky waited until she heard the door close behind her friend before she allowed her knees to buckle. Business her ass. She was ass-over-teacups in love with Ford Adams and up to her ass in trouble. If the chemistry between them before convinced people to buy their products, what would happen now? In the past, she'd only imagined Ford helping her test the products she endorsed on each show. Last night, they had tested all three of today's featured products—together, and thoroughly. Putting her experience into words, sharing it with the viewing audience? She shook her head. She couldn't pull it off. Everyone would know she'd slept with the man.

She yanked the blue dress off its hanger. A sedate sheath, it combined business appropriate with understated sex appeal. From the assortment of costume jewelry, courtesy of yet another shop recently opened in town, Becky chose a string of chunky pearls and a matching bracelet. To complete the look, she slipped on a pair of nude-tone heels provided by the new shoe store. All would be listed in the closing credits in return for their generous donation. Afterward, everything she wore would be sent to a charity in the county seat set up to help abused women escape their circumstances and find jobs to support their families. Adams Manufacturing had hired several from the program and hoped to hire more.

No matter what she had going on in her personal life, the business she and Ford were building was making a difference. Butte Plains had grown. Closed-up shops were reopening as new enterprises. People were moving in, not out, for a change. Ford hadn't mentioned selling or moving in months, but had he noticed the changes in his hometown? He seemed to spend all his time in his office or at home. Even when his friend Scott visited, they rarely hung out together.

A knock sounded on her door. Becky took one last look in the mirror then turned to answer. Ford leaned against the doorjamb, looking like he'd stepped off the pages of *GQ*. His smile was as wicked as ever, but a new, darker flame burned in his eyes as he raked his gaze over her from head to toe. "Lordy, you could make a flour sack look sexy, Becky Jean."

She couldn't help but laugh at his exaggerated southern accent and pseudo compliment. She stepped out, shutting the door behind her. "I'll take your hillbilly remark as a compliment and ignore the fact you just called a very expensive dress a flour sack."

"I did no such thing," he protested, following her down the hall to their new studio. "The dress is gorgeous, but no one could wear it the way you do."

She stopped in front of the studio door and turned. She put her hand up to keep him from bowling her over and it landed on his chest. Before she could move it, he trapped it with one of his own. "Last night was special, Becks."

She tugged on her hand, but he wouldn't let go. "I'm not saying different, but we can't do it again. We shouldn't have done it in the first place."

"Maybe not," he conceded. "But we can't undo what's done, and I don't want to pretend it didn't happen."

"Don't pretend, Ford. Forget. It's what I'm going to do."

She pushed down on the door handle, leaned hard against her shoulder, and the heavy, soundproof door moved inward. With a fake smile plastered to her face, she greeted their recently hired crew.

Well, shit. Ford let the door swing closed in front of him. He'd hoped Becky Jean would have had a change of heart since she'd heaved him out her back door without so much as a good-bye kiss, but clearly, she hadn't. She seemed determined to act as if nothing had changed between them, when he knew different. Everything had changed.

He straightened his tie and shot his cuffs. She thought she could shut him out? The woman had another think coming.

"Let's get this show on the road," he said, entering seconds behind his co-host who began to rearrange the products on the display. Justin gave him a thumbs-up as Ford took his place on set. The young man had risen to the challenge of expanding from one live show to taping multiple shows in one day. He played an integral part in their rapidly growing television network, too. They'd be lost without him as neither he nor Becky Jean knew much about the broadcasting world.

"Ready when you are." Justin looked up from his clipboard. "I'd like to get done early today, if we can, so let's try to do these in one take, if we can."

"Not a problem." By ditching the live broadcasts, they'd gained the ability to edit the shows, which could be a good thing, but not when it came to Becky Jean's candid responses to the things he said and did to provoke her on set. The less retakes today meant less opportunities for her to edit out what he knew would sell the product. "It'll be like the good 'ole days when we were live."

Becky Jean glared at him as she took her spot beside him. "Don't you dare," she hissed at him.

Ford arched one eyebrow and grinned at her warning. Today's shows were going to be the best yet. Now that he knew her body intimately, he had every intention of using his knowledge to arouse and fluster her to the point everyone watching would want what she was getting. Which meant sales would go through the roof.

Justin held his hand up, fingers spread to tick off the seconds. "We're rolling in five, four, three, two, one."

"Good evening, folks. I'm K. Ford Adams and this is B.J. Parker."

Becky smoothed the multi-colored silk over her hips, refusing to look in the mirror again. Why hadn't Amy returned with the nipple cover-up patches she'd sent her for? No one would see Becky's soaked panties, but *everyone* would notice her headlights were on.

She absolutely hated her inability to control her physical responses to Ford's touch, and Lord, did he know just how and where to touch her. Thanks to the night they'd spent together, he knew every erogenous zone on her body, and he'd proved in the first two shows he wasn't above using his knowledge to embarrass her. Justin had even stopped taping in the middle of the second show to adjust the lighting to account for the color in her cheeks. She doubted there were enough filters in the world to counteract the shade of red she would turn when she had to endorse the nipple clamps Ford had used on her.

Damn, they'd hurt, but he'd distracted her through the worst of it then used the pain to give her the hardest orgasm of her life.

She'd run the experience over and over in her mind, searching for the words to convince their viewers to give the tiny little torture devices a try, and come up empty.

Ford won't have any problem coming up with the words. He never did. Fans of the show ate up his sexy-as-hell confidence. The more he made her stammer and sputter, the more products they sold. Parts of their shows were viral sensations, shared over and over again on social media with comments about his hotness and how lucky she was to be his co-host.

Someone tapped on her dressing room door. "We're ready for

you, Ms. Parker." She recognized the voice of the young woman they'd recently hired to assist Justin.

"I'll be right out, Kiley." Becky forced herself to take one last look in the mirror. She made a mental note to order a lifetime supply of the little nipple concealing patches as soon as possible, but for the time being she'd have to pretend her nipples weren't standing up like traffic cones.

All eyes turned on her the second she walked through the door to the set. Holding her head high, she took her place beside Ford then nodded to Justin. "Ready as I'll ever be," she said.

"Good evening, I'm K. Ford Adams, and this is B.J. Parker." Ford launched into the familiar intro on the director's signal. "Last time we introduced you to the *Safety First Restraint System*, designed to allow you complete access to your partner's body while keeping them safe and secure. As you've heard us say on every show, our products are meant for you to enjoy in the context of a SSC relationship—Safe, Sane, and Consensual.

"Still, you have to be a little bit crazy to want to try the items we have for you tonight, isn't that right, B.J.?"

The way his voice dropped when he called her by her on-air nickname reminded her of the way he said her name when he had his hands on her, stroking her to climax. Her cheeks heated and her sex throbbed. "Yes, you do, Ford, but if used responsibly, *the Safe and Snug Nipple Clamps* will provide you with an experience like no other."

Ford splayed his hand on the small of her back, guiding her to stand behind the display table. "You sound as if you speak from experience, B.J. Tell me, have you tried the *Safe and Snug Nipple Clamps?*"

She could do this. She swept her hand over the display, praying the cameras would follow the movement and zoom in on the product while she spoke instead of her flaming face. "Yes, Ford, I have tried them."

He picked up a set identical to the ones he'd used on her the night before and held them in his palm for a close-up. They looked tiny in his hands, but when they'd bit into her nipples, she'd thought a merciless giant had a hold of her. Realizing her real thoughts were *not* a selling point, at least not to her, she decided to keep her mouth shut. Let him sell the damn things.

"They look so delicate," he said, flicking the tiny bells hanging from them. "I'm sure the viewers would like to know more." Ford replaced one of the clamps on its display card then held the other between his thumb and forefinger, squeezing to make the jaws open much like he'd done before placing the first clamp on her breast the night before.

Becky's heart raced, and her knees trembled in tandem with her lower lip. Remembering the searing pain she'd experienced, she barely contained the squeak forming in her throat. "I imagine these would hurt like the devil," he said, his voice dropping lower and taking on a darkly sensual tone that had her clenching her thighs together. She tore her gaze away from his hand, then wished she hadn't. The carnal hunger she saw in his eyes robbed her of speech.

"I didn't know you were into pain, B.J."

"What?" She gave him a questioning look and shook her head. "No. I'm not."

He pinched the tip of his little finger with the clamp, grimacing under the pain. "Ouch! You put these on your nipples?" He removed the toy and gave his hand a dramatic shake.

"Well... I didn't... I mean—"

"Ahh, I understand. You didn't do it yourself, someone helped you." His wicked grin told everyone what they'd done.

Embarrassment ratcheted her body temperature up to flaming. No light filter in the world could compensate for the color in her cheeks.

"Yes," she said, fixated again on the clamp he snapped open and closed.

"I suppose it would make a difference, having someone there to take your mind off the hurt." He clamped his little finger then traced the digit down the length of her arm, leaving a wake of gooseflesh behind. "Did he take your mind off your nipples, B.J.?"

"Yes."

"And did the pain go away?"

She shook her head. "No."

"No?" he asked, feigning surprise at her answer. He'd been there, knew the pain had never gone away, just changed.

"It didn't go away... just became different... less pain and more an ache I felt everywhere."

"Everywhere?" No one with hearing would mistake his one word question, not with the way his gaze dipped low.

She wanted him more than she wanted her next breath. Her nipples were hard as diamonds and probably casting their own shadows under the harsh studio lighting. She grasped his wrist before he could draw another line down her arm with his torturous toy. It was time to turn the tables on K. Ford Adams before he reduced her to a puddle of hormonal goo in front of the world. She brought his hand up between them and removed the clamp. She licked her dry lips first—a warning—then flicked her tongue over his aching pinky—a reminder, she hoped, of the way he'd prepared her nipples before clamping them. "Yes, *everywhere*, Ford. I wish I could explain the feeling better, but any woman who's been distracted by her lover will understand the concept of heightened awareness. You feel as if you're walking a high wire—all your senses are engaged. You're tuned in to every cell in your body. Tense with expectation."

She dropped the clamp to the display table and selected a larger version. She licked his finger one more time then, gaze locked on his, affixed the clamp to it. His nostrils flared and his eyes grew dark. As subtly as possible, she shifted so her stomach brushed his erection below the display table.

"Then you're taken out of your world into another one where there is only you and your lover and the exquisite pain of need." She held his hand between both of hers, stroking her thumb over his palm while she spoke. "You know the feeling, don't you, Ford?"

She knew the look on his face. She'd seen it last night, right before he came. Since she couldn't very well have him coming on set, she lowered her eyes, breaking the invisible connection between them. She turned to the camera. "Any words I could use to describe the sensation of wearing the clamps would pale in comparison to the actual experience. I will say this, wearing them is only half the fun. The other half happens when you take them off." As the words left her mouth, she removed the clamp on Ford's finger. He let out a yelp and tried to yank his hand from her grasp. She held on, massaging his pinky and palm while he dealt with the pain of blood rushing back into the tip of his finger.

She faced the camera with a smile. "The *Safe and Snug Nipple Clamps* are best used with *Safety First Restraint System*. Remember, Safe, Sane, and Consensual."

She smiled until Justin yelled, "Cut," then she dropped Ford's hand and stormed off set.

PART THREE

It is a truth universally acknowledged, that a man in possession of a good fortune, must be in want of a wife.
Jane Austen

CHAPTER TWENTY

"She's killing me." Ford hunched over his scotch on the rocks. His best friend since college, Scott, occupied the barstool next to him.

"We aren't talking about my sister, are we? 'Cause if we are, I'm out of here."

Ford shook his head. "No. Ronnie and I are done." Though he hadn't spoken with her as he'd planned, he believed their relationship had died a natural death. Her lack of pleading with him to come back to take her to any of her society functions proved she'd moved on. "Haven't talked in weeks."

"Can't say I'm sorry or surprised. Never did think you two were suited." Scott finished off his drink and signaled the bartender for a refill.

"Really? Why didn't you say something?" Once, he'd thought he and Ronnie were very well suited. Just went to prove what he knew about relationships. They'd used each other, nothing more.

Scott shrugged then thanked the bartender for the refill she placed in front of him. The woman looked barely legal to work behind the bar, and gorgeous in a way only Texas women could be with her ample cleavage showing, a mane of chestnut hair made for wrapping around a man's fist. Her smile said she'd give you a ride if you were interested. She didn't interest him, but he admitted to being surprised when Scott ignored her, too. He waved the girl away, indicating he didn't want a refill or anything else she might be offering. He'd forgotten their conversation

185

until Scott spoke. "Your relationship wasn't any of my business. Can't say I liked the idea of you with my sister, but she's a grown woman. If she wanted to make a mistake with you, I couldn't stop her, and likewise, I might add." He downed half his drink in one gulp and signaled for another.

Ford finished his drink and signaled for the check.

"So, if it isn't my sister who's killing you, it must be your partner."

Maybe he'd been too hasty in requesting the check. He pushed the paper back to the bartender. "Another round," he said, wagging a finger at both their glasses. Silence reigned until two new glasses sat in front of them. "What makes you say so?"

Scott snorted. "Seriously? Don't you watch your own show? I keep watching 'cause I don't want to miss the explosion when it finally happens. The chemistry between you two is off the charts."

He knew it was, and if the sales figures were any indication, the viewing public knew it, too. He just wished he knew what to do about it. "Wait until you see the shows we taped for next month." *Especially the last one.* She'd spun the tables on him, had him panting and ready to blow in his pants. He'd asked Justin to let him see the final edit, but the bastard refused. He'd suggested they add more phone lines then mumbled something about being a millionaire as he walked away.

Ford stroked his pinky finger through the condensation on the outside of his glass. An image of Becky Jean's tongue licking the hurt away came to mind. He shifted on his stool, making room for his instant wood. Anything would bring the images to mind these days, and every damn time, the results were the same. There would be an explosion alright. It just wasn't the kind Scott had in mind.

"I can't wait. Watching the two of you is better than watching porn."

Ford had nothing to say to his friend's comment. He'd rather watch Becky Jean than porn any day.

"So, have you slept with her yet?"

He'd never told Scott he was sleeping with Ronnie. The man had correctly assumed it at some point, and they'd never really talked about it until today. If he hadn't felt the need to tell his buddy he'd slept with the man's sister, he sure didn't feel the need to tell him the details about his relationship with Becky Jean. "None of your business."

"I'll take your response as a yes," his friend said. "But I don't see what the problem is, unless it was one and done on her part."

Ford stared at his mostly empty tumbler.

"That's it, isn't it? You were her one-night stand?" Laughing like a loon, Scott slapped the bar. Ford could feel the gazes of everyone in the place on them.

"Shut the fuck up, man. This isn't funny."

"The hell it isn't. Fuck-and-run Ford Adams has been caught! I bet you can't even count the number of one-night stands you've had, but all of them were on your terms. My sister lasted longer than any of them, but I'm sure she dug her claws in and wouldn't let go." He guffawed and shook his head. "Damn. Never thought I'd see the day."

Ford fished his wallet out of his back pocket and stood. "Like your record is any better, buddy. We called you Scooter because you scooted out of their beds before they finished coming." He tossed a few bills on the bar to cover their drinks. "See you around."

Scott couldn't be more wrong. Becky Jean had every right to take what she wanted. He'd never indicated he wanted more, and neither had she. What really twisted his short hairs was he hadn't expected her rejection to hurt as bad as it did. Damn it. He wanted more.

~~~

So far, so good. Becky Jean rocked back in her desk chair. It had been three days since she'd made the monumental mistake of taking Ford to her bedroom, and she hadn't relapsed since. Oh, she'd wanted to, and judging by the leering glances and innuendo coming from her business partner, he did, too.

But they couldn't. She couldn't. *Once had been a mistake. Twice would be insane.*

The company was doing exceedingly well. Yes, they were spending lots of money, but their expenditures were nowhere near the amount coming in. If she figured in the new real estate
~~~

acquisitions, and what those would add to their bottom line, Ford had to be well on his way to becoming a billionaire. Hell, he might already be one. Which meant, he'd be looking for a way out soon. He'd never made any promises about staying, and since Adams Manufacturing had a solid future, he had to be planning to return to his other life. The one-year stipulated in his father's will would be up soon. When the date arrived, she could kiss her partner good-bye.

Becky leaned forward and flipped the pages on her old-fashioned desk calendar. Had he already talked to potential buyers? Would he do so without telling her?

She'd known the day would come when she'd have to decide whether to sell or not. The last few months had flown by faster than debris in a twister, leaving her disoriented. If one of Ford's buyers wanted her share, too, would she sell? And if she didn't, would they want her to remain in her current position? She couldn't imagine they would. Anyone who owned the majority of a company would want to bring in their own people to make sure things were done according to their wishes. Her opinion, backed by her very small minority share, wouldn't mean a thing.

Once again, she found herself in a position where none of the choices were hers. Her future hinged on the decisions of someone else. Deep inside, she realized her father's illness had been beyond his control, but the result was the same. Choices had been taken out of her hands. Then Ken Adams had died, locking her into a situation where she had no choice but to help Ford. She wanted the roller coaster to stop so she could get off. She didn't mind a fun ride, but for once, she'd like to choose the ride for herself.

She glanced over the contract in her hand—the one linking Adams Manufacturing to Scott Ramsey's new leather factory for the next ten years. Scott had made a commitment to live in Butte Plains for the next decade, but Ford, his best friend, had made no such commitment. Maybe she'd misread her partner's intentions. It had been months since he'd mentioned selling out. But yet… the calendar stalked her, the one-year mark creeping closer with every turn of the page.

Becky shuffled the papers on her desk. Poised to launch their shopping network into a twenty-four hour business, HR had been working overtime to narrow down possible spokespersons for the various new programs designed to showcase their competitors' products. She'd promised she and Ford would sort through the prospects today so they could be called in for personal interviews. Gathering the headshots and resumes to discuss with Ford, she stopped in her doorway.

Carolyn's distinct voice floated down the hallway. "Like I said, Mr. Adams is in a meeting. You'll need to make an appointment for another time."

The receptionist never raised her voice to a level to be heard this far away. *What the heck?* It wasn't like Carolyn to be rude.

"If you aren't going to tell him I'm here, I'll find him myself!" The clear, cultured, feminine voice reminded Becky of someone, but she couldn't pinpoint who. She changed direction, intending to add her support to the young woman at the front desk. They didn't pay her enough to put up with pushy people. She'd taken one step when a woman turned the corner, heading straight for her. Tall and sophisticated. Beautiful. No, stunning. Perhaps one of the models being considered for the network shows? Deciding right there to remove the woman from the list of possible hires, Becky used her body to block the hallway.

"You can't go in there," she said.

The woman had a few inches on Becky, even without the spiked heels she had on. She stopped, gave Becky the once-over, and, from the expression on her face, found her lacking in everything from appearance to the way she smelled. "And you're going to stop me? I don't think so." The interloper swept past in an invisible cloud of expensive perfume. "Ford Adams? Where the hell are you?"

Becky sneezed then followed the stranger. Rounding the corner into Ford's office, Becky stopped in her tracks. She blinked once, twice, but the image of her partner lip-locked with the strange woman didn't go away.

Carolyn skidded to a halt behind Becky. "I told her she couldn't disturb Mr. Adams."

Becky turned to the receptionist. "It's okay... I think. It seems Mr. Adams knows this woman."

Ford pushed the newcomer away and wiped his mouth with the back of his hand. "What the hell?"

"You have some nerve, Ford Adams." The woman pulled a rolled up magazine out of her designer handbag and waved it in his face.

"Have you seen the cover of Forbes this month?" She tossed the periodical on Ford's desk. "They're calling you The Backdoor Billionaire!"

Ford smiled and reached for the magazine. "Really? That's awesome!"

"Are. You. Kidding. Me?"

Ford scanned the cover, then held it up for Becky to see. "Becks! Did you see this?"

The woman spun around. The way her eyes drilled into Becky made her want to make a cross with her index fingers to ward off evil spirits. "No. We were supposed to get an advance copy." Maybe they had. She didn't have much time for reading magazines these days.

"Who's this?" Evil Woman demanded, half turning to look over her shoulder at Ford.

He cleared his throat and stepped around the woman. "Becky Jean, Carolyn, this is… Veronica Ramsey, Scott's sister. Ronnie, I take it you've met our receptionist, Carolyn, and this is my partner, Becky Jean Parker."

Ronnie. So, the phantom girlfriend materialized. The one who couldn't be bothered to stand beside Ford at his father's funeral or support him in his struggle to save his family business. Unable to meet Ford's gaze, to see whatever emotion might be there, she focused on Ronnie's face and, with clenched fists, held on as the roller coaster nose-dived, leaving her stomach behind.

"Why didn't you just say you were his girlfriend?" Carolyn asked.

Mustering every scrap of professionalism she could find, Becky jumped in. "It's nice to meet you, Ms. Ramsey. We all think a lot of Scott around here." *Can't say the same about you, though. What could Ford possibly see in her?*

"Where *is* my brother?" Veronica stared down her sharp nose at them. She was on a mission. Just what it could be, Becky had no idea. One thing she knew for certain—Ronnie would not fail, and the woman didn't take prisoners.

"I believe he's at the new leather goods factory he purchased. I'm sure Carolyn can give you directions." *Of course, they'd be driving directions, not broomstick directions.*

"No need. I'll give you a ride." Ford reached for his keys in the center desk drawer.

"But, we have to go over these applicants. I promised HR—"

Ronnie's laugh cut Becky off. She turned on Ford. "Are you serious?" This is what you've been doing down here in Butt Plug, Texas, for all these months, deciding which machine operator to hire?"

"Come on, Ronnie." Ford grabbed the witch by her elbow. Becky and Carolyn cleared a wide path to the door. "I'll give you a tour of the town, then we'll hunt up your brother."

As Ford ushered the woman out, Becky heard her say, "Really, Ford? That mouse is your business partner? How have you managed—"

The front door swallowed the rest of the woman's rant, then Becky became deaf to her surroundings. The derisive tone of the woman's voice made her furious. *Mouse?* Who did Ms. Expensive Designer Everything think she was anyway?

"Ms. Parker?"

"Hmm?" Becky forced her attention to the young woman beside her. "What? No worries, Carolyn. You did the best you could."

"Are you going to be okay? I mean, who does she think she is? I guess I just thought you and Mr. Adams—"

"Are business partners. That's all." If she'd ever hoped for more, those dreams had been thoroughly crushed under four-inch stilettos.

"But—"

"But nothing. Mr. Adams had a life he had to temporarily give up to come here. Seems his life has come to take him back."

She hadn't meant to be harsh, but she didn't want to discuss her and Ford's relationship, or lack thereof, with the staff. Besides, as of the moment Scott's sister walked in the door, any relationship other than a professional one between Becky and Ford became impossible. Whatever feelings she had for the man were never hers to have. He belonged to another.

The idea of being the other woman made her sick to her stomach.

Becky waited until Carolyn left before sitting behind her partner's desk. She glanced at his latest drawing and contemplated how her life had come to this. Instead of inventory sorted into domestic and agricultural, she thought in terms of insertables, vibrating, stationary, and portable. She dropped the head shots she'd hoped to discuss with Ford in the center of his desk. This time last year, she'd worried about hiring the right sort of person to operate dangerous machinery, and today? The HR department that hadn't existed a year ago expected her to decide which drop-dead gorgeous models would represent the company on television.

"This is insane." She advanced Ford's calendar two months to today's date then thought better of it and returned the pages to their original position. Did he even realize it had almost been a year since his father passed? All the reminder he needed had just walked in the front door.

She thumbed through the model's photos, selected her six favorites, and moved them to the top, securing them with a paperclip she found in his top drawer. Ford would probably be grateful she'd done the onerous job herself, saving him the trouble of participating in the decision. After all, he had his hands full with the wicked witch of the east.

CHAPTER TWENTY-ONE

After settling Ronnie in the passenger seat of his car, Ford took his time walking around to the driver's side. *What the hell was she thinking, barging in like she owned the place then insulting everyone she came in contact with? Who does she think she is?*

Ford stood beside the door for a moment, willing his anger to dissipate. He'd learned from bitter experience, yelling at her would do no good. The louder he got, the less she listened, and she needed to hear him. But first, she had some explaining to do.

She refused to look at him as he joined her in the car. He cranked the engine, adjusted the air conditioning, and muted the radio before backing out of the parking space reserved for him. In the last few months, his car had spent more time in his company parking slot than it had at the gatehouse he called home. At first, it had been out of desperate necessity. He'd put in long hours trying to coax the company back from the brink of bankruptcy. Once things began to turn around, the hours had been spent dreaming up new products to keep the company moving forward. These days, he spent his time doing what he loved—designing. And he had the time to design because Becky Jean did everything else, and did it well. He wouldn't let anyone come in and insult her the way Ronnie had.

He exited the parking lot and took the longest possible route to Scott's new leather factory. "What are you doing here?"

"I would think my reasons would be obvious."

To some, maybe, but he didn't have a clue. "Maybe to you, but not to me."

"My boyfriend and my brother have forsaken me for this place. I've come to see why, and to take you both home. I'll drag you if I have to."

Ford unclenched his jaw. "First, no one has forsaken you. Scott and I have asked you to visit on numerous occasions. Second, I'm only your boyfriend when you don't want to attend events alone. We had an agreement—no strings, no commitments." He glanced at her. "Don't even try to tell me you've been alone the entire time I've been here."

Before she could respond, he continued, "Third, I can't go back right now. We're expanding at a staggering rate. Becky couldn't possibly handle it all on her own." *Liar.* Becky could handle anything and did on a regular basis. He'd be lost without her, not the other way around.

"That's what employees are for. You hire people to do the jobs you don't want to do, and anything else you do via videoconferencing until you sell. Then it's all someone else's problem."

"Sell?"

He didn't think a block of ice could get any colder, but judging from the frost coming off the woman next to him, it could. "Yes, sell. Remember your original plan? Hang on for the year stipulated in your father's will then sell the factory and come home."

"I don't know what you're up to, but get this straight. I'm not selling."

"Don't be ridiculous." Her laugh chilled him to the bone. "Of course you are. Everyone and everything has a price."

Ford braked hard at a stop sign. He gripped the steering wheel, knuckles white and jaw clenched, as he held onto his patience by the thinnest thread. He didn't believe for a second she missed him. If she had, she would have shown her face in Texas months ago. Coming here had to be an excuse for… something. He just didn't have a clue what.

If he had any doubts his relationship with Ronnie had run its course, she'd erased them today. From the minute she'd walked into his office and kissed him like a drowning victim stealing the air from his lungs, he'd felt nothing beyond anger toward her. He could barely recall the desire that had brought them together the year he and Scott graduated from MIT. She'd attended the commencement ceremony and the party afterward, showering him with the kind of attention he hadn't been able or inclined to turn away. With her love of fashion and everything fashionable, she dazzled, and he'd followed her like a lost explorer followed the North Star. Being outside her orbit for the last few months, he'd found his own way. He liked the direction he was going, even if she didn't.

"No. I'm not." He checked for traffic, and, seeing none, he took a moment to compose himself. "Why are you here, Ronnie? And cut the bullshit about wanting me to come home. If you wanted me to come home, you would have been here a long time ago."

"You don't know anything about me. You never did."

And the inner bitch shows her face. He would have laughed had she not been so predictable. The sooner he found out what she was up to, the better. On the flip side—he knew she wouldn't tell him until she was good and ready.

"Where are you staying while you're here?" he asked, accelerating through the intersection.

"With you, of course."

Oh, hell no!

"This is a small town. It wouldn't be appropriate." He turned on Walnut Street. A large, yellow Victorian stood proud a few blocks down. The old maple in the front yard was majestic in its fall colors. "Scott's at The Yellow Rose. We'll stop in and see if they have a room." If they didn't, he'd kick Scott out, put him up in the gatehouse, and move in with his mother if he had to. He only wanted Becky Jean in his bed, and she probably wouldn't ever speak to him again after today.

"You have to be kidding me. Ford? You are kidding, aren't you?"

Ignoring her whining, he pulled to the curb in front of the only B&B in town. Bright yellow and orange mums lined the recently repaired concrete walkway up to the front porch. It appeared things were looking up for Roseanne. He almost hated to dump Veronica on her. She didn't deserve the punishment. "No, I'm not kidding. Trust me, Ronnie, this is for the best."

Her laugh sounded more like a cackle. Why had he not noticed that before?

"Have you seen the sign at the city limits? Someone changed it from Butte Plains to Butt Plug. It's because of you and your ridiculous sex-toy business, so don't tell me you're worried about propriety. I'm not buying it."

He smiled at the image of the revised welcome sign. *The town's old guard must be beside themselves.*

"Ford Adams! Tell me what's going on! I thought we.... I thought—"

"You thought wrong." Time and distance allowed him to see past Ronnie's outward beauty to the spoiled brat beneath the surface.

She huffed out a breath. "I've waited patiently for you to come home, and I'm sick and tired of it. People understood the reason you had to stay at first, but the company is doing better than ever. There's no reason for you to still be here. Tell me, Ford. Why *are* you still here?"

Unbidden, an image of Becky Jean, her face a mask covering her emotions as Ronnie clung to him, popped into his mind. She'd put up a seemingly impenetrable barrier between them since the night he'd spent in her bed, and, given what she'd seen in his office earlier, he couldn't imagine how he'd get through to her after this.

It's where I want to be. He'd known it for a while, but saying the words out loud would be irrevocable. He'd been happier since coming back to Butte Plains than ever before. He was doing what he loved—with a woman he loved.

His brain skidded to a stop, hung up on the realization he had fallen in love with Becky Jean. He forced air into his lungs and steeled himself for the panic attack sure to follow such an earth-shattering revelation. But instead of panic, a pinpoint of heat sparked in the region of his heart, erupting into a flash fire of warmth and contentment.

No, there was nothing scary about loving Becky Jean—except she probably hated his guts. He'd once heard a person could only hate someone they loved, as both emotions stemmed from passion. And Becky Jean had passion. She'd shown it to him the night he'd spent in her bed. He hadn't imagined the way she'd responded to his touch or the way she'd given herself to him. She felt something for him. Love or hate. Two sides of the same coin.

He could work with that.

"It's where I want to be." His tone brooked no argument. It was high time he set things straight. "You were rude to Carolyn and Becky Jean. Neither one of them deserved to be treated with such callous disregard. You owe them both an apology, and, in the future, I expect you to treat them with the respect they deserve." He didn't wait for her response. Exiting the car, he stalked up the sidewalk, ready to buy the Victorian and evict all the registered guests if it would keep Ronnie out of his home.

~~~

There was no accounting for taste. It was the only explanation for why Ford would be involved with someone like Veronica Ramsey. Ever since the witch had shown up, uninvited, the previous week, Becky's life had been Hell. The half-assed apology the woman had given for the way she'd behaved the day she arrived had been as shallow as a hastily dug grave.

"I swear, if she comes in here asking for more financial data one more time, I'm going to go flying monkey crazy on her."

"Were you talking to me?"

Becky jerked her attention away from the stack of purchase orders on her desk and to the man standing in her doorway. Ford looked good enough to eat, leaning against the doorjamb in his faded jeans and a *Don't Mess with Texas* T-shirt.

"Nope."

Ford's gaze swept her office. "Talking to yourself, then. That's not a good sign." Without invitation, he settled into the one guest chair facing her desk. "So, who has you in such a snit you're talking to yourself?"

How could such a brilliant man be so clueless? Veronica had everyone in the place looking over the shoulder for witches on broomsticks. "Nobody." She shuffled papers around on her desk, hoping if she appeared busy enough, her partner would take the hint and leave. When he gave no sign of moving on, she clasped her hands together on the cleared blotter and changed the subject. "How's the new line of male products coming?"
~~~

"Good, if I do say so myself." When he talked about his work, he looked like a kid in a toy store. A smile lifted both sides of his mouth, and his eyes twinkled with a light from within. She couldn't be mad at him when he looked at her that way.

Becky nodded. "I talked to Scott this morning. He's sending over a contract for the leather goods you designed. Once the paperwork is all squared away, he estimated three weeks until the first shipment is ready. I think direct sales is the way to go on this one."

"No middleman means more profits." He rubbed his hands together. Like either one of them needed more money. "We should slot out some time on the shopping channel to showcase the new line."

"Already done." She sorted through the folders on her desk, picked one out, and slid it across the desktop. "Here are the schedules for the next two months."

"Only two months?"

Becky looked up at him. "You want more?"

"Why wouldn't I?"

"Oh, I don't know. Maybe because you'll be who knows where by then?"

He tilted his head to one side and narrowed his eyes at her. "What makes you think I won't be here?"

"Ms. Ramsey said—"

"She was here? What, exactly, did she say?"

Ford spent most of his time in his office, drawing on his sketchpad or computer, but he still managed to have a clue about most things happening in the office. Could it be possible he hadn't asked Veronica to help him, and he had no idea what his girlfriend had been up to the past week? "She's been here every day this week, asking to see the financial reports, production schedules...."

His face turned a shade of red she'd never seen before, and he clenched his fists at his side.

"Did she say why she wanted the reports?"

"She said you asked her to get them."

A muscle ticked in his jaw. "Did she say why?"

"No. I assumed you were talking to a potential buyer."

His gaze bore into her. "I'm not selling, Becks. Not today. Not next week or next month. Not ever."

"Oh." Her heart did a flip at the use of the pet name he'd given her, only to plummet to her stomach as she realized what he'd said. "Then…? You…?"

"No. I didn't ask her to get them for me. I knew she had to be up to something, coming here, but I had no idea what. I still don't." He tossed the schedule she'd just handed him on her desk. "Shit. I've got to go."

"Ford!"

He stopped in the doorway and turned.

"What's going on?"

"I don't know, but I'm going to find out."

He couldn't remember being this angry, ever. For the last week, he'd ignored Veronica, and since she hadn't bothered him, he'd assumed he'd made himself clear on the subject of selling and going back to New York. She'd shown up the next day, apologized to Becky Jean and Carolyn, and he hadn't seen her since. He'd assumed she'd decided to spend her time visiting with Scott, but in truth, he had no idea she remained in town. *Should have paid more attention.*

Well, he was paying attention now. He grabbed his car keys out of his desk drawer. Whatever plans she had, he would put a stop them.

CHAPTER TWENTY-TWO

"Where is she?" he demanded.

Scott looked up from his cluttered desk, a blank stare on his face as if he'd just woken from a coma. "Who?"

"Veronica. Where is she?"

His friend shrugged. "No idea. Thought you were keeping her occupied."

Ford slapped the doorframe. "Fuck!"

"Something wrong?"

"Do *you* know what she's up to?"

"Up to?" Scott rocked back in his chair. "No. I've barely seen her since she got here. She hasn't taken a single meal at the B&B. I thought you and her—"

"I told you, we're over. Have been for a while." Ford dropped into the old leather visitors' chair—a remnant left behind by the previous owners. He shook his head. "I knew she was up to something when she showed up all of a sudden, but I had no idea."

"What?"

"I just found out she's been poking around in the plant's financials. Even had the balls to ask for copies of reports. She gave Becky Jean the impression I wanted them, probably to give to a prospective buyer."

"Shit." Scott straightened. "And you knew nothing about this?"

"Not a thing. I've been working my ass off this week, working out the kinks in a new toy I plan to unveil at the trade show next week in Vegas. I've barely come out of my office to eat, much less sleep." He raked his hands over his face. "What the fuck is she up to?"

"I've never pretended to understand Ronnie, so don't ask me."

"I've got to find her, put a stop to this shit."

"Did you try The Yellow Rose?"

"Not yet. I'm going there next." Ford stood. "Thanks, man, for listening. I know she's your sister and all, but I could easily strangle her."

Scott snorted. "No offense taken. She's always looked out for herself first and everyone else last. She's definitely up to something. If she shows up, I'll let you know."

"Thanks."

A stop at The Yellow Rose provided no more information on Ronnie's whereabouts. Roseanne confirmed she hadn't seen much of her new tenant. Like Scott, she'd assumed Ford to be the reason. Leaving instructions to call him the minute Veronica returned, Ford headed back to the plant.

With a little luck, the 3-D printer would have spit out his new creation while he'd been gone. If everything went well, he could have enough samples produced in time to hand out at the trade show.

He stopped at Becky Jean's office long enough to tell her not to give Ronnie any more information, and assure her he remembered the trip the following week. They were taking a few interns from the business program at the county junior college over in Plainview to fetch and carry, and several of the new spokesmodels they'd hired for the network shows. Between them, their booth would be well staffed for the week-long event, which meant he'd have plenty of time to spend with Becky Jean.

Neither one of them had had a day off since they'd become business partners, and he planned to take full advantage of the opportunity to get away for a little while.

Becky Jean's brother, Colin, had called a few weeks ago, asking for Ford's help. Turned out, he planned to be in Las Vegas, too. His new record label had booked him and his band as an opening act for one of the major acts in town, and he wanted Ford to help him surprise Becky Jean who had never seen him play in person.

The concert was just one of the surprises he had for his partner. They both deserved to have a little fun.

Speaking of which…. He examined his new creation. It didn't look much different than others he'd seen. It was what went on the inside that made this model unique.

~~~

Ford vibrated with anticipation as he helped the interns put the finishing touches on their booth in the Las Vegas Convention Center. He'd sent Becky Jean back to the hotel to rest up and get ready for their big night on the town. He'd finally told her about the concert tickets after her brother had called to let him know about the giant billboard in front of their hotel proclaiming him the opening act for the next few days. Colin had been disappointed about not being able to surprise his sister, as had Ford, but the concert paled in comparison to the other surprise he had for his partner.

She would have found the toy. If Becky Jean did as his note instructed, it would be worth every penny of bribe money he'd paid the housekeeping staff to have the gift-wrapped package placed in her room while she'd been out.

Since the night they'd spent together, she'd been careful to feature toys on the show she could easily test solo. Technically, his new creation fit into the same category but would be a lot more fun with a partner.

"Ford! What are you doing?"

On his knees organizing the boxes stashed beneath one of their tables, the familiar voice startled him.

"Fuck!" he hissed, extricating himself from the dark cavern created by the tablecloth. He bumped his head on the table, uttered another curse, and stood. Scott's sister and a man he didn't recognize faced him. "Ronnie. What are you doing here?"

"I thought I would surprise you."

"Who's this?" He nodded at the man standing an almost-appropriate distance behind her. It could have been the way he looked at Ronnie like he could see through her clothes that made the gap between them seem intimate.
~~~

The woman glanced over her shoulder and beckoned her companion forward. "Ford, I'd like you to meet Carter Hargraves. Carter, Ford Adams."

The man extended his hand. Out of habit, Ford did the same while he searched his memory for a reason the man's name sounded familiar.

"Nice to meet you," Carter said. "You're a difficult man to reach."

Things clicked into place. Dozens of messages over the last few weeks from the CEO of their biggest competitor, Toy Haven. Messages he'd ignored. "Not if I have reason to speak to you."

The other man raised one eyebrow and smiled. "Can we go somewhere and talk?"

"No." He didn't want to keep Becky Jean waiting. He scanned the booth one last time to make sure everything was in place for the opening the next morning then turned back to his unwanted visitors. "I don't know what Veronica has told you, but Adams Manufacturing has been in my family for four generations. It's not for sale."

Hargraves glanced at Ronnie who smiled and wrapped herself around the man's arm, snuggling up to him like a dancer to a pole. "Don't believe a word he says, Carter. Everything has a price. Tell him what you're offering. He'll change his mind."

Ford glared at the woman then held up a staying hand before either one could utter another word. "Don't bother." He scooted through the gap between the partition separating their booth from the next one and the table. "Ms. Ramsey is mistaken, Mr. Hargraves. If you'll excuse me, I have plans this evening."

"Don't be ridiculous, Ford. Ford! Come back here!"

Seething, he kept walking until the sound of cars breezing past on the street drowned out Veronica's screeching. No doubt she'd used the financial information she'd conned the staff out of to convince their biggest competitor to make an offer for the company. Why, he didn't have a clue. He'd told her in no uncertain terms he had no plans to sell, made it plain he liked his new situation.

His mind reeled, trying to grasp the woman's reasoning and came up empty. "What part of no does she not understand?" he mumbled as he entered the hotel lobby and headed toward the elevators. He keyed in his floor then shook his head to dislodge the anger and disbelief at Ronnie's actions. He'd deal with the woman later. He had much more pleasant things to deal with tonight.

~~~

At Ford's insistence, Becky had left him to finish setting up their booth so she could get some rest before their big night on the town. Unable to sit still, she stood at the floor-to-ceiling windows of her hotel suite and stared at the electronic billboard dozens of stories below flashing her brother's picture every thirty seconds. Yes, she'd timed the intervals. She had known her brother was doing well. He called often enough, but, in the last year, she'd barely come up for air, and had somehow missed his rise to stardom. Well, almost stardom. Soon, he'd be the headliner and some other hopeful would be his opening act.

Tonight would be awesome. First, dinner with Ford, their new business partner, Scott Ramsey, and Becky's best friend, Roseanne Meadows, who had accompanied Scott to Vegas. Her friend still refused to talk about what went on between her and the Yankee, but anyone with eyes could see *something* was going on.

After dinner, the four of them would return to the hotel where they had VIP seats for the concert. Thankfully, she'd had a little warning and had been able to call Amy to help her find a dress for tonight. She'd picked out the black beaded halter-style gown with the slit up the side that both allowed her to move and exposed enough leg to be sexy. Amy had assured her men's heads would turn when she walked by.

Becky squelched a giggle before it made it past her lips. She'd never been to Las Vegas, but she'd heard plenty about the place. Maybe she'd been cooped up in her office for too long, but it felt good to be away — to have a *view* from her window! She loved Butte Plains, but she'd been too busy lately to enjoy her hometown. Even though this was a work trip, she fully intended to squeeze every drop of fun out of it she could — starting tonight.

She spied the gift the moment she stepped into the bedroom. Wrapped in the glossy-white paper and signature red ribbon Adams Manufacturing used to wrap gift purchases for shipment, she knew instantly who it had to be from. *Ford.* She shook her head and placed a fist over her heart to assuage the ache she experienced
~~~

every time she thought about him. *Lord, what now?* Working with him was pure torture sometimes, but she wouldn't trade those times for anything.

He'd said he wouldn't sell his part of the company, but he hadn't said he would stay in Butte Plains either, so she refused to let her heart beat for what it wanted—a lifetime with the man she loved. Plus, he still had a girlfriend, or whatever. Roseanne said the woman had become a ghost around the B&B, evaporating into thin air. Sneaky. She'd led everyone in the office to believe the documents she requested were for Ford, when she wanted them for her own purposes. No one seemed to know where she went every day. Whatever she was up to, it had to be no good.

Becky forced the evil woman out of her thoughts. Tonight, she resolved to have a good time. No thinking about unpleasant things.

She picked up the box, tested its weight in her palm. Light as air, she had no idea what could be inside. The ribbon came away with a light tug on the end of the bow, and a fingernail under the squares of tape on the bottom and sides loosened the heavy paper wrapping. A plain envelope lay atop the nondescript box. Inside, a note from Ford.

Becky,
I designed this for you. Wear it for me tonight?
Love,
Ford

Love? Her crazy heart skipped a beat at the salutation, even though it probably meant nothing. She set the missive aside and opened the box.

Her hands trembled as she lifted the lace thong. Sewn into the triangle of fabric was what could only be a vibrator. She'd seen similar ones in their competitors' catalogues and knew Ford would eventually get around to designing a better version. Besides being incorporated into an actual garment, this one didn't look special. But she knew her business partner—if he couldn't one-up the competition, he didn't waste his time.

"How is this one different?" she said as she examined it. Immediately, she noticed there were no wires, no controller, not even an on/off switch. Another glance at the box confirmed she hadn't missed any parts. She raised one eyebrow, considering the construction again. The wearer would have no control over whatever magic tricks the toy could do.

Was she brave enough to wear it not knowing when Ford would activate it, or what to expect when he did? Maybe.

Becky placed the device back in its box then headed for the shower to wash the grime of travel and booth setup away. Every drop of soapy water carried another of her worries down the drain, leaving her relaxed and in a better mood than she had been in for ages. Her staff back in Butte Plains were competent and capable of handling whatever came up over the next few days. They'd brought enough people with them to staff their booth at the trade show, and they'd been well trained, which left plenty of time for her to have some fun.

And where better to do it than Las Vegas? Sin City?

After moisturizing every inch of skin she could reach with the expensive lotion both Roseanne and Amy had insisted she needed, she dried her hair, leaving it down so it fell in soft curls over her shoulders. Without a moment's hesitation, she stepped into the lace thong Ford had gifted her with. She wouldn't tell him she had put it on. *Let him guess.* A shiver raced down her spine as she speculated about what she would experience when he chose to activate it. Would it even work? It was hard to imagine something so small with no visible signs of a working mechanism would actually do anything. But, knowing Ford, the tiny device would deliver the goods. Whatever they might be.

The dress fit like a dream, and she had to admit, she didn't look half-bad in it. With every move she made, the heavy beading picked up the light, sending it back into the room in tiny sparks. Ford's latest invention rested undetectable between her legs. *Clever.* She couldn't imagine wearing the others she'd seen for hours — they'd simply be too uncomfortable. But it would be easy to forget about this one.

She'd just pulled her hair behind her left ear and secured it with a rhinestone clasp when a knock sounded on her door.

"Just a second," she called out. She slipped her feet into strappy sandals then grabbed her evening purse off the end of the bed. "Sorry—"

The rest of her apology for keeping him waiting died on her lips the second she laid eyes on Ford. The tingling in her lady parts had nothing to do with the device concealed in her panties and everything to do with the man standing before her. *Holy Jesus.* He looked good no matter what he wore, but this…. "Wow."

"You like it?" he said, brushing invisible lint from the jacket of his tuxedo. "I asked Scott to pack up some of my clothes for me the last time he went back to New York. Never thought I'd need this again, but I'm glad he sent it." His gaze traveled from the sparkly clip in her hair down to the slit in her skirt where it lingered before slowly making its way back to her face. She knew he couldn't possibly tell if she wore his gift, but she held her breath anyway, waiting for him to say something about it.

"Just look at you, Becks. It ought to be a sin to be as beautiful as you are." His heated perusal and the sincerity in his voice brought a flood of heat to her face, and lower.

"The dress isn't too much, is it? Amy insisted it would be appropriate for tonight."

"Remind me to give your stylist a raise when we get back. The dress is fabulous, but it's the person wearing it that makes it stunning."

She blushed at his praise. "Stop it." Much more of his praise and she wouldn't be able to function. The fact he hadn't brought up the subject of his gift made her more aware of it nestled between her legs. If that's the way he wanted to play it, she would play along.

Fighting off a massive case of nerves, she checked her purse one last time. Room key. Lip gloss. A single, folded tissue. I.D. Cell phone. Credit card. Cash for tips or a cab if she needed one. "Are we meeting Scott and Roseanne at the restaurant?"

Satisfied she had everything she might need, she pulled the door closed behind her. Ford offered his arm, and she took it, letting him guide her toward the elevators. His mama had taught him well.

"Yes. Is that okay?"

"Works for me. I'm still surprised Roseanne is here with him. I didn't think she even liked him."

Ford shrugged, ushering her into the elevator car ahead of him. He pushed the appropriate button then resumed his place beside her. "I guess she likes him well enough."

"I suppose so." She couldn't help but worry about her friend. What little she'd said about her long-standing guest led Becky to believe she might not like him all that much.

They stepped out of the elevator on lobby level. Ford spun her around to face him. "If there's one thing I know about Scott, it's the women he's been with have all been with him because they want to be. Keep that in mind tonight. Roseanne has chosen to be where she is."

"Okay." She nodded and pressed her lips together. "I'll try to remember."

His words rattled around in her head as she let him lead her from the hotel into the massive attached indoor mall housing some of the best restaurants in the city as well as expensive boutiques and high-end jewelers in a realistic outdoor setting. The lights had been dimmed, mimicking a jewel-toned sunset she would have found romantic if she hadn't been so focused on figuring out what Ford had meant about Roseanne choosing to be there. Of course she had chosen to be there, or she would have stayed at home.

Ford gave his name to the maître d' who then went to check on something. Ford snapped his fingers in front of her face, and at the same moment a sharp vibration jolted her clit. Becky wrapped her free arm around her middle and just managed to stifle a squeal before it passed her lips. Her gaze snapped to Ford's.

Taking both her hands in his, he drew her forward then leaned down and spoke low into her ear. "You're thinking too hard about the wrong things, Becky Jean. What's between Scott and Roseanne is their business. Focus on what matters to you tonight."

With every word he spoke, the device between her legs vibrated, changing in intensity to match his inflection; ceasing with each pause. She gasped as realization dawned and the damned thing reacted to her voice. *Oh Lord. It's sound activated!*

She drew back and her gaze landed on the small American Flag pin attached to his lapel. She'd thought it homage to their Made in America marketing campaign. Clamping her lips shut, she looked up at him.

"I knew you would wear it."

She whimpered as his words, spoken at a conversational level, translated into a series of vibrations she couldn't ignore.

"Do you like it?"

His voice stroked her clit with each word he spoke. She nodded. His invention was evil and ingenious and Lord, the most erotic thing she could imagine!

He let her left hand go and reached into an inner pocket of his jacket. No vibrations accompanied his next words. "The microphone is in the flag pin, as I see you've figured out. Be a good girl, and I'll let you eat your meal in peace."

She raised one eyebrow. "And if I choose to be bad?"

"It's calibrated to pick up loud noises from any distance, or voices within about eighteen inches. You decide if you want me to activate it or not." He smirked. "It's up to you, darlin'."

"Mr. Adams? Your table is ready."

CHAPTER TWENTY-THREE

Ford tucked her arm in the crook of his, leaving her no choice but to go along. He seated her then took the chair next to hers. How close did the transmitter have to be to operate? If he'd sat across from her, would he have been too far away?

She took the menu offered and listened as her partner ordered wine and appetizers from the waiter who had appeared like magic.

"I'm really looking forward to the concert later," Ford said without taking his eyes off his menu.

The concert. The very *loud* concert. Oh, he was an evil one! "You wouldn't."

"Not during your brother's set. That would just be weird."

Weird pretty much summed up her life these days. She'd once lived a quiet, if not boring life. There had been plenty of ups and downs since Kenneth Adams passed away, but thanks to his son, she hadn't been bored a single day. "And it wouldn't be weird to do this in front of our friends?"

He shook his head. "Nope." He looked up as another waiter placed a loaf of artisan bread on a small cutting board in the center of the table. Ford reached for the carving knife and cut off a chunk, offering it to her. Becky declined. "Trust me. If Scott figured it out, it wouldn't bother him in the least. Since Roseanne is with him, I doubt she'd care either."

A cold chill raced down her spine. She opened her mouth to protest that he couldn't possibly know what her friend would think when Ford stood. She followed his gaze to see the couple in question making their way to the table.

Scott held the chair across from her for Roseanne, sinking any chance she had of having a private word with her friend. As he resumed his seat, Ford smiled and winked at her. She stuck her tongue out at him then sat back as he reached inside his coat.

No. He wouldn't.

"How was your flight?" he asked the newcomers. Becky Jean bit the inside of her cheek to keep from whimpering. She clenched her thighs tight which only served to concentrate the sensation. He kept up a running conversation for several minutes. She thought she might die as the microphone/receiver picked up every word Roseanne spoke and several of Scott's, keeping her on the sharp edge of arousal. How in the world would she make it through the concert?

"We're going to debut a new product at the show this week." He turned his attention her way. "Why don't you tell them about it, Becks?"

She thought about begging, but she let her eyes do the job, silently pleading with him to turn the damn thing off. Masturbating in public went way beyond her limits. He reached into his coat and the tension in her shoulders released. She wouldn't rest easy until she knew for certain he'd turned the infernal thing off.

"Go ahead," he said. She let her thighs and stomach muscles relax. "You can probably describe the operation of the *Your Secret is Safe Personal Vibrator* better than I could."

He'd even named the product! She narrowed her eyes at him then quickly shifted gears as he reached for the switch again. He would pay for this! "Hmm. Let me think." She picked up her wine glass and sipped. Over the rim, she caught Scott's amused expression. Immediately, she shifted her gaze to Roseanne who did a terrible job of containing her mirth. A pit opened up inside her, and her stomach slid all the way to her toes. She turned to her partner. "You told them, didn't you?"

"No. I swear." The smile on his face made her want to crawl under the table. "I think you just did."

Shit.

Roseanne laughed out loud. "Oh, God, Becky! If you could have seen the look on your face!" She leaned over the table and whispered loud, "I thought you were going to come right here in the middle of the restaurant." She sat back up and asked Ford, "When can I get one of those things?"

"Stop by our booth tomorrow and I'll make sure you get one. I had enough made up to give one to each of our best-selling retailers. Since it's been tested and approved, I think we can go into production pretty quickly. What do you think, Becky Jean?"

"I think you played a dastardly trick on me."

He flashed her the smile that had sold millions of sex toys via their home shopping television show and made him a billionaire. "They don't call me *Kinky* Ford Adams for nothing, you know?"

Scott laughed. "I saw that! It was the article in *Forbes* magazine, right?"

"I don't know. Do you remember, Becks?"

"*Barron's* called him kinky. *Forbes* labeled him the Backdoor Billionaire."

"That's right." Scott laughed. "God, who would have thought it?"

"Not me." Lifting his wine glass to his lips, he took a sip. "I just wanted to keep the doors open for the year stipulated in Dad's will and not lose everything we had in the process. Never dreamed things would take off the way they did." He turned his gaze on Becky. "I owe it all to Becky Jean. Without her marketing and vision, we might have survived the year, but we would have bled money the entire time."

She could feel everyone's eyes on her. Ford had said much the same to her on numerous occasions, but this was the first time he'd acknowledged her contribution to others. This time when she squirmed in her seat, it had nothing to do with Ford's infernal new device.

"I just put together a reasonable marketing plan. And anyone in the business knows, if your product is inferior, there's nothing in the world you can say to make people buy it."

"Are you saying our products are superior?"

"You know they are. Thanks to you" — she nodded at Ford then to Scott—"and you, too. The two of you have come up with innovative ideas that have the competition scrambling to keep up."

"So tell me about this new one," Roseanne said. "How does it work?"

Ford withdrew a small, square plastic box from his suit coat. It looked like a battery compartment for a toy, but there were no wires running from it, only an on/off switch on one end. "This is the transmitter and control box." He pointed to the pin on his lapel. "This is a microphone." He went on to explain how they would sell it with various types and styles of microphones to suit everyone's needs.

"And the receiver part?" Roseanne asked Becky.

"Is no bigger than a quarter and is sewn into the fabric. You could wear the panties anywhere, and no one would be the wiser."

"Unless you can't control your responses," her friend added.

~~~

Becky wiped tears from her eyes with one hand and held fast to Ford with the other as he maneuvered them to the stage door following Colin's set. She was so freaking proud of her brother! She'd always known he had talent, but his sister's opinion didn't count. The reaction from the audience tonight had confirmed her assessment, though.

The guard scrutinized their credentials before ushering them backstage where another guard pointed them in the right direction. With the familiarity of their years growing up together, she easily found him talking to a group of men dressed in black T-shirts with STAFF printed on the back in bold lettering.

"Colin!" she cried out. Breaking her connection with Ford, she launched herself in his direction.

"Becky Jean!" A smile broke across his face, and he grabbed her up in a hug, nearly crushing her ribs. "God, am I glad to see you."

"You were awesome!" She sniffed as more tears threatened. Colin set her down but seemed as reluctant to let her go as she was of him. "I'm so proud of you I could bust." She wiped her eyes.

"You look like a million bucks in that dress."

She didn't want to think about what she'd spent on her gown. All their lives they'd had to watch their pennies. "Don't get me started on what it cost," she warned.
~~~

"Colin," Ford said, snaking an arm around Becky's waist. He extended his other to shake her brother's hand. "Ford Adams. It's nice to finally meet you. Your sister speaks of you often."

"Nice to meet you," Colin said. "Thanks for helping me surprise Becky Jean, even if I did have to spoil it at the last minute."

"You should see her out front. Every time we walk past the marquee and your photo shows up, she points and shouts, 'That's my brother,' at the top of her lungs." Ford laughed as he hauled her closer.

Colin smiled. "Who'da thunk it? Right, Sis?"

"I never doubted you would make it."

"You might have been the only one, but I'm grateful for your support. Always have been. You're probably the only person who never tried to discourage me from pursuing my love of music."

Becky's heart was so full she was sure it would explode any minute. Colin had always had talent, but in the past few years, he'd grown into it. Success looked good on him. "Dad would be so proud of you."

Colin's smile dimmed, and his eyes glistened. "I know he would. He thought it was his duty to try to talk me out of going to Nashville, but when he failed to convince me, he backed off. Let me find my own way."

"Mom sends her love. She said you promised to fly her out for your debut at the Opry?"

"I did. I want you to come, too, but I figured you could afford your own plane ticket." He laughed, one eyebrow raised.

"Oh, you!" Becky's cheeks grew warm. "Yes, I can afford mine and many, many others, thanks to Ford. He saved the town, Colin. You wouldn't know it anymore. Businesses are reopening. Most of the vacant houses have been bought up and new ones are being built."

"Sex sells, they say." He winked at her and her face flamed.

"I suppose it does."

"I've got some time tomorrow. Ford sent me a pass to the convention. I thought I could come by around lunch? Maybe we could get a bite together?"

"I'd love to! I have to warn you, our products are… are…."

"I know all about your products, Sis. I'm all grown up, remember?"

"Of course you are. It's just—"

"It's time for us to get back to our seats," Ford said. "Say good-bye to your brother. You can take all the time you want tomorrow to catch up with him."

"Bye, Sis." Colin gave her another bear hug. "Thanks again for coming. Noon okay tomorrow?"

"Perfect," she said.

"Colin."

"Ford," her brother said before he turned to greet a group of female fans who'd been waiting impatiently for him to acknowledge them.

They returned to their seats just as the lights dimmed for the headline act.

"How's Colin?" Roseanne asked.

"He looks great! We're having lunch tomorrow. You should come."

Before her friend could answer, the stage burst to life as the renowned country rock band made their appearance. Becky stood along with everyone else to applaud. The opening chords of their first song rocked the building, but the accompanying vibration between her legs had all her attention.

She'd forgotten all about the tiny device in her panties. Now she couldn't stop thinking about it. She grabbed Ford's arm, turned her face into his sleeve, and held on for dear life as his wicked creation pulsed in time with the music. *Holy smoke!* She'd thought it couldn't be more devastating than it had been when he'd turned it on in the restaurant, but boy had she been wrong.

The song ended, and the crowd settled into their seats. Thankfully, Ford turned the thing off while the lead singer spoke to the crowd, but the instant the band fired off again, so did the vibrator. Their second number was a ballad, and while the first song had translated into intense sensations, this one stimulated in soft waves, wrecking her control. Once again, she buried her face in his sleeve and squeezed his arm until her fingers cramped.

"Ford," she pleaded.

He turned slightly, brushed her hair back from her face and leaned in so he could be heard. "Don't fight it, sweetheart. Let it come."

Of course, the microphone picked up every word he said, adding another layer of torture for her to deal with. She squirmed in her seat, and focused everything she had on not coming. *Oh god. Oh god. Oh god. Ford.*

"Quit fighting it, Becks." He stroked her arm from shoulder to elbow while holding her as close as the theater seats would allow and placing soft kisses on the top of her head. She knew the song—had always loved it. It ended on a long, sustained note that warbled and spanned from one octave to another. There was no way she could ride it without coming. She just prayed everyone around her would be too caught up in the emotional ending on stage to witness her surrender to the inevitable.

Ford nibbled on her earlobe then whispered, "God, I love making you come."

As the last word passed his lips, the lead singer let loose, working the syllables up and down the musical scale. His keening wale of love lost forever wrung emotion from the audience who had grown quiet with expectation. Her clit throbbed in time with the music. Every muscle in her body tensed. *No. No. No.* She fought to hang onto the last threads of her control.

With a final burst from his lungs, the singer hit the last note. The crowd erupted, applauding and cheering at the same instant Becky lost her battle. The orgasm barreled through her like a runaway locomotive. She threw her head back, and before the scream rising from her core could make it past her lips, Ford yanked her into his lap and covered her mouth with his. Her entire body quaked with the force of her release, but Ford's hands were on her, his arms bracketing her, holding all the pieces of her together until they somehow reassembled themselves.

The audience rose to their feet—all except the two of them—as the band segued into another of their fast-paced hit songs. Becky jerked, the vibrations almost painful after her intense orgasm. Ford chuckled. Shifting her slightly, he reached into his jacket pocket. She welcomed the ensuing calm between her legs, but on the other hand, her body craved the stimulation. She clenched her thighs, savoring the last lingering internal spasms.

"Better?" Ford asked.

Unwilling to trust her voice, she nodded against his shoulder. She didn't seem to have a solid bone in her body, but the man holding her seemed to be granite from his chest to his thighs supporting her. The thick ridge of his erection gouged her hip—a reminder he'd given, not taken. He held her through two more songs she barely heard for the warnings clamoring in her head. She wanted so much more from this man, but even though he claimed he wouldn't sell his and his mother's share of the company, he hadn't said anything about staying in Texas. She'd foolishly fallen in love with him. Spending more time in his bed would only make his leaving worse, but if he asked, she wouldn't turn him down.

Holding her in his lap while she came down from what had appeared to be an intense orgasm was Heaven and Hell. He had her right where he wanted her, in his arms, but he couldn't do the things he wanted to do to her, with her, in the middle of a concert. If anyone had noticed her behavior earlier, they'd given no indication—save Roseanne and Scott who'd picked up the cues early on and had the decency to look away.

"Is she okay?" Roseanne mouthed.

"Fine," he silently answered.

Becky Jean's friend smiled her understanding. Ford made some hand gestures he hoped conveyed his intention to get them out of there. Roseanne wiggled her fingers in a good-bye gesture, so he figured the message had been received. Scott caught his gaze, leaned in so his date could speak into his ear. He lifted his head again and nodded.

With his intentions known to their friends, he shifted Becky Jean so she could hear him. "Can you walk?"

She looked up at him, confusion marring her features.

"I want to take you someplace private," he said into her ear.

"Okay," she said with a nod.

"Think you can walk out of here?"

Another nod then she stood. Roseanne tugged on the hem of his coat. He turned, and she handed him Becky Jean's small purse. He smiled his thanks, then with a hand on the small of her back, he followed Becky Jean past the others in their row. Once they'd cleared the theater doors, he took over, guiding her through the casino to the bank of elevators that would take them to their rooms.

He paused before pushing the call button. "Unless you'd like a drink?"

She'd worn the vibrator of her own free will, but he'd been the one to force her orgasm. The least he could do would be to offer her the opportunity to slow things down—or heaven forbid—say no. When she shook her head and nodded to the button, his lungs began to work again.

If she'd said no, he would have respected her wishes, but it would have cost him to do it. Nothing short of burying his cock inside her would ease the ache in his groin. She was so damn beautiful, and fuck, he loved to watch her come. He would have nail marks in his arm from where she'd clung to him earlier. Did it make him a bastard to be proud of the marks she'd put on him in the throes of passion? If it did, he'd wear the label.

The doors opened, and, luckily, they were the only ones to enter the car. As soon as the doors closed, he backed her into the corner and switched on the device.

"Do you have any idea what I'm going to do to you?" he asked, letting his invention translate his words into action. He traced the line of her jaw with the knuckle of his index finger then stroked his thumb over her quivering bottom lip. He didn't expect a verbal answer. Instead, he watched her breath hitch and her eyelids flutter shut. He pressed his hips into hers, letting her feel what she did to him.

"I've wanted you since you opened your door this evening looking like a goddess." He paused, adjusted to better feel the vibrations. Satisfied with the new position, he continued. "Your sexy leg sticking out of the slit in the skirt—taunting me." His fingers found her bare thigh. He slipped his hand beneath the heavy fabric to caress her skin. "So hot. So soft. I want to see you… every last inch of you."

Damn. He ground his teeth together and canted his hips away from her. He'd had no idea how powerful his toy could be. If he kept this up much longer, he would make himself come! He made a mental note to have the technical writing department add this position to the instruction sheet to be included with each device then focused on his goal—making his woman come.

His woman. He liked the sound of that. In all his years, he'd never wanted to possess a woman the way he wanted to possess this one. So prim and proper in public, she let loose in bed, and damn if he didn't want to be the last man to ever see her do it.

He ground against her again, slid the hand he'd slipped under her dress around to cup her butt. "I want to taste you." He squeezed her ass cheek. "I want to take a bite out of your ass, mark you as mine."

Becky Jean moaned, and the sound translated into vibration nearly sent him over the edge. He backed away once more, this time promising himself he'd stay away until they got to his room. Then all bets were off.

The car came to a stop. He glanced over his shoulder, noted the floor display. Reaching into his pocket, he managed to turn the vibrator off a split second before the doors slid open to admit two couples dressed for a night on the town. They pushed the button for the rooftop lounge. Ford snaked an arm around Becky Jean's waist and pulled her in close. When the elevator stopped at their floor, he steered her past the rowdy bunch and toward his room.

"You're a wicked man, Ford Adams." Hearing the laughter behind her words, he tossed the keycard on the nearest flat surface then turned to the woman who had made him rethink everything in his life from where he wanted to live to what he wanted out of life. He'd never cared much for the plight of others, but Becky Jean's insistence on hiring local had opened his eyes to the way his decisions affected other people's lives. She made him *want* to be a better person. She made him want. Period.

"I've never claimed to be anything else," he said, stalking her. She took a step back—a halfhearted attempt to get away, at best. He stopped an arm's length from her and smiled. "Admit it, you had fun tonight."

Her face flushed with color, and her lips parted as she prepared to deny the truth.

"Turn around," he said, spinning his finger in the air. "I need to see you."

Her gaze met his for a second—long enough for him to see she wanted to continue what they'd started as much as he did. Then she showed him her back. He stepped in behind her and brushed her hair over one shoulder. "Where the hell is the zipper?"

"Oh! Here." She lifted her arm and pointed to the tiny tab. "Sorry. I forgot."

"No problem." He'd planned on nibbling his way down her spine, but this had possibilities. He grasped the zipper pull and tugged it down until it bottomed out just past the curve of her hip. He caught a glimpse of creamy skin and the band of the panties he'd sent her—and nothing else. Damn, she knew how to do sexy. He slid his hand into the gap in the fabric just below her rib cage, his palm finding soft, warm skin at the small of her back. As he guided her around to face him and took her lips with his, he instantly became a fan of side zippers.

Cupping the back of her head in his free hand, he explored the hills and valleys of her ass with the other. Becky Jean groaned and melted against him which he took as permission to continue his exploration. He'd had his hands beneath dresses before, but there was something sneaky and exciting about slipping in from the side. Like he'd found a secret entrance no one else knew about. Fuck, why didn't every dress have one of these?

Needing air, he dragged his lips from hers but continued to nibble along her jaw. Fingers still entwined in her hair, he tugged her head to the side. He kissed his way down the slope of her neck, loving the way her pulse beat out a wild rhythm, matching his own. He couldn't resist. He opened wide and bit. Not hard enough to mar her perfect skin, but hard enough to get her attention.

"Oh god. Ford." The breathless way she said his name had to be one of the hottest things he'd ever heard in his life. He bit her again, lower this time. She moaned and arched her back so her breasts pressed hard against his chest. He used his chin to scootch the strap of her dress off her shoulder. It slid down and caught on his forearm. He proceeded to kiss and nibble his way south to the tender swell of flesh. Using his teeth, he tugged the fabric lower. Lower. Her scent, magnified by the heat of her body, filled his nostrils as he slowly, slowly, revealed the top of her breast. Then the areola. Then his upper lip skimmed her nipple, and he lost it.

"Fuck, Becks." He grabbed at the dress again with his teeth— captured it and yanked like a beast tearing at the skin of a carcass to get to the meat underneath. The instant her breast popped free of the confining cloth, he attacked, nipping at her beauty, licking, and finally sucking the hardened nub into his mouth.

He couldn't get enough of her. Couldn't get close enough to sate his need. Savage. He knew it but couldn't stop. Yanking on her hair, he bent her over the arm banded around her waist. Her fingernails digging into his scalp were matches thrown on the bonfire raging inside him. Her breathless pleas, "God. Please. Ford. Need. You," were giant-assed logs that incinerated the last vestiges of his control.

He couldn't wait another minute to have her.

Pulling her upright, he took another second to admire the feel of her skin beneath the beaded dress. He'd made a mess of her hair, but what utterly destroyed him was the sight of her breast, bared for him while the rest of her remained perfectly clothed. "God, Becks. I've never seen.... You take my breath away."

"Ford."

Need. It rang in his ears, broke the spell she'd cast over him. He mentally clicked the shutter on the picture before him. Knew it would forever be burned on his brain, and no matter what happened between them in the future, he'd treasure this moment. This memory. "Take that dress the fuck off."

The shrug of a shoulder. A hip wiggle and it fell into a pool of midnight and glittering stars around her ankles. She wore the panties he'd given her and some kind of strappy sandals with heels a mile high, making her legs look longer than fuck. He had things he wanted to do to her with those panties, but they could wait. He needed to be inside her. No gimmicks. No toys. Nothing but her and him and whatever the fuck he was feeling.

"Off." He pointed at her crotch. She hooked her thumbs in the waistband and, with another hip shimmy, added the panties to the pile at her ankles.

He made a conscious effort to breathe as he gazed at the woman before him. The scent of her arousal, heavy on the air, nearly brought him to his knees. His heart kicked and his dick throbbed, anxious to get out of the starting gate. He reached for his belt buckle.

CHAPTER TWENTY-FOUR

How can it take so long to unbuckle a belt?

Becky's gaze followed Ford's hands, silently willing him to move faster. A minute ago, he'd been a wild animal, tearing at her clothes, biting her, sucking her flesh hard enough to extract the marrow from her bones. He'd switched to slow motion. She didn't know how much longer she could remain upright.

She'd been in a constant state of arousal since the moment he'd activated the vibrator in her panties in the vestibule of the restaurant. Granted, the orgasm during the concert had taken the edge off, but the reprieve hadn't lasted long. The elevator ride had put her body back to square one. She hurt. Actually hurt with her need to have him inside her.

Muscle memory. Her pussy knew the shape and size of him. Knew the delicious stretch as he entered her. Knew the regret as he slid back out. Thrilled at the anticipation of feeling the stretch as he filled her again. And had ached for it every minute of every day, it seemed.

"Let me." Carefully stepping free of her clothes, she approached, searched his eyes for a sign of the beast she craved tonight and found it. There. Leashed but straining against his cage. Holding his gaze, her fingers found the button in the center of his chest. He froze. Becky popped the fastener free then went to work on the next one. And the next, until the fabric parted. She flattened her palms on his abdomen, traced the lines of his six-pack. "You're wearing too many clothes, Kinky."

He smirked at the nickname he'd been given by one of the reporters who had interviewed him earlier in the year. Becky turned her hands, brushed her knuckles over his flat nipples. A shiver racked his body, and he sucked in a harsh breath, but he made no attempt to stop her. Her fingers skimmed lower, into the waistband of his slacks. It took nothing to release the hook closure. Less to slide the zipper down.

She read the warning in his eyes — Don't poke the animal. Too late… she already had her hand inside his boxers.

"Becks." His eyelids dropped, a muscle ticked in his clenched jaw. He groaned and rocked into her hand. Once. Twice. "Goddamnit, Becks." His fingers manacled her wrist. His eyes popped open. "Stop."

She knew she should heed the warning, but she couldn't bring herself to do it. For whatever reason, she needed it wild tonight. No holding back. Hot. Messy. Maybe brutal. Sex. She wrapped her fingers around his cock and squeezed.

The beast broke free, took her to the floor. She opened for him, but not far enough to please him. He wrenched her knees up and out. Held her there. With a feral growl, he bent and buried his face in her pussy. The scent of arousal, hers and his, wrapped around them. Becky threw her hands over her head, sought an anchor to ground her as he took her up and up toward a pinnacle higher than she'd ever climbed before. As frightening as it was, as hard as she knew she'd fall, she *needed* to fly off that cliff. Needed *Ford* to push her over the edge. No one else. Just him. Always him.

He took her relentlessly. As if he sensed her need, he feasted on her, bruising with his tongue, scraping her tender flesh with his teeth. Her body belonged to him. The beast controlled her, positioned her where he wanted, took what he wanted — and gave her what she needed.

She felt like one of those giant slingshots being stretched back. Back. Back. Every muscle in her body ached under the strain. For what seemed like an eternity, she froze in limbo. Wound too tight to let go. Wound too tight to remain still. Then he speared his tongue inside her, and the carnality of the act snapped her hold on reality.

The world she knew ceased to exist. She flew into the unknown on the wings of the most explosive orgasm of her life where pain

and pleasure became one. Yet still she reached for something…
something more.

Then he was there, blanketing her with his warmth, his
strength—filling her. "Ford!" She rode the wave with him until
neither one could stop the tide. They came together in a breathless
rush. Becky held on to his broad shoulders and wished the night
would never end.

~~~

With a smile, Becky greeted everyone who stopped at their
booth, handing out the *KeyP Me Safe* keychain/flashlight/vibrators
they'd brought along as giveaways. Somehow, she managed to
answer the questions coming her way, but with Ford standing a few
feet away, thinking about anything other than the night before
proved damn near impossible. More than once, he'd stepped in to
fill in the blanks where her brain had failed her.

The convention was their first opportunity to network with the
various retailers who stocked their products. Since Adams
Manufacturing had launched their own sales platform—going into
direct competition with them—maintaining a good relationship
with them had to be a priority. They'd lost a few with the move into
direct sales, but not all. She had a plan to bring the others back into
the fold with discounted advertising on their Adult Shopping
Network and the promise of exclusive product launches.

But it required her complete concentration on business—
something she could not even pretend to do with Ford so near.
When he whipped out a sample of his latest invention to show to a
potential new client, she excused herself and went in search of
someplace she could be alone. It turned out to be a stall in the ladies'
room, where she closed her eyes and gave in to the memories
tugging at her mind and her heart.

After screwing like mad on the floor, Ford had carried her to
bed where he'd finished undressing then returned to the other
room to retrieve her panties. Wearing nothing but a wicked smile,
he slipped them back on her. Product testing, he'd said as he
searched his phone. A few seconds later, music spilled from a small,
portable speaker on the nightstand.
~~~

He removed the lapel-pin microphone and the wireless control box from his coat and set them on the nightstand before crawling in bed with her.

"I downloaded this music just for this," he'd said. Then he'd turned the device on.

Tears threatened as she recalled the way he'd touched and kissed her while the music played low in the background, converted to a tactile sensation between her legs by his invention. Then, when she didn't think she could take any more, he'd pushed the crotch of the panties to one side and entered her. It had been the complete opposite of their frenzied coupling on the floor, and where the first time had wrecked her physically, the slow, sensual mating to the strains of a symphony orchestra shattered her.

She couldn't even pretend to deny it any longer. She was in love with K. Ford Adams—the kinky bastard. He liked to pretend he didn't care about anything but the bottom line, but she'd seen another side of him.

The new HR department answered to her, so the day Ford had walked in and asked which employees had been there the longest, she heard about it. They day he called them all together and handed them bonus checks—drawn from his personal account—she heard about it.

The day one of their new employees totaled his car on the way to work and Ford went to the hospital to check on the man, she heard about it. And when he paid the deductible on the man's car insurance so he could get a new car, she heard about it.

There wasn't much Ford did she didn't know about. He was a caring and generous employer, and he cared about Butte Plains, too. *Someone* had paid to rebuild the broken-down gazebo in the square, and it sure as heck hadn't been the city council. No, the money had come from Ford Adams. Word had it he walked into City Hall one day and handed the mayor a check—told the man to fix the gazebo and anything else in need of repair. He'd said Adams Manufacturing had a reputation to uphold, and he couldn't do it if his clients saw a rundown town when they came to visit. Everyone knew most visitors to the plant never went past the town square or drove downtown to see the newly repaired antique streetlights or the fresh-as-a-daisy floral baskets hanging from them. Ford had done what he'd done for the people of Butte Plains. He cared. Deeply.

It's why she loved him—not because of the way he made her feel when they made love. Feeling loved and cherished was just a nice bonus.

Becky returned to the booth to find Ford had taken a potential client to lunch, leaving the booth in the capable hands of the staff they'd brought along. She had just finished going over the schedule for the rest of the day when her brother arrived. Colin might not think he'd *made it* yet, but judging from the reaction of the young women in her employ when she introduced him, he'd already made it big. He stood signing autographs for them and the crowd that had gathered, when the last person on earth Becky wanted to see approached the booth.

Determined to be nice even if it killed her, she plastered a smile on her face and greeted the woman. "Veronica. I didn't know you were in Vegas."

The witch smiled and tugged a man forward. Becky supposed he might be handsome, but not like Ford. Jiminy, when had she started comparing every man she met to her partner?

"Becky Jean Parker, this is Carter Hargraves. He's the—"

"I know who he is." An icy shiver ran down her spine. What in heaven's name was Veronica doing with the CEO of Toy Haven? And why would she bring him over to introduce him?

Though warning bells rang in her brain making it difficult hear, she tried her best to be civil. Becky extended her hand. "It's nice to meet you, Mr. Hargraves."

"Can we go somewhere to talk?" he said, taking her hand.

The bells clanged louder. "About?"

"Mr. Hargraves is interested in purchasing your share of Adams Manufacturing," Veronica said.

Becky removed her hand from the man's grasp and turned her attention to the woman beside him. She couldn't have heard correctly. "What?"

"Surely you know Ford is going to sell. Then what will you do? Carter wants your 25 percent, too."

A giant pit opened up inside her, her heart teetering on the edge. "Wait. Are you telling me Ford has agreed to sell to you?"

"Of course he did." Veronica laughed. "You didn't think he would stay in Butt F— Butte Plains forever, did you?"

The brakes on her personal roller coaster car failed. Her heart lurched over the crest and fell all the way to her toes.

"His home is in New York. With me." She delivered the last two words with a deadly smile.

Becky took a step back, right into her brother. "Hey, Sis. Ready to go?"

"Uh."

"Carter Hargraves," the man said. "We saw your concert last night. You're good."

"Thanks," Colin said. "Colin Parker." He leaned around her to shake hands with the woman who had just eviscerated her.

"Veronica Ramsey," she said, her voice dripping with syrup. "You and Becky Jean…?"

"Siblings," her brother said. "She never stops reminding me who's older."

"Listen," Hargraves said. "We were just going to invite your sister to lunch. Why don't you join us?"

A heartbeat later, Becky sat at a table in a swanky Italian restaurant with her celebrity brother and the two people in the world she wished she'd never met. How she'd gotten there, she didn't know. How she would get out without causing a scene, she didn't care. Maybe she could excuse herself to the bathroom and find a back exit. She had her purse. She could call a cab, go straight to the airport and catch a flight to Dallas. Judging from the looks the witch exchanged with her brother, she'd be home before anyone missed her.

A good big sister would warn Colin about Veronica, but she had to admit, she was grateful for deflecting the woman's attention away from her. If he could keep it up, perhaps the conversation she dreaded would never take place.

Attentive waiters came and went, delivering wine, bread, and plates of food she didn't recall ordering. It was as if she looked through a mirror, observing an alternate universe where another version of herself resided. This other Becky smiled and spoke when spoken to. She even ate a few bites when real Becky's stomach felt like a lead ball. She heard Hargrave's offer, but couldn't process it.

The dollar amount sounded ridiculous to someone who still emptied her coin purse into a jar every evening.

Less than a year ago, the cost of this meal alone would have bankrupted her. That she could afford it, and more, staggered her. As she mentally tallied the changes in her life, she knew one thing for certain, none of it meant anything if she didn't have Ford.

Other Becky said, "Ford agreed to sell?"

"He will. He's holding out for a better price," Veronica said. "It's all about the money with him. Always has been."

Funny. Since she'd gotten to know Ford, she'd come to the conclusion the money didn't matter that much to him. He enjoyed his work. Enjoyed being compensated for it, but even when he'd thought the failing plant might eat up everything he had, he hadn't seemed particularly bereft. In fact, he'd seen his predicament as a challenge—one he'd risen to, conquered. Just as he'd conquered her heart.

"I don't have an answer for you today, Mr. Hargraves. I hadn't planned to sell. I need time to think about your offer."

"You won't get a better offer," Veronica stated. Her words were as flat as the line of her lips.

Why did it matter so much to her if Becky sold? It was Ford she wanted, Ford she needed to convince to sell. The proverbial lightbulb flicked on in her head. She knew exactly what Veronica planned. *You lying bitch.* Real Becky straightened her spine. "I've got to go." She cocked her head at her brother then reached for her purse. Colin stood and held her chair for her to rise. Star or not, he had the manners of a Southern gentleman.

"Take my card." Carter reached into his jacket pocket. "Call me when you've made your decision."

Ignoring the card he held out, she said, "That won't be necessary. I've made my decision. I'm not selling. Not unless Ford is."

The shock on Veronica's face told her everything she needed to know. Ford *hadn't* agreed to sell. They were hoping Becky would sign on the dotted line, and they could use her share as leverage to convince her partner to do the same. "Thanks for lunch," she said, knowing full well the bill had not yet arrived.

"What was that all about?" Colin asked as soon as they hit the sidewalk.

"You just witnessed Veronica Ramsey at her best." Wanting to put as much distance between her and the wicked witch of the east, she walked at a brisk pace. "As far as I can tell, no one has ever told her no. It's about time she learned the world doesn't revolve around her."

"I don't know. She seemed nice enough."

Becky stopped so suddenly the guy walking behind her had to take evasive measures to avoid knocking her over. "What? Are you insane?" She fisted her hands on her hips and glared at her brother whose familiar smile goaded her on. "Do. Not. Get. Involved. With that witch, Colin Parker. She's bad news. Spoiled. Entitled. She wants Ford!"

"And she can't have him. I get it, Becks."

"He's mine."

Colin's smile widened. "Yes, he is."

For the longest time, she stared at her brother. Then his words sank in. *Her* words sank in. She groaned and leaned against the nearest light pole.

"You should tell him, Becks."

"I know." She shifted her gaze to the flashing marquee on the casino down the street. "What if she's right and he does want to go back to New York?"

Colin shrugged. "I've been there. It's not so bad. It ain't Texas, but nothing is."

"That's not what I meant, and you know it." She'd go anywhere Ford wanted to go, even New York. "What if he wants to go back to *her*?" She used her thumb to gesture back to the restaurant they'd just left.

"Maybe he just needs a reason to stay." He cocked one eyebrow at her.

She nodded, and for the first time since Veronica had shown up at their booth, her smile came easy. "Maybe he does."

CHAPTER TWENTY-FIVE

"She did *what?*"

"Ms. Parker went to lunch," the nervous intern repeated.

"With Veronica Ramsey and Carter Hargraves?" he clarified, just in case he'd lost his mind and imagined his business partner — the woman he *loved* and *wanted to spend the rest of his life with* — had gone off to discuss selling part of their company to a man who didn't give a shit about his family's legacy, much less the people in Butte Plains.

"And Colin Parker," another intern added with a dreamy sigh. "I didn't know Ms. Parker and *Colin* Parker were related."

Ford growled. Both women took a step back, and Ford gave himself a mental shake. He couldn't blame them, they were just the messengers. He made a conscious effort to school his features into something civilized. Becky Jean would skin him alive if he scared off their help, and they had to man this booth for the rest of the week by themselves. "I'm sorry. I shouldn't have spoken to you the way I did. I'm just surprised, that's all."

"You didn't know Colin Parker was her brother either?" the ditsier one asked.

Ford grabbed control of his temper with both hands. "Yes, I knew he was her brother. I even knew she planned to have lunch with him today. I didn't know about Ms. Ramsey and the other guy."

"That was all of a sudden, I think," the more reasonable one said. *Ashley? Or is her name Amy?*

"What makes you think so?"

Ashley/Amy shrugged. "I don't know. Colin was here then Ms. Ramsey walked up. Everyone else was all, you know" — she made a whirly gesture near her temple — "over Colin, so I don't think they noticed the way Ms. Parker spoke to her. I don't know why exactly, but it didn't seem like a friendly conversation."

Knowing she hadn't had a pleasant conversation with those two helped ease the knot in his gut somewhat. "You weren't impressed by Colin?" he asked, giving her what he hoped appeared to be a friendly smile.

She shook her head. "Oh, no, sir. He's cute and all, but I have a boyfriend back home. Seth is much better looking, and he can sing, too. His band plays every weekend down at the Roadhouse."

The other girl standing behind Ashley/Amy rolled her eyes. Ford resisted the urge to laugh outright. "Seth lives in Butte Plains?"

"He has a place over on Cotton Street."

Ford nodded. As he recalled, nothing but rundown apartments lined Cotton. "Next time Colin is in town, maybe we could get them together. He might be able to help Seth. That is, if your boyfriend is serious about the music business."

Her face lit up like a Christmas tree, and she jumped and clapped her hands. "You'd do that? You're awesome, Mr. Adams!" Then she launched herself at him.

He was trying to extricate himself from her bear hug when a familiar voice did the trick for him. "Amy, how many times do I have to tell you to keep your hands off the boss?"

Amy catapulted away, muttering apologies all around.

"Amy," he said. "Ms. Parker is just kidding." He turned to Becky Jean. "Aren't you?"

"Of course I am, but let's keep the public displays of affection down to a minimum. That's not the reputation Adams Manufacturing wants to project to the public."

So, she did care about the company. He only hoped she cared enough not to sell her share, but if she really wanted out, he'd buy her out himself. Adams Manufacturing had always been a family business. Family should own it.

"It won't happen again, will it, Amy?" He winked at the young lady and she nodded.

"No, sir. Thank you, Mr. Adams," she said. "I can't wait to tell Seth what you said."

Becky Jean's head swiveled between the two of them as if she couldn't decide if she really wanted to know what he'd told the girl or not.

"Glad to help." He'd had enough small talk. He and Becky Jean were overdue for a long discussion. He reached for her hand. "Now, if you'll excuse us, Ms. Parker and I have some business to discuss."

"Call me if you have any problems," Becky Jean said over her shoulder as he dragged her away from the booth.

He would have preferred more privacy for what he wanted to say to her, but the curtained-off storage area in the back corner of the convention hall would do.

"What's this about, Ford?" she asked as he pulled her through a gap in the black drapes.

He came to a stop and spun around to face her. The color he'd noticed on her cheeks when she arrived at the booth had deepened. Images of all the places he'd seen that particular shade of pink on her body flashed through his brain like a brush fire, igniting a matching one inside him. *Where have you been all my life?*

"What?"

"I didn't— Oh. I said that out loud?"

She nodded, studying him as if he'd grown two heads or something. "Are you okay, Ford?"

He chuckled. He'd envisioned this conversation going a lot smoother. He didn't have a clue what he should say next. If he told her he loved her and asked her to marry him, would she think he just wanted to keep her from selling? And if he asked her if she planned to sell, would she think he cared more about the company than he did her? Either way, he was screwed.

"There's something I want—no, need to say to you, but I just figured out there's no good way to say it."

"Oh. My. God!" Her eyes swam with tears. "You *are* going to sell! That bitch was right!"

"No!" When she tried to jerk her hand out of his, he held on tight. "No, Becks." He got down in her line of sight and shook his head. "No. I told you. I'm not selling Adams Manufacturing. Not now, not ever."

His declaration seemed to calm her a bit, but the edge of the woods had never looked farther away. He swallowed hard and said the last thing he wanted to say. "But I understand if you want to sell your 25 percent. It's worth a lot of money. You'd be set for life, you and your mother. You could go anywhere, do anything you wanted, and never worry about money ever again." He squeezed her fingers, hoping she'd hear what he wasn't saying in the words he *was* saying. "Adams Manufacturing has always been a family-owned business."

She sniffed and wiped her cheeks with the fingers of her free hand. "I understand. You want to buy me out." The finality in her statement wrecked him. He'd done a shit-poor job of showing her what she meant to him.

"No. You don't understand at all. I don't want to buy you out." He had to get this right. Holding onto her hand so she couldn't bolt, he dropped to one knee. "I want to marry you. Becky Jean Parker, will you do me the honor of becoming my wife — my partner in life and in business — for as long as we both shall live?"

Maybe he'd laid it on thick, but he wanted her to know he understood exactly what he'd asked her to do. He'd never thought he'd marry. Never wanted to — until Becky Jean showed him what love was. His knee protested to being on the concrete, but he'd get down on both knees and beg if he had to.

"You don't have to marry me, Ford. I'll sell—"

He couldn't listen to another word about selling. Not today. "No. I don't want your share of the company, Becks. I want you. Just you. Say you'll marry me. Please, I don't know—"

"Shh." She shushed him with a finger against his lips. "Why? If you don't want the company, then why?"

It dawned on him then. He'd forgotten the most important thing. *Shit!*

"Ford Adams!" She tried to get away, but he held fast.

"Didn't mean to say that out loud," he said. He shook his head. "I'm making a mess of this, Becks." He stood and took both her hands in his. Closing the distance between them, he rested his forehead against hers. Their gazes met and held.

"I should have led with I love you. I do. Love you, I mean. More than anything. You make me want to be a better person, Becky Jean. I see you and the love you have for other people, and I can't help but want some of your love for myself. I love you. I want to have you by my side, as my wife, my lover, and my partner for the rest of our lives. I won't give up Adams Manufacturing, but I can't run it without you. You are Adams Manufacturing. The only thing you're missing is the name."

He ducked his head and brushed his lips over hers. "Please, say you'll be my wife."

Laughter—joy—bubbled up within her and came out as a hiccup. She'd always dreamed of finding a man to love her, one who respected her as an equal. She could hardly believe her ears, but *that kiss*. It had been so sweet and showed a vulnerability she'd never seen in Ford before, except maybe on the first day when he'd just buried his father then discovered his family legacy had become a concrete block tied around his ankles. She'd fallen in love with him then—or maybe it had been later, when he'd brought her a pocket sandwich and she'd seen the dismay in his eyes at what had happened to his hometown.

She'd known then his emotions ran deep. He cared, even if he told himself he didn't.

They were good together. In the office. On screen. In bed. Lord, were they good together in bed. She flushed just thinking about the possibility of experiencing the kind of passion they had together for the rest of her life.

"I'm dying here, Becks. Say something. Please."

"You're a good man, Ford Adams."

"No," he groaned.

"Of course I'll marry you."

"What?"

"Do we need to get your hearing checked? I said yes. I'll marry you."

"Yes!" He let go of one of her hands and speared a fist into the air. "She said yes!"

"Shh! Ford."

"I don't care who hears me. I want to shout it to the world." He stilled. "Let's go up to the top of the Eiffel Tower. Wait! No. Let's get married. Today. Right now." He grabbed her other hand again.

"I don't want to wait another day to make you mine. We can do the big wedding later if you want. No one else has to know we're already married. Just, please, let's do it today."

"Before you change your mind?" She fought to keep the smile off her face, but her lips had a mind of their own. Teasing Ford was so much fun!

"I'll never, ever change my mind about you, Becky Jean. I love you. I always will."

"I'll do it on one condition."

"Anything you want, sweetheart. Anything."

If she was going to get married in Las Vegas, by George, she intended to do it right. "I want an Elvis wedding."

He laughed out loud. "Anything you want, Becks. Anything you want."

"I want you. Just you."

THE END

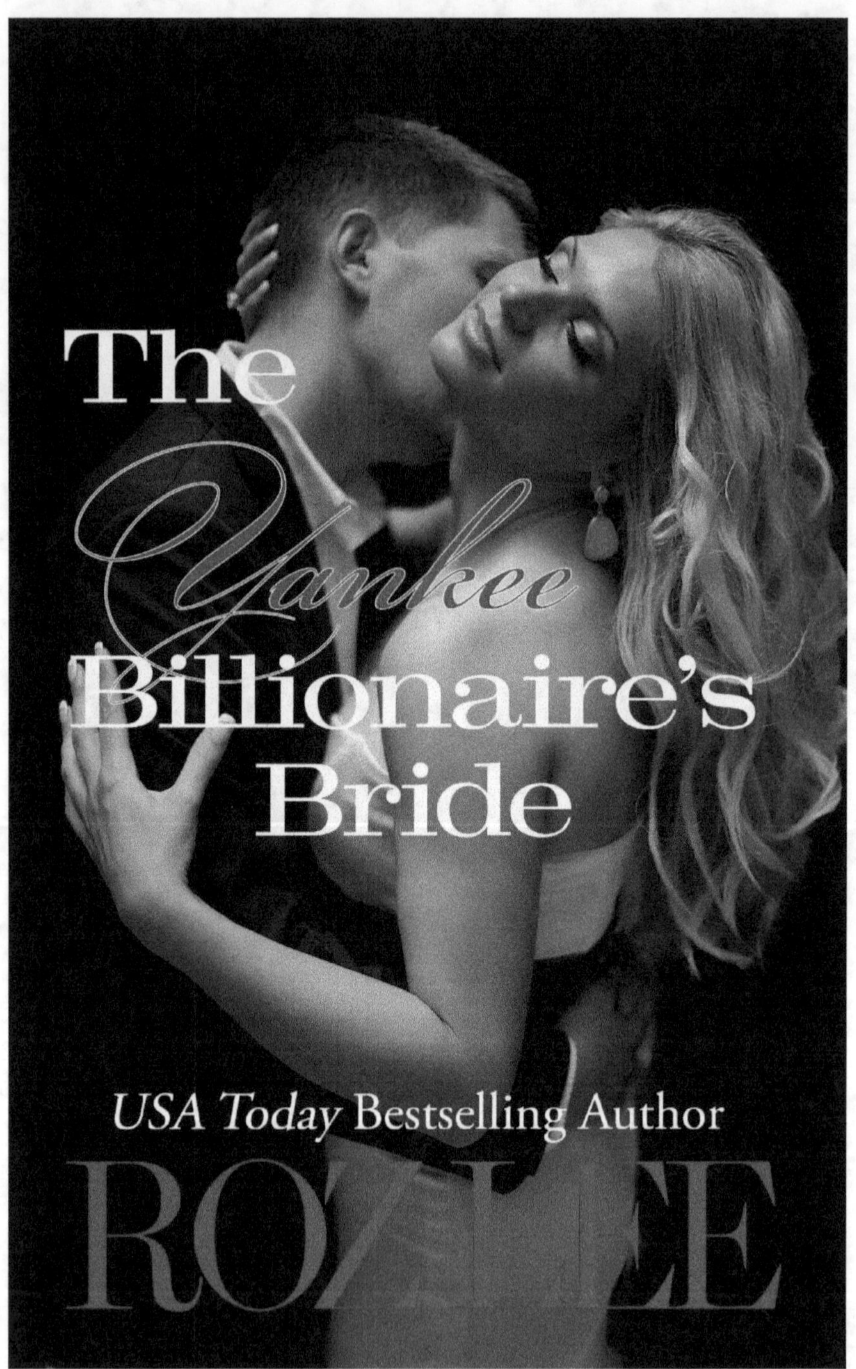

The
Yankee
Billionaire's
Bride
USA Today Bestselling Author
RO LEE

The Yankee Billionaire's Bride

Roz Lee

PART ONE

"If you love someone, set them free. If they come back,
they're yours; if they don't, they never were."
Richard Bach

CHAPTER ONE

Roseanne Meadows stood on the busy Las Vegas sidewalk, watching the limo disappear with the newlyweds inside. Beside her, she could feel Scott Ramsey's gaze boring into her. He knew something was going on in her brain, but, to his credit, he'd said nothing during the wedding. If she knew anything about the man, it was that he wouldn't do anything to ruin his best friend's wedding. Just as she would have cut off her right arm rather than do anything to upset *her* best friend's wedding.

But Becky and Ford were married now, and all bets were off.

"What's wrong, Roseanne? And don't tell me it's nothing because I know you better than that." He should. They'd been sleeping together for months. She'd let him get closer to her, emotionally and physically than anyone else — ever.

"Can we go home now? I think I've had enough of Vegas." Truth. She was finished. Done. Over it. But not over him. Not by a long shot. Maybe she never would be. That hurt more than anything else — knowing he didn't give two hoots about her when every cell in her body ached for him not to be the person she suspected him of being.

"You want to go home tonight? Don't you have a spa date with Becky tomorrow?"

She gave the man the evil eye. That date had been planned

before Becky and Ford had decided on their hasty Vegas wedding chapel nuptials. "Seriously? Becky just got married. Do you really think she's going to want to hang out with me tomorrow?"

"Is that it? Are you worried that you've lost your best friend?"

She'd certainly lost something, but not Becky. Married or not, her childhood friend would never desert her. Roseanne shook her head. "No. I didn't want to say anything to Becks, but I think I might be coming down with something."

"You're sick? Geez, why didn't you say so?" When he wrapped his arm around her waist, pulling her close, it was all she could do not to flinch. Twenty-four hours ago, she would have welcomed his embrace, but that was before. Now, everything he said or did felt false. "Do you need to see a doctor? I'm sure the hotel has one on call."

"I'd rather just go home, if you don't mind?" Home, where she could put this latest failure behind her. Or, at least bury herself in work and pretend Scott Ramsey hadn't ripped her heart out with his bare hands.

"Not at all. Our business here is done." He waved his arm, and the limo that had been waiting for them inched up to the curb. He handed her inside then joined her. After giving instructions to the driver, he made a phone call. "All set. The plane will be ready to go when we get there."

Must be nice. Had it only been a couple of days ago that they'd flown from Dallas to Las Vegas in Scott's private jet to help Ford and Becky at the sex toy trade show? It seemed like years had gone by, or maybe she was just feeling older. And wiser. Scott put his cell phone away and reached for her hand. Roseanne's stomach clenched at the contact, and a groan passed her lips.

"Are you all right? Can I get you anything? We can stop at a pharmacy if you want."

His voice held genuine concern, and, for the millionth time since his sister had cornered her at the convention center and given her an earful, she wondered if she was making the right decision to end her months-long relationship with the Yankee billionaire. Maybe Veronica was wrong. Maybe he just hadn't gotten around to asking her to attend his parents' anniversary party in New York next week. According to his sister, Scott had promised to attend.

In the face of his solicitude tonight, she could give him a few more days. If he didn't ask her to go with him, then she would know everything his sister had said was true. She was nothing more than a distraction for him while he attended to business in Butte Plains. As soon as he could, he'd hand the reins over to a manager and go back home to his high-society parties and glamorous women.

"No. I just think I need to rest. You have to admit, the last few days have been hectic."

"I thought we'd be here for moral support. I had no idea we'd get roped into manning the booth for hours each day."

"I don't think Ford and Becky anticipated how popular their booth would be. I'm sure they thought the interns they'd brought along would be able to handle the flow."

"Agreed. But I'll have a word with Ford if you're ill because of it."

As far as she knew, broken hearts weren't contagious or caused by spending a few hours standing on a concrete floor. "Don't. Please? I'm sure I'll be okay in a few days. I just need to rest." According to Veronica, Scott needed to be in New York by Friday night, which meant if he was going to ask her to go along, he would have to do it in the next few days. Heck, he hadn't even mentioned that *he* had a trip planned, which led her to believe he didn't want her to know about the party. Which meant everything his sister had said was true. Her stomach clenched again. This time, she barely managed to hold in the accompanying groan.

The limo crept along in the heavy traffic crowding the strip. Scott continued to hold her hand, and, rather than argue with him, she let it stay. This was all so stupid. She should just come right out and ask him about the party, but, deep down inside, she needed him to bring the subject up first. If he left for New York without telling her about the family event, she'd know the feelings she had for him weren't returned. They'd been sleeping together for several months. Not exactly living as a couple, but still, their relationship was intimate, and exclusive. Or so she thought.

That was the other bombshell Veronica Ramsey had dropped on her. Scott had a girlfriend, or, to hear her tell it, a fiancé in all but the formal sense of the word. Solange. No last name. None needed. Everyone in the world knew the supermodel with the smile as bright as her name. According to his sister, Scott's family loved Solange and expected the couple to make it official as soon as Scott wrapped up his business in Texas.

At last, they made it to the hotel, packed up their things in the shared suite, and were on their way to the airport and the waiting Gulfstream aircraft.

As soon as they were wheels up, Roseanne disappeared to the bedroom in the rear of the cabin. No invitation to join her was given, and nothing about her demeanor or posture indicated he'd be welcome, so Scott remained in his seat, a drink in hand, and contemplated where their minivacation had gone wrong.

The woman who had occupied the seat next to him on the flight from Dallas to Las Vegas a few days ago was not the same one accompanying him home tonight. He would allow her some leeway for being ill, but that couldn't account for the deep chasm he sensed opening up between them. He was so out of his league with this woman. She was unlike any he'd ever dated. That alone had him wondering what the hell he was doing. None of the others had even come close to making him feel the way this one did — like he would never get enough of her and *afraid* he'd never get enough of her at the same time.

Fuck. I'm so screwed.

He'd known about his parents' anniversary party for months and gone back and forth in his mind whether he should invite

Roseanne to accompany him to the milestone event. In Vegas, his sister had brought up the subject, asking to share the limo ride out to Long Island with him on the big day. He'd agreed, mentioning he might be bringing someone. That's when she'd reminded him of the time he'd made the mistake of taking a date to another such family gathering a few years ago. Before the last good-bye had been said, his mother had been contemplating which set of his grandmother's china she should give them as a wedding gift. He should have expected as much. The woman he'd taken had been just the kind of person his parents expected him to marry — born to wealth, well-educated, and runway model beautiful.

She'd been nothing but arm candy to him. It had taken him months to convince his mother one date didn't equal a marriage proposal.

He couldn't imagine what she would do if he showed up with Roseanne on his arm. She wasn't anything his parents wanted for him. June and Gerald Ramsey would never be impolite to a guest in their house, but there was a big difference between rude and welcoming. He couldn't bear the thought of Roseanne feeling out of place. As genuine and wholesome as homespun cloth, she was ten times better than most of the people who would be at the party, and far above the rest in every way that counted. Which led him to his other fear. His mother was so focused on her kids — particularly him — settling down and producing babies for her to spoil, she might jump to the wrong conclusion and start talking about china patterns again. Lord help him if that happened. No matter what, he wouldn't be railroaded into marrying. One of these days, he'd take the plunge, but not before he was good and ready.

Then there was the very real possibility his parents would inform her about what a screwup he was. No one could say the word entrepreneur quite the way his father could. For Christ's sake, you'd think Scott had become a criminal or something. They were better now than they were when he was a teenager and talked of going to MIT to become an engineer, but not by much. He could count on one hand the number of kids he'd grown up with who had gone on to finish college. As far as he knew, he was the only one to actually use the degree he'd earned. And *gasp*, made money! He'd never understood how that made him the screwup in the family. You'd think his family was fucking royalty or something — too good to get their hands dirty.

Either way it turned out, he'd be screwed. Which was why he hadn't mentioned the party to Roseanne yet, and most likely wouldn't mention it. This was plainly one of those situations where what she didn't know wouldn't hurt her.

CHAPTER TWO

"How're you doing?" Kay Rogers appeared at the door to Roseanne's room. "I brought you something to help settle your stomach." She set a tray laden with tea and crackers on the nightstand. "The guests have checked out—all except Mr. Palmer. He decided to stay another day. Oh, and Mr. Ramsey left for New York. He was awfully worried about you, but I convinced him you'd be fine by the time he gets back."

Roseanne had pretended to be sick in Las Vegas, but the morning after their return, she'd spent more time in the bathroom than in bed, and she'd spent *a lot of time* huddled under the covers. She'd managed to drag herself out of bed the last few days, but this morning, the ailment had returned with a vengeance. Roseanne eyed the food skeptically. "Thank you. What time is it anyway?"

"Almost noon."

"I've got to get up." Roseanne tried to sit up, but her stomach rolled, forcing her to lie back down.

"You don't have to do anything, Ms. Meadows. We've got it covered."

"I hate being useless," she moaned.

"No worries. You just concentrate on getting better. We'll take care of everything else."

"Seriously, I don't know what I'd do without you." Once Ford and Becky's business had taken off, and the rooms at The Yellow Rose were once again full, Roseanne had hired a small staff to take care of the bed-and-breakfast guests, and thank goodness she had; otherwise, she'd be screwed. Kay Rogers was her jack-of-all-trades in charge of making sure the guests' needs were met, and scheduling and supervising the other two new hires—Jamie Higgs, the cook, and Mary Hernandez, the housekeeper. Roseanne made a mental note to add nurse and surrogate mother to the woman's duties. "You deserve a raise."

"I wouldn't turn it down." The woman bustled around the room, straightening things and picking up dirty clothes. "We'll talk about it when you're back on your feet. In the meantime, don't worry about a thing. I'll stay in one of the empty rooms tonight, just in case you need something."

"You are an angel, Kay."

"I know."

Roseanne smiled at the older woman's spunk. The retired school teacher who had never married had taken the job to supplement her fixed income, and, in her words, to keep from going insane. Years of noisy classrooms hadn't prepared her quiet later years. The last few days, she'd earned every penny of her salary, and then some.

Later, Roseanne managed to sit up and sip the now-cooled tea and nibble on crackers, her thoughts turned to Scott Ramsey. Yes, her illness the last few days would have prevented her from accompanying him to New York, but he could have at least told her about the party. Maybe expressed his dismay that she wasn't up to attending. But he'd said nothing.

Despite the difference in their lives—he was filthy rich and she wasn't—they'd been more than compatible in bed. At times, she'd managed to forget Scott didn't actually live in Butte Plains, that his tenure here was only temporary. She didn't want to admit it, but his sister had been right. Scott had no intention of staying in Texas. Which meant she needed to end the relationship before her heart was beyond the point of no return.

The following day she felt better, and the day after that she was even better—almost her old self. Enough at least to fix a couple of sandwiches and meet Becky at her office for a quick lunch. Her friend usually came to the B&B for their weekly lunch date, but, after being out of town for over a week, she needed to catch up on the paperwork that had accumulated in her absence. Roseanne could relate. Though Kay did a great job running the B&B, as the owner, there were still things only she could handle. Then there was the cookbook she'd been working on for the last few months. She'd pitched the idea to some big-time agents, and one of them had actually asked to see what she had so far. She couldn't just let that dream go by the wayside. She had more recipes to perfect and agents to query.

For dessert, Roseanne grabbed two muffins left over from breakfast and a thermos of sweet tea and headed out. Becky had been watching for her and came out to help her carry everything in from the car. "I can't thank you enough for doing this," she said, relieving Roseanne of the heavy thermos. "If I'd known taking a couple of extra days for a honeymoon would double my workload when I got back, I'd have told Ford the wedding would have to wait and hightailed it home."

"You know you wouldn't have done any such thing."

"Maybe not, but, in retrospect, it might have been the right thing to do."

Roseanne followed her friend to her office. The stacks of papers on her desk were indeed impressive, but portable. They moved a couple to nearby shelves to make room for their picnic then got down to the business of eating and catching up on everything that had happened in the four days since they'd seen each other.

"What do you mean? You aren't regretting getting married are you?"

Becky waved away Roseanne's concerns. "Not at all. It's just that we should have thought it through, you know?"

"Enlighten me, please? I don't have the foggiest notion what you're talking about." She poured sweet tea into two plastic cups she'd brought along. Becky drank down half of hers and held her cup out for a refill.

"Ford is like Butte Plains' favorite son, or something like that. People, meaning his mother, have expectations for him."

She was beginning to see. Ford's family had been the pinnacle of Butte Plains society for three generations. Everything they did was news in town. Becky's family didn't run in the same circles, but a mother could be touchy about her only daughter getting married. "And perhaps your mother has expectations for you, too? In terms of a big, splashy wedding with lots of guests and a write-up in the local paper?"

"Yeah, those kind of expectations." She took a big bite of her sandwich, closed her eyes, and moaned as she chewed. "Sweet Lord, what you do to chicken salad, woman. It should be illegal."

Roseanne smiled and took a bite of her sandwich. She did do a good chicken salad, which was why it was going to be one of the recipes featured in her cookbook. "I had extra, so I brought it for you. There's enough for two more sandwiches. Maybe you can figure out how to spread it on bread and then you and Ford can have a picnic lunch tomorrow."

Her friend glared at her for a second before a broad smile broke over her face. "I'm going to ignore that jab at my cooking skills and just say thank you. Though it might be dinner tonight instead of lunch tomorrow. Both of us are buried in paperwork." She swept her hand out to indicate the stacks of folders and papers occupying nearly every flat space in her small office.

"That sucks."

"Sure does. I don't even have time to talk to you about our wedding."

"What's to say? I was there, remember?"

"Oh, not that one. The one we're going to have here."

"Here? As in Butte Plains?"

"Yep. We were hoping we could use your garden at The Yellow Rose. I've got a date picked out." She clicked a couple of keys on her computer and consulted the screen. "Three months from today. How's that work for you?"

Becky had always had a way of talking in shorthand, but this was ridiculous. Roseanne was at least a dozen steps behind in figuring out what her friend was talking about. "Wait. Let me get this straight. You want to have another wedding, three months from now. At my place."

"See, you aren't slow. I don't know what Chucky Bruce was talking about."

Chucky Bruce had been a mean-spirited bully back in fourth grade. His favorite insult was to call someone slow. He'd made the mistake of insulting Roseanne on the playground one day and had paid the price for it. She'd socked him in the nose, proving that at least her fist was faster than his ability to get out of the way. The offended appendage bled like a son of a gun, prompting the school nurse to be called, as well as the principal. Roseanne had taken a three day suspension and a month of helping the cleaning crew after school rather than apologize. Chucky, likewise, had refused to apologize and had received the same suspension and a month of early morning study hall. It seemed he was behind in all his subjects and needed the extra help more than he needed to empty wastebaskets. "Heard he got on with the new waste management company over in Prairieview."

"I heard the same thing." She crunched a potato chip. "Back to my wedding. I know you're busy, but do you think you could handle most of the arrangements? I'll find a dress. Colin said he'd sing. We'll need a band, a preacher, flowers, cake. What else?"

"Invitations, a photographer, a tent, table and chairs for the reception. A caterer if you plan on serving anything more than cake. And security. If your brother is going to be there, someone will have to keep his adoring fans away." They'd all had the pleasure of seeing Colin perform in Las Vegas. The up-and-coming country music star had a large fan base made up of primarily young women who all wanted to become Mrs. Colin Parker. Who could blame them? He was single, sexy, and successful. And a genuinely nice guy, too.

"See? I knew you were the perfect person to put in charge. You're already thinking of things I never would have. Oh, and can we keep the fact that Ford and I are already married a secret for now?"

"You aren't going to tell anyone?"

Becky shook her head. "Nope. We have the video from Vegas. How cool would it be to show it at the reception?" Her friend smiled. "Let everyone in on the secret then?"

"I think it's an insanely great idea." She clasped Becky's hand. "Maybe the two of you could step out for your first dance when the Elvis impersonator starts to sing 'Love Me Tender.'"

"Oh, wouldn't that be fun?" Becky rocked back in her chair, a wicked grin on her face. "We'd just finished saying our vows, so everyone will know when we step into the spotlight in the center of the dance floor while the Elvis sings on the big screen. It's perfect, Roseanne. Absolutely perfect." She clapped her hands like a child who just found out she was going to Disneyland.

"It will be if I can pull this off in three months."

"I never thought I would say this in my lifetime, but money is no object. I'll establish an account to cover all the expenses, so you won't be out a cent of your own money. You'll have full access to the funds. No need to bother me with the details unless you need more. Then, by all means, let me know and I'll put more in the account."

"You don't want to establish a budget?" Like her, Becky had grown up pinching pennies until they screamed. Money had not only been an object — it had been a deep chasm without a bridge.

"I'm tempted, but I honestly don't think it's necessary. Do you remember when we used to have pretend weddings in your grandmother's backyard?"

They'd scattered boxes and anything they could find around the walkways for the "guests" to sit on, and used the rose arbor as a backdrop for the ceremony. They'd also gotten in trouble for cutting her grandmother's flowers to use for bouquets for the pretend wedding party. "How many times did we marry that old momma cat off to your Ken doll anyway? A dozen?"

"At least. I still think that garden is one of the most beautiful places in the entire town. My tastes are simple, and you know that better than anyone. I trust you to create a lovely setting for the ceremony, and another one for the reception. Spend as much as you need, and, for Pete's sake, hire people to do the work. If you're unsure about anything, ask, but I bet you know more about what I'd like than I do."

Roseanne tried to talk Becky into taking a bigger role in the planning, but the woman simply changed the subject. "Have you heard anything from the editor who wanted to see your cookbook?"

She filled her friend in on the latest, which wasn't much, before packing up and leaving Becky to her work. If she was going to pull off a grand wedding in three months, she'd better get moving.

CHAPTER THREE

Scott stood in the foyer of his Manhattan apartment, his gaze taking in the spartan landscape. This used to be home, but it no longer felt like it, if it ever had. The ultra-modern décor seemed cold and uninviting—just the opposite of what the decorator had claimed. He'd been dating the woman for a few weeks when he'd closed on the property. Her references were good—or so his sister had said. He'd been too busy with the design-build company he'd started with Ford to check for himself. If he had, he might have declined her services. But he hadn't, and this was the result. A stark, hard landscape with more sharp edges than a pack of razor blades and not a comfortable place to sit in the entire place.

The apartment had been one of two considered for a spread in a major style magazine, but had lost out to a penthouse owned by some branch of the Saudi royal family. By artist's standards, the place was well-done, he assumed, but by his standards, it looked like a museum where the furniture was the art.

He'd cut the decorator loose shortly after the place was finished and hadn't seen her since. He'd heard through the grapevine she'd finally scored a spot in the magazine. He'd briefly wondered who she'd duped into letting her have her way with their space then promptly forgot all about her again.

He made his way to the master bedroom where he stretched

out on the only soft surface in the entire apartment, his bed, and rested one forearm across his eyes. He'd never been so tired in his life. It wasn't the trip weighing him down, but what he'd left behind. As soon as the wheels had left the runway, he'd wished he'd told Roseanne the real reason he had to go to New York, but the opportunity to do so had passed, and telling her after the fact would only make his omission worse.

Dropping his arm, he gazed at the ceiling. A monstrous lighting fixture that looked like someone had run sheet metal through a giant chipper then let a blind man stick all the pieces back together hung disturbingly low. He'd been assured it was as much art as it was functional, but it still gave him the creeps. He much preferred the antique chandelier that hung over his bed at The Yellow Rose. The soft curves of the armatures reminded him of the best parts of a woman's body, and the soft glow from the candle-tipped bulbs bathed everything in soothing gold tones.

Just thinking about his room at the B&B, he could feel the tension leaving his body. He recalled having the same feeling the first day he'd arrived in Texas. The car he'd hired at the airport had sped across wide open plains and crept through small towns, and, with each mile, the tightness in his shoulders had eased until he'd been able to breathe deeply. If he closed his eyes, he could still smell the fresh scent left behind after a passing shower dampened the dusty sidewalks. There was nothing in New York City that could compare with it.

Just like there was nothing that would compare with the independent Texan who had captured his attention and refused to let go. Roseanne Meadows. Her name fit her. As lovely as any bloom in her garden, she was as open and sweet as a meadow in spring.

Scott groaned and sat up, shaking off the memories. What the fuck? The Texas heat must have scrambled his brains. Why else would he be thinking all that poetic shit about a woman? Maybe the command performance for his mother was a good thing. A couple of days in the Big Apple, and he'd have his perspective back then he could return to Butte Plains, hire someone to run the leather goods factory he'd purchased. In a few weeks, a month tops, he'd be back here for good. In the meantime, he'd hire someone to gut this place. Once he was back for good, he'd decorate it himself.

Scott checked his watch. He had just enough time to shower and dress before he was supposed to meet his sister in the lobby of their building.

His mother had requested his presence tonight at a party to celebrate his parents' thirty-fifth wedding anniversary. Professional excuse maker that he'd become, he couldn't think of a single legitimate reason to miss the affair. If nothing else, he'd be there to show support for his dad. The man deserved some kind of award for putting up with Scott's mother for thirty-plus years. The woman took meddling to a whole new level. Hell, she'd practically made a career out of sticking her nose in other people's business.

Checking his appearance one last time, he picked up the wrapped gifts for the celebrants and made his way down to the lobby where he'd agreed to meet his sister who lived two floors below his penthouse apartment. Expecting to be kept waiting, he was surprised to find her flirting with the new guy, Alan, he thought, at the security desk. The poor kid appeared to be in shock. Who could blame him? Dressed to impress, as always, Ronnie sparkled from head to toe.

"Come on, Ronnie," he said, brushing his fingers over her arm to drag her attention away from the younger man. "We're going to be late."

The doorman anticipated their leaving and held the heavy glass panel open for them. Scott stopped short and waited for Veronica to say her good-byes. When she sailed past him on impossibly high heels and a cloud of expensive perfume, he fell into step behind her. "You didn't get Mom and Dad a present?"

"I'm not an idiot, Snotty Scotty. Of course I did. Raymond put it in the car already."

"How many times do I have to tell you not to call me that?" Scott nodded at his driver who stood next to the limo he rarely used. He preferred the SUV around the city, but the drive out to the Hamptons called for more luxury. Besides, his sister refused to ride in his SUV.

"You'll always be a snot, big brother." She failed to acknowledge the man holding the back door open for her as she ducked into the car.

"Thanks, Raymond." Scott shook hands with his driver. He was one of several the Ramsey family kept on the payroll so no one would ever have to drive anywhere if they didn't want to, and most of his family would rather stay home than be seen driving themselves anywhere. "How's Margaret?"

"The missus is doing just fine, sir. Looking forward to retiring next year."

"That's awesome. She teaches third grade, doesn't she?"

"Yes, sir."

"I don't know how she does it."

"Me, either, but she loves the kids. I think she remembers every one she's ever taught, too."

Scott smiled, thinking of the kind, older woman who had taught him when he was that age. "And no doubt they all remember her, too. I know I'll never forget her."

"I'll tell her you said so, sir."

Dreading the next several hours, Scott climbed in behind Veronica and settled in as Raymond closed the door and made his way around to the driver's seat. A long, narrow box occupied the back facing seat. "Seriously? You got them flowers?"

Ronnie shrugged. "Pink roses. You know how much Mom loves them."

"Mom does, but this is Dad's anniversary, too, you know?" He shook his head. He should have known Ronnie wouldn't give more than a moment's thought to selecting a gift for the occasion. If it wasn't about her, she couldn't be bothered.

"They've got *everything* they could possibly want." She eyed the two small boxes he'd placed beside her gift. "You got them jewelry? How original."

"It's not like I sent my secretary to pick something out. I designed these myself and had them made." He hadn't been sure the jeweler in Butte Plains would be up to the task, but he'd taken a chance and hadn't been disappointed. The man had been in business there for decades, a tribute to his skills, but the downturn in the economy had forced him to reduce his inventory to the lowest price point possible. He'd been grateful for the business, and Scott had been happy to help the old guy out.

Ronnie picked invisible lint from her dress. "Show off. You're such an ass-kisser."

He shrugged and kept his mouth shut. He loved his sister, but take away the shared bloodline, and he doubted they would be friends. He might be an ass-kisser, but to his mind that beat expecting everyone to bow down to him. Less than two weeks ago, she'd shown up in Las Vegas with one of Ford's major competitors in the sex toy market and done her best to convince Becky that Ford had agreed to sell out. It had almost worked. Would have if Becky hadn't seen through the charade. Instead of breaking the couple up, which was Ronnie's goal, she'd forced them together. Thus the hasty wedding at the Elvis is King Wedding Chapel. Yeah, his sister was a piece of work.

"I'm surprised you didn't bring that little mouse you've been seeing. I'm sure she'd fit in just fine."

Every muscle in his body tensed at the sarcasm oozing from her words. "What do you mean by that?"

Ronnie's laugh was pure evil. "You've got nothing in common with her, that's what I mean. She's a hick who runs a bed-and-breakfast, for heaven's sake. Her idea of a party is paper plates and red plastic cups and beer straight from the bottle. I saw the way she dresses." She shivered. "Where'd she get that getup she had on in Vegas? A thrift store? All I can say is she must be something in bed, that's the only reason I can think of for you to be seeing her."

Scott balled his hands into fists. His sister was the last person on earth who should be criticizing another, especially someone like Roseanne. "My personal life is none of your business, and just because she wasn't born wearing a designer outfit doesn't mean anything. She lives within her means, and even if she had all the money in the world, she wouldn't throw it away on overpriced clothes and meaningless parties. And for the record, there's nothing like a cold beer straight from the bottle."

"You're a Neanderthal."

"You're a bitch."

"I'm going to tell Mom you said that."

"Grow up, Ronnie." He turned to stare out the window. It was going to be a long ride.

Curtis, who had been the butler for the Ramsey family as long as Scott could recall, greeted them at the door and directed them to the back of the house where all the guests were assembled. His mother had thrown open the glass partitions separating the indoor and outdoor living spaces, creating one giant area for partygoers to mix and mingle. He left the gifts he'd brought with Curtis and made his way through the already-substantial crowd, searching for the happy couple. Several bars were set up around the perimeter of the terrace. Scott stopped long enough to obtain what he expected would be the first of many drinks he would consume before the night was over. While the bartender mixed the drink he'd requested, Scott continued to scan the crowd. He wanted to find his folks, but he likened attending these kinds of events to a soldier walking into an enemy stronghold with his buddies. Friends were easy enough to identify, but that left everyone else in question. He'd already spotted half a dozen women close to his age. Most were the unmarried daughters of his parents' friends, but there were a few new faces, too. Best to steer clear of them, just in case.

He'd parted ways with Ronnie the second they set foot inside the house, but as he turned to scoop up the scotch and soda the bartender placed near his elbow, he caught sight of his sister and a woman he'd never seen before. Angled away from the masses, the two stood close together and appeared to be deep in conversation. Scott brought the glass to his lips and sipped. Did he even want to know what she was up to? Probably not.

"Well, well. If it isn't the prodigal son." A heavy hand clamped his shoulder. Scott smiled and turned to greet the man of the hour. Gerald Ramsey had aged well. A tad over six feet tall, he had broad shoulders and the blond hair Scott had inherited still hadn't given way to gray. Daily tennis matches kept his body in shape and his skin tan.

"Dad." He clapped his father on the shoulder. "Congratulations."

"It's good to see you, son." The elder man gave his son a pat on the back. He'd never been one to hug his children or show much emotion. Strange, Scott thought as his paternal grandparents had been the exact opposite. Both had been easy with their affections. "Save your congratulations for your mother. How she's put up with me all these years, I'll never know."

"And here I thought it was the other way around," Scott said, half joking.

His father pointed to the glass in Scott's hand then said to the bartender, "I'll have one of those." Then he turned his attention back to his son. "I mean it. It's good to see you. When are you going to come to your senses and come back home?"

"I don't know. Never, maybe." Might as well get it out in the open. Plant the seed and let it sprout.

"You can't be serious." His father's expression remained blank. *Never let them see your drama.* That was always Gerald Ramsey's excuse for avoiding talking about anything serious in a public gathering. He took a sip of his drink. "Is it that woman, the innkeeper that Veronica told us about?"

A ripple of unease crept across his skin. "What did Ronnie say?"

"Not much. Just that you were seeing some working girl down there. Slumming, she said."

I'll kill her. His meddling sister had gone too far. She needed to keep her nose out of other people's business and her mouth shut. "You make it sound like Roseanne hangs out on street corners. She owns a bed-and-breakfast. Yes, she works, but most people do. It's not anything to be ashamed of."

"Didn't say it was, just that this woman is beneath you."

Scott was having a hard time keeping his expression neutral in the face of such absurdity. He clenched his jaw tight and held onto his drink with both hands to keep himself steady. "You've got that wrong. She's way out of my league. Unlike me, she started with nothing and built a successful business that has weathered a huge economic downturn. She's smart and resourceful and not afraid to get her hands dirty. Nothing I've done can compare to what she's accomplished."

"All I'm saying, son, is that you and this woman don't have anything in common. Go ahead, get your fill of her then come back home and settle down with someone more fitting. Make your mother happy and give her some grandbabies." Before Scott could reply, his father said, "Now, if you'll excuse me, I've got to get back to the party before June sends out the search and rescue team. Remember what I said, son. We're counting on you."

Scott watched his dad's tuxedo-clad back disappear into the crowd hovering just inside the open doors leading to the great room. His gaze drifted to the spot he'd last seen his sister. A trio of older couples now occupied the space, smiling politely at a conversation he knew by heart. No one at these things spoke about anything of consequence. Society chitchat. The weather. So-and-so's polo match. Their latest trip to fill-in-the-blank European city. Surrounded by people, he felt alone. He always had—until he'd met Ford Adams freshman year at MIT. His college roommate had never thought Scott was weird because he wanted to do something with his life besides find creative ways to piss away money. The endless balls, parties, and fundraisers had always seemed pointless to the Ramsey's oldest child. He'd rather draw some fantastical invention or take something apart and put it back together than drink and socialize with a bunch of people who had to hire someone to entertain them. And he'd never understood the need for fundraisers. Why pay to go to an event when you could simply donate the same amount of money to the group or foundation in need? He'd heard once about a cause that had sent out invitations to an un-ball. Invitees were asked to purchase tickets for a ball that would never happen. No money was spent on a fancy location or over-the-top decorations. No party planner was needed. No band or DJ was hired. No one had to spend money on a gown or new shoes or to have their hair and nails done. Every cent of the money collected from ticket sales went directly to the organization the nonevent was created to help. Scott had gladly donated a huge sum from his personal account. That's the way fundraising should be.

This glittery party scene wasn't him. It never had been. He tugged on his collar and tried to swallow his distaste at the life he'd been born into. His blood might be blue, but he'd never felt like he belonged among these people. An image popped into his head—his best friend, Ford Adams—working to save his family's business, and loving every minute of it. Designing. Creating. Building something with his intellect, if not his hands.

Then there was Roseanne Meadows. Things were better for her now with Ford and Becky's business bringing people to town, but, being a true entrepreneur, Roseanne was exploring other income streams. He'd seen the notes she kept for the cookbook she wanted to publish. Life had given her lemons, and, instead of folding, she'd made lemon pound cake.

His gaze drifted over the carefully chosen guests. He saw a handful he judged to be happy, and a whole lot more he figured were absolutely miserable based on what he knew of their lives. The vast majority he guessed were just living each day, much like himself, not unhappy.

Was that all he could say for himself? That he wasn't unhappy? *Shit.* How had that happened?

"Scott!" He turned toward the voice so familiar to him. "Gerald said he'd seen you."

"Hi, Mom." June Ramsey never went anywhere, not even to the breakfast nook in her own kitchen without looking her best. For her thirty-fifth anniversary, she'd chosen a floor-length gown in muted gold that made her tan look deeper and her brown eyes sparkle. The cost of her dress alone would probably feed a family of four for a year or more. Weekly trips to the spa and a strict regime kept her looking a good ten years younger than her actual age. She'd never forgive him for messing up her makeup, so he smiled and kissed the air near her cheek. "Happy Anniversary."

"It's good to see you." She studied his face like it was a painting she wasn't sure she wanted to purchase. "You look tired. Is everything okay?"

No. No, it's not. The conversation he'd had with his father had left him on edge. If his mother mentioned anything about Roseanne being unsuitable, he wasn't sure he could keep from causing a scene. Not that he cared what any of his parents' friends thought about him, but there was just enough blue blood in his veins to make him think twice before he ruined his parents' party. He silently thanked the universe, and his mother, for providing the perfect excuse to get the hell out of there. "I'm feeling a little under the weather," he lied, "but I had to come and wish you and Dad another thirty-five years."

"I'm so glad you came, but maybe you should go home, get some rest."

Home. Wherever the hell that was. "I think I will, if you don't mind?"

"Not at all. Did Veronica come with you?"

He glanced over his mother's head. "She's here somewhere. I can send my car back for her."

"Nonsense." She waved his offer off. "We'll make sure she gets home, or she can stay the night."

He hugged her to him, placed another air kiss to her temple. "Love you, Mom. I'll see you soon."

"Love you, too."

As soon as he stepped inside his apartment, he knew he couldn't stay there a minute longer than necessary. It was late, but having boatloads of money meant doors were open to you around the clock. He pulled out his cell phone, scrolled through his contacts until he found the one he wanted. A few minutes later, he was tossing clothes in a suitcase, preparing to head back to Texas, and what he hoped was his future.

CHAPTER FOUR

"You're back."

"I said I would be. You haven't rented my room out to someone else have you?" Scott set his suitcase in the wide foyer of the B&B and smiled at the owner of the inn who wasn't smiling back at him.

"No. I haven't, but maybe I should."

He stood frozen, one hand on the handle of his luggage, the other in his pocket where he'd deposited his keys. What the hell had happened while he was gone? "What are you saying? You want me to leave?"

Roseanne glanced over her shoulder in the direction of the kitchen then back at him. "Keep your voice down. The whole world doesn't need to know our business."

Scott didn't care who heard, but appearances meant a lot to Roseanne, so he lowered his voice to a near whisper. "What's going on?" For the first time since he'd entered the house, he noticed she was wringing her hands—something she only did when she was nervous.

"Did you think I wouldn't find out?"

He cocked his head to one side. "Find out what?"

"Your parents' anniversary party?" She quit fidgeting and squared her shoulders. Her hands became small fists at her sides.

"You know — the one you attended last night?"

Scott sighed and dropped his gaze to the floor. *Shit.* What could he say? *I didn't want to drag you into the mess that is my family? I didn't want you to meet my parents? I didn't want you to get hurt?* All of them true, but obviously not what she wanted to hear, so he pulled out the only plausible explanation he could think of. "You were sick. I thought knowing what you were missing would make you feel even worse."

Her face turned thunderous. "That's bullshit, and you know it. You knew about the party long before I got sick. You could have told me anytime, but you didn't because you didn't want me to go with you. I'm not an idiot, Scott. I know I'm not in your league, but you could have been honest with me. I deserved that much."

"I wanted —"

She held her hand up. "Stop. Just stop. Don't say another word. I have no right to be upset, but I am, which is on me. I let myself think there was more between us than there was. So, thanks for the reality check, and please find another place to stay as soon as possible."

He should have told her about the party when he first heard about it. Roseanne was more than capable of holding her own in his parents' world. A cold, hard truth settled over him. Yes, he'd been protecting her from the pointed barbs his family could throw, but he'd also been protecting himself. He didn't want Roseanne to see the way his family treated him. Didn't want her to know he was, if not exactly the black sheep, the one with the purple stripes — the one his family couldn't understand. Had never made an effort to understand. He'd screwed up, big time. Worse, he had no idea how to fix it. "You can't be serious."

Her features hardened even more, and he got a sick feeling in the pit of his stomach. He'd said the wrong thing. As usual. "I've never been more serious in my life. You've got twenty-four hours. If you aren't out by then, you'll find your things waiting for you on the front porch. Is that clear?"

His mouth had done enough for one day, so he simply nodded.

"Good. We're done." She turned and disappeared into her office. The soft click of her door closing might as well have been the clang of a cell door for the finality of it.

He took the stairs two at a time to his second-story room. It took only a few minutes to toss his things into the duffel bag he'd stuffed beneath the bed. As he looked around the room to make sure he hadn't missed anything, a deep sense of sadness overtook him. Funny, he'd called this place home for a few short months, but had felt absolutely nothing when he'd left the Manhattan apartment he'd lived in for years. He couldn't leave without one last look out the window overlooking the back gardens. His New York apartment had spectacular views, but they were nothing compared to this. The colorful blooms seemed random, but were anything but. They required careful attention which Roseanne lovingly gave them, just as she did everything she did. Whether it was her grandmother's home she'd converted to a bed-and-breakfast, or the cookbook she was working on, or the local civic committees she served on. Everything she did, she did with love.

Did she love him? He'd thought so. She wasn't the type to give herself to a man she didn't have feelings for, and she'd given him everything in bed. The thought of not feeling her skin against his again, of not sinking into her welcoming body, or experiencing the high he felt when she found her pleasure made him wish he could turn back time. Where was a do-over when you needed it?

As he gazed out the window, the old orange tabby cat Roseanne had befriended wandered onto the gravel path in the direction of the back porch where he knew the feline would find a bowl of fresh water and kibble. It had taken weeks to win the cat's trust, but Roseanne had patiently waited for the feline to venture close enough she could touch her. He'd witnessed the process from this very window, falling under the woman's spell the same as the cat had. And like the orange ball of fur, he had no intention of going anywhere.

Butte Plains was his home now. He'd made that decision almost as soon as the jet's wheels had left the ground in New York. There was nothing for him there. Everything he wanted was here, including Roseanne. He'd honor her wishes and find another place to live, but if she thought she'd seen the last of him, she had another think coming. He'd take a page from her own book and win her back with patience and persistence.

~ ~ ~

Roseanne closed the office door and leaned back against it. The last thing she wanted was for Scott to see her crying. He'd treated their relationship like it was nothing, and she didn't want him to know how much that hurt. Her pain was hers, and, like most things in her life, she preferred to keep it private.

That didn't mean it didn't hurt like hell, though. Secure behind the locked door, she sank to the floor and let the tears fall. She'd been a fool to let herself fall in love with a guest. She'd been a fool to fall into his bed, too. He'd been a generous lover, and though she didn't have a lot of experience for comparison sake, he'd more than satisfied her. With him, she'd comfortably explored her sexuality and learned what really turned her on. She doubted she'd ever find another man who made her feel the way Scott did.

She'd let the good times they'd had together blind her to reality. They were worlds apart everywhere but the bedroom. She ran a B&B in a small west Texas town, and he was a billionaire with several businesses and a home in New York. She'd never even been to New York. Her family had never been what she'd call rich. Well-to-do by most standards. Her father was a lawyer and made enough to allow her mother be a stay-at-home mom. They'd had expectations for their only child, expectations she could never meet. Law school had never been her deal. She'd tried and tried to convince them she just wasn't cut out for contracts and legal briefs, but all they'd heard was rebellion. God bless her grandmother's soul, but her passing had provided Roseanne with an opportunity she had grabbed with both hands. She could still hear her father's calm voice telling her she was on her own. "Don't come crying to us for money when this crazy scheme of yours fails. We won't bail you out." Even at her lowest point during the economic downturn, when her financial situation couldn't have looked bleaker, she hadn't even thought of asking them for help. She'd cut expenses, worked her fingers to the bone, and held on until, thankfully, things had started to look up.

Then in walked Scott Ramsey. He'd turned her world upside down. An ill-advised fling with a guest. Another detour in her otherwise orderly life.

Well, she was back on the main road now. If she wasn't good enough for the Ramseys, well, screw them. Though she dearly would have loved to see their faces when they realized their precious son's date was an innkeeper from Butt Plug, Texas! That brought tears of mirth to her eyes. She swiped them away with a sigh.

Reality sucked. She'd been living in a romance novel. But no more. She wasn't Elizabeth Bennett, and Scott wasn't Mr. Darcy. It was time to dry her eyes and get on with life. Maybe someday she'd meet a man who dwelled on her social plane, who loved her for who she was, and would encourage her to explore her slightly kinky side the way Scott had. If not, she'd at least find fulfillment in her work.

That wasn't a four letter word in her vocabulary. She'd always found satisfaction in a job well-done, whether it was tending to the plants her grandparents had lovingly planted, or perfecting a recipe, or simply changing a light bulb. The finished product justified the labor put into the project.

She wiped her wet cheeks on her sleeve then hauled herself off the floor. Her heart ached even more than her throat, which was raw from crying, but both would heal. One sooner than the other, but time healed all wounds, or so they said. Straightening her clothes, she ventured to her new ergonomic desk chair. No sooner had her butt hit the cushioned bottom than her phone rang. She glanced at the blinking light. Her private line. She cleared her throat and pasted on a smile, hoping the physical act of appearing happy would carry over to the words spilling from her mouth. "Hello?"

"What the heck is going on, Roseanne?" Becky Parker-Adams screamed at her.

"Going on?"

"Don't play ignorant with me. Scott just called Ford, wanting to know if he could move into the Adams's gatehouse."

Though it was meant to be servants' quarters, the gatehouse was still one of the largest private dwellings in Butte Plains, and much more modern than The Yellow Rose. Scott would probably feel right at home there. "Is there a problem with him staying there? Ford moved in with you, didn't he?" Rather than stay in the family mansion, Ford had opted to bunk in the gatehouse when he'd come home for his father's funeral. When his stay in town had been extended, he'd opted to stay put. Since Ford and Becky were keeping their Vegas nuptials a secret, he'd quietly moved into Becky's house while maintaining the appearance that he was still living there.

"Of course there's not a problem with him staying there, but there is a problem with him not staying with you. What happened?"

Roseanne knew this conversation would have to take place eventually, but she'd hoped it would be a while before her best friend learned Scott had moved out. She should have guessed he'd call on *his* best friend to solve his temporary housing problem. The best she could hope for was to go with a bit of the truth and save the whole story for a time when it wouldn't hurt so much to tell it. She sighed and dropped her forehead to the desk blotter. "I needed the room, so I asked him to leave. You know I don't rent long-term. He's been here for months. This is an inn, not a boarding house."

"Yes, but—"

"But nothing, Becks." She sat up and pulled the nearest file front and center. "Look, can we not talk about this now? I have a zillion things that need to be done today, and I know you do, too."

"Do you need me to come over?"

She hated the concern in her friend's voice. She felt foolish enough as it was. The last thing she needed to do was confess to Becky that she'd been living a fantasy, dreaming of finding love in the Yankee's arms. No, that was something she'd prefer to keep to herself. At least until her heart scabbed over. Maybe then she'd confide in her best friend. "No. I'm fine. Really."

A long sigh slid across the phone line. "I thought you two were such a cute couple."

"We had some fun together, but we're adults and we have to come in off the playground sometime. Turns out that's today."

After a long silence, Becky said, "You know this conversation isn't over, don't you?"

"I know. Give me a few days, okay?"

"You have until our lunch on Wednesday and not a minute longer. Do you hear me?"

"I hear you. Maybe we could meet somewhere neutral. I don't want anyone else to hear this."

Appeased by her agreement to spill all, Becky suggested a diner that had just opened out on the interstate. The place was noisy and catered to motorists rather than locals. Chances of them meeting anyone they knew were slim, making it the perfect place for a girlfriend chat. Roseanne agreed to the location and, after assuring Becky she was fine, ended the call.

CHAPTER FIVE

It had been forty-two hours and eleven minutes since she'd sent Scott packing, and her heart still felt as if she'd jabbed a knife in it. The worst part was, every time she thought about the man she loved, it was as if she grabbed the handle and gave the weapon a savage twist. At times, she thought the pain would bring her to her knees, but she'd miraculously remained on her feet. Despite her resolve to get on with her life, she'd cried enough to risk serious dehydration.

When the waitress came to take their drink orders, Roseanne requested a pitcher of water. Becky raised one eyebrow — a promise to get to the bottom of her action — then asked for a glass of sweet tea.

As soon as the waitress went to fill their orders, Becky dove in. She leaned forward, arms folded on the table. "A pitcher of water?"

"I need to hydrate. It's hot outside, if you haven't noticed."

"It's not that hot."

"There are other things that can cause dehydration, you know."

The waitress returned. As she placed their drinks on the table, Becky kept her gaze on Roseanne. Her friend was too astute to miss the bags under her eyes or the red rimming her eyelids. She'd tried to hide both, but drugstore makeup could only do so much. Heck, she doubted the stage makeup Becky used when she taped her television show would be a match for her tear-ravaged face.

"A sweet tea and a pitcher of water. Are you ladies ready to order, or should I give you a minute?"

Neither one of them had picked up a menu yet. They did so now, taking the laminated pages from a rack next to the wall and perusing them.

"I'll be back in a minute. Take your time."

Roseanne closed her menu. Her appetite had wavered from nonexistent to insatiable the last few days. She chalked it up to her recent illness coupled with bouts of crying. Becky looked the whole menu over twice before setting it aside. Taking the cue, the waitress reappeared, pad in hand.

"I'll have the double cheeseburger and a side of fries," Becky said.

Roseanne ordered the chicken noodle soup and extra crackers, earning another look from her lunch partner. "What?" she said when the waitress departed.

"You're on a liquid diet?"

"No. I'm just not very hungry. I had a big breakfast." Actually, she'd had dry toast and a few sips of hot tea, and even that hadn't stayed down. Darned stomach. Life's upsets had always affected her physically, but not to this extent. For both her physical and mental well-being, she had to get over Scott Ramsey's betrayal. If talking about it with Becky would help, she was all for it.

"Want to know what I think?"

Roseanne picked up the pitcher and poured herself a glass of ice water. "Not particularly, but you're going to tell me anyway, aren't you?"

"You know I am, girlfriend. That's what friends are for, aren't they?"

Roseanne shrugged and took a big swig. The cold drink instantly made her head ache and her stomach churn. Damn, why hadn't she asked for some bread to nibble on or something? She placed one hand on her stomach and then clamped the other to her forehead, putting pressure on her temples. "If you say so, Becks." There was no use in arguing. Becky couldn't keep her opinion to herself if it was the only thing keeping her from falling off a cliff.

Her friend leaned across the table and whispered, "I think you're pregnant."

Roseanne's head came up so fast she thought it might explode. Becky sat across from her, a Cheshire cat grin on her face. "Are you insane?"

Becky shook her head, the tips of her high ponytail swishing over one shoulder then the other. "Nope. Tell me it's not true."

Roseanne stared at her friend while the possibility whistled through her head like a freight train bearing down on an unprotected crossing. Moments in time played across her mind—moments spent with Scott. They'd always used protection. *Always.* But nothing short of abstinence was 100 percent, and abstinence had not been something they adhered to. Far from it. They'd made love often up until that last day in Las Vegas.

"I can't be." Even she could hear the doubt in her voice. Becky didn't miss it, either.

"You're going to have to do better than that." Her friend sat back, crossing her arms. Roseanne didn't have to see it to know she'd also crossed her legs. The woman smelled victory.

Roseanne reached for her water, but her hand shook too much, so she set the plastic glass down rather than spill the contents all over herself. "We weren't reckless. We used protection."

"They covered that subject in our sex-ed class in junior high. You were there. I sat next to you."

"I know." The class had been eye-opening and embarrassing. They'd giggled about it for months, speculating on what it would be like to have a guy put his "thing" inside you. Becoming pregnant had been a distant and unreal possibility overshadowed by the process that they'd all but ignored it in their girlish excitement. "The only way to be positive you won't become pregnant is to abstain," she quoted in her best imitation of their teacher, Mrs. Roach.

"Did you abstain?" Becky asked.

Roseanne glared at her companion. "What do you think?"

"I think you and Scott were getting it on like bunnies. Every time I saw the two of you together you couldn't keep your hands off each other."

"That doesn't mean I'm preg…pregnant."

"It doesn't mean you aren't, either."

The waitress returned with their meals. Roseanne took one whiff of the food and excused herself. She made it to the restroom in time, emptied the meager contents of her stomach into the toilet then stared at her reflection in the mirror as she cleaned up afterward. She'd been so busy being mad at Scott for not asking her to go to his parents' party she'd ignored the signs. Could her recent illness be morning sickness? Did that last all day? Did it come and go?

She patted her face with a damp towel. The nausea had dissipated only to be replaced by a gnawing hunger she was afraid the soup she'd ordered wouldn't quench. She crumpled the towel in her fist and tossed it in the trash receptacle. Taking a dry towel from the dispenser, she used it to open the door then tossed it in the wastebasket as she exited the ladies' room. Becky was halfway through with her burger when Roseanne slid into her side of the booth.

"You okay?"

"Yeah. I'm starving." She ladled soup into her mouth as fast as she could without actually drinking it from the bowl. As she'd suspected, the light meal wasn't going to cut it. She eyed the mountain of fries Becky had barely touched.

Becky took her burger then shoved the plate across the table. "Help yourself."

"Thanks." She ate like she hadn't eaten in a week while Becky slowly finished her burger. To her friend's credit, she kept her mouth shut until they'd paid and were standing beside their cars in the parking lot.

"When do you want to take the test?"

Never. "Can we stop at the super store at the next exit? If I buy one at Harrington's Pharmacy, everyone in town will know before I get the box open." The local drugstore was handy, but the clerks were the worst gossips in Butte Plains.

"Remember when Billy Proctor had ringworm?" Becky smiled. "Man, that news spread like wildfire."

Roseanne shuddered. "If you think that spread fast, you can imagine how fast this would hit the grapevine."

"Fiber optic technology has nothing on the Butte Plains grapevine."

"So, can we go to the big, anonymous super store?"

"Lead the way, girlfriend. We can use the self-checkout, too. Only the two of us will know."

~ ~ ~

"It's going to be all right, Roseanne." The uncertainty in Becky's tone said otherwise.

Roseanne stared at the little stick that spelled her doom. *No. No, it isn't.* Nothing was ever going to be all right again.

"Scott will do what's right. He's a good man."

Ah, Becky. Your optimism is showing. If there was one thing Roseanne was certain of, it was that she couldn't tell Scott Ramsey. At least not right away. If he stayed in town there'd be no way to keep him from finding out, and chances were Ford would tell him, too. She couldn't expect Becky to keep the information a secret from her husband forever, and, in turn, he'd feel obligated to tell his best friend. "You're putting too much faith in the man, Becks. He had the chance to take me to meet his parents and he didn't even tell me about it."

"What?"

She sat on the closed toilet seat and waved Becky to the rim of the tub then she proceeded to tell her friend what had led to her kicking Scott out of his room at The Yellow Rose.

"This is different, Roseanne. He didn't tell you about a party. You can't seriously contemplate not telling him he's going to be a father."

"He'll find out soon enough, but please, can you keep this to yourself for a while? I need some time to get used to the idea of being a single mom. I've got to figure out how I'm going to provide for this baby."

"Scott's a billionaire. He'll provide for you and the baby."

"I don't want his money. I don't want him staying in Butte Plains because I'm pregnant. He'll go back to New York in a few months...then I'll tell him."

"I don't like it, but as long as you promise to tell him before the baby is born..."

Roseanne crossed her fingers behind her back. "I promise."

CHAPTER SIX

Ford waved the bartender over and ordered two beers, one for him, and one for his best friend who looked as if he'd been sucker punched. He'd never seen Scott Ramsey so depressed. At MIT, his roommate had been known as Smiley, while Ford had often been called Grumpy. The man just didn't have it in him to be down. Or so Ford thought.

"Here. Maybe this will help."

"A legal depressant?" Scott took the offered bottle and drank half of it in one draw. "Can't hurt. Thanks."

"I appreciate you staying in the gatehouse. You don't mind driving my car, do you?"

"Nope. It's a nice ride. You sure your mother won't figure out it's me living there and not you?"

Ford took a sip from his beer. "She won't. I've been living there for months and she hasn't come down the drive to see me. If she wants me, she calls and demands my presence at the house. Just don't answer the house phone, and she'll never know."

"Okay, if you say so, but don't you think it would be easier to just tell her you got married? You're going to have a big shindig anyway, so why would she care?"

"I'm her only child. She's been dreaming about my wedding since I was in diapers."

"I hear you. Mine didn't start that early, but she's making up for it now. If she even sees me with an eligible woman, she starts talking about the china and silver patterns she has stored in the attic." He didn't want to dwell on the fact his parents wouldn't see Roseanne as eligible. His mother certainly wouldn't drag out his grandmother's china for a woman who worked to support herself.

Ford signaled the bartender for two more. "Is that why you didn't take Roseanne to their anniversary party?"

"Partly, I guess."

"How do you think she found out about it, anyway?" He'd already heard the story about Scott getting kicked out of the B&B because he hadn't told Roseanne the real reason he went to New York.

"I assumed Becky mentioned it to her."

"Nope. At least I don't think so. I was invited, as you know, but I forgot to mention it to her, so don't you go and tell her or I'll be sharing the gatehouse with you."

Scott shook his head. "She won't hear it from me." He accepted a fresh bottle from the waitress the bartender sent over and handed her his empty. "So, if none of us told her, how did she find out?"

"Did an invite come to the B&B?"

"Nope. Mom sent it to the leather factory. It's the only address she has for me here."

"Leave it lying around in your room?"

"Nope. It's still in my desk drawer at the factory."

"I don't suppose Roseanne had any reason to go there and snoop around?"

"I can't imagine why she would. Besides, she's as busy as a cab driver on New Year's Eve. The woman has more going on than any of my mother or sister's high society friends."

They drank their beers and contemplated the problem for a few minutes. Ford finally broke the silence. "Did she see your sister in Las Vegas?"

"Not that I know of, but now that you mention it, she acted

funny toward me that last day there."

"The same day Ronnie butted into mine and Becky's business?"

"Yeah. The same day." He took a long draw on his beer. "You don't suppose she got to Roseanne that same day, do you?"

"I wouldn't put anything past your sister. She went above and beyond to try to come between me and Becky, and tried to weasel our company out from under us." He shrugged. "I could believe she spread her poison to your girlfriend."

The conversation he'd had with Ronnie in the limo last week came back to him. "Shit."

"What?"

"Ronnie said some things to me about Roseanne last week on the way out to the estate. I wrote it off as my sister being the bitch she is, but now that I think about it, I wonder if she did have a hand in this."

"Like I said. I wouldn't put it past her, especially after what she did to me and Becky in Vegas." He drained his first beer and started on his second. "I can't believe I dated that woman. What was I thinking?"

"Don't ask me. I never understood what you saw in her."

"You should have said something."

"Would you have listened?"

"Probably not," Ford conceded. "The important thing is that our friendship survived my time with your sister."

"I had faith you'd come around."

"What are you going to do about Roseanne? Are you going to give up on her?"

Scott shook his head. "Can't."

"Yeah, I know how that feels." Ford eyed the content level then took another swig from his beer. "You have a plan?"

"Not really. I've got a few things to prove to her, I guess."

"Like what?"

"Like I plan to stay here for good."

Ford's right eyebrow raised. "Do you?"

Scott nodded. "I do. This place grows on you."

"And Roseanne is here."

"And Roseanne is here," Scott conceded. "She'd be miserable in New York, and if I'm being honest, I was, too. I like it here. I've got room to breathe."

"I used to think all that room to breathe was the same thing as a long road with a dead end in the middle of nowhere."

"It's not. It's opportunity and space to grow. I won't say it isn't a challenge, because it is, but I was so busy staying alive in the city that I didn't have time to explore the things that made me happy. I can make a difference here. This place needs someone with time and money, and I've got both."

"You're going into philanthropy?"

"Not so much philanthropy as entrepreneurship." He drained his bottle and held it up until the waitress saw and nodded. "Roseanne's on a couple of local committees that could use some help." Another round arrived, and they both took the time to sample the cold brews.

"Details?"

Scott leaned in, resting his forearms on the table. "You know that block of empty buildings downtown? The one where the old Cotton Exchange is?" His friend nodded. "I'm going to buy it. I'll set up my office in one of the buildings and rent out the rest."

"Where are you going to find people to rent to? We've seen a lot of growth in the last few months, but everyone wants new construction closer to the freeway."

"As a matter of fact, I was thinking it might be time to relocate our design-for-hire business from New York to Butte Plains. That way we could keep an eye on it. I've already talked to Riley about moving. Fortunately for us, he's between sugar daddies and thinks some Texas scenery might be just the thing. He made some comment about ranchers, cowboy boots, and Stetsons. I didn't ask any questions, just told him I'd discuss it with you and let him know."

"What about the new designer we hired?"

"He wasn't as eager to load up his covered wagon, but he didn't say absolutely no."

"Then I say we do it. Move the whole thing here. If we have to hire a new designer or two, so be it." Ford and Scott clinked their beer bottles together, sealing the deal. "So, your plan to win Roseanne's affections is to move here and become a land baron?"

"It's the only plan I've got. She doesn't believe I'm going to stay. What says permanent resident better than becoming a major land owner?"

"How about a house? Don't get me wrong. You can stay at the gatehouse as long as you want, but it's not the same as putting down roots."

"Got that covered. I put an offer in on that crumbling Victorian around the corner from Roseanne's place."

"Good Lord! I hope you plan to bulldoze it before it falls in on itself."

"Nope. I admit, it's in worse shape than the one you bought and renovated in New York. I've already spoken to a renovation expert in Dallas about fixing it up."

"I can't even imagine how much that would cost."

"More than I'll be paying for the property. I had it checked out. The foundation is solid, and the basic structure is sound. It was built to last, apparently. Decades of neglect have taken a toll, but it can be saved."

"I'll take your word for it. It's too much house for us, anyway, and we're too busy to oversee a renovation of any kind right now. Becky's house is small, but we're content."

"Compared to the houses you and I grew up in, the crumbling Victorian is tiny, but I suspect it will be big enough for the four or five kids I imagine."

"Whoa!" Ford reared back. "You're talking about having a brood with Roseanne, and the woman isn't even speaking to you?

You've got balls, my friend. That's all I can say."

"I told you, she's the one. If I can't win her over, maybe I'll sell the house to you and Becky. Don't tell me you don't want a bunch of kids. I know how much you hate being an only child."

"Yeah, well, we haven't exactly talked about that subject yet. We're young. No need to rush."

"I'm not rushing. I'm planning. There's a difference."

"Whatever. Sounds like you're putting the cart before the horse to me, but what do I know?"

"You know nothing. I thought we established that years ago," Scott teased. Ford was the brother he'd never had growing up, and they behaved like siblings more often than not. Settling in his friend's hometown felt right. "I need you to do me a favor."

"Oh no. Please don't ask me to keep all this from Becky."

"Well, that, too, but I was hoping I could convince you not to invite my parents to your wedding."

"She's going to meet your parents sometime."

"You've met them. Roseanne's blood isn't blue enough for them. They aren't going to approve of her, and I don't want them scaring her off."

Ford shrugged. "I'll see what I can do. It might be too late, though. One of the first things Roseanne did was ask for a guest list so she could send it to someone to hand address all the envelopes."

"Shit." Scott chugged the rest of his beer. "Why do these things have to be planned so far in advance?"

"Hell if I know. I didn't see anything wrong with our Vegas wedding."

"It was legal, so what's the big deal?"

"Asking the wrong person. I'm just following my dad's advice."

"What advice is that?"

"Happy wife, happy life."

Scott nodded. "Sound advice if I ever heard any."

CHAPTER SEVEN

Knowing the source of her illness made it worse, not better. With the help of her best friend, Roseanne made an appointment with a doctor in Prairieview. She came away from the first visit elated and stunned at the enormity of what she was doing. Having been an only child, she'd dreamed of having a big family, but as the years had gone by and no eligible candidates for husband and father had come along, she'd shoved the dream to the back of her mind and focused on living life as it came.

This is my life now, she thought, caressing her still-flat belly with one hand as she steered the car with the other. There was no going back. What was done was done, and she wouldn't change a thing. The kid was probably doomed to being an only child, too, but Roseanne vowed she would do the best she could to raise a happy and healthy child. He or she would have all the love she could give, and then some. She briefly thought about telling her parents, but decided against telling them—for now. They'd just see this as another screwup on her part and demand she hold the baby's father up for every cent she could. Her dad would probably offer to file the lawsuit for her.

She didn't want Scott's money and doubted he'd want anything to do with the child. She would tell him about the baby, but when she was good and ready.

Determined not to take money from Scott, she considered her options. The bed-and-breakfast was doing okay these days, but the earning potential there was finite. Which meant she needed to pursue the cookbook idea. Eventually, she'd need another place to live, too. She could easily keep an infant in her room at The Yellow Rose, but once the child was old enough to sleep in a real bed, she'd have a problem. Converting a guest room to a private room for her kid would reduce the room inventory by one, ensuring the inn would fail. The numbers barely worked as it was. Of course, if she moved out, there would be yet another room to rent, which would offset the cost of renting another house for her and the baby. That also meant there wouldn't be a caretaker on premises. That wouldn't do. Maybe she could convert the garage to an apartment for herself and her child. She mentally calculated the square footage, determined it could work, but the idea met a brick wall. Where would she find the funds for the conversion?

Thinking about all the challenges ahead for her as a single parent made her head hurt. She reached the exit for Butte Plains and smiled at the makeshift nameplate someone had recently added to the exit sign, declaring her hometown to be Butt Plug instead of Butte Plains. The sign alterations had started appearing shortly after Ford and Becky put the town on the map as the home of the now-famous sex toy that had saved Adams Manufacturing from bankruptcy and brought the town back from the edge of extinction. The department of transportation removed the sign alternations regularly, but they always came back. Photos of the signs had gone viral on the internet, which had helped spread the word about the new adult toy and increase sales.

Thinking about Ford and Becky reminded her she needed to stop by the florist and go over the details for the wedding she would be hosting in a couple of months. She did a mental calculation based on what the doctor had told her and concluded she wouldn't be showing then. That was a good thing, as the father of her baby would be the best man to her maid of honor status. If she was showing, there'd be no way to avoid telling him about the child.

Roseanne pulled into a parking spot in front of the floral shop on the edge of downtown. Encouraged by the upswing in the economy, the owners, who had closed their doors a few years ago, had recently reopened. From the number of cars in the lot, business was good. She grabbed the notebook she was never without and entered the store.

"Roseanne!"

"Hello, Mrs. Bullard. I brought my notes on the wedding I spoke to you about. Do you have time to go over them?"

"I'll make time. Let me finish this order, and I'll be right with you."

"No problem. I think I'll wait outside. Just give me a whistle when you're ready." Roseanne had inherited her grandmother's love of flowers, but in the enclosed space the fragrant blooms turned her stomach. Settled on the wooden bench out front, she took a deep breath and willed the nausea to go away. It didn't take much these days to make her gut uneasy, and strong smells were often the culprit. Feeling better, she opened her notebook and refreshed her memory. Becky hadn't been specific regarding her floral choices, but knowing her friend the way she did, pink was a must. She jotted down a few things that popped into her head regarding the arrangements. When it looked like Mrs. Bullard was going to be a while longer, Roseanne flipped to the new section she'd started at the doctor's office and began a new list. In a few short minutes, she had filled an entire page with things she would need for the baby.

Wow. Who would have thought? Overwhelmed with the task ahead of her, she didn't hear the florist approach. "Oh! I'm sorry. I guess I was woolgathering."

"Not a problem. I'm sorry to have kept you waiting."

With her index finger wedged between the pages, she held the notebook up. "As you can see, I kept busy."

"I brought mine, too," the older woman said, indicating the thick binder she held against her chest. "It's nice out here today. Would you mind if we sat here to go over the plans?"

"Not at all. Please, join me." Roseanne scooted over to make room for the floral merchant. They talked for nearly an hour, as neither one wanted to leave anything to chance.

When they were through, Mrs. Bullard closed her binder and sighed. "This is going to be a lovely wedding. I'm so happy for Ford and Becky. They make a beautiful couple."

"Yes, they do, and, thanks to you, their wedding is going to be stunning."

"I appreciate the chance to be a part of their day, and if I might say so, I hope to be a part of yours sometime soon, too."

Roseanne's stomach did a backflip. "Don't hold your breath, Mrs. Bullard."

"I don't know. Lots of new people are moving into town. You never know when the right one will suddenly appear."

"You're a true romantic." Uneasy with the turn of the conversation, Roseanne stood. Mrs. Bullard did the same. For the first time since she'd realized she was pregnant, she wondered what the people in town would think. She certainly wouldn't be the first unwed mother in Butte Plains, but she couldn't recall one who had maintained her reputation in the community. Well, she wasn't going to force Scott to marry her just so people wouldn't talk. This was the twenty-first century, after all.

"It never hurts to look through rose-colored glasses, dear."

"Whatever." Roseanne laughed and forced a smile to her lips. "I've got to be going. Call me if you have any questions; otherwise, we're good to go, right?"

"Right. Scoot on along. I've got it under control."

Well, that makes one of us. "Thanks, Mrs. Bullard. Oh, and I'll have Kay call you to let you know how many arrangements we'll need for the rooms next week." Ever since the florist had reopened, Roseanne had been ordering small arrangements for the rented rooms and the front hallway. She preferred to use blooms from her own garden, but the plants hadn't been able to keep up with the demand. It was a nice problem to have. She hoped she'd be able to continue purchasing the fresh flowers, but if things got real tight with the new baby, the flower arrangements would be one of the first things she'd cut from the budget. Artificial flowers and some essential oils in a diffuser would be less expensive over time.

"I'll order in more yellow roses, just in case."

"Thanks!" Roseanne ducked into the safety of her car and cranked the engine. *Whew!* She put the car in gear and exited the lot. Suddenly hungry and tired, she couldn't wait to get home and be alone for a few minutes. Maybe get in a nap. Her cell phone rang. She pulled over and fished the device out of her purse. There wasn't any money in the budget for a newfangled car with Bluetooth and likely would never be now. "Hi, Kay, what's up?"

"Ms. Meadows, I'm sorry to bother you, but there are some people here from the rental company. They say the tent you ordered isn't going to fit on the lawn. Something about fire clearances. Can you come talk to them?"

Roseanne cupped her forehead between the thumb and middle finger of her free hand and resisted the urge to cry. Breaking down now wouldn't fix anything. "I'm almost home, Kay. Give them some sweet tea and cookies and tell them I'll be along in a few minutes."

"Will do. If I knew what to tell them, I'd save you the trouble."

"No worries. I'm sure it can all be sorted out in a matter of minutes."

"Okay. Drive safe."

Roseanne disconnected and clenched the phone in her fist. She closed her eyes and took a minute to find her center before pulling back onto the road. One more hurdle today then she'd get that nap. One block away from the B&B, she stopped in the middle of the road and stared at the work taking place on the old Victorian she'd admired and worried about for so long. Once a grand lady much like her grandmother's house, only bigger, the place had been vacant for decades and was little more than a ruin. She'd been concerned someone would come in and buy it just for the lot. Judging from the giant equipment on the lawn, that's exactly what had happened.

"Hey! Lady!" A guy wearing a hard hat and dusty work clothes yelled at her from the sidewalk.

Roseanne rolled her window down. "What?"

"You need to move. We've got a dumpster coming in, and you're blocking the way." He pointed at something behind her. She glanced in the rearview mirror and saw the giant truck with the big trash dumpster about a foot off her bumper.

"Okay. I'm going." She rolled the window up and crept down the street. "But I'll be back," she muttered. As soon as she got rid of the tent people, she'd return to the construction site and find out what was going on. If it wasn't too late, maybe the historical society could step in and save the structure. Taking one last look at the place in her mirror, she had the sinking feeling it was too late.

The tent issue proved to be easily solved. There had been a misunderstanding about where, exactly, she wanted them to put it. Once that was corrected, the problem went away. Roseanne took the opportunity to review the placement of the stage, dance floor, and tables with them. Better to find out now if there was a problem than to deal with it at the last minute. Assured everything was squared away with the rental company, Roseanne made her way to the back door and let herself into the kitchen. She grabbed a glass of sweet tea before heading upstairs to her room on the third floor. Winded when she finally collapsed on her bed, she wondered how she would manage the climb when she could no longer see her feet.

Ugh. Something else to worry about! She closed her eyes and willed the tension from her body. A few minutes…then she'd get up.

Beep. Beep. Beep.

Roseanne popped one eye open. The annoying sound

continued, so she sat up, looking around for the source. Eventually, she wandered over and opened the window. The sound grew louder, followed by a loud crash.

"The house!" She'd forgotten all about the construction crew around the corner.

She flew down the stairs, grabbed a water bottle from the fridge, and cut through the backyard to the alley that ran behind her house. The old Victorian looked worse from this angle than it did from the front, and that was saying something. Someone had chopped down the overgrown foliage, creating a path around to the front. Roseanne followed it, coming to an abrupt halt when she came face-to-face with a skid loader.

She placed a hand on her chest to still her wildly beating heart.

"Better get out of the way, lady."

"No. I'm not budging until I speak to whoever is in charge."

"What is this? Some kind of intervention? We have permits."

"I want to see those permits." Everyone at City Hall knew better than to issue a demolition permit for a century-old home without consulting the Historical Society first. She fisted her hands on her hips and tilted her chin up. "Who's in charge here?"

"Hold on." He grabbed a walkie-talkie from a pocket next to the seat and spoke into it. "Randy? We've got a problem here. Can you come take care of it?"

The radio squawked then a voice said, "I'm kind of busy here. Can't you take care of it?"

"No can do, boss. Lady says she wants the man in charge." The equipment operator winked at Roseanne.

"What lady?" the voice asked.

"He wants to know who you are."

"I heard him," Roseanne said. "Tell him I'm from the Historical Society."

He raised one eyebrow and lifted the walkie-talkie. "She's from the Historical Society." Distain dripped from the words.

"On my way."

CHAPTER EIGHT

Roseanne smirked. It was amazing what those few words could accomplish. If there was one thing construction people hated, it was someone with the power to shut them down.

The machine in front of her cut off, and the operator climbed out. "Taking a break," he said.

With no one to intimidate, Roseanne relaxed her shoulders and took a moment to look around. Edging past the machinery, she could see not one, but two giant trash receptacles parked on the front lawn. While she watched, a couple of boards flew out a front window, landing with a thud in the nearest bin. If she was going to save the house, she'd have to work fast. They were already tearing it apart, one board at a time.

The front door opened, and a tall, slender man wearing a hard hat and carrying a clipboard took the rickety steps to the yard at a brisk clip. He wore a dark-green button-down shirt, tan slacks, and tasseled loafers. Stopping to speak with a guy Roseanne recognized as the man from the skid loader, he glanced her way. He clapped the other man on the shoulder, said something she couldn't hear, but assumed was reassuring. Then he focused on her, and, with two trash Dumpsters and an expanse of unkempt lawn between them, she felt his gaze all the way down to her toes.

He approached slowly, as if he had all the time in the world.

Roseanne took a deep breath and held her ground. Lord, he was good-looking! Short-cropped sandy hair peeked from beneath the hard hat which shaded deep-blue eyes. Scruff a shade darker than his hair emphasized the strong line of his jaw. He walked with a rolling gate that spoke of athleticism.

When he spoke, his voice seemed to come from the depths of a very deep well and rolled over her like water from a hot spring. "Hello. I'm Randy Tucker." He pointed to the logo embroidered on the left side of his shirt, which she could now see was a very nice fabric that had probably cost a pretty penny. "Tucker Construction. What can I do for you, Ms...?"

She shook off her attraction to the man. Handsome or not, he was the enemy. "Meadows. Roseanne Meadows. I'm a member of the Butte Plains Historical Society. Do you have a permit to demolish this house?"

"No, we do not have a permit to demolish the house."

"Then I insist you stop, at once."

A dimple appeared in his right cheek. If she'd been in the market for a man, his smile would have overridden her concerns about him tearing down the house. But she wasn't in the market for a man—she'd had one too many of those already. "No can do, Ms. Meadows. We have a schedule to keep."

"I don't give a tinker's damn about your schedule. You will shut down now, or I'll call the police and have them shut you down."

"That won't be necessary, ma'am." He leafed through the papers on his clipboard, found the one he wanted, and released it from the clamp. "We have all the permission we need."

Roseanne snatched the official-looking document out of his hand. "This is a permit—"

"To restore the structure. Yes, ma'am. It might look like we're tearing the place down, but rest assured, we'll replace everything we tear out. We specialize in restoring historic homes and buildings." He reached into his breast pocket, withdrew a card, and handed it over, taking the permit from her at the same time. "Feel free to check out our website."

"Who?" She didn't know what to say. Someone was actually restoring the place? That had to cost a fortune. "Who are you working for?"

"Outfit called BP Investments. We've been hired to restore several structures in town. If you have any questions, you'd best ask them."

She'd never heard of the company. "Do you have an address or phone number for them?"

"Their office is in Dallas, I think. I can give you the number for my contact there."

"Please." She handed him back his card. He consulted his phone, turned his business card over, and wrote on the back.

"Guy's name is Riley Ashworth." He returned the card to her. "Nice fella."

Roseanne glanced at the neat handwriting. The name and number weren't at all familiar. "You said you were hired to renovate other properties in Butte Plains?"

"As soon as we get the deconstruction done on this one, we'll start on the others. A whole block of abandoned businesses on Main Street."

"Is the Cotton Exchange one of them?" She'd admired the structure since she was a kid. Built in 1861, it had been home to many things after the first owners moved out early in the twentieth century.

"You know the place?"

Roseanne nodded. "Everyone at the Historical Society does. You'll need approval from us to remove any of the details from the façade."

"Riley is supposed to be working on that, though the plans I've seen call for restoring the façade to its original condition, as well as retaining most of the interior. Anything that can't be saved will be replaced with new materials as close to the original as possible.

When we're done, you won't be able to tell what's new and what's not."

"I hope you're as good as you think you are."

The moment the words left her mouth, she wished she could yank them back. The man standing before her smiled, revealing a matching dimple on his other cheek.

"I'm good, Ms. Meadows. Real good. You'll see." He tucked his clipboard next to his hip. "Hey, since you're here, I wonder if you can tell me anything about that yellow Victorian around the corner."

He pointed unnecessarily. The Yellow Rose was the only yellow Victorian in the entire town. "I know it. Why?"

"The owner of this property pointed it out as a possible source for inspiration on this renovation. Said the houses were built by the same contractor back in the day. It looks in good shape. Whoever did the restoration on it did a good job."

Roseanne bristled. "The Yellow Rose is mine. It was my grandmother's home, and what you see is original."

"Really? That's even better. What about the inside?"

"A few renovations have been done over the years, and I made some concessions in order to turn it into a bed-and-breakfast, but nothing that would compromise the integrity of the structure." She could see his interest growing as she spoke. Maybe he did have an appreciation for old buildings.

"I'd love to see inside, maybe take a few photos of the moldings and other details? Would that be okay?"

Roseanne nodded. "I suppose, if it would help you restore this one."

"It would. Thank you. There's not much left to go on with this one. When would be a good time to come over?"

She thought about her crazy schedule for a second. "I don't know. I'm in the middle of planning a big event right now, but I suppose I could spare a few minutes. Maybe tomorrow afternoon around one? We'll be in between guests, and the rooms should be turned."

"It's a date, then. Now, unless you have something else to discuss, I need to get my men back to work."

"No. I'm good."

"I'm sure you are. Good day, Ms. Meadows."

She admired his firm butt as he walked away.

When he reached the steps, he let out a shrill whistle then yelled, "Everybody back to work."

An unholy racket began inside the house. Behind her, the skid loader started up again.

Roseanne made her way to the sidewalk, where she turned back and looked at the dilapidated structure with fresh eyes. She fingered the card Randy Tucker had given her. Lots of new people had come into town in the last few months, buying up real estate, hoping to make a profit on it.

"Probably some oil-rich corporation out of Dallas," she muttered.

At least they were restoring and not tearing down. She made a mental note to ask around, see if anyone knew what their endgame was.

CHAPTER NINE

The next day, promptly at one o'clock, the bell above the front door jingled. Roseanne stood and smoothed out the wrinkles in her skirt. She'd gone through several dress selections this morning before choosing this one—a summer-weight sleeveless cotton shift that fit her curves but was simple enough to retain a casual look. She had on strappy sandals with a low heel and she'd pulled her shoulder-length hair into a high ponytail. Daring the day's heat to do its worst, she'd applied a light layer of makeup. She told herself she was doing it to lift her spirits, not because Randy Tucker was coming to see the house. Besides, he was only interested in her house, and she had no business noticing his hunkiness anyway.

"Anyone home?"

His deep baritone sent a shiver down her spine. Must be the hormone cocktail her doctor had warned her about. Satisfied she looked as good as she was going to get, she called out, "Coming!" *Great. Great choice of words.*

She shook her head at her own stupidity then stepped into the hall. Randy Tucker stood there, his chin in the air as he examined the crown moldings in the entryway. His gaze traveled down, landing on her. His eyes widened. A smile brought out his dimples.

"Hello, again."

Roseanne smiled. After feeling like shit for the last few weeks, his admiring gaze lifted her spirits. "Welcome to The Yellow Rose." Maybe if she was nice to him, he might give her a good price on converting the garage to an apartment. If she could find a way to pay for the renovation.

"Thank you. This place is amazing." His gaze returned to the hand-carved woodwork. "All this is original?"

She ran her hand over the ornate newel post. "It is. The kitchen is the only room on the main floor that has been renovated. Everything else you see is just as it was the day my grandparents moved in."

"They were the original owners?"

"Yep. My grandfather passed when I was about six, I think. My grandmother lived here until she passed ten years ago. The house was vacant for two years, until I finished college and moved back. It's been a bed-and-breakfast for the last six years."

He pulled out his cell phone. "Mind if I take some pictures?"

"Not at all." She turned on the ancient chandelier so he'd have better light.

"That's original, too?"

"Yep. I had the electrical inspected. At some point, my grandmother had the place rewired, and the plumbing upgraded to meet modern standards. However, the windows and doors are original. She didn't go so far as to modernize the charm out of the place."

"Your grandmother was a smart woman."

"Would you put that on a plaque? I'm sure my guests will appreciate it when they can't keep warm in the winter or cool in the summer."

"There are ways to alleviate some of the drafts. I'll know more once I see the drafty windows in question."

"I doubt I could afford whatever solutions you come up with. I'm barely hanging on as it is."

He snapped several pictures, including one of the window moldings in the front parlor. "If the energy savings were enough, it would be worth the investment."

"Investment. That's the key word. It supposes one has money to invest, which I don't."

He shrugged. "Maybe sometime in the future, then." He roamed the public rooms, taking photo after photo, both close-up and from a wide angle. When he was done, he asked, "Can I see the kitchen? You said it has been remodeled?"

"Sure. Come on." She led the way into what she considered her haven. Her small staff had completed their work for the day and left, except for Kay who would be back later to check in the guests arriving today. A plate of muffins leftover from breakfast sat in the center of the large, marble-topped island.

Randy let out a low whistle. "Wow. This is amazing."

"The cabinets are original, except for the island. My grandmother had that built about twenty years ago. I had all the old countertops replaced with marble, and put in a new sink and appliances to meet code for a commercial kitchen."

"You and your grandmother did a great job. I'm sure the builder would have used these materials if they'd been available to him." He ran his hand appreciatively over the cold stone counter. "Pictures?"

"Sure. Go ahead." She stood back as he roamed the room, clicking away. She'd had a few guests who loved old houses and wanted to see everything, and learn the history of the place, but none had ever paid such close attention to the details. Randy photographed everything, down to the hinges on the cabinet doors and the shelving in the pantry.

"I can't tell you how helpful this is. My carpenters and designers are going to want to see this place. The photos will help, but nothing beats seeing it in person."

"They're welcome anytime. Would you like to see the guest rooms?"

"Lead the way, pretty lady. I'll look at anything you want to show me."

Roseanne blushed.

He noticed and quickly amended his statement. "Sorry. I meant, I'll look at any part of the *house* you want to show me."

Roseanne's laugh sounded nervous even to herself. This was ridiculous. She was acting like a hormonal teenager when she had zero interest in doing anything with the man. If she were being honest with herself, she wished she was having this conversation with Scott Ramsey. Despite his lack of interest in her, she still loved him, and, thanks to the child she carried, he'd always be a part of her life. She'd made up her mind to tell him after Ford and Becky's wedding. She planned to make it perfectly clear she wanted nothing from him, but hoped he'd at least want to be a part-time parent. If he didn't, well, fuck him. They'd do just fine without him.

"I know what you meant. Come on." He followed her up the back staircase to the second floor. "There are three bedrooms on this level, and one on the third floor." She pointed out the bathroom that two of the rooms shared, mentioning that the Senator's Suite had its own bathroom. Naturally, he wanted to see it all.

"If you don't mind, I'll leave you to look around. I have some phone calls I need to make." There seemed to be no end to the details regarding the upcoming wedding. She still needed to find someone to provide the audio-visual equipment for both the ceremony and the reception. "I'll unlock the other rooms for you before I go."

"That's fine. I don't want to take up all your time. Honestly? I could spend days here, looking at everything, but I'll leave that to my crew. I just need to get enough photos to get them started."

"I'll be in my office." She started to leave. "Oh. Do you need to see the third floor? There's only one room with a small bathroom. The rest is attic space."

"I wouldn't mind seeing the attic. I suspect your room is much like the ones down here?"

"It's directly above us, and nearly identical to this suite."

"Then I'll settle for seeing the attic. Is it open?"

"Never saw a need to lock it. Have fun exploring." She made her way downstairs to her office. She'd heard the phone ring several times since Mr. Tucker had arrived. There were several messages, one about the audio/visual equipment and two others were customers inquiring about available rooms. She returned those first because, without customers, she'd have to close her doors. When she finally got off the phone, having successfully negotiated a price for the delivery, setup, and maintenance of the equipment she needed, she sat back in her chair and closed her eyes.

"You look peaceful sitting there."

Roseanne nearly jumped out of her skin at the sound of the masculine voice so close by. "Oh!"

Randy Tucker leaned casually in the doorway to her office. The smile on his face said he wasn't at all sorry about scaring the bejeezus out of her.

"I'd forgotten you were here."

"Good thing I'm not a serial killer, then."

She allowed herself a smile. "I suppose so. Did you see enough?"

"Not nearly enough," he said, his gaze raking over the modest neckline of her dress. "But enough for now. Mind if I bring some people over in a couple of days?"

"If you could call first, that would be good. I don't want to inconvenience my guests."

"Not a problem." He held up one of the colorful brochures she'd had printed to advertise the inn locally. She kept a few on the table in the foyer for her guests to take with them. "Can I reach you at the number listed here?"

Roseanne held her hand out. "Here. Let me give you my private number." After scribbling her cell phone number on the brochure, she handed it to him. "This time of day is usually good."

"I heard you on the phone. You host special events?"

"This is my first—a wedding for my best friend. I want

everything to be perfect."

"I'm sure it will be. Who wouldn't want to get married in a place like this?"

"The ceremony will be in the garden. We're putting a giant tent on the front lawn for the reception. We'll have a catered meal, dancing, and live entertainment. It's going to be quite a shindig."

"Sounds like it. I saw the garden from the upstairs window. Mind if I take a closer look? My client wants something similar — thus the skid loader you met yesterday. We need access to the rear of the house, so I told them we'd clear the overgrown brush out of the way so the landscapers could get a better look."

"Gardens like mine don't spring up overnight. My grandmother planted most of it when she first moved in. It's taken decades of hard work to get it the way it is."

"May I see it?"

"Sure. I could use a break and some fresh air." She led the way through the kitchen and out the back door. Pausing on the wide porch, she spread her arms out. "This is it."

"Wow." He took the steps slowly, his gaze sweeping from side to side as he took it all in. "You tend to this yourself?"

"Yep. I learned from my grandmother. She was a much better gardener than I ever will be."

"You're doing a great job. No wonder your friend wants to have her wedding here. Have you thought about renting it out for weddings?"

"Up until recently, there hasn't been much call for social events in Butte Plains, but now that the town is growing again, I might. We'll see how this one goes. There's a lot involved." And, with a baby to take care of, her time was going to be limited. Once this one was done, she'd have contacts for the rentals, so maybe she could hire someone to coordinate with the bride and groom. All she'd have to do was collect the money and pay the bills.

"The town is growing by leaps and bounds. I'd think a venue like this could be successful. You should give it some thought."

"I will. Thanks." They strolled the gravel pathways in silence while he took photos. Roseanne wiped a bead of sweat from her forehead.

"I'd better get back. I'm supposed to meet with my designer and head carpenter later. I can't wait to show them these pictures." Roseanne pointed out the shortcut she'd used the other day then watched as he found his way to the construction site. Her grandmother would be so proud to know her home and gardens were being used as inspiration to save another grand old home.

While she'd been out back, Kay had come in through the front. They met up in the kitchen. "Is it that time already?" Roseanne asked.

"It will be soon. Our first guest for the night should be here soon. I just wanted to check the rooms out one more time, make sure everything is shipshape."

"That's a good idea." She told her assistant about letting Mr. Tucker photograph the rooms. "I doubt he moved anything, but just in case."

"Thanks for letting me know. I'll be sure to look for anything out of place on my mini-tour." She folded a dish rag and hung it neatly over the edge of the sink. "If he brings the others at an inconvenient time for you, I'd be happy to show them around. I think it's wonderful that The Yellow Rose will be a part of restoring that house to its former glory."

"Me, too. I don't know who bought the place, but they can't be all bad if they're willing to pay what it must cost to restore the old girl to her former glory."

Kay shook her head. "That must cost a fortune. Just look at what a tract house costs these days."

"I know. It's crazy what people pay for cookie-cutter construction. Give me an old house, drafts and all any day."

"I'm with you. My place isn't anywhere as grand as yours, but it's a far cry from those ugly boxes they're building out near the freeway." She glanced at her watch. "Better go check the rooms. I'll listen for the bell, so don't you worry. I've got this under control."

The older woman hurried off. Roseanne poured herself a glass of sweet tea from the pitcher in the refrigerator, grabbed a muffin from the plate in the center of the kitchen island, and headed to her office. A few more details then she'd call it a day.

CHAPTER TEN

"You were able to tour The Yellow Rose?" Scott had hoped the contractor would take his advice and visit the bed-and-breakfast for inspiration. Roseanne loved her grandmother's home, and nothing short of a dwelling equally as spectacular would ever convince her to leave it. That's why he'd hired Tucker Construction. They had a reputation as the best restoration specialist in Texas.

"The owner herself gave me the tour. Thanks for pointing me in the right direction. I took a zillion pictures. I thought my designer was going to swoon, and my carpenter almost had a heart attack at the thought of having to recreate some of those details."

"If he's not up to the task, find someone who is. Money is no object."

"You sure about that? This is going to cost a fortune. All that woodwork has to be handcrafted. Can't pick that stuff off the shelves these days."

"I'm sure. Whatever it takes. Just send me the bill."

"I will, don't worry. And I'm sure my carpenter is up to the task. His concern is the timeline. He doesn't want to rush."

"I'm anxious to see the place finished, but tell him to take as long as he needs to do it right. And since money is no object, if he knows someone skilled enough to help him, hire him."

"Got it. I'll tell him." He went on about the progress being made, throwing out questions Scott answered or jotted down to think about. Since he planned to live there the rest of his life with Roseanne and their brood of kids, he wanted to do it right.

"Anything else?"

"Just that if you want a garden to rival the one at the bed-and-breakfast, you better hire a damned good gardener and landscape architect."

"Done, and done," Scott said. "Anything else?"

"You still want me to keep your name out of it? Refer any questions to Riley?"

"Until you hear otherwise from me. You okay with that?"

"You're the boss. Talk to you soon." The line went dead.

Scott stared at the screensaver on his cell phone. He'd taken the photo of Roseanne in Las Vegas. It was their first night in the glittering city, and they had tickets to see Becky's younger brother, Colin, perform at one of the casinos on the strip. Roseanne had outshone all the lights along the fabled road in her simple, classic evening gown. He'd begged her to let him take the picture. Other than a few candid shots, it was the only other one he had of her. He kept it front and center so he could look at it anytime he wanted to—a reminder of his goal—to make her his forever. Even if it took forever.

He hated living a stealth life, but he didn't have much choice. As long as Roseanne thought he had no ties to Butte Plains, she wasn't going to have anything to do with him. He couldn't blame her. Her life was here, and it was a good one. He'd never dream of asking her to give it up to move to a place where she didn't know a soul or have any ties with the community. It was much easier for him to pick up and move since he'd never really felt like he belonged in the world into which he'd been born. It was only right that he make a home for himself and the family he wanted in a place of his choosing. And he chose Butte Plains.

The town had grown on him. Ford said like a fungus, but Scott knew better. The town had history. It had character. It had opportunity and challenge. All those things drew him there, made him want to add his mark to the future of the town. In the weeks since he'd left The Yellow Rose, his secretary, Riley, had successfully moved their entire office from New York to Dallas. The two of them had set up a corporation to buy and restore real estate in and around Butte Plains, keeping Scott's name out of the transactions. He wanted to make his mark in the town, but didn't necessarily want the recognition that normally came along with dropping boatloads of cash in a small space. He'd rather see the longtime residents take pride in their hometown and rise to the occasion. He knew they would. The anonymous donation he'd made to the parks department had brought out a lot of enthusiastic people to clean up the town square in order for the city crews to come in and make the repairs necessary to make the place inhabitable again.

Dozens of folks had carried trash bags and sticks sharpened on the end to pick up litter. More had gathered fallen limbs and piled them for the landscapers to push through the chipper. Others had helped scrape peeling paint off the gazebo so it could be repainted. There were new trash receptacles on every corner downtown. Parking spaces had been restriped and light poles repaired. Planters had been purchased and hung from light standards. Newly washed windows sparkled in the sun. Tenants who hadn't done anything in years to enhance the curb appeal of their stores were painting and dressing windows with enticing displays.

Money could work wonders, but it was pride and hope that really made a difference. For the first time in his life, he felt that he'd been born wealthy for a reason.

~ ~ ~

"Did you get it?" Roseanne waved her assistant over to the side porch where she'd taken root while the workers lifted the heavy tent roof into place.

At Becky's request, she'd blocked out all the rooms in the B&B for wedding guests, but her friend had been crazy busy at work and had failed to give her a list of names to go with the bookings. Twenty-four hours away from the I do's and she still didn't have a list, so she'd sent Kay over to Adams Manufacturing to see if she could get it from Becky's secretary while Roseanne stayed behind to supervise the setting up of the tent in the front yard.

"Got it right here." Kay brandished a piece of yellow, lined paper as she approached. "How's the tent going?"

"It's getting there. I thought we were going to have to relocate the water line running from the street to the house, but they found another way to anchor the post in question." That snafu had almost sent her into a fit of tears. Lesser things certainly had in the last few weeks—like the tray of cookies she'd burned while looking at cribs online. She'd cried for an hour over the mess. Thank goodness the experienced workers had found a better way to secure the pole and moved on. Otherwise, she might have cried for a week. Absolutely nothing could go wrong with Becky's wedding. She'd made that vow to herself, and she planned on keeping it. She held her hand out. "Here. Let me see that."

It was a short list. They only had the three rooms, after all. She recognized the first one—a cousin to Ford's mother. The woman had stayed at the inn before and was easy to please. The second one would be a bit of a problem if anyone found out he was there. Becky's brother, Colin, had quite the following among teenage and young adult women. The last names on the list rocked Roseanne back against the porch railing. "Oh, no. No. This can't be right."

"What? Is there a problem? Are you okay?" Kay steered Roseanne to one of the rocking chairs lined up along the porch and helped her sit.

"Did you speak to Becky, or did her secretary give this to you?"

"I talked to Becky. As soon as I told the secretary why I was there, she showed me into Ms. Parker's office. She pulled this out of her desk drawer and handed it to me herself."

No wonder her friend hadn't given her the list until today. Becky had deliberately waited until it was too late to make changes.

Besides, where else would she put up Scott's parents, June and Gerald Ramsey? The new cut-rate motel on the interstate certainly wouldn't do, and Ford's familial home was filled with Adams relatives and family friends. That left one place in town. Her place. *Damn you, Becky Jean Parker-Adams.* Roseanne swiped at the damp line streaking down her cheek.

"Is everything okay? Do you want me to call Ms. Parker?"

"No." She sniffed and straightened her spine. Tears would only smudge the writing, not make the problem go away. She sniffed and blinked a few times to clear her vision. "Nothing to be worried about." She handed the list back. "Put the Ramsey's in the Senator's Suite. Mrs. Ellis likes the pink room on the side of the house. I'm sure Colin won't mind taking the blue room that overlooks the front yard."

"You sure you're fine?" Kay seemed reluctant to leave her, so Roseanne stood and forced a smile for her assistant.

"I'm fine. Everything is fine. Tent is almost up. Our guests are squared away. Mr. McKenna delivered the champagne while you were gone. I didn't know Becky had ordered beer, but there's a bunch of that, too, along with liquor for the bars that will be set up in the tent."

"I hope there's room in the cooler everything."

"If not, can we find some picnic coolers? I'm sure Mr. McKenna will deliver some bags of ice if we need them."

"Good idea. I'll go down to the cellar and eyeball the situation. Don't worry about a thing. If we need more space, I know some people to call."

"You're a godsend, Kay. What would I do without you?"

"Pishposh. What nonsense." She waved away her employer's concern. "You know I'm not going anywhere — except to the cellar."

Soon, the tent was up. Roseanne went over the placement of the stage, dance floor, tables, and bars with the crew before going inside. Out of necessity, she'd put the fact that Scott's parents were going to be staying under her roof for the next few days out of her mind, but the minute she sat down, her concerns came roaring back. Did Scott know? Surely he'd offered them a room in the gatehouse he was staying in on the Adams estate. Maybe he didn't know they were attending the wedding. She dismissed that idea as soon as she thought it. Scott and the groom were thick as thieves. Why else would Ford invite Scott's parents to his wedding?

"Nothing I can do about it now," she muttered to herself. She'd look like an ungracious ogre if she asked Becky to find another place for them to stay. This new wrinkle put her in an awkward position. She'd planned on telling Scott about the baby after the wedding, but with his parents under her roof, she couldn't see doing so. She'd come off as the world's biggest gold digger. She could see it now. "Welcome to The Yellow Rose, and oh, by the way…I'm pregnant with your first grandchild."

Yeah, that would go over well. Ramsey lawyers would descend on her like a swarm of locusts, demanding tests and custody contracts. A sudden pain stabbed at her brain, like she'd drunk an ice-cold beverage too fast. Lord, she'd never thought about Scott and his family wanting custody of her child. She couldn't afford lawyers to fight the kind of battle they could wage. What judge wouldn't see they could provide everything she couldn't? She'd lose custody for sure.

I can't tell them. Not now, at least. Not until I have a lawyer and know more about my rights. She'd take the name of the baby's father to her grave before she'd let a bunch of rich strangers take her child away from her.

She reached for the small directory she kept with names and numbers of business contacts. Her hands shook as she thumbed through the pages until she found the listing she had in mind. Hank was an old friend who had grown up in Butte Plains and now had a law office in Dallas. He'd handled the probate of her grandmother's estate years ago. With a little luck, he'd still consider her a client, as well as a friend, and give her a good rate on advice.

Taking a deep breath, she dialed his number.

CHAPTER ELEVEN

Scott watched the Ramsey jet's wheels touch down on the runway. "Hot damn! Looked smooth as a baby's butt."

"Congratulations," Ford said. "Your new airstrip is officially christened."

"It took long enough. All those permits to reopen the place, not to mention replacing the outdated runway and getting the tower recertified. I was beginning to think it wouldn't ever happen."

"Well, it has, and it's fitting that your parents were the first ones to land here."

Scott nodded. "Yeah. But don't expect them to be enthusiastic about it. They're here to change my mind about making this my permanent home." He glanced around the small but well-appointed building that functioned as the office, waiting area, and control tower. The remodel had been expensive, most of the money going to the tower equipment. Right now, he couldn't justify the money he was spending to keep a full-time air traffic controller on duty, but he hoped traffic would pick up once people learned the airstrip was back in operation and better than ever.

"Here they come." Ford pointed out the window. A golf cart driven by one of his employees headed their way. His father rode in the front next to the driver, his mother in the back. "There's still time. I could ask my mother to put them up at her house. The

Yellow Rose isn't exactly a five-star resort."

"Granted, I wish that invitation to your wedding had never been sent, but since they're here, they might as well see what this town is all about. Besides, my dad grew up in a house almost identical to Roseanne's. He should feel right at home." Scott laughed at his own joke.

"If you say so."

Clearly, Ford wasn't convinced. Scott hated saddling Roseanne with the Ramseys, but he had little choice. He just hoped his parents brought their manners with them. If they didn't, and insulted Roseanne or her home, there might be pistols at dawn. If it came to that, he'd bet on Roseanne any day. His parents wouldn't stand a chance.

Scott pushed the wide, glass doors open. "Mom. Dad. Welcome to Butte Plains Airport."

The older couple's smiles were as plastic as their sunglasses.

"It's good to see you, son." Gerald Ramsey clapped Scott on the back. "Ford! Congratulations!"

"Thank you, sir." Ford and the elder Ramsey shook hands.

June Ramsey followed close on the heels of her husband, giving first her son then Ford a hug. Her gaze scanned the space that constituted the public spaces. "This is so nice, Scott. Look, Gerald." She pointed to a large painting hanging over an arrangement of black leather chairs. "That's lovely."

"It's an original painting by a local artist," Scott said. "I bought several of his pieces for the building. The rest are down the hall and in the pilot's lounge."

"I'd love to see them. May I?" June asked.

"Sure. This way." Scott led them through the building, stopping so his mother could admire the artwork. This, at least, he knew wasn't fake. His mother had always had an interest in art. She'd spent a small fortune on the paintings that graced the walls of their Hamptons estate.

June paused in front of a landscape depicting a West Texas

sunset. The colors were vibrant and the setting serene. "Makes you want to go there, doesn't it?"

"Nothing keeping us from doing that," Gerald said.

"We've never really explored Texas," she said. "Maybe we should."

"Let's get Ford married then we'll see. I'd love to have that painting or one like it."

"I don't know if I want to part with this one," Scott said, "but you can speak with the artist. I think he has more in that series. He'd probably part with one of them for the right price."

"Oh, I'm so excited," his mother said. "Who knew we'd find something like this in Texas?" You would have thought she'd just landed on Mars. Scott kept that thought to himself and showed them to the next room.

"There's a lot more to the state than most people know," Ford said. "Everything from wide-open spaces in the west to dense forest in the east, rolling hills and lakes in the central section, and some of the most beautiful beaches in the world along the Gulf Coast. You could spend a lifetime here and not see it all."

"Then we've got to at least hit the highlights, Gerald."

"I agree, June. Let's get settled in. We don't want to be late for the rehearsal dinner tonight. Gotta meet the filly who convinced Ford to settle down." He winked at his son's best friend.

"Becky is excited to meet you, too," Ford said. "Come on. Scott and I will drop you off at the bed-and-breakfast then we've got to run a couple of errands before the shindig tonight." They made their way out to the parking area where Scott's new Land Rover waited for them. Someone had already piled their luggage in the back.

"Scott said the wedding and reception will be on the lawn?" His mother peered over her designer lenses at Ford.

"That's right. The Yellow Rose has one of the most beautiful gardens in the county, maybe in all of Texas. The owner is also Becky's best friend, Roseanne Meadows. Her grandparents bought the house when they first married and put in the garden. Roseanne has done a great job of keeping it up since she inherited and turned the house into a bed-and-breakfast."

"It reminds me of Grandmother Ramsey's house," Scott said.

"Is it as drafty as my mother's home?" Gerald asked.

As he'd feared, they'd left the better part of their manners in New York. Scott shrugged. "You always said those were ghosts, not drafts."

"That's what Granddad always told me. It was a crock of shit but kept me from complaining about how cold the place was."

"Well, as hot as it is this summer, you won't have to worry about drafts at The Yellow Rose," Scott said.

"Please tell me it's air-conditioned." Gerald pulled a handkerchief from his pocket and wiped imaginary sweat from his brow.

"Trust me, Dad. You're going to love it." Scott glanced in the rearview mirror at his dad, his expression warning the older man to hush.

Ford mouthed, "It's not too late," then turned to look out the windshield when Scott shook his head.

They pulled into the driveway of the inn a few minutes later. The giant tent on the front lawn kept them from seeing the front of the house, but the side view was almost as impressive.

"Oh my," June exclaimed. "I see what you mean, Scott. This is so much like Grandmother Ramsey's house." She walked around to the wide steps leading to the front door.

"I stayed here the first few months I was in town," Scott said. "Wait until you see the woodwork. It's all hand carved." And worth a fortune, he now knew. The man he'd hired to replicate the moldings for the house around the corner was charging him an arm and a leg.

Ford bounded up the stairs and opened the front door. A bell jingled, alerting the staff.

"This is beautiful," June said, running her hand over the

stained glass insert in the door, depicting a bouquet of yellow roses. "Is this original to the house?"

"Yes, it is." At the sound of the familiar woman's voice, Scott looked up. Roseanne stood in the entryway, looking tired but beautiful. She wore tan slacks and a sleeveless blouse in cream. Her hair was pulled up in a high ponytail, revealing tiny gold earrings and the slim column of her neck. When she extended her hand to his mother, he noticed her nails were painted a pale pink—probably to match the dress she would wear tomorrow as Becky's bridesmaid. "My grandmother said she wanted that window, and the only way she could get it was to buy the whole house. So, she convinced my grandfather to purchase it for her as a wedding present."

"That's so romantic," June said, taking Roseanne's hand. "I'm June Ramsey, and this is my husband, Gerald."

"Roseanne Meadows. Welcome to The Yellow Rose."

"I grew up in a house very much like this one," Gerald said. "Cold as a well digger's ass in the winter and hot as Hades in the summer."

"Then you know all about the quirks of an old house," Roseanne said. How she managed to keep her smile in place, he'd never know.

"You mean the creaking floors?"

"And the wavy glass in the windows," Roseanne added. "All the windows in the house are original, handmade glass. I thought about replacing them with modern, double-pane windows but decided the energy savings wasn't enough to sacrifice the historic detail."

"Humph."

"Gerald!" June scolded her husband.

"Let me show you to your room." Roseanne started up the stairs, leaving them to follow.

Scott caught Roseanne's gaze when she stopped and opened the door to the Senator's Suite. Had she purposely arranged for his parents to sleep in the same bed where he and Roseanne had made love countless times? Judging from the smirk on her face, yes, she'd done it on purpose.

He followed his folks into the room and hefted the two suitcases he'd carried onto the bed. Ford came in with two more. His parents thought packing light meant no dark-colored clothing.

"Is this all there is?" his father asked as he took one step into the bathroom, coming back out as if he expected the room to have miraculously expanded.

"You have a full bath, queen-sized bed, writing desk, and armoire. You'll find extra towels stacked in the armoire." Roseanne recited her innkeeper's speech with mechanical precision.

He could almost see her calculating which object in the room would make the biggest dent in his father's head.

The paperweight. No sooner had he thought it than her gaze landed on the blown glass object sitting on the desk. She'd never in a million years actually bash him on the head, but he gave her kudos for thinking it. She wasn't going to take any guff off his parents, and that pleased him to no end.

"We'll be fine," his mother said, ushering them out in that way she had of being polite while still telling you to fuck off.

They went. The last one out, Scott paused. "Rehearsal is at six. No need for you to be there. Dinner will be in the dining room downstairs. See you then."

As soon as he and Ford were in the car, Scott said, "That went well."

"It went better than I expected."

Scott backed out of the driveway and pointed the SUV north. "First, tell me where we're going." Becky had made him swear to keep Ford on task today and tomorrow, and he was taking his duty seriously.

"Back to the airstrip. I chartered a private plane for Becky's brother."

"Where's he staying?"

"Same place as your parents."

"Oh, boy. That's going to be interesting."

"It's not as interesting as the reason you didn't invite Roseanne to your parents' party, so give."

Scott braked for a four-way stop. He let another car turn in front of him before proceeding through the intersection. "Let's just say I had my head stuck up my ass at the time. That's my only excuse."

"That's a valid excuse. Are you going to tell her about the house or the buildings you bought?"

"Not yet. As long as I'm living in your mother's gatehouse, I'm still a temporary resident. Once I've got my roots sunk deep, I'll tell her."

"So, you're going to stay even if she doesn't come around?"

"Yep. Everything I want is here. My woman, my businesses, my best friend…and his wife. The great state of Texas is stuck with me. Is there a test I have to take to officially become a Texan?" He swung the car into the parking area at the airstrip. Other than the cars parked in the spaces reserved for employees, theirs was the only vehicle in the lot. He hoped that changed soon as others in the region learned the airstrip had reopened.

"It's called a driver's test. Pass that and you're official."

"I did that last week. Even registered to vote and bought a Lone Star Flag for the pole I'm putting up at the house."

"Sounds like you've got it covered, except for the accent. You might want to hire a speech therapist."

"Hey, I've picked up a few things. I can say y'all, over yonder, and thar as in, that thar is a plane." He pointed at the sky where a sleek jet angled toward the runway.

"That's a good start," Ford said as he reached for the door handle.

"Damn straight it is." Scott opened his door.

PART TWO

"Even the rich are hungry for love, for being cared for, for
being wanted, for having someone to call their own."
Mother Teresa

CHAPTER TWELVE

The big day had finally arrived. Roseanne had done all she could do, for the time being. Becky looked radiant in her designer gown, and Ford could have walked off the pages of GQ in his hand-tailored tux. From the bouquet of imported pink roses to the custom-made cake and sparkling champagne to be consumed later, no detail had been overlooked or compromised on. Roseanne had worked diligently to make the garden behind The Yellow Rose B&B a showplace fit to be the backdrop for the intimate gathering of friends and family, but as she listened to the groom pledge his eternal love, she let her gaze wander to the rose-covered trellis shading the happy couple. She'd used every gardening trick her grandmother had taught her, and her fingers had suffered, but the vines eventually submitted to her will, blooming beautifully to form the most romantic setting she could imagine.

Roseanne pressed the rumpled tissue to the corner of one eye then the other. Becky would never forgive her for having raccoon eyes in the post-ceremony photos, but damn, hearing her best friend pledge to love, honor, and cherish, even though it was only for show, had her fighting to keep the waterworks at bay. She'd been maid of honor at Ford and Becky's impromptu wedding in Las Vegas a few months ago, so it wasn't like she hadn't had time to get used to the idea, but that had been different. Yes, she'd been happy for the couple then, but in their haste to wed, they'd skimped on most everything that made a wedding special. Not so today. Though they could afford a much more elaborate affair, they'd gone for small and elegant instead.

Someone cleared their throat. Roseanne looked in the direction of the sound, and her gaze locked with her counterpart across the makeshift altar. The best man raised one eyebrow and cocked his head toward the bride and groom. Roseanne turned to see the officiant holding his prayer book out, his finger tapping the page.

Crap! She gave her best friend an apologetic smile and dropped the groom's ring in the center of the book. Across the way, the best man repeated the process with the bride's ring then captured Roseanne's gaze again. She looked away before the devilish smirk on Scott Ramsey's face lured her in. She'd fallen for it more times than she could count, but no more. There was much more at stake now. She couldn't afford the luxury of giving in to her desires. She'd done so before and look where it had gotten her — pregnant and single.

She returned the best man's gaze with a hard stare then focused all her attention on the smiling couple as they, without hesitation, professed their love for one another before God and as many people as could squeeze into the Victorian garden.

After a highly inappropriate kiss, Ford and Becky Adams faced the crowd then stepped off the small, raised platform. Amid cheers and applause, they made their exit. Steeling herself for Scott Ramsey's touch, Roseanne wrapped her fingers around the arm he offered, and, focusing on the retreating bride and groom, allowed the love of her life to escort her down the flower-strewn path to the bed-and-breakfast she called home.

"I should spank your ass for that," Scott said.

Despite her resolve to remain unaffected by him, his softly spoken comment hit its mark. Arousal tingled across her skin then made a beeline to the juncture of her thighs where it set up a primal drumbeat. Every step, every swish of pink chiffon against her skin exacerbated her condition until she thought she might expire from want of something she'd willfully given up. Once again, she questioned her decision to end their relationship. She missed their physical connection almost as much as she missed talking with him. He was smart, and funny, and a good storyteller. To say they were compatible in bed would be a gross understatement.

She caught a glimpse of his parents in the small crowd gathered to witness Ford and Becky's nuptials. Reality crashed down on her shoulders. Scott was more like them than he was like her. *And therein lies the problem.* Different worlds had collided and created a new universe.

The best she could hope for would be for Scott to go back to New York with his parents after the wedding. She'd wait a few months then call him and tell him about the baby. Just so he'd know, not because she wanted anything from him.

She risked a glance at her escort. From the moment she'd laid eyes on Scott Ramsey, she'd been a goner. Too handsome by far, he usually played his gorgeousness down by wearing T-shirts and worn denim. In his designer tux, he took her breath away. She had to get away from him before her last brain cell died from lack of oxygen. Officially a member of the wedding party, she had other responsibilities she needed to tend to before she could relax and be the perfect maid of honor Becky deserved for the remainder of the evening.

Removing her hand from his forearm took the last of her willpower. "I've got to check on the dinner," she said, putting distance between them before she gave in and told him everything. "I won't be long."

She'd make a pass through the kitchen while the guests made their way to the front lawn for cocktails under the big tent that had been set up for the occasion. Once she knew the help hired for the night had everything under control, she'd return to the garden to pose for pictures with the bride and groom.

~ ~ ~

Scott stood rooted to the spot as Roseanne entered the house, closing the door with authority. Not exactly slamming it—she'd never disrupt the proceedings in such a way. He loved that she was too much of a lady to let her personal drama intrude on her friend's moment. None of the women who ran in his social circles back home in New York would think twice about creating a scene at another person's wedding.

He wandered back to the rose arbor where the bride and groom posed for photos. For a guy who'd left home for greener pastures, vowing never to return, Ford looked like a proud bull standing in sweet clover. When the photographer called for the groom's parents to join the couple, Scott noticed the momentary lapse in Ford's good mood. His father's death had brought him home to Butte Plains a little over a year ago, and he still grieved the man's passing. If not for the stipulation in the will that Ford keep the family business in operation for twelve months before selling or closing, his friend would never have hung around long enough to get to know the woman he'd just pledged to love, honor, and cherish for the rest of his life.

And I wouldn't have met Roseanne.

Thoughts of the vexing woman should have soured his mood, but he couldn't help himself where she was concerned. He wanted her. He needed her. He would have her. Again.

Ford's voice cut through the night. "Scott Ramsey! Get your ass over here."

Scott stepped forward. "You sure you want my ugly mug in your pictures? You know you're going to have to look at them for the rest of your life, don't you?"

"He knows," the bride said. "I cautioned him to choose his best man wisely for that very reason."

"And I still chose you, so get over here," Ford said. "Let's get this done so I can dance with my bride."

Scott took his place beside his best friend and smiled for the camera while, inside, his gut churned.

"Hey, Roseanne! Get over here!" Ford waved his hand and yelled over the heads of the guests who'd wandered back, cocktails in hand, to observe.

"I'm coming!" came the breathless reply. Scott hid a juvenile snicker behind his hand.

The crowd parted, allowing Roseanne through, but the moment she breached the front line, she stopped short. The bride and groom weren't alone. Scott Ramsey stood beside Ford, his gaze locked on her. A familiar fire burned there, threatening to reduce her resolve to cinders. Past experience told her it didn't take much to ignite his fire, but she wondered what she'd done this time.

A part of her reveled in the knowledge she affected him so easily—payback for what he did to her. But another part of her realized that women who played with fire often got burned.

"Stand here beside me," Becky urged, sweeping her train behind her with one hand while she held fast to her husband with the other. "We'll get one of the four of us then I want one of you and Scott together."

Oh Lord. She'd expected the photo with the small wedding party, but not the one of her and Scott together. She'd thought she was through touching him for the evening. Would it look strange to put a foot or two of distance between them? Of course it would. That's why, when the bride and groom stepped from the arbor, she allowed Scott to pull her close with an arm around her waist.

Following the photographer's instructions, they angled slightly so the back of her thigh pressed against the front of Scott's. He placed one hand on her hip, steadying her. Holding her bouquet of pink roses in her hands, she couldn't even swat at Scott's other hand where he'd molded it to her ass.

While the man with the camera fiddled with the lens or some such, Scott leaned in so his warm breath fanned across her neck. "Do you remember the day we met? I wanted you then. I want you even more now."

Roseanne stifled the groan rising in her throat and, hoping to dislodge his hand, shuffled on her feet. All she managed to do was stroke her ass against his wide palm, causing him to grip her hip tighter. "Be still and smile at the camera."

She smiled at the camera, but through the lens of time, she saw the day, the exact moment Fate put this man in her path. She'd been in her office, trying to add two and two and make five, or more, if possible. The sagging economy had reduced business at the B&B to a fickle stream, flush when rain poured down on the citizens of Butte Plains, dry as dust when it didn't. She'd had a full house the week before due to the funeral for Kenneth Adams, Ford's father, but until the next storm, she didn't have a single booking. Then in walked Scott Ramsey, a Viking from the frozen north. A Yankee sent to steal her heart. He'd done that, and so much more.

"All done." The photographer's dismissal sent a wave of relief through her body, but, as she lifted her foot to step from the casual embrace, Scott's arm snaked across her front, dragging her hard against his front. The heavy ridge of his erection pressed against her ass, making her all too aware of her own needs. The very same ones that had landed her in her current predicament.

"I don't want to let you go." His words whispered across her skin. "You want me, too. Don't even try to deny it."

She couldn't. Wouldn't. He'd never believe her anyway. Desire wasn't their problem.

"Let me go," she said, pulling at his wrist. "I've got to get everyone seated so the staff can serve dinner before everything gets cold."

"When this is all over, we need to talk."

For the span of a heartbeat, she thought he knew her secret, but then he gave her rear end a playful slap and said, "Go on, Little Bo Peep. I'll help herd the sheep into the tent."

She went. As fast as possible without spooking the guests into a stampede. Safe inside the kitchen, she willed her racing heart to calm. He couldn't know. He simply wanted to press his case for them being a couple one more time. Perhaps lure her into his bed again. It wouldn't be difficult. It seemed the same hormones that made her weepy and sick also made her horny, and there was no one she wanted to be with except Scott Ramsey. He stirred her libido like no one else ever had—a fact she kept reminding herself was no reason to marry the guy.

Like he would have me. She glanced out the window. Scott made a good sheep dog. Only a few stragglers remained in the garden, but her baby daddy was on the case, rounding them up and steering them to the path leading around to the front yard.

Roseanne turned and held up her hand, fingers splayed. "Five-minute warning. Start with table one and work your way back." She found the head caterer and pulled her aside. "I'll be at table one. If you have any problems or questions, send someone to get me."

"Don't worry about a thing, Ms. Meadows. We've got it under control," the older woman said. "My staff has done this a hundred times or more. You just go. Enjoy the rest of the evening. We'll serve and cleanup then be out of here before you know it."

CHAPTER THIRTEEN

Roseanne did a quick tour inside the tent, making sure the bartenders had everything they needed and that the DJ understood the schedule. Becky's brother, Colin, sang a song during the ceremony that he'd written for the couple and planned to sing a couple more songs—just him and his guitar—after dinner. He was also acting as the Master of Ceremonies.

Satisfied everything was in place, she took her seat next to the bride. Scott occupied the seat on the other side of the groom. Becky and Ford's mother's, Becky's brother, and Ford's aunt rounded out the head table which was covered with a white tablecloth overlaid with shimmering pink taffeta. The bride's bouquet rested in a vase in the center, flanked by smaller arrangements of pink and white roses alternating with pink and white tapers. The other tables were similarly decorated. Crystal stemware and silver flatware reflected light from chandeliers hanging from the tent struts that were strung with pink tulle.

"There you are," Becky said. "I haven't had a chance to thank you for all you've done."

"No thanks necessary."

"Well, you're getting them anyway. Everything is beautiful—just like I knew it would be. Ford and I can't thank you enough."

"She's right," Ford said. "I'm simply amazed. Have you

thought about becoming a wedding or event planner? You could do it, you know?"

"That's very nice of you to say, but I've got enough on my plate as it is. Still, if you need my help putting something together for Adams Manufacturing, just let me know. I'll give you the friends and family rate."

"What about me?" Scott said. "Can I get the friends and family rate, too?"

Roseanne caught Becky's curious look but refused to take the bait. "Locals only, Mr. Ramsey."

"What if I was a local? Would I qualify then?"

More than you know. More than you know. Becky kicked her under the table. Roseanne shot her a look meant to silence her. The last thing she needed was Scott picking up on the nonverbal clues flying between her and the bride. He wasn't an idiot. He'd know something was up, and he wouldn't stop until he found out what it was. "Since you aren't then I see no point in speculating."

A team of waiters arrived with their plated meals, and the conversation turned once again to the wedding.

"This is out of this world," Ford said, as he stabbed another slice of Tournedos of Beef Forestiere. "Is this your recipe, Roseanne?"

"Everything on the menu is from one of my recipes." She dipped her fork into her Chateau Potatoes. "I was fortunate to find a caterer who was willing to prepare my recipes instead of insisting on their own."

"I know," Becky said. "The food at these things is usually blah, but oh my God"—she savored a bite of Creamed Carrots and Minted Green Pea Timbales—"this is beyond delicious."

Everyone else at the table complimented the cuisine except Scott who seemed to be attacking his plate like a starving man. Roseanne couldn't think of a better compliment.

"Are you going to put these recipes in your cookbook?" Ford asked. "'Cause, if you are, I'm going to buy Becky a copy."

"Hey!" Becky elbowed her husband. "Are you saying I can't cook?"

"No. I'm saying you can't cook like this." He smiled at his bride, taking the sting out of his words.

Becky shrugged. "He's right. I can barely boil water, much less prepare something this good." She took a sip from her wineglass. "Ford would benefit from the recipes more than I would. He's a great cook."

Scott looked up from his empty plate. "I keep hearing about this cookbook, but I haven't seen it yet. What gives?"

"Roseanne is working on a cookbook," Ford said. "Isn't that right, Roseanne?"

She glanced around the table. All eyes were trained on her. "It's a silly dream," she explained. "I've been querying agents. If I can't find representation, I might self-publish the book."

"What do you need an agent for?" Becky's mom asked.

Roseanne briefly explained what she knew of the publishing industry then turned the conversation back to the bride and groom, where it belonged. Pretty soon, questions about their honeymoon plans were flying, as well as hints from their mothers about the grand babies they hoped would be arriving soon. Roseanne remained silent, picking at the last of her meal. As soon as Ford's mother had brought up the subject of babies, Roseanne had lost her appetite. Feeling as if someone were watching her, she glanced up. Her gaze collided with Scott's and held.

The waiters returned to clear the empty plates. Colin stood. "That's my cue. Got to get this party started."

Roseanne pushed her chair back. "I'll just make sure the DJ—"

"I've got it, Roseanne," Colin said.

"You're sure?" She sat back down.

"Positive. You just work on your maid-of-honor toast. I'll call you up when it's time."

As instructed, the wait staff delivered individual personalized tissue packs along with coffee and scoops of homemade butter pecan ice cream. Colin took to the stage, and everyone settled in to listen to another original song he'd written for the occasion. He followed that up with a toast to his older sister and her husband. The first tissues came out as he spoke of his sister's unselfishness that allowed him to pursue his love of music while she gave up her dream of working for a large marketing company in a big city. There wasn't a dry eye in the place as the guests lifted glasses of expensive French champagne to the bride's happiness.

Scott took Colin's place at the podium. His eloquent toast spoke of the family we choose as opposed to the family we're born with, emphasizing the fact he thought of Ford as a brother as well as his best friend. Roseanne used the corner of her napkin to collect the tears forming in her eyes as he held his champagne glass aloft. "To friends, the family we choose."

She tipped her glass along with everyone else—only the liquid never met her lips.

Since the men had toasted to the bride and groom individually, Roseanne raised a toast to the couple, wishing both of them a lifetime of love and adventure. As she lifted the champagne flute, she signaled the audio/visual technician. Suddenly, the lights dimmed and a giant screen deployed behind the stage. The guests' reactions were priceless as, one by one, they figured out what they were watching on the screen. When Elvis began to sing "Love Me Tender," a single spotlight lit the center of the dance floor, and in that beam of light, the newlyweds swayed to the music.

Cameras flashed all around, capturing the couple's first dance then Scott took Roseanne's hand and led her to the dance floor. Pretty soon, the parquet square was filled with dancing couples.

As soon as the song ended, the DJ began an instrumental version of the same song, playing it low so everyone could hear the vows Becky and Ford had spoken to each other in Las Vegas. The crowd in the tent cheered when the couple kissed on screen and reenacted the scene right there in the middle of the dance floor surrounded by friends and family.

Roseanne sniffed back tears.

"Here. I saved some of my tissues for you." Scott handed her a nearly full packet of tissues bearing the custom logo Ford had designed for their wedding. "Do you always cry this much at weddings?"

She dabbed at her eyes and used his chest as a shield while she blew her nose. "I don't know. I've only been to two — both of them for Becky and Ford."

"The guests are eating this up," he said. "I was afraid there might be a mutiny when everyone found out they've been married for months."

Ford and Becky were somewhere in the center of the mob that had surrounded them, as the video faded to black, and the date and location of the wedding filled the screen.

"The bride and groom are so happy, everyone has already forgiven them for keeping the secret," Roseanne said.

"I suppose. Can't imagine doing this more than once, though."

Roseanne choked back a sob. She'd dreamed countless times of becoming Scott Ramsey's bride, but no more. The thought of someone else walking down the aisle, speaking sacred vows with him, nearly brought her to her knees. She stumbled. Scott caught her easily, holding her close. "God, I knew this was too much for you. Let's get you to your seat."

"I'm fine," she protested as he supported almost her entire weight. "I can walk."

"Just let me help you."

She couldn't do otherwise without causing a scene, so she let him half carry her back to their table. As soon as she was seated, he shoved a water glass at her.

"Drink this. Better lay off the champagne until you get some food in your belly."

He'd noticed she'd barely eaten her meal but failed to notice she'd only lifted her champagne glass to her mouth. She hadn't even allowed the liquid to touch her lips. "I was saving room for cake."

"You have someone taking care of the cake cutting, right?"

"Ford and Becky's moms asked if they could be in charge of that. Everything is set up, or it should be."

"I'll check. You sit here." He stood. "What am I looking for? A knife. Some forks and plates?"

"Good grief. It will just take me a second." She stood then gripped the edge of the table as the room began to spin.

"Fuck!" Scott caught her by the elbow and eased her back into her chair. "You aren't going anywhere, unless it's to the hospital."

"I don't need a hospital. I'm fine. I just need to rest a minute."

"You've been overdoing it."

"I have not. It's hot in here, that's all."

"How about a walk in the garden, then? I'll bring you back in time for the cake cutting. I promise."

Roseanne looked around. The DJ had taken over from Colin, and everyone was having a great time, including the bride and groom who were slow dancing to a rock tune that had everyone else bopping around like wind turbines with broken wings. Even Scott's parents were out there, dancing like no one was watching, as the saying went.

"Come on. It's going to be a while before anyone even remembers there's a cake."

Fresh air sounded heavenly. "Okay. But we have to keep an eye on the time. I promised the neighbors the music would be over at a decent hour." She stood slowly, allowing her body time to adjust before she headed for an opening in the panels forming the walls of the tent. Outside, she instantly felt better. Summer nights in Texas couldn't exactly be called cool, but the slight breeze helped.

"Maybe we should open some of the side panels on the tent. I didn't realize how hot it had become until I stepped out here."

"I'll take care of it." He steered her around to the back of the house where the chairs for the ceremony still occupied most of the walkway. "You sit here and don't move until I get back. Promise?"

"I promise. Just get those panels open before someone faints from the heat."

"Will do. Be right back."

CHAPTER FOURTEEN

Roseanne picked up a program that had been left on an adjacent chair and fanned herself. She hadn't been all that hot until Scott had taken her out on the dance floor. It wasn't physical exertion that had heated her blood, but being in his arms. The heat of his body pressed up against hers had sent her libido into overdrive. Couple that with the heat of all those bodies in such close quarters, and you had a recipe for disaster. Lucky for her, Scott was big and strong enough to support her; otherwise, she would have collapsed right there on the dance floor.

She could see it now. Someone would call the paramedics and, before they gave her any meds, she'd have to tell them she was pregnant. Thank goodness Scott hadn't insisted she get medical help; otherwise, her secret would be out, and not in a good way. *I'll tell him. Just not tonight.* No way was she bringing her personal drama out. Absolutely nothing was going to ruin Becky and Ford's big night.

Scott returned with two bottles. He cracked the seal on a bottle of water bearing a pink label that read Becky + Ford and the date surrounded by a heart, and handed it to her before opening the bottle he'd snagged for himself. He sat beside her. "I opened panels on two sides. The air is flowing better now. Everything is fine. I think you can take a few minutes to catch your breath."

"Thanks. I've been going nonstop since early this morning. I guess I didn't realize how hard I'd been pushing myself." She took a sip of water. The cool liquid felt good going down.

"Ford and Becky wouldn't want you to make yourself sick."

"I know. I'm sure I'll be fine. The fresh air is helping."

Scott took a sip of his beer. "Damn. This is good." He held the bottle up to the light so he could read the label.

"It's called *You're the One*. It was brewed especially for tonight by a local brewer—Lucky Lady Brewery."

He took another swig and smacked his lips. "Never heard of it."

"It's new. I went into McKenna's Liquor store to talk to Mr. McKenna about placing an order for the bars for tonight, and to ask if he could recommend some bartenders. He'd just received a delivery from Lucky Lady. He said the stuff was really good, so I took a couple of bottles to Ford. He loved it, so I contacted the owner to see about getting a supply for tonight."

"How did you get them to brew a special batch for tonight?"

Roseanne shrugged. "The owner is a woman—Julie Davis. When I told her what I needed it for, she offered. Made the special labels and everything for a reasonable price."

"It's excellent for a small batch brewery." He finished the last of the beer and let out a loud belch.

"Good grief." Roseanne bumped shoulders with him. "At least try to be civilized."

"Why? There's nobody out here but us."

"That was gross."

"That was manly."

"Disgusting." She stifled a laugh. He always knew how to lighten her mood.

"Maybe it was," he conceded. "Sorry."

"Apology accepted."

Ribbing over, their conversation died. Music from the front yard filled the silence between them. Finally, Scott asked, "Tell me about your cookbook."

"I've written one already, and I have enough recipes for several more. I'm trying to find a literary agent, but so far I haven't had any luck. Becky thinks I should self-publish, but I'm not sure I'm up to doing all the work that's involved in something like that. Not and keep the bed-and-breakfast running. I'm going to give it a little more time—see what shakes out—before I decide what to do."

"You're a fabulous cook. I miss the breakfasts you made when I was staying here."

"Thanks. The cook I hired a few months ago is still using my recipes."

"So, not much has changed except that you aren't slaving over a hot stove every morning."

She nodded. "I spend most every afternoon in the kitchen, trying out new recipes and perfecting old ones. I'm sure you've sampled some of my test products. I usually unload them on the unsuspecting employees at Adams Manufacturing."

"That's where all that good stuff in the break room comes from?"

"Yep."

"I'd pay you to drop some of that off at the leather factory. My employees would love it."

"I could do that, but I won't accept payment for it. It's either throw it out, which I can't bear to do, or foist it off on someone else."

"Foist on my employees anytime you want."

"Thanks. I'll do that." Roseanne stood. "I better get back. It's getting late. If I round up the mothers of the bride and groom, can you corral the happy couple? That would save me some time."

"Not a problem. Want me to drag them over to the cake table?"

"If you don't mind."

"Not at all." He put his hand on the small of her back and kept it there as they strolled around to the front yard. The respite had done her good, but the feel of his hand resting possessively on her back reminded her of what they'd once had, and the secret she kept from him. He was a good person, would make an excellent father—if he wanted to. She'd seen the effort he put into getting that old leather factory up and running. If he put even half that much enthusiasm into being a parent, he'd be a good one. But he'd be in New York, and no matter how deeply she believed he'd be a good parent, she couldn't imagine him being a long-distance one.

Inside the tent, she went in search of Ford and Becky's moms. The two of them had inhabited the same city for over two decades, yet they'd never met until recently. From two distinctly different socio-economic groups, they'd orbited the same world, one at the very center, the core, the other on the periphery, so insignificant as to be invisible. Now, they were on equal footing by virtue of their children marrying. As Roseanne watched them collaborate on the details of the cake-cutting ceremony, she couldn't tell which one had traveled the farthest to get to where they were now. They made it look easy, the woman who had been born to wealth, and the one who had scraped by even in the best of times, working together for a common goal—grandkids.

Neither one had been discreet about their wishes. Both widowed, their children grown, they were ready for grandparenthood.

~ ~ ~

Scott spotted his prey. He wove his way through the crowd on the dance floor to where Ford and Becky held court. They looked exhausted but deliriously happy at the same time. He hated to be the one to tell them the night was almost over, but someone had to. This shindig couldn't go on forever. He tapped his best friend on the shoulder.

"You trying to cut in?" Ford asked.

"I would, but Roseanne said it's time to cut the cake."

"Already?" Becky asked. "Seems like we just had dinner."

"That was over an hour ago," Scott said. "The natives are getting restless. They want cake."

"Then, let them eat cake," Ford said, taking his bride by the hand. "Lead the way. We'll follow."

Scott cleared a path to a table set up near the stage. Draped in the same shimmering pink tulle as the guests' tables, it was topped with a huge, four-tiered cake. A ribbon made up of real pink roses cascaded across the top layer and wound down and around to the bottom, reminiscent of the bride's classic gown which gave way in back to a long, ruffled train.

Mrs. Adams and Mrs. Parker teamed up to toast the couple then stepped aside to let them cut the cake.

"Thanks for getting them over here." Roseanne appeared at his side.

"No problem. Where'd you go?"

"I ran to the bathroom. All that water."

Scott chuckled. "At least you aren't dehydrated."

Ford and Becky took turns smashing cake into the other's mouth. As usual, everyone cheered and laughed at the ridiculous custom. Scott knew if he ever got to smear frosting and cake anywhere on the woman at his side, he'd make every effort to lick it all off. From the look on Ford's face, he was having the exact same thought regarding his bride.

"I'm hungry, though. I've had my eye on that cake ever since the bakery delivered it this afternoon. I can't wait to find out if it's as delicious as it looks."

"It does look good." He applauded along with everyone else as the couple intertwined their arms and sipped from champagne flutes engraved with Mr. and Mrs. "Why don't you go sit at the table? I'll grab us a couple of slices."

"Thanks." She walked away.

He'd never seen her look so tired. Maybe it was the stress of putting on such a big event, or that coupled with the heat, but he planned to keep an eye on her. He'd find some excuse to check on her tomorrow, and if she wasn't looking better, she was going to see a doctor. That was all there was to it. He dodged the newlyweds and snagged two slices of cake. He waved off the filled flutes offered to him and grabbed another beer for himself and a water bottle for Roseanne from the bar.

Roseanne was alone at the table. Scott could account for everyone except Colin. He hadn't seen Becky's brother since the video had ended. He'd probably snuck out to meet old friends or something.

"Here you go." He held out the drinks. "Water or beer?"

"I think I'd better stick with water." She took both bottles, placing the beer on his side.

"Probably a good idea," he said as he handed her a plate and fork. "I've got a feeling there are going to be a lot of people here who are going to wish they'd made the same decision come morning."

Roseanne laughed. "Don't you know it? Have you taken a look at the liquor bottles at the bars? A lot of them are almost empty. They weren't small bottles, either."

"And that doesn't take into consideration the amount of champagne and beer that's been consumed."

"True."

They ate in silence for a few minutes then Scott asked, "Is the cake as good as you thought it would be?"

Roseanne forked up another bite. "It's fabulous. I wasn't sure the bakery could duplicate my recipe for such a large batch, but they did a great job I think."

"This is your recipe, too?"

"You like it?"

"It's incredible. I've been to dozens of weddings, and, to be honest, I usually pass on the cake. They're like eating sawdust. I have to say, I'm surprised."

"I'm just full of surprises, Scott Ramsey."

He smiled and took a drink from his beer. "I'm sure you are, Roseanne Meadows. I'm sure you are."

CHAPTER FIFTEEN

Scott sighed. He'd lost track of Roseanne again. She'd nibbled at her cake then excused herself to check on some minor detail. Wandering the tent, looking for her, he almost ran into Ford who had somehow become separated from Becky. "Have you seen Becks?"

"No. Have you seen Roseanne?"

"Can't say that I have." The groom shoved an empty beer bottle into Scott's hand. "Take this, would you? I need to find my bride and drag her out on the dance floor again before the DJ packs it in for the night."

"Don't you have a plane to catch?" Scott looked around for a place to ditch the empty bottle.

Still searching the crowd, Ford said, "Thanks to a very generous friend who loaned us his private jet, we don't have to rush. He assured me the plane wouldn't leave without us."

"Just bring my plane back in one piece, and you're responsible for cleaning the interior if necessary."

Ford smirked. "Thank goodness the seats are leather."

"Go on. Find Becky and dance the night away if you want. The jet will be waiting whenever you get there. Oh, and if I haven't already said it, congratulations. I wish you all the best."

"Thanks, man. I always thought 'the one' was a myth, but

Becky changed my mind." With that, he headed off like a man on a mission. Scott silently wished him well.

A few couples remained on the dance floor, some more skilled than others. Snagging another of the craft brews from the bar set up in the corner, he took a satisfying swig. Whoever the owner of Lucky Lady was, she knew how to brew a good beer. It wouldn't take much to expand the business well beyond the confines of Butte Plains, if she chose to do so.

Why wouldn't she? The business man in him calculated the profits to be made with wide distribution and came up with a number sure to entice any entrepreneur. He sure as hell planned to go wide with his leather goods. He'd signed a contract with Ford and Becky to feature his line of apparel and implements for the BDSM lifestyle through their home shopping network. Next week, he'd be meeting with a popular brick and mortar retailer about carrying his more mainstream products in their stores. Add in his own direct-purchase system, and the sales projections were through the roof.

A murmur swept through the crowd. Scott looked up in time to see the bride and groom take to the dance floor. Scott smiled to himself. Ford had found his woman; it was time he did the same.

He set the empty beer bottle on a service table near the rear entry then made his way down the worn red-brick path that wound around the side of the house to the gardens where the ceremony had taken place. The tiny white lights Roseanne had strung through the branches of the century-old oaks twinkled in the occasional soft breeze, reminding him of Central Park in the summer. Adding to the ambiance, candles in jelly jars dotted the gardens, peeking out from under rose bushes and summer blooms he couldn't begin to identify. Everything about the simple décor screamed romance.

Scott stopped on the pathway, turned, and scanned the back of the house. Lovely in its old age, the Victorian had nothing on its owner who stood silhouetted in the wavy handmade glass of the kitchen window. Roseanne belonged here, in this place, and in this time. She loved the old house she'd inherited from her grandmother, and the house loved her, if that were possible. She nurtured it, and, as if to say thank you, it sparkled like a gem for her.

He blinked, and when he looked again, she'd moved off to take care of some other imagined emergency or such. She'd eventually come back outside, if for no other reason than to snuff the candles. Deciding to wait for her, he crammed his hands in the trouser pockets of his tuxedo and strolled the path.

"The party is in the front yard, Mr. Ramsey."

At the sound of her voice, Scott spun to face the woman he couldn't get out of his system. She stood a safe distance away, but close enough he could make out the lines of fatigue bracketing her eyes and her mouth. He wanted nothing more than to sweep her into his arms and carry her away so he could take care of her.

He smiled, hoping the darkness prevented her from seeing the raw need that had to be obvious on his face. "I thought you were coming right back. Is everything okay inside?"

She nodded. "We're almost out of beer, but we have enough champagne to fill a swimming pool, so I told the staff to push that a little harder."

"The beer is very popular. I hope you kept a case back for Ford and Becky to take home."

"I kept two, actually. Locked them up in the cellar." She glanced toward the path leading around the house. "I need to go check on things in the tent, see if I can move things along."

He fell into step beside her, and they made their way around to the front yard. "Are they doing the traditional garter-and-bouquet-throwing thing, or are they bucking tradition once again?"

"Despite the Vegas wedding, they're very traditional people. Why don't you see if you can round up some single men, and I'll round up the single women, and maybe we can get this show on the road?"

Scott mock saluted her. "Will do."

He couldn't take his eyes off her. She seemed to have gotten a second wind, bustling about, herding the guests like a true cowhand so they didn't even realize they had no choice. Her cheeks flushed from the heat and exertion, and he couldn't help but remember when she'd had that look for an entirely different reason. Lord, what she'd done to him. He couldn't get her out of his mind, or his heart.

She'd wrangled the crowd to form a corral of sorts with the bride and groom in the center then taken her place along the rail to watch the age-old custom of stealing a garter from the bride.

Scott stood in the center of the small group of unattached bachelors he'd gathered, watching.

Becky looked like she'd rather crawl under the nearest table than bare her leg for everyone to see, but Ford wasn't going to be denied. Seating her like a queen in the chair Scott had placed center stage, Ford dropped to one knee in front of his bride. Their gazes locked. Ford lifted her foot, caressed her ankle. The onlookers cheered him on as his hands crept beneath her gown, slowly advancing toward his goal. The two seemed locked in their own intimate world, completely oblivious to the fact that several dozen people watched their every move. What should have been a light moment had become a sensual testament to the couple's connection.

Realizing he'd been holding his breath, Scott forced the air from his lungs, and, feeling guilty for watching such an intimate exchange, he sought out Roseanne. One hand pressed to her heart, she dabbed at the corners of her eyes with a tissue. She'd seen it, too, that almost magical bond the bride and groom shared. *Look at me, sweetheart. Look at me.* As if she'd heard his thoughts, she scanned the circle, coming to a stop on him. Heart hammering, he met her gaze. *We have it, too. We have it, too.*

Wolf whistles erupted all around him. He looked up just in time to see something flying through the air. Instinct took over. He put his arm up to shield himself. Someone jostled him to the side.

His arm lowered to protect his body from the new, closer threat. Something brushed against his hand. His fingers closed into a fist, trapping the offending object a split-second before he realized what he'd captured. His gaze went to his hand, to the scrap of blue satin and white lace peeking out between his fingers. *Shit.*

The other single men clapped him on the shoulder, congratulating him on a job well-done. Several off-color remarks were made, but all he could think about was that, in a few minutes, he'd be taking Ford's place in the center of the circle in order to place the bride's garter on the leg of a yet-to-be-selected single woman. There was no hope for it; he had to go along with the silly custom. Smiling, he tucked the garter halfway into his breast pocket, letting it dangle out for all to see. The guests cheered the move before turning their attention once again to the bride and groom.

Across the circle of guests, Roseanne assembled the single women into a knot. Amid cheers and whistles, Becky tossed her bouquet over her shoulder. It soared in a high arc, coming down in the midst of the group. Fingers grasped and came up empty as the pink nosegay defied their best attempts to snag it. Scott lost sight of it as it dropped behind the head of one of the taller women. Gasps and groans from the assembly told him someone had finally managed to get their hands on the flying flowers. As the group parted, gently shoving the woman with the winning hand to the front, Scott once again held his breath.

Someone shoved him forward. He stumbled, righted himself, and looked up. He saw her feet first. Strappy silver sandals gave way to trim ankles and shapely calves that disappeared under a tea-length pink skirt. His gaze traveled up to where the bride's delicate, pink bouquet shook in the woman's hands. Hands that had driven him crazy more times than he could count. Hands he desperately wanted to feel on him again.

Roseanne. He smiled.

CHAPTER SIXTEEN

Oh, shit.

Roseanne eyed the roses she hadn't meant to catch. Somehow, they'd ended up in her hands anyway. Stunned, she allowed the others to shove her toward the front.

Becky squealed with delight then rushed over to grab her in a bear hug. "I'm so happy! Go get him, girlfriend!"

Roseanne forced a smile to her lips. She'd rather eat the bouquet than allow Scott Ramsey to place that garter on her leg in front of all these people, but she had no choice. This was Becky's big day, and she wouldn't ruin it for her.

"Okay. Okay. Give me some room." She wiggled out of the bride's embrace. Striding across the open floor was the one man she was genetically programmed to want. Too handsome for words, especially in his custom-tailored tux, she felt her resolve vaporizing.

"Hurry up," Becky urged, giving her a little shove. "The sooner you get this over with, the sooner I can get on with the honeymoon."

And the sooner Scott goes back into his hole.

Okay. I've got this.

She forced her feet to move toward the chair in the center of the room. Scott met her halfway, extending his hand. Steeling herself for his touch, she placed her fingers on his palm. The electric current she'd come to expect when they touched hummed through her body. Her heartbeat ratcheted into the stratosphere while the blood coursing through her arteries thickened to molten lava.

"I've got you, sweetheart."

Her eyes met his. The desire she saw there had to mirror her own, yet, like a moth drawn to the flame, she couldn't look away, couldn't save herself. She'd known the second she saw the bouquet in her hands that she was going down, that she didn't have the fortitude to resist him if he put his hands on her again.

She let him guide her to the chair. Clutching the roses hard enough to crush the stems, she sat. Dimly aware of the catcalls and cheering going on around them, she couldn't tear her gaze away from Scott. He didn't seem to notice their audience any more than she did as he went down on one knee in front of her. His fingers closed around her ankle, a warm, tender shackle that made her weak with need. In his eyes, she saw recognition. He, too, recalled the times she'd lay naked and open to him while he placed the restraints on her ankles and wrists.

"Relax, baby." He held her ankle fast with one hand while the other reached for the garter dangling like some erotic trophy from his breast pocket. "I'll take care of you."

His promise, spoken only for her ears, went straight to her most tender spots. She gripped the seat of the chair with her free hand to keep from squirming.

Gaze locked with hers, he maneuvered the elastic band over her foot then slowly, with both hands, inched it past her ankle, over her calf. She held her breath as his fingers scorched a path over her knee to her thigh, pausing there. Hidden beneath her skirt, his hands branded her skin, claimed the sensitive flesh as his own. The heat in his eyes guaranteed the promise his hands made.

One more time. What would it hurt? She craved to feel the press of his skin against hers one last time. Needed to know the touch of another human being, know the heat and urgency of desire.

Slowly, his hands retraced the path they'd taken, until her foot once again rested on the floor. Eyes still locked with hers, he rose and placed his lips on hers. Just a gentle brush of warm skin on numb skin, but it brought a cheer from the crowd and snapped Roseanne out of her lust-induced coma. She jerked when his lips brushed the shell of her ear. "Your room in five. If you aren't there, I'll come looking for you."

What else could she do? She nodded. Taking her by the elbow, he drew her to her feet. With his arm supporting her waist, they smiled and waved at the cheering crowd.

Becky rushed forward, placing a kiss on her cheek. "We're going to go change clothes. See you in a few?"

Roseanne nodded. "Take your time."

"You okay?" Scott asked.

"Yeah." She twisted out of his embrace. "I need to check on something in the house."

"I'll come with you."

She dropped the bridal bouquet on the small table in the hallway then they took the back stairs to avoid any guests who might wander into the house. The DJ had put on a dance favorite that probably kept most of them occupied, but Roseanne wasn't in the mood for interruptions. On the second landing, Scott caught up to her. Putting his hand possessively on her ass, he propelled them to the third floor.

She opened the door. He kicked it shut behind them at the same time his arm snaked around her waist, pulling her back flush against his front.

"Got to have you." The words rumbled from his chest, the vibration equally as arousing as the words themselves.

"Oh, God." She'd lost her mind, but she didn't miss it one little bit. Her body fit itself to his, muscle memory and longing making her pliable.

His free hand found her nape. His fingers worked their way around to her jaw while his thumb exerted pressure on the back of her head. She dipped her chin to her chest. With her hair piled high in a fancy updo, he had full access to the sensitive skin on the back of her neck. He pressed an openmouthed kiss below her ear. A shiver ran down her spine. "You taste so good. I could eat you up."

She groaned, imagining him doing just that. "Please." If she didn't get relief soon she'd combust.

"On the bed." They crossed the distance together then he spun her around and took her face in his big hands. His heated gaze said it all, and hers answered back, lowering to his lips. He took her mouth in a kiss that sent the lava in her bloodstream rocketing along. She reached out, grabbed fistfuls of starched cotton to ground herself. It didn't work. Her head spun and her hips moved, seeking the hard ridge beneath his fly. His lips left hers. "Sweet Jesus, I've got to taste you."

She nodded. He lifted her like she weighed nothing and tossed her on the bed. Wishing they had time for restraints, she grabbed for the footboard, holding on as he pushed her skirt to her waist. A low growl came from his throat then he reached for her panties. They were gone in an instant. He shoved her thighs apart, opening her to his gaze. "Fucking beautiful," he said.

He lowered himself between her legs. The first brush of warm breath against her skin had her bucking her hips off the bed. Knowing she needed to cede control, he seized it. Wrapping his arms around her thighs, he yanked her to the edge of the mattress and buried his face in her pussy.

She cried out and, closing her eyes, gave herself over to the incredible sensations created by his talented lips and tongue. He knew how to drive her wild with need, drawing his tongue over her swollen flesh, slow and easy, until every nerve ending in her body tingled then flicking her clit or thrusting deep inside her. She clutched the footboard with one hand and the quilt top with the other as he took her to the peak and beyond.

Pleasure, sharp and oh, so glorious, shot through her. Her body convulsed, fought his firm but gentle restraint until, at last, the crisis passed and she floated back to earth. She felt his smile against her thigh as he placed a sweet kiss there, just inches away from her core.

Like he had all the time in the world, he stood and carefully smoothed her skirt back over her wet center. "These are mine," he said. She blinked tears from her eyes and, in the dim moonlight streaming in the window, saw her panties dangling from his index finger. "You can keep the garter."

Her circumstances hit her like a sledgehammer. A tent full of people were on her front lawn. The bride and groom had gone to change into travel clothes, and, instead of handing out origami doves filled with birdseed, she'd selfishly been playing hanky-panky with the best man!

"I've got to go." She pushed herself upright.

"Roseanne." He blocked her way.

"No." She shook her head. Lord, she must look a mess. "This was a mistake."

"You don't really believe that."

She placed her hands on his stomach and shoved. "Get out of my way, Scott. I've got to go."

He stepped back. She sprang for the door, but before she convinced the temperamental old doorknob to turn, his words slammed into her. "This isn't over, Roseanne. *We* aren't over."

Yes, we are. Her feet pounded on the back stairs to the rhythm of her heartbeat. She hit the last landing and sprinted for the powder room off the front hall, praying that none of her guests were using it. She'd be screwed if someone saw her this way—eyes filled with tears, lips swollen, hair probably a rat's nest, and sporting a full-body blush. There'd be no doubt what she'd been up to, and anyone who knew her would know who she'd been up to it with.

The gods must have been watching out for her. She dashed into the powder room, locked the door, and faced herself in the mirror. "Dear God."

It took her a good ten minutes to finger-comb her hair into some semblance of normality and another five to erase the raccoon smudges under her eyes. Her dress had a few more wrinkles than before, but all in all looked pretty good—considering. She wished she'd thought to grab a fresh pair of panties, but she hadn't. Only one person would know she wasn't wearing any, and if he so much as smirked at her, she'd hit him over the head with a chair.

When she finally emerged from the powder room, she found Ford and Becky waiting in the front parlor to make their grand escape.

"We were wondering where you were," the bride said. "Is everything okay?"

"Fine," she lied. "If you'll just give me a minute, I'll make sure everyone is ready to send you off in style."

"Can't we just skip this part and disappear out the back door?" Ford asked.

"No, you can't skip this part," Roseanne said. "If they don't see you leave, they'll stay here all night, and I promised the neighbors we'd shut this down before midnight."

"He's kidding." Becky gave her groom a kiss on the cheek. "Aren't you, darling?"

Ford shrugged. "Sure. Just kidding, Roseanne."

His reluctant acquiescence amused her. She smiled and held up a finger. "Give me a minute. I'll come open the door for you when we're all ready."

She ducked out, closed her eyes, and breathed in the fresh, night air, willing it to settle her nerves. When she opened her eyes, Scott stood in the open tent panel, hands in his pockets, staring at her. "Are they ready?"

Roseanne nodded. "Yes. I have the birdseed packets here." She pointed to a couple of baskets filled with the paper birds she'd left on the porch swing.

"I'll tell the DJ to make the announcement." He turned and headed into the tent. Helping her, despite the way she'd ran out on him.

Placing a hand on her stomach, she refused to think about how she'd left him. He'd given her an explosive orgasm, and she'd given him nothing. Yet here he was, helping her bring the evening to a conclusion. Maybe Becky was right. Maybe she should tell him tonight.

When the last guests had departed, she expected to see him waiting for her, but he was nowhere to be found.

CHAPTER SEVENTEEN

Roseanne opened the refrigerator and groaned. She'd tried her best to forget about catching the bride's bouquet, but she couldn't deny the evidence. Someone, probably the caterer, had put the flowers in the refrigerator to preserve them. Damn Becky for insisting Roseanne take part in the ridiculous tradition. Folks in Butte Plains took that kind of crap seriously.

The best she could hope for would be that everyone who saw her catch the bundle of pink roses would be unable to recall anything that happened last evening. Otherwise, everyone in town would know about her misfortune before the tent came down later today. The Butte Plains grapevine worked that fast. Thank God no one knew what had happened *after* the spectacle on the dance floor.

Roseanne groaned. How stupid could she be? But she'd never been able to resist Scott when he looked at her the way he had when he slipped the garter onto her leg. His kiss had incinerated her last bit of willpower. No more. She'd made that clear afterward. He'd caught her at a vulnerable moment — that was all. She'd succumbed to his charm, to the sexy way he growled when he kissed her. Damn. Why had he done that? He'd known she would melt.

Moving the flowers aside, she found the carton of milk she had come looking for. Taking it out, she shut the refrigerator door, blocking the blooms from sight. It was early. Jamie wouldn't be in to begin prepping for breakfast for at least another hour. Hopefully, her guests would sleep in. Ford's aunt had turned in right after the wedding cake had been served. Mr. and Mrs. Ramsey had danced until the very last note of the very last song before calling it a night. If there was one thing those two were good at, it was partying. According to their son, they had plenty of experience.

She had no idea what time Colin had gone to bed. She'd lost track of him right after the DJ took over. He was a grown man, and thus, not her responsibility. He could do as he pleased. She just wished he'd been there to see the bride and groom off on their honeymoon. If Becky had noticed his absence, she hadn't said anything. She'd been excited to get on the plane Scott had provided to take them to Paris. She'd also had a lot to drink, like most of the guests. Well, she had ten days ahead of her. Plenty of time to get over a hangover and still see the sights.

A knock on the back door startled her, causing her to spill the milk she'd been pouring into a glass. She turned. Through the window, she recognized her early morning caller.

Colin Parker, his bow tie hanging loose and his tuxedo jacket slung over his shoulder, smiled. "Hey, Roseanne. I forgot my key. Can you let me in?"

Hands on her hips, she frowned at him. He'd abandoned his sister on her wedding night only to come prowling home like a satisfied tomcat the next morning, begging for forgiveness.

"Ah, come on, Roseanne. Let me in."

She flicked the dead bolt—all the help she was going to give him—and stepped back. He twisted the handle and stepped inside.

"Thanks. I've been sitting out there for hours, waiting for someone to wake up." He opened the refrigerator and stared inside just like he used to do when he was a kid and followed his sister everywhere, including to Roseanne's grandmother's house. "Not many leftovers," he commented.

"That's a good thing. There's plenty of cake." She motioned to a couple of large boxes stacked on the corner near the coffeemaker.

"It's good. You should try it."

Colin groaned and shut the refrigerator door. "Did she notice I wasn't there for the cake?"

Roseanne shook her head. "I don't think so, but she'll eventually see the pictures." Meaning he wouldn't be in any of them.

"She won't hold that against me. She knew I wanted to see some old friends while I was here."

"Your friends only come out at night? Is that why you couldn't have waited until today?"

He popped the lid on the top box, eyed the contents then opened cabinets until he found a plate.

"There's a knife in the wood block to your right. Forks are in the drawer right behind you in the island."

He nodded. "Same place they were when we were kids." He plopped a generous slice of cake on his plate then licked his fingers before opening the drawer containing the flatware.

"Same flatware, too."

He examined the fork he'd chosen. "I'll be damned. Sure looks the same."

"Where were you?"

"Went to see some old buddies of mine. You remember the Watson twins? Bobby and Tommy?"

"I thought they were in jail."

He shook his head as he chewed then swallowed. "Not anymore. They own a music store now. All legit. You've seen it. Music City over on Woodlawn?"

"That's their place?" Recently opened, they sold musical instruments, gave lessons, and hosted local talent on a stage out back on weekends. Even without a liquor license, the place had become very popular. "Explains why they don't sell alcohol at their events."

"They served their time and learned their lesson. Maybe they'll never have a liquor license, but they don't need one. Place was hoppin' last night."

"I'm sure it was." She drank the last of her milk then rinsed and put the glass in the dishwasher.

"I just came down to check that everything was okay for my cook to come in and make breakfast this morning. Looks like the caterers did a good job of cleaning up, so I'm going back to bed for a few hours." She pointed a finger at her guest who she loved as if he was her own little brother. "Don't you dare leave your mess for Jamie to clean up." She turned to leave.

"Hey. Wait a sec."

The serious tone of his voice stopped her. She leaned against the newel post on the back stairs. "What?"

"I met someone last night. Name's Julie Davis. You know her?"

"I've heard of her. Why?"

Colin shrugged. "Just wondering. She's new in town, right?"

"She's been here about a year, I think. Bought the Scoggins' place when they retired from farming and turned it into a boutique brewery. Did you have beer at the reception?"

"Yeah. That was hers?"

"Yep." She put her foot on the next step. "That's all I know about her. Remember what I said about leaving a mess." She climbed the stairs to her room on the third floor. By the time her head hit the pillow, she'd forgotten all about Colin staying out all night and his questions about the owner of Lucky Lady Brewing Company.

CHAPTER EIGHTEEN

Fuck.

Scott had spent yet another restless night, thinking about the few moments he'd had alone with Roseanne. He hadn't meant for things to go that far, but the volcano had been stirring for two days. Seeing and touching her, even innocently at the rehearsal, had been the catalyst, setting his blood on fire—reminding him of exactly what he'd lost.

Looking like a sweet, pink confection last night, she'd made his mouth water. Everyone could have their addictions—alcohol, nicotine, name your drug. Roseanne was his addiction. He lived to touch, smell, taste her. He'd been in withdrawal since she'd come to her senses and kicked him out of her life. He didn't deserve her. It had been only a matter of time before she figured it out.

She'd forgotten for a few minutes last night, and so had he. He'd earned the blue balls he'd suffered most of the night. He should have kept his hands to himself, should never have followed her up those stairs. Should never have let his needs overrule his brain. But if last night turned out to be his last memory of the way she sounded when he made her come, of the heaven between her legs, he'd cherish it until his dying day.

But today was another day in his quest to be the man he wanted to be. Even if Roseanne never saw him as anything more than a Yankee carpetbagger, he'd do what he could to make her town the place she envisioned. There was no time to lose. He needed to find the right tenants for the buildings downtown, and if nothing else had come from last night, he'd had an idea.

He'd spent the morning researching his prey. He'd been surprised to find very little about the owner of Lucky Lady Brewing Company. The people he'd talked to all said she wasn't a local and that she kept to herself. No one knew where she came by the funds to buy the property she occupied or to start up a microbrewery. That didn't mean the Butte Plains grapevine wasn't ripe with speculation, but Scott wasn't interested in imaginative guesswork.

Scott consulted the GPS one more time. A large, white barn with a green shingled roof loomed in the distance next to a smaller, but every bit as impressive, farmhouse. He slowed, checked the number on the oversized mailbox perched on top of the stump of what had once been a very large tree. It had taken some investigative work, but he'd eventually located the old Scoggins place, which meant he'd found the home of the Lucky Lady Brewing Company. He flicked the turn signal on, and, with a whispered prayer that the homeowner didn't shoot trespassers, he crept up the driveway.

As he approached the house, a large, black dog bounded out from the shade of a century-old oak to meet his car. He didn't know much about dogs, but this one, with its wagging tail and lolling tongue, appeared friendly enough. Scott parked next to a vintage pickup truck that bore the logo he'd become familiar with, and cut the engine. When no one greeted him with a shotgun, he decided his luck was holding.

"So far, so good," he muttered as he opened the car door.

It wasn't the first time he'd questioned his sanity regarding everything Butte Plains, Texas. He'd risked a small fortune on the leather factory, the old, abandoned airstrip, and still another on the real estate downtown. Thanks to Ford and Becky's success with Adams Manufacturing, vacant properties were being snatched up by savvy investors, and he'd plunked the money down before considering what he would do with the extra square footage. He intended to use the Cotton Exchange building for his new offices. One space would become the new offices of Ramsey and Adams Designs. He had plans for the space between the Cotton Exchange and the corner, but the way things were going, he wasn't sure they would ever get off the ground. That left the corner property, and, after last night, he knew exactly what he wanted to occupy the space. According to the few people who knew the brewer, the chances of convincing her to open a tasting room in his vacant location were roughly the same as an armadillo crossing a freeway without getting run over. In other words—nil.

When no one answered the door at the house, Scott followed his nose around the beautiful old structure to the barn he'd seen from the road. The friendly black lab trudged along behind him as he traversed the well-worn path that led to a pedestrian door on the west side. Through the multi-paned window, he could see most of the operation inside. He knocked. He was about to give up and try again another day, when a woman appeared in the window. If this was Julie Davis, she was much younger than he'd thought—mid-twenties, he'd guess. Younger than him by half a decade, at least. He smiled and waved.

A striking woman, she looked comfortable in jeans and a pastel plaid shirt left open to reveal some sort of girly white undershirt thing. She wore athletic shoes, and had her long, blonde hair up in a ponytail that swung back and forth as she strode toward the door. The scowl on her face when she jerked the door open wasn't a good sign.

"Yes?" she said, keeping one hand on the doorknob while the other held a clipboard against her chest.

Scott wasn't sure if her displeasure stemmed from the interruption or from having company in general. More than one person had described the woman as a recluse. He wondered if her lack of community interaction had more to do with being busy than anything else. He'd never given much thought to the brewing process, but what he could see of this small operation looked like a lot of work for one person.

He held out his hand. "Scott Ramsey, Ms. Davis?"

She dipped her head in acknowledgement but made no effort to shake his hand. "I'm Julie Davis."

So this was the owner of Lucky Lady Brewery — a Texan if her soft drawl was genuine, and he believed it was. He'd long since learned the slow dialect had nothing to do with the person's intelligence. Something in her tone warned him not to underestimate her. He dropped his hand to his side.

"What brings you all the way out here, Mr. Ramsey?"

"I was wondering if I could have a minute of your time. I have a business proposition I'd like to discuss with you."

She glanced at her clipboard then looked over her shoulder. His gaze followed hers to a giant tank. Steam rose from a large open hatch on the top. "Look, I don't know what you're selling, but I'm not buying. Now, if you'll excuse me? I've got to keep an eye on the temperature of that vat."

"What I've got to say will only take a minute," he pressed. "Could you monitor the vat and listen at the same time?"

She rolled her eyes at him then swung the door open wide. She pointed a finger at the dog. "No, Bud. Wait." The dog, tongue hanging out and tail wagging, sat. She turned her attention back to Scott and gestured for him to enter. "Come on. I don't have time to argue with you."

Scott stepped inside and was immediately hit with a wall of humid air, thick with the smell of something earthy. He took in the impressive facility. Clearly, there was more to brewing beer than cooking up some hops, or whatever it was they used. Besides the dozen or so giant stainless steel vats and tanks, he noted a small bottling station to one side. A stack of flattened cardboard sat next to what he assumed was a labeler. One entire wall of the place from floor to ceiling was lined with industrial shelving, on which sat pallets stacked with supplies. He noticed a small forklift parked in the corner. He might not know the brewing business, but recognized expense when he saw it. Ms. Davis had spent a lot of her, or someone else's, money on her equipment. As he made his way over to where the owner of the Lucky Lady Brewing Company stood, he wondered if she considered this a business, or if she was just another rich girl with a hobby.

"Nice place," he said.

She consulted a couple of gauges on a panel then glanced at her clipboard again. "Talk, Mr. Ramsey, or leave. I'm busy."

Scott raised one eyebrow at the curt comment and cleared his throat. "Like I said, I have a business proposition for you."

"Go on," she said, not taking her eyes off the steaming vat. "Just be ready to move fast. That's boiling water in there. Sometimes it splashes over."

She didn't move, and, not wanting to look like a wimp, neither did he. "Are you familiar with the Cotton Exchange building downtown?"

"I've seen it. Looks like it was an impressive place back in the day."

"I own it, and the buildings on either side of it. I'm moving my offices into the Exchange building. I'm thinking the corner space would make a good tasting room for Lucky Lady."

The side glance she gave him might have meant anything from she was interested, to wishing him to hell. At long last, she focused her attention on the gauges again. She hadn't ordered him to leave, so he waited with one eye on the open hatch, from which boiling water could erupt at any second, and the woman who controlled the micro-universe he'd entered. After a minute or two, she jotted something down on her clipboard and turned to him.

"What makes you think I'd want to open a tasting room?"

He nodded at the row of stainless steel vats. "This looks like a pretty expensive hobby."

"It's not a hobby."

"I know less than nothing about this business, but I do know you can't be making money on the volume you're currently producing and selling. At best, that's a failing business model. You have an excellent product, and this town is in need of a place for folks to unwind. Recent notoriety is bringing tourists and people looking to relocate. Now would be a great time to hitch your wagon to the train before it leaves the station."

She smiled and turned to study her gauges. He got the impression she wasn't an impulsive person. Wonder what brought her here? Why a brewery? At last, she spoke. "If I wanted to hitch my wagon to anything, it wouldn't be a train, at least not the kind that leaves a station. You aren't from around here, are you?"

"New York. But I live here now."

She nodded. "Carpetbagger?"

He bristled. "No." Shook his head. "Hell, no."

"Gonna take more than that to convince me otherwise."

What is it with the women in this town? Maybe he should take an ad out in the local paper, listing his references and his intention to become a permanent resident. Maybe then she'd believe he wasn't trying to take advantage of her or the people of Butte Plains. "You provided the beer for Ford Adams's wedding. I was the best man. Ford and I are partners on several business ventures and friends. We met at MIT, went into business together in New York. He can vouch for me."

"The Adams family goes back a long ways in this town."

"They do." He nodded. "Oldest and biggest employer in town."

She sighed and wrote another note on her clipboard. "Look, I can't say I'm not interested in expanding, but I'm busy right now. Can we talk another time?"

"Sure. No problem." He fished a business card out of his wallet and handed it to her. "Call me when you have some time. I'll give you a tour of the space then we can sit down and talk about the details—rent, renovations, marketing."

She slid the card beneath the spring-loaded clamp on her clipboard. "I could spare some time in the next week or so. I'll give you a call."

"Thanks." He took another look around and decided he needed to do some research on the brewing process before they met again. "I'll just let myself out."

While he waited for the brewer to grant him an audience, Scott kept busy with the other projects he had going on—anything to keep from knocking on Roseanne's door and begging her to reconsider. He believed in the old saying, actions speak louder than words. When Julie Davis finally did call several weeks later, they met downtown the next morning. "It doesn't look like much," he said as he worked on the old lock, willing it to open. "But it's solid. I've had two different engineers look over every inch of the place. If you're okay with keeping the historic look, then everything else is just cosmetic."

The door gave way, and he allowed Julie to precede him. There was just enough light coming through dirty windows to illuminate the dust particles they'd stirred up.

CHAPTER NINETEEN

The owner of the Lucky Lady Brewery stood in the middle of the big front room and slowly spun in a circle, taking in the ancient hardwood floors, the wide expanse of windows and the tin-clad ceiling. "What was this originally?"

"Records show the first tenant was a general store. They went out of business around the beginning of the century, the twentieth century," he clarified. "After that, a women's dry-goods store moved in. They occupied the space for nearly eighty years before calling it quits. A couple of small stores tried to make a go of it here over the next few decades, the last being a floor tile business that closed ten years ago."

"So, the space has been vacant since the turn of the century? The twenty-first century?"

"That's right."

"What's going to happen to it if I don't open a tasting room in the space?"

Scott shrugged. "I don't know. I'll have to find something else to put in here. Maybe a restaurant or an old-fashioned soda fountain. It needs to be something that will bring people this far off the freeway to sit for a while, maybe stroll down the sidewalk and visit the other stores."

Julie walked to one dirty window and looked up and down the

street. "Someone has done a lot of work out there. Was that you?"

"A lot of local people pitched in to help. I mostly provided the funds. The people who grew up in this town are committed to bringing it back to life. So am I."

"This is a far cry from Manhattan."

So, she'd done her homework. "It is, and that's what I love about it."

She nodded and looked back out the window. "I'd want to brew some micro batches on site. Would I have any trouble with doing that?"

"Trouble?"

"Zoning. Licenses?"

"No problem on the zoning. I've already spoken to the city planner about that and been assured they won't stand in the way of any business that wants to claim this corner as their own. As for a liquor license, that would be up to you to acquire."

"Can I see the rest of the place?"

An hour later, they sat across from each other at the new diner out on the highway. Scott would have preferred someplace quieter, but Julie insisted. When they were through talking, she was heading to Dallas to pick up some supplies and could just hop on the freeway from there.

Julie pushed plates out of the way, making room for the pad of paper she had brought along to take notes on. "Look." She scribbled furiously, drawing a rough sketch of the main floor of the building. "See? There needs to be a bar here. Then over here" — she drew more lines—"there needs to be tables, maybe long ones, picnic style."

"Here. Let me show you what I had in mind." He swung the pad to his side of the table. She handed over her pen, and he drew another rough sketch. Before he finished, Julie slid in beside him and grabbed the pen from his hand.

"No." She shook her head. "I see what you're getting at, but that won't work."

Scott surrendered the pad. She tore off the top sheet and began sketching on a new page.

"This is the tasting room, right? So the bar has to be here because that's the only place we would have access to the keg storage area."

"What if we did this?" Scott hunched over the pad to draw his latest idea.

Wanting to see better, Julie ducked her head so their faces were only inches apart. Scott scooted over to make room for the leggy blonde. In the short time he'd known her, he'd come to the conclusion that the dumb blonde jokes didn't pertain to her. She was smart and beautiful. If he hadn't given his heart to another, he'd find her earthy scent and coltish figure attractive. But he had given his heart, and though he noticed Julie's qualities, he just wasn't interested, and as far as he could tell, her only interest in him had to do with the property he owned, which made working with her easier. Heads together, they worked for the better part of an hour, drawing, revising, and troubleshooting before reaching a tentative agreement on the layout of the key elements of the design.

"Can you do that?" she asked.

"I'll talk to my restoration expert and see. If it can be done, do we have a deal?"

"I'll want my attorney to look over the paperwork before I sign anything, but yeah, I think we have a deal." Her smile nearly blinded him. She placed a hand on his forearm then before he could stop her, she leaned in and kissed him on the cheek. "I've got to go."

She tore the top few sheets off the notepad, left them on the table. Faster than a dust devil, she packed up her stuff, leaving him sitting there with a pile of crude design notes and the bill.

~ ~ ~

Roseanne was starving—something she was all too familiar with these days. Seems she was either sick at her stomach or hungry. This was a hungry day. She'd stayed up too late the night before then slept in this morning, causing her to have to rush to get to her doctor's appointment in Prairieview. There'd been no time for breakfast. She'd had to wait nearly an hour to see the doctor who rushed in after delivering a baby at the hospital across the street. It was a good excuse but hadn't done Roseanne's stomach any good.

The billboard advertising fresh pastries at the next exit made her mouth water. Taking the next exit, she pulled into the parking lot for the flashy new diner. She grabbed her wallet and went inside. Next to the cashier, a glass case containing all manner of delectable goodies caught her attention. She spent a minute scanning the contents, deciding which one, or two, to take home with her. Her gaze locked on the thick chocolate brownie topped with chopped nuts. "I'll take two of those, please."

While the cashier bagged her selection, Roseanne checked out the dining room. Not too many locals came this far out to grab a bite to eat, but a few did. Her gaze skimmed over the crowd, stopping on one head in particular. Scott Ramsey sat in a booth about halfway back along the front wall, his back to the door, his head bent as if carrying on a private conversation with the blonde next to him.

Brownies forgotten, Roseanne stared at the couple. They sure looked cozy, sharing the same side of the booth, practically breathing the same air. She inhaled deep, willing her stomach to ease, remembering what it had been like to breathe the rarified air around Scott Ramsey. It had been weeks since she'd seen him, but she knew firsthand how he could draw you in, make you feel like you were the only woman in the world. Even with all the food smells permeating the air, her nostrils knew his scent. Knew the heat that radiated off him.

"That will be five dollars and thirty-one cents."

"Oh. Sorry." Roseanne fumbled with her wallet. She handed over a ten dollar bill, her gaze wandering back to the couple in the booth while the clerk counted out her change. Suddenly, the couple sat up and began talking. In profile, she could see it was a friendly conversation, animated and pleasant. The woman leaned in and placed a cutesy kiss on Scott's cheek, stunning Roseanne with its familiarity. How many times had she pecked him on the cheek when they parted company? Too many to count.

"Your change, miss."

Roseanne jerked her attention to the young man behind the counter. "Yes. Thank you."

She took the change, stuffing it absently in her pants pocket. She grabbed the white pastry bag, planning to make her escape before Scott or his mystery woman saw her. Without checking to see if either one had left the booth, Roseanne made a dash for the door and her car. She'd just put the vehicle in gear when the diner door opened again and the blonde stepped out. Head down, she dug in her purse for her keys. Roseanne knew her. Had done business with her.

Julie Davis. She truly was a Lucky Lady.

~ ~ ~

It had been two weeks since she'd seen Scott having an early lunch — or was it a late breakfast? — with Julie Davis, and she refused to think about it. Much. In fact, she'd relegated herself to only thinking about her baby's daddy with another woman three times a day — morning, noon, and night.

Her thoughts weren't rational. She knew they weren't, but she couldn't stop them. She'd tried, immersing herself in work. The garden hadn't been this weed-free in years, the closets had never been cleaner, and the woodwork had never been shinier. Kay had scolded her more than once for doing the job she'd hired Maria to do, but Roseanne couldn't sit still.

So, when it came, she welcomed the call from Randy Tucker. Showing her beloved home to his carpenter and designer gave her something to do besides dwell on the fact that she really, truly, was going to be a single mother. She'd finally admitted to herself that in the back of her mind she'd hoped Scott would come begging for her forgiveness. Having met his parents at Becky's wedding, she had a better understanding of why he hadn't asked her to go to their anniversary party. Talk about a piece of work. If Scott hadn't been the spitting image of his father, she'd swear he had been adopted.

But that didn't excuse his behavior. He should have told her about the party. Let her decide if she wanted to go or not, but the fact that he hadn't invited her to a family event proved how little their relationship meant to him. Since she'd booted him out of her house, he hadn't made a single attempt to talk to her, other than at the wedding, when he'd had no choice.

She could still feel his arousal pressed against her backside, feel his breath on her neck, hear the desire in his voice as he held her close while the photographer snapped photo after photo of the happy couple and their entourage. *He didn't have to proposition you.* She'd practically dragged him back to her bedroom. That was true, but knowing he still found her desirable didn't mean squat. He'd already found someone else to have lunch or, gag, breakfast with. Just went to prove women were a dime a dozen in his eyes.

The bell on the front door jingled. *Right on time.* Roseanne joined Kay in the foyer to welcome their guests.

"Mr. Tucker," she said, offering her hand. "I didn't know you were going to be here, too."

Taking her hand, his eyes appraised her with a warmth she hadn't felt in a long time. "Couldn't resist another chance to look at a lovely lady."

Roseanne wasn't sure if he was talking about the house or her. She smiled and nodded. Randy Tucker was handsome, and his manners were impeccable. As a woman, she could appreciate those qualities, but she simply wasn't interested. She'd already made one bad choice, and getting involved with Tucker while she carried another man's child would be idiotic. She gently took her hand away, silently offering an apology for not reciprocating his interest. Maybe in a few years, when the wound wasn't so fresh, she'd consider dating again. Find some nice guy who could love her and her kid.

Pipe dream. That's what that is.

"As it turns out, something has come up," she lied. "I've asked Kay to show you around. She knows almost as much about the house as I do." Another lie, but she wasn't the least bit sorry. Ever since she'd seen Scott with Julie Davis, she'd felt as if she were on a sinking ship. It was time she focused on survival, and that meant delegating the less important duties to others. This was one of them.

Kay stepped forward. "Welcome to The Yellow Rose. If you'll follow me? We'll begin the tour in the kitchen. I have a pitcher of sweet tea and a plate of scones, if anyone is interested."

The group filed past, Tucker staying behind. "I meant what I said. I came to see a lovely lady. It's a darned shame she's busy. Maybe we could have dinner instead?"

Roseanne clenched her hands into fists and searched the floor for a polite way to say no.

"Just dinner. No expectations, just conversation and some food you don't have to cook. I'd love to pick your brain about the restoration I'm doing downtown."

She shook her head. "The offer is tempting, but no. I…can't."

He dipped his chin. "I see. Well, if you change your mind, you have my number."

"I do. Thanks for understanding."

"Guess I better get in there before all the scones are gone, then."

Roseanne laughed. "Yes, you'd better."

She watched him go then returned to her office, shutting the door behind her. She had a few things to go over before she met later that day with the attorney she'd engaged to look into her rights as a single parent.

PART THREE

"You may all go to hell, and I will go to Texas."
Davy Crockett

CHAPTER TWENTY

Roseanne rushed into her best friend's office, skidding to a stop in front of her desk. "Becky! Guess who I just got off the phone with?"

Becky Adams sat back in her chair and smiled. "Don't know, but I bet you're going to tell me."

"An agent! She called me out of the blue. Said I queried a friend of hers who no longer handles nonfiction, and she passed my letter on to her."

"That's great, I guess. What did she say?"

"She wants to represent me!" She couldn't help it. She squealed. "She said she'd send a contract, and that I should have an attorney look it over. Oh my God. I can't believe an agent actually called me!"

Becky laughed. "I told you someone would, didn't I?"

"You did, but I didn't believe you." Running out of steam, she finally sat, clasping on the edge of Becky's desk to ground her. "Who would want to represent little ole me? It's amazing."

"Not so much amazing as exciting. What else did she say?"

"Oh, Lord." She closed her eyes and tried to recall the entire conversation, but parts of it were lost to her. She'd been too keyed up to grasp it all. "She said she'd seen the sample chapter I sent and loved it. She said everyone loves a bed-and-breakfast, and who wouldn't want to make those scrumptious meals for their family or guests." Her eyes popped open. "And she said she knows two publishers who have been looking for just this sort of project." Roseanne forced her hands to her lap. "Is that cool, or what?"

"It's super cool," Becky confirmed. "I knew you could do it. You can say I told you so anytime now."

"Okay. Okay. You told me so, smarty pants."

"What's next?"

"I need to find a lawyer to look at the contract. She said she'd email me a copy then overnight the print version." She dug her phone out of her pocket to check her email. "It's here! Oh my God. I can't believe it. This is really happening."

"We have a lawyer we use to handle all of our contracts. I could ask him to take a look, if you want."

"Wow. Yes, that would be great."

Becky picked up the handset on her desk phone. "Email me that file and I'll print it out for him."

Roseanne forwarded the email while her best friend talked to the lawyer. When Becky ended the call, she opened the email, and, in a few seconds, the printer behind her desk began to whir. It wasn't long before it spit out several sheets of paper. Becky scooped them up, smacked the stapler head to hold them all together, and passed them over the desk.

"Here you go. You know where the new offices are, don't you? Take the long hallway that goes off to the left when you go in the studio building."

"I remember. The conference room is down that hall, too."

"That's the one. His name is Pete Shannon. His office is about halfway down, before you get to the conference room."

"I can't thank you enough, Becks. You're the best friend ever."

"Have you thought any more about the other big thing in your life?"

Roseanne sobered. "Every minute of every day. But you already know that. What you really want to know is if I'm going to tell him anytime soon."

"You know I think you should."

"He's moved on, Becks."

She leaned forward, crossing her arms on the top of the desk. A deep crease formed between her eyebrows. "What are you talking about?"

"I saw him with a woman. They looked awfully cozy, and it was the middle of the day." She got up and shut the office door. The only other office at this end of the hallway was Ford's, and he usually worked with headphones on, but you never knew when someone would drop by. Becky kept an open-door policy with her employees.

"Spill, girlfriend." Becky was all ears as Roseanne told her about seeing Scott and Julie Davis at the diner out on the interstate.

"I don't believe it," Becks said.

"I saw it with my own eyes. I bet he's working his way through every single woman in town. Maybe some of the married ones, too."

Becky sat back in her chair again. "I'm sorry, Roseanne. Ford said he was a good guy, and I took his word for it."

"Not your fault. I knew he was a damned Yankee, but I still fell for his charm. Just my luck to get knocked up in the process."

"Do you want me to talk to Ford? If he knew, he wouldn't let Scott get away without at least paying child support."

Roseanne shook her head. "No, please don't say anything to anyone. I've consulted an attorney. He says I need to tell Scott eventually." She sighed. "Truthfully? I don't want his money. If he can't be a hands-on father to his child, then I don't want anything else he has to offer."

"Okay." Becky sounded skeptical. "But put me on record as objecting to this plan of action. The baby is just as much his responsibility as it yours."

Roseanne waved the papers in her hand. "I should take these over, see what your lawyer has to say. If this agent can sell the book to a publisher, and she says she can, maybe I'll have the means to support the baby myself. Then I really can tell Scott Ramsey where he can go."

~ ~ ~

"What do you think?" Scott and Ford had just completed a walk-through of the newly completed office space that the company they had founded together in New York would now occupy on Main Street in Butte Plains.

"It's fantastic." Ford ran a hand down the original molding surrounding the front door of the century-and-a-half-old building. "Makes me want to renovate my office at the plant."

"Why would you want to get rid of the institutional green paint and the layers of dust? It would destroy the character of the place." Scott chuckled at his own joke.

"Seriously? Right? Besides, I think the dust is all that's holding the place together," Ford said, laughing along with his friend. He sobered. "Becky gave me a new desk chair for my birthday. I love it, and I know her heart was in the right place, but it doesn't go with the desk, or anything else in the room."

"Nothing goes with anything in that office. Face it, Ford, every Adams for the last hundred years has left his mark on that room. Maybe it's time you left yours."

Ford nodded. "Maybe it is." He looked around at the beautifully restored building, taking in all the details. "You know, the original office was in the building we turned into studio space. My great-grandfather built the current building and moved his office there. We've got two factories going now, a distribution center, a television studio, and we're thinking of opening a retail outlet on a piece of land out by the highway. It would be nice to consolidate all the corporate structure in one place."

"Have you seen the buildings over on the next block? I bet you could pick up the entire block for a song. Lots of square footage."

"Can I afford it?"

"Shut the fuck up. It's an investment in the future of Adams

Manufacturing and Butte Plains."

"You sound just like the mayor."

"You mean the part-time mayor slash Realtor."

"Yeah. Him." Ford, hands on his hips, took one last look at the new space. "Okay. Let's go take a look."

They stopped on the corner. Ford pointed to the windows blanked out with brown paper. "What's going in there?"

"Lucky Lady Brewery's new tasting room." The light changed, and they crossed the street.

"Wow. How did you make that happen? I hear the owner is a recluse."

"Her name's Julie Davis. I don't know that she's a recluse, just a workaholic. Runs that entire microbrewery all by herself. We've finally come to terms on the lease. Waiting for the Historical Society to agree to the interior restoration. Once they do that, and the city issues permits, we'll get started on the project."

"Using the same company?"

"Yeah. Tucker Restoration out of Dallas. They did a great job on our office space, and you should see how the house is coming along. It's costing a fortune, but it's worth every penny to see the place come alive again."

They stopped at the next corner, looking south down Elm Street.

"The whole block is empty?" Ford asked.

"Yep. I looked at it when I was thinking about buying downtown. Would have bought it, but I figured the most bang for my buck was on Main. However, you don't need that kind of exposure. A block over from the action would be perfect for your corporate headquarters. There are still a couple of storefronts available on Main. You could open a factory outlet store downtown."

"It would be good to have a way to get rid of manufacturing overruns." Ford crossed the street to get a good look at the abandoned buildings. "This could work for our offices. What about parking?"

Scott led Ford to the end of the block to a large, vacant lot piled with old tires and derelict appliances. "Parking garage, right here."

"Think the city would let me build a parking structure here?"

"I think they'd let you build anything you want as long as you clean the place up. It's an eyesore. Throw in some free parking on the ground level for tourists and shoppers, and they'll probably pitch in the building permits for free."

"It's something to think about, for sure. Let me run it by Becky. She knows more about our financial situation than I do, but I think she'll go for the idea. She hates our current situation."

"I've gotten to know the folks in City Hall pretty well. If you decide to do this, let me know, and I'll see if I can get some concessions for you."

Ford laughed and shook his head. "Look at you. All chummy with City Hall. You probably know more about real estate in this town than the Realtors. You've really settled in here, haven't you?"

"I guess I have." He kicked at a pebble on the sidewalk, sent it skittering into the street. "My apartment in New York sold last week. Made a shit-ton of money on it." He lifted his chin toward the empty block of buildings. "If you don't want to buy it, I will. Lease it back to you, renovated of course, for a dollar a month or something. If you want to buy somewhere down the road, I'd make you a good deal on it."

Ford whistled low. "That's a deal I don't think we can pass up. Let me talk to Becky."

"Sounds good. Seriously, I'm okay either way. These buildings are fabulous. They deserve to be saved."

CHAPTER TWENTY-ONE

They walked back to the new offices of Ramsey and Adams Design and Engineering where they'd left their cars. Scott waved good-bye to his friend. Alone, he opened the door to the empty storefront two doors down. Bouncing his keys in his hand, he let his eyes adjust to the dim light coming in the dirty windows and tried to envision the space in another way.

He wondered if Roseanne remembered telling him about her idea. It was a lazy Sunday. The weekend guests had checked out, and the bed-and-breakfast was empty except for them. They'd spent the afternoon in bed, making love slow, lingering afterward to cuddle and talk. He'd listened to her dreams for the future, tucking them away to examine later when her body wasn't there to distract him.

"This will do," he said to the empty room. It had been a hotel in another life. The commercial kitchen in the back was a relic, but that could be replaced easily enough. He stood in the center of the front room, imagining the way she'd set it up. A few tables here in the front room so people strolling along the sidewalk could see inside. The old guest rooms upstairs restored and converted to dining rooms.

A tea room. High tea in the afternoons, just tea and pastries the rest of the day. Roseanne's baked goods were to die for.

The back would be Roseanne's personal domain. Her test kitchen. No more grabbing a few hours each day in the kitchen at the B&B to work on her recipes. She could experiment all she wanted and hire others to prepare and serve the tea menu.

It would fit perfectly into the backdrop of downtown and, with the aid of the other businesses moving in, would have a steady clientele.

He'd already hired a PR firm to promote Butte Plains as a weekend destination. With the new airstrip, they were promoting the town to private plane owners' groups. Who knew there were flying clubs out there had fly-in meetings? The PR people were working with the new hotel by the freeway and Roseanne's bed-and-breakfast to provide a group rate for certain holiday weekends to encourage the clubs to visit. Ads were being placed in travel magazines across the country, but primarily in the South and Southwest.

He locked up and headed to his car. He had a golf course in need of a new owner to check out.

~ ~ ~

It was happening. It was *really* happening!

For once, Roseanne's stomach was queasy for another reason besides being pregnant.

"Are you packed yet?" Becky called from the hallway. "It's time to go."

"Done." Stuffing one last-minute item into her suitcase, she closed the lid and zipped up the case she'd borrowed from her best friend.

"We've got to go, girlfriend. You've got dinner reservations tonight. Don't want to be late." Becky stood in the doorway to Roseanne's third-floor room.

Roseanne sat on the bed next to her borrowed suitcase. "Please come with me tonight. I'm begging you. My agent said it would be okay."

"Nope. I'm going to order room service then enjoy the hell out of an expensive bottle of wine and that gorgeous soaking tub in our suite. Besides, you don't need me. Your agent and your editor will be there, fawning over you like you're some kind of big shot, which you are. This is your deal. You worked hard for it, so enjoy. Besides, after my meeting tomorrow morning, the two of us are going to celebrate in style."

"Okay, okay." She stood and slid the luggage to the floor.

"Leave that," Becky said. She leaned out the door and yelled, "Ford! Come get Roseanne's suitcase."

Loud footsteps sounded on the back stairs.

"I can—"

"Nonsense. Ford can carry it down twice as fast as either of us could."

"You haven't told him, have you?"

Becky swiped her finger across her chest twice. "Cross my heart." She gave her friend the evil eye. "But I'm going to if you don't tell you-know-who soon."

"Tell who what?" Ford asked, huffing from climbing all the way to the top floor.

"Nothing," Roseanne and Becky said in unison.

Ford reached for the handle on the luggage. "Got it. None of my business." He disappeared, case in hand. The women shared a look they'd perfected over years of friendship. The discussion wasn't over, just tabled until they were alone and had plenty of time.

"Let's get this show on the road before I chicken out." Roseanne headed for the door, Becky on her heels.

Roseanne had only traveled in such luxury one other time— when she'd flown with Scott in one of the Ramsey family jets to Las Vegas. The one Ford had chartered for his wife and her best friend for this trip to New York City wasn't quite as elaborate on the inside, but it came close. Before they left the ground, the flight attendant offered them an array of drinks. Becky chose champagne while Roseanne opted for fizzy water in a pretty bottle.

"I don't know how I can thank you and Ford enough for doing this for me."

"No thanks needed. This is a business trip for me, too. I've needed to meet with these people forever, but Ford didn't want me to go alone, and, with everything we've got going on right now, one of us needs to be in the office. You couldn't have sold your cookbook at a better time for us." She lifted her champagne flute. "I thank you for that from the bottom of my heart."

Roseanne raised her water bottle in salute. "The fact that you're getting a whole weekend in a luxury suite in New York has absolutely nothing to do with your enthusiasm for this trip, I suppose."

"Not a damned thing, sister."

Takeoff went smoothly, and soon they were at cruising altitude. Roseanne reclined her seat and tried to enjoy the moment. She couldn't believe how much her life had changed since that trip to Las Vegas. She'd ended her relationship with Scott only to find out days later she was pregnant. By all appearances he'd moved on—she'd seen the evidence with her own eyes. So even if she did want him back, that was out of the question. Almost paralyzed by the daunting task ahead of her, she'd still managed to orchestrate Becky and Ford's wedding. Then, the calls had come that made all the difference. First, an agent then the call that she'd sold Roseanne's first cookbook to an editor at a major publishing house in New York. The advance they were offering wasn't enormous, but substantial, her agent called it.

At any rate, the money would allow Roseanne to rent a small place of her own where she'd have room to raise her child. This trip was so she could meet her new editor and discuss their marketing and book launch plans. She got butterflies in her stomach every time she thought about it. Or was that the baby moving around?

She placed her hand on her belly which was now gently rounded. Easy still to hide, but not for much longer.

"You know you're going to have to tell him, don't you?"

"I know." Roseanne sighed. She should have known Becky wouldn't let the subject drop. "I will. I've put it off because my lawyer suggested I draw up a custody agreement to present to Scott when I tell him. Be proactive. Until I sold this book, I didn't have the money to pay him to prepare the papers. I'll have him get started on it as soon as I get home."

"I know you were counting on Scott going back home, but, from what Ford says, he isn't going to do that. He wants to stay in Butte Plains."

Roseanne huffed and stared out the window. "I bet he'll run far and fast as soon as he finds out he's going to be a father. No way will he stick around for that."

"I don't know. I sort of think you need to give him the benefit of the doubt."

Roseanne shot her a look. "Seriously?"

"Yeah, I'm serious. You met his parents at our wedding. They're nothing like him. I can believe he was protecting you when he didn't take you to their party."

"Maybe he thought he was protecting me, but that still doesn't account for him not telling me about the party and letting me decide."

"Turns out the decision was made for you anyway, and not by Scott, but by Scott's baby. Talk all you want about not being allowed to make your own decisions, but remember you aren't giving him any choices, either."

"I know." She wasn't being fair to Scott, but every time she thought about telling him, legal papers in hand or not, her stomach rebelled. What if he stayed in Butte Plains because of the child? What if he married someone else and had more kids? God, she'd have to live in the same town with him the rest of her life — see his other kids grow up with a full-time father. How would she ever explain that to her child? She closed her eyes and searched deep for strength. "I'll tell him, Becks. I swear I will."

~ ~ ~

The car and driver Ford had hired to cart them around town met them at the airport. Roseanne had thought it was even more excess, but as soon as she saw the traffic and crowded sidewalks, she changed her mind.

"How does anyone ever get anywhere in this city?" she asked.

"Don't know," Becky said, tipping her head to get a better look at a building. "Ford had a house in Westchester and rarely went into the city. I can see why."

"Me, too." She'd never seen so many people in one place, and all of them appeared to be in a hurry to get somewhere else. "Where do you think all these people are going?"

"I have no idea. Work? School? Shopping? All those things we use our cars for."

Roseanne shook her head. "It's crazy. I don't know how they stand it. I like my space." At a stoplight, she saw a woman pushing a stroller across the busy intersection. Mother? Nanny? Instantly, she thought about the child she carried. What if Scott won custody? Somewhere amid all these buildings that blocked the sun was the place he called home. Would he want to bring the baby here to raise? Would he hire a stranger to look after their child while he darted around the city, racing to nowhere? Her hand went to her belly, seeking comfort for herself and silently reassuring the child within.

"Are you okay?" Becky placed a hand on Roseanne's arm. "Is the baby alright?"

"I'm fine. We're fine," she corrected.

"You looked like you were in pain."

She shook her head. "No. I was just thinking. If Scott sues for custody and wins, he'd probably want to bring the baby here. People like him don't raise kids. They hire nannies to do that for them. I can't let that happen."

"First, I don't think you have anything to worry about. Scott seems like a reasonable person. Besides, we're talking about Texas. What judge would let a single dad take a child away from its mother and haul off halfway across the country with it?" She shook her head so hard her ponytail slapped against her cheeks. "Not going to happen. But," she said, "kids are resilient. They adapt to their surroundings. I'm certain there are plenty of happy, healthy children growing up here."

"Ugh. That's not what I wanted to hear."

"I know it's not, but I think you're projecting sins on Scott without any grounds. You won't know what his intentions are until you tell him about the baby."

Roseanne shot her friend a warning look.

"Okay. I'll shut up. But you know I'm right."

They passed a glass-faced tower that seemed to have no pinnacle. So cold and impersonal, reflecting, deflecting. Windows with no soul. Roseanne wiped a tear from her eye. She couldn't wait to complete her business and get back home.

CHAPTER TWENTY-TWO

Roseanne followed the maître d' as he threaded his way through the crowded restaurant to a small room on the second floor. Her dinner companions were already there. They stood and introduced themselves.

"Roseanne, I'm so happy to meet you. I'm Liz Rothstein."

This was the agent she'd spoken to several times on the phone. Roseanne smiled and extended her hand to the woman who might have been five feet tall, weighing in at maybe a hundred pounds with a halo of dark, frizzy hair that framed her narrow face. She had a booming voice that made her seem larger than she actually was. "It's nice to meet you, Liz."

"And this is your editor, Paula Ramone." She indicated the other woman at the table. The two women couldn't have been more different. Paula towered over the diminutive agent and, thanks to her generous curves, probably outweighed her by fifty pounds. She'd pulled her straight, glossy black hair to one side, holding it in place with a jeweled clip.

"Hello, Roseanne. It's nice to meet you."

The two shook hands. "My pleasure," Roseanne said, taking the seat across from the two women. She grabbed the neatly folded napkin at her place setting, spreading it across her lap to give herself a moment to calm down. She'd had all of ten minutes to enjoy their hotel room before she'd returned to the car for another hair-raising trip through man-made canyons filled with cars and people.

"How was your trip?" Paula asked.

"Uneventful. Which is exactly what you hope a plane ride will be, right?"

The women laughed. "True," Liz said. They exchanged polite conversation while waiters in white coats and black slacks bustled around them, bringing baskets of bread and dishes of fragrant olive oil seasoned with cracked pepper.

"I hope you like Italian," Paula said. "This is one of the best places in the city to get authentic Italian food."

"She should know," Liz said.

"Italian, through and through," Paula confirmed. "But that doesn't mean I can't enjoy other types of food. As a matter of fact, I'm a food junkie. Your recipes really caught my eye, Roseanne. And the concept is something I think every hostess can relate to whether you have guests you want to pamper or just want to do something special for your family."

"Thank you. We try to pamper our guests at the bed-and-breakfast. If they wanted a cold, impersonal experience, they'd stay at a chain hotel. They choose The Yellow Rose because they want more."

"Exactly!" Liz said. "Plus, your recipes aren't so complicated that it takes a trained chef to prepare them."

"I've found that complicated doesn't always mean better."

Waiters appeared with platters of steaming dishes they placed in the middle of the table for everyone to serve themselves. "Like Italian food. A few key ingredients and you have a simple, but delicious meal. Help yourself." Paula pointed to each dish, naming them as she went. Roseanne's mouth watered.

"It all looks delicious." She ladled a generous helping of spaghetti with meat sauce onto her plate, topping it off with a slice of garlic bread.

"Wine?" Paula lifted the bottle that had been opened and left on the table to "breathe."

"No, thank you. I think I'll stick with water."

"Liz?"

"Sure." She held her glass while Paula poured.

"You sure?" Paula asked again.

Roseanne waved her offer away. "Positive. But, thank you."

They focused on filling their stomachs for a few minutes, breaking the silence with the occasional comment about the food which was delicious. Roseanne hadn't experimented much with Italian dishes, but she vowed to give it a try when she got home. She especially loved the array of desserts that arrived as they were taking their last bites.

"Oh, yum!" She wiped a glob of sweet cheese filling from the corner of her mouth. "This is fabulous."

"Cannoli is my favorite," Paula confessed. "I could eat my weight in them, which is saying something." She laughed and reached for her second one.

With the help of her dinner companions, Roseanne tasted all the confections and felt ready to burst when the waiters came to clear the table. "You know I'm going to go home and try to recreate everything I've eaten here."

"I can send you some of my family recipes if you want."

"I want." Roseanne beamed. Family recipes were the best. "Most of the recipes in my book are adaptations of my grandmother's recipes. She was a fabulous cook, but ingredients have changed over the years. There are healthier options and, in some cases, more flavorful ones."

"Which brings us back to business," Paula said. "Normally, something like this would take years to get out, but we've had some setbacks with one of our usually reliable authors. That's bad for us, but great for you. We want to fast-track your book—get it out in time for the holidays."

"I don't know what to say. This is—"

"A big, freakin' deal," Paula said. "I've already sent the recipes to an independent test kitchen we use. They'll work up all the crap no one wants to know about their food—calorie count, fat, and salt numbers. The art department has been working overtime on a cover. I have some ideas to show you, see what you think."

Roseanne's head swam. Everything came at her too fast for her to keep up.

Paula continued on, oblivious to Roseanne's state of mind. "We'll launch big with some cooking shows. I've got contacts at the Food Network, so that shouldn't be a problem. I'm positive I can get you a spot on all the major morning shows. Then we'll hit all the major markets, New York, Chicago, Dallas, Los Angeles. Their local morning shows followed up by signings at the large retailers. If we have time, I'd like to squeeze in some signings in the satellite cities, too."

Satellite cities? What the hell are those? Television appearances and book signings all over the country? What had she signed on for?

"Oh, and my people, *your* people, are working on some magazine interviews, too. What do you think? Sound good?"

Roseanne knew she must be staring like a loon, but she couldn't find words.

"That's an ambitious plan," Liz said. "Are you sure you can pull it off in time for the holidays?"

"It's going to be a tall order, but yes, I think we can."

"I can't do it."

"What?" Both women screeched at the same time.

"I said, I can't do it. Maybe some of it, but not all."

"Why not? Do you understand what kind of opportunity this is? This is the kind of marketing package usually reserved for top-tier authors. We're doing you a favor. A big favor." Paula's tone had reached the same temperature as the ice in Roseanne's water glass, and sounded just as brittle.

Roseanne twisted her hands in her lap. She'd never imagined something like this happening.

"Roseanne." Liz reached across the table. "Are you okay?"

"I'm…fine." She took a deep breath then let it out. "I appreciate the opportunity, but I can't do that kind of tour."

"Why?" Liz's normally booming voice held nothing but concern now. "Tell us why."

"Because I'm pregnant." A glass shattered somewhere behind her. Roseanne ignored the commotion and continued. "The baby is due around Christmas."

Both women stared at her, their mouths open in shock.

"I'm sorry. I would have told you, but it…. I didn't—"

"How could you have known?" Liz said. She turned to Paula. "What can you do?"

"I don't know. I'll have to go back to the team and see what we can salvage from this." She made no attempt to hide her disappointment. "I wish I'd known."

Roseanne opened her mouth to apologize again, but Liz cut her off. "There's no way she could have known you would do something like this. You should have told me. I could have told her, and then we wouldn't be in this mess."

"Liz said it would be next year before the book came out, at the earliest."

"That's the normal timeline, yes," Paula said.

"This isn't her fault."

"No, I suppose it isn't." Paula signaled for the waiter. When he arrived, she asked for the check. They sat in silence until the back and forth was done and the bill paid. Paula stood. "It really is a pleasure to have met you, Roseanne." She turned to the agent. "Liz. I'll be in touch."

"I'm so sorry."

"Don't be. Like I told Paula…this isn't your fault. She knows better than to do something like this without checking with the author first. The contract is signed. If they want to launch on an accelerated timeline, that's their business, but you are under no obligation to participate in the tour."

"My contract says that?"

"It has an out for extenuating circumstances. I'm sure your attorney noted that clause."

Roseanne nodded. "Yes. He mentioned that, but—"

"I know. Don't worry about it. She'll fume about it for a day or two then she'll revise the schedule. If she insists on the early release date, then we'll agree to a fair amount of promotional appearances. You can do the morning show interviews from home via satellite link. Surely there's a television station near you?"

"As a matter of fact, my best friend and her husband produce their own home shopping show. They recently launched a new network. Maybe you've heard of it—The Adult Shopping Network?"

"Who hasn't heard of it? They call him The Backdoor Billionaire, right?"

"Yes. His name is Ford Adams. He married my best friend, Becky Jean Parker. They have a state-of-the-art studio, and I think they have satellite access. It's just a few blocks from my house."

"That's perfect! I'll email Paula and give her that information. You could even pre-tape interviews for some of the smaller markets, and I'll do my best to keep the personal appearances confined to a decent geographical range to minimize travel. Would that work for you?"

"I think I could handle that." She'd have no choice but to tell Scott about the baby if she was going to be on television unless she could convince them to do tight, headshots only.

"Then it's settled. I'll have a talk with Paula, get this straightened out. Don't worry."

CHAPTER TWENTY-THREE

It had been a week since her trip to New York, and she hadn't heard a thing from her editor or her agent. She tried not to think about it. No news was good news, right? When she'd returned to the hotel and told Becky what had happened, she'd insisted on calling the attorney who had looked over the contract for Roseanne. He'd confirmed that yes, she had agreed to make personal appearances and participate in marketing the book, but that in no way obligated her to do anything that would be detrimental to her health or well-being. In his opinion, asking a woman in the last weeks of her pregnancy to traipse around the country to sell a book fell under the "asking too much" umbrella, especially since the timeline Roseanne had agreed to had been changed on her without notice.

The confirmation made her feel better about the whole thing, but she was still afraid they'd find some way to weasel out of the contract based on her inability to fulfill her end of the marketing plan. When Kay knocked on her office door, she welcomed the interruption. Anything to keep her mind occupied so she didn't dwell on things she couldn't control.

"What is it, Kay?"

"There's a gentleman here to see you. He said it was personal."

"Who is it?"

Kay shrugged. "No idea. He's not from around here, I can tell you that. Too slick. Lawyer would be my guess."

Roseanne's heart sank. Her worst fears had come true. They'd found a way to break the contract. She opened the top drawer of her desk to grab a tissue from the box she kept there, giving herself a moment to fight back the tears. She could be a watering pot later. Right now, she needed to be strong, assertive. Her attorney had assured her they couldn't use her pregnancy as a reason to nullify the contract. "Would you show him to my office, please?" She'd meet him on her own turf where she held the position of authority.

"Yes, ma'am. I'd be just as happy to show him the door."

Out of necessity, she'd told Kay about her pregnancy. The woman hadn't been surprised. She'd seen Roseanne's battle with morning sickness and fatigue, and lately she'd noticed her expanding belly. Always loyal, she'd become Roseanne's protector, taking on more responsibility and putting in more hours.

Roseanne smiled. "I appreciate the offer, but he'd only come back another time. Best hear what he has to say so I can deal with it."

"If you say so."

"I say so. Show him in."

She quickly dabbed the extra moisture from the corners of her eyes and ran a hand over her hair, smoothing an errant strand back in place. Whatever he had to say, she'd hear him out then call her attorney and fill him in. Together, they'd come up with a plan to respond.

Kay appeared in the hallway, followed by a man wearing a three-piece suit and carrying a briefcase that screamed expensive lawyer.

"I'll be in the kitchen, Ms. Meadows. If you need anything, just holler." The way she emphasized the word anything brought a smile to Roseanne's lips. All she'd have to do was raise her voice, and Kay would come running, rolling pin in hand, most likely.

Remaining seated, she said, "Thank you, Kay." She shifted her gaze to her visitor. "I'm Roseanne Meadows. You wanted to see me?"

He stepped inside. "My name is Roland Meiser." He slid a card from an inside pocket of his suit jacket and handed it to her. "Senior partner at Meiser, Swift and Harding in New York City."

Roseanne took the card, glancing briefly at it before dropping it on top of the stack of purchase orders she'd been sorting before he arrived. "What's this about, Mr. Meiser?"

He swung his briefcase into his lap and opened it. "I'm here to make you an offer."

What? "I don't understand. An offer? From whom?"

"I represent the concerns of the Ramsey family." He held out a sheaf of papers. Roseanne made no attempt to take them.

Her blood ran cold. "Again. What is this about?"

He dropped the papers on her desk and stood. "You have forty-eight hours to respond before the offer is off the table for good."

"And if I refuse this offer?"

"Then my client has instructed me to file for sole custody of the child you carry. You will never see your child, Ms. Meadows. My client has the means and the clout to have the child removed from your care the moment it takes its first breath. Don't make the mistake of thinking you can fight us on this. You will lose. Take the offer, Ms. Meadows." He stopped in the doorframe and turned. "I look forward to hearing from you soon."

She couldn't speak. Couldn't breathe. Couldn't move. Her gaze landed on the stack of papers he'd left on her desk. The Ramsey's. Scott. It was too much to process. If she didn't take the offer. What offer? Reaching out as if afraid the paper might strike at any moment, she dragged them forward. Slowly, she forced her fingers to function, lifting the papers from the desk. It took a moment for her vision to clear enough for her to make out the neatly typed words.

She read. Then read again. Words with no meaning floated

before her eyes. Settlement. Paternity. Cease and desist. Forbidden. Claim.

No. No. "Noooo!"

"Roseanne! What's the matter? Is it the baby?"

Kay. Sweet Kay holding her. "I've got to go."

"No, no you don't. Everything's going to be alright. Should I call the doctor?"

Doctor? "No. I've got to go. See that bastard."

"Who? The doctor?"

"No. I've got to go." She stood, forcing Kay to step back.

"I'll drive you. Let me get my purse." When Kay returned, Roseanne held the papers in her fist, her only tether to reality. "Where are we going?"

"I don't know. Where he is." Where would he be? She didn't have a clue where he spent his days. "The leather factory?"

"I know where that is. My cousin used to work there."

Roseanne nodded.

"Okay, then. Is my car okay?"

Another nod.

The drive went by in a blur of color and sounds muted and silenced by the noise in her head—the whirlwind of legalese designed to tear her life apart.

"We're here. Do you want me to come in with you?"

She searched the parking lot, spied his car in a VIP spot. "I don't care." It didn't matter who heard what she had to say. She'd climb up on the roof and shout it to the world if it would make a difference.

She'd been here before. Nodded to the receptionist and continued down the hall to the office he'd claimed for himself when he bought the place. Behind her, she heard Kay say, "No, she'll just be a minute."

A minute. A lifetime. What did it matter? She stopped in the doorway. Scott Ramsey stood behind the desk, a cardboard box open in front of him—the desktop clear, the walls bear. Leaving.

Going back to the cesspool he'd crawled out of.

He looked up, saw her. A smile on his lips that faded as his gaze swept to her swollen belly — the pregnancy unmistakable now. "Roseanne. Sweetheart." He came toward her. "What—?"

She threw the papers at him, stopping him in his tracks. "Who the hell do you think you are? Who do you think I am? Offering me money to keep my mouth shut, to disappear into some hellhole so you can go on with your life as if nothing happened? You're despicable, Scott Ramsey. I wouldn't put your name on my child's birth certificate if someone held a gun to my head. You can tell that slimy lawyer of yours there's no charge for that, you bastard. You can keep your money. I don't want any part of it. That's the deal. The only deal you're going to get, so don't even think of suing for custody. Good luck finding me or my child if you choose that route."

Don't cry. Not now. Not yet.

"Roseanne!"

His voice spurred her on. She could barely see to walk, but she refused to cry where he might see. She'd shed enough tears over him. Never again.

"Come on. Let's get out of here."

Kay. Sweet Kay. In the car. Going. Going. Away. "Thank you."

"He's the one?"

Roseanne nodded. She closed her eyes, letting the tears fall.

~ ~ ~

Scott stood in the parking lot, legs braced apart, hands on hips, watching the car disappear with Roseanne in it. *What the fuck?* His brain scrambled to make sense of the last few seconds. He'd been packing the few things he kept in the office in order to move to his new digs in the old Cotton Exchange building. Then, as if he'd conjured her up, Roseanne stood in his doorway. Beautiful, angry, and…pregnant.

Pregnant. How the fuck had he missed that? His blood heated. He'd done that to her. Him. His baby. Their baby.

Pride, love, pure happiness coursed through his system. He'd have to call Tucker and set his ass on fire to get the house finished. They'd need a nursery. Maybe the small room next to the master suite.

"Mr. Ramsey?"

What? "What is it, Penny?"

"There's a phone call for you. It's your father. He says it's urgent."

The world stopped spinning—stilled on its axis. Everything Roseanne had said in his office came back to him in a rush that nearly brought him to his knees. The papers. *"You can tell that slimy lawyer of yours there's no charge… You can keep your money."*

What money? He clenched his fists. His mouth felt like the Sahara as he ground his molars in an effort to keep his rage inside. His parents had somehow found out about the baby. He knew it all the way to the marrow of his bones. What had they done? "Tell him I'll call him back. Oh, and there are some papers on the floor in my office. Gather them up and bring them to me."

"Yes, sir."

The door closed behind him with a whoosh. Gaze fixed on infinity, he could see Roseanne's rounded belly as clear as day. Knew he'd do anything. Beg. Denounce his trust fund to be a father to his child.

But first, he had to find out what the hell was going on.

CHAPTER TWENTY-FOUR

"Where to?" Kay asked. They'd been driving around in circles for half an hour because Roseanne had refused to go home.

"I don't know. Home, I guess." Guests would be arriving soon, and there was no one there to greet them. Now, more than ever, she needed the inn to run smoothly. She'd need every cent she could scrape together to fight for her child. "Can you handle things by yourself this afternoon?"

"You know I can." Kay steered the car into the driveway. They walked around to the back and let themselves in through the kitchen. "I don't know about you, but I could use something cold to drink. And a cookie, maybe?" She pulled two glasses from the cabinet and filled them with sweet tea from a pitcher in the refrigerator.

Roseanne sat at the island, her hands rubbing her belly, silently telling the life within that everything would be all right. She'd find a way. Kay placed a glass in front of her then nudged the plate of cookies Roseanne had made that morning into her line of sight.

"You need to eat something. Keep your strength up."

"Thank you. For everything." Roseanne reached for a cookie. "I don't know what I would do without you."

"Good thing I'm not going anywhere, then," the older woman said.

Roseanne chuckled at the now-familiar verbal exchange. Though true, it had become their little joke. Roseanne depended on Kay, and her assistant treated her more like a daughter than an employer. They were lucky to have found each other when they had, and they both knew it.

"Things are going to get weird around here," she said.

"What did the lawyer want?"

Over sweet tea and cookies, Roseanne filled Kay in. It was only fair the woman know what was happening since it ultimately could affect her job. If Roseanne had to disappear with her child, everything she'd built for herself would be destroyed, including the bed-and-breakfast.

"Oh, honey. That's just awful. How can people be so cruel?"

Roseanne shook her head. "I don't know, Kay. I really thought I knew Scott, but apparently I was wrong. Very, very wrong."

"Are you sure he's a part of this?"

"He was packing up his office." She met the woman's gaze. "He's going back to New York."

"Oh."

"Yeah. The bastard is running, but, just to make sure his mistake doesn't come back to bite him in the ass, he sicced his lawyer on me. Buy the lady off. Make sure his name is never mentioned in regards to his bastard child. Well, not a problem. I would...wouldn't...."

"Oh, honey." Kay embraced Roseanne. The tears she'd held at bay finally broke through the dam, spilling out in gut-wrenching sobs she had no ability to control. "It's going to be okay. Just you wait and see."

She wanted to believe that, but she was no match for the likes of the Ramseys. Money meant power, and, compared to them, she had nothing. Nothing but her determination to stay as far from them as possible.

When she finally gained some control, she could barely hold her head up. Rage, fear, and grief had stolen her strength. Kay helped her to her room and made sure she was tucked in bed. With orders to rest, Roseanne closed her eyes and slept.

She woke with a mouth as dry as cotton. The room had grown dark, but sounds coming from the floor below told her their guests for the night had arrived. Glancing at the clock, she saw she'd slept most of the day away. Her stomach rumbled, reminding her she needed to eat—not for herself but for her child. Easing her way out of bed, she stretched and gingerly made her way to her private bathroom. After a quick shower, she pulled her hair back and dressed in leggings and a flowing top that didn't scream pregnant woman.

Taking the back stairs to the kitchen, she hoped to avoid seeing anyone. She should have known Kay would be there.

"There you are. I made dinner for you. It's not much, just soup and some of that bread you made the other day. I used that recipe you were working on last month. I hope you aren't sick of Minestrone."

"No. I'm not sick of it." She'd adapted the iconic Italian soup, adding meat and thickening the sauce to make a hearty main dish version. "Thanks."

"Not a problem. Have a seat. It'll just take a few minutes to heat it up." She turned a burner on beneath a giant stockpot then set about getting a bowl and utensils.

Roseanne helped herself to a glass of water, drinking it down in one long gulp before refilling it and sitting down to wait for her meal. If she got to keep the advance the publishing company had paid her, she would have to consider using a portion of it to make things easier for her assistant. Kay had spent too many nights sleeping on the loveseat in Roseanne's office. Maybe she would consider moving into the owner's suite on the third floor once the garage had been converted to an apartment for her and the baby.

The child seemed to do a somersault, startling her and bringing back into focus the painful reality she now had to live with. Scott didn't want anything to do with his child.

A buzzing sound drew her attention to the corner of the island. A cell phone vibrated on the polished marble surface.

"It's been ringing all afternoon. I put it on silent so it wouldn't disturb the guests."

"Who?"

Kay shrugged and continued to stir the soup. "Don't know. None of my business."

Roseanne retrieved the phone, waiting until she was seated to punch the button that would bring the screen to life. *Scott.* Twenty-seven times. He'd left a couple of voicemails and a few dozen text messages, too. She set the phone aside. Whatever he had to say could wait until she had eaten. Maybe even forever. "Everything go okay with check-in?"

"Yep. Couple in the front room were late getting in, but everyone is settled now. The couple in the Senator's Suite want to talk to you about having their daughter's wedding here in the spring. Said they saw pictures of the Adams's wedding in some magazine and thought this would be the perfect place."

"I'll talk to them tomorrow. Anything else?"

"Nope. You going to be alright this evening? I can stay if you think you need me."

"I'm good." If Scott decided to come over instead of harass her by phone, she'd call the police. She didn't have to take any shit from him or his family. "Thanks for everything. I don't know what I'd do without you."

The older woman slid a bowl of soup and a generous slice of homemade bread in front of her. "Good thing I'm not going anywhere, then."

~ ~ ~

How the hell did his life get this fucked up?

Scott read the offer again. And again, his blood pressure hit the roof. He'd tried countless times to contact Roseanne, let her know this was bullshit and to forget about it, but she hadn't answered a single one of his calls or texted him back. He had no idea if she'd listened to the voicemail messages he'd left. He could only hope she had.

He'd wanted to go to her, tell her in person, but as soon as he'd read the papers she'd thrown at him, he'd known the only way to end this was in person. As the wheels of his private jet skidded on the runway, he gripped the armrests and steeled himself for the confrontation to come. If the people who shared his blood couldn't accept him, the woman he loved, and the child they'd created, then they could go to hell. And they could take their money with them. He had enough of his own. More than they knew. Maybe more than all of them combined.

While he'd worked hard and made wise investments that had netted him a sizeable fortune, they'd spent. Lavish parties. Expensive toys, vacations, and clothes. None of that meant anything to him. He'd rather barbeque in the backyard with a few friends than put on a tux and mingle with a bunch of people who thought they were better than anyone else. He'd gladly give up his jet for a car and a long trip with Roseanne along the back roads of Texas. Give him a pair of jeans and an old T-shirt, and he would be a happy man.

Pretenses were for those who had no identity of their own. He knew exactly who he was, and, in a few minutes, his family would know, too.

He rented a car at the airport. He'd called no one. He was here for one reason, and when he'd completed his task, he would leave. Maybe forever. That was up to them. He no longer cared what decision they made as long as they left him the hell alone. Because, as soon as he cleared this matter up, he was going home. To Texas. To Roseanne. To his child. To the future he had always wanted.

He didn't ring the bell. Didn't wait for Curtis to let him in. Who the hell needed a butler? Open your own damned door. How difficult was that?

"Mom! Dad!"

Curtis, his brows raised in alarm, appeared at the end of the long, center hallway. "Mr. Ramsey! We weren't expecting you."

No shit. "Where are they?"

"I believe Mrs. Ramsey is upstairs. Mr. Ramsey is out at the putting green. The weather—"

"Tell them both I'll be waiting in the library. If they aren't there in five minutes, they'll be hearing from my attorney tomorrow."

Curtis dipped his chin. "As you wish." Then he was gone, leaving Scott standing in the middle of the marble monstrosity his parents called a home. He shook his head. He couldn't wait to move into the old Victorian he'd purchased. Tucker had assured him the renovation would be complete in two weeks. He'd laughed and asked for a realistic estimate. "Okay, four weeks," the man had said. "Promise."

His sneakers squeaked on the polished floor as he made his way to the library. Lined with books and furnished with warm leather chairs, it was the only room in the house he truly liked. Though smaller, the library in his new house would look much the same as this one, and double as a home office he would share with Roseanne—if he could convince her to marry him. After the stunt his parents had pulled, he couldn't predict what would happen when he asked her. Once, he'd had no doubt.

He'd screwed that up all on his own. His intentions had been good. Spot-on as this latest debacle proved. He'd been right to protect Roseanne from his family. If she'd let him, he'd protect her for the rest of their lives.

At the sound of footsteps on the marble floor outside, Scott turned. His parents entered through the double doors together. If he'd had any doubt they were in this together, their united front banished it.

"Scott, darling," his mother said. "We're so glad you're home."

"Son," his father said. "You should have called. We would have sent Robert to pick you up."

"I'm perfectly capable of driving myself. As a matter of fact, I'm capable of doing a lot of things. Like choosing where I will live.

What I will do with my time and my money. I can even dress myself and cook my own food." He nodded. "Shocking, I know. I even do my own laundry."

"Scott—"

He held up a hand to stop his mother. "You know what else I can do? I can choose who I want to be my family."

"Now, son—"

"Don't. Don't call me that. You've lost the right." Scott clenched his fists to keep from picking up something and throwing it across the room. Venting his anger like a spoiled child would only convince these two they'd done the right thing. "How dare you make decisions for me concerning the people I love? How dare you assume I have no right to raise my own child? What did you think you would do with the baby if Roseanne refused to take your money? Huh? Did you think you'd sue for custody then ship the kid off to boarding schools for the rest of its life? Pretend it didn't exist?"

He could see from the look on their faces he'd hit that nail on the head. His stomach turned. "Let me tell you how this is going to go. You are going to call your lawyer and tell him this was all a big mistake. You're going to tell him to destroy everything to do with this ridiculous proceeding. He's to forget he ever laid eyes on Roseanne Meadows. Then you're going to forget you ever met her, and while you're at it, you're going to forget about me. I don't exist as far as you're concerned. Don't try to contact me. Ever. Is that clear?"

"Perfectly, brother of mine."

Scott's gaze shot to his sister who stood in the doorway. He had no proof she had anything to do with this, but he had his suspicions. Trouble might as well have been her middle name. "Ronnie."

"So you knocked up the little innkeeper." She shrugged and stepped into the room. "No big deal. Happens all the time." She moved like a cat on the prowl. He tracked her movements, determined not to become her prey again.

"You will speak with respect where Roseanne is concerned, or you won't speak at all. And it is a big deal to me. That's my child you're talking about, not to mention the woman I love."

"Love? Really, Scotty? She's a mouse. Don't you think you've toyed with her enough? It's time to cut your losses before you find yourself living in that mouse hole of a town, playing daddy to a litter of squeaky kids."

He dug his nails into the palms of his hands. He'd never struck a person in anger before, but if she didn't stop talking, she might just be the first. Woman or not. "Shut up while you still can, Ronnie."

"Mom and Dad did you a favor. Why can't you see that? You know, Solange has been asking about you? She's yours for the asking. Think about it. She'd be the perfect wife for you. She's beautiful. She has her own life. She wouldn't drag you down."

He'd dated the supermodel for several months and couldn't recall a single moment of their time together. All he remembered was feeling like a noose had been looped around his neck, the end of the rope held tight by his mother and his grandmother's goddamned china. "You want me to marry her so the two of you can continue fucking each other without anyone knowing."

"What?" his mother screeched.

"Here now!" his father bellowed.

"Fuck you." This came from his sister.

Bingo. He'd nailed that one, too. "Don't worry. I'm not going to tell anyone as long as you and them" — he indicated his parents who were now staring at their youngest child — "leave me and my *family* alone."

"We're your family, dickwad."

"No. You aren't. Family doesn't try to make their grandchildren disappear. They don't manipulate their children's or sibling's lives. I'm done with all of you. As Davy Crockett said, 'You may all go to hell, and I will go to Texas.'"

He shoved his way past his speechless parents and fuming sister. Veronica chased him to the front door, alternately swearing at him and begging him not to say anything about her relationship with Solange. He had nothing left to say, so he kept his mouth shut. Halfway back to the airport, he pulled into a service center and peeled his fingers from the steering wheel. He went in and grabbed a cup of coffee and a donut. The coffee tasted like dirty water and the pastry might have been cardboard. He didn't care. The caffeine and sugar gave him the energy to continue on toward the new life he'd chosen for himself.

Returning to the freeway, he thought about what he'd just done. He wasn't happy about cutting ties with his family, but it was the only way he could see to go forward. He wouldn't poison his new life with the negative energy he'd lived with his entire life. He wanted more for Roseanne and his son or daughter. But first, he had to convince Roseanne to talk to him. Or at least hear him out. Until he could accomplish that, his life would be on hold.

CHAPTER TWENTY-FIVE

"Becky?" Scott stood in Becky Jean Parker-Adams's office doorway, his fists clenched almost as tight as his jaw. He'd had exactly twenty-four hours to think about the fact he was going to be a father, and that others had known and kept it from him. One of those people sat before him. "Have you got a minute?"

She smiled and shoved her computer keyboard tray under the desk. "Sure. I could use a break."

Scott stepped inside, shutting the door behind him. Becky raised an eyebrow, but kept her smile in place. He understood her first loyalty would be to Roseanne, and, though he was certain Becky had known about the baby for some time, it was her love for her best friend that he was counting on today.

"Mind if I sit?"

"Not at all. What's on your mind? Is this about the new offices? Ford told me you'd shown him some space downtown."

He sat in one of the ancient chairs in front of her equally ancient desk. "No, this isn't about the office space, though you really should consider relocating your corporate offices. Having everything under one roof would make life a lot easier for you."

"I agree. That's why we're going ahead with the purchase of the property you brought to our attention. We had your man, Mr. Tucker, walk through it with us. It's not going to be cheap, but renovations are possible."

Scott nodded. "I'm glad to hear that." He met her gaze head-on. "Is there some other news you would like to tell me? Maybe something I should know but is being kept from me?"

She held his gaze for a moment before she closed her eyes and sighed. "I told her she should have told you. How did you find out?"

So, she did know. "She came to my office yesterday, basically to tell me I could go to hell."

Becky sat forward, her eyebrows knit together. "Why would she do that?"

"Because my parents' lawyer paid her a visit. Presented her with an offer—money enough to live on for a few years in exchange for filling in unknown under father's name on the birth certificate and never acknowledging to anyone that I'm the father. The papers she threw at me said if she didn't accept the offer, they'd sue for custody and she'd never see her child again."

Becky's mouth hung open. Her eyes had grown wide and her face pale. "You can't be serious."

"I had nothing to do with it. I didn't know she was pregnant, and I haven't got a clue how my parents found out. The only time they met her was at your wedding, and it certainly wasn't obvious then."

"No, it wasn't. She's only recently begun to show." Becky slumped in her chair.

"How far along is she?"

"Five months."

He did the calculation in his head. "Before Vegas."

Becky nodded. "Yes. She found out shortly after the Vegas trip."

"She was sick. Morning sickness?"

"Yeah. She didn't know at first. I actually figured it out and had to convince her to take a test."

He'd missed experiencing that with her, and so much more.

"She's been to a doctor?"

Becky opened her mouth to speak then shut it. She studied him for a moment then tried again. "You really should be talking to her about this. It's not my place—"

"No, it's not your place. However, Roseanne made it clear yesterday she doesn't want to see me. I swear to you, I didn't know. None of the things my parents threatened in those papers will ever happen. I won't let them happen. I intend to be a father to my child, but, first, I have to talk to Roseanne. I need your help to do that."

She picked up a pen and twirled it between her fingers. "Ford said you're planning to stay in Butte Plains."

"I am. This is my home now, even if things don't work out between me and Roseanne, but I can tell you, I want them to."

"Okay." She nodded. "I believe you. I always thought the two of you were good together, but she's my best friend. Just because you're Ford's best friend doesn't mean I'll cut you any slack. You've hurt her before. If you do it again, I'll make it my job to make your life here a living hell. Understood?"

"Understood. Now, will you talk to her? Convince her to hear me out?"

"I'll do my best, but there might be an issue."

"What kind of issue?"

"I thought I was the only person besides Roseanne to know. She hasn't even told her parents."

"Or me."

"Or you. She might think I told someone…maybe Ford, and that he told you. It would be a logical assumption."

Scott rolled his shoulders to ease the growing tension there. "I see what you mean."

"I hope she knows I would never do anything like that, but hormones seem to rule her these days. I'll do my best, if she'll talk to me."

That was the most he could hope for. "Thank you. You'll let me know how it works out?"

"I'll call you after I've talked to her—if I talk to her." Scott rose. He'd made it to the door when she stopped him. "Oh, and, Scott?"

"Yeah?"

"You'd better figure out how your family got wind of this. Roseanne isn't going to take kindly to having these people looking over her shoulder."

~ ~ ~

Damn. She shouldn't have left those papers in Scott's office. Not that she'd ever forget what they said, but her lawyer would want to read them for himself. She ran a finger over the raised lettering on the business card the Ramsey's shyster had left behind. Her attorney could call and get all the details he needed. If she never saw or heard from a Ramsey again, it would be too soon.

She didn't know where she was going to get the kind of money she'd need to fight the Ramsey's, but she would. Absolutely no one was going to take her child away. She'd work ten jobs if she needed.

She had to make some decisions about the running of the bed-and-breakfast. The more she thought about it, the more it made sense to convert the garage into an apartment for herself and the baby, or a future caretaker. That would open up all the bedrooms in the house to guests, increasing potential income. The first step would be to get an expert's opinion on the garage conversion. She dug through the top drawer of her desk and found Randy Tucker's business card. If anyone would know if her idea would work, it would be him. She'd been flattered by the personal interest he'd shown in her, but one look at her now would squash that. Too bad. In another life, she probably would have gone out with him.

Before she could talk herself out of it, she dialed the number on the card. Expecting it to go to voicemail, she jumped when the line connected, his voice sounding distant. "I'll be right back. Don't do anything until I tell you to." A moment later, he spoke into the phone. "Randy Tucker. How can I help you?"

"Mr. Tucker. It's Roseanne Meadows. From The Yellow Rose Bed-and-Breakfast?"

"Oh, hello. How are you?"

"I'm fine. You?"

"I wish just once a client wouldn't change their mind in the middle of a renovation, but, other than that, everything is good."

"Oh. I'm sorry. I mean, I thought I'd get your voicemail. I can call back later."

"No problem. I needed to get something out of my truck anyway. What's up?"

"I was wondering if you could come by sometime—no real hurry—and give me some advice. I'm thinking about converting my detached garage into an apartment. I don't know where to begin or if it's even something that could be done."

"You'd have to check with the city to make sure it's allowed. No use spending money on architectural drawings if the city won't approve the construction."

"I hadn't thought of that." A car door opened in the background. After a short interval, it slammed shut.

"I'm just around the corner from you. I could drop by in about an hour and take a look. No sense going to all the trouble of checking with the city if the building isn't structurally sound to begin with."

She could feel a headache coming on. None of the things he'd mentioned had even occurred to her. "Would you mind? I'd really appreciate it. I don't want to waste a lot of time and money on a dead end."

"Let me make sure my crew is clear on the changes the owner wants to make then I'll be over. Expect me within the hour, okay?"

"Perfect. Thanks, Mr. Tucker."

"Randy. You can call me Randy."

"Thanks, Randy."

"See you soon, Roseanne." The line went dead.

The interest he'd clearly shown in her when they first met hadn't gone away. She caressed her belly. *It will soon enough. Just wait until he gets a good look at me now.*

When he called to say he was on his way, Roseanne met him in front of the garage. Painted yellow with white trim to match the house, the two-car structure hadn't been touched in decades other than to add a fresh coat of paint when needed. The matching barn-style doors had long since succumbed to gravity, hanging slightly off-kilter.

"Sorry to keep you waiting," Randy said, stepping through the break in the hedges that led to the alley.

"Not a problem. Seriously. This could wait."

His gaze took her in, stopping briefly on the mound beneath her shirt she could no longer hide. "I don't know. Looks like you'll be needing an extra room pretty soon."

Heat rushed to her cheeks. She hadn't gotten used to people's reactions yet, especially from those who knew she wasn't married. Placing a protective hand on her belly, she summoned her inner strength. "Yes, I was thinking I could turn this into an apartment for myself. That would free up the room I'm currently using for another guest room. I just don't know if it's feasible or if I can afford to do it. It's worth checking into, I guess."

"What kind of timeline are you thinking?"

Roseanne shrugged. "I don't know. I guess it depends on how much it would cost. I'd have to see about getting financing to cover it then there's the city. I have no idea if they'll let me convert the garage or not."

"Well, let's take a look. There are a few key things to watch out for when you're thinking of doing something like this." He walked to the corner of the building. "I'd say you have about five hundred square feet, give or take." His gaze went to the roofline. "Not enough clearance there to make a second story, but you might get another two hundred square feet of loft space. My best guess is it would be a total of around six hundred square feet finished. Not huge, but enough for the essentials."

"I could put in a kitchen and a bathroom, right?"

"There's electricity," he said, pointing to the overhead wire running from the pole in the alley. "What about water and sewer?"

She shook her head. "Not that I know of."

"That would be something to figure into the cost. Let's have a look inside."

Roseanne kept the door hinges oiled, so the big door swung easily, as long as she lifted the end up so it didn't drag in the dirt. They stepped inside. Randy paid no attention to the boxes stacked around the perimeter. Some of them still contained things Roseanne had brought with her when she'd moved back from Florida years ago. Others were things her grandparents had collected over the years. She'd always said she would go through them, but hadn't found the time yet. If she were to go ahead with the construction, she'd have to find time. Everything in here would have to be moved. That meant she'd need a new storage place for the gardening tools and lawn mower, too.

"The roof looks sound, inside and out, but I'd have to get up on it to really tell."

"It's at least fifteen years old. I think my grandmother had it replaced at the same time she had the one on the house redone."

Randy nodded. "It should be okay, then. That would save you a lot of money." He poked around at the exposed studs. No one had ever bothered to finish the walls. "The wood looks to be in good condition. No rot that I can see. No evidence of termite damage. You'd need to reinforce the joists if you were to put a loft in. Electrical isn't up to today's code. That would all have to be redone. Depending on the floor plan you choose, you might have to put in more windows. Every bedroom has to have an accessible window in case of fire. You'd have to seal up the front, get rid of those garage doors and put in a regular door."

"That sounds like a lot of work and expense."

"On a place this size, it wouldn't take all that long. Three weeks, maybe four. If you want, I can draw up a rough estimate. Something you could take to the bank for the loan."

Looking at the project through his eyes made it seem

impossible. Why had she ever thought this could be a solution to her problem? "Let me think about it. I guess I should check and see if the city will let me do it first. An estimate at this point would be putting the cart before the horse."

"I know it sounds like a lot, but it would be a piece of cake for an experienced contractor. See what the city has to say, and if they're okay with it, let me know. I think I know this guy who owns a construction company, and he just happens to have a crew in the neighborhood. I bet I could talk him into giving you a good price."

She could feel heat blooming on her cheeks. "Thank you. I wouldn't expect any favors. That's not why I called you."

"I know, but you've been a big help to me on this project. Thanks to you, your neighbor is going to have an authentically restored home. I owe you."

"You don't owe me anything. How's the house coming? Almost finished?"

"We're getting there. We'd be done upstairs if the owner hadn't thrown a curveball yesterday."

"Oh?"

"Yeah. Said he wanted to add a door between the master bedroom and the guest room next to it."

"Why would they want to do something like that?"

"Word is they just found out they're going to have a baby. They want to use the guest room as a nursery and thought a connecting door would be convenient."

It had to be a coincidence. That was all it was. "Did you ever find out who the owner is?"

"Nope. All my communication is through Riley. Hey, did you ever contact him?"

She shook her head. "No. Once I saw what you were doing with the house, I forgot. You said the company owns more property in town?"

"Yeah. A whole city block downtown and some other stuff we aren't involved with. We just finished the building they're going to use for their offices. That Cotton Exchange must have been something back in the day. It's pretty special now."

"I remember you saying you were going to do that restoration, too. I'd love to see it."

"You should stop by sometime. Riley said they'd be all moved in by the end of this week. I'm sure he'd love to show you around."

"Thanks. I might do that. I need to go downtown anyway to talk to someone about the zoning issue."

He glanced at the screen on his phone. "Sorry, but I've got to run. I need to locate a vintage pocket door so my crew can get it installed. All of a sudden, the owner wants this place done yesterday."

"Must be the new baby. I know I'm sure thinking about the future."

"Anything you need, Roseanne. Just let me know."

She fought back tears as she watched him disappear through the break in the hedges. She'd detected nothing but genuine kindness in his words and manner. Her heart hurt with the realization a virtual stranger had more compassion for her circumstances than the father of her child. Why hadn't she met him first? He was the kind of guy she should have fallen in love with, but love wasn't something one controlled. Just the opposite. It made otherwise sane people do insane things.

No need living in the past. What's done is done. Time to look to the future. She replaced the lock on the garage doors and headed back to the house to contemplate her next move. Should she go downtown and ask about the zoning? That was the first hurdle. If she couldn't get a permit to convert the garage, she'd have to come up with another solution to her problem.

"Then that's where I'll start," she mumbled to herself. She'd just reached the back porch when her phone rang. She recognized the ringtone assigned to her best friend and hesitated. She'd tried not to think about how Scott had found out about the baby, but unless he'd seen her recently, which to her knowledge he hadn't, then someone had to have told him. Since the only other person in town who knew was Becky, it stood to reason her oldest friend had let the secret slip. Maybe to her husband who was Scott's best friend. She'd said from the beginning Roseanne should tell Scott. Well, now he knew, and look how that had turned out.

Roseanne hit the ignore button and slipped the phone into her pocket. She needed a little more time before she forgave Becky.

CHAPTER TWENTY-SIX

It had been weeks since she'd been downtown. Construction trucks bearing the logo of Tucker Restoration lined one side of Main between Second and Third. Though the windows of the old corner store were covered in heavy paper, the door stood open. Roseanne peeked inside. An army of people were busy restoring the ancient wood trim while still others worked on what appeared to be a bar against the far wall.

She'd missed more Historical Society meetings than she'd been able to attend in the last six months. From the looks of it, she'd missed quite a lot. All along the block, windows sparkled in the sunlight, sidewalks had been repaired, light poles bore a fresh coat of paint, and baskets filled with vibrant flowers hung from new brackets. If not for the modern vehicles parked along the road, she would have thought she'd stepped back in time to the turn of the twentieth century when cotton had ruled this part of Texas.

Moving along, she came to a stop in front of the old Cotton Exchange building. The window still held the original glass, imperfections and all, but, now, the ornate gold lettering declared the building to be the home of BP Investments, Inc.

She pressed her face close to the glass, but not close enough to leave a smudge, and peered inside. The front part appeared to be some sort of waiting area. Large, masculine leather chairs were arranged into seating areas around tables that looked like slices from giant tree trunks. Plush rugs covered wide-plank hardwood floors and defined the arrangements. "Wow." Someone had spent a truckload of money to make the place appear casual yet elegant.

A tall, slim man walked into the room. He carried an electronic tablet in one hand, which he consulted as he negotiated the furniture. Roseanne jumped back. The man glanced up, saw her standing outside, and smiled at her. He set the tablet on a large, wooden desk at the back of the room then headed toward her, motioning for her to enter.

She shook her head. She really shouldn't. City Hall would be closing down for lunch soon, and she wanted to make her inquiries and get home before today's guests began arriving. Not that Kay needed her to be there, but it was her inn, and she felt responsible for everything that went on there. Before she could convince her feet to move, the man opened the front door—original front door, she noted.

"Want to take a closer look? It's okay. I think just about everyone in town has been in the last few days to see the place. We're still moving in, but I'd be happy to show you around."

"Really? It wouldn't be too much trouble?" Why was she even asking? She was dying to see what they'd done with the place. "I'm a member of the Historical Society."

"Then you have to come in. It's the law or something, isn't it?"

His smile and good humor lifted her spirits. What would it hurt to spend a few minutes checking out the restoration? "Okay. If you're sure? I don't want to get in your way."

"I'm positive. Have you lived here long?" he asked as she walked past him into the room.

"All my life. Well, most of it anyway. We moved to Florida when I was in high school, but I came back as soon as I could."

"Then you probably know some of the history of the building and the others on the block."

She nodded. "I do. This was a five-and-dime when I was a kid. I guess the dollar stores are the modern day equivalent." She ran her hand over the rich wood panels that still graced the walls. She pointed to the ornate marble stairway off to one side. "I used to love that staircase. It looked like something out of a fairy tale, or so I thought when I was ten. I'm glad to see it survived."

"I was given permission to murder anyone who dared mar that staircase, or any other original pieces. I'm happy to say I didn't have to kill anyone. Tucker Restoration did a wonderful job of bringing the place into this century without destroying the history of the building."

Roseanne laughed. "The owner must really like his historical details."

"He does."

The familiar voice froze her in her tracks. Her heart did a somersault just as the baby decided to shift positions. She gasped and, arm outstretched, braced herself against the wall.

"Roseanne!" Scott flew to her side. "Are you okay?" He took her elbow and guided her to the nearest chair—a big, tan leather job that looked like it could seat a football team. "Riley. Get Ms. Meadows a glass of water."

"Yes, sir." The other gentleman scooted off to do as Scott commanded.

"I'm fine. I don't need water." She tried to wrench out of his embrace, but, with one arm around her waist and the other firmly holding her elbow, she didn't have a chance. She sat where he indicated, hoping he'd move away, giving her a chance to escape. No such luck. He sat on the edge of the cushion, effectively trapping her in the chair.

"You're pale."

"I'm fine. I just didn't expect to see you here."

"I thought— Becky didn't talk to you?"

She shook her head. "No. Why?" She remembered the earlier call she'd sent to voicemail. She'd never even checked to see if she'd left a message. "Is she okay?"

"She's fine, or at least she was when I saw her this morning."

"Then why would you think she and I would have talked?"

Riley came back with a cut crystal glass filled with water and ice. Scott took it then handed it to her. "Why don't you go see how things are going down the street?" he said with a nod toward the door. "I'm sure I can handle anything that comes up in the next few minutes."

"Sure thing, boss. Oh, and Randy called. Something about a pocket door. He said you should call him."

"I'll take care of it."

Riley swung his hips as he made his way to the door. "Okeydokey, then. I think I'll take my lunch break while I'm out. Don't wait up for me."

Scott waved to his employee, and when the man was out of sight, he turned to Roseanne, a big smile on his face that vanished quickly. "What's the matter? Is it the baby? Are you having contractions?"

"Fuck you, Scott Ramsey. How dare you act like you care a fig about my baby."

His expression turned thunderous. "That's *our* baby, and I care a hell of a lot more than a fig, whatever that means."

"I didn't come here to argue with you." She made an attempt to get out of the chair, but between the deep cushions and Scott's big body wedged in beside her, she couldn't leverage herself out. "Move!"

"You aren't going anywhere until we talk."

"I'll call the police. This is kidnapping."

"It's nothing even close. You came into my place of business of your own free will."

"And you won't let me leave. That's kidnapping."

"If Becky didn't talk to you, why are you here?"

"Randy said the building was finished. I just came to see it. I didn't know—" She cut herself off as something Riley had said finally penetrated her brain. "You! The pocket door. You're the one who bought the Victorian around the corner from me."

"Guilty as charged."

He'd told Randy to add a pocket door between the master bedroom and the guest room next to it because he wanted to make the smaller room into a nursery. "If you think you're going to take my child away from me and raise it on the next street over, you really are insane. I'll fight you until my last breath then I'll come back from the dead to haunt you." She made another attempt to get up. "Get out of my way!"

"Hold on, Roseanne. You aren't going anywhere until you get it through your thick skull that I'm not your enemy. I bought that house months ago, along with a lot of other properties, to prove to you that I'm not going anywhere. I have a Texas driver's license, which Ford assures me makes me almost a Texan. I own property here. When you saw me at the factory yesterday, I was packing things to move in here."

"I thought—"

"You thought I was going back to New York. I know. You didn't give me a chance to explain."

Could she have been wrong about him? "Why do you want a nursery?"

"I thought it would make it easier on you to have direct access to the baby's room. Is that a crime?"

She shook her head. "You expect me to live there? I have a home, Scott."

"You have a business. It's not a suitable place to raise a kid, not with strangers coming and going all the time. I bought the house for us, before I knew about the baby, but it's yours, with or without me."

"Scott—"

"No argument. The house is in your name, anyway."

"Why did you do that?"

"I thought it would make a nice wedding gift."

"You were going to ask me to marry you?"

He nodded. "In Vegas. Then you got sick and asked to come home."

She recalled the reason she'd felt sick that night—or at least the reason she'd thought she felt sick. "You didn't tell me about the party."

"My parents' anniversary?"

She nodded.

"I didn't want to subject you to their brand of hospitality. You've met them, and after that visit from their lawyer, surely you can understand why I didn't want you anywhere near them."

His parents had been civil when they'd been in town for Ford and Becky's wedding, but just barely. They hadn't even left a tip for the housekeeper when they checked out, despite being a pain in the ass, complaining about everything from the size of the bath towels to the creaking floors. "I guess I can, but still, you should have told me. Let me make up my own mind."

His brows met in the center of his forehead. "For the record, how did you know about it in the first place?"

"Your sister made a point of telling me in Vegas. I'm sorry, but she's a piece of work."

"I know. Can you believe Ford dated her?"

"No. She's a viper."

"Takes after my parents."

"Can I ask you something?"

"Shoot."

"How did you find out about the baby? Did Becky tell you?"

"You told me."

She recalled the stunned expression on his face. "No way. You mean you didn't know until yesterday?"

"Didn't have a clue, which makes me wonder how my parents found out."

"Well, I sure as hell didn't tell them." They both thought about the problem for minute. "Wait. I was in New York last week. You think they could have seen me and I didn't see them?"

"It's a big city. Lots of people. Why were you there, and where did you go?"

"I went to meet with my agent and my publisher. I sold the cookbook I've been working on." She grabbed his arm and squeezed. "You didn't have anything to do with that, did you?"

"I might have called an old friend, made a suggestion. What's your agent's name?"

"Liz Rothstein with the Greenberg Agency."

"Never heard of her or her agency."

"Are you sure?"

"Positive. Even if my friend did put a bug in someone's ear there, I can tell you those people don't sign contracts as favors to anyone. They think your book will sell, or they wouldn't buy it."

"Uh-huh. I don't believe you, but I've got other things to worry about."

"Like finding out how my parents knew about the baby before I did. You can't imagine how pissed off that makes me."

"I would have told you —"

"But my sister came along, stirring up trouble. It's what she does best."

"I didn't know in Vegas. I honestly was sick. Turns out it was morning sickness."

"And you weren't showing at Ford and Becky's wedding. I would have noticed."

She didn't need a mirror to know her ears and neck were turning red. He couldn't have gotten a better look that night. "It didn't even occur to me that you might notice."

"All I remember is how beautiful you were. You were a vision in pink, and when I touched you… Well, I had to have you."

"When you touch me —"

"What?" His fingers skimmed her arm from wrist to elbow.

"What happens when I touch you?"

"You know." His hand moved slowly along, barely touching her skin.

"I don't." He leaned in. His lips brushed the shell of her ear. "Tell me, sweetheart."

"I...can't." If he got any closer, she might combust. That was what he did to her.

Hot breath stirred the hair tucked behind her ear. "It makes you hot, doesn't it?" He took her earlobe between his lips and sucked gently on the sensitive skin. "At the wedding...you were hot for me. Wet." He nibbled down her neck to her collar then back up. "When I put the garter on your leg, I could smell your arousal. You wanted me then, didn't you?"

Her actions had proved that point, so there was no need to deny it now. "Yes."

His tongue traced her carotid, making her pulse jump like a racehorse out of the chute. "I still have the panties I took off of you that night."

God, she had felt like such a slut going back to the wedding without them. Every brush of air against her swollen, slicked skin had reminded her of the mistake she'd made. Mistake.

She gathered all her strength and pushed against his chest. He sat back, his face a mask of confusion. Well, she'd clear that up for him. "Yet, two days later you were out with another woman. Did you have my panties with you then? Were you thinking about me then?" She heaved herself past him and stood. "I don't think so."

CHAPTER TWENTY-SEVEN

"Roseanne." He stood, his hands outstretched, pleading with her. "Honestly, I don't know what you're talking about. What woman? Where?"

"Don't." She held her hands up, palms out. "Don't deny it. I was there. At the diner. I saw you, Scott. Me. With my own eyes."

She knew the second comprehension dawned on him. His facial muscles sagged, and his gaze dropped to the floor. "Yeah. Did you think no one you knew would see you out there by the freeway? Is that why you took her there?"

"It's not what you think."

"I think you're screwing Julie Davis. That's what I think."

He planted his fists on his hips and glared at her. "That was a business meeting. Julie came downtown earlier to look over the corner space as a possible location for a tasting room. The diner was her idea because she had to go into Dallas for supplies after our appointment. We had our heads together over a sketch pad. Would you like to see the original drawings she did that day? Or the architect's final drawings that came from that meeting? How about we go over there and I'll show you how the construction is coming along? Oh." He reached in the front pocket of his jeans. "Yes, I had your panties with me that day. I carry them with me every day."

She stared at the ball of white lace and satin sitting in the palm of his hand. She didn't know what to say. He had an answer for everything she threw at him, and they all sounded plausible. Had she been wrong about him? About everything? "Why?"

"Why do I carry them?"

She nodded.

"To remind me of what's at stake here. To remind me of my goal."

Her gaze me his. "You're goal?"

"To get you back. I'm nothing without you, Roseanne. You never believed I'd stick, but you were wrong. This is my home, and not because I own property or have a Texas driver's license, but because this is where you are. I bought the leather factory, this building, the airstrip, for you. You love this town, every crumbling brick of it. I'd restore the whole damned place for you if I could."

"You would?"

He stuffed her panties back in his pocket. "I'd do anything for you, Roseanne. Anything. You want me to beg you to take me back? I'll do it. I rented about a dozen billboards along the freeway. I'll have them plastered with signs begging you. I'd run naked down Main Street just to see your eyes light up. I love you."

"You do?"

"More than is wise. I told my family to fuck off because of you. That lawyer who came to see you is probably trying to figure out a way to cut me out of my inheritance as we speak."

"Oh, Scott. No!"

"I don't care, Roseanne. My parents have never understood me. My grandparents did. They were good people, kept my parents in line. But once they were gone…well, things changed. My parents' expectations for me are so far out of line with what I want for myself, I can't see them ever coming together."

"But, the money."

"Means nothing to me. I have plenty of my own, and they can't touch my trust funds. At the rate they're spending their own money, there won't be anything left to inherit when they're gone anyway." He shook his head. "I don't get it. If they were spending it on a good cause—"

"Like bringing a dead town back to life?"

He smiled. "Yeah, like bringing a dead town back to life, I wouldn't have a problem with their spending. But all they can think about is themselves. I'd much rather invest in Butte Plains. Did you see how great Main Street looks? That was community volunteers. I bought the supplies, but the people in town did the heavy lifting. I respect their work ethic, Roseanne. The town has been through hard times, but the people who live here, like you, haven't given up. They're bringing it back to life themselves. They just needed a little help."

"You're enjoying this, aren't you?"

His smile lit up the room. "I am. Do you remember when you told me about this building? How you used to come here when you were a kid?"

"I remember."

"I decided to buy the building then. I have to admit, I wasn't planning on buying an entire city block, but, once I started looking into it, it made sense."

"So, Lucky Lady Brewing will have a tasting room on the corner. Your offices are here? What are you going to do with the space in between?"

"Want to see what I have in mind?"

"Sure."

"Let me get the keys, and the plans I had drawn up." He started to head upstairs but stopped on the first tread. "Want to see what we did upstairs?"

Why not? She'd always dreamed of what this building could be in the right hands. "Okay." Following him up the ornate staircase, she marveled at the condition of the woodwork. "Is this all original?"

"It is. Took forever to get all the layers of paint off, but it was worth it, don't you think?"

"Yes. It's beautiful. All this was made by hand."

"Over a hundred and fifty years ago. It's a testament to the craftsmanship and quality of wood they used that it's still here."

"And you. If you hadn't bought the place, no telling what would have happened to it."

"You gave me the idea, so all this is your fault."

They reached the switchback landing. Scott stopped and waited for her to catch up. She placed her fingers on his arm. "Seriously, Scott. You aren't spending your entire fortune on my dream, are you?"

His gaze bored into hers. "I would, if it would bring you back to me, but no. I haven't even made a dent in it. Besides, I expect to make it all back, except for what I'm spending on the house. That's for you and the baby."

And maybe for him, too, but she wasn't ready to go there just yet. "Thank you." She stepped past him and continued to the second story.

"What do you think?" He came up behind her. "The infrastructure is all new, wiring, plumbing, but, otherwise, it's exactly the way we found it."

"It's…beautiful." Low, natural wood walls separated the front room into individual work spaces occupied by vintage desks topped by ultra-modern computer systems. Most had ergonomic chairs behind the desks, but a few still had old-fashioned wooden ones. An office sectioned off with the same low, wood walls topped with frosted glass took up the entire back wall. "Your office?"

"My office. Want to see?"

It was modern and historically perfect in every way possible. Roseanne circled the massive carved oak desk, taking in every detail, including a photo of her that had been taken at Becky and Ford's first wedding in Las Vegas. The photographer had caught her in an unguarded moment when she'd smiled at something one of them had said.

"You were so beautiful." He'd followed her around the desk.

He picked up the frame and gazed at the photo. "I didn't think it was possible for you to be any more beautiful, but I was wrong. Pregnancy suits you. You're radiant."

"I'm a blimp."

"No. You don't know what it does to me to see you like this. My child growing inside you. A child conceived of our love. No matter what happens between you and me, I'll always love and care for you and the baby. I'll always be right here, Roseanne."

She ducked her head to keep him from seeing the tears gathering in her eyes. "Thank you. You'll be a good father."

"I'm going to try my best. That's all anyone can say, right?" He opened the center desk drawer and grabbed a set of keys from the tray. "I'll just get the plans." A moment later, they headed back down the stairs. He held the front door for her then, after unlocking the building next door, ushered her into the dilapidated space.

"Yikes!"

"It looks worse than it is," he said. "There's about fifty years of dust on everything, as best as I can figure out. The last tenant moved out around 1960."

"Before we were born."

"Try to see beyond the dust. Picture tables scattered around. Maybe chandeliers hanging from the ceiling and a fireplace on that wall. We'd polish the hardwood floors, maybe put some rugs under the tables. White tablecloths, those little vases with pastel roses in them." His arm swept the space, painting a picture for her. "And in the back room, a commercial kitchen big enough for an army of pastry chefs to keep up with the demand."

She could see it. She had seen it. His words were her words. She placed one hand on her belly and the other over her mouth to hold in the sob threatening to escape. This was her tearoom. The dream she'd only told one person about in all her life—him.

"Hey, hey," he said, hurrying to support her with an arm around her shoulder. "Don't cry."

She dashed tears from her cheeks, but her emotions had stolen her voice.

"I thought you'd be happy."

She nodded. "I am," she cried. "These are…hap-happy tears."

"You like it? You want to see the plans? I wasn't sure what size tables you wanted, so I had the architect draw his rendering with some big ones and some small ones, too." He steered her to a set of sawhorses with an old door on top. He rolled the plans out, anchoring the curled edges with blocks of wood he found on the floor.

Roseanne stared at the top page—the architect's vision for what the inside would look like. He'd captured every detail she had envisioned, weaving them together to create her dream. "It's perfect. Absolutely perfect." God, she'd become a watering pot. She couldn't stop the tears from falling.

"Check out the kitchen. There's room for you to have a test kitchen for all your recipes…so you can do more cookbooks." He flipped the page over to reveal a kitchen fit for a five-star restaurant. "See, this would be your test kitchen over here. It's separate from the tea room kitchen but could be used on special occasions if you needed the extra equipment and space."

"Like for wedding or bridal showers. Or birthday parties."

"Those are great ideas. Ways to maximize the earning potential of the space. You could host things like that during hours you would otherwise be closed. This space was originally a hotel. You could use the guest rooms upstairs as private dining rooms."

"Scott."

"What, sweetheart?"

"This is…"

"For you." He placed his hands on her shoulders and smiled gently down at her. "This is for you, Roseanne."

"But you could rent this space—"

"Who said I wouldn't be charging you rent?" He chuckled. "I'm a businessman, not an idiot."

"Oh."

"But, for my wife, I could maybe discount the rate. You know…for services rendered?" He winked at her, and his grin made it clear what kind of services he had in mind.

"Are you…asking?"

His thumb brushed a tear from her cheek. "This isn't the way I imagined asking, in a dusty old building, but yeah, I am asking." He dropped to one knee and took her hand in his. "Roseanne Meadows, would you please, please marry me?"

Her inability to catch her breath didn't have anything to do with the dust clogging the air. Scott had stolen the air right out of her lungs, just as he had stolen her heart and owned her body. A million things raced through her mind at lightning speed. She'd judged him falsely, assuming things about him that weren't true, while he had seen her for who she was and accepted all of her. She didn't deserve him.

"Roseanne, please," he begged. "All I want is to make you happy. Oh, crap! I almost forgot." He released her hand to dig in his front pants pocket. "I have a ring."

"You do?" If he'd gone to the trouble of getting a ring, then this wasn't some spur of the moment insanity. He'd *planned* on asking her to marry him. Her heart swelled with love for him.

He stood and held a small box out to her. "Open it. Please?"

The small leather-clad box with gold pinstripes around the edges looked old, but she could tell it had been taken care of. She opened the hinged lid and gasped. "Oh, Scott. It's lovely."

"It was my grandmother's engagement ring. She left it to me. I found it when I cleaned out the safe in my apartment."

"You cleaned out your safe?"

"Yeah. The weekend of my parents' anniversary party. Cleaned out the safe, took what I wanted from the place, which wasn't much, and put my apartment up for sale."

"Why?"

"Because it wasn't my home any longer."

She held his gaze, silently questioning.

"My home is wherever you are."

"Scott," she breathed.

He cupped her hand, turning it so he could look at the ring, too. "I didn't think I'd find someone who would want this old thing, but when I looked at it that night, I knew it was meant for you. It's old, nothing like the ones they make today. If you don't like it, I'll buy you anything you want."

"It's perfect." She'd never seen a more beautiful ring. The yellow marquis-cut diamond set in an antique gold filigree band winked at her in the dim light of the old hotel.

"Marry me, Roseanne."

"I shouldn't."

"Why not? What can I do?"

"I shouldn't, but…but I am. If you're sure."

"I've never been more sure about anything in my life. You're the one, sweetheart. The only one I'll ever want. The only one I'll ever need."

"I want you, too. I need you." It had taken her long enough to admit it, but once she did, a weight lifted off her shoulders.

"Is that a yes? Please tell me it is."

She smiled up at him. "That's a yes, Mr. Ramsey."

"Thank God." Suddenly, he dropped to both knees and pulled her close so he could wrap his arms around her hips. He pressed a soft kiss to her belly. "Did you hear that, buddy? Your mom said she would marry me."

"Scott." She ran her hands through his hair. She'd missed touching him, missed these tender moments they'd always been so good at. He looked up at her. "I love you both. So much."

"We love you, too. So much."

Finally, he rose to frame her face in his hands. He pressed his lips to hers, sealing the deal. "How soon can we get married?"

"How soon do you want to?"

"Yesterday works for me."

"I'll see what I can do." She went up on tiptoes and brushed her lips over his. "I've missed you."

His lips quirked up on the corners. "Why, Ms. Meadows. I do believe you're propositioning me."

"I always knew you were smart. So what's it going to be, mister? Are you going to take me up on the offer?"

"Damn right I am."

THE END

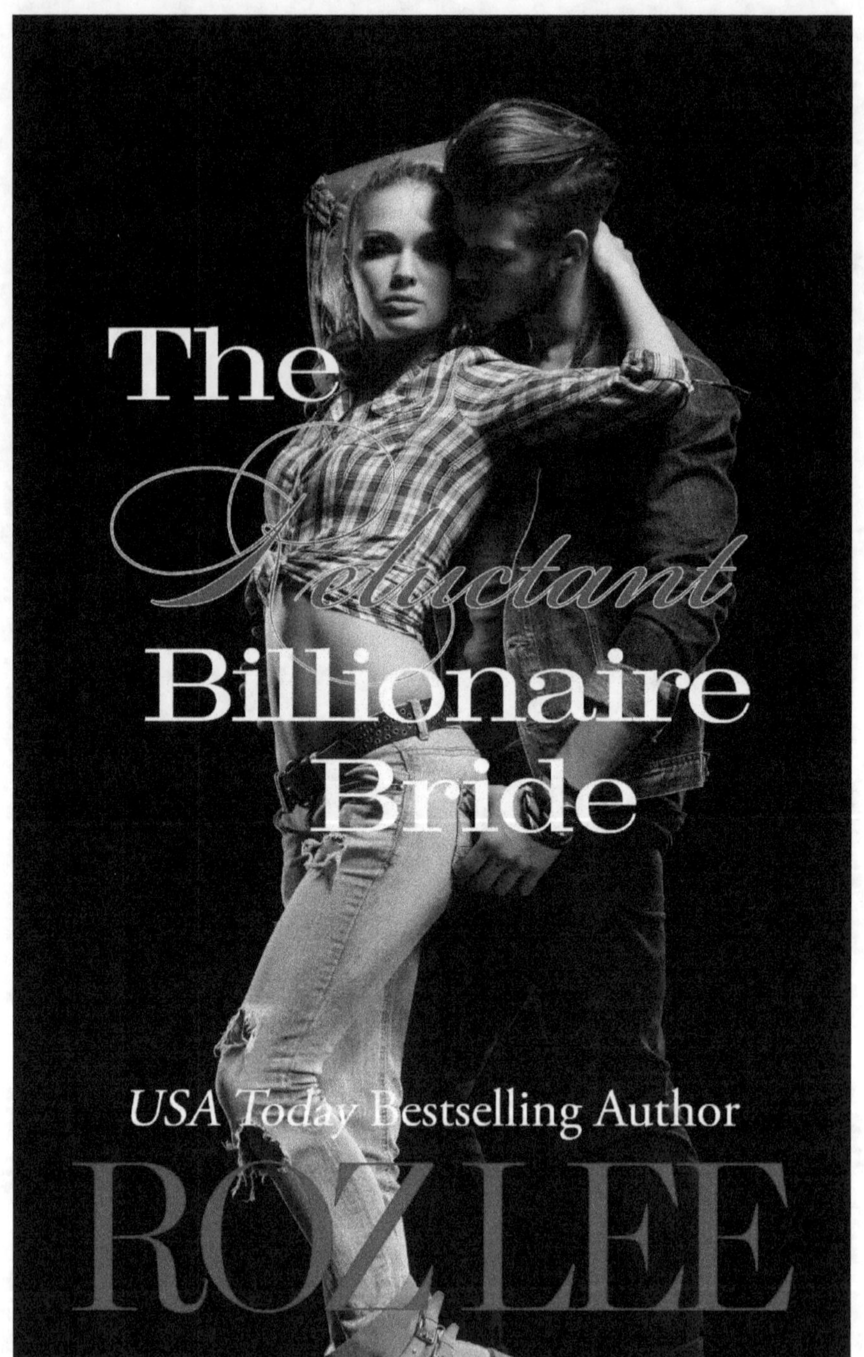

The
Reluctant
Billionaire
Bride
USA Today Bestselling Author
ROZLEE

The Reluctant Billionaire Bride

by

Roz Lee

Dedication

To the lucky lady whose experiences inspired this story.

Acknowledgments

I owe a lot to many.

To my family for putting up with my habit of taking real life situations and twisting them to fit the story I want to tell.

To my readers for encouraging me to keep telling my stories. Without you I'm not sure I'd continue to torture myself.

To my editor, Laura Garland, for her dedication to getting it right and for her willingness to slog through the mess I send her in order to find the manuscript I *intended* to send.

I couldn't do it without any of you.

CHAPTER ONE

Julie stood in the shadowed doorway separating the workroom from the tasting room. The opening-night crowd swarmed around the bar, couples mostly, with a few singles mixed in. The locals she'd hired to be the face of Lucky Lady Brewing Company smiled at the patrons as they cashed in the free drink cards they'd handed out liberally all around Butte Plains for the last few weeks. In the half hour or so she'd been standing there, she'd seen at least a dozen customers return, paying for their next drink. "Who would have thought?" she mumbled.

A flash of light reflected off the vintage glass insert in the front door, illuminating her hiding spot and nearly blinding her. When her eyes adjusted, she crept forward again, scanning the faces for the newcomers. Scott Ramsey spied her first, waving an arm to get her attention. She waved back, letting him know she'd seen him.

"Quite the crowd," he said, joining her in the small alcove. "Congratulations."

"It's all your fault." A few months ago, she'd been content with the challenge of brewing craft beers. McKenna's Liquor took whatever bottled goods she sent over, never pushed for more than she could deliver, and didn't ask questions she didn't want to answer. It had been the perfect setup for a woman who valued her privacy as much as she did.

"I'll gladly take the blame," Scott said, eyeing the filled-to-capacity room, "but this is all you."

Julie shook her head. "All I did was provide a custom brew for your friend's wedding. You were the one who came up with the idea to open a tasting room." She'd been less than enthusiastic about the idea—until she'd seen the space he had in mind. Over a hundred years old, the structure had housed several businesses over the years but had retained its character. A sucker for vintage architecture, she'd fallen in love with the building. Perhaps it wasn't the wisest thing to base a business decision on, but if the opening-day crowd was an indication of things to come, it appeared to have worked out.

"Maybe." He shrugged. "But look at this place. You turned a pig into a purse."

Julie smiled. "Be careful. Your Yankee roots are showing."

"What?" The transplanted New Yorker feigned innocence.

"I made a silk purse from a sow's ear. If you're going to fit in around here, you're going to have to work on your vocabulary. Your money will only get you so far."

He dipped his chin, acknowledging her barb. "Words of wisdom I'll take to heart." The front door opened again, and they both turned to look. A trio of women—young enough they needed to be carded—walked in. Scott returned his attention to Julie. "Roseanne said you had something for us to sample?"

"Yep." Pushing through the saloon-style swinging door, she beckoned him to follow. "Come on. Your bride-to-be called earlier. She's going to be a little late. She had to go over to The Yellow Rose—something about a guest arriving without a reservation."

"I'm surprised Kay would need her help. Wonder what the problem is?"

"No idea. Not my problem." She stopped in front of a worktable holding six capped green bottles, sans labels. "Voila!

My first attempt at nonalcoholic beer."

"These are for us?" Scott asked.

"I wouldn't do this for anyone else." She'd been working night and day on this brew ever since Scott and Roseanne had asked her to come up with something the pregnant bride could drink at their upcoming wedding. The challenge had been something she'd mostly enjoyed, but the time had come for a second opinion, and she was having doubts. She chewed on her bottom lip.

"I'm not making any guarantees. Could taste like rattlesnake piss for all I know." Not exactly true. She'd tried it and thought this version good enough to bottle a few samples, but you never knew what someone else might think.

Scott's phone belted out a synthetic version of Mendelsohn's "Wedding March." He held up his index finger. "Hold on a sec. I gotta take this."

"No problem." Julie leaned a hip against the worktable, crossed her arms, and studied her toes while her guest pressed the phone to his ear.

"Roseanne, honey. What's up? Uh-huh." Scott glanced at Julie. "Just showed up? You didn't know he was coming?"

Julie shrugged her shoulders, indicating she didn't have a clue what was going on, as she listened to the one-sided conversation.

"Okay. I'm sure Julie won't mind if I bring the bottles home." Holding Julie's gaze, he raised an eyebrow in question.

She shook her head. "Not a problem. I'll just box them up for you," she whispered then went in search of an empty box, leaving Scott to finish up his phone call with his fiancée. From past experience, she knew they usually ended their conversations with a bunch of mushy fake kisses and sappy endearments. It was enough to make a single woman with no prospects sick.

She certainly wasn't looking for a relationship. The microbrewery she'd started when she moved to Butte Plains was all the lover she needed. Sure, it made demands on her time, but that was as far as it went. She owned it, not the other way around, and as long as she stayed behind the scenes, she could reap the benefits of her little hobby brewery, and no one would connect Julie Davis with the person she'd been before her life went to Hell in a handbasket. And, it kept her busy. Gave her a reason to get up every morning.

She'd held various food industry jobs since she turned fifteen and got a job washing dishes at the restaurant across the street from the apartment building she'd grown up in. The extra income had been a welcome addition to their single-parent household, plus, her mother who was a waitress at the restaurant could keep an eye on her teenage daughter.

Dishwashing had led to waitressing then, when she'd turned twenty-one, she'd learned to tend bar. The extra tips she'd earned behind the bar helped pay her way at the local junior college where she'd received an associate's degree in business management. To celebrate completing her last exam, she'd purchased a lottery ticket and a full tank of gas on the way home. Handing over the cash for her purchases, she laughed with the cashier, a funny little man by the name of Marty, about all the things they'd do if they struck it rich. Never in her wildest dreams did she think she would actually win a lottery jackpot or believe the casual conversation could put her in danger. Her conversation with Marty Scruggs was one she almost didn't live to regret.

She'd all but forgotten about the lottery ticket she'd purchased and hung on the refrigerator door with a cheap magnet advertising a local auto repair shop. Her mother had seen it though, and while she'd dressed for her first day shift behind the bar, her mom checked the winning numbers.

For as long as she lived, she'd never forget the scream that brought her running from her room, her black uniform slacks forgotten on the floor as she hurried to do battle with whoever was murdering her mother.

She found her mom sitting at the tiny kitchenette table, her eyes filled with tears, her whole body shaking. Nearly incoherent, it took several minutes to understand what her mother was saying.

"You won!" she said. "You won!"

"I won what?"

Jan Harris waved a crumpled slip of paper in the air. She'd grabbed it, realizing what it was at the same time her mother engulfed her in a rib-crushing hug. "Oh, baby. You won!"

She'd extricated herself from the embrace and smoothed the slip of paper out on the table. "How many numbers did I get right?" She rarely played the lottery, allowing herself one two-dollar play a couple of times a year—usually on her birthday or when she'd passed a particularly difficult class. She'd won a few dollars once by matching three of the winning numbers. She'd cashed in the winning ticket and bought her and her mom both milkshakes at Sonic to celebrate the win. "I want a chocolate malt this time. How about you?"

"Hon, you can buy the whole damn drive-in! You won!"

Laughing, she'd stared at the ticket. How much had been up for grabs last night? Several hundred million, she recalled, but in truth, she hadn't paid much attention to the jackpot total when she'd purchased the ticket. Why would she? The odds of winning more than enough to add malted milk powder to a milkshake was roughly the same as reaching for the sky and coming up with a handful of stars. In other words—zilch.

"It says here there was only one winner for last night's drawing. Did you buy the ticket at the usual place?"

Her mom was breathless, but at least forming whole sentences now. She thought about the question. "The gas station on Travis Highway. I always stop there on my way home from school."

Mom held up her cell phone. On the screen was a photo of the self-service station she knew well. "Is this the place?"

"Yeah, but, Mom, hundreds of people, no, thousands, probably bought tickets there this week. That doesn't mean I won."

"The numbers, baby. Look at the numbers."

Willing to humor her mom but still excited to see if she'd won enough to maybe put a down payment on a new car, she said, "Read them off to me and I'll check them against the ticket."

Her mom read them slowly. She ticked each one off before moving on to the next. "Let me see," she said, reaching for the cell phone. "Are you sure those are last night's numbers?"

"Positive. See for yourself." Jan handed over the phone and began dancing around their small kitchen. "A billionaire! My daughter is a billionaire!"

"Mom." She'd laughed. "Stop being ridiculous!"

"I'm not being ridiculous. I'm celebrating. You're a billionaire!"

"I'm not…" The breath froze in her lungs. There on the screen was the date of the draw. She held the ticket up, found the same date printed beneath the numbers. The same numbers displayed on the screen. "There's got to be a mistake."

"No mistake, sweetheart! You won." Her mom sat down and reached for a pen from the Mason jar filled with writing implements they kept against the wall with the napkin holder and salt and pepper shakers. "Hurry up and sign it on the back, so no one can steal it and claim it's theirs."

She'd signed what had been her legal name at the time, Jennifer Harris, on the line marked with the X.

If she'd known the horror awaiting her because of that ticket, she would have stuffed it down the garbage disposal and said good riddance. But she hadn't. And she was Julie Davis now. A woman with no past and a lonely future ahead of her. Who said money couldn't buy happiness?

CHAPTER TWO

Could one kiss change a person's life?

Colin Parker knew the answer to the question was yes. If it was the right kind of kiss with the right kind of person.

He'd spent months trying to make sense of one kiss. Even went so far as to write a song about it. The song, and indirectly the kiss, had already changed his life almost beyond recognition.

Now, here he was back in Butte Plains to see if reality was as good as his memory, and to restore some sanity to his life. But first, he had to find a place to stay.

Colin leaned against the marble-topped island in the kitchen of The Yellow Rose Bed and Breakfast. His older sister's best friend, Roseanne Meadows, owned the place, and he was counting on her to let him hide out there for a few weeks. At least long enough for him to locate a permanent home for himself.

The thought of staying in his old room at his mother's house made his dick shrivel up, and there was no way he was going to beg a room from his sister. There wasn't a house big enough to accommodate a bachelor and a newlywed couple at the same time. He could only imagine the kind of things the average newlywed couple could get into, much less a couple who owned the hottest sex-toy business going. Imagining his sister being half of said couple was enough to make him break out in hives.

Having ruled out staying with his mother or his sister had left only one option. The Yellow Rose. He'd stayed here for a night or two for Becky's wedding, which had been held right here in Roseanne's garden. It wasn't the kind of place people would expect a single man to stay — which made it perfect.

"What's the problem, Roseanne? Why can't I stay here?"

"Kay told you why. We're booked solid for the next two weeks. Why don't you stay at your mom's…or with Becky and Ford? I know either one would be happy to have you."

He rolled his eyes. "Come on, Roseanne. You know why."

His sister's very pregnant best friend folded her arms over her gigantic belly and tapped the toe of one sandaled foot on the tiled floor while she thought his statement through. "Okay. I get it. A grown man might have issues staying with his mom. And Ford and Becky are still in the newlywed phase. Sometimes, I can hardly stand to be around them."

"Then you'll help me out?"

She let out a frustrated breath. "There really isn't room for you here. Kay wasn't exaggerating, we're booked up."

He opened his mouth to protest when she held up an index finger to silence him. "But, if you won't consider one of the new hotels out on the interstate —"

"You know I can't stay in one of those places."

"I suppose not. Which leaves one option."

Her grin made him rethink his decision to return home. "What?" he asked.

"My place. Well, it's mine *and* Scott's."

Roseanne and Scott had clearly put the cart before the horse, getting pregnant before deciding to marry. Becky had told him the two were living together now. "Seriously? How is that better than staying with Ford and Becky?"

"Our house is three times the size of Ford and Becky's. You'll have the entire third floor to yourself. Plus, if I'm cooking, there will be enough for you, too."

The promise of a steady diet of Roseanne's cooking made his mouth water in anticipation. She'd always been a good cook, and her recently published cookbook based on the recipes she served to her guests at The Yellow Rose had been on the bestseller list for over a month. Still, he should protest. It was the polite thing to do, and Heaven knew he'd been raised to be polite. "Are you sure? Shouldn't you ask Scott?"

"Scott will be thrilled to have another guy around, but don't think you have to hang out with him. Just knowing he's not the only Y chromosome in the house will make him feel better."

Colin huffed out a laugh, his lips curving into a smile. "It's a girl, isn't it?" He motioned toward her extended belly.

"Shh!" she said. "No one is supposed to know!"

Poor Scott. Outnumbered already. "My lips are sealed." He pushed away from the island and stretched his six-foot-two frame. His escape from Nashville had taken its toll. He needed a couple hours sleep and a beer. Not necessarily in that order. "Where is this house Scott bought for you?"

"You heard about it?"

"You know Becky can't keep a secret."

She led the way out the back door, through the neatly trimmed hedge separating the garden from the alley. "That's why I haven't told her the sex of the baby. She'd blab it all over the place and ruin the surprise."

He followed her around the corner and through a gate in a tall wooden fence. "Aren't you and Scott the ones who are supposed to be surprised?"

"Yes, but neither one of us likes surprises."

Colin was shaking his head at Roseanne's version of logic when she stopped in front of an enormous Victorian. His head swiveled, getting his bearings. "I thought this place would have fallen down by now."

"It almost did, but thanks to Scott, it's going to be here for another hundred years or so."

"Wow."

"I know. Impressive, isn't it?"

"Talk about an understatement." He took in the wide wraparound porch, the stained-glass windows he thought might be original, and the quirky paint job so typical of Victorian houses. "How big is this place?"

"Around five-thousand square feet. Six bedrooms and five bathrooms plus a library and two parlors."

"Holy cow!"

"Yeah, I know. I'll never be able to keep it clean, but Scott has an answer for everything."

"What's that?"

"Money. Hire someone, he says. Come on." She started up the walkway. "I'll get you a key to the front door. Take your pick of rooms on the third floor. I'd show you myself, but I can barely make it up to our room on the second floor these days."

"Not a problem," he said as he got his bearings in the newly renovated home. "How about I take care of the third floor while I'm here. I still remember how to make a bed."

"It's a deal." She handed him a key she'd taken from a drawer in the front parlor. "Make yourself at home. Help yourself to anything in the kitchen. We've got a grocery delivery service in Butte Plains now. Would you have ever thunk it?"

"Not in a million years," he said. "This place has changed since Ford came back to town." For the first time, he was beginning to question his decision to make this his permanent home. He wanted peace and quiet, not urban sprawl.

"It sure has, mostly for the good, though. Lucky Lady Brewing Company just opened a tasting room on Main Street. Grand opening is today."

An image of the owner of Lucky Lady burst into his brain like fireworks on the Fourth of July. Julie Davis. He'd met her at Becky's wedding then, later afterward, he'd seen her at a local music venue two of his high school friends had opened on the outskirts of town. They'd spent hours talking and listening to the amateur performers, some of which weren't half bad, before calling it a night. Well, actually, they'd been ushered out of the place in the wee hours of the morning. Waiting on the back porch of the B&B because he'd forgotten his key, he'd scared the crap out of Roseanne when she'd come down to start breakfast for her guests.

"You remember Julie Davis, don't you? You asked me about her the morning you almost scared me to death."

No way was he telling Roseanne how many times he'd thought of Julie since Becky's wedding. She'd run straight to his sister with the information, putting an end to any privacy in regards to his love life. Yeah, maybe coming home wasn't such a good idea after all.

"I remember her. Why?"

"She owns Lucky Lady Brewing Company."

"And?" She was fishing for information, only he wasn't going to take the bait.

"She provided the beer for the wedding."

Grateful for the opportunity to change the subject, Colin shrugged. "It was a beautiful wedding. You did a great job."

"Thanks. Kay wants to make weddings a regular thing we offer."

"You should."

Roseanne waved away the suggestion. "I don't know. It's a lot more work than it looks like it is."

"So, when are you and Scott tying the knot?"

"Soon. We're having a little affair here in a couple of months."

"Before the baby arrives, I hope?"

"It will be cutting it close, but yeah, that's the plan."

"If you need someone to sing, I'm your man."

"Thank you so much, Colin. Does this mean you'll still be here then?" That was the million-dollar question, wasn't it? "If not, I'll come back. It's the least I can do for you taking me in like this."

"Nonsense." A blush bloomed on her cheeks. "You're practically family. Our house is always open to you."

"Well, I'd better go get my truck." He added the key she'd given him to the keyring for his new truck. "Okay if I park in the drive?"

"Yep. Scott uses the bay on the left, so park on the right side."

"Thanks, Roseanne. I really do owe you one." He leaned down and kissed her on the cheek before heading out.

CHAPTER THREE

"Everything okay?" Julie set the six-pack of nonalcoholic beer on the worktable.

"Yeah. Seems we have an unexpected houseguest," Scott said, pulling the cardboard container toward him.

"I can't believe Roseanne would invite a perfect stranger into your home. Why not just send them down to one of the hotels on the interstate?"

"He's not a stranger. It's Colin Parker, Becky's brother."

It took a second for Julie to unlock her muscles. Everyone with ears knew Colin Parker. He'd been an up-and-coming country artist a year ago, but he'd recently had several songs hit the top of the charts and stay there. He'd become a household name, and one of the most eligible bachelors in Nashville. "Colin is staying at your house?"

"Apparently so. That's what Roseanne was calling to tell me. I think I'm supposed to keep it on the down-low, so don't mention it to anyone, okay?"

"My lips are sealed." *Bad choice of words*, she thought as memories of how her lips had parted for Colin's kiss. They'd just closed down a local music venue and been on their way to their respective cars, which turned out to be the only two left in the parking lot, and occupying adjacent lined spaces. The conversation they'd started hours ago inside continued as they sat on the hood of Colin's rental then, as the lights illuminating the parking lot winked out, revealing a sky growing lighter by the minute, he'd cupped her chin, turning her to face him.

He'd given her plenty of time to say no, but, looking into his blue eyes and seeing the man she'd come to know so well, she'd done the opposite of what she'd meant to do. She'd leaned in, offering up her lips for what had become in her mind as *The Kiss*.

Her toes had curled and heat had consumed her body as their lips and tongues dueled it out. He'd broken the connection. It sure as hell hadn't been her. She'd been too lost in the moment to think clearly. Thank God Colin hadn't been as affected. He'd gently ended the kiss then, being the gentleman he'd been raised to be, helped her into her car, and watched as she drove away. In the wrong direction.

She'd gone three blocks before she realized what she'd done and righted the situation. Embarrassed to be seen heading past the venue, she'd gone miles out of her way to get home. Yeah, she'd keep her lips sealed this time. There wasn't any reason to see Colin while he was in town. It wasn't like they were friends. She hadn't heard a word from him since he'd returned to Nashville. Granted, he didn't have her private number, she kept that unlisted, and changed it every few months, just to be on the safe side. Out of necessity, the brewery's phone number was available to the public, though. If he'd wanted to reach her, he could have done so.

Scott picked up his six-pack. "Guess I'd better be going. We'll let you know what we think of these."

"Thanks. I can bottle the remainder and slap on some labels in plenty of time for the wedding." She stopped herself from adding, "Tell Colin I said hello," before Scott exited out the back door, avoiding the crowd out front, but it was a close thing.

The last thing she needed was to see Colin Parker again. Just remembering the way he'd walked her to her car, without a word, and sent her on her way, should be enough to bring her to her senses. And if it wasn't, the fact he couldn't go anywhere these days without a bevy of fans and/or paparazzi following him should do the trick. The last thing she needed was to have her face splashed all over social media. The new life she'd worked so hard to build would come crashing down.

<div align="center">~~~</div>

He was taking a chance coming here, but as soon as Roseanne had mentioned Julie's new tasting room was having a grand opening celebration, he'd had to come. The place was interesting—a mix of old and new he could appreciate. He'd done some carpentry to pay the bills and knew quality work when he saw it. Half restoration and half modernization didn't come cheap, not if it was done right, and this had been done right. He couldn't recall a time when the corner building hadn't been vacant, which meant Julie had probably invested a small fortune in the renovation.

Colin made his way to the bar, expecting to find Julie there, her full lips smiling, making the customers feel at home. Not seeing her, he tilted his sunglasses down enough he could look over the top of them and scanned the room. The woman he'd come to see was nowhere in sight. Maybe she was working behind the scenes. A place like this had to have a storage room.

Politely edging his way up to the bar, he signaled one of the women serving foam-topped glasses of beer to the eager patrons stacked two deep.

"What can I get you?" the bartender asked.

Colin skimmed over the offerings listed on a blackboard behind the bar. "I'll have the…Don't Cry in My Beer?"

A smile broke on the woman's face. "It's a pale ale. You okay with that?"

"What would you recommend?"

"How about I bring you a sampler? Then, you can make an informed decision."

"Sounds like a good plan." He plunked a twenty-dollar bill on the counter. The barkeep swept it up, headed to the cash register. A few minutes later, she set his change down, along with a wooden plank on which six small glasses of beer sat in equally spaced cutouts.

"This one is Don't Cry in My Beer," she said, pointing to the glass on the far left. It was so pale, he figured he could read a book through it. "And that one" — she pointed to the dark brew on the far right—"is Stuck in the Mud."

"Looks strong."

"It'll grow hair," she said. "Looks like you still have all your hair, so how about trying the one in the middle? It's called Kissed at Sunrise. Better get it before it's gone. People are really liking it."

Kissed at Sunrise? The name reminded him of the last time he'd been in town. The sun hadn't exactly been up when he'd kissed Julie on the hood of his rental, but the heat from their lips touching had damn near burned him to a crisp. "I'll have one of those," he said, without even trying the sample. When she returned, he had to smile at the overflowing mug she placed on the bar in front of him. "Any chance Julie is around somewhere?" She had to be. This was the grand opening of her new tasting room. Who wouldn't want to be around for that?

"Julie?"

The barkeep brushed a long curl over her shoulder, revealing for the first time her name tag. Avery, it said. "Julie Davis. The woman who owns Lucky Lady Brewing Company."

"Oh, her!" Avery needed to keep her day job. An actress she was not. "Do you know her?"

"We've met," he said. "Would you mind checking to see if she's here?"

"Give me a minute." She held up an index finger. "I'll be right back."

~ ~ ~

Julie counted the aluminum kegs stacked on industrial racks

in the storage room. They'd been through a lot already but weren't in danger of running out. That would be a disaster! She was glad she'd opted for draught only beer in the tasting room. The commercial dishwasher she'd had installed could handle the glassware, as was evidenced by the volume today, but the bottling process for such enormous quantities would require her to add staff at the actual brewery, something she had no intention of doing.

Remaining a one-person operation limited her growth potential, but it was the way it had to be. She'd built the brewing room inside one of the barns on the old farm she'd purchased, which meant it was steps away from her home. After Scott Ramsey had come visiting, without an invitation, she'd had an electric gate installed at the end of the driveway, along with a surveillance system which allowed her to see and speak to anyone wanting access to the property.

It meant she had to stop what she was doing in order to let delivery trucks in and out, but having the peace of mind that came with controlling her environment, and her privacy, had allowed her to keep Lucky Lady Brewing Company in business. And, to expand.

She didn't need the money, but having grown up pinching pennies until they squealed, the idea of losing money, even when she had it to spare, made her physically ill. The brewery had repaid her initial investment, allowing her to pay for the renovations for the tasting room out of the profits. So far, so good, for a hobby she enjoyed, and kept her from becoming a total recluse. As long as she remained out of the public eye, she'd be a lucky, and safe, lady indeed.

A blast of sound from the tasting room had her looking up from her calculations. The woman she'd hired to manage the place, Avery Harper, closed the connecting door behind her. "Sorry to bother you, boss, but one of the customers is asking for you."

"Can you handle it, Avery? I trust your judgment."

"I appreciate your confidence in my abilities, but he's not asking for the owner, he's asking for you—Julie Davis."

Julie squared her shoulders. "Me?" Her heart raced. She'd been so careful to keep her face out of the media coverage the tasting room had generated. "What did you tell him?"

"I said I wasn't sure if you were still here." She placed a hand on the door handle. "Want me to tell him you left?"

Julie clenched her mechanical pencil with both hands. Lots of people knew her as Julie Davis. Nearly everyone in Butte Plains did. It could be a reporter from the local paper. They'd offered to do a short piece on the opening. Or it could be Randy Tucker, the contractor whose awesome renovations had made the tasting room a modern space, while retaining the historical character of the building. He'd promised to come by today. Still, she couldn't be too careful. "What does he look like?"

"Tall, dark, and handsome, though he's wearing a baseball cap and sunglasses. Inside."

"Cowboy boots and a button-down shirt?" She'd never seen Randy Tucker in anything but boots and dress shirt.

"Don't know about the boots, but he's wearing a T-shirt. Looks like he found it in a rag bin."

That didn't fit the description of anyone she knew. "I'll take a look on the security camera." She slid off the stool she'd been sitting on and headed to the small office Randy had built into one corner. It was both the manager's office and home to the expensive surveillance equipment she'd purchased. "Come point him out to me."

Avery stood over Julie's shoulder as the two women surveyed the crowd in the other room. "There," Avery said, pointing. "He's still at the bar."

Julie jerked her gaze to the monitor on the far right. Her breath caught. She supposed his choice of attire was his version of camouflage, but she'd recognize him anywhere. Colin Parker.

What was he doing here?

"Do you know him?"

She nodded. "Yeah. I know him."

"Want me to get rid of him?"

"No. Just tell him I left for the day."

"Are you sure? He's kinda cute."

Too cute. Too well-known. If he got out of there without someone recognizing him, it would be a miracle. "I'm sure. As a matter of fact, you won't be lying to him. I am going home." She grabbed her purse off the shelf where she'd left it earlier. "Give me a few minutes head start before you go back out there. Okay?"

"Not a problem, boss."

"And stop calling me boss," Julie said, giving Avery a hug. "It makes me feel old."

CHAPTER FOUR

Avery disappeared through a door at the end of the bar. Colin took a sip of the foaming beer. His eyes lit with appreciation as his tongue swept over his lips to catch every drop of the cold brew. *Damn, that's good.* He took another sip, savoring the bittersweet flavor. The taste vaguely reminded him of a sunrise, full of promise with a hint of warning. Things could get really hot before the sun set again.

How many times had he thought about the kiss they'd shared? A million, it seemed. He'd even written a song about it. "Hello, Sunshine, Goodbye" had gone platinum a few months ago and rocketed his career to the stratosphere.

Watching the door for Julie wasn't doing any good. Watched pot and all that, so he spun around, taking in the packed room. His gaze touched briefly on every face. He was shocked to realize he didn't know a single one. It hadn't been very long ago he'd known everyone in Butte Plains, and they'd known him. Things really had changed in his hometown. Wondering if the growth was a good thing or bad, he shifted his gaze to the street outside the old but crystal-clear glass window.

A few people strolled by—strangers. Tourists? He'd heard Roseanne's fiancé, Scott Ramsey, had launched an advertising campaign designed to attract people out of Dallas to their little neck of the woods. It was an easy day trip by car from the Metroplex with plenty of things to do once you got here. Like have a brew at the new Lucky Lady Brewing Company tasting room followed by a stroll down Main Street to do a little shopping in the various antique stores and boutiques filling the once-empty storefronts.

Before Ford Adams returned to town and transformed the family business, Adams Manufacturing, into a successful sex toy conglomerate, Butte Plains had practically become a ghost town. It was just one of the reasons Colin had been chomping at the bit to get out of there. Since he'd decided to come home, he was a little disconcerted at the changes he saw. Where had the peace and quiet he'd once hated, but now craved, gone?

A flash of movement outside caught his attention. Everyone else was taking their sweet time, except for her. He caught a glimpse of the woman's profile as she turned her head to check for oncoming traffic. *Julie Davis.* Judging from the way she darted across the street, against the light, the minute there was a break in traffic—another thing Butte Plains didn't used to have—she was in a hell of a hurry.

Colin took another sip and contemplated the brewmaster's fine ass as she hustled in the direction of the new parking garage on Second Street.

He felt a tap on his shoulder. Turning, he smiled at Avery. "Not here?" he asked, knowing full well the woman in question had recognized him on the security camera mounted near the ceiling and hauled ass out of there to avoid seeing him.

"Sorry. I guess she went home. It's been a long day."

Tell me about it. "No problem. I'll catch her another time." He left Avery a generous tip—it wasn't her fault her boss got cold feet—and took one last sip of Kissed at Sunrise before heading to the pickup he'd left in the new parking garage a block over. Slipping into the driver's seat, he pushed the ignition button. A blast of cold air from the dash vent smacked him in the face. He chuckled at the irony. Slapped twice today. Once by Julie Davis. Once by the air conditioner.

Pulling carefully out into the traffic on Second Street, he mentally checked one thing off his "Reasons to return home" list. Reconnecting with Julie Davis wasn't going to happen. And here he'd thought that kiss had been pretty damn good. So good, it had sent him running back to Nashville.

A heavenly scent drew him through Roseanne's front door and straight to the kitchen. There were definitely advantages to bunking at her house instead of his sister's. Becky couldn't cook to save her life. Yet… "What are you doing here?"

Becky stepped away from the industrial quality stove, a wooden spoon in her hand. "I think that's my line." She brandished the spoon like a weapon. "Were you even going to tell me you were in town?"

Were all big sisters such a pain in the ass? "Yes, I was."

"When? On your way out of town? Does Mom even know you're here?"

He felt his cheeks turning red. "Not yet. I was going to see both of you tomorrow."

"Tomorrow." She wagged the spoon under his nose. "That's just great. I have to find out from my best friend my brother is in town, and oh, guess what? He's staying at *her* house, not mine!" Her anger seemed to evaporate. "Way to make me feel loved, little brother."

The sad expression on her face made him feel like the worst brother on the planet. How did she do that? "I'm sorry, sis. You know I'd stay with you and Ford, but face it, you just got married, and your house is kind of small." The only two bedrooms shared a common wall, and there was only one bathroom. Cozy for two, but not so much for three. They had gobs of money between them. Why they were still living in the old bungalow Becky had bought years ago was beyond him.

"You know you're always welcome."

"I know."

She smiled. "Just bustin' your chops, bro."

"You are the worst big sister in the world. I don't know why I love you." He crossed the room to place a kiss on her forehead.

"You love me because I'm the only person in the world who doesn't fawn all over you like you're some kind of celebrity."

The image of one sexy brewmaster came to mind. Apparently, Becky wasn't the only female who thought he wasn't the best thing on two legs. "You could be right. I can always count on you to keep me grounded."

"It's item number one in the big-sister manual."

He eyed the giant pot on the stove. "You aren't cooking, are you?"

Becky frowned. "No. Just minding the pot while Roseanne and Scott…well, whatever they're doing is none of my business."

Colin held both hands up, palms out. "Please, spare me that image! I've got to be under the same roof with these people."

"You have options. Don't pretend you don't."

He held up one finger. "Your house. Which we've determined is not an option." A second finger went up. "Mom's house." He frowned. "Think about that for a while."

Becky made a silly face. "Okay. I can see how it might be awkward for you."

"And last." A third finger joined the other two. "One of those cheap hotels out on the interstate. I don't want to toot my own horn, but get real, sis. Even I'm entitled to a little privacy now and then."

"Scott will kick you out on your ass if he finds paparazzi on his porch."

"I know, and I'll be careful. With a little luck, I'll be out of here soon."

"What do you mean? You just got here."

"I mean out of their house and their hair." He paused for dramatic effect. "I've decided to move back to Butte Plains."

"Oh. My. God!" Becky launched herself at him, hugging him tight while her feet danced a jig. To be on the safe side, he moved his toes out of reach. "I can't believe it!"

He carefully extricated himself from her embrace. "I've got to find a place to live. I want some acreage. Maybe an old house I can fix up. A barn I can convert to a recording studio. And privacy. That's my number one requirement."

"Wow. You've given this some thought, haven't you?"

"Yeah. I've been thinking about it for a while. With the local airport up and running again, I can commute to Nashville when I need to, or anywhere else I need to go. Most of my work is done at home or in the recording studio anyway."

"Don't forget touring." Becky adjusted the flame under the cook pot then resumed stirring the contents.

"I haven't. But it would sure be nice to have a place to come home to. I hate my apartment in Nashville."

"Do you have a place in mind?"

He shook his head. "No. There are a couple of old farms on the market, but nothing I saw really meets all my criteria." Spying a door with a glass panel with the word "pantry" etched into it, he headed toward it. He could use a snack before dinner, 'cause God only knew when that would be served.

"Maybe I can help." Scott Ramsey's voice preceded him down the old servant's staircase and into the kitchen. "I know every piece of land for sale in the area."

"He should," Roseanne said, joining them. "He's been buying it up like they aren't making any more."

"Well, they aren't," Scott said in his defense. "You sure you want acreage? There's more to choose from here in town."

Colin shook his head, his snack forgotten for the moment. "I've thought about it, but no. I need space."

"And some privacy," Becky said. "I've seen the headlines in the trashy magazines. You've become their favorite subject."

He couldn't deny it. The paparazzi were everywhere in

Nashville, and if they couldn't uncover a real story, they made one up. "Apparently, I have. Is it too much to ask to just be left alone?"

"Speaking as someone who has had a few run-ins with the kind of people you're talking about," Scott said, "I can sympathize. Since I took myself out of the New York social scene, things have calmed down for me a lot."

Scott was one of *The* Ramsey's—an old money family whose pictures regularly appeared in the social columns. "The key is to fly under their radar. Don't do anything to draw attention to yourself. And, it helps to live in a place like this where they wouldn't normally think to look."

"Unfortunately, Butte Plains is widely known to be my hometown. I never thought to keep it a secret until it was too late. It's only a matter of time before one of those vultures starts wondering where I've gone. That's why I need something with acreage. And a fence."

"There's one place I can think of…if you aren't afraid of a little work."

"I'm pretty good with my hands, and anything I can't do myself, I can afford to hire out now. Where is this place?"

"You know where the Scoggins used to live?" Scott asked.

Colin glanced at Roseanne. "Didn't you say Julie Davis bought the Scoggins place?" Just saying her name made his body react in a most uncomfortable way. Trying to seem casual, he moved to put the kitchen island between them.

"She did," Roseanne said. Concern in her voice, she asked Scott, "She isn't selling, is she?"

"No. No way. She's pretty well ensconced there with the brewery set up and all. I'm talking about the place adjacent to hers. There's an old farmhouse, a couple of barns, and about a hundred acres of pastureland, if I recall correctly. They don't want to break it up into smaller parcels, and there aren't many buyers who want that much land."

"Whose place is it?" Becky asked.

"I can't remember the name," Scott said. "But if Colin is interested, I'll see what I can find out. I don't think it's actually listed for sale."

Living next door to Julie Davis might be the death of him, but with a hundred acres, the likelihood of seeing her, even once in a while, was slim. "I'm interested. See what you can find out."

CHAPTER FIVE

Colin vaguely remembered the Scoggins family farm but knew he'd recognize it if he saw it. Besides, it was a nice day, and what else did he have to do?

With a cup of coffee from the new establishment on Main Street, aptly named Wide Awakenings, he headed out of town, in the opposite direction from the freeway. *The farther off the main roads, the better*, he thought as he passed several new housing developments going up on what had once been farmland. How long would it be before urban sprawl made it out to Julie's place? He didn't know how much land she had, but if he bought the adjacent hundred acres, then she sold out to a developer, he'd be screwed.

As he maneuvered along the winding two-lane farm-to-market road, he recognized several farms he knew had been in the same families for generations. Some had fallen into disrepair, but, for the most part, they hadn't changed a bit since he was a kid growing up in Butte Plains. He wondered how many of the kids who had lived on these farms and gone to school with him had stayed to take on the family business. Some, perhaps, but it was hard to make a living farming unless you had thousands of acres and deep enough pockets to survive the lean years when crops failed due to drought or too much rain or any of the other million reasons a field might not produce.

Not much different than the music business. Who knew why one song made the charts and stuck, and why another didn't? Hell. Farming might be the way to go, except once a successful crop was sold, that was it. No more income. If you had a record take off, the money kept coming in long after it dropped from the charts.

Just keep on keeping on. Words he'd learned to live by in those early years when he'd first moved to Nashville with nothing more than a handmade guitar and a dream. He was one of the lucky ones who had risen from the masses to make a living doing what he loved. So many of the artists he'd met waiting tables by day and playing dives by night were still there. Caught in a web they couldn't seem to break out of.

He knew the Scoggins place the moment he saw it. The house had been part of the North Texas landscape for over a century, and if he recalled correctly, the youngest of the Scoggins kids had been a year or two ahead of his sister in school. Colin checked his rearview mirror before stopping in the traffic lane to get a good look at the property. A barn, not much newer than the house sat a good distance away. The only new structure, a huge, metal-sided building, sat behind the house.

So, this was the home of Lucky Lady Brewing Company. The only thing setting the place apart from the other old farmsteads he'd passed was the fancy new gate at the end of her paved drive and a small sign bearing the Lucky Lady logo. Apparently, Julie Davis liked her privacy, too. "A girl after my own heart."

A battered, old farm truck approached from the other direction. Colin checked his rearview again then accelerated, leaving Julie's place behind. A short distance past her driveway was a dirt road with nothing but a couple of strands of barbed wire attached to bois d'arc posts to act as a gate.

Colin pulled off the road and got out. The drive took a sharp turn and disappeared around what appeared to be a natural rise in the land. No structures were visible from the road, at least not from this angle, but he imagined the house and barn were somewhere up there, beyond the rise. Which, if he was right, meant the house couldn't be more than a stone's throw from Julie Davis's house. That gave him pause.

Hoping to get a better look at the house, he returned to his truck and resumed his drive. It wasn't until he'd turned around and headed in the direction he'd come that he spied the house. The old Queen Anne style farmhouse sat exactly where he'd thought. He wouldn't mind having Julie as a neighbor. The gate she'd put up testified to her love of privacy, but what if she expanded the brewery? Besides the paparazzi finding out where he was, the last thing he needed was a large-scale production going on next door. There'd be trucks rolling in, day and night, and workers. *Shit.* It would be a nightmare of the first order.

Or, she could sell to a developer. He'd have tract houses popping up like prairie dogs right next door. He couldn't decide which scenario would be worse.

Maybe this isn't even the place. The house appeared abandoned. The paint was peeling, and if his eyes weren't deceiving him, several windows were broken out. Tufts of grass were coming up in the ruts of the dirt driveway. It was by far the worst looking place he'd seen on this road.

Colin continued on, taking note of the land on the other side of Julie's place. The house on the other property was newer than Julie's, or the one he'd just seen by about a century. Sleek and modern, it was far from abandoned. Miles of fencing divided the place into smaller pastures where horses grazed, each in their own space. Who the heck had that kind of money out here? He'd have to ask Scott. If anyone knew, he would. Despite being a recent transplant to the community, the man seemed to know everything and everyone. In the long run, it didn't really matter who lived there. This wasn't the property Scott had spoken to him about. No way. He'd specifically said there was an old farmhouse, and this one was not old.

Maybe he should look for something else. Living within a stone's throw of Julie's house wasn't the best idea. She obviously didn't want to see him. Sort of awkward since one of the reasons he'd decided to look for a place in Butte Plains was because of her. Colin slapped the steering wheel with the palm of his hand. It was that damned kiss. One fucking kiss, and he'd lost his freaking mind.

In hindsight, perhaps putting her in her car immediately after — without a word, if he recalled correctly — might not have been the right thing to do. But, damn it all to Hell, she'd short-circuited his brain. It's what he told himself, anyway. The truth was too hard to admit in the light of day. Something so profound could only be examined in the darkest part of the night when he was alone with the memories of a perfect sunrise kiss. Then, and only then, did he accept he'd been scared out of his mind.

He'd never felt anything like the feelings that rocketed through him when their lips touched. He'd understood on a cellular level that Julie Davis posed a threat to everything he'd ever wanted. Just one kiss and he knew he'd give up Nashville and his dream of making it big in the country music industry for one night in her bed. He hadn't had much to drink, but his realizations had sobered him up quick, fast, and in a hurry.

Distance hadn't done a thing to dim the memory of the kiss, and time had only given him the opportunity to realize what a complete and utter moron he'd been. On one of those dark and lonely nights, unable to shut the memory down, he'd turned to his guitar. Instead of banishing the memories, they'd come out in the form of words and lines of music he'd written down without even thinking about it. He'd woken up on the sofa the next morning with a sore neck and a hit song to show for it.

Since the release of "Hello, Sunshine, Goodbye," he'd had several tunes hit the top of the charts. His fan base consisted of mostly women, his manager told him, who loved a guy who could admit he'd been wrong. Colin hadn't been wrong, but he'd keep his knowledge to himself. Taking Julie to bed the morning he kissed her *would* have been wrong. She wasn't a one-night-stand kind of woman, and it was all he'd been able to offer her at that time. His career had simply meant too much to him then, and Butte Plains still looked better in his rearview mirror than through the windshield—even if the sexiest woman alive lived there. He'd done what was right for both of them, and, despite the way she'd ditched out on him yesterday at her new tasting room, he still held out hope she'd give him another chance.

~ ~ ~

"Good news," Scott said as they sat down to another of Roseanne's delicious dinners. It had been nearly a week since he'd promised to inquire about the old farm he'd mentioned to Colin. In the meantime, Colin had looked at several other properties with a local real estate agent and come up empty. Real estate was drying up in Butte Plains, thanks to his sister and her husband. The business they'd resuscitated had infused new life into the entire area. Good for the town, but not so good for him.

"I could use some good news about now."

Scott held the chair for his fiancée then took the one beside her. "I spoke with the owner of the property I told you about the other day. She said she might entertain an offer."

Colin perked up. "Really? Fantastic!"

"She has some conditions, though." He helped himself to a large scoop of mashed potatoes then passed the dish to Colin. "You might not be interested once you hear them."

"I'd agree to just about anything right now. I've looked at half-a-dozen properties this week, and they're all crap." He ticked off their shortcomings. "No land. No house. A contaminated well. Hell, one of them was landlocked. The owner has been fighting to get legal access through a neighboring property for the last thirty years."

"Seriously?" Roseanne passed a basket of homemade rolls.

"Can they prevent a person from accessing legally owned property?"

Colin took a couple of warm rolls but kept the basket nearby. "It's some sort of family argument. Began a couple of generations ago, I guess. The land was divided between two brothers who hated each other in hopes they would, as the agent put it, find common ground and learn to get along. They never did. The one with access to his property refused to let his brother clear a road to his property. He even bought all the surrounding property just to spite his brother. The landlocked parcel has since been passed down to another generation, but still no luck in procuring an easement across the relative's land."

"Good luck selling, then," Scott said.

Colin shrugged. "Even if I could get a good look at it, I wouldn't want it. No one has set foot on it since the will was probated. The real estate agent had a satellite photo. It's a mess. Thanks, but no thanks." He bit into one of the fresh rolls and moaned as the buttery yeast flavor burst on his tongue. "I've died and gone to Heaven!"

Roseanne laughed and passed him a dish. "Try it with some of this cinnamon butter."

"Careful, woman. If you keep feeding me like this, I might not ever leave."

"You'll leave," Scott said. "Just wait until the baby gets here. Crying babies and dirty diapers trump food, no matter how good it is."

Colin shuddered and made a face. "Please, spare me! What does the woman want in return for selling the property? I've got cash, and I'm willing to throw in a pint of blood if it will convince her to sell."

"Two conditions. First, you can't bulldoze the house. She wants it restored."

Colin let the first condition sink in. "And?"

"You can't subdivide the land. She doesn't want it turned into a housing development."

"I don't have a problem with keeping all the land, but I need to see the house before I agree to restore it. If it's structurally sound, then I'm willing to talk."

"You should take someone with you to look at the house. Someone who knows what to look for."

Colin raised one eyebrow. "I suppose you know someone?"

Scott smiled. "Yep. Randy Tucker. He's done a lot of work for me, including restoring this house and my new office space downtown. He did the work on the new Lucky Lady Brewing Company tasting room, too."

Having seen two of the three places Scott had listed, Colin didn't need further convincing. "Send me his number."

CHAPTER SIX

Colin wrestled the post and wire gate out of the way. One look at the neglected driveway and he decided to leave his truck where it was and walk up to the house. Fixing the driveway went on his mental list of needed repairs. As he approached the house, he knew the list was going to be a very long one. He didn't need a restoration expert to tell him the porch wasn't safe, and the siding needed paint. One of the two chimneys looked like it might fall at any moment.

While he waited for Randy Tucker to arrive, he moved cautiously from room to room, falling in love a little bit more with each space he entered. He caught a glimpse of something moving outside and went to take a better look. A large black dog dashed across the yard, intent on following the trail of something only he could smell. The dog disappeared into the tall weeds just as another flash of movement caught his eye. Colin smiled as Julie Davis carefully navigated her way through the barbed-wire fence separating the two properties. Dressed in worn denim and a T-shirt bearing the Lucky Lady Brewing Company logo, her blonde hair pulled into a high ponytail, she took his breath away.

Memories, never far from his thoughts, of the kiss they'd shared came roaring to the forefront with a vengeance. His dick grew hard and his fingers itched to feel the silk of her hair threading through them. He'd have to make peace with her somehow if they were going to be neighbors. He wouldn't apologize for the kiss, but he would apologize for the way he'd sent her off into the sunrise by herself. She deserved to know why he'd done it, even if it meant admitting his cowardice.

Maybe if she knew the truth she'd give him a second chance.

Just as he lost sight of her on the downside of the rise the house sat on, someone rapped on the front door. "Come on in," he called out. "It's open."

Colin nodded at the man who stepped inside. "You must be Randy Tucker. I'm Colin Parker. It's nice to meet you." The two shook hands.

"Same," Tucker said as he took in the once-beautiful home. "This is quite the place. Needs work."

"Tell me something I don't know." Colin laughed. "She looks like she has good bones, but I'm no expert."

"Looks can be deceiving." Tucker ran his hand over a dusty doorframe. "I'll be straight up with you. Even with good bones, this is going to cost a small fortune to restore. It would be cheaper to gut it and start over with new materials than to try to save what's here."

Colin shook his head. "Starting over's not an option. It's either restore it or walk away from the property." He explained about the seller's stipulations.

"Okay, then," Tucker said. "Let's have a look around. I'll take some notes, and I should be able to give you an estimate in a couple of days. Some things will be nonnegotiable, meaning they have to be done for various reasons — to meet current building codes or for safety reasons. Other things will be optional. Maybe you'll want to do them now or wait a while — spread the expense out over a few years."

"You think it'll be that bad?"

"Won't know until I get a better look at the place. Want to show me around?"

They walked through the house. Randy asked questions in each room to determine what Colin hand in mind for each one, offering ideas when Colin came up short on vision. Tucker climbed into the attic then took a look under the house. By the time they were done, their shadows cut a long swath across the front lawn.

"Good news." Tucker stood on the far side of the driveway to get a look at the front elevation. "The structure appears to be sound. I noticed some cracks in the plaster walls, which might mean we need to do some leveling, but we're talking a minor repair compared to having to redo the entire foundation."

"Then I'm not crazy if I buy this place?"

"Not by a longshot. I won't lie. It's going to cost a lot of money to fix it up."

"I've got money. I'd just like to have some left over when I'm done."

Tucker laughed and held out his hand. They shook hands. "I'll call you in a couple of days, and we can get together and review the estimate. Then you can decide if it's the place for you."

"Sounds good." Colin watched as the restoration expert disappeared around the curve in the drive. He didn't want to tell him, but he'd made up his mind to buy the place the minute he saw Julie Davis crawl through the fence.

~ ~ ~

Julie tallied up the invoices for the third time. Her concentration had been shit this morning, and she knew exactly where to place the blame — on Colin Parker's shoulders. With a little luck, he'd go home to Nashville in a few days. She'd done a credible job of banishing him, and *The Kiss*, from her thoughts over the last few months, but knowing he was in town — and looking for her — had brought those memories back in a rush, making her knees weak and her heart race.

He was bad news. Too good-looking for his own good, he was also a talented singer/songwriter with a huge following. The baseball cap and sunglasses he'd sported at the tasting room hadn't been a fashion statement. They'd been a necessity. They might fool most, but she'd known it was him instantly. He was too popular for his visit not to draw attention soon. Someone would recognize him and word would spread. Before long, the paparazzi would show up, followed by his fans.

"All the more reason for me to stay right where I am until he leaves town, don't you think?" she asked Bud, her black Labrador retriever. The dog, sprawled on the floor at her feet, didn't move a muscle. She reached down and rubbed the top of his head. He opened his eyes and rolled to his side, feet outstretched. "Sorry," she said with a smile. "I hate to disturb your nap, but I could use some fresh air. How about you?"

The dog raised his head then laid down again. Bud wasn't much company, but he was all she had. He listened when she needed someone to talk to, and he never offered his opinion unless treats were involved. Health codes prevented him from being inside the brewing room, but she made up for the time apart by accompanying him on long walks as often as possible. Thanks to her forty acres and the hundred acres adjacent, which had been vacant for at least a decade judging by the decay of the old house on the property, Bud never ran out of things to sniff and places to explore. She'd inquired about buying the adjoining acreage when she'd purchased her place, but the family hadn't been ready to part with the land their ancestors had farmed up until the late 90s. She hated to see the house continue on its downward spiral, but there wasn't anything she could do about it. The owners would sell when they were ready. Not to her, though. She didn't need a second house or more acreage to take care of. The house she had was plenty big enough for one human and one dog, and she had no interest in expanding the brewery beyond its current footprint. With a little luck, her neighbors would sell to someone interested in restoring the house to its former glory. If they let her continue her walks with Bud on the property, she'd consider it a bonus.

"Come on, lazy." Julie stood. "Let's get out of here for a few minutes." The moment her hand touched the door knob, Bud scrambled up and pushed past her, his toenails clicking on the old wood floor. She'd put as much sweat as money into making the small house her own, and she loved every square inch of it. It wasn't huge like the old Victorian next door, but it felt like a mansion compared to the small apartment she'd grown up in. Opening the door to wide-open spaces instead of a busy street lined with ageing apartment buildings and even older businesses never got old.

Julie took a deep breath, filling her lungs with clean air. Satisfied to let Bud lead, she followed him around the house and across to the neighboring property. Once under the sagging barbed-wire fence, he took off running. Julie took her time, carefully maneuvering over the rusted wire. She'd ruined several pieces of clothing, trying to get from one pasture to the next and wasn't ready to ruin another today.

"Bud!" she called. "Wait up!" Unconcerned about the dog—he knew where he was going and how to find his way home—Julie sauntered past the old farmhouse and down the well-worn path the dog had taken. He loved to chase the ducks that called the old stock tank on the property home. They'd never let him catch them, and she doubted he'd know what to do with one if he did catch it. She thought he just liked to see them flap their wings and hear them squawk.

Julie found Bud right where she thought he'd be and sat down on a grassy patch along the bank of the man-made water hole to watch the show. Bud's ears flapped and his tongue lolled out as he danced along the edge of the water, barking at the ducks who had all gathered in the middle of the tank, totally unconcerned for their safety. With any other Labrador retriever, they'd be in trouble, but not with her dog. He had to be the only retriever on the planet who was afraid of water.

"Give it a break, Bud. Maybe they'll come to the bank if you shut up for a little while." As if he understood, the dog stretched out next to her, and, in a few minutes, his snoring brought a smile to her lips. "Good idea," she said, lying on the grass. The paperwork on her desk could wait while she took a few minutes for herself. She closed her eyes and let the peace of the place settle over her.

~ ~ ~

Colin sat on the steps leading up to the porch and let his imagination take flight. He could see himself sitting here with his guitar, playing for friends or quietly composing in his head. Something about the property lowered his blood pressure, though he knew he'd probably want to blow the house to smithereens long before the renovation was complete. He'd have to find a place to stay until the house was livable. He'd want to keep a close watch on the process, which meant he'd need to be nearby. His gaze swept the open horizon. Other than the old barn, there wasn't a thing in sight. Unless he looked around the corner.

Standing, he stretched then walked around to the side yard to peer at his neighbor's house. It wasn't anywhere as large as this one, but it had to have at least two bedrooms. A smile broke across his face as the craziest idea he'd ever had formed in his mind.

She'd never go for it. Not in a million years, but if there was one thing Colin had learned from his time in Nashville, it was that you didn't get anywhere if you didn't take a risk now and then. Producers and record labels weren't going to find you if you hid in your room, and sexy brewmaster's weren't going to invite you to live in their spare room if you let them run away every time they saw you coming.

He eyed the spot where she'd come through the sagging fence then let his gaze follow the path she'd taken. Unless she'd reentered her property somewhere else, she had to still be on his side of the fence. With his fledgling idea still forming in his head, he set out in the direction he'd last seen Julie Davis' fine ass going.

"You can run, but you can't hide, woman."

The trail was nothing more than a path created by feet repeatedly trampling the overgrown grass into submission. Colin mentally added a tractor with a deck mower to his list of necessities. He'd earned extra money in high school, cutting and baling hay for some of the farms in the area. Most of the other teenagers who'd hired on to do the dirty and exhausting work had hated it, but he'd found it oddly soothing. Like everyone else, he'd despised loading the square bales onto a trailer then unloading them again in the barns, but driving the tractor had been fun. The rhythmic swoosh and slice of the mower blades cutting through the dry grass, and the hum of the engine providing a steady backbeat had been music to his ears.

The place would make a great hay farm, he thought as he stood at the edge of the rise the house sat upon and looked out over the rest of the property. It had been cleared for farming except for a spot to the north where a copse of trees remained. Farmers in the early days rarely relied on cash crops to feed their families. They'd purchased staples like flour and sugar but provided their own meat and vegetables. And where there was livestock there was water. He'd bet his new boots those trees surrounded a stock tank.

He knew he'd been right! As he got closer, he felt the dip in temperature and the rise in humidity. His nose twitched at the slightly fishy smell. It wasn't uncommon to have these man-made tanks stocked with channel catfish. The bottom-dwellers supposedly helped keep the water clean by eating everything from dead fish to algae. Catfish were sort of a regional delicacy around these parts, too. Colin had never been a fan of the fish, fried or otherwise, and since he didn't plan to keep livestock, maybe he'd just have the tank filled in. Wondering what the work was going to cost him, and if he could do it himself, he didn't realize how close he'd come to the water until he caught a glimpse of it up ahead. The clear water sparkled like a diamond surrounded by emeralds. The trees he'd seen from the rise would shade the tank in the heat of the day, but, this late in the afternoon, were silent sentinels on the far bank. A wide band of lawn variety green grass carpeted the perimeter of the rocky shoreline. Half-a-dozen white ducks huddled together on the bank opposite while the two interlopers he'd come in search of, apparently unaware of his presence, lay sprawled on the grass not twenty feet from where he stood.

Colin's chest shook with silent laughter. She had some watchdog. He hadn't exactly tried to disguise his approach. Even the ducks had raised their heads to determine the threat posed by his arrival before tucking their bills under their wings to resume their afternoon nap. But not this dog. He hadn't moved an inch. From where he stood, Colin could hear the canine's snores. He shook his head at the sight. What a life. Nothing better to do on a sunny afternoon than trespass on your neighbor's property for a little siesta time.

For about two heartbeats, he considered leaving them to their naps, but he couldn't do it. This time, trying to be as quiet as possible, he moved forward until he could see Julie's face. With no makeup, and relaxed in slumber, she looked like every guy's girl-next-door fantasy come to life. He could attest to the kissability of her lips, and the softness of her curves in his hands. She'd allowed him enough liberties during their one kiss to know her breasts were a perfect handful, and her hips generous enough to hang on to.

God, how he wanted her. Had since he'd first laid eyes on her at his sister's wedding. Kissing her had confirmed everything he'd suspected. She could be *the one*. The realization had been about as frightening then as discovering an alien blob was eating its way through small Texas towns, and Butte Plains was next on the menu.

Adjusting the instant hard-on he'd gotten the minute he saw her, he took a seat beside her. Too far away to touch, but close enough to fuel all manner of fantasies involving him and her and a patch of green grass.

Every soft puff of air from between her lips made him harder. Every tiny movement she made brought on fantasies of her moving beneath him while he made love to her. How could just watching a woman sleep be such torture?

Snapping off a too-long blade of grass, he systematically destroyed it by peeling off one strip at a time until nothing remained but the thick spine down the middle. It was either fidget or kiss his sleeping beauty awake, and he knew one thing for certain. One kiss wasn't going to be enough. Not this time.

He bent to select another blade of grass to torture when she stirred beside him. Snapping off the perfect specimen, a blade about a foot long and nearly an inch wide, he turned. Expecting to find her still asleep, he smiled when, eyes still closed, she stretched her limbs. The thin fabric of her T-shirt pulled tight over her tits, and the hem rose up enough to show a strip of pale skin above the waistband of her jeans.

The blade of grass he'd picked was no match for Colin's fist. *Shit.* Keeping his hands to himself was going to take more self-control than he possessed. But he'd find it somewhere. Like everything else he'd ever decided to do, he wouldn't fail in this. If it took until the end of the world, he'd convince Julie Davis to give him a chance.

CHAPTER SEVEN

Julie stretched as the last remnants of her recurring dream evaporated into what they were — figments of her imagination. Why, oh why did she have to keep reliving *The Kiss*? Her lips remembered it like it had been yesterday, and her subconscious continued to dredge it up on a regular basis — usually when she was tired or stressed. In the dream, they didn't stop with one kiss.

Why couldn't she be one of those people who didn't remember their dreams? She recalled every detail from the feel of his lips on hers, to the heat of his bare skin pressed against hers as they moved together as one. How many times had she woken up with an ache between her legs, reaching for a man who wasn't there? Who never would be. Never *could* be.

The warm earth and soft grass felt good — so good she didn't want to wake up, but she sensed the sun going down, and she didn't want to try to navigate her way home in the pitch black on a trampled grass trail that rambled wherever a certain black lab's nose had taken him.

Recalling the stack of documents she'd left on her desk, she groaned. There was nothing she hated more than sitting at a desk all day, crunching numbers. But with her investment advisor arriving tomorrow, she hadn't had a choice. She needed to know which investments were paying off, and which weren't. Rich people didn't stay rich by sticking their head in the sand. Winning the money had been easy. Keeping it was the trick. Her associate's degree in business wasn't nearly enough to qualify her to manage a billion-dollar estate, but it was all she had to draw upon to wrangle a bevy of lawyers and advisors who profited when she did. So far, they'd all done well. She couldn't complain, but dreams like the one she'd just had could derail her.

Single women everywhere had to be careful. There were all kinds of creeps out there, but as a single woman with money, she had to be even more careful. She'd learned that lesson the hard way. She doubted Colin Parker was out to get her money. Surely, he had plenty of his own since his career had taken off, but damn—*The Kiss*! What she'd give for a do-over. She'd push him away. Tell him to keep his hands and those damn intoxicating lips of his to himself!

She'd been content with her lot in life—resigned to keeping men at arm's length in order to protect her secret. Then Colin Parker had walked into his sister's wedding, and she'd nearly forgotten her self-imposed rules. Recovering just in time, she'd left as early as was socially acceptable, ending up at a new music venue on the outskirts of town. Ironically, the owners were a set of brothers whose criminal records prevented them from selling alcohol. But they'd quickly built a reputation for drawing some of the best musical talent around, and the place was packed most nights. It had been the perfect spot to spend an anonymous evening. Until Colin Parker walked in.

He hadn't been crazy famous then, just up-and-coming famous. The locals who'd recognized him hadn't treated him like the celebrity he was now. In hindsight, it was the he's-no-big-deal attitude that had given her a false sense of security. She'd let him get close. Had danced with him to a couple of songs then ended up talking with him until they'd been kicked out so the brothers could lock up. They'd continued their conversation on the hood of his car. One thing had led to another, which led to *The Kiss*.

A whisper of movement—nothing more than a rumor on the otherwise still air—put all her senses on red alert. She'd seen signs of wildlife in the area. Coyotes weren't unheard of, and the occasional deer. Maybe the water had attracted a raccoon? Could just be one of the ducks looking for bugs in the grass. Lay there and pretend to be asleep, or run for her life?

A shift in the air currents brought an unexpected scent to her nostrils. The only animal who smelled like that was the male of the human species. One particular male to be precise. Heart racing, Julie jerked upright. And there he sat, his gaze heating her from the inside out. Or maybe it was the remnants of her dream talking.

Colin Parker sat a safe distance away—if she were a rabbit, but she couldn't move as fast as the little puffy-tailed fur balls inhabiting the area. If he wanted, he could grab her before she was able to scramble to her feet. Her stupid heart wanted to believe he'd had ample opportunity while she slept to cause her harm, while her brain warned her not to listen to a damn thing her heart had to say. Choosing not to be stupid, she went with her brain.

"Are you stalking me?" she shrieked. She tried to put more distance between them, but Bud, sprawled out on her other side, had no intention of moving. With the water at her feet, she was left with one option. She crab-walked backwards then pushed to her feet.

Colin watched her retreat but made no move to follow her. "Simmer down," he said, turning to face her. "I saw you come this way earlier, and when you didn't return, I thought I'd see if you were still out here."

"Sounds a lot like stalking." Without taking her eyes off him, she moved closer to her dog. Bud raised his head, sniffed the air once then stood. He stretched into a perfect downward dog yoga pose before padding over, tail wagging, tongue hanging out, to nose at Colin Parker.

Petting Bud as if they were the best of friends, Colin glanced up at her. "Stalking implies I've been following you, and I have not. I was minding my own business when you trespassed on my property. I simply wanted to make sure you had returned home safely."

"Wha-what do you mean, *your* property?"

Colin pushed Bud off his lap and stood. Brushing dog hair and grass from his jeans, he said, "Well, it's not mine yet, but it will be soon. I've decided to buy this place."

Her mind raced to make sense of what he'd just said. "I didn't know it was for sale." Was that the best she could come up with?

Colin shrugged. "Officially it's not, but the owner is willing to sell to the right person."

"And you're the right person." Julie snickered. "Yeah, right."

"Apparently, I am. I've agreed to her price contingent on being able to meet her conditions. I came out today to see if the house could be restored. I saw you from the kitchen window when you came through the fence."

"That was hours ago."

"I told you, I was checking out the house. Even had a restoration expert out to take a look." He tucked his hands in the front pockets of his jeans and looked a little embarrassed. "It needs *a lot* of work."

She hadn't been inside, but she saw the outside every day. The exterior was enough to scare most buyers off. She called Bud to her side and began walking up the path the two of them had made through the tall grass. She didn't look to see, but knew Colin followed. When the old house came into view, she stopped. "Is it worth saving?"

Colin stopped beside her. "Randy Tucker says it is."

"Did he also tell you it's going to cost a fortune?"

"He did. I won't know an amount for a few days, but I suspect his estimate is going to make my checkbook weep."

Julie laughed, listening to her heart this time. He hadn't been stalking her. Her brain argued with her again. "Why this house, this place? There must be others that don't need this much work."

"I should have bought something last year, but coming home was the last thing on my mind at the time. Since then, the real estate market has dried up. People are snatching up everything in sight. Scott Ramsey told me about this place, said he knew the owner. So, here I am, looking to buy an extreme fixer-upper."

"You said the seller has conditions?"

"She wants it in the contract that the buyer has to restore the house. She doesn't want it torn down or left to fall down. And, she doesn't want the land sold off or subdivided."

"As your future neighbor, I hope you agree to her conditions."

"I will. Randy assured me the house is sound despite all appearances to the contrary."

"He does good work."

"I'm staying with Scott and Roseanne. He did a beautiful job on their old house, and I saw what he did with your tasting room."

"You've been there?" she asked.

"You know I was."

"If you're implying *I'm* stalking *you*—"

"I saw you hightailing it out of there a few minutes after your bar girl went looking for you."

Heat crept into her cheeks. She didn't know what to say, so she kept her mouth shut.

"I don't blame you. I wouldn't want to see me either if I were you."

He was right, she'd been avoiding him, but she'd like to know why he thought she was. "Why would you think I'm avoiding you?"

For the first time since they'd been standing there, he turned his attention away from the house to look at her. "I'm sorry, Julie. If I had it to do over again, I would have put you in my car and taken you back to the B&B with me. Sending you home alone after…well, after that kiss was the cowardly thing to do."

Her brain decided enough was enough. Her stupid heart was going to get her in big trouble with this man if she didn't watch out. For crying out loud, he was going to be her neighbor! She had to keep their relationship in perspective. Telling him she'd been hurt and disappointed, and that her subconscious had repeatedly gone where she physically hadn't, wouldn't do. Instead, she mustered every bit of fake indignation she could come up with and prayed he wouldn't see through her pathetic attempt at acting. Chin held high, she said, "It was the right thing to do. I hate to deflate your giant ego, but I wouldn't have gone with you."

Liar. Liar. Liar. Her heart kept up the mantra all the way to the fence and across her yard to her back door. She certainly would have gone with the up-and-coming country musician, but there was no way she was going to make the mistake of falling for the man he was now. He came with a cruise ship full of baggage, all labeled *paparazzi,* and Lord knew, she had enough baggage of her own. She didn't need any of his.

~ ~ ~

"Well, that went well," Colin said to his new old house as Julie Davis disappeared inside her own. He hadn't jumped her, and she hadn't run. Small victories, but he'd take them. She was lying when she said she wouldn't have gone to the B&B with him. He'd bet his first platinum record she would have. She'd been as into their kiss as he had been, and he knew willing when he saw it. She'd been willing. If not for the yellow streak down his back, he would have taken her to bed somewhere. Maybe not at the B&B since he'd left the place without a door key, but somewhere.

Colin had to turn on his headlights in order to see how to fasten the rickety gate in place. He mentally added proper lighting to the electric gate and new fencing he'd need. He'd probably dream of dollar signs stalking him tonight. Fiduciary nightmares would be better than dreaming about kissing Julie again. If he'd never kissed her in the first place he'd still be in Nashville, living the carefree life of a bachelor—albeit a poor one.

He let himself in to Scott and Roseanne's house with the key Roseanne had given him and made his way up to his room on the third floor. He'd chosen one at the rear of the house partly because it was decorated in shades of green, and partly because his hosts' bedroom was one floor below on the front of the house. He'd thought this would be better than staying in his sister's small house with her and her new husband, but Scott and Roseanne weren't much better. They weren't newlyweds, but they were more lovey-dovey than he'd expected them to be, given Roseanne's pregnancy.

Tossing his keys on the dresser, he sat on the edge of the bed and pulled off his shoes. He'd made progress today on two fronts. He'd found a place to live. Granted, it was a dump, but Randy had convinced him it could be saved. And, he'd apologized to Julie.

They were on speaking terms now—a plus in his book. Convincing her to let him bunk at her place while his was under construction was going to take some doing. She had every right to be wary of his intentions because his intentions were questionable.

He intended to have her in his bed. From there, the intentions were quite clear in his head. He'd honed them in his dreams every night since the kiss. He knew exactly how he'd strip her clothes off her. He knew exactly how he would tease her nipples and drive her to the edge with his fingers between her legs. He knew every way he would make love to her.

God, he was hard just thinking about touching her. And, he was damned tired of fucking his hand instead. His newfound fame brought a lot of unwanted attention from his female fans. He couldn't count the number he'd declined to sleep with over the last few months. They were everywhere, seemingly crawling out of the woodwork in restaurants and outside the local venues he loved to play. Some had even found out where he lived and shown up on his doorstep. He'd turned them all down because of a memory he couldn't banish no matter how hard he tried.

He should have known Julie Davis wasn't like the others. His success didn't impress her because she'd taken the time to actually get to know him. Her opinion of him wasn't based solely on the lyrics of a song he'd written. Unfortunately, the opinion she had of him wasn't a good one. Why else would she have gone out of her way to avoid him?

As he headed to the shower in the en suite bathroom, he hoped his apology today had elevated her opinion of him.

CHAPTER EIGHT

"Colin!" Becky rolled away from her desk and stood. "What brings you by?"

It was the first time he'd been to her office since he'd returned. Adams Manufacturing seemed to grow larger by the day. He took in his surroundings. She'd redecorated since his last visit the week of her wedding. "Not much." He chose one of the fancy upholstered chairs facing her and sat. "Thought I'd stop by and say hello."

His sister cocked her head to one side. "What's going on, baby brother?"

"What makes you think anything is going on?"

"Get real, Colin. You hate places like this." She waved her hand around to indicate her office. "You're allergic to corporate America. Last time you were here you said the walls gave you hives."

"You said you'd redecorated. I had to come see, didn't I?" He loved messing with her. Always had. She was so easy to rile. The last time he'd been here she'd been anxious about what her wedding guests were going to say once they found out the event they were attending wasn't the real thing. He didn't think anyone would care one way or the other, so to distract her, he'd made the crack about her ugly, outdated office. The strategy had worked.

She'd gone into big-sister lecture mode, and, as he'd predicted, the wedding guests thought the video of their secret Vegas nuptials they played at the reception was a hoot. Elvis impersonators tended to make people smile.

"Not buying it. Come on, spill."

He grinned. "Or what? You'll get out the thumb screws?"

"We have something similar," she said. "I'm sure with a little adjustment—"

"Don't say it!" he begged. Just thinking about some of the possible words that could come out of his sister's mouth made him cringe. He'd come to terms with her selling sex toys, but he sure as heck didn't want to talk about them with her. "Please don't say whatever it is you were going to say."

"Then tell me."

"Okay, okay." She'd won the first round. "I bought a house this morning."

Her squeal had him covering his ears. As she rounded the desk, arms spread wide, he stood and allowed her to grab him in a bear hug. He hugged her just as hard, happy she shared his excitement.

"Whoa, there. Who said you could hug my wife?"

At the sound of Ford's voice, Colin placed a kiss on his sister's head then set her away before turning to his brother-in-law who leaned against the doorjamb, a huge smile on his face. "She hugged me first." Colin moved to shake hands with the older man. "Good to see you again."

"Likewise." His gaze slipped to his wife. "What was that high-pitched shriek about?"

Becky wrapped an arm around Ford's waist and kissed him on the cheek. "Baby brother bought a house today! He's back in Butte Plains for good!" She turned her no-nonsense gaze on Colin. "You are staying for good, aren't you? This isn't just an investment?"

Colin nodded. "Yep. I'm here for good. It's going to be a

while before I can move in, though. The house needs extensive renovations."

Becky wanted all the details, so, over coffee in the employee break room, Colin filled them in on the property and his agreement to renovate the dilapidated house.

"Sounds like you'll have your hands full for a while." Ford stood and stretched. "Glad to have you home." He glanced at his watch. "I've got a meeting in a few minutes. You'll let me know if you need anything?"

"Sure thing." They shook hands, and Ford left.

"You can count on me, too," Becky said. Colin stood when she did. "I need to get back to work, too." She hugged him again. "I'm so glad you came by to tell me. Mom's going to be so excited. She's missed you."

"She was the first one I told, and yeah, she's glad I'm home, too."

They stopped outside the door to Becky's office. "Seriously, Colin. If you need anything—"

"I'll let you know. I promise."

~ ~ ~

The place was officially his. Colin sat on the porch of his new home, looking out at the overgrown landscape because it was the least daunting of possible views. This, he could do something about. He'd nearly bought out the local hardware store this morning, filling up the bed of the new pickup truck he'd purchased just before leaving Nashville. While the grading crew worked on getting the driveway ready for construction vehicles and delivery trucks to access the property, he planned on taming the yard. His new tractor and deck mower would be delivered in a few days. Then he'd tackle the rest of the property. Once the yard was cleared and he could see what he had, he'd decide if he needed to install some privacy landscaping along with the new horse fencing and electronic gate he'd already contracted.

First things first. He unloaded a giant rubber trash can from his truck and began filling it with the debris he could see—plastic bags that had blown in from the road—faded soda cans and beer bottles, evidence the abandoned house had been scouted out by the local teenagers at one time.

After gathering up all the trash he could see, he unloaded the self-propelled mower he'd bought and went to work on the yard surrounding the house. It was slow going, but the blades did a good job of knocking down the knee-high vegetation, which he had to admit was more weeds than grass. Something else to add to the landscaping list, he thought.

~ ~ ~

Julie glanced at the clock on the nightstand and groaned. Nine a.m. She rolled over and stuffed a pillow over her head to muffle the noise coming from next door. Normally, she'd have been up for hours, checking on the brewing vats, but last night had been another one of *those* nights. Colin Parker and his infernal kiss had invaded her dreams, and she'd woken in the middle of the night, hot, horny, and unable to get back to sleep until nearly dawn.

The sound of a lawn mower, punctuated by the occasional clunk followed by a loud curse, finally drew her out of bed and to the window. Her room, located at the rear of the house above the kitchen, overlooked the neighboring property.

A shiny new red pickup truck sat in front of the old barn. "I guess he really did buy the place," she said to Bud who sat in the middle of her bed watching her and probably wondering when she was going to take him out to do his morning duty. She was about to oblige him when Colin Parker, walking behind a lawn mower, turned the corner of his new house.

"Oh. My. Lord." Jesus, did he have to mow shirtless? Quickly, she stepped to the side so he wouldn't see her ogling his wide shoulders and six-pack abs. He looked even better than her subconscious had imagined he would look, and she'd thought she'd done a pretty good job, based on her limited exposure to the man. "Honey," she said to herself, "you weren't even close."

He got to the corner of the house then turned the mower, cut a swath over to the driveway before turning toward the front of the house again. Julie knew she should look away, but the view from the back was as mesmerizing as the view from the front. Wide shoulders tapered to a slim waist, and, Lord have mercy, a fine ass encased in tight denim! She sighed. Why couldn't the place have sold to a hairy, pot-bellied, tobacco-chewing farmer instead? Those images might have given her nightmares, but she'd take them over the dreams she knew she'd be having based on her new knowledge of his anatomy.

Bud stood and wagged his tail. "Okay. Okay. Give me a minute to put on something decent," she said. "Then I'll take you out. But no going next door. Do you hear me?"

She was watching her first cup of coffee dribble into her favorite mug when she heard another clunk, followed by an even louder clunk which was followed by a curse loud enough to be heard by people in town. Just as she grabbed her mug, the mower cut off. Silence. Blessed silence. Opening the door, she stood aside as Bud rushed out. He wasted no time hoisting his hind leg to do his business against the Rose of Sharon bush. Then he was off like a rocket, headed for the fence separating her place from Colin's.

"Bud!" She raced down the steps and across the yard. "Come back here this minute!"

By the time she reached the fence line, her dog stood next to her new shirtless neighbor. His hand was on Bud's head, giving the dog the attention he sought, but the man's gaze was on the door of his new pickup.

Julie managed to avoid the sharp barbs and got through the fence without tearing her clothes. "I'm sorry," she said as she approached the two. "Bud doesn't have any manners."

Colin continued to look at the truck as he replied, "He's a good dog. Not a problem."

"Well, he shouldn't just run up and demand to be—" Her

gaze followed Colin's. "Oh! That's not good."

"Hit a damned rock," he said.

"I heard." Fine lines radiated out from the point of impact to create a sunburst effect on the grapefruit-sized dent in the door panel. "It can be fixed, can't it?"

"Yeah, it can. Just thought it would be a while longer before I dented it up."

"Welcome to life on a farm," she said. "Have you seen my truck? I left it out in a hailstorm last summer. It looks like a giant golf ball now."

The corners of his lips lifted slightly, and, for the first time since she'd joined him, he tore his gaze away from the damage to his vehicle and onto her instead. His blue eyes seared her skin as they traveled from her toes to her nose, while his smile grew broader. His laugh was deep and genuine. "That's yours?"

Julie nodded.

"Damn near laughed my head off when I saw it in town the other day. You should park it inside."

She pointed at the dent in his brand-spanking-new truck. "And you should take your own advice, neighbor."

Colin looked at her as if deciding if she was serious or not. Then his smile grew even wider. "Touché, neighbor. Maybe we could get a package deal on detached garages." He pointed at the old barn. "I need the barn for my tractor and stuff."

"And I have a garage. I'd left the truck out because I knew I'd need it later on. The storm took me by surprise. Luckily, my Camaro was in the garage."

"There go my plans to try to get a two-for-one deal on a garage." He didn't look the least bit disappointed.

"Maybe you can negotiate a deal for a new barn *and* a new garage?"

"Or maybe I'll have a garage added onto the recording studio I'm going to have built."

"Recording studio?" Images whirled through her mind like a

tornado on steroids. People coming and going at all hours. Loud music, and God knew what all.

"Yeah. I need a place to work. You didn't think I was retiring, did you?"

She didn't know what she thought, but she knew she hadn't considered the possibility he'd be recording next door to her. "No. I guess… Well, I guess I thought you'd record in Nashville, or at least in Dallas. Not here." She let her gaze wander past the old barn to the expanse of open land. "Where are you planning to put this studio?"

He must have picked up on the tone of her voice because his reply sounded a bit defensive and his smile had vanished. "Why? Afraid you'll have to listen to some country music?"

Country music star or not, she had a right to know what his intentions were since they were neighbors. "I like country music, but I don't want to listen to it all night. Some of us have to sleep, you know."

"Duly noted. I'll make sure the banjo-playing rednecks are off the front porch at a decent hour."

Infuriating man. Julie planted her fists on her hips and glared at Colin. "You know that's not what I meant, but thanks anyway." She glanced at the dent one more time. "And try to keep the cursing down, too, while you're at it."

The damned fence snagged her blouse as she went through. She swallowed a curse rather than give him the satisfaction of knowing how little his cursing had actually bothered her. She'd found it amusing, but she'd never tell him. The arrogant bastard. Why, oh why had she ever thought he could be *the one*?

Not in a million years. Not if he was the last man on the planet. Not if…well, not if!

CHAPTER NINE

That hadn't gone well.

Colin jerked his gaze from the spot in the fence where Julie Davis, her dog, and her fine ass had just gone through. Raking a hand through his hair, he dislodged several pieces of grass then kicked the dent in his door for good measure. "Well, fuck!"

Damn it all to hell. What had begun as a day full of promise had deteriorated at record speed.

Lowering the tailgate, he pulled a water bottle from the cooler he'd brought along and sat down. It wasn't even 10 a.m. and he was sweating like a pig. He'd caused serious damage to his new truck and pissed off the one person in Butte Plains he seriously did not want to piss off. Not only was she his neighbor, which called for diplomacy, but he'd damn near hung the "the one" label on her. He glanced at his watch. Yep. The driveway people were late. He couldn't wait to see what else this day had in store for him.

The cold water felt good as it went down. He finished off the bottle and got another one which he pressed to the back of his neck. It had been a long time since he'd worked this hard, and then he'd done it for the money. No one was paying him to do this, so why was he killing himself? His gaze swept the yard. Weeds and all, it looked a hundred times better without the trash and the overgrown grass. If he tried real hard, he could envision the house the way it had looked in the drawing Randy Tucker had done to illustrate the changes he wanted to make.

New porch posts and railings. New steps. New, energy-efficient windows, custom-made to look identical to the existing ones. A new paint job. And those improvements were just the beginning. Gutters. Roofing. New siding where he'd found dry rot and termite damage. He'd even sketched out a new landscaping plan and recommended a local guy to do the work.

Thus, Colin was out here putting in sweat equity. The landscaper's quote just to clean up the yard—never mind create new flowerbeds and repair the crumbling walkways—had been a shock. Thus the pickup load of lawn and garden equipment and the sweat. Whatever he saved on the yard he could put into the house.

He finished off the second water bottle then tossed the empties into the almost-full trash can.

The driveway contractor arrived just as he finished mowing. After talking to the supervisor to make sure they were on the same page about what was to be done, Colin assembled his new weed whacker. If his neighbor was afraid his music would be too noisy, she probably wasn't too happy right now, either. Between the whir of the weeder's gas engine and the heavy equipment blading the drive, even he was wishing for a set of noise-cancelling headphones.

~ ~ ~

Colin walked into the Lucky Lady Brewing Company Tasting Room, his gaze sweeping the tables for Scott Ramsey and Ford Adams. His brother-in-law had called earlier and invited him to join them for a beer. Craving some normalcy in his life, he'd grabbed his Mustangs baseball cap and a pair of sunglasses, and headed out.

Spotting them sitting at the table farthest from the wide windows, he smiled and joined them. "Hey." Taking off his sunglasses but leaving the hat on, he sat with his back to the room. He'd let his hair grow some since he'd been home and it now curled up at his collar. His ratty T-shirt bearing the Butte Plains Farmers logo labeled him a local as opposed to a celebrity. As a disguise, it would have to do.

"Hey, yourself." Scott lifted the mug in front of him. "We got a head start. Hope you don't mind."

"Not at all."

Avery, the bartender who he'd met the time he'd come in looking for Julie, appeared at his elbow. "What can I get you?"

Colin glanced at the menu inside a plastic stand situated in the center of the table. "I'll try the Kissed by Sunrise again."

"Coming right up."

"Again?" Ford asked.

Colin shrugged. "I came in here right after I got home. Thought I'd give the place a try."

"It's become a favorite for locals and tourists," Scott said. "Just as I predicted."

"You had something to do with this?" Colin waved his had to indicate the tasting room. It was quickly filling up with the after-work crowd.

Scott explained how he'd pitched the idea to Julie. "She didn't want to do it, but I convinced her she could run it from behind the scenes. Looks like it's paying off for her."

"I would say so," Ford said. "You have to get here early if you want a table."

"How's the house coming?" Scott asked, changing the subject.

Ever since construction had begun on his house, Colin answered more questions than a two-year-old could ask. "Good, I guess. I don't have anything to compare with, though." He frowned as his phone vibrated in his pocket. Reaching for it, he asked, "Is it normal to have to answer a zillion questions a day?"

"Pretty much," Scott said. "You going to answer that?" He pointed to the phone Colin held in his hand.

"I think I'll finish my beer first. Every time they call, I have to drop what I'm doing and drive out there to take a look. Wish I could just delegate the responsibility, but I'm sure I'd live to regret it if I did."

"Why aren't you staying in the house?" Ford took a long drink from his glass.

"You haven't seen the place," Colin said. "It's a dump. They've stripped out all the electrical and plumbing. Dust everywhere. I have to wear a mask just to walk through the rooms." God only knew what was in the dust. He didn't want to sound like a prima donna, but he couldn't risk his voice by breathing in toxic waste.

"What about renting a travel trailer?" Scott waved at a couple who'd just walked in. Colin had never seen them before. Did the man know everyone in Texas? "You'd have all the comforts of home but still be on-site," he continued.

"When I'm on tour, I practically live in one of those things. Don't know if I could stand it as long as the renovation might take. I thought about trying to rent a room from my new neighbor, but I don't think she's too happy with me right now."

Both men stared at him.

"What?"

"What did you do to piss Julie off?" Scott asked.

"Wait." Ford held up one hand. "Julie Davis is your neighbor?"

"Yeah. Her property adjoins mine on the south side. I could throw a rock from my backyard and hit her house." He turned to Scott. "Let's just say, she's not happy having me as a neighbor."

"Huh." Scott took a sip of his beer.

"You could always put up a tent. Camp out," Ford said. "Maybe she'll feel sorry for you and let you rent a room."

Colin froze, his beer halfway to his lips. "You're a genius! Why didn't I think of that?"

"Are you nuts?" Scott's raised voice drew stares from the

other customers. "You've got hot and cold running water, a soft bed, and air-conditioning at our place."

"I know, it's crazy, but it might work."

Scott stared at him. "This is about more than being close to the work site, isn't it?"

"Maybe," Colin conceded. He spoke to Ford. "You think the new sporting goods place down the street sells tents?"

"Probably, but if you're looking for sympathy, you don't want to look too comfortable."

"True."

"I've got just the tent you need," he said. "Finish your beer and I'll show you."

"How old is this thing?" Scott held a handkerchief over his nose as they stared at a rotting bundle of canvas in the cobweb-infested basement of Ford's ancestral home.

"Twenty-five years, I guess. My dad bought it when I was a kid. We were going to do the whole family camping thing, but my mom refused to go. I set it up a few times in the yard, but, other than my solo adventures, it hasn't been out of the basement."

"It's perfect." Colin dragged it to the edge of the shelf. "Help me get it out of here."

"I'll hold the door for you," Scott said.

CHAPTER TEN

It had been nearly a week since her dust-up with Colin, and the construction noise was driving her straight up the wall. The sun was barely up when Julie opened the door to let Bud out and found a plastic grocery bag hanging from the handle of her storm door. Still in her summer pajamas, which consisted of a worn-out tank top and a pair of boxer-style shorts, she made sure none of the guys working on Colin's house were looking then stepped out on the porch to grab the bag.

While the dog took care of his business, she went inside and opened the bag. She couldn't help but smile at what she found inside — a pair of noise-cancelling headphones!

She had to give the man credit, he knew how to apologize. She'd often wished she had a pair when she was trying to study while her mother watched television in the other room. The fancy headphones had been way out of her budget then, so she'd made do with a cheap pair of earbuds from the discount store. She hadn't thought about them in ages — well, not since she'd moved here. Up until Colin bought the place next door, she'd had no need for them. With all the construction going on within spittin' distance of her house, she could put them to good use.

Bud scratched at the door, wanting in and to have his breakfast. Still smiling over the headphones, she opened the door.

The dog flew in, tail wagging in anticipation of being fed. "Wait just a sec," she said to her loyal canine, her full attention trained on her neighbor's yard. "What the heck does he think he's doing?"

Just then Colin looked up from his task and waved.

Julie waved back then, realizing she was still in her pj's, she jumped inside and slammed the door.

After measuring kibble into Bud's bowl, she ran upstairs to dress. Ten minutes later, she was standing on her side of the fence, watching the famous country music star erect a canvas monstrosity in his yard. "What's the tent for?" she asked when he finished pounding a stake in the ground.

"It's my temporary residence," he said as if living in a tent made perfect sense. "Until the house is livable. Randy says it'll be a couple of months, maybe three."

"You're going to live in a tent for two or three months? That's crazy."

"I don't have many options. I need to be close to the construction. They're really trying to get it just the way I want it, so there are lots of questions to answer. Most of the time, I can't visualize the problem over the phone, so I end up driving out here to take a look. I'm wasting their time and mine, so I decided to camp here. This way, I can work on the landscaping when I want to and do my own thing the rest of the time."

"What are you, nine years old?" She eyed the structure. It could sleep at least ten people and was tall enough in the center even Colin could probably stand up inside it. "Reliving your childhood?" Yeah, it looked older than both of them combined.

"Hey, my family had a lot of fun in this tent when Becky and I were kids. It brings back fond memories. So, yes, maybe I'll be reliving my childhood for a few months, but that's not necessarily a bad thing in my book."

"Seriously, Colin?" The thing couldn't possibly still be waterproof, and there was a tear in one of the screens. She pointed it out. "The mosquitos and God knows what else are going to eat you alive. Not to mention you have no place to shower. What will you do for food?"

"No worries." He dug around in a plastic storage container sitting off to one side for a minute then stood, brandishing a roll of thick tape. "I've got duct tape! Do you have any idea how useful this stuff is?"

Oh, she knew. Nearly everything she'd owned had been held together by duct tape at one time or another. Replacing items had been a last resort, and, even then, they'd often had to decide if they could live without the item or not before sacrificing the funds to buy a new one. More often than not, the new one had come from a thrift store. "You've lost your mind," she said, turning and stomping home. She was going to laugh her head off the first night he ended up sleeping in his pickup because his ancient tent leaked like a sieve.

~ ~ ~

Colin watched his new neighbor stomp off in a huff. He'd got her good. This wasn't the same tent his family had used for their camping trips when he was a kid, but it was about the same age and twice as big. Some of his other camping supplies he'd found in his mother's garage, like the old camp stove and gas lantern, while the cot, sleeping bag, and new battery-operated lantern were purchases he'd made at the new outdoor supply store about a block down from Lucky Lady Brewing Company's tasting room on Main Street.

He'd told Julie the truth about the questions. They *were* driving him nuts, and because he often couldn't imagine what they were trying to get across to him over the phone, he spent way too much time on the road between here and Roseanne and Scott's house.

He'd rolled into town with a week's worth of clothes and the same guitar he'd left with all those years ago. Only the vehicle was different. Not sure the old pickup he'd restored in high school would make the return trip, he'd purchased a new one and made the drive rather than risk someone recognizing him at an airport or rental car company. The rest of his stuff, including the old pickup, would be here when they got here.

In the meantime, he'd be perfectly happy camping out. He had everything he needed, including peace and quiet every night after the workers left. He could roam the property for inspiration or get out his guitar to amuse himself. Hell, he might even find a new song or two if he looked inside himself hard enough. But most of all, he'd be close to Julie.

Once the tent was up and furnished to meet his needs, he went to work on the landscaping in the backyard. After removing the old clothesline, he cut down the shrubs that had grown high enough to block the light to some of the downstairs' rooms.

Colin used the hem of his T-shirt to wipe sweat from his eyes then grabbed a cold water bottle from his cooler.

"Wow. The yard sure looks better." Randy Tucker, restoration expert extraordinaire, stood at the corner of the house looking like the professional delegator he was. "I saw the light coming in through the windows and had to come take a look."

"Thanks." Colin twisted the cap off the bottle and downed half the contents. "Think they'll grow back or should I yank the trunks out and start over?"

"If this was my place, I'd remove the trunks then you can train the new plants to the shape and size you want them."

"I was afraid you were going to say that." He finished off the water then chucked the empty bottle into a nearby trash can. He counted the stumps crowding the foundation. "It's going to take forever to dig all those out."

"You could hire it done," Randy said.

"I could. Or I could enlist some help."

Randy took a step back. "Don't look at me. I've got workers to supervise."

Colin laughed. "Nah. Wasn't thinking of you."

"Whew." Randy wiped imaginary sweat from his brow.

"What's with the tent?"

"It's my new home until you get my house finished, so make it quick, will ya?"

"Why didn't you rent a motor home or a travel trailer?"

"I figured it would feel too much like being on tour, and that's one of the things I'm trying to get away from." And, no one, especially not Julie Davis, was going to feel sorry for a guy living in an expensive motor home with all the amenities. But Tucker didn't need to know all Colin's reasoning.

"Okay. Have it your way, but your tent looks like it could leak."

Colin eyed the old canvas structure. It probably did leak. In fact, he was counting on it. "You think?"

"Wouldn't surprise me in the least." The contractor shook his head. "Well, I've got to get to work. Gotta take some measurements so I can get my carpenter started on those new kitchen cabinets."

"Don't let me keep you, then." He waved his hand toward the tent. "As you can see, there's not a minute to waste."

"You might want to reconsider the motor home idea," he called over his shoulder.

Colin shook his head, a smile on his lips. Nah. The tent was perfect. Besides, he was counting on Julie being neighborly and not letting him suffer out here for long.

CHAPTER ELEVEN

Colin leaned on the handle of his shovel and wiped sweat from his brow. When he'd come up with the idea to camp out in his yard, he'd expected the adventure would last a few days before a Texas-sized rainstorm would convince Julie to let him stay in her spare bedroom until his house was habitable. He should have consulted a meteorologist. Then he would have known the weather gods had other plans. Texas was known for its rapidly changing weather. So, where the hell was it?

He downed his third bottle of water that morning and scanned the bright-blue skies. Not a cloud in sight. He'd strip naked and dance around the yard chanting if he thought it would break this cycle of relentless heat.

"How's it going?"

Colin turned to greet the man in charge of restoring the house. "You tell me."

"The house is coming along. We should be finished on schedule." Randy Tucker's gaze swept over the yard. "The patio looks good. The fire pit was a good idea."

"Thanks." He'd spent the better part of the last week on his knees, laying the individual paving stones for the fire pit and patio. "I've got friends coming over tomorrow night for a little informal get-together. There'll be beer, hot dogs, and maybe a song or two. Stop by around seven. Oh, and it's BYOLC."

Tucker frowned. "What's BYOLC?"

Colin smiled. "Bring your own lawn chair. The new patio furniture won't be here until next week." He lifted his shovel and jammed the tip into the hard-packed earth. "With a little luck, I'll have the pergola up by then."

"You're still determined to do this yourself?"

The physical activity was the only thing keeping him from thinking about his sexy neighbor all day long. He hadn't seen much of her since the day he'd put the tent up. Her dog still came over now and then, always stopping for a pet before heading to the pond to chase the ducks. "Once I get the holes dug for the posts, I have some old friends who are going to help me build the structure."

"Do any of you know what you're doing?"

Colin shrugged. "Maybe. Maybe not. Bobby and Tommy will be here tomorrow night. I'm sure they'd appreciate any tips you might be able to give them."

"Bobby and Tommy Watson? The guys who own the music store in town?"

"Yeah. You know them?"

"We haven't officially met, but I've been to their after-hours event a few times."

The Watson twins had gotten into a spot of trouble after high school and spent a while in jail. When they got out, they opened a music store in the old gas station their grandpa left them. They made a decent living these days selling instruments and giving lessons. On weekends, weather permitting, they hosted local talent on a stage they'd built behind the store. The kiss that changed his life took place in the Music City parking lot. The brothers' criminal records kept them from getting a liquor license, but the lack of alcohol hadn't hurt their business. "We all graduated high school together. Used to get together and play music. When my mom would kick us out of our garage, we'd go to theirs, and vice-versa. I can guarantee you, if they get to pickin' tonight, the music will be good."

"I'll think about it." Randy gestured at the house. "I'd better get back to work. Guy who owns this place is chompin' at the bit to move in."

With a smile, Colin bent to his task. He had a pickup load of shrubs to put in before his friends arrived for tonight's cookout.

~ ~ ~

Julie crooked her finger, pulling the edge of the curtain just enough to sneak a peek at her sexier-than-hell neighbor. Again.

Damn. This was getting to be a habit. She'd lost count of the number of times she'd dropped everything to spy on Colin this week. At first, she told herself she was checking to see how the landscaping was coming along, but peeking once a day would have been more than enough to satisfy her curiosity as to what plants he was putting where.

Nope. This was more than idle curiosity. This was lust. Pure and simple. Well, maybe not *pure*. That would be stretching things a bit too far. She'd had more impure thoughts this past week than in all her adult life combined. Why did the man have to be so good-looking? And fit. He wasn't a rhinestone cowboy. Not with muscles like the ones she'd been admiring all week. A physique like his came from good old-fashioned hard work.

She had to admit, he'd done an excellent job with the landscaping, which appeared to be almost finished. Good thing, too. She'd lost too much time peeking out her bedroom window. When he put the last of the new shrubs in, he'd move on to the front of the house. Out of sight. And hopefully, out of mind.

Like she could forget him. She'd be doing ordinary things — like picking up a case of empty beer bottles — when an image of Colin bent over, laying brick pavers in an intricate pattern around the fire pit would pop into her mind. Then she'd spend the next hour reviewing every mental image she had of the man. He'd even invaded her sleep, starring in the most erotic dreams she'd ever had.

Julie watched him dig the last hole and pop the plant in. All the while, she told herself the show was coming to a close. Might as well watch until the end. Right?

"Probably smells to high heaven," she grumbled to Bud who had followed her upstairs and now was sound asleep on the rug next to her bed. "Just look how dirty and sweaty he is." She shook her head as he wiped his brow on a sleeve then went down on his knees and began to backfill the hole by hand. "He'll never get the dirt out from under his fingernails."

But, damn, he had a fine ass. Even if it was encased in filthy denim.

Disgusted with herself, she let the curtain fall from her fingertips. She'd just tidy up a bit before going downstairs.

As she gathered the dirty towels and clothes she'd left scattered about and piled them into a basket to take downstairs, she congratulated herself on her willpower. And look, hadn't she turned an unscheduled looky-loo trip upstairs into something useful? She grabbed a soft cloth from the linen cabinet and began to dust her bedroom furniture. When she got to her nightstand, her arm brushed the window curtain aside—just enough. And just in time.

Colin held the water hose in one hand and, with the other, whipped his dirty T-shirt off and turned the water on himself. Julie gave up all pretense and stared. Water cascaded over his head, over his wide shoulders, and down. Down. Down his sexy-as-hell back. Washing away the dirt and sweat. Leaving a wide expanse of firm, tanned, wet skin over flexing muscles as he rinsed his hair.

It wasn't the well water, which she knew would be cold, making her shiver, but the raw masculinity on display. She crushed the edge of the curtain with fingers itching to play in the water. To explore all those fascinating planes and angles.

Slowly, head tilted back, he turned. Water ran in rivulets over hills and through valleys outlining the tightest six-pack she'd ever seen. Flat planes arrowed down past jeans that, stretched from a hard day's work, hung low on his hips. So. Low.

Julie licked her lips. Imagined lapping at the water, drinking her fill. She forced her gaze up toward the source of the water, pausing to admire his well-defined pecs. Just then, he shook his head, sending diamond droplets flying in a wide arc, breaking the trance she'd been in.

She blinked, and her gaze clashed with his. "Oh!" Her free hand flew to her mouth. Embarrassment heated her skin. Colin smiled wide then, with a wink, he turned, cranked the spigot off, and walked away without another look.

Julie yanked the curtain into place. "Damn him!" She stomped over, picked up the basket of dirty laundry, and clunked down the stairs. "Damn arrogant ass!"

She dropped the basket on top of the machine then grabbed the edge with both hands to steady herself. After a few deep breaths, she felt better, more in control. Forgetting all about the laundry, she grabbed a beer from the refrigerator and went to the front of the house — as far away from Colin Parker as she could get and still be indoors.

How long had he known she was there? A few minutes? Or had he known she'd been watching him all week?

She groaned and let her head fall against the sofa cushion, only to jerk it back up as the movement reminded her of the way he'd stood just moments before.

Would these new images ever go away?

"Not in this lifetime," she muttered.

God. Caught looking like a schoolgirl in the boys' locker room. How embarrassing.

Even worse, he knew!

He knew!

She couldn't do it again. No more peeking. "No more." She shook her head.

"No more," she confirmed.

~ ~ ~

Colin smiled as he walked to his tent. Smiled as he gathered clean clothes. Smiled all the way to the stock tank. Smiled as he stripped out of his dirty clothes. Smiled as he walked in up to his knees then dove into the deeper water. He'd been pleasantly surprised to find out the tank was fed by a natural spring. The constant flow of fresh water kept the pond clean and the water cool even on the hottest of days, making it the perfect place to rinse off after a day of back-breaking work.

As he stepped out on the grassy bank and lay down to air dry, thoughts of his sexy neighbor once again came to mind. God, she was cute. She'd been watching him all week. Just a peek, now and then. But he'd known and let her have her fun. Thinking about her made his body react, and since the only person likely to find him out here was Julie—and she hadn't set foot on his property since the day he'd set up the tent—he saw no reason not to take the edge off. It had been too long since his dick had seen any action, and being close to Julie every day, knowing she was watching him and not being able to do a damn thing about it, was driving him bat-shit crazy. It was also one of the reasons he worked himself into the ground every day.

But today, just like every other day, as soon as he stopped working, his thoughts turned to her, and his body ached. He'd done a good job of ignoring it, but a man could only take so much, and Colin Parker had reached his limit.

With one arm serving as a pillow, he bent his knees, dug his heels into the soft earth, and stroked himself. Closing his eyes, he let his imagination run along the same path it did every night, and, soon, he was making love to Julie, her lithe body rising up to meet his as he drove into her wet heat over and over again. Imaginary lovers could never be as good as the real thing, but when he finally exploded, splashing ribbons of hot cum over sun-touched skin, he welcomed the relief.

He lay there, letting his heart rate return to normal, and wondered how much longer it would take to break through the wall Julie had erected between them. Remembering the first time he'd caught her peeking at him from an upstairs window, he smiled. She hadn't cut a door in the wall, but she was peeking over it. It wasn't much, but it *was* progress.

He just didn't know how much longer he could live like this. Wanting. Needing. Imagining what he couldn't have. Might never have. He'd thrown nearly every asset he had into the property next door to hers, and the idea of living so close to her yet so very far away was flat-out unacceptable.

His skin cooled as the sun dipped below the trees forming a living fence on the far side of the stock tank. Diving back in, he rinsed away the evidence of his lonely loving. Using the clean shirt he'd brought along as a towel, he dried himself off then pulled on his last clean pair of jeans. After donning a clean pair of socks and his work boots, he headed up the hill to his makeshift housing.

CHAPTER TWELVE

Invitations weren't his style, so he'd put the word out to a few friends, trusting them to spread the news about his little get-together tonight. There could be anywhere from two or three people who showed up or there might be two dozen. Or more. It didn't matter to him. He had a couple of packages of hot dog wieners and a couple of cases of beer. Everything else would take care of itself just as it had when he'd been in high school. He and his friends had gathered almost every weekend night on the shores of the local lake. Everyone knew to show up with a guitar and something to eat or drink. They'd all gone home, stomachs and hearts full to the brim. Tonight wouldn't be any different.

As the cars began to arrive and his backyard filled up with lawn chairs and picnic coolers, he kept an eye on the house next door, hoping to catch a glimpse of his neighbor. He'd spent most of the day outside, laying the last few pavers and tidying up the area. Mostly, he'd spent his time watching for the sexy brewmaster next door. Her dog had come over a couple of times, but Julie had remained out of sight.

He knew every one of the people gathered on his lawn, had known most of them his entire life. It was good to see them all again, but there was one person missing. If he could catch Julie looking out the window, he'd signal for her to join them. Then, the night would be perfect.

His friends didn't disappoint. Everyone brought something to share. Besides hot dogs cooked on the makeshift grill he'd made out of an old grill rack he'd found in the barn balanced on a couple of sticks of rebar stretched across the fire pit, they dined on homemade potato salad, fruit salad, chips and dip. Someone had picked up brownies from the diner out by the freeway, and another had brought homemade chocolate chip cookies. There was beer and wine for the adults, and those who'd brought the next generation with them provided age-appropriate drinks for them.

Colin made the rounds, paper plate in hand, spending a few minutes with each guest, getting to know the new additions — wives, husbands, and kids he'd missed meeting while he'd been in Nashville. He'd almost made the complete circuit when another pickup came up the driveway. All heads turned to see who the late arrival could be. Randy Tucker ambled around the corner of the house, a small cooler in one hand, a guitar case in the other.

Colin smiled. "Randy," he said, taking the insulated bag from him and setting it on top of his own cooler. "I didn't think you were going to come."

"Almost didn't."

Colin nodded at the case the man had in a white-knuckled grip. "You play?"

"A little. Don't know why I brought it." His gaze assessed the group gathered around the fire pit then returned to Colin. "I'm an amateur by your standards."

Colin chuckled as he clapped Tucker on the shoulder. "No worries. Some of these guys have been playing all their lives and still can't find a tune in a well bucket. Have you eaten?"

"Yeah."

"There are some damn good brownies around here somewhere." He looked around, found the person he wanted, and crooked his finger at her. "Chrissy. Come here, there's someone I want you to meet." She was the only female who'd come alone, and she'd set up camp next to him. They'd known each other forever, and because she played guitar as well as anyone he knew, she'd been part of his circle of friends as long as he could remember. They'd dated a few times in high school, but nothing had ever come of it.

The long-legged blonde stood and tossed her paper plate in Colin's solitary garbage can before joining them. "Hey," she said, giving Tucker the once-over.

"Hey," Tucker said.

"Randy, meet Chrissy Baxter. Chrissy, this is Randy Tucker. He's the restoration expert I hired to fix this place up. Tucker, Chrissy is an interior decorator by day but moonlights as a Dallas Cowboys Cheerleader. She also plays a mean six-string—unless she's lost her touch."

"I haven't lost anything, and the name is Christine." She glared at Colin then turned her star-powered smile on Tucker. "It's nice to meet someone who doesn't think I'm still six years old."

From the look on the restoration expert's face, he didn't think she was a child. Far from it. Nevertheless, Colin protested. "I don't think you're six. Sixteen, maybe."

"Shut up, Colin Parker, or I'll tell Mr. Tucker about the time you—"

"Whoa. Stop right there." Colin held his hand up. He knew where she was going with her comment and put a stop to it. That was the problem with people you'd shared a sandbox with. They knew things. Embarrassing things. "If I concede you're all grown up now, will you keep an eye on Randy for me?"

"Sure. Come on," she said, grabbing the guitar out of his hand. "I brought an extra chair."

Chrissy hadn't lost her touch. Her fingers flew over the guitar strings, keeping up with Colin and shaming most of the others. If anything, she'd improved since the last time he'd heard her play.

How long had it been? Probably the night before high school graduation. They'd all gathered out at the lake for one last jam session. Some of his friends had gone off to college, others had taken jobs. A few had gotten married—thus the kids running around. Colin had loaded his battered suitcase and the guitar he'd made in woodshop in the pickup he'd bought with money he'd earned working odd jobs and hightailed it out of town like a posse was after him. He'd been halfway to Nashville before the ink dried on his diploma.

Someone threw another piece of scrap lumber on the fire. Sparks danced in the air, flickering out, ash floating down while all around, friends took turns choosing the song. Most knew them all and joined in. Others played the parts they knew or could pick up on. Everyone sang when they felt like it. No one criticized. Colin had honed his skill around campfires like this one, playing with friends who didn't care if he missed a note or changed the lyrics to suit himself.

He'd missed this in Nashville. Sure, he'd made friends and sat around playing music with them, but it hadn't been the same. There'd been an agenda lurking like a dirty river beneath every jam session. Professional jealousy came in many forms and could cut to the bone. He couldn't count the number of people he'd called friend who'd abandoned him the minute he'd achieved what they considered success. And for every one of them, there'd been two to take their place. People who wanted to be his friend. Some had hoped his success would rub off on them. Others had wanted to ride his coattails to the top. A few had wanted to sabotage his career. For what reason, he had no idea.

Then there had been the women. There'd been a time when having beautiful women throw themselves into his path would have made his day. But those last few months, there'd only been one woman on his mind. Glancing up at the window he knew gave her the best view of his property, he tried not to let his disappointment show.

Dammit. His impromptu show with the water hose had scared her off. Or, more likely, winking at her had done the trick. He shouldn't have let her know he had seen her. Doing so had given her one more reason to avoid him.

Suddenly weary, he strummed the last notes of the familiar country ballad then set his guitar aside. Others followed suit. Still others stood and stretched then began to pack up their belongings. Tomorrow was Monday, and most of them had jobs to get to. Wishing the night wasn't over but knowing it had to be, he raised his voice so everyone could hear him. "Thanks for coming out tonight. Same time next week?"

He'd never meant for the night to be anything but a one-time event, but the positive responses coming from his invitation made him smile. Once the construction was completed, he'd probably spend most days out here all alone, so the idea of making tonight a regular weekly event sounded like fun. He could already feel the creative juices that had all but dried up in Nashville beginning to flow again. A booster shot once a week could only be good for his career.

Waving goodbye to the last car to drive out, he tossed some more wood on the fire and picked up his guitar. It was late, but when his muse visited, he knew enough to listen to what it had to say.

~ ~ ~

"You don't know what it's like." Julie sat at the giant marble-topped island in the center of Roseanne's new kitchen while her friend worked her magic with her new copper-clad coffee-making monster. The thing looked like it belonged in a high-end coffee shop, not someone's kitchen.

"I can imagine," Roseanne said as she set a mug filled with a delicious-looking concoction in front of Julie. "I've heard Colin play, remember? And I can imagine who shows up out there. We have some very good musicians in town. Some are amateurs only because they want to be."

Julie knew the statement to be true. The first week Colin had hosted his Sunday night jam session, she'd spent the evening wearing noise-cancelling headphones. The next week, she'd opened her bedroom window just enough to let the sound in. Last night, she'd moved an easy chair closer to the window and with the lights off, snuck a peek or two. "I'll give you that, but do they have to play every Sunday night? Don't these people have jobs?"

Roseanne chuckled as she set her beverage down and joined her friend at the island. "Most of them do, I suppose. What time did the hoedown break up last night?"

"Ten o'clock." Just as it had the previous two Sundays. She could live with everyone leaving at ten. It was what happened after that kept her awake. After his guests left, Colin sat outside and played all by himself. She didn't know what he was doing, but his clear bass voice carried, and, short of putting on the noise-cancelling headphones he'd given her, she couldn't help but hear.

"Ten doesn't sound so bad." Roseanne took a sip of the latte she'd fixed for herself. "If he has another one, you should go over."

Julie shuddered. "I don't sing or play. I'd be out of place."

"That's nonsense if I ever heard it. Colin wouldn't give a damn. And what's one more guest? You said everyone brings food to share. I'll make my coconut cake or a plate of double chocolate brownies for you to take. Throw in some of your newest brew, and trust me, no one there will care whether you can sing or play."

"There might not be a next time." *Liar.* She'd heard Colin extend the invitation just as he had the week before. For all she knew, it would turn into a regular thing, and she'd be sentenced to spending every Sunday evening for the rest of her life listening at the window.

"You know Colin would welcome you."

She hadn't exactly been the nicest neighbor since he'd pitched that ridiculous tent in his yard. "I don't know. I gave him heck about his tent."

"It's a tent. By definition it's temporary housing."

"I know, but you should see it. It's a good thing we're having a dry summer. If it rains, he's in big trouble."

"Don't look now, but trouble is on the way. Weather dude says we're in for a big storm sometime next week."

CHAPTER THIRTEEN

"He's nuts," she muttered to Bud who took up most of the floor space in her kitchen while she stepped around him to cook. "It's raining cats and dogs out there." And had been for most of the day. From her bedroom window, she had a bird's-eye view of Colin's yard. The place was a mud hole, and the roof of his tent was collecting rainwater in several places. Every now and then, he'd poke the sagging canvas from inside, sending water cascading off the roof. As she dropped a dirty spoon in the sink, her gaze drifted to the window. "Oh. My. Lord."

"Bud. You won't believe what he's doing now." She watched for a minute longer before she closed her eyes with a sigh. "I can't believe I'm going to do this."

Julie slipped on her mud boots and grabbed an umbrella. "Wait here, Bud. I'll be right back."

Colin joined her at the barbed-wire fence separating their properties. "What are you doing out here?"

"I came to ask you the same thing," Julie said. "Are you nuts? You can't cook in the rain."

"Sure you can," Colin said, though there wasn't much conviction in his words.

She motioned to the camp stove he'd set up on a set of sawhorses. One side had sunk into the mud, leaving the stove sitting at a precarious angle. How he thought he was going to cook on it, she didn't know. "Put that away and come over. I've got enough for two."

A few minutes later, Colin Parker arrived on her porch, soaked to the bone and carrying two plastic grocery bags. "Here," he said, handing her one of the bags. "My mama would tan my hide if I showed up for dinner without bringing something to share."

"You didn't— Oh!" She pulled the bottle of wine out and examined the label. Having tended bar, she recognized the winery, if not this specific wine. "You shouldn't have."

Colin held the other bag up. "Well, I was hoping your hospitality would extend to the use of your shower. I'm chilled to the bone."

He'd left his muddy boots in the mudroom, but the legs of his jeans were covered in black goop. Water dripped from his hair and shirt onto what had been a clean floor a few minutes ago. Now she understood the expensive wine. She closed her eyes again, praying for patience. When she opened them again, his eyes pleaded with her to take mercy on him.

"Okay, okay. But if you get mud all over my house, I'll leave you out in the rain next time." Julie turned to check on the meatloaf in the oven. "I've only got one bathroom. It's at the top of the stairs." She pointed to the staircase leading off the kitchen. "Towels are in the cabinet next to the vanity."

"Thank you. I won't leave a speck of mud anywhere. I promise."

Julie bent to look through the oven's glass panel. When she stood, the sight of long, hairy legs and a tight ass encased in white cotton briefs streaking through her kitchen almost caused her to drop the wine bottle she still held. Carefully setting the bottle down, she grasped the edge of the countertop with both hands, letting her head fall between her hunched shoulders. "Oh, God. What have I done?"

It's just dinner, she rationalized. *I can do this.* The old pipes groaned, confirming he'd found, and was using, her shower. Her mind automatically merged the images she'd stored of him working shirtless in his yard with the new image she had of his other half. She'd already seen him half-naked taking a shower from a water hose. It was a short leap from there to imagining him naked in *her* shower, water and ribbons of soapy suds cascading over the hard planes of his torso and the corded muscles of his legs.

Julie shook her head to dislodge the image her subconscious had conjured up. Lord, how many women would give anything to have Colin Parker naked in their shower? Millions, probably, which was all the reason she needed to bring herself down to earth. The plastic bag of clothes he'd brought with him was just a tip of the iceberg. The man had baggage. Lots and lots of baggage. She didn't need the kind of complications he brought with him. Having him as a neighbor was going to be bad enough. It was a done deal, though. He was moving in, already had if you counted the tent, and she wasn't going anywhere. Moving the brewery was out of the question. She'd given some thought to the logistics of their situation. Tonight would be the perfect time to discuss some of her concerns and ideas with her new neighbor.

He entered the kitchen just as she was dishing up the sliced meatloaf and whipped potatoes. She handed him a plate and motioned to the flatware drawer she'd left open. "Grab a fork. We can eat in here, if you don't mind?" One of the things she liked best about her house was the large eat-in kitchen. She'd had the dining room enclosed, and the space had become her office. She had a smaller one off the brewing room, but she ran the business out of her home office.

"Man, this looks and smells great," Colin said, taking a seat at the scarred table she'd picked up at an antique store. "Thanks."

Julie set her plate down across from Colin then headed for the refrigerator. "Something to drink? I have iced tea and beer."

"Beer sounds good."

She popped the tops on two unlabeled bottles, tossed the caps in a wastebasket sitting next to the refrigerator then joined Colin at the table. He turned the bottle a full turn. An eyebrow raised in question.

"It's a full-bodied ale for fall and winter," she told him. "I haven't named it yet."

"Am I the first to try it?"

"Besides me, yes. Let me know what you think."

The moment the rim of the bottle touched his lips, Julie's brain went into overdrive. Memories she'd tried so hard to suppress came rushing back. The feel of his lips on hers. The heat that had started with a spark and grown to a conflagration in a matter of seconds. Heart racing, she forced her gaze down to the plate she'd prepared for herself. She picked up her fork and dug into the mashed potatoes. How many times did she have to tell herself he wasn't *the one*? Hell, he wasn't even a contender. Colin Parker was a threat to the nice, quiet—safe—life she had worked so hard to build.

"Wow." Colin smacked his lips then raised the bottle for another taste. "This is fabulous."

"Thanks." She sipped from her own bottle. It was good. Probably one of the best she'd brewed yet. She could see making it a seasonal tradition if it sold as well as she thought it would. "Look, Colin, I've been thinking."

"About?" He took a bite of the meatloaf, humming his appreciation for the flavor.

"For starters, the fence. I'm thinking we should have something more substantial than we have now. Old barbed wire isn't much good for anything. What do you think? I'd be willing to pay for half of it."

"I've been thinking about our fence, too. We can't have you tearing your clothes on the barbs. I'm having horse fencing put up across the front of my property. I could ask them to extend it along our border, with a gate of course, so you and Bud can come and go as you please."

"Sounds like a good idea, but I was thinking of something a bit different. I'm sure you would like your privacy—"

Colin set his fork down and trained his gaze on her. "I like my privacy as much as the next guy, but also don't want to look at a brick wall when I'm in my backyard. If I'd wanted a damn wall I would have bought a place in town."

Julie set her fork down, too. She didn't know what had got his dander up. She'd only been trying to do the neighborly thing and allow him some privacy. "I'm not talking about a brick wall. Just a privacy fence. A six-footer should do it. And there's no need for a gate. Bud has plenty of room to roam over here."

The old wooden chair groaned as Colin straightened his shoulders and glared at her. "Horse fencing or nothing."

"Why are you being so stubborn? A privacy fence will give you peace of mind."

"It'll give me a headache."

"You're being ridiculous. You live next door to a brewery. A six-foot-tall fence will insulate you from my business and provide privacy for you. Isn't that why you bought the property?"

"I knew there was a brewery next door when I bought the property, and, yes, I was also looking for privacy, which I have. Some additional fencing along the front, along with an electronic gate, similar to the one you have at the road will ensure it." Colin pushed away from the table and stood. "Thanks for the shower and dinner."

Julie sat, rooted to her chair, as Colin stalked past her. What had seemed like a reasonable conversation had taken a sudden turn she struggled to comprehend. When her brain finally caught up, she bolted for the mudroom.

"Wait!" she called. But it was too late. Halfway to the fence that had caused so much trouble, his clothing was already soaked. "Dammit."

She slammed the door shut then leaned against it. Bud sat in the doorway between the mudroom and kitchen, watching the goings on with interest. "Stubborn ass." Bud woofed. Julie patted him on the head. "You and I are in agreement, Buddy. It will serve him right if he catches a cold."

Returning to the kitchen, she sat to finish her meal, but the nearly full plate across from her mocked her every bite. It was just a fence. With a gate. No need to get riled up about it. So why had they argued?

Appetite lost, she reexamined every word said since he'd come strolling into the kitchen in tight jeans and an I heart Nashville T-shirt and bare feet. His wet hair stood out in all directions, making her want to run her fingers through it — to tame it.

"This is ridiculous," she said. Bud's ears perked up, and his tail wagged. "I provoked him, Bud. It was either make him mad or jump his bones." Elbows propped on either side of her plate, she dropped her forehead into her upturned hands. Somewhere along the way, she'd convinced herself a wooden fence between them was the answer to her problem. Out of sight, out of mind. She could see it now for the sorry excuse it was. She'd tried to build a fence around her heart, and when the strategy hadn't worked, she'd come up with the idea of a fence between their properties. But deep in her heart, she knew a fence wouldn't work, either.

It was *The Kiss*. She'd wanted more from him then, and nothing had changed since. She still wanted Colin Parker. Wanted to feel the heat of his skin, run her fingers through his adorably mussed hair, feel his lips on hers, and so much more. *Down that road be dragons*. She raised her head, and her gaze landed on his unfinished meal. Her brain conjured up an image of his broad shoulders and firm ass, soaked to the bone, fleeing her house.

"Talk about dragons," she muttered. She'd shown her fangs and spit flames at him and quite possibly reduced the fragile bridge between them to cinders. All because she couldn't forget *The Kiss*. It had taken on a life of its own in the months he'd been gone. He'd admitted he should have taken it further instead of sending her off alone, but since his return he'd said nothing about wanting a relationship. He hadn't wanted one then, and he didn't want one now. Getting into the self-inspection, she had to admit the lack of interest on his part hurt. The man probably had dozens of women in Nashville throwing themselves at him. She'd been a distraction. Someone to pass the evening with after his sister's wedding. A way to amuse himself until he could get the heck out of Butte Plains.

He was back now, and her neighbor. It was time to get over *The Kiss*. Nothing could ever have come of it anyway. He was a paparazzi magnet, and she was camera shy — for good reason. Being seen with Colin Parker a few months ago hadn't carried any risk, but things were different now. He could put up an electronic gate and miles of horse fencing, but none of it would keep a determined photographer from taking pictures. Hadn't she just read about a Hollywood type who was suing a photographer for using a drone to take photos of him swimming in his own pool? No fence was going to protect Colin from a sophisticated privacy breech.

Neither one of them could stay behind their locked gates forever. Eventually, they had to come out, and Lord help her if they were together. Photos would be taken, and the safety she'd worked so hard for would be lost.

Colin's unfinished meal mocked her. Behind their locked gates, they could still be friends. Couldn't they? He'd been perfectly reasonable to propose the new horse fence to replace the rusty barbed wire. It would look nicer than a six-foot-tall privacy fence. And it was generous of him to allow Bud to continue romping across his property. He loved chasing the ducks at Colin's stock tank.

"I was an ass," she said to Bud. "Do you think I should

apologize?" Bud barked once, voicing his approval. "Guess there's no time like the present."

CHAPTER FOURTEEN

Colin shed his wet clothes, tossed the sheet of plastic he used to keep his bedding dry onto the floor, and lay down. He'd been an ass. Why did he let her rile him so? "Goddammit." He brushed a drop of water from his forehead. She'd been right about the tent leaking, and he'd been right about her taking pity on him, though she'd only invited him in for a hot shower and a meal. *Fuck.* Out of dry clothes, he was cold, hungry, and miserable, and he had no one to blame but himself.

He'd seen the way she looked at him when he walked into the kitchen after showering. She'd wanted him, and he'd wanted her just as much, but he'd wanted a hot meal, too. The ginormous gas grill he'd ordered had been placed on backorder. He'd managed a few things on the fire pit, but if he never saw another hot dog or can of beans or, Heaven help him for saying it, steak again as long as he lived, he'd be happy. Damn, her meatloaf had been good, and the whipped potatoes to die for. But the most delectable thing at the table had been Julie.

Shit. She looked good enough to eat, and he'd planned on having her for dessert. He wasn't a Neanderthal. He knew women appreciated the buildup. Foreplay. And there was no better foreplay than sharing a meal together. He'd seen the way she watched his lips when he brought a bite to his mouth, and Lord knew he'd been watching her eat.

God, those lips. He'd never forget the way they felt beneath his, and, fuck, how many times had he imagined them wrapped around his dick? A million, at least. Every damn time he took himself in hand, for sure. It was his favorite fantasy, and one he'd practically worn out the last few months.

It was going to have to last him a lot longer. He'd let her talk about erecting an ugly privacy fence between their properties get to him. She was shutting him out, just like he'd shut her out when she'd come to see his tent. He should have known his behavior would come back to bite him in the butt, and damned if it didn't hurt like a son of a gun.

He closed his eyes and listened to the staccato sound of rain drumming down on the camp stove he'd left outside. There was a song in there somewhere. Something about loneliness or stupidly letting go of *the one* in order to pursue other goals only to find out later she didn't want you.

But she did. He wasn't a clueless teenager any longer. He'd had some experience with women. He knew when one wanted him, and, by God, Julie Davis had had that look in her eyes when he joined her in the kitchen. His horny subconscious hadn't imagined it. So, why all the talk about putting up fences? There wasn't a fence big enough to keep in the sound of his weekly jam sessions. Hell, she watched and listened from an upstairs window. One he now knew was in her bedroom.

No, she wanted to build a fence because she didn't *want* to want him.

Now, there was a song. A fucking sad song, to be sure.

He'd have to change her mind. How, he didn't know. Maybe it was a case of just having to wear her down. Dismantle the fence she'd put up between them, one picket at a time.

"Colin! Are you in there?"

He sat up, cursing as a drop of water meant for his forehead plopped on his shoulder and proceeded to roll down his bare chest. Fucking rain. He would have ditched the tent at the first sign of rain and bunked in his new old house tonight except the floors had just been refinished. The place stunk to high heavens, and stepping on the floors would be like stepping on a giant glue trap.

"Julie?" He reached for his wet jeans and struggled into them. He was trying to button the fly when she appeared on the other side of his duct tape-patched screen door. "Hey." He unzipped the panels to let her in. "What are you doing here?"

"You didn't finish your dinner." She held out a plastic container with one hand. With the other, she produced a bottle of beer from the pocket of her raincoat. "Peace offering?" Her gaze seemed to follow the path of the water droplet making its way along the same path as his happy trail.

Goddamn. She had that look again. He manhandled the top button through the hole in his waistband and mentally said, "Fuck it," to the rest of them. His dick was so hard, and the jeans too wet to make them work. "Thanks." He took her offerings and motioned for her to sit on the dry end of his cot. "I shouldn't have left the way I did. You were just trying to be a good neighbor."

"I wish that were true." She began to remove her coat.

"I wouldn't if I were you." He waved his hand holding the beer at the ceiling just as a big, fat drop of water let go of the canvas. It plopped right where his head had been a minute ago. "I can't vouch for the integrity of my ceiling."

She ditched the coat with a shrug. "I'll take my chances." She perched on the cot, her hands nervously skimming over her thighs. "I came to apologize. I don't know what got into me. I'm not usually rude to guests."

Colin removed the top on the plastic container. Inside was the meal he'd left behind and a set of plastic utensils. "I was the one being rude. As you said, you were just thinking of me, of my needs." As much as he wanted her meatloaf, he wanted her more.

"Again, I wish that were true." She watched as he brought a

forkful of tasty meat to his lips. "But I was thinking of my own needs."

Colin jerked his gaze to hers. "I'd like to hear more about your needs." If that wasn't the cheesiest line ever delivered, he didn't know what was. Her cheeks turned an adorable shade of pink, and he couldn't help but wonder if he'd find the same shade in a more intimate part of her. His dick throbbed, making its needs known.

"You don't want to know. I mean, you didn't then. I can't imagine you would now."

Whoa. If not for the lump of meatloaf stuck in his throat, he would think this was a dream. But it wasn't. She looked as nervous as a cat in a room full of rocking chairs, but he admired her guts. Julie Davis wasn't a wilting daisy. Hell, no. She was a rose, thorny, but worth the risk, and damn if he hadn't already risked it all. His manager had warned him this move could be career suicide, but he'd done it anyway. Because of this woman. He set the container on top of the cooler/chair/table. Taking her face in his hands, he brushed his thumbs over her cheekbones. The heat of her blush made him want to feel the same heat surrounding his cock. "I'm sorry about the way we parted back then. You know—after my sister's wedding? I wanted you so much then it scared me. I've wanted you every day since. I want you now." He dragged one thumb over her lips. "It was more than just a kiss."

"Was it?" Her hot breath caressed his thumb.

"You know it was." His gaze dropped to her lips. "Should we give it another try?"

"Probably not." She swayed toward him. One hand landed on his chest, branding him while her lips parted in invitation.

"Probably not," he agreed, meeting her halfway.

Their lips touched, tentative at first, but the spark he remembered was still there, hot enough to ignite even the wettest timber into flame. When her hands snaked over his shoulders and speared through his hair, he took the kiss deeper — and sank into the fire. Need and want consumed him. He was toast, and though the realization should have scared him, it didn't. Not this time. Julie Davis was his.

When she moaned and pulled away from him, his heart crashed to his feet. "Too many clothes," she said. Seconds later, her tank top landed on the floor. Struck stupid by the sight of her breasts encased in snow-white lace, he didn't realize her dilemma until she cursed. "Fuck. I can't get this loose."

"No hurry." He cupped her breasts, amazed at how they fit so perfectly into his palms. "I'll help you with it in a minute." His gaze met hers. "I've dreamed of this moment for so long. Let me just look at you for a second."

"But—"

"Shh." He rubbed her nipples through the lace and smiled when they responded to his touch. "We'll get to it. I promise."

"I need—"

"I know, sweetheart. I need it, too, but there's no rush now. Is there?"

"Um," she moaned as he gently squeezed her mounds. "Do that again. Please."

Colin wrapped one arm around her to support her then dipped his head to her chest. His tongue played across one lace-covered nipple then the next before he selected one to graze his teeth over. Her fingernails dug into his scalp. "Oh. Oh, Colin." Her head fell back, her hair brushing across his hand. He nipped at the other nipple then soothed it with his tongue. She writhed in his embrace, thrusting her chest toward him, begging for more.

"I love lace, especially white lace," he said, palming her soft globes. "But it's time for this to go."

With practiced fingers, he worked the back closure loose. "Keep your hands right where they are." He drew first one strap then the other over her shoulders and down to the crook of her arms so her bra hung between them like clothes on a line. He liked the feel of the lace against his skin, but the view was better this way. Her rose-tipped breasts were high and firm. His prior examination had assured him they were the real thing. Artificial wouldn't have been a deal breaker, but he was damn glad they weren't. He cupped her right breast, brought it to his mouth, and licked the rosy tip. When he blew on the wet flesh, it drew up tight and hard. Shit, she was beautiful, and he said so. "You are so fucking beautiful. I could do this all day." To prove his point, he applied his tongue to her left breast then blew on it, too.

"Colin." His name, spoken like a plea confirmed it was time to move on. She needed more, and Heaven knew, he needed all of her.

"Lie down, sweetheart. You are definitely wearing too many clothes."

Her hands slipped from his head to his shoulders then trailed down his chest as he lowered her to the foot of the cot, where hopefully, the roof would hold and not drench them both, though no amount of water was going to put out the fire burning inside him. "Hurry, Colin."

The tight, knit pants she wore hugged her calves and ended just above her ankles. He dug his fingers in under the waistband and tugged. Julie wiggled her ass and down they went, revealing a band of white lace that spanned her hips and dipped between her legs.

"Good God Almighty. Are you trying to kill me?"

She kicked her legs free of the pants then her gaze followed his. "They're just panties." Her thumbs hooked the sides. Colin covered her hands with his.

"No. Leave them on."

"They're in the way."

"No, they aren't." He pulled her hands free. "Hands above your head, sweetheart. Don't move them until I tell you to."

His tone brooked no argument, and she did as he said, but not without protest. "Bossy much?"

"Only when it comes to your pleasure." *And mine,* he thought as he bent over her. He pressed his nose to her crotch and inhaled. Damn, there couldn't be a more intoxicating scent. He couldn't wait to taste her, but there was plenty of time. In the gray light of dusk, she looked like an offering from the gods, spread across a cot that should have been a magnificent bed to match her beauty. *Next time,* he vowed to himself. Next time they'd have a soft mattress and pillows, and every luxury, but for now, this would have to do.

She lifted her hips, and he dug his chin into her pubic bone. "What did I say? There's no hurry, sweetheart."

"God, Colin, you're killing me."

"One kiss at a time," he said, placing a kiss along the top edge of lace. "One kiss at a time."

CHAPTER FIFTEEN

She was dying. Hands clasped above her head, she lay spread before him, and all he wanted to do was kiss her. His lips seared her skin as he worked his way across her belly, first one way then the other before dropping lower and doing it all over again. If he didn't get to her aching center soon, she was going to grab him by the hair and smother him with her pussy.

Each time she protested, he pressed her thighs wider, his callused fingertips sending shivers of need through her system. When he finally kissed his way to the crown jewel of her sex, she begged for mercy. "Please, Colin. I need you."

"I know, baby. I know." His hot breath fanned the flames of her desire, and she lifted her hips, seeking a satisfaction she feared only this man could provide.

Then his lips were on her through the lace of her panties. His tongue flicked at her clit, and she saw stars. Not an orgasm, but damn close. She moaned her frustration and urged him on with a pump of her hips.

"So beautiful." He breathed the words across her heated core then his tongue grazed her covered slit from bottom to top. "And, oh, so good. I need to taste you, sweetheart."

"Please, Colin. Oh, God, please!"

He pulled the lace down to her thighs then lifted one leg in order to slip the panties off, leaving them hanging from the other leg. She didn't care about the panties. All she cared about was feeling his lips on her, finding the pleasure his kisses had promised. She didn't have long to wait. He pressed her legs wide, opening her to his gaze. "Fucking beautiful," were the only words he spoke before his open mouth covered her.

Dear Lord! His lips and tongue were everywhere from her clit to her pussy and even to the place she'd always thought forbidden. But nothing was forbidden with Colin. It all felt good. No, better than good. The scruff of his beard against her sensitive skin added to her pleasure as he nipped and sucked and licked at her. She couldn't remain still, and he didn't stop her as she sought her pleasure, fucking his face.

His tongue teased her, dipped inside then flicked out to dance attendance on her clit before he closed his lips around the nub and sucked. Julie thrashed on the cot, making the old wooden frame creak and groan beneath her. Rain drummed on the canvas above them, a soundtrack to the storm brewing inside her. She was so close. So close. "Colin." She begged for something she couldn't name. A need unfulfilled.

Then he speared her with two fingers and she was even closer to the great unknown. She whimpered her need, and his fingers began to move. In. Out. In. Out. Gentle then harder. And harder. Faster. His teeth grazed her nub. She shattered as the most powerful orgasm she'd ever had tossed her on wave after wave of pleasure, and all the while Colin placed open-mouth kisses on her mound, her clit, her thighs. When, at last, she lay weak and spent on the cot, her breathing ragged, he slipped his fingers from her. She tried to clamp her legs closed, to hold him inside her, but his shoulders kept her open to him.

"That was the most beautiful thing I've ever seen," he said, the reverence in his tone, convincing. "I need to be inside you."

"Yes. Hurry, please."

"I need a raincoat—a condom," he clarified.

"I know what a raincoat is," she said. "Just hurry the fuck up. I'm freezing."

Colin rocked back on his heels as his right hand went to the pocket of his jeans where he kept his wallet. "Shit." Had it fallen out? He looked around on the floor, shoved his boots out of the way. Still nothing. Then it hit him. "Fuck!"

"What's the matter?" Goose bumps had formed on her delectable flesh, and her nipples were hard and turning purple in the cool moist air.

"My wallet is in the jeans I left at your house."

"I'll bring it to you tomorrow." The annoyance in her voice gave way to a gasp as she realized what his missing wallet meant. "Oh."

"Yeah, oh." Colin rubbed both hands over his face, forcing his libido into submission. He knew he was clean, and couldn't imagine she wouldn't be, but there were other things to consider, and he didn't take chances.

Julie scooted back on the cot enough so she could sit up. With one arm wrapped tight around her shivering torso, she used the other to push her hair out of her face. "Let's go." She reached for the waterproof jacket she'd worn earlier.

Still fighting the lust gripping him tight, it took a few seconds for Colin to register her meaning. "You want to go to your place? And—"

"Don't you want to?"

"Hell, yes. I just thought..."

"Don't think too much or I might change my mind."

At her words, his big brain shut off and his little brain took over. He helped her into her jacket then gathered up her clothes, stuffed them in a plastic grocery bag which he tucked under his arm, and ushered her out into the dark rainy night. The light above her porch acted as their beacon. He held the barbed wire while she climbed through before following.

Safely inside, she hung her wet jacket on a peg in the

mudroom then, stark naked, padded over to the stacked washer and dryer on the other side of the small room. When she bent to retrieve his muddy jeans from a laundry basket, his heart pumped another liter of blood to his groin. Damn, she was going to be the death of him, but God, what a way to go!

"Here." Turning, she held his wallet out to him. His gaze swept over her beauty, pausing briefly on the neat patch of curls at the juncture of her thighs then again on her still-erect nipples. "Are we good?"

"Huh?" She waved the wallet under his nose. "Oh, yeah. Thanks." He prayed he had a condom in there. He could still remember his dad's voice asking him if he had protection before he went out on a date, and in the same breath admonishing him to think before he used it.

He eyed the small packet nestled between two twenty-dollar bills and breathed a sigh of relief. The voice of reason smacked him upside the head. Did he really want to use it? There was only one answer to his question. Hell, yes. He'd never wanted to use it more than he did right that second. He held the condom up. "I've only got one. Let's see how long we can make it last."

"Last one in bed is a rotten egg." Julie took off running. Colin did his best to keep up, but his hard-on crammed into wet jeans restricted his movement. When he shut her bedroom door behind him to keep Bud out, she was already tucked under the covers. "Do not bring those wet clothes into my bed."

"Wouldn't dream of it," he said, tossing the condom to her. "Hang onto that, will ya?"

Julie scooped it up from where it fell on the bed beside her then her gaze returned to him. Colin unbuttoned the one button he'd managed to fasten when she'd called out to him earlier. At the sight of his tighty-whities, she licked her lips. His dick twitched in anticipation of having those lips wrapped around it. Maybe later, after they'd used his one condom, he thought. Then they'd have to get creative.

"Want to see more?" he asked.

"Yes, please."

Her brazen answer pleased him. She knew what she wanted and wasn't afraid to ask for it. If she'd spoken up all those months ago, he wasn't sure he would have had the strength to send her home the way he did. Then again, he wouldn't be the person he was today if he'd stayed in Butte Plains. Shaking off thoughts of the past like raindrops, he hooked his thumbs under the waistband of his briefs and pushed them and the jeans past his hips to his thighs. His cock sprang free. The appreciation in her eyes was like throwing gasoline on a match. His restraint went up in flames.

Colin kicked his jeans and briefs off in record time then dove beneath the covers with her. She snuggled up to him, her ice-cold hands a welcome shock that allowed him a brief moment to think. "I want you so bad I don't think slow is going to be possible."

"We can do slow later," she said as her hand found his dick under the covers.

He grabbed her wrist just as she closed her fingers around him. "This is likely to be over before it begins if you follow through."

"That bad, huh?"

"Sweetheart, you have no idea."

"Then you'd better get this on." She held up the condom.

He snatched the packet out of her hand and kicked the covers down so he could see. He had only one chance to do it right. Any mistake and the party would be over. For the first time ever, his hands shook as he ripped the foil, thankfully leaving the contents intact. Rolling it on was sheer torture as every touch activated nerve endings already on edge. Suited up at last, he pulled the covers up over them and reached for her. Their lips met in a kiss that heated his blood as their tongues dueled. He moved so she was beneath him and settled between her legs, his cock pressed into her stomach. God, she was soft. His hands roamed, learning every inch of her. He couldn't get enough of her curves. Breaking the kiss, he tasted his way down her neck to her shoulder then down her chest to the swell of her breasts.

"Colin." He loved hearing his name on her lips, especially when she said it all breathless with a hint of impatience.

"Let me love you, sweetheart." He closed his lips around one nipple while his fingers teased at the other one. She cradled his head in her hands and arched into him. Lord, she tasted sweet. He switched breasts, lavishing attention on the other one the way he had the first. Her fingers played through his hair then closed into fists. When she tugged, he released her nipple.

"Oww!" he cried out playfully. "Too much?"

"Can we…can you…*now*?"

"I thought you'd never ask." He shifted so the head of his cock slid between her folds and nestled at her entrance. He could feel her wet heat through the thin latex barrier and, for the first time ever, wished the condom wasn't necessary. Colin planted his hands on either side of her, angling his body so he could see her face as he entered her. Instinctively, she brought her knees up, opening herself to him, and, in that moment, he pressed forward until her soft tissues caressed the head of his cock.

"Oh," she breathed. "You feel so good."

The strain of trying to go slow, to give her time to adjust to his size was eating away at his sanity. He counted to ten in his head then gave her another inch. His cock twitched and his balls drew up tight against his body. Shit. He was going to come and he hadn't even done anything. He wasn't going to last a minute at this rate. "Look at me, sweetheart."

When she opened her eyes, he mustered every ounce of self-control he had and said, "You feel too good, baby. I'm not going to last long."

She nodded. Her tongue darted out to wet her lips, and he almost lost it. He'd had more control than this when he'd been a virgin and Cindy Holcomb had laid on the bench seat of his old pickup and hiked up her skirt to reveal her bare snatch. He'd nearly driven off the road then recovered enough to drive to a secluded spot. It was the first time he'd used the condom in his wallet. The whole thing had lasted less time than it took for the radio DJ to play a Top 40 hit. Here he was, over a decade later, and he was going to come before Julie even took all of him.

"I want to feel you, all of you, inside me. I don't care how long you last, just let me feel you."

Her plea did nothing to ease the need clawing at him, but hearing her voice helped him focus on her pleasure rather than his. He'd make this good for her even if it killed him. "Eyes on mine," he said. When their gazes locked, he inched slowly forward until he was fully seated inside her welcoming body.

"Good God Almighty," he whispered. "You feel so good." Every cell in his body called for him to move, to pull out and thrust back in, over and over again, but as good as doing so would feel, it would be the beginning of the end, and he never wanted this to be over.

"You feel good, too." She wiggled her hips, and he saw stars.

"Don't, baby. Don't move." He could feel sweat beading on his forehead as he kept his need to move in check. "You'll make me come."

"Really? I could do that?"

"Easily," he said through his clenched jaw. Colin closed his eyes and concentrated on his breathing. *In. Out. No! Shit.* His entire body shook from the effort it took to remain still and just feel the wonder of being connected to Julie in this most intimate of ways. He'd never felt anything like it. He didn't want to move, but he had to. *Had to.*

Pulling out until only the tip remained inside her, he slid into her welcoming heat, and, once again, held himself still. "So good, baby. You feel so damn good."

"I need you to move, Colin. Please. It feels so good, but I need—"

"Me, too, baby. Me, too." Drawing their pleasure out wasn't going to happen. He'd given the effort everything he had and failed. It was time to let go. Time to give in to his desires. His hips rose and fell in a rhythm as old as time, driving him closer to release with each repetition. Not wanting to go over the edge without her, he reached between them. He knew he'd found the right spot to massage when her back bowed and she pressed her head into the pillow, exposing her lovely neck to him. Colin bent to trace the column from chin to the hollow at the base.

"Come for me, baby."

"Colin," she breathed.

"It's okay, baby. I've got you. Let go."

"Oh. Oh!"

Colin kissed his way around to the long-corded muscle running from her jaw to her shoulder. "Give it to me, baby."

He scraped his teeth across her skin then opened wide and clamped his teeth gently on her neck. Julie's body tensed then she flew apart, her hips bucking, her inner muscles convulsing around his cock. He buried his face in the crook of her neck, trying to hold on to his last measure of control, but the guttural sounds she made, and the way her fingers dug into his ass as she came shredded his intentions. Holding her tight, he lost the battle he'd been waging and gave in to his most basic and primal urges. His hips jerked, no sign of the rhythm he'd built his life around, and, with a cry from deep within, he came harder than he'd ever come in his life.

CHAPTER SIXTEEN

As sanity returned, Julie took a quick inventory. After an explosive orgasm, Colin's cock still felt warm and solid inside her like the last piece of a puzzle. The contrast between his skin and hers felt right, even if he was heavy. She let her legs and arms slide down to the cool sheet. When he rolled off her, she clamped her legs shut to ease the ache of loss there. He wasn't her first, but it was definitely the first time she'd felt so empty afterwards.

Without a word, Colin climbed off the far side of the bed. She admired his naked ass as he made his way to the en suite bathroom and closed the door. While water ran, she pulled the covers up over her and closed her eyes, trying to commit the last few minutes to memory. Who knew if or when they'd do it again, and how could it possibly be as good the next time? She didn't have much experience to compare with, but she had enough to know what she'd felt this time was different. More. Better. Life changing. She almost, *almost*, didn't want to try it again, certain a repeat performance wouldn't live up to the original. But, hey, even if it fell short, it would still be spectacular.

Hearing the doorknob turn, she turned her gaze to the door. Would he dress and leave, or join her in bed even though they'd used the only condom they had?

"Mind if I stay here tonight?"

"After what we just did? I'd be a damned ungrateful bitch to turn you out into the rain, wouldn't I?"

Colin grinned as he dove beneath the covers and pulled her close. "Yes, you would." He kissed her lightly on the mouth. "You were incredible. I'm sorry I didn't last longer."

"Don't apologize, please. I had two of the best orgasms ever. No complaints here."

"I aim to please," he said, rolling to his back and taking her with him so she lay on her side, her head resting on his shoulder. His callused fingers stroked her arm as he spoke.

"Like I said, no complaints."

"I'll go into town tomorrow and get more condoms."

"I didn't say it was good enough to repeat, did I?" she teased.

"What? Are you crazy?"

Julie giggled at his outrage. She ran her hand through the light hair on his chest that had felt so good as it rubbed against her nipples. "You want to do it again?"

"Hell, yeah. Don't you?"

"Yes. I'd like that very much."

"Then it's settled." He squeezed her tight in his embrace. "I sure wish I brought more condoms with me, but, after the way we parted last time I was here, I wasn't sure you'd let me in your bed."

"I wanted you then," she confessed.

"I wanted you, too, but—" Colin sighed. "I was scared."

"Of me?"

"No. Yes." His body grew tense. She waited for him to continue, to explain why he'd left the way he did. At last, he took a deep breath and let it out. "I was afraid if I made love to you, I'd never go back to Nashville, and I had to return. I'd invested too much in building my career to let it slip away. I knew I was taking a chance I might regret later, and I did regret it, every day, but I had no choice. I couldn't come home to Butte Plains a washed-up country singer wannabe. What would I do? Work the assembly line at my sister's sex toy plant? I would have hated my life, and I would have made you miserable in the process."

"I wish you'd told me why then. I was dazed and confused and horny. I even turned the wrong way out of the parking lot and had to double back in order to get home. When I did get home and had time to think about what you'd done, I got mad. Were your ears burning?" she asked with a smile. "I think I called you every name I could think of then started making up new ones."

Colin rubbed one ear. "That's what was wrong! I thought I'd gotten an ear infection or something. Darn near went to the doctor, but it cleared up on its own."

"Eventually, I chalked it up to experiences best not repeated, and the name-calling stopped."

"Until I showed up at the tasting room, looking for you. I could swear my ears were getting a workout then."

"Nope. Must have been someone else calling you names." She tried to hide her amusement, but it spilled out in waves of laughter.

"It was you, then." Colin rolled her beneath him and began to tickle her ribs. Before long, he was kissing her, and his hands gentled, seeking out her most intimate places. "I can't get enough of you," he said as he pushed two fingers into her slick opening.

Julie spread her legs wide for him then dug her nails into his shoulders as his touch ignited a desire she'd thought quenched by their earlier lovemaking. "God, that feels good," she moaned.

"This time, it's all for you, baby. Just relax and let me make you come."

His cock, hard and heavy pressed into her thigh. She wanted him inside her but knew they had to be reasonable — take precautions. With no plans to enter into any kind of relationship, she'd quit taking the pill when she moved to Butte Plains, and Heaven only knew who he'd been with. She refused to think about all the women in Colin's life. Right now, she was the only one in his bed — well, her bed — and nothing else mattered. Especially when he was doing such wonderful things to her body.

With his free hand, he palmed her breast then teased the nipple to a hard peak before taking it into his mouth. Flames engulfed her from the inside out as he licked and tugged on the sensitive bud while, below, his talented fingers stroked and strummed until she began the familiar climb to the top of the cliff. His teeth grazed her nipple at the same time his thumb flicked her clit. It was not enough and too much at the same time. She didn't even try to stop herself from falling from the cliff. Then she was flying through space, grasping for anything to anchor her to earth.

"That's it, baby. Come for me."

"Colin," she gasped as pleasure gripped her body.

~ ~ ~

Could a guy die from blue balls? He was about to find out.

Watching Julie fly apart under his hands was one of the great wonders of his life and one he wouldn't trade for anything — even a cure for blue balls. He'd gladly suffer for her pleasure. As her body relaxed, he withdrew his fingers from her snug channel then rolled to his back, taking her with him. He managed to pull the covers up over them then tried to focus on the woman wrapped around him instead of his throbbing cock. No one had ever called him a selfish lover, and he would be damned if he was going to turn into one now. Julie was spent. Once she was asleep, he'd take a cold shower. Then he'd buy the biggest box of condoms he could find tomorrow, so this wouldn't happen again.

"That was amazing." Her warm breath on his skin combined with her soft curves pressed up against him almost sent him into orbit. "Thank you."

"Anytime, sweetheart. Anytime." He meant it. He'd be her booty call 24/7.

She raised up on one elbow, as she placed her hand on his chest her hair brushed his skin, sending shock waves through his body. "But what about you? It hardly seems fair."

"Don't worry about me."

Her fingers played through the smattering of hair on his chest then tracked lower, following the trail to his happy place.

"Careful." He grabbed her wrist, stopping her before she could wrap her hand around his boner.

"I could do something to help." Her fingers, stopped but not trapped, danced across his abdomen.

Colin groaned and clenched his jaw. "I'll be okay. You should get some sleep."

"Sleep is overrated." Escaping his grasp, she took his shaft in hand.

It was all he could do not to come immediately like some green kid getting his first hand job in the back seat.

"You're so hard." She worked her hand up and down his length. "Does it hurt?"

"In the best possible way," he replied through gritted teeth. His focus entirely on one part of his anatomy and what she was doing to it, he barely registered the cooler air brushing over his body when she kicked the covers off.

"I want to taste you. May I?"

"What? Huh?" He forced his eyes open. She wasn't where he thought she was. It took only a moment to see she'd shifted down the mattress so her face was even with his groin. *God almighty.*

"May I?"

"May you what?"

"Taste you." She pumped him once, twice.

Colin fought through a fog of need to make sense of her words. When his brain finally figured it out, he choked out a response. "God, yes." Then her lips were on him, sliding down his length, engulfing him in a hot, wet heaven. "Jesus, woman!" He rose to his elbows. No way was he going to miss seeing this.

Her fingers were wrapped around the root of his shaft, her rosy lips stretched tight as she worked her mouth up and down. Slowly. Colin sucked in a breath and held it until his lungs burned before he let it out in measured increments synced to her pace. At this rate, he was going to pass out either from lack of oxygen or from overstimulation. Christ, he couldn't watch and feel at the same time, not and survive. If he had to choose one, he chose feeling. Closing his eyes, he dropped back to the mattress and let her take him to paradise.

It was a short trip. He'd been halfway there before she even touched him. It had been a fast climb to the precipice from there. In minutes, an oath exploded from his lips at the same time he came against the back of her throat.

Colin clamped a hand over his chest, grateful to feel his heart still beating beneath his palm. "I thought I'd died and gone to Heaven," he said, only half joking. For a second, he'd thought he'd seen the pearly gates beckoning him home.

Julie crawled up and cuddled against his side. "I did it right, then?"

He chuckled. "Sweetheart, if you'd done it any more right you'd be calling 9-1-1."

"Think you can sleep now?"

"Hell, yeah. How about you?"

His answer was a light snore. It took some doing, but he managed to pull the covers up without disturbing her. Colin closed his eyes, and, in seconds, he was asleep.

CHAPTER SEVENTEEN

Julie woke, slightly disoriented. Colin Parker lay sprawled across her queen-sized bed, his hair mussed and his cheeks scruffy. He was sexy and adorable at the same time. She quickly decided it was a lethal combination and spelled the death of her regular schedule if she didn't move soon. A whimper outside the door was the catalyst that propelled her up and to the bathroom. She took care of business, donned a robe then eased out of the bedroom. Bud nudged her hand with his wet nose.

"Hi, Budster. You need to go out?" The dog wagged his tail and headed down the stairs. Julie followed, wincing as rarely used muscles complained of last night's activities. She let Bud out, scooped some kibble into his bowl then popped a pod in the coffee maker. It was unusual for her to have more than one cup in the morning, but this morning she wished she had one of those pods capable of producing a whole pot. If Colin stuck around, she'd have to pick some of those up at the store. And, find the carafe that had come with the machine. It was…somewhere.

She let Bud in and was checking her emails on her phone and working on her second cup of coffee when Colin came downstairs. He'd pulled on the only clothes he had upstairs, the jeans he'd worn to get from his tent to her house in the rain. She tried not to stare at his bare chest, but how could she not? Wide shoulders tapered to a trim waist and slim hips that fit perfectly between her legs. He was all hard muscle and golden tan skin her fingers itched to touch. Touching would lead to other things, which brought about another realization. They'd used the only condom they had last night. Which had led to other things. Her cheeks heated as she recalled how exciting those *other things* had been.

"Good morning." He crossed the room and bent to kiss her lightly on the lips. "You taste like coffee."

Julie forced her lascivious thoughts away and stood. "Want some?" She headed for the coffee maker. "It takes about thirty seconds."

"Please," he said, rubbing the dog's ears. "Has he been out?"

"Yep, and fed." Geez, they sounded like an old married couple. Julie's heart did a flip-flop. What the hell was she thinking? It was one night. One spectacular night, but still. She handed Colin the filled cup then resumed her seat at the kitchen table. He took the chair across from her and sipped the hot beverage. She guessed he wasn't much of a morning person. It wasn't a deal breaker, but it was a reminder of how little they knew about each other.

"What have you got planned today?" she asked.

He nodded at the window where bright sunlight streamed in. "Looks like a good day to work on the landscaping." His gaze went to the vintage cat clock on the wall above her head. "I've got a guy coming out this morning—finally—to give me an estimate on an electronic gate."

"Time for breakfast?"

Colin shook his head. "Nope. I'll grab a power bar. He's supposed to be here soon." He stood, drained the last of his coffee then set the cup in the sink. "Thanks, though. Another time?" His smile and the wicked sparkle in his eyes told her how much he'd like a repeat.

"Rain check?"

He groaned. "Please don't talk to me about rain. I'm up to my ears in mud as it is." He took her in his arms and drew her close. "But, yeah, I'll take a rain check."

His kiss stole her breath then he pulled away. She followed him to the door. Standing on the second step, he held the glass storm door open and leaned in for another kiss. Then he was gone, loping across her yard, dodging puddles. She watched until he put one hand on the top of a fence post and propelled himself to the other side. Closing the door, she leaned against it for a moment as memories of the night before flitted through her mind. If she had a brain in her head, she'd tell Colin Parker to get lost. To never come darken her door again. But, apparently, she'd lost her marbles because she had no intention of telling him any of those things.

~ ~ ~

Colin couldn't wipe the smile off his face as he vaulted over the fence and crossed the yard to his tent. In the sunshine, the relic didn't look so bad, and truth, after last night, it would forever hold a special place in his heart. In his haste to get to Julie's place, and find his only condom, he'd left the front flap unzipped. He saw the fresh muddy footprints on the floor first. With all the rain yesterday, there was plenty of mud inside, but most of it had dried, and the prints he was seeing now were not his.

Maybe one of the workers had come looking for him? That was probably it. Shrugging it off, he went in search of the only clean T-shirt he had left. His sister had given it to him a few weeks ago when he'd taken her out to lunch. It was sold exclusively at their sex toy outlet store and bore a screen-printed photograph of the actual Butte Plains city limits sign. Shortly after Becky and Ford's success with their Backdoor Locking System butt plug, some ingenious person had modified the freeway marker to read Butt Plug city limits. In the photo memorialized on the shirt, they'd also added the word assholes beneath the Population 3469. The highway department had been quick to remove the qualifying word in regards to the inhabitants, and, thankfully, whoever had added it had not seen fit to do it again. However, it didn't matter how many times they fixed the name of the city, within hours it would be modified again. They'd eventually given up, it seemed, and people on the interstate regularly passed through Butt Plug, Texas.

Colin found the shirt in one of the plastic bins he used to hold his meager food supplies. He considered turning it inside out but figured everyone had seen the sign, so what would it matter. He was out of clean socks, so he put on the least nasty ones he could find then slipped his feet into his boots. Intending to make use of his sister's washer and dryer when he went to town, he stuffed his dirty clothes into a garbage bag and set it next to the entrance. Heck, he could probably score a box of condoms from his sister—wait—he'd ask Ford instead. Getting sex supplies from his sister was too weird to contemplate, even if selling the stuff had made her a millionaire. Thinking of all the other interesting things he might score from his brother-in-law, he exited the tent with a smile on his face.

Would Julie like to experiment with some of the stuff his sister sold? Hell, he'd bet she already had one of their fancy vibrators. They were so popular, they'd even made the national news when they came out.

Colin shook his head. Who would've thought? He was chuckling and smiling to himself when he rounded the corner of the house and came face-to-face with a man he didn't recognize. His first thought was it had to be the gate contractor, but there was something about the way the man dressed that put Colin on alert. "Who are you?" he asked, not caring if he sounded friendly or not.

"So, you are living in a tent," the man said, which pretty much guaranteed he wasn't the man Colin was expecting.

"I said, who are you?"

"Just an interested party." His gaze darted over Colin's

shoulder to Julie's house. "A little too wet for you last night? Or just wet enough?"

Every muscle in his body tensed. How long had this scum been hanging around? Had he seen him leave Julie's house? Damn paparazzi. "You're trespassing." He'd put signs up on the gateposts and every other fence post along the road frontage. The man had to have seen them. Colin retrieved his cell phone from his back pocket. "You've got thirty seconds to get off my property before I call the police."

"Hold your horses. I'm going." He took a few steps toward the empty driveway then stopped and turned to face Colin. "Nice shirt, by the way. I'll see you around."

Colin pocketed his phone as he watched the intruder saunter down the empty driveway. He must have walked from the road, which meant he could have been snooping around for hours. *Shit.* He hadn't seen a camera, but everyone with a cell phone these days had one.

Where was the gate guy? Hell, would a gate even keep the scum out? Maybe he needed to rethink his security measures. He'd once thought any publicity was good publicity, but not since the celebrity rags had started making up stories to go with the photos they snapped. He'd been romantically linked to women he'd only spoken to for a minute or two at a social event and broken up with more women than he'd actually dated. Heaven only knew what they'd make of him living in a tent. He could see the headlines now — *Country Star Colin Parker — Broke, Homeless, and Living in a Tent!* They'd make no mention of the house, clearly under construction. No. That might actually make sense. No story there.

So, maybe the tent was a bit extreme, but it worked for him on two levels. It kept him near the construction zone, and it had garnered some sympathy from Julie. She was talking to him now, and more, which was all good in his book. Still, he needed to call his publicist and give him a head's-up. Maybe he could get something out there to explain the tent like — *Colin Parker Communes with Nature on Camping Trip.* Yeah, that sounded good. He'd wait and call at a decent hour. No need to roust Cameron out of bed yet. The situation only existed in Colin's mind — at the moment.

Hearing the faint sound of a car starting, Colin gave the departing scumbag a one-finger wave goodbye then climbed the newly built steps to his house. If last night's humidity hadn't messed up the dry time for the floors, he should be able to walk on them this morning. He liked to walk through the house before everyone got there. He wasn't checking up on them — just getting a feel for his new living space. It was already beginning to feel like home, which was a good thing, wasn't it?

Thankfully, the floors were dry, but the smell of stain and polyurethane remained, so he went through the house, opening every window. He was standing at the window in what would be the master bedroom, looking out at the property next door, when Julie appeared on the pathway leading from her house to the brewing room. Bud ambled beside her, looking as if he'd made the trip a thousand times and was bored with it. If there wasn't so much going on over here during the day, he'd gladly let the Labrador retriever hang out with him.

The sound of multiple trucks coming up his drive drew his attention away from the window and what was rapidly becoming his favorite subject, Julie Davis. Hustling down the stairs, he greeted the men, and one woman, Emma, who he was told was one of the finest wood carvers in the state of Texas. They went right to work while Colin went to what would be his kitchen. Devoid of cabinets or appliances, they'd set a piece of plywood across sawhorses as a makeshift countertop. Colin plugged in the coffee maker he'd purchased from a local thrift store for a buck, filled its tank with water from a gallon jug then tossed the old filter, and put in a new one. As he scooped grounds, he thought about Julie's coffee maker and wondered what the next generation would think of this pot in a few years?

He snapped a picture of the appliance with his phone and posted it to his Instagram account with #oldschool.

Pouring the first cup for himself, he smiled at the sounds of progress going on throughout the house. Nail guns. Saws. Someone had turned on a radio, and country music filled the silence in between. Maybe he *was* old school. He liked the craftsmanship of days gone by. He liked pouring coffee from a glass carafe. Liked smelling it as it aged on the hot plate like fine whiskey in an oak barrel. Hell, he'd bet somewhere someone was working on a single pod thingy-jig for alcohol. Aged in plastic. He'd have to ask Julie what she thought of the idea in regards to beer. Everything was evolving. Even country music.

When it came to country music, he was definitely old school. He didn't much care for the so-called crossover tunes that straddled the fence between country and pop music. He was country all the way, and, so far, he couldn't complain. He'd done well singing his style of music. Seems there were still people out there who shared his views, and, as long as there were, he planned to keep writing and singing. He just preferred to do it away from prying eyes.

He wandered out to the front porch and leaned against one of the new posts. Grateful for the shade as the sun had already turned the temperature up to "bake," he looked out over his land. He'd grown up in town but had always dreamed of owning land, having room so he wasn't knocking elbows with his neighbors. If the house next door had belonged to anyone else besides Julie Davis, he would have left this one to rot and found another place to buy. But the idea of knocking any of his body parts with Julie's had added value to the place, in his opinion. After last night, he knew he'd gotten a bargain. Hell, he would have paid twice the price and promised to cover the rundown house in gold foil.

A dark-green pickup bearing the logo of a local fence company came up the drive. Colin set his Styrofoam cup on the porch railing and hustled down the steps to meet the contractor. The sooner he got the electronic gate installed and a new fence up, the better off he'd be. Paparazzi were like cockroaches. If you saw one out in the daylight, you could bet there were a hundred more you didn't see.

CHAPTER EIGHTEEN

Colin waved goodbye to the fence contractor then went inside to see if anyone had any questions for him. After clarifying that, yes, he wanted the crown molding replaced in all the bedrooms, he grabbed his bag of dirty laundry and headed into town. Expecting Becky to be at work, he was surprised to see her car in the driveway, so he rang the doorbell instead of using the key she'd given him—in case he changed his mind about the tent situation.

His sister came to the door wearing the same ratty bathrobe he remembered from her high school days and looking a little green around the gills. He retreated to a safer distance. "Whoa. Sorry. If you're sick. I'll go to Mom's to do my laundry."

Becky held the door open wider. "Come on in. I'm not contagious."

Colin held his ground. "Beg pardon, but are you sure?"

She gave him what he called the stink eye and said, "Last time I heard, pregnancy wasn't contagious."

The comment rocked him back on his heels. It took him a second to recover then he dropped his dirty laundry on the porch and grabbed his sister in a bear hug and swung her around, whooping and hollering as he did so.

"Put me down," she yelled, pummeling his shoulders with

her fists like she used to do when they were kids, and he swung her until she nearly puked. She was his big sister in age only. In every other way, he was bigger than her, and had been most of his life.

Colin relented, settling her feet firmly on the hardwood floor. "Best news I've had all day. Hell, all week. All month!" he proclaimed. He grabbed his bag of laundry, dragged it inside, and shut the door. "Does Mom know?"

"No. Just you, me, and Ford, for now, so don't you go blabbing it around town."

Colin's eyebrows met in the center as he glared at his sister. "You weren't going to tell me, were you?"

Becky sat on one end of the sofa and brought her knees up under her. Colin took the chair opposite and waited for her answer. "No," she finally said. "I wasn't going to tell you. Not yet."

"Why the hell not? And why haven't you told Mom?"

Becky's tired gaze met his. "I wasn't going to tell you because you ran to Mom with every secret I ever told you."

"I did not." Damn. He sounded like a toddler caught plucking petals off his mother's rose bushes.

"What about the time I told you not to tell Mom I'd lost my library book?"

Colin opened his mouth to defend himself, but she was right. He'd run straight to their mother with the news.

"And what about the time I told you Roseanne and I were really going to the skating rink instead of watching a movie at her house?"

He was guilty that time, too. "I was a kid, Becks. And you were always so perfect. Tattling on you made me feel like less of a screwup."

"I could go on, but I think I've made my point."

"I'm sorry I was such a horrible little brother, but I'm grown up now. I can keep a secret." He trudged down the hall to the laundry room. As he emptied the bag into the washer and added detergent, he smiled to himself. He was going to be an uncle! He loved kids and would shout the news from the rooftop if he could. His smile turned to a frown. He set the dial on the machine then returned to the living room where his sister was stretched out on the sofa. "Tell me again why I can't say anything?"

Becky looked everywhere but at him. His gut clenched as a horrible thought took root in his brain. "Is there something wrong? Are you sick?" He might have been a lousy little brother, but he loved his sister. "Oh, no!" His heart did a somersault. "Is the baby okay?"

She turned her gaze on him and rolled her eyes. A giant smile broke across her face. "Gotcha!" she said. "You are such a worrier."

"And you are a wretched sister." He pushed her feet to the floor and sat down. "I'm going to tell Mom." Becky's laugh was infectious. The corners of his lips twitched as he refused to laugh at his own gullibility.

"The truth is, we'd rather—*I'd* rather—wait to tell Mom until I'm past this morning sickness phase. You know how she is. She'd be over here all the time. They say misery loves company, but in this case, it isn't true. I'd rather suffer alone."

Colin nodded. She was right. As soon as their mother knew, there'd be no getting rid of her. She could hover with the best of them when one of her kids was sick. "I get it. I'll keep my mouth shut."

Becky thanked him with a slice of a chocolate cake Roseanne—of course, she knew about the baby—had sent over, and the two of them talked about the baby and how the remodel on his house was coming along. At last, his laundry was done. He stuffed everything into the bag and set it beside the front door. "You'll call if you need anything, right?"

"Right," she said. "And you'll do the same?"

"Sure. Are you any good with a hammer?"

His jest brought a big smile to her face. "You are such a brat, Colin Parker."

"But you love me anyway."

"Yes, I guess I do."

After admonishing her to take care of herself and his nephew—he was certain it would be a boy—he took his laundry and left. He made another stop at the grocery store for condoms, beer, and bottled water then headed home. He was passing Julie's place when she pulled out onto the road in the old pickup she used to make deliveries. They waved to each other, and he continued on to his place where a crew was setting fence posts for his new gate.

Seeing the workers reminded him of the man he'd encountered this morning. He'd yet to call his publicist so he could start a damage control campaign. *Better to be proactive than reactive*, he thought. He pulled up Cameron's number on his cell phone and pushed the call button. It went straight to voicemail. Instead of leaving a long message, he asked Nashville's premier publicist to return his call then turned his attention to the man waiting on the porch.

"Randy," he said, extending his hand to his restoration expert. "What brings you out today?"

~ ~ ~

Julie waved at Colin as she pulled out onto the road with this month's delivery for McKenna's Liquor Store safely resting in the bed of her pickup. Where had he been?

Her cheeks grew warm as she considered the possibilities. They'd only had one condom last night. He'd promised to get more today. As the flush on her cheeks spread to the rest of her body, she wondered if perhaps a new truck, one with air-conditioning, might be a wise investment. She'd opted for the old truck because it had character, never once considering its flaws. Windows rolled down on her partially restored vintage transportation, she made the familiar drive practically on autopilot. She'd managed to shut out memories of last night long enough to complete the shipment and prepare the invoice she would leave with the cases, but seeing Colin again, even for such a brief moment, brought them flooding back in.

She'd always been one to daydream. Hazards of growing up with next to nothing, she supposed. As a child, she'd daydreamed about being part of a perfect family with a mom and a dad. Maybe a sister. Never a brother, though. Boys were a mystery to her, and she'd heard they had cooties. Cooties. No one had ever seen one, could not describe one, but knew, without a doubt, they were bad. Contagious even. Transmitted with a mere touch. Maybe even a look.

She laughed at the memory. Colin Parker didn't have cooties. Cuties. He had cuties. He probably wouldn't appreciate being called cute, but he was. Take the tent thing, for example. It was boyishly cute the way he was living in a tent next to his home while it was under renovation. Crazy, but cute. Restoring the old home—seriously cute.

He also had a cute butt. And a cute smile.

"Face it, Colin. You're cute," she said into the wind buffeting her through the open window.

What wasn't cute was his celebrity status. She knew better than to get involved with someone like him. It couldn't possibly lead to anything good, but last night had been oh so good. Better than good. The best ever.

She didn't have much experience, but she couldn't imagine sex could get much better. How could anyone stand it if it did?

She pulled up to the loading dock at McKenna's, dropped the tailgate then knocked on the door. Mr. McKenna himself appeared, and, in a few minutes time, they'd transferred the cases from her truck to his stockroom.

Julie checked the time on her cell phone. She needed a few things at the grocery store then she had to hurry back to the brewery. The temperature on one of the vats had been fluctuating lately, for no apparent reason. She needed to keep an eye on it and determine if it was something she needed to call a repairman for.

Bidding Mr. McKenna goodbye, she hopped into the cab of her pickup. She could spare ten extra minutes at the store. She'd grab a couple of steaks and some big potatoes to bake. Maybe some fresh salad greens. She and Colin hadn't made any plans, unless you counted his vow to obtain more condoms as plans. If he wasn't coming over again, they wouldn't need the protection, would they?

She'd just pulled into the parking lot when a familiar tune filled the cab. She picked up her cell phone and swiped her finger across the screen to answer the call. "Hi, Mom. What's up?"

They'd always been close, and though they'd both moved far away from their old apartment in Houston, they still talked several times a week. She'd wanted her mom to come live with her, but she was too independent to do so. Julie had established a sizeable trust for her with some of her winnings and purchased a condo in a swanky over-fifty community for her. The woman who had sacrificed so much so her daughter could have a good life enjoyed leisurely days learning to play tennis and golf with her new friends. One thing that hadn't changed about her was her love for those trashy celebrity magazines found in the grocery store checkout lanes. She mostly read the online versions now, on her iPad.

"Are you seeing Colin Parker? Is he as adorable in person as he appears on T.V.?"

"How? Wait. What?"

"It was you in the picture, wasn't it?"

Despite the heat that had built throughout the day, Julie shivered. "What picture?"

"It's in the *National Star*. It sure looks like you. Looks like your house, too."

"My *house*?" She felt like she'd been swept up in a tornado. Spinning, her mind reached out, trying to grasp something solid.

Something that made sense.

"You haven't seen it, then?"

"No. You know I don't read those rags."

"They aren't rags." Her mother's familiar protest was something solid. She held on to the ridiculous phrase and willed her brain to sort through the rest.

"My picture is in the *National Star*? Today?" She quickly switched the call to speaker then opened the internet browser. Moments later, she found the website. And stared at the front-page photo. Of herself, on her porch, barely dressed and kissing a half-dressed Colin Parker. This morning. The photo had been taken a few short hours ago.

"Jennifer?" No matter how many times she reminded her mom she'd changed her name, and the reasons why, she still called Julie by the name she'd given her at birth.

"Mom, I can't talk now." She stared at the photo. "I'll call you later, okay?"

"Okay, but it'll have to be late. It's game night at the clubhouse."

"Fine. Late. Have fun. I love you." Not waiting to hear her mother repeat the words, Julie ended the call.

This was bad. Really, really bad. She scrolled down, searching the accompanying article for her name, and breathed a sigh of relief when she was identified only as Colin Parker's sexy and accommodating neighbor. It wasn't a particularly flattering description, but at least they hadn't mentioned her name or her association with Lucky Lady Brewing Company.

She clicked on the photo so it filled the entire screen. Holy hell. This was bad. Very, very bad. She'd expended too much effort making Jennifer Harris disappear to let some rag newspaper resurrect her. She was Julie Davis now. A small-time brewer. A reclusive sort with no past and few friends. No matter how good the sex was, Colin Parker couldn't be one of those friends.

With trembling hands, she flipped through the contact list on her cell phone. Agent Wilkins had said to call him if she had any concerns. This was more than a concern. Panic hovered on the edge of her nerves, threatening her ability to reason. If anyone could accurately assess the threat the photo posed to her new life, it would be the FBI agent in charge of her case.

"Agent Wilkins." Even though she hadn't heard his voice in over a year, hearing it now was like balm on an open wound.

"Agent Wilkins. It's me, Jennifer Harris."

"Julie!" His use of her new name confirmed his continued interest in solving her case. "How are you?"

"Not good. That's why I'm calling. The *National Star* has a picture of me on their website."

The sound of keys clicking on a keyboard assured her he was bringing the site up as they spoke. There was a pause then he asked, "How did they get it?"

She kept the explanation short, explaining she'd had no idea there was anyone around besides her and Colin Parker. "How worried should I be?"

"There are several things you have going for you. They didn't identify you, so your new identity is still intact, and unless your kidnapper reads the *National Star*, he'll never see the photo. When was this taken?"

"This morning. My mom saw it and called to let me know."

"I'll make some phone calls. See if I can get it taken down, but if someone has already downloaded it to their computer, we might be too late."

A chill raced down her spine. "Meaning, it could show up somewhere else."

"Exactly. We simply don't have the resources to troll the internet, looking for one photo. It could pop up on a fan's social media account or a blogger could pick it up. I'll see what I can do, but don't be surprised if it shows up again. Colin Parker is news, especially in the country music world."

"What can I do?"

"Stay as far away from him as possible, and call me if you see the photo anywhere else."

Deep down, she'd known she couldn't have a relationship with Colin, but hearing Agent Wilkins confirm her belief made her heart ache. Would she be alone for the rest of her life?

"I will. I promise. And thanks."

"You deserve to have a life, Julie. I told you we would find him, and we will. In the meantime, keep your head down and your eyes open."

Ending the call, she folded her arms on the steering wheel and rested her forehead on top. She had more money than she could spend in several lifetimes, but the only things she wanted were the things it couldn't buy.

CHAPTER NINETEEN

At the sound of a door slamming, Colin looked up from his latest project—assembling his new gas grill—to see Julie striding across her lawn. Even from this distance, he could tell she was pissed. He ran a quick mental checklist, searching for what he could have done and came up empty. He'd only seen her once since leaving her house in the wee hours of the morning. She'd waved at him in passing—like normal people do. So, what had crawled up her butt and put that look on her face?

Straightening, he placed his crescent wrench on top of the unintelligible instruction sheet and hustled over to the fence where she'd come to a complete stop. When she wouldn't cross the line into his yard, he knew her attitude had something to do with him. He just couldn't imagine what.

"Hey, neighbor," he said. "What's up?"

"What's up? Seriously?" Her expression radiated anger, but her body language was pure defensive. Arms crossed in front of her, shoulders hunched, she was braced for an argument. "You are bad news, Colin Parker. I knew it from the beginning, but I ignored my instincts. It was my mistake. I won't make it again. Stay away from me."

She was halfway to her house when his mouth caught up

with his brain. "Wait! What's this about? What did I do?"

Julie stopped and turned to him. The pain he saw on her face slashed him to the core. Leaping over the fence, he caught up to her moments before she reached her porch. "Julie. Wait. Whatever this is, we can fix it. Just tell me what happened? Was it something I did?"

"You can't fix this. No one can."

"I don't believe you. There isn't anything that can't be fixed." Except his broken heart. He could feel it cracking with every word she spoke in that final, fatalistic tone. What he'd thought was infatuation he now knew was so much more. He was in love with her. Had been since their first kiss. "Give me a chance. Please."

Her hand was on the handle of the storm door. Two more steps and there would be a physical barrier between them in addition to the invisible force field she'd put up. It was time to lay it all on the line.

"Julie. Stop. Give me a second." To keep from grabbing the door and yanking it out of her hand, he took a step back.

She took another step then turned. Framed by the edge of the door and the doorjamb, she looked fragile. Broken. Just like him. He ran his fingers through his hair, trying to think. If he told her how he felt, would it make a difference? Maybe not, but as the saying went, nothing ventured, nothing gained. "Somehow, I imagined the first time I said these words to a woman being a bit more romantic. Dinner. Candlelight. Dessert. But staying away from you isn't an option." She visibly stiffened. Colin held his hands up, palms out, and took another step toward his yard. "I'm not a stalker."

She moved again, slipping farther away from him, her eyes wide with something. Fear? God, he hoped not.

"I don't know what I did. You have to know I'd never do anything to hurt you." The invisible wall between them was growing ice crystals. It was now or he might never have the chance to tell her. He cleared his throat, forced his gaze up to hers.

"I love you."

~ ~ ~

His words hit her like a baseball bat to the chest. She tightened her grip on the aluminum door handle and dug the fingernails of her other hand into the wooden doorframe. How many nights since their first kiss had she dreamed of hearing him say those words to her? She should have been ecstatic, what woman wouldn't be? Excruciating pain radiated from her shattered heart as the words she'd refused to even think in regards to Colin Parker died in her throat.

I love you, too. Oh, god, how she loved him. But her past and his future were rivers too wide and mountains too high to cross. Still, she owed him some explanation for her sudden turnabout. Was it possible he hadn't seen the photo? Even if he had, he had no way of knowing the danger it put her in. He couldn't fix her situation. But he could stay away from her.

"Julie?"

God, he was waiting for her to say something. To return the sentiment. She couldn't. If she did, he'd never let her hide from him again. "The *National Star.*"

His eyebrows rose high on his forehead. "The picture? It won't happen again. I promise."

"Keep the reporters away from me. If you love me like you say, then do this one thing for me. It's all I ask."

"I—"

She didn't let him finish. Closing and locking the outer door, she crossed the porch to the inner door and repeated the process. The little house had become her sanctuary. It had given her the sense of security she'd needed so badly but now felt like a leaky sieve, every hole in the porous sides filled with watchful eyes.

Sagging into one of the kitchen chairs, she closed her eyes and willed her breathing to calm. She'd lost so much more than her privacy. She'd lost her heart, too.

After what had happened to her after she won the lottery,

she'd come to terms with living alone for the rest of her life. In the deepest recesses of her mind, she'd hoped one day the danger would become something in the distant past, and she would find someone she could trust. She'd never imagined her heart would have ideas of its own—that it would give itself to someone she absolutely couldn't be with.

Life with Colin would be like living in a fishbowl. Unless she hid in an underground bunker, there would be photos of him and her together, and that was unacceptable.

Sometimes, she wished she'd never won the jackpot. If she hadn't, she wouldn't be living this covert life far away from the only family she had. Despite her degree, she might still be tending bar or waiting tables. Honest, but hard work. She might have met someone by now and gotten married.

But her someone wouldn't be Colin Parker, and she couldn't imagine loving another the way she loved him.

~ ~ ~

He should have run over the reporter with his truck when he had the chance! Instead, he'd let him walk away, thinking a phone call to his publicist would be all the damage control he'd need.

You're an idiot, Parker. He pulled the article up again on his computer, clicking on the photo of him kissing Julie so it filled the screen. The photographer had captured the exact moment when he'd changed the angle of the kiss, and, for a split second, Julie's face was clearly visible. Even though they hadn't identified her, it was enough for her to tell him to get lost.

Before last night, he might have accepted her decision, but not now. Not when he knew every fantasy he'd had about holding her, making love to her, had been so far off the mark. They'd been excellent fantasies, but nothing compared to the real thing. He'd been with enough women to know what he and Julie had shared last night had been special.

He was hard just thinking about the feel of her skin, so soft and warm—the sounds she made when he touched her in just the right place — the way her body responded to his — the incredible feeling that he'd come home when he was balls deep inside her.

Their connection had been more than physical, and though she hadn't responded in kind when he told her he loved her, he knew she did. She'd said it with her body last night.

So, why had the photo upset her so? He couldn't say he liked having his personal business on the internet, either. All the other photos in the spread had been of him and his temporary living quarters. Sensationalism at its best. Take something no one would give another thought and twist it so it seemed to be more than it was. Ironically, they'd made more of his dilapidated tent than while wearing nothing but dirty jeans, he'd been kissing his next-door neighbor at a suspiciously early hour. Given the carefree bachelor lifestyle he'd lived in Nashville, he guessed they figured it was par for the course for him. Living in a patched-together tent — that was something they could twist until it fit their narrative.

One thing was for sure. He had no intention of letting one photo keep them apart.

~ ~ ~

It had been several weeks since she'd confronted Colin about the photo of them kissing on her porch after a night of what she had to admit was spectacular sex. Since then, she'd managed to stay on her side of the fence. She'd rarely peeked out any windows, and she'd worn the noise-cancelling headphones he'd given her to drown out the music coming from his yard every Sunday night. She still took Bud out and walked to and from the brewery building several times a day. It was hard not to notice things. Like, he'd taken down the tent. The lights she'd seen on inside the still-under-construction house told her he'd moved indoors.

His Sunday evening gathering had grown into a full-on event a dead person couldn't miss. Once, when she'd gone out to buy groceries, she'd noticed a teenage boy with a cooler and a lawn chair, manning Colin's new electronic gate. At least he'd followed through on the gate installation, but a teenager was hardly what she'd call security.

Heading home from a long day inside the brewing building, she let her gaze drift to the large group gathered on the other side of the fence. Unable to believe her eyes, she came to a complete stop. Sitting in the spot vacated by the eyesore tent was a shed on a trailer. Had he bought a storage shed and it hadn't been unloaded from the trailer yet? As she watched, a couple of people approached, going around to the opposite side. Only then did she notice the metal stairs visible beneath the raised trailer bed.

"Oh, no. He didn't." She moved closer, her gaze focusing in on the small sign discreetly placed on the back wall of the shed. *Butte Plains Sanitation Solutions.*

He'd put a portable toilet practically in her yard!

"No. No. Oh, hell no!"

She closed the distance between her and the fence line in a few angry strides, Bud hot on her heels. "Colin Parker!"

About a hundred pairs of eyes turned her way, but there was only one set she was interested in. A sci-fi tractor beam couldn't have zeroed in on her prey faster. In less than a second, their gazes met, sending a shiver of awareness along her spine, making her lady parts tingle, and igniting a rage inside her that burned hotter than the flames rising from his fire pit.

Colin stepped from the crowd, his lips quirked up on one side as he made his way over to her. He looked every bit the successful country artist he was in worn denim, an expensive but understated western shirt, and boots polished to a mirror shine. A white cowboy hat sat atop his head. He'd had his hair trimmed since she'd last seen him, and just the right amount of scruff covered the lower half of his face, giving him a sexy outlaw look she found near impossible to resist. Her dog made no effort to resist. Bud slipped beneath the bottom strand of rusty wire and, tail wagging, ran up to greet their neighbor.

Colin bent to scratch Bud behind both ears before acknowledging her presence. "Julie," he said, tipping the brim of his hat in greeting. "What can I do for you?"

Seriously? He had to ask? "You can get your outhouse out of my backyard. That's what you can do." She mentally congratulated herself for sounding rational when her insides were a mixed-up mess of rage and horny as hell.

Colin glanced briefly at the toilet-on-a-trailer then to her, his smile never wavering. "It appears to be in my yard, not yours. Is there something else I can do for you?"

She could think of a thing or two. In fact, she'd thought of little else the last few weeks, but she'd decided to go cold turkey when it came to Colin Parker. No matter how miserable it made her. It was the right thing to do. It was the *only* thing to do. Her life depended on it.

"Are you kidding me? Take a good look, hotshot. You. Have. An. Outhouse. In. Your. Yard!"

He did as she said, taking a good, long look at the trailer before speaking again. "Yep. I believe you are correct. I have an outhouse in my yard. *My* being the operative word. Honestly, I don't want all these folks traipsing through my house to use my one functional bathroom. So, it's either an outhouse or send them off into the bushes." His smile grew brighter, if it was even possible. "Or, I could send them over to your house."

Julie's eyes narrowed. "Don't. You. Dare."

"See, that's what I thought you'd say. So the outhouse stays." He turned, took two steps toward his guests then spun around. "You're welcome to join us. There's plenty of food." With another tip of his hat, he left her standing on her side of the barbed-wire fence and returned to the party.

Julie watched his rear end, magnificent in jeans, strut across the yard. Only after he was swallowed up by the mass of people gathered under his new pergola did she realize her dog had followed him. She could try calling Bud to come with her, but doing so would only focus attention on her. The dog knew where his food bowl was. He'd make his way there as soon as people stopped feeding and petting him, which she could see was already happening.

With a huff, she turned her back on the party and headed to her previous destination—home. As she stood staring into the refrigerator, trying to decide what she would have for dinner, the smell of grilling meat from next door still in her nostrils, her thoughts turned to the person she couldn't stop thinking about.

Infuriating man. Why couldn't her neighbor be ordinary? Reasonable? Just some average guy who liked to play his guitar? Why did he have to be a star with millions of adoring fans?

Why does he have to live next door to me?

For the first time since she'd settled in Butte Plains, she thought about moving. Colin wasn't going anywhere, obviously. She could live here in a perpetual state of irritation, needing what she couldn't have, dodging him and the media attention he brought with him. Or she could move.

It wasn't her first choice of action. She liked living in Butte Plains. Though she didn't have many friends—a conscious decision on her part—she did have a few.

Julie pulled the ingredients for a grilled ham and cheese sandwich from the refrigerator then took a small frying pan from the bottom cabinet. She buttered the bread, stacked ham and cheese then topped it with another slice of bread. While the sandwich browned on the first side, she helped herself to another of her yet-to-be-named brews. This one was her first attempt at producing a lager. She'd spent countless hours researching methods and familiarizing herself with the brewing process before finally committing to giving it a try. Several months later, she'd finally bottled her first batch.

Twisting off the cap, she brought the bottle to her lips. The cold brew slid down, silky smooth with the slightest hint of a rough edge. "Not bad," she said, realizing after she'd spoken her dog had abandoned her for the evening. She took another sip then flipped the sandwich over to brown the other side. Next door, the music portion of the evening had begun. It seemed everyone who owned a guitar, banjo, or other acoustic instrument brought them along to Colin's shindig. What had begun as a casual get-together had grown beyond recognition.

Which drove her thoughts around to the portable outhouse he'd brought in. Since they lived outside the city limits, there wasn't much she could do about it other than complain to him and hope he got rid of it, but, as he'd pointed out, the alternatives weren't good.

Julie plated her sandwich, added a handful of her favorite brand of potato chips then sat down at the kitchen table to enjoy her meal.

CHAPTER TWENTY

Colin helped Randy Tucker with the tricky transition from one note to the next then picked up the tune again with the guitar he treasured more than just about anything he owned. He'd made it himself in woodshop at Butte Plains High School. The project had spanned his sophomore and junior years—something unheard of before, but he'd convinced the teacher to let him do it instead of making cutting boards and salad bowls, the two most popular woodshop projects.

As he strummed and sang along with the old favorite one of his guests had chosen, he let his thoughts drift. He thought about the woodshop he'd begun work on in the old barn. Once his equipment arrived, he planned to start on a new guitar. Something with inlaid designs on the body. This time, he'd use real opals for the fret markers along the neck instead of plastic replicas.

His brain took the leap from a benign subject to one guaranteed to send his blood pressure spiraling out of control. Damn Julie Davis and her delectable neck. Hell, he ached to taste every inch of her. What was with her, anyway? He wasn't sure if she was his muse or his Kryptonite or a mixture of both. Memories of their one night together fueled his dreams, while the wall she'd built between them brought him to his knees.

He'd had high hopes when he'd heard her call out his name earlier, but those had been quickly dashed by the furious look on her face when he'd gotten close enough to see her clearly. He'd wanted to drag her through the fence and show her how much she meant to him more than he'd wanted his next breath, but her body language had told him he'd probably find his dick wrapped in rusty barbed wire if he tried, so he'd fallen back on sarcasm, and if he recalled correctly, pure arrogance to get through the conversation. *Not your best moments*, he thought as he picked up the rhythm of the next song. Thankfully, it was one he could play in his sleep, so he continued to let his mind drift. Too bad it only drifted one way.

His gaze landed on Bud, Julie's Labrador retriever who had taken up residence next to his chair and gone to sleep. If the dog was still here when everyone left, he'd see it got home safely. And maybe he'd get another chance to talk to Julie. Since the sleazy reporter had trespassed and taken a couple of pictures, he'd had a new fence installed along three sides of his property and a state-of-the-art electronic gate to keep unwanted guests out. So far, it was working. He'd convince her he valued her privacy as much as he did his own. And find out why the hell she was so obsessed about it in the first place. There had to be more than she was telling. If she didn't trust him, they didn't have a chance of making a relationship work. Bud stirred, looking up at him with brown eyes he couldn't resist. Bowing out of the song, he petted the dog's head. Shit, he even loved her dog. What the hell was he going to do?

Colin glanced at the house next door. There was still a light on in the kitchen and another was on upstairs. He stood and signaled the Labrador to follow him.

She answered the door, wearing an oversized T-shirt that hit her mid-thigh. Colin's gaze swept over her from her bare feet to her long blonde hair cascading over her shoulders in soft waves. *Breathe. In. Out. Keep your clammy hands to yourself.*

Shit. He hadn't been this nervous the night he'd shown up to collect Sherry Rigs for their first, and it turned out, only, date. He'd been sixteen when Sherry's mother had met him at the door, wearing a pink silk kimono meant for a much smaller woman. She'd invited him in to wait for her daughter, but his feet had felt like lead weights and he'd opted to stay where he was. He'd often wondered what would have happened if he'd followed her inside. He'd never know. Sherry and her mother had moved a week later. No warning. Just up and left.

Standing on Julie Davis's porch, he knew all the way down to his bone marrow — if she invited him in, he'd follow.

Bud didn't wait for an invitation. Tail wagging, he scooted past his mistress and disappeared around the corner. Julie smiled as the dog breezed past her. "Thanks for bringing him home."

"No problem. I owe you an apology."

She cocked her head to one side, silently questioning.

"Earlier." He shifted his feet. "I was rude. I'm sorry. You have every right to be concerned about the toilet trailer. I'll move it tomorrow. I could put it on the other side of the barn. A few more steps won't kill anybody."

"Thanks. For the apology, and for moving the outhouse. It's just—"

"Uncouth?" He smiled. "I wasn't here when it was delivered. Randy's guys let them leave it there. I just never thought—"

"No harm done," she said, clearly intending to shut the door in his face.

"Julie. Wait." The door stopped its forward motion. "Please?"

She leaned against the doorjamb but kept one hand on the door.

"Can I come in? Just to talk."

For the briefest of seconds, he saw indecision cross her face then she straightened and took a step back. His heart pounded. He tested his feet to make sure they'd move when the time came. Then she opened her mouth. "Not tonight, Colin." And closed the door. The dead bolt sliding into place signaled the end of their short-lived relationship.

When the light above the porch went off, he forced his feet into action. He stopped long enough to pick up his guitar and let his guests know they could stay as long as they liked then he went up to his newly completed master suite. As he stripped and climbed into bed hours earlier than usual, he told himself it was because the next day would be a long and busy one. He wasn't retreating to lick his wounds. But as the hours ticked by, and the music from his yard dwindled and the last car drove out, he gave up on sleep. Reaching for his guitar, he sat in the moonlight. Words and notes came in a slow rush as he poured out his anguish to the night.

~ ~ ~

He felt like hell and probably looked the part, too. There wasn't a damn thing he could do about it except hope it got better on its own. After pulling an all-nighter writing, he'd downed two cups of coffee and taken a cold shower before the limo he'd hired for the day buzzed the gate. When he'd booked this gig to sing the national anthem at this afternoon's game, he'd envisioned Julie sitting beside him on the way to Dallas. He'd screwed his plan up in royal fashion, so, instead of a beautiful woman accompanying him, he had Ford and Scott.

He wasn't at all surprised when they'd accepted his invite at the butt crack of dawn. What red-blooded American male didn't want to play hooky for a day to see the Texas Mustangs baseball team take on the New York Knights in post-season play? Especially if they could watch the game from the owner's private box? It was just one of the perks that came along with the gig. There would be an interview in the press box with the live commentators and a chance to meet the team in the locker room after the game. Win or lose. The national exposure would be good for his career, if he didn't botch the anthem. The Mustangs' organization provided ample time to rehearse before the stadium opened its gates.

"You look like shit," Ford said as the driver closed the limo door behind him. "Late night?"

"You could say that." Long night would be more accurate, but he really didn't want to get into it with his brother-in-law.

"Becky and I are going to have to make it to your shindig one of these days."

"You know you're welcome. Come early, though, if you want a good seat." He couldn't believe how popular his Sunday night get-together had become. Even before Julie had gone apeshit over the portable toilet, he'd considered building a small amphitheater on the far side of the stock tank. He'd have to look into getting a road built and providing parking and a more permanent bathroom facility, but it might be worth the time and expense. He'd seen firsthand last night how annoying the music could be when you just wanted to be left alone. He couldn't blame Julie for being disgusted with his weekly parties. If he were in her shoes, he'd be pissed, too.

The limo came to a stop, and Scott joined them before the driver could get his seat belt unfastened. Ford and Colin both groaned when they saw the New York Knights shirt he was wearing.

"What?" he asked.

"You know we're sitting in the owner's box, right? The *Mustangs* owner's box?" Ford reached around, yanked a Mustangs cap out of his back pocket, and settled it on his head. "And you call yourself a Texan now," he grumbled at his best friend.

"Hey, I've been a Knights fan all my life. You can't expect me to change my loyalty so quick."

"We damn sure can," Ford said.

Colin tuned out the friendly argument. If it kept Ford from digging deeper on the subject of his lack of sleep, he didn't have a problem with it. Whoever said misery loved company had it all wrong.

"Hey, big shot." A jab to his ribs woke Colin from the first good sleep he'd had in two days.

"What?" He sat up, rubbed his hands over his face then helped himself to a water bottle from the cooler built into the wide armrest. "Are we there yet?"

"Not hardly," Ford said. "We just wanted to know who canceled on you at the last minute. We're grateful for the invite, but it was a little last minute."

He took a long pull on the plastic bottle before answering. "Nobody." It was the truth. He'd never gotten a chance to ask Julie, so she'd never had a chance to cancel on him.

Both men laughed like they knew something he didn't. "I never got around to asking. So, no. No one canceled."

"See," Scott said. "I told you we weren't his first choices."

"Hmm," Ford said. "You have any ideas about who his first choice was?"

"If I had my guess, I'd say it was his sexy next-door neighbor."

"Julie Davis? The Lucky Lady Brewing Company girl?" Ford asked.

"She's not a girl," Colin said before Scott could confirm Ford's statement.

"Oh, see," Scott said. "He's got it bad for her. You did see the photo of them kissing, right?"

"That was her? How do you know?"

"Just shut the fuck up," Colin interrupted again. "I thought about asking Julie, but she guards her privacy like a virgin in a harem guards her purity." He clearly needed more sleep. He'd never meant to say those words. Not to anyone, let alone the two happiest men in Butte Plains. They had their women and thought everyone else needed one, too. Well, he didn't. He'd done just fine without one so far. And hell, if he couldn't have Julie, he didn't want a poor substitute.

"Sorry," Scott said. "But have you ever thought she might

have a good reason for flying below the radar? There are a lot of assholes out there. It's hard being a woman, especially a single one."

Colin turned to gaze out the window. Could Scott be right? Was Julie hiding from someone? He hated to think of her watching over her shoulder or that someone had done something to make her so cautious.

Colin finished his water bottle and reached for another one. His movement must have been the signal because Ford and Scott changed the subject back to baseball, arguing about which franchise had the better team, Dallas or New York. At least they were leaving him the fuck alone.

CHAPTER TWENTY-ONE

Julie pulled into the driveway of Roseanne and Scott's newly renovated Victorian just around the corner from The Yellow Rose, Roseanne's very successful bed-and-breakfast. It was hard for Julie to decide, but she thought this house might be more beautiful than the other. The color palate of this one was more to her liking. Yellow was okay, especially for a Victorian home, but this subtler blue-gray, trimmed in at least four complimentary colors ranging from green to purple, made the place look like an elaborate birthday cake. Julie liked cake. Always had. She'd become a big fan of the coconut cake Roseanne served at The Yellow Rose. She sure hoped it was on the menu for today's impromptu get-together.

Roseanne had called bright and early this morning to invite Julie to spend the day with her and Becky. Seemed Colin was slated to sing the national anthem at the Mustangs playoff game this afternoon and had invited them to go along, leaving the women with an unexpected day to themselves. Julie wasn't sure what all was on the docket, but Roseanne had mentioned high tea and pedicures. After spending another Sunday evening alone while a party raged on the other side of her fence, she didn't even have to think before accepting the invitation. Though she hadn't spent much time with either woman, she could use a little company. Maybe some girl talk would help her forget the hurt she'd seen in Colin's eyes when she'd refused to let him in last night.

He'd never understand her reluctance to be in the spotlight. She'd done everything short of plastic surgery to make her former self disappear. She'd changed her name, moved to another part of the state, and bleached her hair blonde. And, she kept in touch with the FBI agent who had been in charge of her kidnapping case. Thanks to him, she'd lived to claim her lottery winnings, but the man who'd abducted her and tried to force her to sign over the winning ticket was still out there somewhere. When it became clear the FBI knew who he was, he'd abandoned his scheme to claim the billion-dollar jackpot for himself. After promising he'd see her again, he'd left her bound and gagged in a derelict building outside of Houston. It had taken nearly forty-eight hours for them to locate her. They'd never found her kidnapper.

Shaking thoughts of those harrowing days when she'd thought she'd never live to spend a single penny of her winnings, she followed the walk to the wide steps leading up to the wraparound porch. With its cheerful hanging baskets and comfortable-looking rocking chairs, it was one of the most inviting places she'd ever seen.

Julie rang the doorbell and waited.

When no one answered, she peered through the side window.

"Hmm." She turned around and her gaze fell on Roseanne's new mom-mobile—a brand-spanking-new minivan with every bell and whistle available. A person's car in their driveway most of the time meant they were home, but it was a short walk, especially via the shortcut through the alley, to the B&B. Roseanne had said she'd be here, but perhaps something had come up and she'd walked over to her place of business.

Julie eyed the arrangement of rocking chairs to her right. She could walk over to The Yellow Rose, or she could make herself comfortable. Becky would be here shortly, too. She looked forward to getting to know the other woman a little better.

Settling into the nearest rocker, she closed her eyes and let the peaceful setting lull her almost to sleep. This was the life, she decided, and began to calculate what it would take to build a sitting porch onto her house. At the sound of glass breaking somewhere in the house, Julie jumped up and pressed her nose to the window. She had to cup her hands around her face in order to see inside, but when she did, she gasped. "Roseanne!"

She dashed for the front door, and when the knob turned easily, she thanked God Butte Plains was still the kind of town where people didn't lock their doors all the time, and rushed inside. "Roseanne!" she yelled, approaching the woman she'd come to call friend. The pregnant woman lay sprawled on the floor between the open-concept kitchen and the living area, the shattered pieces of a teacup and saucer scattered about.

"Oh my God! Oh my God! Roseanne!" Julie shook her friend's shoulder. When she didn't respond, Julie whipped out her cell phone and dialed 9-1-1.

Later, as she paced the waiting area of the local hospital emergency room, waiting for word on her friend's condition, she was so glad she hadn't decided to walk over to The Yellow Rose. Who knew what even a few minutes delay could have meant in terms of the baby and Roseanne's survival?

Roseanne's fiancé and baby daddy, Scott Ramsey, had gone to Dallas with Ford and Colin. The men weren't expected home until late. Julie didn't have Scott's number anyway, so, knowing Becky had needed to go into the office for a few minutes to clear her day, Julie requested the number for Adams Manufacturing from directory assistance then dialed and asked for Becky Adams. The nice lady on the switchboard connected the call to Becky's office. "It's a family emergency," she informed the girl who answered. "I need to speak with Becky immediately. Tell her it's about Roseanne." She prayed her friend's name was enough to get Becky on the phone.

"Julie, what's wrong? Did something happen to Roseanne?"

Julie quickly told Becky what little she knew. "I didn't know how to get in touch with her fiancé, so I called you."

"You did the right thing. Thank you." She promised to inform Scott then assured her she would come straight to the hospital. "I'll be there in ten minutes. Call if you hear anything."

She promised, knowing they'd tell her nothing. She wasn't family, and could barely claim friendship with the woman, though the budding friendship had come to mean a lot to her. When she'd first moved to Butte Plains, she'd craved isolation. Anonymity. But as the months passed with only Bud and the occasional delivery person to talk to, meeting Roseanne had made her feel a part of the community. As long as her kidnapper was still out there, she wouldn't totally give up her reclusive ways, but she missed having friends she could trust.

Roseanne's best friend made a beeline for Julie, wrapping her in her arms. "Oh. My. God. Are you all right?"

"I'm fine. A bit shaken." She hadn't realized the state of her nerves until she'd spoken.

Becky led her to a section of plastic chairs and sat with her. "I can't even imagine what you've been through, but I'm so glad you were there."

"Me, too. When I think what could have happened to her if I hadn't…"

"Don't," Becky said. "Let's not borrow trouble."

Julie agreed. "No. We've got plenty already. I was so scared. Roseanne—"

"Is going to be fine. We have to believe that." Becky held her purse in a white-knuckled grip. "Have you heard anything?"

"Not a thing. I'm not family. I've asked, but they won't tell me anything."

Becky stood. "Let me see what I can find out. Ford has donated so much money to them since his dad died, they named the new heart wing after his father."

A few minutes later, she returned, her face red. "They won't tell me anything, either."

"What about Scott? Will they tell him anything?" Their wedding was weeks away so, technically, Scott wasn't related to Roseanne, either.

"If they don't, he'll tear the place apart when he gets here. He and Ford are on the way home. He did say he'd call her parents on his way here. They're in Florida. He's sending his jet to get them."

"That's good. She'll want to see them." Julie knew she'd want to see her mom under the same circumstances.

"Do you have any idea what happened?"

"I haven't got a clue." She explained how she'd arrived, expecting Roseanne to be waiting for her, but it seemed no one was home. "So, I sat in one of the porch rockers to wait. I'd been sitting there for a few minutes when I heard what sounded like glass breaking. The sound came from inside the house. I didn't think. The door was unlocked so I ran inside." She'd never forget finding her pregnant friend surrounded by broken glass and unconscious on the kitchen floor. "I found her in the kitchen and called 9-1-1."

Becky gripped Julie's hands tight. "I know I've said it before, but thank God you were there. I would have been, but with Ford gone today, there were a few things at the office I needed to take care of before I could leave."

Julie covered Becky's hand with hers. "You couldn't have known, so don't go down that path. I was fortunate not to have anything I had to do today, so I was able to go over a little early."

At the sound of the electric doors swooshing open, they both turned. Scott Ramsey blew in like a tornado, his best friend hot on his heels. Scott's gaze swept the room, landing first on the reception desk then on the two of them. Becky stood, dragging Julie to her feet, too. "Scott."

His long legs made short work of the distance between them.

He was a handsome man, no doubt about it, but, today, the only thing anyone would notice about him was the worry etched into his features. "Where is she? Is she all right? The baby?"

"We don't know." Becky clenched her purse in a white-knuckled grip. Ford put his arm around her shoulders, dragging her tight against him. "They won't tell us anything."

"They'll tell me." Turning on his heel, Scott crossed to the reception desk.

They didn't have to strain to hear the conversation. After Scott's initial exchange with the administrator on duty, their voices had risen.

"She's my fiancée. And that's my baby she's carrying. I don't give a rat's ass about your policies. You're going to tell me where she is, and I'm going to go see for myself."

"If you try, I'll call security, sir, and have you escorted off the property."

From where they stood, it was clear Scott was about to explode. Becky slid from Ford's arm. A moment later, she dragged Scott to the far side of the waiting room. "Sit," she told him, indicating one of the hard plastic chairs. "Ford knows people." She gave her husband a pleading look. "See what you can do. Please?"

Much to Julie's relief, Scott sat, but his gaze followed Ford to the reception desk. Julie wished she could hear what was being said, but, this time, the conversation remained civil, their voices low.

"I can't believe this." Scott wrung his hands and both legs bounced. The man was a ticking time bomb.

"I know it's frustrating, but I'm sure we'll have news soon." Becky placed her hand on Scott's arm.

"Not soon enough for me."

"You made good time getting here." Julie tried to distract him from the conversation taking place across the room. "Roseanne will be happy to see you."

"If they ever let me see her."

"They will. Just wait and see."

Ford ended his conversation and headed toward them. Scott sprang to his feet, catching up to his best friend in two long strides. "How is she? Can I see her? The baby?"

Ford's smile was reassuring. "Calm down, buddy. I spoke with her doctor. He said she's going to be fine, and a nurse is coming to get you in a few minutes. Looks like you're going to be a father today."

"What?" Scott's face turned ashen. "The baby is coming? Now?"

"That's what they told me."

A nurse in full surgical scrubs came through the doors leading into the main section of the hospital. "Scott Ramsey?"

"Here! I'm Scott Ramsey."

"Ms. Meadows is being prepped for surgery. Come with me, please." She turned and held the door open for him while Scott remained frozen on the spot.

"You aren't going to be one of those men who faint, are you?" Ford asked.

"No." He took a deep breath and let it out. He squared his shoulders. "Hell, no."

The three of them watched Scott Ramsey step past the nurse, and the door closed behind him. Ford turned around. "Everyone is okay. There are some complications with the pregnancy, and the doctor thinks it's wise to deliver the baby by Cesarean today."

"You're sure Roseanne and the baby are okay?"

"Her doctor said she would be fine."

"What can we do?" Becky asked.

"Sit down and wait?" Ford said. "I don't have a clue how long something like this takes."

"Not long, I wouldn't think," Julie said. "Is there anyone we should call?"

"Yes," Becky said. "I forgot to ask Scott if he got in touch with her parents. Do you know?" she asked Ford.

"He spoke to them right after we left Dallas. He had to send his family's jet from New York, so I don't think they've left Tampa yet."

Becky nodded. "Okay. I'll call and update them on the situation." She turned to Ford. "Can you call Kay at the B&B and let her know she'll have to handle things for a while?"

"What can I do?" Julie asked.

"Can you call my brother? Leave a message if you have to, but I'm sure he'll want an update."

This wasn't the right time to tell Becky the last person she wanted to call was Colin Parker, so she nodded and said, "Sure. Not a problem."

"Perfect." Becky already had her cell phone out, searching her contacts for the Meadows' number in Florida.

CHAPTER TWENTY-TWO

Colin retrieved his vibrating phone from his pocket and read the text message from his neighbor. It sounded like Roseanne and the baby were going to be all right, and, thankfully, Scott had arrived just in time. He never would have forgiven himself if the man had missed the birth of his child or, Heaven forbid, something worse had happened to Roseanne. If Colin nailed the anthem the way he knew he could, there would be another opportunity for Scott and Ford to see a game from the owner's box and meet the team members.

The manager for the pregame activities motioned him forward. Colin slipped the phone into his pocket and took his place at the microphone set up in front of home plate. As the stadium announcer introduced him, he waved at the cheering crowd. These were his people, mostly. There were a few people in the stands who wore Knights colors. Country music wasn't big in New York, but, here in Texas, this close to his hometown, people knew his name.

Because of the delay between when the words left his mouth to the time they came through the speakers lining the stadium, he wore an earpiece that fed the prerecorded music to him. All he had to do was concentrate on what he heard through the earpiece and ignore what he heard coming from the speakers. Not an easy thing to do, but he'd done well in rehearsal. He felt naked without his guitar, but unless you were Jimi Hendrix, you didn't play "The Star-Spangled Banner" on a guitar.

Cameras clicked away. Every step he'd taken since he stepped out of the limo had been recorded. Given the way she'd reacted to the photo the sleaze reporter had taken of her and him together, Julie would have hated this. For once, he was glad he hadn't asked her to come along. Scott's theory about her need for privacy gripped him in the gut. He couldn't think about that now. The countdown began in his ear, and he thrust everything from his mind except remembering the complicated verse.

~ ~ ~

Julie stepped outside to make the call but opted to send Colin a text message instead. Call her a chicken if you wanted, but she'd rather strut around the parking lot naked clucking than hear Colin's voice on the other end of the line. No doubt he'd probably prefer the less personal text as well. Especially after last night.

She'd been a bitch about the portable toilet. And though she'd accepted his apology, she'd been a bitch about that, too. Not waiting for a reply, she returned to see if there was anything else she could do to help. Becky and Ford sat off to one side of the waiting room, their gazes trained on a flat-screen television mounted on the wall. Julie glanced up. Colin Parker waved at the crowd as he walked out onto the field at Mustangs Stadium to sing the national anthem. Julie's heart kicked into overdrive as she stared at the screen.

"Come on," Becky said, her arm circling like a windmill on steroids. "Colin's going to sing the national anthem!"

Becky patted the faded orange seat beside her, and, not seeing any way out, Julie sat. Becky had every reason to be proud of her brother. He'd accomplished a lot for someone his age. And, from what she'd heard, he'd done it all on his own. He played and sang only songs he'd written himself. Nearly every recording artist out there hired songwriters or licensed original work to record. "The

Star-Spangled Banner" was probably the first song he'd ever sung on a public stage he hadn't written himself. Clearly, his reasons for not covering other people's work wasn't because he couldn't do it because he nailed the anthem. By the time he'd sung the last notes, Julie was a heartbeat away from jumping up from her seat and pledging allegiance to the flag.

Becky clapped and bounced in her seat. "Good job, Colin," she shouted at the TV. "He did great, didn't he?" She didn't wait for an answer. "I wish I could have been there, but oh" — she calmed — "I wouldn't want to be anywhere but here right now."

"Colin wouldn't want you to be anywhere else," Ford said. "He would have come home with us, but it was too late to cancel out."

Julie didn't want to hear another thing about Colin. "Becky, do you think it would be okay if I went over to Roseanne's house? There was broken glass — I don't want Scott to have to deal with it when he gets home." She'd been too upset to notice, but she suspected there had been food left out, too.

"I hadn't given it a thought. Would you mind?"

"Not at all. I'm going stir-crazy sitting here waiting." And she felt like a third wheel. Becky had Ford to lean on. She had no one.

"Me, too," Becky admitted, "but I can't leave. Not until I know Roseanne and the baby are okay."

Julie stood. "Then I'll go over and clean up. Call me if you hear anything. I can get some things for Roseanne if Scott doesn't want to leave her side."

"I'm sure they'd appreciate it. I'll call you. It shouldn't be much longer."

The EMT's wouldn't let her ride in the ambulance, so her pickup was in the hospital lot. Grateful to have something to do besides wait and listen to Becky go on about her brother, Julie drove across town. Like nearly everyone else in the area, she followed the Mustangs' season. The truck's radio only got a few stations clearly. One of those, thankfully, carried the games. She'd just pulled into Scott and Roseanne's driveway when the game announcers introduced their special guest for the inning—Colin Parker.

Great. Just Great. She'd texted him to avoid hearing his voice and now this. She should turn it off and get on with her business, but the moment he said hello to the announcers, her butt glued itself to the seat. They spoke briefly about the Mustangs' one-run lead and the home run by Jason Holder that had put them in the lead before turning the between-pitches conversation to Colin's rendition of the national anthem and his singing career, tying the whole thing back to his roots growing up in Mustangs' territory and his recent return to the area.

"Is it true you're living in a tent?" one of the announcers asked.

Colin chuckled. "Not anymore." He went on to explain about the house he'd purchased and how it'd needed extensive renovations before he could move in. "I still don't have a working kitchen, but I've got a bedroom and a bathroom now. I'll tell you, though, when those saws and nail guns get going during the day, I almost miss my leaky tent."

Julie smiled at the easy way Colin explained what the tabloid reporter had tried to make sound crazy at the worst, eccentric at best. They talked briefly about how Colin had worked hard to get where he was. He'd told her some of his story the night of his sister's wedding, but she hadn't realized until then how much he'd overcome to get to where he was now.

What would he think of her if he knew she could buy him ten or twenty times over with money she'd done nothing to earn? Another reason to keep her distance from him.

Colin got a plug in for his latest release before the inning ended and they cut to commercial. After removing the key from the ignition, Julie grabbed her purse and went inside. The sooner she got this done, the better. She'd need to go home and let Bud out before she returned to the hospital.

~ ~ ~

Colin followed the Mustangs' employee assigned to make sure he didn't get lost or swamped by fans. He was glad the interview was over. He hated talking about himself. His publicist, however, was probably doing cartwheels right now. He was constantly telling Colin to be more open about his life. "People relate to that shit," were his exact words. It didn't make him feel any better about answering the questions he considered intrusive. He loved singing, would do it for one person or a stadium full, it made no matter to him. But when it came to discussing his life off stage, he figured it was none of anyone's damn business but his own.

Like the fucking tent story. He'd be answering questions about it for the rest of his life. It wouldn't have even been a story if that damn reporter hadn't published the photo of him kissing Julie. Thank God his publicist had gotten the message across—no questions were to be asked today about the kissing photo. Julie didn't deserve to have her face and name linked to him in a sordid way. There'd been nothing sordid about the night they'd spent together—consenting adults and all—but some people could find a way to make something out of nothing.

Was he guilty of blowing things out of proportion? Making something of one kiss on the hood of a car and one night of the best sex he'd ever had when they had been nothing to Julie? Sitting in the luxury box with a perfect view of home plate, sipping a beer that wasn't anywhere as good as the ones Julie brewed, he couldn't focus on the game. He stood and yelled when everyone else did, but he didn't have a clue what was going on down on the field. Just like in Nashville, he was surrounded by people, but alone.

~ ~ ~

Julie had just finished cleaning up the broken teacup when Becky called. "Becky? How is Roseanne? The baby?"

"She's fine and so is the baby."

"Well, don't keep me hanging. Is it a boy or a girl?"

Becky laughed. "It's a girl!"

"I bet she's beautiful. Do you think the new parents would mind if I came to see her?"

"Mind? Are you kidding? They've been asking where you are! I told them, of course, and they're grateful for your help, but they do want to talk to you."

She couldn't imagine why they'd want to talk to her, except maybe to thank her for being in the right place at the right time. No thanks were necessary. "Tell them I'll be there soon. Is there anything Roseanne needs from home?"

"Funny you should ask. I have a list. Can I text it to you?"

"Sure." She glanced at the food intended for the tea party that didn't happen. Maybe she could package some of it up for the new parents and their guests to share. It would be a real shame to let the coconut cake go to waste. "I'll need a few extra minutes, but I'll be there. Promise."

"Perfect. Thank you again. I don't know what we would do without you."

In her eyes, she hadn't done anything extraordinary, but it felt good to be a part of something so special, even if she was only the errand runner. Friends pitched in wherever they were needed. Though her friendships with Becky and Roseanne were new, they felt solid. And that felt darned good.

CHAPTER TWENTY-THREE

Julie was still smiling when she punched the code into the keypad and the gate at the end of her driveway slid open. She couldn't believe Roseanne and Scott were going to name their precious daughter after her! Julie Rebecca Ramsey. A sweet bundle of joy named after her mother's best friend and the woman who had come to Roseanne's rescue.

Julie wiped a tear away just as something darted across the road, illuminated briefly by her headlights. Heart pounding, she hit the brakes. Bud! What was he doing out? Hands gripping the steering wheel, she quickly scanned what she could see of the property. Nothing seemed out of order except her dog was out running around. He'd been sleeping on the kitchen floor when she'd left. Had she left a door open?

No. Absolutely not. After the picture had surfaced in the *National Star*, she'd taken to locking her doors, even if she was just crossing the yard to the brewing house. No. She'd closed and locked the door when she left, and she didn't have a doggy door. The only way Bud could have gotten out was if someone had let him out. And no one in Butte Plains had a key to her house.

Bud stopped in the glare of her headlights, tail wagging and tongue hanging out. Stupid dog. He never met a stranger. She slid the car into Park and opened her door. One foot on the drive and one still in the car, she called for her pet to come. Bud loped over and jumped in the car, barreling over the console to the passenger seat. Julie closed and locked the door then backed down the driveway and out of the gate. Stopped on the side of the road, she dialed 9-1-1 to report a possible intruder. Assured help was on the way, she placed another call to Agent Wilkins.

~ ~ ~

"Is that your place?" the limo driver asked.

Colin jerked awake. The lack of sleep last night, coupled with the busy day, had finally caught up with him on the way home and he'd drifted off to sleep. Sitting on the edge of the seat, he peered out the window. "What the hell?" He couldn't tell if the flashing emergency lights came from his place or Julie's from this distance, but he knew. "Nah. Must be my neighbor's place." If it had been his, someone would have called him.

His gut clenched. What was going on? Scott's words came back to him, "Have you ever thought she might have a good reason for flying below the radar? There are a lot of assholes out there. It's hard being a woman, especially a single one."

Hard on the heels of that thought was Julie's voice telling him to leave her alone—all because of a damn photo in the *National Star*. Had she been right to be angry? Had it put her in danger? Had *he* put her in danger?

Christ! He'd never forgive himself if he had. "Hurry up."

When they finally pulled into his driveway, he got out and punched in the gate code himself rather than give it to the driver. He tipped the driver, tossed the bag of Mustangs gear he'd been given on the porch, and ran around the side of the house.

Julie's place was lit up like a circus. The sight of an ambulance amid about a dozen police cars and several fire trucks nearly brought him to his knees, but the need to know if she was okay gave him the strength he needed to cross the yard and hop the fence. He was halfway to the ambulance when two men in tactical gear, rifles raised, stopped him in his tracks.

"Whoa! Whoa!" he said, raising his arms. "I'm Colin Parker. I live next door. Is Julie okay?"

Another man approached, and while the other two held him at gunpoint, this one searched him. After examining the ID in his wallet, the man asked, "Where were you today?"

"I was in Dallas at the Mustangs game."

"Someone can vouch for you?"

"About forty-thousand in the stands and probably millions who watched on TV. I sang the national anthem."

The new arrival signaled for the other two to point their weapons somewhere else. Colin breathed a sigh of relief as they followed orders. The officer handed him his wallet, and Colin slid it into his pocket. "What's going on? Is Julie okay?"

"She's fine. Can't say as much for the brewery, though. Ms. Davis is over there." The man pointed toward the brewery where Julie stood wrapped in a blanket, watching as uniformed police did whatever the hell they did, and firemen trekked in and out of the door. A tall man in a suit stood next to her. "She could use a friend about now."

He didn't know if he qualified as a friend, but he kept the thought to himself. "Is it okay if I go over there?"

"Be my guest." He stood aside, clearing the way.

Swallowing hard, Colin crossed the yard. Red and blue lights flashed across her pale skin. She looked lost and vulnerable wrapped in a blanket while the air around her was typical Texas late summer—hot and humid. Not wanting to spook her, he angled his approach, hoping she would see him in her peripheral vision. His strategy worked. As he grew closer, she turned her head. Her first expression was alarm but then quickly changed to relief as she recognized him. Fast on its heels was the same hard mask she'd worn when she told him to get lost.

"Julie," he said. When she ignored his arms opened to her and trained her gaze on the commotion taking place, he dropped his hands to his sides. "What the hell happened?"

"Nothing for you to worry about," she said.

He let his gaze sweep the chaos in her yard. "Sure looks like nothing to me."

The big man next to her spoke. "You must be her neighbor — Parker, isn't it?"

"Colin Parker. And you are?"

"Special Agent Garret Wilkins, FBI."

"FBI? What the hell? What's going on?" He turned to his neighbor. "Julie? Why is the FBI involved?"

"It's none of your business, Colin."

"Seriously? My next-door neighbor's house and business were vandalized and the place is crawling with Federal Agents and it's none of my business?"

Still refusing to look at him, Julie pressed her lips in a hard line. Colin turned to Wilkins. "Maybe you can tell me what's going on since Ms. Davis seems to think an army of law enforcement, including the FBI in her yard, is none of my business."

"Someone broke into Ms. Davis's house and the brewery this afternoon. They caused quite a bit of damage. I understand you were out of town today."

"Dallas. I just got home. There were supposed to be people working on my house today. They would have been here until about five."

Wilkins nodded. "I've got people chasing them down now."

"You don't think one of them —"

"We just want to speak with them. Make sure they are who they say they are. Maybe one of them saw something."

"Then you haven't caught the people who did this?"

"No, but we will."

Colin trained his gaze on Julie who hadn't contributed a thing to the conversation. A thought occurred to him, and his heart sank to his toes. "Bud. Where's Bud?"

"He was running loose when Ms. Davis came home," Wilkins

said. "She put him in her car. After we cleared the house, we put him inside."

"Thank goodness. He's a good dog."

"Not much of a watch dog," Wilkins said.

Colin agreed. "No, he's not a watch dog." Just then, a firefighter wearing a captain's hat approached.

"Ma'am. We weren't able to stop the evacuation from the vats. Someone took an axe to them. Looks like a total loss."

Julie nodded her understanding. "Thank you for trying."

"Our pleasure, ma'am. We hope you're up and running again soon. We're all big fans of your beer."

"That's nice of you to say, but I don't know—"

"If you need help cleaning up, whatever, give me a call. The name's Singleton. We'd be happy to help."

A single tear tracked down her cheek. Julie wiped it away with her fingers. "Thank you. Your support means a lot."

"No problem. It's time for us to get out of your hair." With a tip of his hard hat, Captain Singleton turned and walked away and began issuing orders to his men.

Slowly, the fire trucks left. Then, one by one, the police cruisers followed until it was just a handful of FBI forensics people and the three of them standing in the yard. "Do you have someplace you can stay tonight?" Wilkins asked.

Julie shook her head. "No place I could take Bud. I'll be okay here."

Colin couldn't believe his ears. "What the hell? You are not staying here tonight." He looked at the FBI agent. "She can stay with me."

For the first time since she'd seen him walking across the yard, she looked right at him. "No."

He tried to rein in his temper. She was being ridiculous. "I only have one bedroom and one bathroom. They're yours tonight. I'll get my cot out of the shed and sleep on it. Bud is welcome, too." He looked at Wilkins. "I don't have much else in the house yet, but the alarm system has been installed."

"Mind if I check it out first?"

"Not at all." He dug out his keys and his phone. "I can disarm the alarm from here." He found the app on his phone, and the outside lights came on at his house. "Good to go. Is it okay if I take Julie in her house to get a few things for her and Bud?"

"Yeah. Tell the agent inside I said it was okay." Wilkins looked at Julie. "You can't stay in your house tonight. This sounds like a good alternative for you and the dog until we catch this guy."

"I'd rather get a hotel room."

"A hotel isn't a good idea. We don't know where…this person is. There aren't many places to stay around here."

Julie nodded as the truth sunk in. "Okay." She glanced at Colin. "Let's go."

CHAPTER TWENTY-FOUR

She might as well have sat out under a tree all night for all the sleep she got in Colin's bed. He'd insisted on changing the sheets, but his scent remained to tease her with things she wanted but couldn't have. Seeing his things in the one bathroom they had to share didn't help. Neither did knowing he slept on the other side of the wall.

Then there were the creaks and moans the old house made. Hers made them, too, but she had grown used to those. Last night, sheer exhaustion had made her drift off to sleep over and over again, only to be awakened by the sound of the house settling. Rationally, she knew what the sounds were, but she lay awake listening anyway, just like she had for months after that rat bastard had kidnapped her.

To say she was dragging this morning was an understatement. On any other weekday, she'd have been up for hours. Other than Bud, who Colin assured he would take care of, she had nothing to get up for today. Her brewery was gone. Destroyed by a lunatic with a grudge. Agent Wilkins had told her not to set foot outside alone until she heard from him. She checked her phone for missed calls or messages. Nothing.

Julie dragged herself out of bed and to the bathroom. After showering and dressing, she went downstairs. The house was quiet today — not a construction worker in sight. That, she knew was her fault, too. They'd probably been told to stay away until the FBI cleared them.

Had her worst nightmare been here all along? Working on Colin's house? The idea made her insides turn to ice.

She found Colin in the kitchen, sitting at a table made from an old door propped up on sawhorses. The scent of fresh coffee hung in the air. Bud's food and water bowls occupied a spot under the window where she assumed Colin's new sink would eventually be. She consciously avoided the window since she knew it overlooked her yard.

"Morning," she said, eyeing the carafe of dark liquid. "Where's Bud?"

"He's sleeping on the front porch. Help yourself." Colin motioned to a stack of Styrofoam cups next to the coffee maker. "My dishes are somewhere — Arkansas, I think, along with everything else I own."

He wasn't in the best of moods this morning, understandable. Her cloud of doom had cast a shadow on his life, too. She poured herself a cup of coffee and joined him on the only other stool in the room. She blew on the hot liquid then took a sip. "Moving truck get lost?"

"Hell if I know. Maybe they're taking the scenic route."

She half smiled at his attempt at levity. "I owe you an explanation."

"I take it this has something to do with the photo in the *National Star*?"

"Yes, but it's not your fault. I blamed you, but it was only a matter of time before he found me. Who knows if he saw the photo or not? Crazy people are resourceful."

"Christ, Julie, what are you tangled up in? The freakin' FBI is involved!"

She straightened her spine. "I'm not a criminal."

"What, then? An informant? A witness?"

She shook her head. "Those would fall under the U.S. Marshall's Service. I'm a victim. Agent Wilkins is in charge of my case. My *unsolved* case."

"Fuck, Julie." Colin ran both hands through his hair. "I'm sorry."

She sipped at her cooling coffee before continuing. "Do you remember a couple of years ago—there was a huge lottery jackpot? One person won over a billion dollars?"

"Yeah. It made the national news. There was a follow-up story a few months later when the jackpot was claimed by a corporation."

"Lucky Lady, Incorporated."

"Jesus! That was you?"

Julie nodded.

Colin's brows knit together. "What was last night all about? Is someone trying to get your money?"

"Not anymore. Now, he's just trying to kill me."

CHAPTER TWENTY-FIVE

"So," she wrapped up her story, "I legally changed my name, incorporated as Lucky Lady, and moved to Butte Plains. Scruggs never mentioned my mom so I don't think he knew I lived with her. But, to be on the safe side, the corporation bought a condo for her in Houston and I moved here, to Butte Plains. It's been three years. I've become complacent. Put myself out there too much. I don't know how he found me. Maybe it was the photo in the *National Star*. Maybe it was something else."

Colin stood and paced the empty room. "I don't know what to say, Julie." He stopped and looked at her. "Julie isn't your real name."

"It's my legal name. Mom still calls me Jennifer. I don't think she'll ever get used to the new name."

"Jennifer," Colin tried it out. "Would you rather I called you by your real name?"

"No. Too many people knew Jen Harris won the lottery and want a piece of it. The mentality seems to be that I didn't do anything to earn it; therefore, everyone I've ever said hello to in my life is entitled to some of it. I'm sure Ford and Scott have met the same kind of people, but they earned their money." She shrugged. "It's different. So, I'll stick with Julie Davis from now on. Only a handful of people know she's rich."

"So, you're what, a billionaire?"

"I wasn't at first. By the time Uncle Sam got his share, the payout was well under a billion. Thanks to some really good investments, I'm worth over a billion now."

Colin whistled low. "I never would have guessed. You don't act like you have a lot of money."

"Thanks. I try not to. After a few initial purchases — a condo for Mom in a retirement community and the land and brewing equipment — I've hardly touched it for myself. Most of the principle is tied up in investments — stocks, real estate and such. I give myself a living allowance out of the interest then the rest gets rolled over into the investment accounts. And, I give a lot to charity. The new gazebo in town square? That was me. The improvements to the youth facility? Me. I could go on. The list is long. After what happened to Roseanne, I'm thinking about making a donation to the hospital. The maternity wing, to be specific."

He stared. He couldn't help it. She looked like the girl next door, but she wasn't the same person he'd thought she was. "Your charity is admirable," he said for lack of something else to say. He gave to charity, too, but he'd never be able to match what she could do.

"I'm sorry my shit fell on you. If it's any consolation, I'll sell you my property for a reasonable price."

"What? Why would you do that?"

"I can't stay here, Colin."

"Why the hell not? They're going to get the asshole who did this, and when they do, things will return to normal. You can rebuild the brewery. You have friends here."

She shook her head. "You aren't listening. Even if he's caught, nothing will be the same for me. There's something about won money. It makes people crazy. It's as if it's found money, like picking up a twenty-dollar bill on the sidewalk. You were fine before you found it, so you'll be fine when it's gone. All you're going to do is spend it on something frivolous anyway, right? Might as well give some of it to insert name here."

"I don't think that way, and neither does my sister or her husband. And you can't think Roseanne or Scott would care if you have a dime to your name."

"You're missing the point. I feel like there's a target on my back. Sometimes, like right now, I wish I'd never won it. You know what the irony of this whole situation is?"

"No. What?"

"If that bastard only knew how much trouble gobs of money is, he wouldn't have been so eager to get it. It's a hell of a lot of work. Even with an investment broker I trust, there are reports to read and decipher, decisions to be made—constantly." She sighed. "I used to dream about what I'd do if I never had to worry about money again, and here I am, worrying about money all the time. I'm diversified enough, so the failure of one investment won't break me, but that's no reason to be complacent. Maybe I should give it all away—to charity I mean. Life sure would be simpler."

"I sort of understand. I don't have the kind of money you do, but I'm doing okay for myself these days. But along with the money came fame. Like you, I dreamed of what it would be like to reach my goal, now I spend most of my time trying to stay on top. I won't. Fame isn't like money. You can't bank it or invest it for a rainy day. All I can do is hope there are more days of sunshine than there are rainy ones. And keep doing what I do until the rain sets in for good."

"I never wanted fame. Still don't want it."

"What *do* you want?"

"I don't know anymore."

"Meaning you knew once?"

"Yeah." She glanced out the window at her home. "I'd lived my entire life in a ratty apartment building in a questionable part of town. I wanted my own place out in the country. And I wanted to own my own business. Be my own boss for a change."

"You have those things, Julie."

"Had. But even before last night, I'd decided it wasn't enough." She turned to him, her eyes filled with sadness. "I won the lottery, but I lost all my friends in the process. After the kidnapping, they all knew about the money. Couldn't keep it a secret any longer. Things became awkward. It's the best way I know to describe what had been normal relationships up until then. People who never had a problem talking to me before didn't know what to say, how to act around me. I was the same person they'd known forever, but the money made me different somehow. Suddenly, I was alone, except for the people who wanted something from me—a donation to their favorite charity or foundation. They had no interest in me. If I didn't have money, they never would have spoken to me. And when I told them no, they went away. Then I was really alone.

"I told myself it was okay. I was better off alone. I picked up Bud from a rescue group. He's been my constant and only companion for three years. Bud was enough for a while. Then I met Roseanne and Becky. And you. And I began to think maybe I could have a real life here, with friends and maybe more."

"The kiss," he guessed. "I was a nobody last year. A wannabe country singer."

"You were safe," she confirmed. "Then you came home and you were on top of the world. A celebrity with a huge following and a contingent of paparazzi."

"You should have told me you were hiding out. I would have understood."

"And done what? Locked me away in an ivory tower? I don't want to live like that."

"Do you hear what you're saying? You don't want to live the life of a recluse, but you're afraid to go public. You can't have both. There's got to be a compromise, Julie. Look at Ford and Becky. Or Scott and Roseanne. They've all got scads of money and *they* aren't hiding from life."

"I'm so confused."

"Well, take your time. You're welcome to stay here as long as you want."

"I-I can't—"

"Why the hell not?"

"The forensic team will be out of my house by now. I'll turn on the alarm. I'll be fine."

The idea of her alone in the house while that crazy person was still out there somewhere was wrong. "I'm not letting you stay over there by yourself."

"I'm not staying here."

"Then I'm going with you." Before she could protest, he continued, "I'll stay in your guest room."

Her cell phone rang. She picked it up from the makeshift table and glanced at the caller ID. "It's Agent Wilkins. I have to take this."

Colin nodded then his cell phone chimed. Yanking it from his pocket, he walked into the adjacent room to take the call from Randy Tucker. "Hey. What's up?"

"Sorry about the delay today, but there's good news."

"I could use some about now."

Randy laughed. "I bet you could. Everything quiet next door?" When the restoration expert had called earlier to find out why the FBI wanted to interview him and all the people he had working on Colin's house, Colin had told him about the vandalism next door.

"Looks like everyone finished up and left."

"I'm glad to hear it. Most of my crew has been cleared to return to work today. If it's okay with you, of course."

Colin's gaze swept the unfinished front parlor. "The sooner this place is finished, the better."

"Getting antsy?"

"You could say that."

"Thanks for being patient with me and the crew. We should

wrap things up in about two weeks. Maybe less. Oh! And be on the lookout for your kitchen cabinets. They're supposed to be delivered today."

"You mean I'm going to have a kitchen soon?"

"End of the week. Promise."

"Sounds good." He didn't cook much, but he was tired of eating takeout and keeping beer and lunchmeat in a cooler.

Colin ambled back to the kitchen where he found Julie standing at the window, coffee cup in hand. "That was Randy. His crew checked out. They're all who they claimed to be."

"I'm glad." She turned and leaned against the wall so she faced him. "Agent Wilkins told me things should return to normal on your side of the fence today."

"I don't think anything has been normal over here since I bought the place, but yeah, I know what he means." Colin found his abandoned coffee cup and topped it off with the last bit in the carafe. "I know it's chaos here, but you really shouldn't be alone until they catch this guy."

"That's what Agent Wilkins said, too." She smiled and shook her head. "Let me clarify. He didn't say your place was chaotic. He thought I shouldn't be alone."

"Did he offer any solutions?"

"He suggested I stay here for a while."

"And you said…?"

"I would glue myself to you for a couple more days, but no more. If they haven't found him by then, I'm going back to my house."

Colin brought the Styrofoam cup to his lips and sipped the hot brew in order to hide his smile. *Thank you, Agent Wilkins.* "I was thinking you might be able to help me some while you're here."

"How?" She held her hands up, palms out. "I don't do construction. End of discussion."

He let her see his smile this time. "I had something else in mind." His gaze swept the room. "My kitchen cabinets are supposed to arrive today. I need appliances. Randy picked out some options for me to choose from, but I haven't had time to go look at them. Would you mind helping me decide?"

She caught her bottom lip with her teeth.

"I won't let you out of my sight. I promise. We'll go straight to the appliance store and come straight home."

"I guess it would be okay. But later, I need to do some work of my own. Do you have Internet access?"

"Yep. I've got Wi-Fi, too. My mom said I could have my dad's old desk. If you're up to it, we can swing by and pick it up on our way home. Then you'll have plenty of space to work."

"Okay, but we need to be careful. Agent Wilkins said he could be anywhere, watching for me."

"I doubt he'll expect you to show up at my mom's house or an appliance store today. But we won't take unnecessary chances. You can wear my cowboy hat and sunglasses. I'll even borrow one of the construction guys' trucks. Can't get much more incognito than that."

CHAPTER TWENTY-SIX

Colin's hat was at least a size too big for her head, but after she'd caught her hair up in a bandana and stuffed it underneath the crown, it stayed in place. Wearing his aviator-style sunglasses and one of his plaid shirts she'd knotted at her waist, she would be difficult for anyone to identify through the tinted glass on the truck they'd borrowed. Still, her heart raced as they drove through the gate and onto the main road.

"Not a soul in sight," Colin said as he navigated the two-lane winding road toward town.

"That's good, I guess."

"All the law enforcement responding last night might have chased him off."

"Maybe, but I don't think he's done. When he ran last time, he expected me to be dead before anyone found me. I don't think he's going to stop until I am dead." She curled her hands into tight fists as the reality of the danger she was in gripped her.

"Or until he's caught." Colin reached across the seat, covering her hand with his. He pried her fingers loose then gave them a squeeze. "He made a mistake coming here. The people of Butte Plains don't put up with people like him."

"He's nuts, Colin. I don't want anyone here to get tangled up with him."

He gave her hand another reassuring squeeze. "Even me?"

She caught herself before the words, *especially not you*, sprung from her mouth. He'd already said he loved her. Letting him think she returned the sentiment, which she did, would only make it worse for both of them when she left. She forced indignation into her voice and said, "Not even you, Colin."

"Well, that's reassuring. For a second there, I thought you didn't care if I lived or died."

"Please. Can we talk about something else?"

"Like what?" He glanced her way. Unable to meet his gaze without breaking down and telling him the truth—she'd give herself up to the maniac trying to kill her if it meant saving his life—she turned and looked out the passenger side window.

"I don't know. Tell me about your new kitchen. How can I help you pick out appliances if I don't know what style the cabinets will be?"

Colin made a turn and headed toward the freeway where most of the warehouse-type stores had sprung up. They drove for a while in silence then he began to tell her about his kitchen. Staring out the window, she caught a few words. *Country. Farmhouse sink. Copper.*

What was she doing? She should rent a car and get as far away from Butte Plains as possible. Staying here, traipsing around town, even in disguise, was putting herself and Colin in danger. Damn. Why had she ever let her guard down in the first place? *Because I felt safe here.* Her new identity had given her a false sense of security. Allowed her to make friends. To get close to people. Too close.

Colin poked her in the arm. "Julie?"

"What?"

"I didn't think you heard me. I asked you what you thought about the copper accents Randy plans to put in the kitchen."

"Oh." Damn. She'd been so lost in her own thoughts she'd missed most of what he'd said. She had two choices. Admit she hadn't been listening, or answer and hope she didn't sound like an idiot. "Well, I like copper accents, so you're probably asking the wrong person."

Colin nodded, seemingly satisfied with her response. "Okay, then. I thought it sounded kinda weird, but if you don't see a problem, I won't say anything."

A few minutes later, she pointed to a nondescript warehouse ahead on the right. "There it is."

Colin steered the truck into the parking lot. "Doesn't look like much." He put the truck in Park and cut off the engine.

"I came here to buy the coolers for the tasting room." Julie opened her own door and hopped out. "Come on. You won't believe this place."

An hour later, they returned to the truck with a receipt for their purchase. "Thanks for coming along." Colin braked and looked both ways before exiting the parking lot. "I probably would have just tossed a coin if you hadn't been here to help me decide."

Julie smiled. "No thanks necessary. You were right. I needed to get out and do something."

"You up for one more stop?"

"Actually, I was thinking maybe you could drop me off at the tasting room while you go to your mom's. I doubt I'd be much help loading furniture anyway."

Colin gave her a sideways look. "I can load the desk myself, but are you sure you want to risk going there?"

"I need to talk to my staff sometime, and the sooner the better, I suppose. If I *were* to rebuild the brewery, which isn't to say I *will* rebuild, it would take months to return to full capacity. I don't see how I can keep the tasting room open. We'll run out of stock long before I can replace what's there."

"Can't this wait until they've caught this guy? He went after the brewery. He might go after the tasting room next."

"All the more reason for me to shut it down now before

someone gets hurt."

"You can't tell them over the phone?"

"No. I can't. I hired these people. I need to tell them in person, and they all should be there in the next few minutes to prepare to open for the day. And you've seen the kind of security the place has. There are cameras everywhere. Inside and out."

"Cameras aren't considered protection."

"No, but door locks are. I'll stay in the office where I can monitor all the video feeds while I talk to everyone. If I see anything at all unusual, I'll call 9-1-1."

"You're sure you'll be safe? You won't leave the storage room?"

"Promise."

"Okay, then. I'll drop you off, but I won't be gone long."

"I don't need much time. I just need to speak to them in person. Rip the Band-Aid off."

"I'm sorry you're having to do this."

"Me, too. But I don't have a choice."

Colin insisted on going in with her. As she'd predicted, her manager was already there, preparing to open for the day. Julie made the introductions. "Avery Mitchell, Colin Parker."

"Nice to see you again," Colin said, extending his hand. "As you can see, I found her."

Avery laughed as she shook hands with the country star. "Indeed you did. It's nice to officially make your acquaintance. I can't believe I didn't recognize you. I'm a big fan."

Wasn't everybody, Julie wondered as Colin posed for a selfie with her manager? The man couldn't go anywhere without someone asking for a photo or an autograph. He'd spent most of his time at the appliance store, smiling for cameras while she looked over his choices and made a decision. He was going to have one very nice kitchen. If hers wasn't almost as nice, she'd be jealous.

"Thanks for the selfie." Avery blushed like a schoolgirl.

"My pleasure," Colin said, sounding like he actually meant it. Julie walked him to the door.

"How do you do it?" she asked.

"What?"

"You know. Smile and act like it's no big deal to interrupt your day for a picture."

Colin put his hands on her waist and pulled her in close. It seemed like forever since she'd felt his hands on her, and damn, it felt good. "It's easy. It *is* a big deal. Without fans, my career is nothing but a hobby, and hobbies, by definition, don't pay. It's people like Avery who make it possible for me to have a kick-ass kitchen and other creature comforts I've come to enjoy. Smiling for a couple of pictures is small thanks for what they give me."

"Well, you made Avery's day. Maybe her whole week."

"What about you? I'd like to make your day, too."

"You already have."

His brows knit. "How so?"

"You got me out of the house, out of my funk. Just being here and seeing what I've built makes me want to rebuild the brew house."

"Hearing you say that makes *my* day." He touched his forehead to hers. "I hoped you'd come around. Butte Plains needs you. I need you."

"Do you really?"

"I really, really do." The low timbre of his voice danced over and through her like a static electric charge, putting every cell in her body on alert. "And once this is all over, I'm going to do whatever it takes to make you see you need me, too."

Aware Avery could probably hear, if not see them, she simply nodded to acknowledge his words.

"I've got to go. I'm going to swing by and grab Ford out of the office to help me load Dad's desk. Then I'll come get you. Can you do what you need to do in say, an hour?"

"That should be plenty of time."

He kissed her on the tip of her nose before letting his hands drop from her waist. "I hate leaving you here, but the sooner I get going, the sooner I'll be back."

"I'll be fine. And I'm not alone, so don't worry about me."

CHAPTER TWENTY-SEVEN

Julie locked the door behind Colin, set the alarm then leaned against the door for support. If they found the creep who was trying to kill her, she had no doubt it wouldn't take much on Colin's part to convince her to give a relationship with him a chance. But if the guy disappeared again like he'd done before, it might be years before he resurfaced. In the meantime, staying here put everyone around her in danger. She couldn't let that happen. She'd done nothing but think about her options since they'd left Colin's house. Being her own boss at Lucky Lady Brewing Company had been fun, but she could hire someone to run the brew house just as she'd hired Avery to run the tasting room. She had the means to hire middle management people to bridge the gap between her and her employees. Avery and the others she employed would keep their jobs. Heck, she'd probably need at least two people, maybe three to do everything she did at the brew house.

Where would I go? The idea of leaving Texas was a nonstarter. Houston was out. Her mother lived in Austin. Maybe she could find a place in East Texas. They'd visited an old friend of her mother's in Athens once. It had seemed like a nice place to a ten-year-old at the time.

"Are you okay?"

Avery's concerned voice snapped Julie out of her musings. She pushed away from the door and rolled her stiff shoulders. "I'm fine. Just needed a couple of minutes to get my head on straight."

"Lord, don't I know what you mean?" Avery said with a grin. "Colin Parker is one fine-looking man." Her grin disappeared. She crossed her arms and glared at Julie. "Girlfriend. Why didn't you tell me who he was when he came looking for you?"

"I was surprised you and everyone else in the place hadn't figured it out by then. He wasn't wearing much of a disguise."

"Speaking of disguises—what the heck are you wearing?" Avery hadn't heard about the incident last night or she would have said something. It had been late, but with social media being what it was these days, she couldn't believe the destruction of Lucky Lady Brewing Company's brew house hadn't blown up the Internet.

She pinched at the flannel plaid and knit her brows. "What? This? Haven't you heard flannel is the new silk?"

"Nope. What gives, boss lady?"

Julie sighed. "Let's have a seat in the office and I'll tell you." She waved Avery into the seat in front of the video monitors and took the only other chair in the small space. From her vantage point, she could talk to her manager and see all the video feeds at the same time. She didn't expect Marty Scruggs to show up—he had a history of running when law enforcement got too close—but she wasn't going to take any chances.

"There was an incident at the brew house last night. Someone broke in and destroyed the place. As a precaution, I'm shutting down the tasting room for a few days."

"Wait! What? Run that by me again. Someone destroyed the brew house? Were you there? Are you okay?" Her gaze swept Julie from head to toe then locked on her eyes. "How did I not know this?"

"I'm fine. I wasn't home at the time." She went on, describing her day from the time she'd left to have tea with Becky and Roseanne, to finding her pregnant friend passed out and the hasty trip to the hospital. It seemed like it had been days since she'd paced the ER waiting for news about Roseanne's condition, but it had been less than twenty-four hours. Avery's mouth hung open as Julie related the story of coming home to find Bud running loose and the frantic call she'd made.

"Why'd you call the FBI? Why not just call 9-1-1?"

"That's another story."

"I've got nothing but time." Avery sat back, arms crossed.

Julie filled her in on the sordid story. At this rate, everyone in Butte Plains was going to know who she was before the last jelly donut was sold at Hanson's Bakery. Her cover had been blown all to smithereens.

"So…you're a billionaire." It wasn't a question.

Julie shrugged. She could almost see the wheels turning behind Avery's startled expression.

"Wow." Avery shook her head. "So, you're just going to close up shop and let this asshole get away with this?"

Julie blinked. "What choice do I have? Opening up today or anytime in the near future puts you and everyone who works here in danger. Not to mention our customers."

"Well, bless your heart." Avery patted Julie on the knee. "It's so sweet of you to be concerned, but that's not how we roll in Butte Plains." She stood, squaring her shoulders and sticking her chin in the air. "Do you have a photo of the lowlife who's after you?"

"Um. Yeah, I can get one." Though she'd be happy if she never saw his face again. She scrambled to process what Avery had said. Giving up, she asked, "What do you mean that's not how you roll?" She had a bad feeling about this. A real bad feeling.

"I mean, let the asshole bring it on!" She pulled her cell phone from the pocket of her jeans. "Excuse me," she said, brushing past

Julie to get to the door. "I've got to make a few phone calls." She turned and called over her shoulder. "Find his photo for me."

Oookaaay. Avery disappeared into the front room, phone pressed to her ear. Julie didn't know why, but she followed the other woman's order and soon sent a copy of Marty Scruggs' Wanted poster to the office printer. The ink wasn't dry on the black-and-white printout when a knock sounded on the door.

"I'll get it." Avery sailed in, heading for the door. "You got the photo I asked for, hon?"

"Yes." Julie stared at the face of the man she'd half expected to see everywhere she went since the day he'd left her to die in an abandoned warehouse.

"Good girl!" Avery opened the door to admit half-a-dozen people. In half an hour, what Avery called, The Butte Plains Cavalry, filled the room. Tables were set up and blocks of time spoken for. Copies of the Wanted poster were made and distributed to the hodge-podge group of citizens.

"We're real sorry to hear about your troubles, Ms. Davis," the portly gentleman wearing a three-piece suit said with a smile. "But don't you worry about a thing. You're one of us now. We won't let anything happen to your tasting room."

Julie muttered a thank you as the man wandered off to help the organizational efforts. Avery elbowed her in the side. "See? We're good. That was Harvey Thornberry. He owns the dry cleaners and the laundromat."

Which explained the perfect creases in his slacks. "And the others?"

"Locals." She pointed out a couple of other business owners and a few housewives.

"Friends of yours?"

"Yep. Your friends, too." She'd never seen such an outpouring of support in her life, and it touched her beyond belief. These people answered the call to help a fellow citizen even though they'd never met her. A lump formed in her throat, and she felt the hot burn of tears massing for an assault on her equilibrium. This was exactly the type of community she'd hoped to find in Butte Plains, and her past had shown it to her and taken it away all in the same day.

Life didn't play fair. At least, it hadn't with her.

At the sound of the door opening again, Julie's heart dropped to her toes then rebounded when she recognized Duncan McKenna, owner of McKenna's Liquor. She'd been doing business with him since she'd bottled the first batch of Lucky Lady beer. He'd been one of the first people in town she called friend.

"Julie." He took her in a big bear hug. "Are you okay? I heard what happened at your place last night. Awful. Just awful."

"I'm fine, Mr. McKenna. Thanks for asking."

"The sooner we get this guy off the streets, the sooner you can get Lucky Lady up and running again. My sales have gone through the roof since I started carrying your beer."

She couldn't help but smile at his statement. "I'm glad to hear that." She didn't want to make promises she couldn't keep, but she hated to disappoint the man, too. "I'll do my best to get the brewery back on schedule as soon as possible." And she would, even if it meant hiring someone to run the place for her.

"It's all I can ask." He gave her hand a little squeeze. "Now, if you'll excuse me, I need to see what my assigned time is. Don't worry. If this guy comes around, we'll be ready for him."

She didn't doubt it for a minute. But would Marty Scruggs be stupid enough to make an appearance? He had to know there were FBI agents all over the place looking for him. Not to mention local cops and, now, the Butte Plains Cavalry. He'd have to be really stupid to show his face around town.

The door opened again and in walked Colin Parker. Heads turned. Conversations stopped as everyone gawked at the country star. A heartbeat later, everyone turned back to what they were doing, and the noise level went up again. Colin's gaze found her, and, without preamble, he crossed the room and took her in his arms. "What's going on? Is this the Cavalry?"

"You know about this?"

"Heck, yeah. Everyone in town knows about the Cavalry. I can't believe I didn't think of calling them myself." He shook his head. "I'm an idiot."

"No, you're not."

"I should have thought of this. Who did, by the way?"

"Avery."

"Smart girl."

"I don't know. Is this legal?"

"More or less. We've always had a small police department. The Cavalry has been around for as long as I can remember. They help out with parades and stuff. Rumor has it they used to carry guns. A few of them still do, but only the ones who are volunteer sheriff's deputies. Back in the day, they provided security for a couple of president's who came to town to campaign."

Her gaze swept the assembled group. Julie wondered which ones might be armed. She focused in on one very old lady carrying a purse that looked like it weighed a ton and was big enough to hide a cannon. Lord help her. She forced her gaze away from the pistol-packin' grandma and focused on the conversation. "I can't imagine anyone coming here to campaign, much less a presidential candidate."

Colin raised his eyebrows. "This was a hoppin' place years ago when cotton was king."

"I feel like I'm putting these people in danger." God, she couldn't live with herself if someone got hurt because of her.

"Don't worry. They're well trained. They all go through a training class at the police department once a year. They take their mission seriously."

She could see the truth in Avery's statement. They were a surprisingly well-organized bunch. For the foreseeable future, there would be a small contingent of Cavalry members inside the tasting room during operating hours and more patrolling the surrounding area the rest of the time. She had lost count of how many people had told her not to worry about a thing. "We take care of our own," seemed to be their motto.

"Are you ready to go? I need to get this pickup back to its owner."

"Since this is beyond my control…let me speak to Avery then I'm good to go."

~ ~ ~

It had taken the better part of an hour to get Julie out the door. Everyone wanted to wish her well and assure her the tasting room was in good hands. Alone at last, Colin asked, "Heard anything from Agent Wilkins?"

"Nothing." The hat he'd loaned her hid most of her expression, but the defeated tone of her voice told him plenty.

"I'm sure they're busy…doing whatever it is they do."

"I know. Agent Wilkins is a good person. He won't stop until he's turned over every rock."

"Have you decided what you're going to do?"

"Yeah. I think."

God, was he going to have to drag it out of her one word at a time? "Care to share with me?"

The brim of the hat caught on the seat, holding the hat in place when she turned her head to look at him. He couldn't help but laugh at the hat sitting crooked on her head. "Ugh!" She yanked the offending Stetson off and settled it in her lap. "This thing is driving me nuts!"

"It makes you look like a kid playing dress-up."

"I'm not a kid, and I'm tired of playing dress-up." She plucked at the old shirt he'd loaned her. "I'm also tired of hiding."

Colin's ears perked up. "What does that mean, exactly?"

"It means, I'm going to sleep in my own house tonight. And tomorrow, I'm going to order new equipment for the brew house."

He hardly dared, but he had to ask. "So…you're staying?"

"For now. One of the Cavalry guys gave me the name of a private security firm. I'm going to call them, see if they can set up patrols around my property and recommend additional security measures I can take. Even if I decide to move, I'd hire someone to run the brewery. After what happened here last night, I couldn't expect an employee to live here without providing the best security possible."

Colin clamped his jaw so tight he wouldn't be surprised if he needed dental work on his molars. She couldn't seriously be thinking about moving. About leaving. He worked his jaw loose and tried to turn the steering wheel to dust with his bare hands instead. "Extra security sounds good." It was the best he could do and not have to apologize later.

"I'll try my best to see they don't impose on your lifestyle." She gave a little laugh and turned to look out the window on her side. "You might want to rethink the fence we talked about."

"Why? Are you trying to tell me something, Julie?" He flexed his numb fingers before wrapping them around the wheel again. "If you are, then just spit it out. I'm a grown man. I can take it." *I think.*

Her next words were spoken deliberately. As if he couldn't catch them all if she delivered them normally. "I'm saying, a wall between our properties would provide you with the privacy you insisted on having."

There had to be something wrong with her hearing. He'd told her he loved her. Not two hours ago, he'd held her in his arms and confessed how much he needed her. "I also said I didn't want a wall. Or a damn privacy fence between us." He enunciated the next words as clearly as he could, considering his jaw hurt like hell from clenching his teeth. "I don't want anything—N.E. thing—between us."

He felt her gaze boring a hole in the side of his head, but he refused to look her way. Refused to apologize for his feelings. He loved her, dammit. What part of *I love you* did she not understand?

"I'm sorry, Colin."

The pain evident behind those three simple words cut through his anger and straight into his heart. *Fuck.* He was being an ass. "What do you have to be sorry about?"

She shrugged. "I don't know. Everything, I guess."

"Everything?" He couldn't believe his ears. Was she lumping him and what they'd shared into her blanket statement? "Even the time we spent together?"

Heat bloomed across her cheeks, and she turned her gaze to her hands clasped tight in her lap. "None of this would have happened if I hadn't let you spend the night."

Christ almighty! "And you're sorry I spent the night?" He peeled one hand off the steering wheel and ran his fingers through his hair in an effort to keep the top of his head from blowing off. "Jesus, Julie. You can be sorry about a lot of things, but not the things we did together. Never that."

When she didn't respond, he silently chastised himself for being an insensitive clod, but dammit all to Hell, she'd enjoyed their lovemaking as much as he had. He pulled off the road, punched in the code to open the gate, and proceeded up his driveway. He backed the bed of the truck up to the front porch, and, before cutting the engine off, he tried one last time to reach her. "I've got a good imagination, Jules, but I didn't imagine the way you responded to me. It was more than just sex for both of us, and you know it. Yes, what happened the next morning was unfortunate, but shit happens. You either shovel it out of the way or get buried by it. You're letting it bury you, and I can't for the life of me understand why you'd rather be buried by shit than be with me."

He slammed the truck door shut with more force than necessary then took the porch steps two at a time. A couple of guys came out of the house to see what was going on, and Colin enlisted their help getting the desk moved into what had been the ladies' parlor but was now going to be his office. When he went outside to move the truck, Julie was gone.

"Well, shit."

CHAPTER TWENTY-EIGHT

Julie slammed the door hard enough to rattle the glasses in the wall cabinet ten feet away. Out of breath from sprinting across two lawns, she clutched the countertop and inhaled deeply. Lord, what a mess she'd made of everything.

She'd spent so much time the last few years lying about…well, everything, she'd apparently lost the ability to speak the truth even if it meant an end to her lonely existence.

What had she been thinking? Apologizing for loving Colin? Because that's exactly what she'd been trying to do. Only he'd seen through her lies—saw the truth eating away at her—and called "bullshit."

Tears spilled over, and she pushed away from the support of the counter. Making it as far as the kitchen table, she collapsed into a chair. Elbows on the table, she propped her aching head in her upturned palms. "Stupid. Stupid. Stupid," she chastised herself.

"I always knew you were a stupid bitch. 'Bout time you figured it out."

Like someone had jolted her with electricity, Julie stood, putting the chair between her and her worst nightmare. Time and life on the run had not been kind to Marty Scruggs. His clothes weren't much more than filthy rags, and, from the odor assaulting her nostrils, it had been some time since he'd showered. His thin hair, once dark, appeared gray beneath layers of dirt. One thing hadn't changed—his crazy-as-fuck eyes. She shivered as the beady orbs scanned over her.

"What do you want, Marty? Do you want money?" Unlike the last time she'd seen him, this time she had access to plenty of money. She'd give him every last dime she had if it meant she'd never have to see him again. "I've got money. Lots of it. It's yours. Just leave me alone."

"You think all I want from you is your money? Money that should have been mine all along?" He took a step toward her. Julie took a step back, realizing too late she'd boxed herself into a corner. There was nowhere for her to go. "You owe me, bitch."

"I-I don't owe you anything." His nostrils flared, and she knew she'd said the wrong thing. Holding one hand up like a stop sign, she said, "Money. I owe you money. Nothing more."

He took another step forward. Julie pressed herself into the corner and gripped the back of her chair. If he came close enough, could she get the chair up and use it as a weapon? She mentally took inventory of her kitchen, inwardly cursing when she realized she'd have to get past Marty to get her hands on anything else she could use as a weapon. *Dammit.* She had no one to blame for her predicament but herself. She'd left the security of Colin's side rather than face the truth.

Colin was right. Their night together had been spectacular. Denying it wouldn't make what they had together go away. Her brain immediately flashed to the day he'd stood on her steps and said he loved her. She'd let her anger and her fears overrule her heart. She should have told Colin she loved him. She should have taken a chance on a life with him. Marty Scruggs probably would have found her. He *would* have. It was clear to her now. One way or another, the beady-eyed nutcase would have found her.

"I'm going to do what I should have done when I had you tied up in that warehouse." Julie watched in horror as he reached behind him and pulled a carving knife from his belt. The light streaming in the window caught the blade, temporarily blinding her. When she raised her hand to shield her eyes, she saw he'd taken another step closer. Panic threatened to overwhelm her, but she wasn't the same person she'd been when he'd snatched her from the gas station all those years ago. Naively thinking she could reason with him, she'd made it easy for him to take her. Whatever he had in mind now, he'd find she wasn't going to meekly go along. Knife or no knife.

"Come out from there, little miss rich girl, or I'm coming in after you." He made a sweeping motion with the knife. "You're gonna take those clothes off, or I'll cut them off. Don't care if I prick you a time or two in the process. I've been dreaming of seeing you bleed for years."

She could see the truth of his statement in his eyes. He'd been content to leave her alone to die a slow death before, but she'd lived. He wouldn't make the same mistake twice. "I'll transfer the money to you. All of it. Just don't hurt me."

"I don't give a shit about the money!" Spit flew as he screamed at her. "You think this is about money, bitch? Well, it's not. It's about you living all high-and-mighty while I've been living under rocks and hiding out. If you'd given me the money then, none of this would be happening now."

"I couldn't give you the money then." She hadn't claimed the jackpot before he'd kidnapped her. She'd signed the ticket and placed it in her mother's safe deposit box while she'd consulted an attorney about the best way to protect herself and her mother once they claimed the prize. Marty had made the mistake of grabbing her on a holiday weekend when the bank had been closed. He'd told her if he couldn't have the money, then she couldn't, either. Then he'd slipped through the hands of the FBI, leaving her to die. "I can now. Let me go. I'll go to the bank and get a cashier's check. Better yet, I've got mobile banking on my phone, I'll do it from here." She whipped her phone out of her back pocket and held it up for him to see.

"I ain't stupid, girl. Rich people like you got money squirreled away everywhere. I bet you don't have enough in your checking account to buy lunch, much less set me up. That's why we're going to do this my way." He held the knife up, letting the light play off the blade. "I'm going to take what I want. What I should have taken when I had the chance. And you're going to give it to me. Right here on the kitchen floor. Hard and fast and you're going to like it, aren't you?"

She was running out of time. She could feel it in her bones. He didn't want money this time, but she'd be damned if she let him have what he did want. As she moved to return the phone to her pocket, she pressed the button on the side five times in rapid succession before slipping the device into place. *Please, God. Don't let the S.O.S. feature be a hoax.*

"Come on out of the corner, missy. Give me what you gave your rhinestone cowboy next door."

At the mention of Colin, her blood ran cold. "I'm not giving you anything."

"Saving it for the man-whore? Word is, he screwed every cunt in Nashville. You were just one more notch in his guitar."

Julie shook her head. "No." She willed her trembling legs to hold her up a little longer. "How? How did you know?"

Marty's yellow-toothed smile made her stomach turn. "Saw you. You think that reporter was the only one spying on his stupid tent."

Good God. The only way he could know she'd begged Colin to fuck her was if he'd been there. Listening outside the tent. Which meant he'd seen their half-naked sprint to her house because their only condom had been in the wallet Colin had left there. Right then and there, Julie made up her mind. If she got out of this alive, she was going to tell Colin how much she loved him, and she didn't give two figs about the paparazzi. Let them take all the pictures they wanted. It was a small price to pay to be with the man she loved.

She focused on the maniac across the room from her. Marty Scruggs might get what he wanted today—but she'd do everything in her power to see he paid dearly for everything he took.

"I ain't gonna say it again, girl. Come out of the corner and take your clothes off. He saw it all. I'm gonna see it, too."

"Come and get it, you bastard. 'Cause I'm not *giving* you anything. You want it, you gotta come and get it."

"Goddamn." He smiled as he approached. "I knew this was gonna be fun."

Julie tensed as he gripped the edge of the table with both hands and yanked it to the side, exposing her pressed into the corner, a pathetic chair in her grasp.

"Maybe your fancy cowboy will still want you when I'm through. Maybe he won't."

Doing her best to ignore the knife he brandished at her, Julie prayed for a chance to make an escape. To get to her, he had to get the chair away from her. Which meant he had to reach for it at some point. He'd expect a struggle. She'd only have one chance. A split second to react.

Wait for it.

Wait for it.

~ ~ ~

Colin checked the Caller ID on his cell phone. Signaling the cabinet delivery guys standing in his kitchen to give him a second, he pressed the receive call button and put the phone to his ear. "Agent Wilkins. What's up?"

"Where's Julie? She's supposed to be with you!"

Guiltily, he glanced out the window at the house next door. "She was, but I guess she'd had enough babysitting. She went over to her place a few minutes ago. Why?"

"Because the 9-1-1 dispatcher just got an S.O.S. from her phone."

Colin's heart stopped. Was she in danger? Had that Scruggs bastard come back? Had she walked in on a trap? If so, it was all his fault. He'd been an ass—again.

Agent Wilkins continued, "When they couldn't make contact, they called me. I'm en route, along with several locals. We need you to open her gate."

Colin nodded.

"You hear me, Parker?"

"I hear you." He was still wrapping his head around the realization he might have pushed Julie into the hands of a man who wanted her dead. She might already be harmed. How long had she been gone? Five minutes? Ten? Hell, he couldn't recall. He'd gone in to get someone to help him unload the desk and when he'd returned to the truck, she'd been gone. Before he'd moved the truck, the delivery van with his kitchen cabinets had rolled up the drive. Shit. She might not be at her house. He could have snatched her right from his yard and taken her anywhere. "I'll get the gate open. But she could be anywhere around here. I'll get my guys to start searching."

"Don't do anything stupid, Parker. This guy is dangerous. He's got nothing to lose, and he knows it. I didn't tell Julie, but he's wanted for a series of rapes across the state. After he left her for dead, he went completely off the rails. We've been one step behind him for years."

"Shit!" He grabbed one of Tucker's men by the sleeve and held on as he ended the call. "Get here, quick. I'm sending someone to open Julie's gate right now." He pocketed his phone and turned to the guy he'd waylaid. "I need you to go open the neighbor's electronic gate. The code is LUCKY. Figure out a way to keep it open. The cops are on the way."

"Cops?"

"Yeah. The guy the FBI questioned you about? He's back. They think he has Julie, and they could be somewhere on the property next door. Go out the front door and stay on the driveway until you're out of sight of both houses then cut across to Julie's driveway. Got it?"

"Yes, sir."

"And keep your eyes open," Colin called after him. "This guy is probably armed!"

The carpenter was hardly through the front door when Colin yelled for everyone else in the house to assemble in the front room. Quickly explaining what he wanted, he admonished them all to be careful as they searched his property. "The cops are on the way. Assist them any way you can."

"Where will you be?" one of the painters asked.

"Next door."

"I'll go with you." Colin's gaze went to the back of the crowd. Randy Tucker stepped forward. "Go, people. Call me if you see anything unusual, but do not engage this guy unless you have no choice."

"You don't have to come with me," Colin said.

"No, I don't. But I think you know something you aren't saying, so I'm not letting you go over there by yourself."

"I saw something in the kitchen window. Like light reflecting off a mirror or something. Julie's in the house. I'm certain of it. I just don't know if she's alone."

"Let's go find out." Tucker headed for the door, Colin on his heels.

They darted around behind several trucks to get to the old barn Colin was using to store construction supplies. Skirting around behind it, they came out some distance from Julie's house. Having been in Julie's kitchen, he knew he could approach from that angle and not be seen from the kitchen window. He pointed out the storm door. "That opens onto the porch/mudroom and laundry room. There's another door inside leading to the kitchen. If we can get onto the porch, we should be able to hear what's going on inside."

"Those old porches are notorious for squeaking floorboards,"

Tucker said.

"This one is pretty solid. The latch on the storm door might be a problem. As I recall it's pretty tight. Makes some noise when it opens."

"What about the front door?"

"Don't know. Never even seen it."

"Maybe we should give it a try first. We'd have the element of surprise on our side if we could get in that way."

"Good thinking, Tucker. If it's locked, there's always the back door."

"Let's go, then."

"Cops should be here soon," Tucker said as they made their way to Julie's front door.

"Not waiting." Colin put his hand on the old-fashioned door handle and began to press down on the thumb latch.

Tucker put a hand on Colin's wrist, stopping him. "Pull the door toward you to release the pressure on the latch."

Colin nodded his understanding. The house he'd grown up in had the same kind of latch. He'd learned the same trick to minimize the sound, practiced it hundreds of times in his teenage years. With the same patience he'd used to avoid his mother finding out he'd been out all night, he tugged the door tight against the jamb and pressed the thumb latch. It gave with the faintest of sounds. Colin inched the door open enough to see inside.

The door opened onto a small parlor, again, not unlike the house he'd grown up in, only the furniture in this one was new and appeared hardly used. He'd have to be inside to see down the hallway leading to the kitchen. "Clear."

"Careful," Tucker admonished. "Those hinges are old. Who knows when they were last oiled?"

From what he'd seen of Julie's house so far, he knew she'd put some money into it. He'd be surprised if the rarely used front door hinges had escaped her notice. He was betting everything on her having seen to the maintenance of the hinges. Julie had quickly become his everything, so, to be on the safe side, he pushed the door open a fraction of an inch at a time. When he'd created a gap big enough for a grown man to sneak through, he stopped. "I'm going in. Hallway to the kitchen is to the left, behind the door."

"Does she have hardwood floors?"

"Yeah. Why?"

"Take your shoes off. Your socks will make less noise, but you'll have less traction." He shrugged. "It's a tradeoff."

Colin ditched his shoes. Tucker did the same. "I'll be right behind you."

Colin sent up a silent prayer for the help to be on the way but, at the same time, worried the arrival of law enforcement could escalate the situation—if there was a situation inside. He hoped to God Julie was all alone in the kitchen. He could live with scaring the crap out of her as long as she was safe.

They snuck inside and, with Colin leading the way, crept down the hallway toward the kitchen. A man's voice stopped them in their tracks.

"I ain't gonna say it again, girl. Come out of the corner and take your clothes off. He saw it all. I'm gonna see it, too."

"Come and get it, you bastard. 'Cause I'm not *giving* you anything. You want it, you gotta come and get it."

That's my girl! She had to be terrified. Her voice shook, but she wasn't going to give up easily.

"Goddamn. I knew this was gonna be fun." The nasty tone of the man's voice, followed by the sound of furniture scraping on the floor, had Colin moving forward only to be stopped by Tucker's hand on his arm.

"You can't go charging in there," Tucker whispered in his ear. "You getting shot or worse won't do her any good."

"Let me go," Colin snapped as he wrenched his arm free. He dropped his head against the wall and took a deep breath. He was not going to stand by while some lowlife raped and murdered his woman, but Tucker had a point. He couldn't just rush in there. He had no idea what exactly he'd be walking into. A rash move on his part could escalate things beyond all control. He needed a distraction. It suddenly occurred to him there was another way into the kitchen. Signaling Tucker to follow him, he backtracked to the front door. He pointed to a wide staircase. Using a combination of cryptic hand motions and whispers, he laid out his plan. Tucker nodded and gave Colin a thumbs-up to indicate he understood and approved.

Tucker mouthed, "Good luck," right before he snuck out the front door. Moving as fast as he dared, Colin made his way up the stairs, cut across the wide sitting area on the second floor then crept down the rear staircase. Making it to the corner landing where the stairs turned and descended into the kitchen, he paused to listen. Relief swept over him, and his lips lifted on the corners as Julie's curses met his ears. From the sound of it, she was doing a good job of holding the guy off, but how much longer could that last? She was determined, but her options were few.

As if on cue, Tucker banged on the front door then barged into the front room. "Ms. Davis!" he called out, making his presence known.

"In here, Mr. Tucker!" Julie said, her voice quivering.

Taking advantage of the distraction, Colin cleared the final treads and burst into the kitchen. His gaze fell first on Julie. Like a circus lion tamer, she held her would-be attacker at bay with a chair from her kitchen dining set. Scruggs' attention, which had been on the opposite doorway, swung around. Suddenly, Colin was face-to-face with the knife-wielding man.

Scruggs lunged toward him.

Julie screamed, "No!"

Colin jumped back, avoiding the thrust of the blade just as Julie lifted the chair high and brought it down on the assailant's head.

Wood splintered. Blood gushed from a cut on the man's scalp.

Brandishing what was left of the chair, Julie swung again, catching the bastard in the side of the head.

Dazed, Scruggs dropped the knife and grabbed his head with both hands. Like a slow-motion scene, his eyes rolled back in his head and his knees buckled.

Tucker rushed in, nabbed Julie from behind, and pulled her out of the way. Colin swept his foot out, sending the knife out of reach just as Scruggs crumpled to the floor at their feet.

Julie's chest rose and fell with her rapid breathing. Her eyes wide, she glanced over her shoulder at Tucker then at Colin before her gaze landed on Scruggs.

The sound of sirens approaching rapidly seemed to break the spell holding them suspended in time.

Tucker released Julie's arms. "Nice shot," he said. "Remind me never to piss you off!"

Julie reacted like she'd been bitten by a diamondback rattler. Whirling on Tucker, she placed both hands on his chest and shoved. He stumbled against the table and tumbled into one of the remaining chairs. Before either man could react, she turned on Colin.

"What the hell were you two doing?"

Judging from the fury making the veins on her forehead pop out and the cute-as-hell way she was standing, legs wide, fisted hands riding on her hips, he doubted she'd appreciate the only answer that popped into his head — *saving your ass, thank you very much.* He stepped around the heap of sorry excuse for a human being lying on the floor. "What does it look like we were doing?"

"It looked like you were trying to get yourself killed!"

Damn, she was sexy when she was riled up, and she seemed to be riled up almost all the time around him. And if he had his way, he planned to keep her riled up for the next fifty years or so. But first things first. "Would it have mattered to you if I had?"

The first tear he'd seen from her since setting foot inside the kitchen spilled over her eyelid, leaving a damp trail down her cheek. Her lips quivered, and the mask of bravado that had carried her through the last few minutes fell away. Barely a whisper, she said, "You know it would have."

Colin opened his arms. She came to him, pressed her damp cheek against his chest, and wrapped her arms around his waist. Enfolding her in a tight embrace, he thanked God for making her strong and brave when she needed to be and so damn special the rest of the time. Resting his chin on the top of her head, he held her until the approaching sirens stopped and officers swarmed into her small kitchen.

CHAPTER TWENTY-NINE

The sun had set by the time Agent Wilkins wrapped up his investigation and congratulated Julie on a job well done. Through the endless hours of explaining over and over again how she'd come to clobber Scruggs over the head with a kitchen chair, Colin had been by her side. He'd held her hand. Fetched tissues, coffee, water, and snacks. He'd even fed and walked Bud who, oblivious to everything going on, had been living the highlife at Colin's house all day.

Tucker had told his side of the story and left earlier, vowing to check in on her soon.

Julie waved goodbye to her favorite FBI agent as his car disappeared down her driveway. She stood for a moment, face turned to the vast starlit sky, and breathed in freedom. For the first time since she'd won the lottery, she was truly free. Her secret was out, and there were no more monsters lurking in the shadows.

There was, however, one person she'd kept in the dark for too long. She shivered, recalling the moment Colin had burst into her kitchen—unarmed! She'd almost had a heart attack. Yes, he'd frightened her, him and his buddy Tucker, crashing in like bungling idiots, but it had been the realization that with one well-placed jab of Scruggs' knife, she could lose him forever that had scared her out of her wits. When Scruggs had turned on the man she loved with all her heart, she'd done the only thing she could — she'd attacked. And she wasn't going to apologize for it because, in his own way, Colin had been trying to save her. Truth be told, he had. Her arms had about given out on her, and she hadn't known how much longer she was going to be able to keep her predator at bay. Scruggs had had the upper hand, and he'd known it. He'd been waiting for her to weaken then he would have made his move. Up close, she wouldn't have had a snowball's chance in Hades against the knife he'd held.

So yeah, she owed her life to Colin and Tucker. Rubbing her upper arms where they still ached from holding the chair aloft, she sighed into the warm night air. It was time for her to come clean with Colin. Maybe, just maybe, if she apologized for all the mean things she'd said to him, he would forgive her. Then maybe he'd find a way for her to repay the debt she owed him.

He was waiting for her in the kitchen which, she noted, minus one chair and one large knife missing from the block she kept on the counter, looked as if nothing of import had gone on there. Arms crossed, and one hip leaning against the counter, she suspected he'd been watching her through the window above the sink the whole time she'd been outside.

"Figure anything out while you were out there?" he asked.

"I think I saw the big dipper," she said with a shrug. "Or it could have been my imagination."

"You have a good imagination."

She cocked her head to one side. "What makes you think so?"

"I don't know. Maybe it was the way you *imagined* you could hold a maniac off with a *kitchen chair* until help, which might or might not have been coming, got here." He sounded mad, but the way his lips quirked up on one side said otherwise.

She took a step closer. "I didn't imagine anything. I did what I had to do, and I had sent out the S.O.S. on my phone. I didn't imagine that."

"No. You didn't imagine calling for help."

She took another step, closing the distance between them another foot or so. "And I didn't imagine the things I said to you this morning or after you almost got yourself killed by a bat-shit crazy man with a knife."

Colin frowned, his shoulders tensing. "No. You didn't imagine any of those things. You were actually quite eloquent both times."

"I owe you."

This time, it was Colin who cocked his head in inquiry.

Julie continued. "I owe you an apology. I shouldn't have shut you out earlier. I was afraid. I'd been in my self-imposed exile so long, I'd forgotten what it was like to have friends...to have relationships. You were the first person I'd let get close. It scared me."

"Apology accepted."

"And, I shouldn't have yelled at you after. The truth was, my arms were worn out. I don't know how much longer I could have held him off. You saved my life, but all I could think about was he might kill you before I had a chance to tell you I love you."

She said it, and he didn't move a muscle. He just stood there staring at her until her cheeks flushed and she dropped her gaze to the floor.

"That's a nice apology, but as you said, you owe me."

Her gaze snapped to his.

"What do you want from me, Colin? Money?"

"Hell, no! I don't want your money. You can keep every penny. You might have won it, but you earned it. It almost cost you your life. Twice. It's yours to do with as you please. Keep it. Give it away. I don't care."

"What, then? What do you want?"

He stepped forward, closing the gap between them. Toe-to-toe, he reached for her hands, entwined his fingers with hers. "I want the spirited woman who, armed with nothing but a wooden chair, tamed a maniac. I want the woman who survived the unspeakable then went on to build a new life for herself. I want the woman who naps on the bank of the pond with her dog when she should be working. I want the woman who gave herself to me in a leaky tent on a rainy night. I want the woman who built emotional walls to protect herself but found the courage to tear them down.

"I want you, Julie. Just you. I love you. Say you'll marry me."

It would be so much easier to give him the money, but it wasn't what he was asking for. He didn't want anything she *had,* but he did want *everything she was.* She'd spent years guarding both. She loved him. She really did. But was he asking too much? "That's a mighty big price to pay for saving my life, don't you think?"

"It's only fair," he said. "I saved your life. Save mine. Be my wife. I'll even throw in a new chair to replace the broken one. And if I screw up, you can brain me with it."

"Are you going to screw up?"

"And lose the only thing in this world I can't live without?" He shook his head. "Not on your life."

Could she live without him? Her heart two-stepped up into her throat, nearly choking her, and she knew the answer was no. From the first moment she'd laid eyes on him, she'd known he would mean trouble. She'd been right. He said she'd torn down the emotional walls she'd put up, but the truth was, he'd barreled right through them and made a beeline straight to her heart and made it dance.

Mind made up, she pulled her hands out of his and rose onto her toes. She draped her arms over his shoulders, cupping her hands around the nape of his neck. "Okay, cowboy. You throw in a new chair, and we've got a deal."

He wrapped his arms around her, pulling her against his hard body. They fit together like a pair of old boots, and being in his arms felt just as comfortable. "Say it, Julie. Say you'll marry me."

"I'll marry you, Colin Parker. Just say when."

"Tomorrow."

"Tomorrow it is," she said, and sealed the deal with a kiss.

THE END

ABOUT THE AUTHOR

USA Today Best-Selling author Roz Lee is the author of over thirty romances. The first, The Lust Boat, was born of an idea acquired while on a Caribbean cruise with her family, and soon blossomed into a five-book series originally published by Red Sage. Following her love of baseball, Roz turned her attention to sexy athletes in tight pants, writing the critically acclaimed Mustangs Baseball series.

Roz has been married to her best friend, and high school sweetheart, for over four decades. They have two daughters and are the proud grandparents of three adorable grandkids. Roz and her husband live in the wilds of New Jersey with their Labrador Retriever, Bud which is code for Big Unruly Dog.

Even though Roz has lived on both coasts, her heart lies in between, in Texas. A Texan by birth, she can trace her family back to the Republic of Texas. With roots that deep, she says, "You can't ever really leave."

When Roz isn't writing, she's reading or traipsing around the country on one adventure or another. No trip is too small, no tourist trap too cheesy, and no road unworthy of travel.

Website – www.RozLee.net